Small Sacrifices

ISBN: 1-4564-2026-7
ISBN-13: 9781456420260

Small Sacrifices

Mari Bauer

2010

I

Maddy Sheridan leaned back in her broke-in office chair, put up her feet on the desk and kicked off her shoes. She popped the top on her Coke Zero and took a deep swig from it then covered her mouth when a burp slipped passed her lips. She looked around covertly to make sure no one observed her "less than lady-like" deed. Coast was clear. Well it wasn't like anyone here at the paper had any delusions about her manners. She was the chameleon; she could fit in any situation and "appear" to be right at home. One of the great skills of being an investigative reporter, she talked to people and could get things out of them without them even knowing they were divulging anything. And then there was just Maddy, outspo-ken, nosey, driven and what she would like to think "down to earth."

She was restless. There was no big story knocking at her door. Her latest quest...uncovering the dirt behind a possible city cover up. She hated pissing off members of the city council, they always made her life a living hell, well not a liv-ing hell but sure made her life was inconvenient.

She sat back in her chair and flipped through her notepad. What to do, what to do? She dug out her cell phone from her holster case connected the belt-line of her blue jeans and checked for messages. She started at a blank screen. Well that sucked. Her nose crinkled up and a smile spread across her lips. Jackson Parker. Jack was a detective at SCPD, darkish brown hair and brown eyes with gold specks. When he would throw his head back and laugh it was like music to her ears. He had rakishly good looks...and was her best bud and best source. Let's see what kind of trouble Jack could get her into. Maddy pushed #3 on speed dial and pushed the speaker button. AC/DC's *Highway to Hell* blared out her speaker-phone. She laughed. He changed it; *Its only Rock N Roll* no longer fit his image. He must be having one of those weeks.

"Maddy...what's up?" the man on the other end answered.

"Yo Angus, was just about to ask you the same," she teased.

"I'm kind of in the middle of something here. Can I call you back later?"

He was up to something. She slid down in her seat, all fun aside. "What you got?"

"Maddy, please, it's official police business, you know I can't talk about it."

"Jack, since when has that ever stopped you? You know me, come on man, I need a fix here," she pleaded.

There was silence on the other end of the line, "Damn it girl. One of these days you are going to get me fired or killed."

She smiled into the phone, "Pleeeeease."

"My car's parked at 1245 Parkland Place. There is a file in there I need. Please bring it to the house at that address." Jack sighed. "Be smart about it."

"I loves ya Jack!" she snapped the phone shut. She gathered her materials and took off.

It was late August. The midday sun was beating down and the humidity was high. Summer in Iowa—90° one day 70° a couple days later. She popped the lock on her little silver Chevy Cobalt. The guys up at the bullpen made fun of her car; they called her the silver bullet. Not because the car was fast, obviously she wasn't built for speed, but because with Maddy behind the wheel, in the six months Maddy had her, she had a climbing track record of animal kills to her name ranging from more birds than Maddy could count, a couple rabbits, a squirrel, a skunk, to the latest victim, a pit-bull. Maddy swore the last was in self-defense. "He was chasing me," she protested. All she did was turned the car around and returned the favor.

Maddy spotted Jack's black Impala. It was parked on the side of the street, two squad cars were parked in front and behind. Their lights were off so it wasn't a hot scene. She parked her car on the opposite side of the street and got out. She went to Jack's car and peered in the window. As instructed she reached in, grabbed the file and went in search of Jack.

The house was a small stick frame house, painted beige with dark brown trim. She figured it for a two bedroom, open kitchen—dining room/living room, single bath. Based on the nicely manicured lawn, the inside would be immaculately cared for.

When Maddy walked up the sidewalk to the open front door she was met by a uniformed officer. He was kind of a short, portly man in his early thirties, dark hair, and a ruddy complexion. "Hey Bobby, what's up? Jack wanted me to deliver this." She held up the file.

Bobby reached out for it, "I can give it to him."

She pulled her arm back, "no...you don't understand, he said for *me* to bring it to him." She waited for him to let her gain entrance.

"What do we got here?"

"Missing persons." Bobby sighed and stepped aside. "You know the rules Maddy."

She dashed past him and smiled back at him, "Don't touch anything. I know, I know."

The house smelled of lavender. Maddy had a keen sense of smell; scent was always one of the first things she noticed. Just as she had predicted the room opened up into a small living room furnished with a brown micro suede couch and love seat, glass coffee table, matching end tables, and your usual unremarkable lamps. The room was neat with the exception of a couple Cosmos and a Readers Digest spread out on the table. A partial glass of liquid sat on a coaster on the table. A candle that had long since melted away and burned out was on a candle plate. The wax had spilt over the plate's rim and on to the table. Lavender of course. Off to the left was a dinette set, nothing fancy. Her house assumption was erroneous, a solid wall with a doorway led into the kitchen.

Past this door way she heard voices. One of those was Jack. She followed the voices into a galley kitchen where she found Jack conversing with the driver of the other squad car, Sgt. Russ Petersen. Russ was an older guy with graying sideburns and dark salt and pepper hair. He was a medium sized man, about 5'8", 5'9", dark features and harldy ever smiled. Russ looked at Maddy and nodded a greeting and turned his attention back to the detective finishing his report to Jack. "No sign of forced entry, no sign of a struggle. How do we even know she disappeared from here?"

"Melted candle on the coffee table, half full glass near it," Maddy stated flatly as she handed Jack the folder.

Jack looked at her with a raised eyebrows creasing at the same time. The disapproval look.

"Sorry, was just a simple observation.... And the lamps were left on...." She shut her mouth.

Russ glared at her and then looked back at Jack, "Does she really have to be here?"

"Maddy shut up or I will have to ask you to leave," Jack said as he was writing something down in his note pad. When Russ was looking towards the back door, Jack glanced up at Maddy and winked. She answered by sticking out her tongue.

As the two men continued to converse in a quieter tone, Maddy walked around the kitchen. The kitchen was updated but not what you would call modern, almond fridge, matching electric range, no dishwasher, fake granite counter tops, tile floors, clean enough but not spotless. "Where's the dog or cat?"

Both men looked at her, "Huh?"

She pointed to the floor at the end of the counter. "Food and water bowl. Small animal." She bent down and picked up a little chunk of food that was on the side of the bowl. Kibbles and Bits, this was a bit. "Dog."

Both men looked at each other and shrugged their shoulders.

"Bet you feel stupid." Maddy began to walk around whistling softly.

"Maddy..."

"Don't touch anything," she waved him off.

Off to the side of the back door was a small laundry area where the washer and dryer fit snuggly together. She sniffed. That wasn't dryer sheet smell. Dog, dirty dog. She knelt down and called, "Here puppy, puppy." She listened. An uneven vibration, just barley audible was coming from behind the dryer. Then it whimpered. She knelt down and saw a little tuff of silver and gold quivering against the wall. She didn't know if the little guy was stuck, but it sure was scared to death. "Jack help him, he's stuck behind the dryer."

"Oh for crying out loud. I think you can handle it."

She shook her head, "Nope can't do it." She raised her hands in the air, "No touchy."

Jack gave an exasperated sigh and asked her to step aside. He nudged the dryer away from the wall and reached back to grab the dog. The pup gave a low growl and a high-pitched yip as it snapped at him. Jack reeled on his heels and fell back. "Damn, feisty little shit. You want it, you grab it!" He moved out of her way.

Maddy sat on the floor cross-legged so she would be less intimidating to the dog. He was just a little thing, smaller than the average cat. His features were so tiny, so delicate, so hairy–not furry—hairy, beady little black eyes underneath bushy looking eyebrows. It was a less than manicured Yorkie. It gave a little whine and then barked at her. Maddy made a kissy noise and patted the floor in front of her. The dog stood, its ears perked up and wiggled its stubby little tail. "Come here puppy..." It slowly moved closer, cowering with its body slouched, its head held low but still looking up at her. Maddy reached out with her palm down and dangled her fingers. The pup licked her fingers and then shocked her by jumping into her arms eagerly covering her face with doggy kisses.

Russ stood in the doorway. "Humph, no accounting for tastes."

Maddy glared at him, "You know Russ, you can be a real ass. Did you take lessons for that or does it just come naturally?"

Jack helped Maddy to her feet. When he reached too close to the dog it gave a low growl. Maddy looked at Jack and raised her eyebrows. "Maddy, do me a favor. Take the pup outside and wait for me by my car."

"But..."

"Please Maddy..." he appealed to her to defuse what could be a sticky situation. And Maddy understood. She knew Russ did not like her nor thought she had any place at crime scenes. If he pushed it Jack could get in trouble for allowing it. Obediently she scooped up the pup and left.

While Maddy waited for Jack to join her, she sat down at the base of a tree just past the parking area near Jack's car. She released the Yorkie who wouldn't leave her side. She examined it closer. It was a he. His coloring was a little off for a Yorkie. His topcoat was silver instead of the normal black while the hair on his head and lower body was pale gold. He was way past grooming time. His ears were not cropped as standard to the breed, but he was a pure bred. A blue collar circled his neck, attached were three tags, one rabies, one license, and one nametag—Rufus. "Rufus," she spoke softly and scratched gently under his chin. "How long have you been alone sweetie?"

"His master was reported missing this morning." Maddy jumped. She hadn't heard Jack approach. Jack leaned up against the car, dug out a pack of cigarettes and a lighter and lit one.

"That's a really nasty habit," she commented. "Give me one." He tossed her the pack and the lighter. She pulled one out and lit it, inhaling it deep with in her lungs and then choked. She tossed him back the smokes and lighter still coughing.

"You need to quit trying to run with the big dogs, Maddy. It really doesn't suit you." Rufus cocked his head when he heard the word dog. "No offense Rufus," Jack said in a serious tone.

Maddy flicked the cigarette into the gutter. "Point well taken. So what are we looking at Detective?"

Jack shook his head and laughed. He opened his passenger side door and sat down, pulling out the folder and opened it up. "Her name is Vanessa Granger. The last time anyone has made contact with her was nine days ago. She is an office manager over at Tyler Construction and has been on vacation. That's why no one reported her missing until she didn't show back up at work. They tried calling her both at home and her cell. When she couldn't be reached they contacted her sister. Her sister didn't want to be bothered—never checked things out, and finally her best friend came to the house to check things out for herself. She found the house unlocked, Granger's purse and keys on the bedroom stand and her car in the garage."

"How about her bags? How do you know she even returned home?"

"Well as you so smartly pointed out, the evidence in the living room that she had been there. Russ may not have noted it but *I* did. Her bags were in her bedroom on the floor and had been unpacked. So she had to be home before she disappeared."

"Do you suspect foul play?" she scratched Rufus' tummy.

Jack shook his head "Technically we have no reason to, but Maddy...this is the second woman to turn up missing in two months. This is Sioux City, not L.A."

"So you think they might be related, this Vanessa and Cynthia Stewart?"

"Maybe."

Maddy thought for a moment. "Jack how do we even know she left? Were her bags empty because she had unpacked or because they were never packed? Without really knowing, how will you determine when she did go missing? Could have been a couple of days ago, could have been nine days ago."

Jack was jotting down things in his note pad. "Definitely something that needs checking into." He tossed his pad to the side. "I've told you this before Maddy, but you really are wasting your talent being a reporter, you should have been a cop."

Maddy threw her head back and laughed, her long, curly, coppery colored hair bounced softly around her shoulders. Her emerald green eyes sparkled. "My talent lies in writing, that's what I do. Being snoopy is just one of the side effects. Besides you and I both know I don't have the restrictions you do. I don't have to worry about stepping on people's rights." She laughed again. "I'm the press, I am suppose to be annoying."

Jack's phone went off in his pocket. He pulled it out and flipped it open. He got out of his car and walked to the far side of it. Maddy heard a muffled conversation then the phone click shut. Jack returned to her. "Listen Maddy, I have to head back to the precinct. I will send you over some info on the two cases. If you could write up a story on the missing women maybe we can gets some leads from the public. You want to put the dog in the back of the car?"

Maddy pulled the dog close to her, "Why? What do you want Rufus for? What are you going to do with him? He doesn't even like you!"

"Mads, he belongs to the vic. I will call her sister and have her come and get him. In the event Vanessa turns up, I am sure she will want her dog back."

Maddy snuggled her face into Rufus's hairy head. "Good-bye little man. You be good." She reluctantly placed him gently in Jack's back seat. When she shut the door Rufus jumped up against the window looking at her with those deep dark eyes, whimpering, pleading with her. She couldn't take it. She had such a soft spot for animals.

"I'll talk to you later," she turned to leave.

Jack grabbed her by the shoulder and turned her to face him. He was surprised to find a tear sliding down her cheek. "Hey...hey what's with the tears? You've only been around this dog for less than an hour. Where's the hard nosed reporter I know and love?"

She sniffed and wiped her eyes. "I don't know. I'm sorry. I just feel like he needs me." She laughed weakly. "I'm just being stupid. Female thing I guess. I'll talk to you later. Take care of him okay?"

"I will." She didn't wait for him to answer. Jack watched her walk to her car and didn't look back before she started it and took off.

Maddy drove downtown to a little diner a few blocks from City Hall. She was meeting with her source for expose of a couple of city councilmen.

Maddy climbed the steps up to the Journal's entrance. This City Council angle had potential, but it really wasn't what she wanted to do. But hell when it comes to a job, you can't always do just the things you are interested in doing, She looked at her watch. 4:37, close to quitting time and for once she couldn't wait. She breezed into the bullpen with her bag flung over her shoulder.

Just as she was headed toward her office, Max Sutton hollered at her that the Chief wanted to see her. Sutton was an idiot. Mr. Master columnist, yeah right.

Maddy knocked on the door of Andrew Collins, her editor or as known around the paper as the Chief. He was an older gentleman in his early 60's, balding with graying on the sides. He wore dark wire rimmed glasses that shielded pale blue eyes. She had the utmost respect for him. He could be hard nosed, unyielding, and what some would call a hard ass. That was not the Chief she knew. Yes, he was a no nonsense kind of guy, but he had a good nose for a story and could separate the bullshit from good shit. He saw in her as a raw talent for digging up dirt and encouraged it. He said she wasn't afraid to get her hands dirty and even had a knack for wallowing in it. However he did keep her on a loose rein and was not afraid to pull her back in if she got too far out there.

She heard him grunt from the other side of the door that she took as a sign of admittance. She entered the cramped little office and plopped down on an older office chair that had arms on its side. She slid down in it and crossed her knees. "You summonsed?"

"You are slouching. Would it kill you to act like a lady?" Chief eyed her over his glasses.

"No, only when the occasion calls for it." She eyed him, "Is this a new requirement?"

Chief shuffled some papers in front of him. "What do you have on this council story?"

She reached in her bag and pulled out her note pad. "I met with Mark this afternoon. Looks like we have a couple of councilmen having in-prompt-to meetings at the country club regarding land purchasing and housing developments."

"What do you think? Is it worth pursuing?"

She wrinkled up her nose, "Something smells about it all, and yes there could be something to it. I need to do some checking, but a good part of this needs to play out before I can prove anything.

She shut her notebook, "There is however another matter..."

Chief looked at her expectantly, "And..."

"We have another missing woman." She waited for his response. He just sat there and looked at her, not quite what she was hoping for. "Vanessa Granger was reported missing, last seen nine days ago. Cynthia Steward two months ago? Is any of this ringing a bell?"

He didn't even look at her. "So? What makes you think there's a connection? One of your gut feelings I suppose?"

She shook her head, "No, but Jack thinks there could be. I don't know if it's because the closeness of time period or if it's something he hasn't told me. He wants me to run a story on them. See if any leads come in. He said he would send me over the files."

"See where it goes, but don't forget your assignment." He then nodded his head in the direction of Maddy's office. "One of Jack's lackeys dropped a package in your office." He turned is attention to his keyboard. She had been dismissed.

The bullpen was awfully quiet when she walked past. No one looked up at her or acknowledge her. She shrugged her shoulders and let the thought pass. When she entered her office there was an object sitting on her chair. She swung her chair around. On it was a small tan kennel cab. The animal inside yipped at her and started to dig aggressively at the door. She knelt down so she was eye to eye with it. "Oh my God!" She flipped the lever on the door, the pup jumped in her arms and climbed his way to her face. "Rufus! Where did you come from?" She held him back from her so she could take a look at him. He had been given a bath and a light trimming. The hair on the top of his head was tied back with a red ribbon. "What have they done to you?" She pulled the ribbon out. "That's just wrong!"

There was a manila envelope on her desk with her name scribbled on it in Jack's handwriting. Taped to the top of the kennel was a folded piece of paper. She pulled it off and opened it. Someone had taken a photo of a Yorkie wearing a t-shirt and Photo Shopped printing on the t-shirt. "I break under Cobalts". Maddie felt her temper flicker. She took the paper and stood in her doorway looking at her co-workers. No one would look up. Two of them were typing away at their keyboards, one was "on" the phone, and Sutton was doodling on a piece of paper. It wasn't until he snickered that all the others cracked up. She grabbed Rufus and Jack's folder and went to leave. She stopped momentarily in front of Sutton. She wadded up the paper and threw it letting it bounce off his head. "Fuck you!"

2

Maddy unlocked her car and set Rufus down on the passenger seat and then opened Jack's envelope. In it were two files, one for each of the missing women, and a note scribbled on a piece of paper. *Here is what I have on our vics. See what you can make of it and when you put together a story for print, please let me read it first. I hope you don't mind me leaving Rufus with you. The sister wants no part of him and said to take him to the pound. I thought you would make a better foster parent for him. Jack."*

She gave the files a passing glance and then stuck them back in the envelope. She would look at them closer when she got home. She grabbed a CD from her visor and popped it in the CD player. Melissa Etheridge's *I Want to Come Over* began to play. She hit eject and replaced a CD with a Matchbox 20 mix. This was more into her mood. Music was a form of therapy for her and *Push* was more fitting to her mood.

She looked over at Rufus. He was quietly sitting on her seat, cocking his head from side to side as he stared at her. She reached over and scratched his chin and he in turn licked her fingers. Such a sweetie.

She put the car in gear and headed out of the city. Maddy lived on a nine acre spread 45 minutes from the city. She liked to keep her worlds apart, her career life versus her personal life, never the two shall meet. Some might find this odd, but it was just something she needed to do. She liked the commute. In the mornings it helped her organize her day and in the evenings it helped her let go of her day. Right now she was thinking about her co-workers. She was still a little pissed about the dog incident, but if she thought about it what they did was funny, would have been funnier if it hadn't been done to her. Yes, she was a poor sport. She shrugged it off and lost herself in the music for the remainder of the drive.

Maddy turned down the white pine lined lane into her acreage. She pulled in front of the garage and looked down toward the barn. Four horses were standing at the gate watching her. She was tired and wanted to get started on those files. She decided she would drive down to the barn and get chores done and over with. Once down there she got out and left Rufus in the car with the a/c running. When she opened the barn door the scent of hay and horse manure struck her. Dim light from two small windows and a brighter light from the back barn entrance was her only means of seeing, but once her eyes became accustom to it she could focus. She grabbed a couple of buckets and scooped oats from a dark green 33-gallon trashcan. She checked the water tank, half full, that could wait until tomorrow. She closed the barn up, walked over to the pasture gate and dumped the grain, spreading it out in to the long trough. She watched as one horse pushed another out of the way according to their pecking order.

When she returned to her car, Rufus was patiently waiting, his face pressed up against the passenger side window. She got in and drove back to the house. She grabbed the files and stashed them in her shoulder bag then scooped Rufus up in her arms. She was welcomed with more licks to the face and dog breath. She laughed as she nuzzled him.

Maddy took the steps two at a time, pulled the screen door open and pushed the inner door open. She was met by Jack, her one-year-old sable sheltie, staring up at her with his beady eyes that almost seemed to penetrate her. She loved his sweet nature and playfulness, but when he looked at her like this, he was just creepy. Rufus struggled in her arms and she set him down on the floor. She expected the customary sniffing and maybe some posturing on Jack's part, but instead the dogs met nose to nose, both tails wagging vigorously. It wasn't long when Jack grabbed a tuff of Rufus's hair and pulled him with him. They began to wrestle and then they took off to other parts of the house. Wow, that was a shock, although a nice shock.

She entered her bathroom and pulled some clothing off a towel rack. She slipped out of her work clothes, threw them in the hamper and slipped into a pair a grey cotton capris and a tank top. She ran a brush through her hair and then pulled it back into a ponytail with a hair tie. She turned on the hot water facet, pulled a washcloth from the pine linen hutch and scrubbed the makeup off her face. Much better.

Maddy padded barefoot into the kitchen and removed the files from her bag and set them on the table. She pulled a glass from the cupboard, went to the fridge and poured herself a glass of black tea. She popped the lid off a tub and picked two slices of lemon from it and squeezed them into her tea. From a catchall drawer she plucked out a yellow sticky pad.

She slid into one of the oak kitchen chairs, took a sip of tea, and pulled the files to her. She looked at Cynthia Stewarts file. First she studied her photo. She had amber colored hair about shoulder length, curling under slightly emphasizing high check bones, pale blue eyes, pointy nose and full lips. The file said she was 5 foot, six inches and weighed 130 pounds. You might not call her looks remarkable but pleasant. The file said she was 31, a teacher at Jackson Middle School, lived alone at the River View Apartment complex. She disappeared from her home on July 16, last seen returning to her home at approximately 6:15 PM. She had been reported missing by her boyfriend, Kent Peters. He had stopped by her apartment that evening as they were going out for a late supper when she returned from a church service. Her apartment was open and she was nowhere around. As with Vanessa, her purse, car keys were left behind. He tried to call on her cell phone, but there was no answer. He fell asleep on her couch while waiting for her and when he awoke in the morning, Cynthia was still not home. He called the cops and reported her disappearance. She flipped the folder. It yielded nothing more. That's it? That's all he gave her to go on? What was she suppose to do with that?

She grabbed Vanessa's folder. At least with this one she had a little more to go on. She opened it flat on the table and pulled out the photo of the woman whose home she visited today. Vanessa was a small petite woman of 5 foot two, 118 pounds, blonde hair, blue eyes, actually on the pretty side. She was 33. Vanessa was reported missing this morning by her friend and co-worker, Sandy Morton, after she went to Vanessa's home and found it empty. Vanessa's sister had been informed and reported she hadn't seen or heard from her in months. She was employed by Tyler Construction as an office manager for the last 4 years. Single, no known boyfriend and pretty much kept to herself. Once again the file ended abruptly.

Jeeze Jack was really holding out on her. What's with that?

She closed Cynthia's folder since there really wasn't much she could do with what she was given so she would concentrate on Vanessa. She grabbed her sticky note pad and a marker. Tapping the pen on the table she opened her mind to any questions that popped in her head. The fist being when did she actually disappear and how could Maddy find out?

Just then Rufus and Jack came tearing in the room, Rufus tugging at Jack's long white mane.

Rufus...Vanessa wouldn't leave the dog home alone while she went on vacation. Jack mentioned nothing about anyone taking care of him, hell they didn't even know he existed. *Check boarding kennels* she scribbled in a note.

It was reported both girls were called on their cell phones, which resulted in no answers. Did they not answer because the phones were turned off or did the phones go to voice mail? *Talk to boyfriend and friend.* Where are the phones? If she could get her hands on the phone she could find out the last time the women actually used them. She thumped her head with the palm of her hand. Duh! Jack could pull the phone records, but would he share the information with her? It was highly unlikely. She smiled to herself. She had her secret means of getting records, all kinds of records. However she would need their numbers and their carriers. *Get phone records.*

"Where did Vanessa go on vacation and who did she go with?"

She opened the files back up and jotted down Cynthia's boyfriend's name and home address and the name of the friend that called in Vanessa's disappearance.

Another thing, Vanessa's home. The yard was well maintained. If she remembered it correctly it appeared to be just mowed. This might not mean anything as it was a good possibility she hired a lawn service. However the appearance in the home was a different story. The burned out candle indicated, of course, that it had been burning for quite some time—hours. The glass on the table, a wine glass, still had some fluid in the bottom of it. Either there had not been much in the glass or it had ample time to evaporate. And then there were the blinds, they were drawn shut, which could and more likely meant it was evening. The lit up lamps reinforced this theory. Rufus's dog bowl was empty of food and water. The water bowl was dry, yet there was some kibble on the floor. Maddy honestly believed Miss Vanessa was missing for only a day or so.

Maddy reached for her glass of tea and took a big swallow. She then put the sticky notes in each of the corresponding files, bent down and put them in her bag. When she straightened up in her chair she came face to face with Rufus...on her table. "What the hell are you doing up here?" The little dog wagged his stubby tail and ran his tongue across her nose and lips. She spat and wiped the dog kiss off her face with the back of her hand, grabbed the pup and put him on the floor. "No dogs on the table!" she scolded him, her finger wagging in the air. He cocked his head and licked around his mouth, barked and took off after Jack. She slid all the chairs deep under the table. Vanessa was not a vigilant dog owner. Rufus had no manners.

She put her hands on her hips and stretched her back. She grabbed her tea and strode into the living room, set her tea on the coffee table and plopped on the couch, put her feet up and squirmed until she felt comfy. She grabbed the remote and flicked on the television. As she was channel surfing an image of Cynthia Stewart caught her eye and she stopped. It was on a local channel from the city. As she watched the newscast she began to fill agitated as she listen the anchorman report the disappearance of Cynthia and Vanessa. "What the hell..."

Maddy grabbed her cell and punched the number three. After a few frames of AC/DC Jack picked up. "Maddy! What's up? How's Rufus?"

"Why in the hell did you ask me to write up a story about these missing women when you were just turning it over to the network?"

The phone was silent for a few moments. "I didn't, Maddy. My Captain did. He felt it needed more immediate and broader coverage."

She held the phone in front of her and glared at it, then brought it to her ear again. "I see."

"I see.... That's what you always say when you really don't see at all. Now Maddy, don't be like this. I'm sorry; it was out of my hands. Do you understand?"

His voice was trying to sound soothing but was coming across as irritated. Irritated? Why should he be irritated, she was the one who was pissed? "Don't you dare try changing things around as if I did something wrong!"

"I never said or implied such a thing," he protested. "Are you still going to write the story?"

She took a deep breath and sighed. "I'll tell you what Jack, why don't you send over your nice little news release and I'll assign it to one of the lackey's." And with that she flipped the phone shut. "Asshole."

Man this day sucked. Jack jumped on the couch and plopped his body down on her, resting his alligator nose on her lap. She stroked him behind his ears while he soulfully looked up at her. Rufus stood on his hind legs with his front paws on the couch beside her. Jack raised his head and barred his teeth and let out a low growl. Rufus backed down. Maddy threw her head back and laughed. About time Jack showed some balls and staked out his territory.

She backed into the couch, flipped the channels some more and settled on the Food Network. After an hour of Iron Chef she tuned off the TV. All that food and now she was hungry. She made a quick summer sausage sandwich and was heading for the door to let the dogs out when her cell phone went off. Just as she flipped it open her foot stepped in something cool and wet. "Shit! Damn it Rufus!"

"Maddy?"

"Hold on Jack." She grabbed a paper towel and dropped it over the puddle. She went out the door and sat on the steps to keep an eye on the boys. "That dog!" she hissed. "He's like a mountain goat, gets on the table, and pees on the floor and he's only been here a few hours!" Then she paused, "What do you want?"

"Sheesh, do I dare? Doesn't sound like you're in the best of moods," he chuckled. Dead silence. "Listen Maddy, I'm really sorry about what happened earlier."

"You called me for that?" Her tone was flat.

"I don't want you angry with me."

She let him squirm a little before she said, "Don't worry about it Jack. I'll get over it, I always do."

"Rufus giving you a hard time? You want me to take him back?"

She watched to two dogs chasing each other, having a good time. "No, he just needs to settle in. I'm just not used to a dog with no manners."

Jack paused. "Will you still work this case with me?"

"What do you need me for?"

"Because you're good. You and I both know you are better at getting to the facts than most the men on the force." Then he laughed, "and you're much better looking than all of them."

Maddy smiled but didn't comment on the last statement. "Do I get full disclosure?"

"I will give you what I can. You know I have limitations, I could get fired."

"Don't worry about it, I have my own ways. Just keep me in the loop."

"How do you get your information? Some of the info you get takes a subpoena yet you seem to walk right into it."

She would rather not be having this conversation. Even though they had been "working" together for two years there was so much he didn't know about her. He knew who she was as a person, but nothing about her personal life and her past. It was not information she shared. She trusted Jack more than anybody, yet it wasn't enough. Once again she would side step, "A good reporter never reveals her sources."

"The forever elusive Maddy," Jack laughed, that deep throaty laugh that made her feel warm inside. "You could commit the perfect crime and the best interrogator couldn't crack you."

She looked at her sandwich in her hand and at the two pups now sitting patently at her feet. She tore it in half and tossed it to them. She watched them scarf it up. She hadn't realized a minute or so had lapsed. "Jack...."

"Maddy...what's up with you? You are not acting like yourself tonight. You want to talk about it?"

She pulled the hair tie from her hair and ran her fingers through it and sighed. "I don't know. Just a mood is all. Call it PMS if you want to. Listen Jack, I have a headache (she lied) and am tired. I'm going to call it a night."

"Okay, hey can we meet for lunch tomorrow?"

She tried to remember if she had anything going. "I think it will be alright, I call and let you know okay?"

"If you do, change your plans, I'm better company," he teased. "Pleasant dreams Maddy."

"Night Jack," she whispered, "and Jack..."

"Yeah?"

"Thanks."

"Always Maddy, always," and the phone went dead.

As she was driving to work the next morning, Maddy was thinking about the night before. She hadn't slept well. Something was eating at her and she couldn't pin point why. She shrugged it off and mentally organized her day. First she would take a trip to Tyler Construction and talk to Sandy Morton, and then she would make a trip to Vanessa's house. She would meet up with Jack for lunch, after she would follow up on leads she got during the snoop session.

It was 9:05 when she pulled into Tyler Construction's parking lot. She checked her appearance in the rear view mirror then smirked. Why bother, she didn't care how others thought she looked. The main office was a yellow brink one level building with large tinted windows at the entrance. Maddy pushed against the heavy medal door that opened up to a reception area where a heavy set red headed lady sat behind a dark wood counter with a computer area off to the left side. She leaned against the counter. "May I speak to Sandy Morton?"

The woman pointed to the nameplate on the counter, "That would be me. What can I do for you?"

Maddy pulled a business card from her bag and placed it on counter and slid it across to Sandy. "I'm Maddy Sheridan with the Journal. I would like to ask you some questions about Vanessa Granger."

The woman held up the card and then glanced up at Maddy. "You're the press, why should I talk to you?"

"Because I am trying to help find her. Detective Jackson Parker gave me your name. Please Miss Morton, I am not out to exploit Vanessa, just to find out where she is and what happened. Here let me show you something." She took out her cell phone and showed Sandy a picture she had taken of Jack and Rufus this morning. "Recognize this dog?"

Sandy held the phone in her hand and studied the photo. "That's Rufus. Why do you have him?"

"I'm am playing foster mom until we can locate Vanessa. Her sister wanted to put him in the pound," Maddy explained.

Sandy gave a look of disgust. "Wanda...she is such a selfish bitch. She wouldn't even go check on Vanessa when we called. Do you believe that?"

Maddy grabbed her note pad and her pen. "What is Wanda's last name?"

"Miller, lives down in the Singing Hills area," she paused as thumbed through her Rolodex and jotted down a number. "That's her home phone, but you would be wasting your time on that one."

"Where did Vanessa spend her vacation?"

"She flew down to Galveston for a week, then she was just going to dink around home. She called me when she landed in Omaha last Wednesday. Then it was like she just dropped off the face of the Earth."

"Did she make it a habit to call you often?"

"Well, she didn't call everyday if that's what you mean. But when she didn't show up at work this Wednesday when she was supposed to and she hadn't called me, I was concerned. And when I called her, I couldn't get a hold of her, either by cell or her landline, that's when I really got worried. I called Wanda. She just said Vanessa was a big girl and could take care of herself." Sandy shook her head. "That is one cold woman."

"Then you went to Vanessa's to check on her?"

"Yes, I did. When I got there her car was in the garage. I rang the front doorbell and got no answer. When I tried the door it was unlocked so I went in and called her name. I went from room to room. She was nowhere to be found. Her car keys and purse were on the bedroom dresser."

"What about her cell phone?"

Sandy shook her head, "Nope, didn't see it."

"What about the dog? Where was he?"

"Didn't see him either."

"Can you give me her cell number and do you know the carrier?"

She jotted down the number on a slip of paper and handed it to Maddy. "She's on Verizon."

Maddy was pleased Sandy was so forth coming, "Sandy, can you tell me about Vanessa? What was she like, her personality, her likes, dislikes, affiliations?"

Sandy sat back in her chair and took a few deep breaths. "She's quiet, very consceious, friendly to those she knows. She's very shy, volunteers in the community, active in her church. She doesn't go out much socially."

"How about a boyfriend?"

Sandy laughed, "Heavens no. She's scared to death of men!"

"How about family?"

Sandy shook her head, "No, her parents died a couple of years ago in a fire. All she has is Wanda and to the best of my knowledge they don't speak to each other."

Maddy kept writing as Sandy talked. "Do you know why?"

"Couldn't tell you. Vanessa never talked about it."

Maddy closed her notebook and held her hand out and shook Sandy's. "You've been most helpful Sandy. I really appreciate you taking the time to talk to me. If you think of anything more that you might find helpful, please give me a call."

Sandy flipped Maddy's business card between her fingers. "Miss Sheridan, do you think she is still alive?"

"Let's hope so," she said over her shoulder as she went to leave. Then she remembered something, "Sandy, who took care of Rufus while she was gone?"

"Tri-View Vet Center."

"Thanks."

Maddy sat in her car and did a mental checklist and absorbed the information Sandy Morton had given her. Maddy did the 411 on Tri-View Vet Center and placed the call. "Hi, this is Wanda Miller. My sister, Vanessa Granger, left her dog Rufus with you while she went on vacation. I was supposed to pick him up for her, but I was out of town. I haven't been able to reach her. Could you tell me if Rufus is still there?...No?...Could you tell me when she picked him up? Tuesday morning? Great, thank God. Thank you, bye." She snapped her phone shut, a smile written on her face. She looked at her watch. 9:45. Good she still had lots of time. She needed to call Jack to firm up her plans for lunch.

She took out her cell and hit speed dial. It only took a few seconds for him to answer. "Hello?"

"Good morning baby cakes, how ya doing this morning?"

"My, my...isn't this a change from last night? You sound like your old self again."

She decided not to respond to his comment. "Are we still on for lunch?"

"As long as you want to."

She laughed. "Now you're the one who said if I had any plans to break them. Where do you want to meet?"

"McDonalds," he said in all the seriousness he could muster.

She looked at her phone and then said, "I'm sorry, I think you must be mistaking me for one of your hot dates."

He laughed. She smiled to herself. God she loved that laugh.

"You pick, I'm easy."

Now it was her turn to laugh, "So I've heard. How about Perkins on East Gordon."

"Not sure I like that comment," Jack replied in good nature. "Perkins it is. 12:30 okay."

"Works for me, see ya then." She snapped her phone shut.

Now off to 1245 Parkland Place. Maddy was singing along to Gwen Stephanie when she parked her car opposite to Vanessa Granger's home. The place was quiet. One would never have known it was a possible crime scene with the exception of the yellow police seal on the front door. Can't enter that way, couldn't break the seal. She hoped the back door would be more useful. She looked around the neighborhood; all was quiet. She snuck around to the backyard and saw the back door that she knew led into the kitchen. From her pocket she pulled a pair of latex gloves and slipped them on. Could never be too careful when it came to messing with crime scenes. She ran her fingers along the doorsill. No key. She sat on the steps and looked around her. Please say there was a hidden key. She really wasn't good at picking locks. The back walk was lined with flagstone and hostus. One of the flagstones was a little off from the others. Bingo! When she pried up the stone a small black key box was smashed into the soil beneath. It looked like it had been there a long time; hopefully Vanessa hadn't changed her locks. She took a twig and freed the box and popped it open revealing one silver key. Damn she was good.

The lock turned easily under the guidance of the key and door creaked open. As she suspected the door opened into the laundry room where she had found Rufus the day before.

She kicked off her shoes to make sure she wasn't tracking anything in. She walked softly through the house. Everything was pretty much the same as it was the day before. Maddy was looking for a computer. She was sure Deputy Dufus wasn't smart enough to confiscate the computer to disseminate it. Sad but true. She found a laptop in Vanessa's bedroom. She pulled out the desk chair and booted up the computer. She pulled down the bookmarks, yep there it was, Verizon Wireless. Online bill pay here we come. It only took seconds to sign on to the sight. She crossed her fingers that the computer remembered the password. She pulled the scrap of paper from her pocket and punched in the phone number. The account with password popped up. Yes! She pulled up the billing records. She didn't have time to read through the records now so she sent it to the printer. She needed to get out of here before she got caught. Last thing she needed to do was to get caught trespassing at a crime scene. Jack would kill her. As soon as the document finished printing, she shut down the computer, took her prize, slipped out as she came in and replaced the key from where she found it.

When she returned to her car she let out a sigh of relief. Her adrenalin was on high status. It was such a rush being bad!

It was 12:45 when she pulled into the full Perkins parking lot. She scanned the lot and spotted Jack's Impala parked off to the side. It was vacant, he must be inside. Shit, now she was going to have to hear about punctuality.

She gave the hostess Jack's name and was led to a booth in the back where Jack was patiently waiting. He was tapping a knife on the table. A soda, no doubt Dr. Pepper was in front of him and a glass of tea with a slice of lemon was placed opposite of him. Two menus were placed on the table between them. She slid into the booth and opened her mouth to apologize.

"Don't bother," Jack spoke softly and took a draw from his soda. "I don't want to know."

Maddy picked up the menu and studied him from over top of it. Okay now what do you say to that? "Jack..."

"Maddy, I don't want to fight with you, especially about something so stupid and normal as you being late." He picked up his menu and appeared to be reading it. "So what have you been doing with yourself this morning?" He didn't look up at her.

"You're so rigid," she commented. "I've been working, that's what I do on the days I work."

He shot her a look. "You've been investigating the disappearances?"

"Why would you say that?"

"I went to question the Granger woman's friend. She said she had already talked to you, that I referred you to her." His voice was cool and low.

She set down the menu. "Jack, why do you act so shocked. You know me well enough to know how I work. Why are you so pissed about it?"

He set down his menu and ran his fingers through that gorgeous thick brown hair. Maddy secretly took a deep breath. If he only knew what thoughts ran through her head about him. No, she smiled to herself, it was a good thing he didn't. "I have a feeling she was more forthcoming with you than she was with me. I don't really like you getting a jump on me interviewing witnesses. I thought you were going to keep me in the loop."

She took the lemon from her glass, squeezed its juice into her tea then dropped the lemon into her glass. She took her straw and pushed the lemon deep into her glass. She was taking her time, choosing her words carefully. "I'm not sure what it is you want me to tell you, Jack. Yes, I spoke to her, didn't get anything that we didn't basically already know." She reached out and took his hand in hers and grinned, "Show me yours and I'll show you mine."

He covered her small delicate hand with his large one, squeezed it and held it tight. When she tried to gently pull it away, he held on. When she looked at him puzzled he asked, "How do I know you will be totally on the level?" He loosened his grip but didn't let go, instead he traced the lines of her palm with his forefingers.

What was he doing? Maddy jerked her hand away from him. "You don't!" she snapped.

"Does my touch repulse you that much?" His eyes met hers.

"No...I never said that. You're just messing with my head. Don't mind fuck me, Jack."

Maddy didn't notice that the waitress was standing by them. She didn't know how much of the exchange she heard. She asked if they were ready to order.

Maddy ordered a mushroom Swiss and a side salad while Jack ordered an omelet with hash browns.

"Skipped breakfast," he commented when the waitress left.

The silence between them was deadening. Maddy was twisting her straw wrapper between her fingers. She was confused. Jack and she have never played games with each other. They hadn't worked a case together in a couple of months but had kept in contact. Things had always been laid back and relaxed between them. Now it seemed like there was an undercurrent between them and it was getting in the way of their ability to work together and their friendship. At least she thought so. Was it her? Was she sending him singles?

"Listen Jack, you know how much you mean to me," her voice was but a whisper. "You're my best friend, the only person I trust. I don't want to loose that."

He took another sip from his Dr. Pepper. "I know you won't let me into your private life, you have made it perfectly clear." He was trying not to sound harsh; he didn't want her to bolt. "I believe...you and I, we have a special connection..." he sucked in a deep breath and slowly let it out. "Are you attracted to me at all?"

Maddy's head flew up and her mouth dropped. He was her friend; she could not lie to him, not about real things anyhow. She felt her cheeks grow hot.

Jack's head dropped. "Never mind, you saying nothing is saying everything. Forget I ever asked, okay?"

Her voice was shaky when she spoke, "No wait. I will be truthful with you, but I ask that you respect what I tell you, okay?"

"Yes."

She rubbed her temples. How did a simple lunch turn into this? "Do I find you attractive...yes...very much so. But you have to understand something. I don't do romantic relationships. I just can't. This relationship, our friendship we have is all I am capable of giving. What you mean to me Jack, I don't want to risk it by... well love affairs end, friendships, deep friendships don't."

The waitress had arrived with their food and placed it in front of them. Before Jack took his first bite he said, "Fair enough."

"I got a time line and background," Jack said as he stuffed fork full of omelet in his mouth.

Maddy relaxed. "Sister is going to be no help. Rufus was picked up from kennel Tuesday morning. We know she made it to Omaha, so she definitely made it back from her trip. Did you find a cell phone?" She waited for his reaction.

He stopped mid-chew, "No."

"How about with Cynthia?"

"No."

"Got any leads from your "newscast"?"

Jack chuckled, "No."

Maddy laughed and flicked the shredded straw wrapper at him. "Some great detective you are."

"How do you know about Rufus?"

"Called the vet center he was bordered at."

"And they just handed you the information?"

She looked up at him with her green eyes sparkling, smiling sweetly, "Of course not, I lied."

"I'm going out on a limb here, but I am assuming your are working some angles you don't wish to share with me at this time?"

"Yep"

"Thought as much, but you will fill me in when the time comes."

"Yep. I always do."

He picked up a jelly packet and tossed it at her.

She picked it up. "Mmmmm.... strawberry. If I were to get into a sticky situation, strawberry would be my choice."

They finished their meal with light conversation, the tension have melted away. Jack paid the bill and they walked out together. Jack walked with her to her car. Maddy took out her keys and stood to face Jack. It felt kind of awkward.

"Don't freak out on me here, Maddy." He pulled her close and wrapped his arms around her and held her tight. He whispered in her ear "You mean a great deal to me, Maddy. I will be honored to be whatever it is you need me to be."

Maddy's face was crushed against his chest. His cologne was intoxicating and the feel of his body next to hers, wow! As he began to release her from his embrace he softly kissed her forehead.

They both heard the buzzing coming from Jack's pocket. He took out his cell phone and flipped it open. "Parker...where...how long ago? They on the scene already? Yeah. I'm at Perkins East. I will be there in 10." He flipped the phone shut.

Maddy watched him. "What is it?"

"We got a body, I gotta get going."

She started following him to his car. "What are you doing?"

She reached for the door handle of his car. "I'm going with you," she stated flatly.

He looked at her like she was nuts. He was torn between his job and he need to fix things with her. "Okay, but you do as I say and you stay in the car, got it?"

She slid into the seat, "yeah, yeah I got it."

He slid in behind the wheel and looked at her, "Maddy, I mean it."

She smiled up at him. "I know you do."

3

Jack was whipping out of the parking lot on to Gordon before Maddy could even get her seat belt on. He had flipped on his emergency lights and was driving west.

She settled down into her seat. "So are you going to fill me in?"

"A body was discovered at Bacon Creek Park behind the dog run. One of the dogs escaped outside the run area. When the owner finally located him, the dog was diligently digging at a mound of dirt which resulted in uncovering a body of what appears to be female," Jack explained.

"One of our vics?" Maddy's blood was pumping.

Jack shot her a sideways glance. "How the hell would I know?"

"Damn Jack, mellow out!"

"Listen Maddy, you really have to listen and do what I say. This is a murder investigation. You just can't go strutting around like you own the place. DCI is already on the scene. Its not just my case anymore, I won't be lead detective now. It's the state's case now."

"They just can't come in and take over!"

"They can and they have. I will still be working the case but as a grunt," he replied disdainfully.

She watched him. His face was tightly drawn and he was chewing on his lower lip. His knuckles were white as he gripped the wheel. He really was perturbed.

Maddy rode in silence. They drove up a small service road, which led to a rural area known as Bacon Creek Park. It was very nice recreational area where a creek had been dammed up to make way for bass fishing, had a swimming area, offered canoeing, camping and ample walking paths. They had taken an area and fenced it off so people could bring their dogs to run. This was the area Jack had referred to.

The park had been closed off to public traffic. Jack flashed his badge and the unies waved him through. Police cars, both marked and unmarked, lined the road. The Crime Scene Unit was already on the scene as well as the morgue wagon. Officers could be seen making a trek back and forth from the vehicles to the scene.

Jack turned the car off but left the keys in it, "In case you get hot." He got out and took off his jacket and threw it in the back seat. A hint of perspiration was already revealing its self down his back and under his arms. He shut the door behind him and then looked through the window at Maddy. "Maddy stay!"

As he walked in front of the car and began to walk up the grassy hill, she poked her head out the window. "Woof!"

Jack glared at her, he was not amused and to top things off, he flipped her off!

Damn, he was really stressing. Was he that freaked out because DCI was in the mix or was there something else to this. He wasn't even sure if this body had anything to do with the missing women.

Maddy sat in the car for what seemed like an eternity. She could have this much fun at the office, at least she could move around. All the action was up there and she couldn't get a taste of it. Out of boredom she began to snoop around Jack's car. Of course he wouldn't have anything fun like a pair of handcuffs, or a gun, not even a taser. What kind of cop was he? She popped open the center council and dug through it. "My, my, my...what do we have here?" she smiled as she held up a clearance pass. She didn't think about her promise to Jack, only now she could get close to the action. Surely he would understand, she was just doing her job anyway she could.

Maddy reached over and turned the ignition on and rolled up the windows. She got out and locked the car behind her. She untucked her blouse and attached the badge to its hem and proceeded to walk up the hill. A couple of unies gave her the once over, but when she flashed the badge they let her walk on by. Her nerves were hopping with excitement. What was wrong with her, getting off on seeing a dead body? As she moved through the crowd of cops, she began to smell decomposing flesh, which once you've smelt it, it was forever imprinted in your brain. When the scent grew almost stronger than her stomach could tolerate she knew she was close to the source. She managed to poke her head between some plainclothes cops to see what was going on.

The area had been taped off in grids surrounding the site. The grave was shallow, approximately three feet deep and six feet long. During the course of unearthing the body, mounds of soil were piled around the body. CSU personnel were carefully moving debris away from the body while a couple of photographers were diligently taking photos of the body and scene at every conceivable angle. The body in the grave was definitely that of a woman, small in stature. Her body appeared to be wrapped in some kind of gauzy material and it was hard to see any real detail. On thing Maddy noticed however was the girl's hair, it was very long, and a dark chestnut color.

"She's not one of missing vics," she said flatly before she even realized it. Several men turned and looked at her with a surprised and questioning look.

Maddy felt one pair of eyes burning into her. Jack. Their eyes locked. His were bearing down on her, his face flushed red and she was sure it wasn't from the heat. She saw Captain Thomas pull him aside and say something.

Jack quickly moved through the crowd and was soon escorting her out by her elbow. His grasp on her was tight and even hurt a little bit. She tried to pull away. "I can walk back on my own," she snapped.

He didn't release her. He didn't speak to her. He wouldn't even look at her. He took her to his car. "Give me my keys."

She handed them to him and he popped the locks. "Get your purse."

She knelt in and grabbed it. When she turned around to face Jack, he grabbed the clearance badge, snatched it off her shirt and threw it in the car not caring where it landed. He got on his radio and called for Bobby Russell to bring a squad car around.

Maddy had never seen Jack so angry with her before and she knew better to even open her mouth.

Jack spun her around to face him. "Maddy, you knew. I told you how important this was and it was not the time or place for your bullshit. I took you at your word, I trusted you. Now my ass is in hot water with the Captain, you made me look like a total dumb fuck to the DCI officers. I should have known better to bring you here, that I couldn't trust you. Stupid move on my part"

Bobby pulled up in a cruiser. Jack opened the passenger side door and practically shoved her in the car. "Escort Miss Sheridan to her vehicle, Bobby. Thank you."

Maddy started to say something but Jack cut her off. "Don't Maddy, don't make it worse by opening up your mouth. There is nothing you can say or do right now that's going to fix things. Just leave." He turned and hiked back up the grassy hill.

She told Bobby that her car was parked at Perkins and then sat quietly going over what happened in her mind. She had fucked up big time. This could be it; Jack was probably done with her. An hour ago he was asking if something was going on between them and now he couldn't stand the sight of her. Most times she didn't give her antics much thought, but she was feeling remorse over this one.

Bobby glanced at her with a smirk on his face. "You get the feeling you've fallen from grace?"

"Shut the hell up, Bobby," was all she said to him. They rode the rest of the way in silence.

After he dropped her off, she dug out her keys, got in and started the car, cranking up the a/c. She sat there for several minutes staring off into space. Her eyes blurred up and a tear slid down her cheek. She messed up and this could cost her Jack. This is why you don't care too much about people, you just end up screwing things up and it hurts like hell. She wiped her face with a tissue and put her car into gear and headed back to the Journal.

When she arrived back at her office she knew she probably should fill the Chief in on what had been happening, but she just didn't have the heart for it right now.

Maddy pulled out the phone records she had heisted off Vanessa Granger's computer. Thank God Jack knew nothing about this. She laid the sheets in front of her and scanned the calls. Obviously Vanessa qualified for the low volume plan. There were no text messages and less than a hundred calls. The last outgoing call was Tuesday evening, three days ago at 6:15. She picked up her desk phone and dialed the number. "Trinity 1st Reform Church, may I help you?" came a woman voice on the other end.

"Who did you say this was?" The woman repeated herself. "I'm sorry, I have the wrong number," she stammered and hung up.

The remaining calls were short incoming calls from two different numbers. With out verifying it she would guess they were from Sandy. Just for the hell of it she ran a few of the numbers through a reverse lookup. Nothing significant caught her eye.

Maddy had been messing around with the phone records for a couple of hours when there was a knock outside her office door. Chief stood in the doorway looking at her with an odd expression on his face. "What?"

He came in and shut the door behind him and sat on the corner of her desk. "I just got off the phone with a little birdie."

"Really?" she started shutting down her computer. "And I bet it sang like a canary."

Chief chuckled and rubbed his hand over his stubbly chin. "Yep. Supposedly one of my reporters breached a murder scene and had to be escorted off the premises. Any truth to this?"

She kicked back her chair and leaned forward. "Appears to be true." She couldn't meet his gaze.

"Maddy what are you knocking yourself out for? You took a risk—you took a gamble. That's how we play the game, you know that. You wouldn't be the reporter you are today without doing some outlandish things. You've done worse without blinking an eye."

She was quiet for a moment, chewing on her fingernail. "I know, I took a gamble and got into the scene, but at what cost, Chief? I may have won the hand, but I think I lost the game."

Her mentor put his hand on her shoulder. "You mean Jack? That man's put up with your shit for the last couple of years. Do you really think this is going to scare him away?"

She shrugged her shoulders. "I don't know. I really fucked up this time. I might have possibly put his job on the line. His Captain jumped on him right there in front of everyone including the DCI." She looked up, "You know what the sad thing is? I had promised him I would stay in the car. He made it very clear to me how important it was I stay put and don't do anything dumb. But I did it anyhow and never gave it a second thought until everything blew up. What kind of person does that make me?"

Chief put his finger under her chin so she had to look up at him. "That makes you Maddy Sheridan, impulsive, reckless, but all in all you're a good, compassionate person who is always looking for the truth, even at a cost."

Maddy's cell phone, which was on her desk, began to vibrate. She quickly snatched it up hoping it would be Jack. It was Mark, the city administrator. She set it back down on the desk.

"You better get that, you still have other stories to cover." Chief got up and opened the door to leave. He turned to look at her, "Listen Tiger, everything will work out. You'll see."

She flipped her phone open, "Hey Mark, what's up?"

"You need be at the country club around 6:00. I heard off the grape vine the gang is getting together for a few drinks in the clubhouse. Maybe you might pick something up."

She took a deep breath. Yes, life and career must go on. She looked at her watch 5:45. "Okay, I will be there. What am I looking for?"

"Observe and report," he laughed. "I don't know hon, you'll just have play it how you see it."

After she hung up, she got up and went to the ladies room. Standing in front of the mirror, she studied her appearance. The day's wear and tear was showing. She took her makeup bag out of her purse, applied some mineral base to her skin, touched up her eyes with some mascara and applied a thin layer of lipstick. She smacked her lips together to even it out. She pulled the hair tie from her hair, ran a brush through her coppery locks and then shook her head so it fell naturally around her shoulders. "Okay, show time."

Maddy grabbed some files off her desk, flipped the light and locked the door. Twenty minutes later she was parking her car at the country club.

She had to adjust her eyes to the dim bar lights. She scanned the room searching when her focus came to a stop at a table of three men sucking down some drinks and being jackasses. How did Mark think she was going to get any information from these guys? It didn't look like private out-of-session meeting, just some pompous businessmen getting a buzz on.

She took a seat at the bar as close to the table as she could and ordered vodka sour. She wasn't much of a drinker and knew she should have ordered a soda, but she was feeling down and belting down a few drinks might just do the trick.

The bartender proved to be a very nice guy with some great stories. He had her laughing so much she felt much better...or was it the eight mixed drinks she had? At that point who cared? She ordered another drink and looked at her watch. 9:15. Damn where did all the time go? "Last one Randy. I need to hit the road."

"No you don't sweetheart. You want me to call you a cab?"

Maddie laughed and slammed her hand down on the bar. "Hon, I live about an hour from here." She pulled out her wallet and looked at her cash. "Not enough here to take a cab to home," she giggled. "Damn."

"You got some one I can call? Do I need to take your keys?" Randy grabbed the bar phone.

Maddy took out her cell phone. "Better text," she laughed some more. "Slurred speech might give it away." She punched the number 3 but instead of hitting send she pulled up the text option. She didn't know what was tougher, focusing on the keypad or having the dexterity to find the letters. Finally she typed out, "Jack where are you?" and it hit the send button.

Seconds later her text alert went off. "What do you want?"

She giggled like a school girl and typed, "You."

Alert "Maddy, unless you have something important, leave me alone. I'm on a date."

"Where and with who?" send.

Alert "None of your business. What do you want?"

Her body pulled back and she gawked at the phone. Wow he was still really pissed. "Sorry! I'm drunk and I can't drive home." Send.

This time it took a couple of minutes before the alert went off. "Jesus Maddy. Where are you?"

"At the Country Club bar." Send.

She sat at the bar sipping her final drink, several minutes passed and no text. Was he really going to just leave her here? She pulled up her contact list looking for someone that could help her. She didn't want it to be just anyone because she didn't just wanted any one to bring her to her home.

From behind someone tapped her shoulder startling her. She dropped her phone. She bent down to pick it up almost falling off her bar stool. From her vantage point from below two pairs of legs stood behind her. One she recognized as Jack's black shoes and his grey dress pants. The other was a set of black stiletto shoes adorning nicely sculpted legs, which she followed up to meet the proverbial tight fitting black dress. The woman had a tiny waste, ample boobs, slender neck, narrow face, high cheek bones, pert little nose, doe eyes, and to top it off, honey blonde hair pulled back in a loose bun on top of her head. "Barbie!" she said out loud.

Randy gave a muffled laugh from behind the bar.

"How long has she been here?" Jack asked Randy.

He shrugged his shoulders, "I don't know, since before 7:00."

"How much she had to drink?"

"That's her ninth."

He turned to Maddy. She noticed his jawbone was twitching. Not a happy camper, not at all. She tried to be serious which only made her laugh more.

"What are you even doing here?"

She brought her fingers to her lips, "Shhhhhhsssshh. I'm spying. I'm spying on those guys." She pointed at the table where the councilmen had been sitting. It was now vacant. "Hey, when did they leave?"

Randy wiped the bar in front of her. "About an hour ago."

"She got a tab?" Jack asked Randy. Randy showed it to him and Jack laid a twenty on the bar. Randy threw Jack Maddy's car keys.

Jack helped Maddy off the bar stool and guided her out of the club. "You're just lucky we happened to be having dinner here."

Maddy turned and waved to Randy.

"Good night Maddy, it's been a pleasure," Randy smiled and waved.

The cool air felt good on Maddy's face. The wind was picking up and the smell of rain was in the air. She loved rain at night. Hell she loved rain anytime.

Maddy turned her head to face Jack's date. "Sorry, I screwed up your date." She held out her hand for a handshake. "I'm Maddy."

The woman glared at her withholding the return. "I know who you are," she replied coldly.

"This is Stella Rogers, my girlfriend," Jack stated flatly as he leaned her up against her car. "Now stay...for once."

Jack guided Stella away from Maddy and she could hear them talking in low voices. She saw him hand Stella his car keys. "Take my car home, I'm going to drive Maddy home."

"Can't you just call her cab?" Stella whined. "You don't owe her anything after what she did to you today!"

He told her? Nice, real nice.

"She doesn't live in town, now please, Stella, I will make it up to you." He leaned in and gave her a slow kiss and a swat on the butt. Stella squealed in delight.

Maddy looked away. She got a sick feeling in her stomach and she didn't think it was from all the alcohol.

Jack unlocked her car and guided her into the passenger seat. Just as Jack slid into the driver's side the rain began to fall. His knees fit snuggly underneath the steering wheel. "Damn you are short." He moved the seat back.

Maddie watched Stella as she did a fast walk across the parking lot covering her head with her quaint little handbag. She began to laugh hysterically and rolled down her window. She crawled half way out; the warm rain pelted her face. She began screaming, "Stelllla.....Stellllaa...."

Jack grabbed her by the belt loop of her pants and pulled her back in the car. "What the hell are you doing?"

She laughed, "Don't you get it.... Stella...from *A Streetcar Named Desire*? It's funny," she laughed some more. "Don't you think?" She looked at him and giggled.

"Sit back and shut up, get your buckle on and roll up that window."

"Sheesh, where's your sense of humor?" She did as commanded, rolling up her window and snapping on her belt. She sat there quietly; every so often laughing under her breath as some bizarre thought crossed her mind. Then she noticed they weren't moving. "What ya waitin' for?" she asked.

"I don't know where you live." He looked straight a head, his voice void of any emotion.

"You sure know how to dampen a party...or is that the rain?" she laughed. No comment from the driver's side. "Oooookay fine. Head east on 20."

He put the car in gear and drove through the city in silence, the streetlights whizzed by. Friday night in the big city, people out having fun, couples doing their thing. Yeah, high times on a Friday night.

They had been driving for a little over a half an hour, passed through two small bedroom towns and were now on the long stretch before they reached Maddy's turn off. Maddy's stomach began to lurch and her head begin to spin. No, Lord, please don't.

"Jack, you need to turn off on the next gravel," she pleaded.

"Why?" it was the first time he looked at her since they left.

"Because I don't want to puke in my car okay?" she snapped.

He quickly turned off and drove about a quarter mile and pulled over. Maddy unbuckled quickly, opened the door, leaned out and threw up, and threw up, and threw up. She felt as if her socks were going to come up through her throat.

She wasn't sure how much time passed before her stomach settled down. She leaned her body back in the car and pulled the door shut. Her head was still spinning.

Jack pulled out a handkerchief from his pocket and handed it to her. "How you feeling?"

She took the handkerchief from Jack, wiped her face then spread it out and covered her face then leaned her head back. "Like I wish I could die."

For the first time since lunch he laughed. "I take it you're not a drinker."

With every heart beat her head pounded. "Really? What gave you your first clue, Detective?"

"Simple deduction hon." He folded up the center council. "I know there's not much room but come here."

She lifted the cloth and eyed him cautiously, "Huh?"

He patted his legs, "Lay down, and rest your head."

"I can just recline my seat."

He grabbed her arm and pulled her down so her head was resting on his lap. Good thing he was tall, kept her head from hitting the steering wheel. "You know this can be misconstrued as being kinda kinky."

Jack reached into his pocket and pulled out his phone. He played with some buttons until the right screen came up. "What's your address?"

"Why?"

"GPS" he showed her the screen. She gave it to him. "Now just close your eyes."

Maddy adjusted her body until she had some semblance of comfort and rested her head on Jack. She stared at the glow from the dash board as her thoughts jumbled together. She felt something touch her head and tensed until she realized it was Jack's hand. His fingers softly stroked her rain soaked hair. His touch was soothing. The last thing she remembered before she passed out was thinking what a fucked up day it had been.

"Maddy," Jack whispered softly. "We're here."

She leaned up in the seat a little too quickly. "Oh shit, stop the world, I want to get off." She blinked a few times to focus. From the light of her headlights she saw Jack and Rufus standing together in the doghouse. The falling rain glistened in the beams of the lights.

"Do you want me to carry you in?" Jack asked.

She held her fingers to her temples. "Don't be stupid, I can make it."

Jack got out and came around to her side of the car and helped her out. Her legs felt like noodles and she began to waiver. Jack put his arm around her waist and held her up, leading her to the house.

"You got a key?"

"It's open. Let the dogs in too please." Then she stopped. "Shit, I need to feed the horses."

"You can do it in the morning. Come on let's get you inside." He guided her through the yard gate, up the steps, and opened the door. The dogs scooted in between their legs and stopped in the kitchen briefly to shake off the rain and then took off to parts unknown.

"Wait," Maddy pulled away from him and darted into the bathroom; which was just off the kitchen.

Jack could hear her retching. He stood in the doorway watching her and laughed.

She looked up and wiped her mouth. "Fuck you. Do you have to stand there and watch? There's pop in the fridge, I am sure you can find the living room. The remote is on the coffee table. Now go away and leave me to die in peace."

Finally she felt as if there was nothing left to come up. She had thrown up on herself, her clothes were damp and she knew she had to smell awful. Maddy stumbled into a standing position and leaned in and turn the water on in the shower. She pulled a couple of towels out of the hutch and a set of nightclothes. She stripped down and climbed in. She set the water on cool, letting it spray on her face and soak her hair. She leaned against the wall and closed her eyes.

Jack peered into the living room dimly lit by the kitchen light. He saw a lamp and flipped it on. The room was nice and homey. Maddy had it split into an area for watching television and another sitting area that appeared to be for maybe reading, but that part didn't appear to get much use. A large, inviting, brown overstuff couch was in the center of the room, a cherry end table, which the lamp sat on was on one end, matching coffee table in front. A matching love seat was tucked away in a corner, the other matching end table and lamp beside it. He flipped on the other lamp. Along one wall was a huge matching cherry entertainment center that housed a 42" flat screen TV. The shelves above it were lined with knick-knacks of horses and a few framed photos. One was a silver 8x10 of two children. They were sitting on some steps of a building both with their arms wrapped around what appeared to be a brown border collie. The girl had straight reddish brown hair that framed her face and deep brown eyes. She looked to be around seven years old. The little boy was had wavy brown hair and brown eyes and appeared to be around three. Both were smiling sheepishly at the camera. More pictures of the two kids at younger ages also adorned the center. He heard the water turn off and quickly sat on the couch and flipped on the TV.

Maddy came out of the bathroom rubbing a towel vigorously through her hair. She threw the towel back in the bathroom. She grabbed a glass from the cupboard, went to the fridge and filled it with cold water. She brought the blue packet to her mouth and ripped it with her teeth. She was standing in the kitchen doorway when she dropped in the two large tablets. They plopped in the water and began to fizz.

"You must like throwing up if you're going to drink that," Jack commented.

She swished the liquid around in the glass mixing it thoroughly then downed it. "At least there would be something to come up." She observed Jack sitting on the couch. He had kicked off his shoes at the door. His jacket was draped over one of the kitchen chairs, wet she assumed. He was sitting on the couch with Jack draped across his lap and Rufus perched behind him on the back of the couch. Damn dog. Jack had slipped off his tie and placed it on the coffee table. His shirt was unbuttoned half way down his chest. She sucked in a quick breath. "You look...em...comfy." Then to the dogs, "Jack, Rufus, down. You're all wet."

Both dogs jumped to the floor.

"Jack? Should I be honored or insulted?" he asked with a smile spreading across his face.

Maddy sat down on the opposite end of the couch. "Don't flatter yourself. His name is Captain Jack Sparrow. It was already on his papers when I bought him. Now if you looked like Johnny Depp..." she grinned, "that's a different story."

"Where'd you get him?" He was making light conversation, avoiding what they needed to talk about.

She slumped down letting the couch swallow her and propped her feet on the coffee table. "I bought him at a garage sale."

"A garage sale? You're kidding."

"Nope...Okay Jack, I realize I am not exactly thinking clearly, but I would feel more comfortable if we cleared the air about today."

Jack muted the TV and sat quietly, as mute as the TV.

Okay, she would go first. "What I did today was far beyond out of line. I don't have an excuse. I am truly sorry and hope that I haven't destroyed our relationship." She waited for a reaction.

Jack leaned forward and ran his fingers through his hair, something he did when he was uncomfortable. "Listen Maddy, I am not going to lie to you and tell I wasn't thoroughly pissed at you. We won't go over that I did give you a direct order. But I got a total ass chewing by the Captain. I was totally humiliated in front of the DCI. Some day I had hoped to make into the DCI. Now I wonder if this incident will follow me. I went from being the lead detective on this case to just another officer." He was quiet for a long moment. "Maddy you won't be able to tag along to crimes scenes anymore. At least not for a long time. I have been given strict orders."

Maddy felt tears stinging her eyes. No, she would not cry. "I understand," her voice quivered. She turned and looked away from Jack so he couldn't see her face.

Jack reached out and took Maddy's hand. "That doesn't mean I won't be a source of information and get you what you need for stories. You'll still be able to do your own investigating. Its not like you use that much from me anyhow. I am just an anchor point."

The room was silent for a couple of minutes. Maddy still wouldn't look at him.

"I wasn't going to tell you this Maddy, but I will do so in good faith. I don't want to discuss what I am going to tell you, just give you the info. Is that understood?"

She nodded.

"The woman in the grave is Miranda Mitchell. She is 28 and disappeared from her home in North Sioux. Her last visual was at her home 20 days ago. I will send you what I can get on Monday."

"Thank you," she murmured.

"There is something else. We found another grave about a hundred yards from the first sight. The body appears to be buried the same way. We haven't ID'ed her yet. I think we are looking at a serial killer, Maddy. And because the crime has crossed state lines, the FBI will be in on Monday. Now remember, no discussion, okay?"

Maddy took it all in. She had so many questions but she wouldn't ask. Not tonight. "Okay."

Maddy chewed on her nails, her eyes focusing on the silent TV. Her eyes were full of tears but as long she didn't blink they would stay put. Jack still held her hand in his. He tugged on it, "Come here Maddy."

She pulled away and rose to her feet moving to stand by a large picture window that was in the sitting area. Lighting flashed illuminating the sky and thunder rumbled in the distance. Jack stood behind her wrapping his arms around her and kissed the top of her head. "No more work talk okay?" Her body shook in his arms. He spoke into her hair; she could feel his breath on her skin. "I'm sorry, Maddy. I never meant to hurt you."

She reached up and wiped her cheeks with the back of her hand. "You didn't do anything, you don't need be sorry. Everything that has been done is of my own doing." She leaned back against his chest feeling comfort in it.

"Maddy, how come we just don't hang out together?" He felt her body go rigid. "Relax, lets go sit on the couch." He led her to it and they both sat down. He put his arm behind her but did not rest it on her shoulders.

"My worlds need to stay separate—career—personal. I have to have it that way," she spoke softly.

"And I am career to you?"

She cleared her throat. "I...I don't know. We haven't worked a case in a couple of months. We hardly seen each other, only touched base. Seem like no big deal, we've always been like that. Now this time...we've been working this case for two days and look at us. Something just feels different. I don't know who's sending more mixed messages, you or me. You have less patience with me. Am I that much worse? And here we are, in my home, my sanctuary."

"And that makes you uncomfortable?"

She looked up at him, "A little."

She stretched over to give him a kiss on the cheek, he turned his face at the moment and she caught him at the corner of his mouth. She blushed, "Whoops, bad aim," she laughed nervously.

He shifted his body so he could face her better. "Let's see if we can fix that." He leaned forward until his lips ever so softly touched hers. They lingered. She was surprised how soft they were yet they had a sense of command about them. Her breath caught in her chest, her heart was pounding erratically. He pulled away. He cupped his hands around her face and searched her eyes for what she was feeling. She saw the sparkling gold flecks in his. "Do I scare you Maddy?"

This time she leaned in to him and kissed him, softly at first and then deepening, he matched her passion. He ran his fingers through her long hair; she wrapped her arms around his neck pulling him nearer. The kiss seemed to go on forever, yet not long enough. They parted lips and he pulled her into his arms. "You didn't answer me, do I scare you?"

"More then you know. You understand I can't give you what you want? I can't give you a romantic relationship. I can't give emotionally what I don't have to give. If I could, believe me Jack you would be right there in front. Can you be my friend, my best friend?" she searched his eyes for the answer.

He leaned forward and kissed her forehead, "Your very special best friend. As I told you today, I will be whatever it is you need me to be." Then he kissed her again lightly. "You need to get some sleep."

She showed him the guest room and went off to her own room. The alcohol was still filtering through her system. She began to wonder if tonight even happened. She slipped between the sheets and drifted off to sleep.

Early morning birds and the sound of two pups barking woke Maddy up from her slumber. She open one eye, rolled over and put the pillow over her head. Her head felt like it was splitting. She could still here Rufus and Jack barking outside. What the hell? What were they doing outside? Slowly the memory of last night began to seep back into her brain. The bar, Randy, Jack...Shit! Jack! She shot out of bed and ran across the hall to the spare bedroom. It was empty, bed made nice and neat. She could have sworn he spent the night here. How drunk had she been?

She padded to the kitchen and noticed the backdoor was open up to the screen door. She peered through the screen and her heart skipped a beat. Jack was sitting on the steps, his back turned away from her. His broad shoulders were framed in a nice snug white t-shirt, which also accented his nicely muscled tan arms. His hair was all wavy, not the smooth comb she usually saw. He was taking turns throwing toys to the boys.

The kiss...she touched her lips. Did it really happen? She wasn't going to bring it up.

She filled two glasses with orange juice, stopped to grab a couple of aspirin, and pushed the screen door open with her knee. Jack looked up and smiled and moved out of her way. She handed him one glass and then sat down beside him. She popped the pills in her mouth and took a gulp of juice.

After Jack took the glass from her he took a sip. "Got a headache Maddy?"

She threw him a dirty look, "Well duh."

He set the glass down and leaned back with his right arm behind her. "Would you like me to go cook you some bacon and eggs?"

She choked on her juice and sent it spraying from her mouth. She jabbed him with her elbow. "Asshole!"

He threw his head back and laughed, "Damn, the language you use. Such a lady!"

She smiled despite the throbbing in her temples. "So unlike Barbie huh?

Puzzled he glanced at her. "Barbie?"

She nudged him with her knee. "Stella, silly. I bet a swear word has never passed her sweet perfectly shaped lips...unless she's one of those weird chicks that likes to talk dirty in bed." She teased.

"Let's just say she doesn't have quite the handle on the English language as you do. Why do you call her Barbie?"

She looked at him in disbelief. "You're kidding right?"

"No, really, why do you call her that?"

Maddy took another swallow of juice. "Oh come on, she's your girlfriend. She's perfect, pretty, nice body, perfectly cultured. She will make the perfect up and coming DCI agent's wife. She's respectable." She glanced over at him. He was looking off into the distance. She knew he heard her. "Open mouth, insert foot. Seems more and more lately the more I say, the worse I sound. I'm sorry. I'm sure she's very nice, otherwise you wouldn't be with her."

Jack whistled and patted his hands on his knees. Captain Jack and Rufus tore across the yard. He quickly picked up a small squeaky toy and gave it a toss. Rufus got to the little mouse first and Jack grabbed him by the ear and took off.

"We need to quit apologizing to each other all the time. We think what we think. Saying sorry doesn't make it so." Jack picked up his pack of cigarettes from beside him and took one out and lit it. He held the pack out to her and when she pulled back he laughed. "Glad to see that nasty habit was short lived."

"About Stella," he took a puff, "We've been dating for a couple of months. She's all right. She fun to hang out with, athletic, likes a lot of culture. She's not crazy like you," he laughed.

"Not like me..." she said softly.

"It wasn't an insult. You are just two totally different women."

"Jack, you don't have to explain yourself to me. You have a life without me and that's okay. No worries," she smiled weakly. "When do you want me to bring you back to the city?"

He snuffed out his cigarette and set the butt beside his foot. "You don't have to. My brother Rick and his family are going to the lakes. He's going to swing by Stella's and pick up my car and drop it off here...if that's okay with you?"

"I guess. Stella's really going to love that. Her disdain for me was very apparent. Now she's going to know you spent the night here."

He shrugged. "She'll get over it and if not...tough."

They sat quietly for a few moments. Maddy glanced over at him. He appeared to be taking in his surroundings. She was so used her acreage she didn't give it much thought, so she tried to look at it from his perspective. "I have the best view of the world from right here on these steps. I see the best sunsets every day of the year; I can watch an upcoming storm from here because of the clear view to the west. Seen some really spectacular thunderstorms. I can watch the horses run and kick up. Like I said, this is my sanctuary."

"You really do have a fantastic home. You're lucky. It's peaceful and cutoff from everything...especially the ugliness. I can kind of understand why you want to keep it all to your self." Jack smiled and put his hand on Maddy's leg. "By the way, I went down and fed your horses. Might not have been the right amount. They looked pretty happy so I am sure it was too much."

"I'm sure it's fine. Thank you." She put her hand over his and gave it a soft squeeze. "What would you say if I told you that you are the only person from *that* world that has ever been here?"

"I'm honored."

She kicked him with her toe, "Don't be, you weren't invited and was out of necessity."

"Can I ask you a favor?"

"Maybe."

"Can I spend the rest of this weekend here....with you?"

"Why?"

"It's away from the city, away from what happened this past week, and what will happen next week. But most of all, I want to be with you. I want to be with Maddy, the woman, not Maddy, the reporter." He searched her face.

Maddy carefully considered his request. It was totally against her rules. But she wanted to be with him too, away from work and all the rules of having to put up fronts. It would be nice to be able to talk to each other without having to be careful who was listening or watching. "Say I agree to this. You have to agree to some things."

"Okay."

"We take this time to just enjoy each other's company. Don't interrogate me. In other words don't ask me personal questions about my past. I reserve the right to remain silent. If I want you to know something, I will tell you. Please don't think I am saying this to be bitchy, but my privacy is sacred to me and I am not going to tell you why...Oh yeah, and no sex."

"Damn!" he snapped his fingers together. "That was the deal breaker."

Maddy felt his eyes bearing into her. "Go a head and ask, doesn't mean I'm going to tell you."

"I don't want to break the rules right off the bat," he laughed. "Its just odd. I have known you all this time. I always got the impression you were like this open book, what you see is what you get. I mean you are smart, witty, wonderful sense of humor; your powers of observation are amazing. I thought that was the whole package. Now after two years I am discovering there is a whole different part of you I didn't know existed. But you don't want anyone to know. I pick up fear when that gets threatened, but I won't analyze you and won't pry." He waited for the shoe to drop. "Well...what are you thinking?"

She shook her head, "Major, major mistake...you really blew it now..." she brought his fingers to her lips, "You forgot to say sexy!" and she bit him playfully.

He grabbed her and put her in a headlock.

"Hey! Hey! Watch the head!"

Jack loosened his hold and pulled her face toward him. Before she knew it their lips were locked. Her hand came to rest on his chest. She could feel his heart beating beneath the soft cotton. His tongue parted her lips and the kiss deepened. Desire and fear is what she felt. She pulled away..."Whoa there. That's not a friendly kiss."

"I just wanted to show you I don't have to tell you I think you are sexy."

Maddy rose to her feet. "Behave. Well Detective, just because you are taking the weekend *off* doesn't mean I am. I have work to do."

"Oh for the paper?"

She laughed, "No, this place doesn't keep its stellar looks by itself. I need to go get dressed. You can tag along or you can be a couch potato." She did the once over on how he was dressed. "You can't help me dressed like that, what are you going to do for clothes?"

He grabbed his cell and made a quick call to his brother and asked him to pick of some clothes and toiletries from his house.

His brother Rick arrived a little over an hour later dropping off Jack's car and a bag for the weekend. Maddy stayed in the house and watched through the bathroom window. Jack had wanted her to come out and meet his brother and his family but she refused. She told him that was more personal than she was prepared to get. He just shrugged his shoulders and said okay.

She could see the likeness in their faces between the two brothers but that is where it ended. Rick was obviously older, maybe a little taller, but his stature was smaller. His hair had a hint of gray around the temples and he wore wire-rimmed glasses. Purely white collar, guessing an accountant or finance officer. The two men chatted for a while and as they did two kids, 8 to 10 years old got out and ran around the car. Rick and Jack gave each other hug then Rick said something to the kids, they got in the car and left.

Maddy had changed into blue jeans and a sleeveless t-shirt. She had pulled her hair back into a ponytail, took a baseball cap and pulled the tail through the opening in the back.

Jack also changed in to jeans and a red t-shirt then slipped into a pair of sneakers. She eyed him up and down and nodded in approval. She thought he was sexy in a suit, but it had nothing on blue jeans and a tight t-shirt.

They spent a good part of the day mucking stalls, moving bales, grooming the horses and checking for injuries. Maddy took her yearling into the round pen and worked him while Jack watched. He enjoyed seeing her communicate with the animal. She controlled the bay with subtle body language, the horse eager to please her. When she stood still the horse would stop whatever he was doing, turn to face her, then come to her and lick her hand when she reached out to him. Jack was impressed.

They had just finished up a light lunch and was returning outside. While they were inside the sky had grown dark and sound of thunder could be heard in the distance. Maddy pulled Jack down with her to sit on the steps and watch the storm roll in. Her senses felt electrified by the tension of the stillness of the air.

"Maybe we should head in," Jack started to rise.

She grabbed his arm, "No...not yet, come on you gotta feel this." The air temperature dropped, a dull roar could be heard coming closer. She saw the trees to the southwest begin to whip in the wind, which quickly washed over them. Seconds later a sheet of rain cut loose and drenched them. "Okay," she stood and grabbed the door handle, "now!"

While Jack was taking a shower Maddy prepared a meatloaf for supper and stuck it in the fridge until cooking time. She wrapped a couple of potatoes for baking and set them on the counter. She poured two glasses of tea and set them on the table and waited for Jack.

When Jack opened the bathroom door he was shirtless with a towel wrapped around his neck. He was wearing a pair of sweat pants and was shoeless. "Put a shirt on," she commented. He stood and gave her a questioning look. She laughed, "You can't walk around like that, I'm only human."

He stood over her and wrapped the towel around her and was going to kiss her when he felt a sharp piercing on his ankle. "What the hell?"

Rufus had a mouthful of Jack's sweat pants viciously attacking him. Jack kicked him back and the dog lost contact but was back growling, barking and biting. Maddy grabbed him and quickly threw him in the bathroom and shut the door.

When she came back Jack was sitting on a chair eying the little puncture wounds Rufus had left on him. She slipped back in the bathroom trying to keep Rufus from escaping. She grabbed the first aid kit and slipped back out. Rufus continued to scratch and bark at the door.

"I don't understand, he's been around you all weekend and seemed fine." She dapped peroxide on his ankle. "Superficial, you'll survive."

"Maybe he suffers from split personality." He took a few band-aids and applied the to the little tears. He glanced at the bathroom door. Rufus could be heard growling, scratching and barking, but it wasn't at the door.

Maddy cracked the door and looked in. Rufus had crawled in Jack's bag and was going to town ripping into things. She threw a towel over him and picked him up. She carried him out of the bathroom and to her bedroom and closed the door. When she unwrapped him he was panting heavily and was shaking. She rubbed him on his shoulders and he slowly calmed down. Soon he was licking her face. She poked her head out and called Jack, the dog, and shut them both in her room.

She returned to the kitchen. "I need you to go back in and take another shower. This time don't put on any aftershave or cologne."

"Why?"

"Just do it."

Fifteen minutes later he came back out of the shower. Maddy went over and sniffed him. Zest soap. Perfect. She went in and grabbed his bag and set it in the spare room, then let the dogs out of her room. She scooped Rufus up and brought him out to the kitchen. When she held him out to Jack he moved back. "What the hell are you doing? You want him to rip off my face next."

She stuck Rufus's face up to Jack's. The dog began to lick him vigorously. Jack took the dog, a little cautious at first, but when the pup responded with affection he relaxed.

Maddy sat down beside him. "You stunk."

"Huh?"

"It was never you he was reacting too. It's your cologne."

"How do you know?"

"When I checked on him in the bathroom he was attacking your bag. You were wearing that scent on Thursday at Vanessa's house, but not last night, not until after the first shower."

"Yeah but he didn't have that strong of reaction to me on Thursday."

"The scent wasn't as strong. You know what I think? I think the person who abducted Vanessa wears this scent. I think he must have hurt her or threaten her, thus threatening Rufus and he got protective. So now he associates that scent with the event."

"The dog goes nuts at the smell of Polo. Amazing...kind of out there, but nonetheless amazing. Now if Rufus could just tell when and what happened we'd have something."

"She was abducted Tuesday night, sometime after 6:15."

"How do you know?"

"The last activity on her cell was at 6:15. She placed a call to Trinity 1st Reform Church. The activity started again when Sandy was looking for her."

"And you know this how?"

She took a gulp of her tea. "I pulled her cell phone records."

Jack gave a sigh and scratched the back of his head. "I'm not going to ask... until Monday.

Things were a little awkward between them for the remainder of the day and they were careful not to talk about the case. That was the deal. After a quiet supper, they curled up on the couch together, watched a movie and fell asleep.

The ring of Jack's cell phone startled them awake Sunday morning. Maddy moved so he could get up. He looked at the caller Id. "Shit, it's Stella."

She started to get up; Jack grabbed her and sat her back down. "Don't you want some privacy?"

"No," then he answered the phone. "Hello?"

The volume on his phone was pretty high; she could hear both sides of the conversation. Cool.

"Where are you? I thought you were coming over last night," she heard Stella ask Jack.

"I decided to get away for the weekend. I needed a break," Jack replied calmly.

"I could have come with you. I won't get see you hardly at all come Monday." Maddy cringed at the sound of Stella's whinny voice.

"No, Sweetie, I just need some space from the city." Sweetie?....eeeew.

"You were fine Friday night. This is because of her isn't? Are you with her?"

Maddy held her breath to see what he would say.

"Yes," Jack told Stella without an ounce of hesitation.

"You've been with her since you left here? That's why your brother picked up your car?"

"Yes Stella. We'll talk about it when I get back."

"Fuck off!" Phone went dead.

Jack clicked the phone shut. His cheeks filled with air and he slowly blew it out. "Well....that went well don't you think?"

Maddy looked down at her hands trying to suppress a smile. "Guess that depends on your perspective." She threw him a quick glance. "You okay?"

He flicked her with his fingers, "Quit pretending you didn't enjoy that."

She covered her mouth with her hand and then scratched her chin, "Well... actually..."

"You are one cruel bitch!" he feigned disbelief.

"Oh come on," she laughed. "You could have lied to her and your credibility would have remained intact."

"Listen to you," he shook his head, "credibility doesn't come from lying."

"It does if you know what you're doing."

Jack leaned forward and put his head in his hands. "I don't want to know if you have practice that with me. I like to think I am an honest person. Anyhow, either Stella will get over it or she won't. Being here with you this weekend has given me a lot of insight as to what does make me happy, and honestly, being with Stella doesn't." He smiled, "That was kind of fun."

Jack's phone went off again. He looked down at it and answered as he got off the couch. He went in the kitchen and made sure he was out of earshot. Maddy couldn't hear anything but Jack's muffled voice. His tone sounded serious. Must be work. She knew he was going to have to leave earlier than expected, but she also knew that came with the territory.

She got up and stretched then she folded up the throws they had covered up with the night before. Jack came back into the room with a frown on his face. Maddy wrapped her arms around him, stood on her tiptoes and give him a kiss on the cheek. "You don't have to say a word."

"FBI will be here this afternoon. The Captain wants me to help get things organized. Autopsies are back and forensics is back. So the grunt work begins." He hugged her and buried his face in her hair taking in the smell of her.

"You ever work a case this big?

"Nope."

She hugged him tighter. "Then don't look at it that you are going to be their grunt. Look at as a learning experience. And it's exciting hon, you'll be right there in the midst of the investigation. I'd kill to be there." She poked him in the ribs and he jumped. "You'll be running with the big dogs, Babe!"

While Jack was getting his things together, Maddy let the dogs out and made a pot of coffee. She took a travel cup out of the cupboard and filled it. Jack came out with his bag looking like a lost pup. "Oh Honey," she hugged him and gave him a kiss. "It can't be that bad can it?"

He kissed her forehead. "No I guess not."

She handed him the travel cup and he smiled. "It's been great being here with you this weekend." His hand caressed her cheek and his lips softly brushed hers. "I probably won't see you tomorrow, but it's not for lack of wanting to. I'll give you call though."

"You do whatever it is you need to do. I will be there when you need me."

They walked out to his car together, hugged again, and then Jack left. She felt lonely already, and that was not a good thing. She didn't like nor want to feel the need to be with someone. Allowing Jack to get this close to her this weekend was a mistake, but it was one she would make all over again.

She busied herself for the rest of the day doing laundry and cleaning her house.

At 8:00 she decided to call it an early night. She had showered, let the dogs in and was just locking the door when her cell went off. She grabbed it off the table and looked at the ID. "Caller ID blocked." That was odd. She answered, "Hello?"

"Hello Minnie." She dropped the phone, sunk to the floor and sobbed.

4

Maddy's hand was visibly shaking as she poured the hot, strong coffee into her travel mug. She didn't sleep well. Her mind kept returning to the phone call. Why did he call her now? Two years without hearing a word, why now? She needed to detach. This man from her past could no longer control her. He destroyed her once before because she let him and she's be damned if she would let him do it again. She let the dogs out and hit the road.

Normally she would be planning her day, but she didn't want to think so she popped in a CD and turned it up loud enough that it drowned out her thoughts.

Maddy pulled her office keys out and was about unlock her door when the Chief popped out of his office and flagged her over. Now what? He waited at his door, ushered her in and shut the door behind them. He sat down behind his desk and motioned for her to do the same. There was no smile to greet her. "What's going on?" she asked tentatively.

He picked up a thick, bounded package from off his desk and gave it to her. "This was delivered by a police courier. You are to take it back to your office and study it. A car will be here at 11:00 to pick you up."

She nervously fingered the string on the package. She recognized the type of package. It was a crime packet. "I don't get it, it doesn't make sense. Yesterday I got escorted from a crime scene now they want me to look at it?"

Chief shrugged, "Well evidently they want something from you. Use it to your advantage."

Maddy returned to her office and opened the packet. She cleared her desk of all items and then dumped the contents on its surface. Among the contents were many photos, autopsy reports with attached photos, and crime reports. What the hell? First she grabbed the photos. These were shots of the burial finds from Friday. She spread them out in front of her. They were clipped together by victim. She picked up the first, identified as 28 year old Miranda Mitchell. The body—head to toe, was wrapped in thin gauze like material (what she had seen Friday). The body was placed directly in the ground face up. The next picture the gauze had been cut aside. The woman was dressed in what appeared to be an ivory colored frock. Blood, although not excessive, stained the front from her neck to her abdomen. What struck Maddy was the way she was posed. Her arms were crossed and her hands overlapped just below her sternum, and wrapped around her hands...a rosary. Whoa! She looked over the other photos of the grave scene. She resorted both sets of photos to do a comparison of the two gravesites. They were duplicates with the exception of the rate of decomposition. Mitchell disappeared just under three weeks ago. Her body was still fleshy despite insect activity. The unidentified body was badly decomposed. Although still fleshy, decomp was in an more advanced stage than Mitchell's which could put her demise a few weeks prior to Mitchell's. Decomp stage could put Jane Doe's TOD in Cynthia's range but based on body build and hair color it was ruled out.

She then grabbed the autopsy reports and photos. Maddy studied Mitchell's report first since it had the freshest details. She took out the photo of the body prior to the corner's first incision. The first thing that caught her eye was the deep gash across the woman's throat. Okay, her throat had been slit. An incision had been made vertically from the above her breastbone to just above the point where her rib cage ended. Another lateral incision cut just above the breast line intersecting near the heart. Coincidence or planned? Red lines were present around her neck (below the slash), around each wrist and each ankle. Little red gashes ran along the lines. Ligature marks.

She reached for the autopsy report. Cause of death, exsanguination, she bled out due severing the jugular vein, carotid artery, and trachea. That was one hell of a deep cut. The thoracic incisions were ante mortem as were the ligature injuries. Based on the lividity she had been moved. She had been deceased approximately two to three weeks.

Victim Jane Doe revealed like injuries and same cause of death. Approximate time of death somewhere around six to eight weeks. She was victim number one unless another body turned up.

Mitchell had disappeared in the same manner as Cynthia and Vanessa. She was reported missing within 48 hours of her last known contact. The relevance of disappearance with the two missing women was never brought to light.

A search through missing persons was in the process hoping to turn up the identity of Jane Doe.

Maddy jumped when she heard a knock on the door. She looked up. There was a young man dressed in a black suit standing patiently in front of it. He had short, cropped red hair, pale complexion and a splash of freckles. Just a babe in the woods. She jotted down the last of her findings and closed her pad.

Maddy poked her head out, "Can I help you?"

"Miss Sheridan, I have been sent here to pick you up and bring you back to police headquarters," he said straight-faced. He reminded her of a guard at Buckingham Palace.

"By who?"

He didn't answer, just stood looking like a mannequin for a men's clothing store. She gathered the materials she had spread out on her desk and put them back in the packet. She grabbed her bag and followed the guy out of the building. He led her to a black Suburban and opened the passenger side door for her. She got in and buckled herself in. She turned to the guy and studied him; he acted like she wasn't there. "You act more like secret service than FBI," she stated flatly. "What's your name?"

"Agent Andrew Whittmer."

"What do you guys want with me?"

"Your guess is as good as mine. I'm just following orders of the Special Supervisory Agent." He put the vehicle in gear and drove off.

"And who would that be?"

"You'll find out soon enough. Why do you ask so many question?"

Maddy shot him a look of disbelief, "Well duh, Sherlock. I'm a reporter, that's my job."

They rode the rest the way in silence. When he pulled into the parking area Agent Whittmer turned to her, "I've known you a very short time, but I pride myself on being and good judge of character. I don't care for you. You are cocky and a smart ass and I don't know what the hell you are doing with this investigation. But who am I to question a commanding officer?"

"Wow, astute and obedient," she smirked as she pushed past him.

Whittmer caught up with her. "Follow me," he said coldly. He led her upstairs to one of the interrogation rooms, which puzzled her breifly until a different guy brought in some paper work for her to sign. It was a waiver of confidentiality. It was to secure her silence so that she couldn't use anything she learned from this meeting or any subsequent meeting pertaining to this investigation in the course of her employment at the newspaper. Damn, this was crippling, but what could she do? She signed—the chief was going to kill her.

Maddy was given a visitor's badge then led to the briefing room where she took a seat as far back as she could. She was really uncomfortable with this situation. She did not like interaction with the FBI; with past experience it was not something she felt it could mean anything good for her. She sat quietly as members of the SC police force filtered in, one of them being Jack.

Jack walked past her and then turned and did a double take. "Maddy? What are you doing here?"

She was fidgeting with the corners of her crime packet. "The FBI drug me in here." She looked up at Jack and pleaded, "Jack, I don't want to be here. Can't you get me out of here?"

He lightly touched her hand, "Sorry Mads, I can't help you. It's not my ball game anymore."

She had such a foreboding feeling about this. Her past was coming back to bite her in the ass. She looked up at him. "Jack, you need to distance yourself from me...please?"

He looked confused but didn't question her. He went and sat on the opposite side of the room.

After about five minutes the room filled in with some uniformed officers, a handful of detectives, DCI and 5 FBI agents, one of those being Whittmer, the toad, she thought. The room was filled with muffled voices and she got more than one wondering glance. The voices quieted down when Jack's captain came with another man, another FBI agent.

When Maddy saw the man, she recognized him and gasped. She closed her eyes and looked away. "Lord, you cannot be so cruel," she said silently to herself.

The Captain introduced the man as SSA Bryan Mayland. He would be heading up the investigation and everyone working the case would ultimately be answering to him.

Mayland welcomed everyone, gave some background on himself, his team and their experience with serial abductions. Three of the agents were from the local field office out of Omaha. The remainder, she assumed came straight from Quantico. He would brief everyone on the basics of the case then meet with the detectives working on the case.

Maddy tuned out the briefing. She probably knew more than they did anyhow. It was Mayland that had her attention, not what he was saying but what the hell was he doing there. Mayland, or rather Bryan was the man who called her last night. Ten years ago, they had been lovers; ten years ago he left her to go back to his wife so he could be with his stepson. Nine years ago she found out he had a mistress along with his wife. Two years ago he surprised her with a phone call which rekindled feelings she thought were long dead. Two years ago his mistress found out he was having a long distance love affair with her and gave him an ultimatum. Two years ago he chose the mistress and didn't even have the decency or respect to tell her. The mistress did and told her not text him nor call him ever again. She hadn't heard a word from him until last night. He destroyed her twice; it would be a cold day in hell before he would do it again. That was their history in a nutshell.

She studied him. Ten years had not been kind to him. He was a tall man, about 6'1", his dark hair was thinning and was graying at the temples. He wore wire-rimmed glasses, which vaguely hid pale hazel eyes. She could see shadows beneath his eyes and his face was slightly flushed, evidence to her he was still drinking? He was a little heavier through the middle, middle age spread or more evidence of the alcohol, she didn't know. Once he had been handsome, charming, sweet, sexy, protective, supportive, her knight in shining armor...once. She closed her eyes and listened to his voice. She loved his voice. It was deep...and sexy. It could be soothing to her, erotic, or cuttingly cruel. Like him.

She was brought out of her revere by the sound of moving chairs. The non-essentials were being asked to leave. She got up and moved for the doorway. She was about to slip out and make a run for it when she heard Bryan's booming voice. "Sheridan, stay." Damn! Man what was it with men commanding her like a dog!

He asked everyone to move to the front part of the room and to take out their crime packets. Maddy followed his instructions.

"Everyone has had ample time to study your packets," Bryan walked back and forth in front of them. He was observing them, sizing them up. She knew the game. She sat there staring at him, her arms crossed, her chin pushed out in defiance.

He stopped in front of Detection Johnson, a co-worker of Jack's. "Tell me what you see Detective." So they guy told him, what he visually saw—two dead women, mutilated.

Next he stopped in front of Jack. "The victims have been bounded, tortured and killed perhaps part of some ritual. More than likely the abductions were planned ahead, he targets single woman between the ages of 25 and 35. There's no evidence of sexual assault. Tox screens aren't back yet so we don't know if they were drugged. At the current time I would say what we have is inconclusive to have an accurate reading on what's going on here."

Maddy secretly smiled. Not bad Jack, not bad. Not quite what he was looking for but you did well.

She was on to his game. Bryan loved power; he loved control. He was asserting his control by showing how inexperience or incompetent those below him were.

He was standing in front of her now—she could feel him. "Sheridan?"

She looked up at him, all wide-eyed and innocent. "What?'

"Let's get your read?"

"My read, Agent Mayland?" she held her voice steady. "I'm not a cop, just a lowly reporter."

Jack coughed, she glanced at him and he discretely shook his head no. Sorry Jack, this is one I do know how to handle. She winked at him.

She looked back at Bryan, he saw the exchange between her and Jack. She looked past him. Maddy flinched when Bryan slammed his hand down on the desk in front of her. He leaned down so his face was just inches from hers, his voice low, "Don't fuck with me, Maddy." He stood back up and said, "Now let's try this again, Miss Sheridan. Let's just pretend you know what you're doing."

"Asshole," she hissed. She took out the two autopsy photos and the two-gravesite photos, took a deep breath and begun, "The COD of both vic was exsanguination. The vertical and horizontal lacerations were antemordem and suggests torture. The vics were bound with something jagged and sharp, perhaps razor wire. The slitting of the throat was climatic.

The torturing suggest that the unsub is a sexual sadist. It's not the torturing that gets him off, but it is the suffering of the victim that is sexually arousing." She paused at looked directly at Mayland. "There is no greater power over another person than that of inflicting pain on her to force her to undergo suffering without her being able to defend herself."

She looked back down at her packet, "The unsub selects his victims. Based on what we know so far, all the victims were taken from their homes, no sign of forced entry, which suggests the victims know the unsub. His victim of choice, so far, is Caucasian, single, female, between 110—140 lbs, between the ages of 25-35. Hair color and body build are not factor, nor is their occupation or education.

He is of the organized dichotomy. The crimes are premeditated and carefully planned. He is antisocial but knows right from wrong, is not insane and shows no remorse. He has advanced social skills, plans his crimes, displays control over his victim using those social skills, leaves little forensic evidence or clues, and often engages in sexual acts (in this case the torturing) with the victim before the murder.

When he is finished with the victims, he doesn't just dump the body, but gives them a burial. He cleans them and dresses them for burial. Before he lowers them into the grave he lines it with gauze. Once in the graves, he poses the body." She held up one of the grave photos. "He crossed their arms and wraps a rosary around their hands which leads me to believe there is a religious factor going here. He then wraps the material around them and covers them with dirt. All this is contingent that these cases are connected."

She stacked the photos up in a pile then looked up at Bryan. "Does that satisfy your morbid curiosity?"

Bryan was leaning against the wall. A slow smile spread across his face. "Its nice to see you haven't thrown away all your skills." Then he turned to talk to the room. "I hope all were taking notes. Miss Sheridan's profile on our unsub is close except she left out he is male, Caucasian between the ages 35-45."

Maddy felt every eye on her. God what they must think of her, she sounded like a textbook. It had been a long time since she had to do a profile, but not long enough. That was the part of her life that was dead to her. Damn him. The mind fuck had begun. He would unnerve her, find a weakness and then go in for the kill. Talk about a sadist.

Now she was pissed, hell what did she have to loose? "Mayland," he turned to face her. "Now that I have performed for your little dog and pony show, its my turn. Why in the hell did you bring me down here? To humiliate me? Didn't work, did it? I have nothing to do with any of this. I'm a reporter, not a cop. You could have just as well called on any of your FBI minions," she waved her hand in their direction. "That's their job, that's what they get paid to do." She stood up and grabbed her bag and her packet.

Bryan grabbed her by the arm, "This is who you are Maddy. It's in your blood, you can't hide what your are."

"Fuck you!" She jerked her arm away from him and walked out the door.

Her heart was racing, her blood was boiling and she needed to get away from him. Maddy heard foot steps running up behind her. Thinking it was Bryan, she quickened her steps. A hand touched her shoulder and she turned, and struck out her fist striking out against her pursuer's face. "Jesus Maddy!" Jack caught her hand in midair.

He braced her up against the wall, her chest was heaving, and her nostrils were flaring. "Jack, the smartest thing you could do right now is to stay away from me, as far as you can. Please, I don't want you to get hurt, please. Go back; don't let him connect you with me. Don't give him any ammunition." Panic rose within her.

"Hurt me? He's not going to hurt me. Maddy what the hell is going on here? How do you know that guy? How does he know you? And that...that...profile..."

he was looking at her in disbelief. "FBI? You? Who are you? Do I even know you at all?"

She touched his cheek and searched his eyes wishing she could give him all the answers. "Go back to the room Jack. I really need to get out of here..." She slid past him and ran to the elevator.

"Maddy..." he called after her.

Since she had no ride back to the Journal, Maddy rode the bus. It was a humbling experience but it beat hoofing it. She bypassed her office and went straight to the Chief. She didn't knock, just barged in and shut the door behind her. She threw the crime packet on his desk and sat in the chair across from him. Chief was flipping a pencil between his fingers calmly waiting on Maddy.

She started biting her nails. That seemed to happening a lot lately. They were comfortable in their silence for a few minutes when Maddy finally broke it. "How much do you really know about me?"

"More than you think I do, but I respect your right to do what you had to do to survive both emotionally and mentally. This guy from the FBI...I take it you worked with him."

She nodded, "For a few years. Bryan Mayland. He's dangerous to me."

"Physically?"

"No, maybe dangerous is the wrong word, toxic is more like it. Don't get me wrong; he is very good at his job. It's the predator in him. He gets immersed in the hunt, feeds on it. It just seems he has this sick need to prey on me. I finally feel like I have escaped him. Years go by and boom, there he is. He tears me down until I'm broken and then he's gone, leaving me in this pile of rubble." She thought for a moment. "He made me profile the kidnapper in front of the other agents, the detectives....Jack. Why?"

"To expose you, essentially blow your cover, to show you that no matter where you've gone, who you've become, he can bring you right back to where he wants you."

"Yeah, I guess."

Chief picked up the crime packet, "So how'd ya do?"

She smiled and laughed weakly, "Little sloppy and disorganized but for not doing it for 7 years, pretty damn good."

"How'd you get out with this?" he patted the packet.

"Caused a scene and cut and ran. Can't use it though, had to sign a confidentially agreement."

"Good way to keep you off the story. Maybe it's for the best. You got vacation time coming. Perhaps you should go see your sister in Houston, get out of here and keep you safe 'til this all blows over."

"No fucking way! I don't need what's in there, besides I got it committed to memory. I can do my own digging, my own investigation. When the story breaks, I'm breaking it. This is who I am now. No one is going to take that away from me," she said vehemently.

"Where's this leave Jack?" Chief had taken his pencil and was doodling on his desk pad.

"Jack has to stay away from me. Bryan will crush him, ruin his career. I can't be responsible for that."

"Jack won't. He'll want to know what happened down there," he paused. "He deserves some answers. Maddy, your world, as you know it is gone. Thanks to Mayland, part of your past has leaked into your present. You are going to have to deal with it or run away and start over again."

Maddy hated to admit it but the Chief was right. She couldn't pack up and start over again. She was comfortable with her life here, at least she had been. "I need to clear my head."

"Do what you need to do Maddy. What do you want me to do with this?" he patted the packet.

"Lock it up somewhere. After all the bullshit Mayland put me through, he's not getting it back. I earned it!"

As she was walking back to her office Max Sutton handed her a Coke Zero. "Peace offering," he said smugly.

She smiled softly, "Thanks Max" She unlocked her door and sat down in her chair. She popped the top on the Coke and downed part of it. Her mouth was so dry. She was staring at her desk pad, Cynthia and Vanessa was scribbled in the corner. Was it only Thursday since her life began to go haywire? She wished she had never called Jack, she wished she had stuck with the boring City Council story. Even if she had, would Bryan still be here?

She heard a knock on her door, when she looked up Bryan was standing in her door way. He had his jacket thrown over is shoulder, his sleeves were rolled up revealing hairy arms and his tie was loosened. "Not a very profession look G-Man," she commented. Detachment, she had gotten good at it. Stay calm, you slip, he gains control she told herself.

"I'm off for a while." He was leaning against the doorframe.

"That's nice. Why don't you go play in a minefield? Go anywhere you want, just get the hell away from me." She took another sip of her coke and set it down on the desk.

Bryan casually came in and sat in the chair opposite of her desk. "You really don't mean that." He looked around her office assessing it, forming an opinion. Besides a few framed prints, there were a few Iowa News Association awards to her credit on the wall. "Quaint, but you could have done better for yourself."

She felt herself start to bristle. Chief popped his head around the corner. "Maddy, who's your friend?" She knew he knew.

She nodded toward Bryan, "Special Supervisory Agent Bryan Mayland," then nodded the other direction. "That's my boss."

Bryan stood and shook Chief's hand then sat back down. "I just came to visit an old co-worker."

"She's one of our best investigative reporters. Should be in the big city, but we're honored to have her on our staff."

Bryan nodded, "Yes, she always was a master at words. That's why she made such a good liaison. She's wasting a natural talent."

Maddy watched the exchange. They were sizing each other up. Bryan was trying to dominate and Chief was blocking every step. Damn she really had to respect the guy now.

"Everyone is entitled to his own opinion...*even you*." The Chief turned to Maddy. "Don't forget that appointment, I don't want to have to rescheduled. Send a text if you are running late."

Maddy smiled, "I will let them know if I need to."

He nodded and left the room.

She turned her attention to the man across from her, "Bryan, why are you here? I thought you gave up fieldwork to just do training. How come you decided to go out in the field?"

"Saw the case come across on the notification list and thought it would be a good opportunity to come see you." He was watching her.

"Oh? Feeling a little like a good mind fuck do you?" she stood behind her desk and leaned over so her face was close to his, "Got news for you asshole, I'm sitting this one out."

Bryan leaned back and laughed hard. "You have such fire, it's such a challenge to rein that in. You have to admit, profiling got your blood pumping."

Maddy sat back down; keeping the desk between them seemed like her best strategy. "Second nature, but doesn't mean I want to do it. Why did you feel the need to make me do it in front of other people? Was it to make them feel inadequate or me? What purpose did it serve? I'm not law enforcement, I'm not part of the investigation."

"You can't tell me you haven't been poking your nose into it. As for having you there, I wanted you to see you belong in field, not behind a desk. It's a nice little charade you've built here, but it's mundane. You need real excitement to make you feel alive...you need me."

She had been taking a swig of coke when he said that and she choked. Then he laughed uncontrollably. It hadn't taken him long to give her his agenda. "Don't flatter yourself."

"You got something going with the cowboy detective?" he asked tentatively.

"Huh?"

"Parker, what's up with that? You with him?"

"I'm not *with* him as you put it. He is a friend. Leave him out it, he's got nothing to do with you and me."

"So you admit there is a you and me?" he sounded hopeful.

"I am saying we have history, therefore a relationship. I never said it was a good one."

Maddy rocked back in her chair a couple of times and then leaned forward with her elbows coming to rest on her desk, her chin resting on her hands. "How'd you get Donna to let you off your leash? I bet she has no idea where you are." She lowered her voice down to a whisper, "I bet you told her it was a secret mission and you would be incognito right?"

"I have no one back there to answer to," Bryan took out a pack of cigarettes and pulled one out.

"Liar." She snatched the cigarette out of his hand. "It's the law, no smoking in public places."

"I have never lied to you," he protested.

"Bullshit!" she scoffed. When green eyes met hazel eyes, his didn't flinch. Maddy took a deep breath and exhaled it slowly. "Bryan, I don't want to play, I just don't have the desire nor the strength to do this again."

Maddy felt her phone vibrate in her pocket. She slid her hand in, pulled it out and looked at it. Jack's name was flashing with each vibration.

"Aren't you going to answer it?"

"It can go to voice mail." She set it down on her desk.

"I don't know if I should be flattered or think you're a slacker," Bryan smiled.

Maddy jumped when her desk phone began to ring. "Shut up," she snapped. She picked it the handset, "Sheridan."

"Maddy, I need to see you," the familiar voice demanded. Shit! Jack!

She turned in her chair so she had her back to Bryan. "I'm sorry, I have someone in my office at the time. May I call you back or would you like to schedule an appointment?"

"An appointment? What the..." there was a pause, "He's there isn't he? Mayland is with you. Maddy what the hell is going on?" The agitation in Jack's voice was apparent.

Maddy lowered her voice, "Yes, that is correct. However I do believe we should have a face to face to go over that information to verify its validity."

Silence on the other end of the phone. "After work?"

"That might work, I will check my schedule and get back to you. Thank you for calling, I look forward to meeting with you." She hung up the receiver before he could reply.

She turned her chair back to face Bryan. He was leaning back with his legs splayed in front of him, his arms crossed at his waist.

"Quit that smirking," her eyes narrowed, "For two cents I would love to drag my nails across your face and wipe that look off it."

Bryan threw his head back and laughed, it was a laugh that pulled a little at her heartstrings. "Do I even need to ask?"

"I was just thinking, that would have been foreplay for us at one time," he chuckled.

Maddy felt the blood rush to her cheeks, "Bryan, you are..." Her cell phone vibrated on her desk. She held her finger up to him and raised the phone to look at the ID. Unknown caller.

"Sheridan," she answered.

"Miss Sheridan, this Sandy Morton. I'm sorry to bother you, but I can't get any answers from the police."

"I'm not sure if I can, but I will if I can, Sandy."

"The two bodies.... Was either of them...Vanessa?" The woman's voice had a tremor.

Maddy glanced at Bryan, he was looking at her walls...again, and she would guess he was listening, again. "Yeah, Sandy, about that, no they weren't there. Are you still at work?"

"Yes, why?"

"Because you sound like you could use someone to talk to, do you want me to stop by?"

She could almost hear Sandy smile across the phone. "I would like that." Maddy told her she would stop by and snapped the phone shut.

"Bryan, I really do have work to do, so if you don't mind, could we wrap up this little...whatever you want to call it?" She stood up from her desk and moved around to the front where she came face to face with this man who had stolen her heart, the man that had broken her heart...twice. She extended her hand to him.

Bryan grasped her hand, but instead of shaking it he used it to pull her close to him and he wrapped his arms securely around her. Her hands were pressed snuggly against his chest. He buried has face in her hair. His breath was hot against her ear. "You're mine Minnie..."

"No!" she pushed hard against his chest but he had her locked in his embrace. Their faces were just inches apart. "Minnie died two years ago when you left her without saying a word, not even a good-bye."

His hand slid up her back and grasped the back of her head gently by her hair and pulled her face into his. His lips crushed down on hers, commanding but not harsh, demanding a response from her. And despite her resolve she opened up to him and returned his kiss with a passion she thought was gone. Her arms crept up around his neck; her fingers ran through his hair pulling him to her. She couldn't breath, she couldn't get away, and she couldn't get close enough.

It was Bryan that finally broke the kiss, but still held her close. "Maddy," he spoke softly, "I want you to know, with all the crazy bullshit that has happened in our lives, I have always loved you...and I will never lie about that to you."

She tried hard to read him. She wanted to believe him, but ultimately it came down to one thing, he would disappear again. "Bryan..."

He touched her lips with his finger, "No, just leave it at that for now." He brushed his hand along her cheek. "You and me, Minnie, we're fire and ice."

Maddy's heart was pounding in her chest and she felt like her body was turning to mush. "It's safer for me to stay frozen," she touched his lips softly with hers, "I can't be burned by your fire Bryan...not again."

He lightly released her from his embrace. He held her arms with his and looked down at her. "You're afraid, but you have to trust me."

She broke eye contact with him, "No Bryan, I don't. I can't."

They were interrupted by Maddy's office intercom. She pushed the button, "yes?"

"Maddy, there is a woman coming up to your office and she doesn't look happy. I thought I would give you a head's up."

Maddy barely had her hand on the doorknob when the door was pushed open and Stella stood before her. She was dressed in a navy blue business suit, form fitting, well tailored, stiletto shoes. Didn't her feet ever hurt? Her blonde hair was loose but not a hair was out of place. Maddy bet if she touched it, it would probably break. She wondered if Jack ran his fingers through it would he be able to get them out? "Barbie," she whispered under her breath then louder she said "Stella... can I help you?"

Stella's eyes went from Maddy to Bryan back to her again. "I don't appreciate you conning Jack into spending the weekend with you. I can see through your pathetic ploys to get him into bed with you, He doesn't see it, but I do," she said vehemently.

Maddy smiled and laughed, "Jack's a big boy and he can take care of himself. I don't think he needs your permission if he wants to go on a little *slumber* party. Sometimes a guy just needs to escape from all his *problems.* If you're that insecure in your relationship with him, maybe you need to re-evaluate how serious he really is about you."

The next thing she knew Stella's fist was flying in her direction, she saw it coming, closed her eyes and waited for the impact. It didn't come. When she opened her eyes, she was surprised to see Stella tiny wrist being securely held by Bryan's large hand.

"I think you need to leave before I entertain charging you with assault," he said to her. Bryan was guiding her out of Maddy's office.

Stella turned to Maddy and hissed, "Stay away from Jack...Bitch."

Maddy poked her head out after Stella, "Yes, I'm a bitch, it comes so naturally to me, like my hair, my boobs...my personality." She smiled sweetly. "Have a nice day!"

Stella jerked her arm away from Bryan. "Let go of me asshole!" She stormed off down the hall, her heels clicking on the marble floor. They could be heard echoing all the way to the elevator.

Maddy leaned against the wall and laughed, "Bryan, you never told me she knew you. But then again with those heels, she's right up your alley."

"Shut up," he gave her a quick kiss. "I have to get back to work, stay out of trouble." He popped in her office and grabbed his jacket and took off down the hall.

Maddy yelled after him, "If you hurry, you can catch her in the parking lot!"

He flipped her off over his shoulder.

She laughed, turned around and noticed the room had gone quiet and everyone was staring at her. "What...like you've all never seen at cat fight before?" She slipped into her office and shut the door.

Maddy sunk down into to her chair and closed her eyes. Lord what a day. Being true to form, whenever Bryan was part of her life, her world was like a roller coaster. He was right though; he made her feel alive, which wasn't necessarily a good thing. For every high there was definitely a low.

She grabbed her bag, flipped off her light and locked her door. She was off to see Sandy. She needed to get back on track, get her mind back on work and less on the personal chaos.

She pulled the Cobalt into Tyler Construction's parking lot. There were hardly any cars there. Didn't anyone work at this joint? She got out of her car and walked toward the office. When she opened the door she was met by a cool blast of air. "Ooooh that feels so good!"

Sandy was at her computer typing away. When she saw Maddy, she slipped off her glasses and stood to greet her. "Miss Sheridan, thank you so much for coming."

She smiled, "Call me Maddy, please. How you holding up?"

"Not so good," her voice was shaky. "I'm sorry but it just feels the police are handling this so...inhumanly. I mean Vanessa is my friend; she's not just "the missing victim." You are sure she was not one of the bodies they found?"

Maddy nodded, "100% sure. I can't give you the details, but I can guarantee that information.

"Do you know anything more? Can you tell me that?" Sandy grabbed her bottle of water and took a drink.

"This is what I know, it doesn't come from the police, and so it's not official okay?"

Sandy nodded.

"The best I can calculate she went missing probably sometime Tuesday evening. Did she have things she usually did on Tuesday's?"

"Vanessa is a loner. She is quiet, very shy and keeps to herself. We don't see much of each other outside of work, but talk a lot here at work. It's just the two of us here in the office most of the time. The most socializing she ever talked about was she plays on the Internet a lot."

"Plays?"

"Chat rooms. I think she finds it easier to talk to people there because she can be anyone she wants to be. I don't care for it, I think meeting people on the Internet is dangerous."

Sandy had peaked Maddy's interests "Has she ever met anyone from the net?"

"Not that she ever told me. You think it could be related to her disappearance?"

"Anything is possible. I have to ask you a question, its not the most above board thing to do."

"If it can help find Vanessa, I don't care," Sandy's eyes lit up in anticipation.

"You have a key to her house?"

"Yes," she waited for Maddy's request.

"I need her computer. Can you to get it for me? If you don't feel right about it, its okay." Maddy watched for Sandy's reaction.

"I can get it," she said without batting an eye.

"Do you think her disappearance is related to the others?" she asked.

"The police are looking at it that way. The DCI and the FBI are investigating now. Hopefully that will lead to a resolution quickly," Maddy explained.

"Yeah I saw that on the news. When are you going to write something about it?"

"For the time being, I am barred by "the powers that be". I have been privy to sensitive information and because of that I more or less have a gag order on me. But trust me, anything I uncover in the course of my own investigation is fair game. From this day forward, I am pretty much on my own."

"Please let me help you," Sandy had become animated. "I am good at researching. I can check facts out for you, do whatever, you just tell me what you want."

Maddy smiled, "You are a good friend, Vanessa is lucky. Let's get our hands on her computer first, see what we can find on there."

Maddy text alert went off. She pulled her phone out of her case. She looked up at Sandy, "Do you mind if I take this?"

"No, no, go ahead. I need to shut down anyhow." Sandy sat back down at her computer station.

Maddy flipped her phone open. The text was from Jack. "Where are you? I thought we were going to meet up."

She typed in a reply, "I'm sorry, I had to go on an interview." Send

Alert "Thought you were going to call."

"I got called out." Send.

Alert "Are we still going to meet up?"

"Not sure when I am going to be done." Send

Alert "You're avoiding me, Maddy."

"Don't be stupid, Jack. I do work for a living." Send

Alert "So I take that as a no, I won't be seeing you."

"Take it anyway you want Jack, I gotta go." Send

She waited a couple of minutes for a reply and when none came she stuck her phone back in the case. She smiled weakly at Sandy. "Men."

Maddy and Sandy discussed their plan of action. Sandy would drive over to Vanessa's and go into her house under the rues of watering plants. Yes, granted the police seal was still up, but Sandy could play dumb if she got caught. Sandy locked up the office and they walked out to their cars together agreeing to meet up tomorrow. If Sandy had any problems, she would notify Maddy.

Maddy headed east out of town. She couldn't wait to escape this world and get back into her own. Today had been an eventful and terribly long day. Way too emotional. Bryan crept back into her thoughts. No, that wasn't entirely true. He hadn't really left them. It was starting again. He consumed her. He had this power over her that was hard for her to fight. She knew if she surrendered to it she would be lost again. Too bad she wasn't the kind of person who could have a fling and keep her emotions in check. But when it all came down to it, she did love Bryan, always had. But that love had been destructive and she couldn't see it having any other outcome. She needed to get a check on her emotions for Bryan. It was only a matter of time before he disappeared into thin air.

Then there was Jack. She felt they had gotten so close over the weekend. It was fun spending time with him without feeling threaten. The man meant so much to her. They were friends, she trusted him explicitly, and no matter what she told herself, she was incredibly attracted to him. Even though she told herself she couldn't have a relationship with anyone.

Jack...she hadn't been very nice to him today. She had left him hanging with a lot of unanswered question. But if she told him the truth, would he feel betrayed? Would he ever believe in her again? She didn't know and she was terrified to find out.

Maddy cranked up her music and drove the rest of the way home.

When she arrived home she slipped into the house and changed into some riding clothes. She put the pups in the house so they could get out of the heat and then went down to the barn. She grabbed a lead rope and went out to the pasture and whistled. All four horses came running but it was the big sorrel gelding, Buddy, she wanted for her mount. She clicked the rope to his halter and led him into the barn. She tied him to the post and gave him a little sweet feed to munch on while she groomed him. The finishing brush glided over his bulging muscles sweeping bits of horsehair and dust in its wake. She put her nose to his skin and breathed in. Mmmm the smell of horse flesh. You couldn't describe it to anyone. Only a true horse person understood and appreciated it. She sprayed him down with fly spray, sprayed some in her hands and did his eye area and ears. She threw the saddle blanket and saddle on his back. She tightened up the cinch and the girth. She slid the halter off and the bridle over his head and tightened it. She led Buddy out of the barn and mounted him. Moments later she was riding in the wind down a gravel road. Her ride was choppy at first but soon her body fell into rhythm with Buddy's canter. She pushed the horse for two miles and then slowed him down to a walk for the return ride home. Horse therapy, you can't put a price on it. Her mind was focused on her surroundings looking for things her horse might react to. If it wasn't on that it was on her horse, reading him.

Maddy turned up her lane and trotted Buddy toward the barn. It was then that she spotted the black Impala sitting next to her car. Jack. The moment of truth.

5

Jack's car appeared vacant. As she rode Buddy at a walk to the barn she scanned her yard and found Jack sitting on the ground playing with the dogs. Funny, she thought she had put the dogs in. He looked up at her but made no attempt at contact. She dismounted and led Buddy into the barn. She grabbed the halter and lead rope, unbuckled the bridal and slid the halter over his nose, then tied him to the ring. Maddy was just pulling off the saddle when she saw a shadow darken the barn entrance. From the corner of her eye she saw Jack. He came in and sat down on the ledge of the door.

Maddy hoisted the saddle on its stand and put the blanket over it to dry. She reached in a canister and pulled out a couple of peppermints. Buddy's ears perked up and he stretched his neck out so that his nose was pointed towards her hand. She couldn't unwrap the mint fast enough before the gelding lipped her hand and crunched on the candy. She brushed him down quickly then turned him out through the walk-in gate.

She looked over at Jack as he sat silently watching her, which made her feel pretty edgy. She grabbed a hay hook and dragged two bales out into the alleyway and pushed them up against the wall. She sat down on one and pulled her legs up underneath her.

"What are you doing here, Jack?"

"You wouldn't come to me so I came to you." He pulled out a cigarette and lit it up.

"What if I don't want to talk?"

Jack inhaled deeply and blew out the smoke. "Maddy, I'm not here to play games with you, I won't. This is me, Jack, the guy you said you trusted more than anyone. So let's cut the bullshit. Are you going to level with me? Because if you aren't, I'm going to get up and leave and when I do...we're done." His voice was calm, too calm even.

She studied his face. It was kind of hard to get a good read in the dim light of the barn, his jaw was tense, and a narrow crease shadowed his brow. His brown hair was sticking out in tuffs, he had been running his fingers through it again. His day had not gone well either. The only difference between their days—he knew nothing, she had all the answers.

"You might not like what you find out." She pulled a piece of straw from the bale and chewed on it nervously, "Then what? Either way I loose."

"Christ Maddy, give me a little more credit. You make such a big deal out of trust, then damn it, do it."

She stretched her legs and shifted her weight on the bale. "Come over here and sit with me."

He flicked his cigarette out the door and then moved to the bale next to her. "How do you want to do this?"

"You ask what you want to know. I will answer the best I can, what I can. My only request is, don't interrogate me and don't push if I tell you to stop." She looked over at him for acknowledgment. He nodded.

"All this time I've been telling your with your skills you should be a cop and you blew me off like it was a big joke," he shook his head. "How you must have laughed at me. All this time and you're a Fed. Why? What are you doing here? Why are you pretending to be someone you're not?"

"I'm not pretending anything," she protested. "And I'm not FBI."

"Semantics Maddy, that's what you're giving me. Explain to me what happened today."

Maddy took a deep breath and blew it out slowly. "Many years ago, I did work with the FBI. I was a liaison between the agents working a case and the local law enforcement, I ran interference with the press, helped communicate with the families of victims, studied possible case files, just assorted stuff."

"Bullshit. Call it what you want, Maddy, you were an agent. And you weren't a liaison; you were a profiler. I saw you in action today."

"Don't be silly, Jack, I just watch a lot of *Criminal Minds*."

He shot her a dirty look.

"Listen Jack, I am not going to into detail about that part of my life. I did it, lived through some bad shit, and I had to get out. I had to save myself, so I quit. Eventually I started over. One of my degrees is in English and I did my time at some larger metro papers doing the crime beat, but it was still too close to what I was running from. One of the publishers I worked for knew Chief, pulled some strings and here I am. Up until this last week, I was quite content being here. I never told you, or anyone else because it's not important and nobody's business. It's in the past and that's where it needs to stay. I'm sorry if that's not enough of an answer for you Jack. I am not trying to be evasive with you; I just can't and won't go back there. Do you understand?" She reached out, her hand was shaking, and her fingers grazed his hand.

Jack wrapped his fingers lightly around hers. "Maybe in time you will trust me enough that you could tell me everything."

"Jack it not a matter of trust. If I talk about it, it becomes real again, I just can't."

Maddy gave Jack a sideways glance. He was chewing on his lower lip nervously. "And?"

"What's the story behind you and Mayland?" he asked.

Her heart sank. This shouldn't be part of the tell-all agreement, this was her personal, private life and she didn't want to share with anyone. "If I told you we have history, would you be able to leave it at that?"

Jack released her hand, slid to the edge of the bale and pulled himself to his feet. He brushed himself off with his hands.

Maddy's heart began to race in a panic. "That's not fair Jack! I have never asked you about your personal relationships, never made any demands. Granted you had a right to ask about my professional past, but you're going to walk out on me because I don't wish discuss Bryan with you?"

Jack looked past her at Buddy messing around by the water tank. "So it's Bryan, now..." he nodded his head slightly. He returned to his perch on the ledge of the barn door and lit another cigarette. "When I first saw you in the briefing room this morning, you were terrified, I wasn't sure why, but then discovered it was him. Maddy, the man brought you into an investigation because he had an ulterior motive. He treated you like shit, he taunted you, belittled you, and bullied you. To what means? I am assuming you worked for him. If he wanted your opinion or take on the case, he could have asked you in private. He didn't need to parade you in front of the squad. The range of emotion he evokes from you..." Jack ran his finger through his hair. If he kept that up for much longer his hair was going to fall out. "fear, anger, defiance and more fear. Watching the two you this morning was like watching a toxic chemical reaction. Hell Maddy, you were afraid for me. For him to evoke so much emotion, the man has to mean something to you."

This would have been so much easier to explain to him if Bryan hadn't stopped by her office today. Despite the fact that Bryan had stirred up old emotions she had to keep in mind the wake of disaster he leaves behind when he vanishes from her life. And she knew he would once again vanish, as quickly and unexpected as he appeared. Bryan was her past, Jack was here and now.

Despite her claims of not wanting personal involment with Jack, there definitely was something there—something undeniable. The time she spent with him this weekend, she enjoyed his company, she enjoyed his touch and even though she hated to admit it, desired his touch.

Jack snuffed out his cigarette then came back and sat beside her on the bale. They sat there in silence. Maddy's visual attention was focused on a cobweb on the opposing barn wall as it danced in the breeze that was moving through the barn.

"So you have nothing to say?"

Maddy groaned as she pulled her knees up to her chest and buried her head against them. "It's not that I have nothing to say, I just don't know what or how to say it."

Jack gave a nervous laugh, "Funny you are rarely at a loss for words."

She gave him a weak smile. "Okay," she started out slow. "Bryan and I worked in the same unit with the FBI. He had already had 10 years in with the Bureau. When we met he was separated from his wife. We started hanging out after hours." She couldn't help smiling a little as she looked back at that time in her life. "God we were so close, we would talk for hours and hours, some times all night. We shared things about our lives that we told no one. We laughed, we cried, and we fought, Lord did we fight. I was going through a tough time emotionally and he was there for me. I loved him so very much, and he loved me. But I could never say he was mine. He wouldn't give me that. Told me to 'keep things in perspective.' I learned to hate those words and couldn't understand why he kept reminding me of that. The first time we were "together" was on his birthday. I had given him a box full of lots of little gifts, each that a special meaning. That was the first night he told me about his stepson and how much he missed him. He was hurting and I hurt for him. Anyhow to jump a head, he got this big bonus in February and decided he was going to use it to go see his son who was in Moldavia with Bryan's estranged wife. When he returned he informed me he and his wife were going to try to make it work for the sake of his son—at least until his son turned 18." The smile had faded from her lips and her heart was aching as if it happened such a short time ago instead of ten years ago. "I told him I would wait for him, be his mistress, whatever. I just couldn't bear to loose him. He said no, we had to cut off all contact with each other—no phone calls, no email, no anything. I honored his wishes. It broke my heart but how could I fault a man who was doing the "honorable" thing? So I let him go. Hell, I had no choice."

Jack took Maddy's hand. "I'm sorry, that must have been very hard on you."

"Ha!" she sneered, "not as hard as finding out a year later he had a mistress. We lived in different cities by then and by some fluke a few years later I met her on the Internet, not knowing who she was at the time. What are the odds? I got to know her fairly well. As the years went on Bryan would drop me a quick email just to see how I was doing when I knew he could care less. I never answered back. He had no clue that I had become friends with his mistress and when she made me aware of who she was, I didn't want him to know. She was a nice lady, too nice for him. She knew about me, we even compared notes. Sometimes I wonder if it wasn't a set up, that she sought me out.

A couple of years ago he found out. I became his quest," She looked at Jack, "This part is too fresh to go into detail so I will give you the jest of it. Bryan had changed. He went through hell with his wife (according to his mistress); his son was a drug addict. He had been assigned on many difficult cases, some pretty grizzly. His partner bled to death in his arms after being shot in the head by an unsub. He himself had been shot in the incident. This Bryan had aged beyond his years. He was jaded, bitter, paranoid, mistrusting, and a heavy alcoholic. And those were just his traits I could understand. But with this new Bryan, he was deceitful, manipulative, controlling, obsessive, and possessive and my all time favorite name for him—The Master at Mind Fuck. And yet I still loved him." Maddy put her forehead on her knees again. She when she looked up she quickly wiped the tears from her eyes. "Jack can we just leave it at that?"

"How did you end it?" he asked softly.

"I didn't. His mistress did. I never heard from him again...until now."

"Nothing? No explanations? No goodbye?"

She shook her head and the tears began to fall. Once the leak started the dam broke. Jack wrapped his arms around Maddy and pulled her close, sobs racked her body. "He hurt me, he hurt me so bad." She buried her face in his chest, his shirt damp with her tears. "And the worst part is...I knew better, I saw the red flags, but I just ignored them, I just let it happen. I let him tear me down, let him break me. He destroyed me and I gave him the weapon."

"Jesus Maddy," He took her by the chin so she was facing up to him. Her eyes were red, her cheeks tear stained. She squeezed her eyes shut tight and more tears spilled. Jack kissed each eyelid, then his lips traveled down each cheek. He just wanted to make her pain go away.

With each kiss Maddy felt that the warmth of his lips made her stronger, made the pain ebb a little slower. She turned her head until her lips came into contact with his. She could taste the salt of her tears, the faint hint of tobacco, and the sweetness of Jack.

Her heart quickened, but it still ached. She cared enough for Jack not to let Bryan destroy them. She pulled away from him and laid her head on his chest. She could feel his heart pounding in his chest as it rose and fell with each breath. She pushed herself up so she was sitting upright on the bale. With the bottom of her shirt she wiped her cheeks and her eyes, "Hay fever," she laughed.

Jack pulled a hanky out of his pocket and handed it to her. She laughed as she took it from him and dabbed her eyes. "I sure hope when you give me these, they're not used."

He nudged her, "Of course they are, you think I would waste a clean one on you?"

She blew her nose in to it and handed it back to him. "You are such a gentleman."

He held it between his thumb and index finger, "You are so gross, why can't you act more like a lady?" He shook his head.

"Oh that reminds me." She stood up and gave him her hand to pull him up from the bale. "Barbie came to see me today." She dusted off his back then turned around so he could do the same for her.

"Barbie?...oh you mean Stella?...Christ, what did she do? As if this day could get any worse."

Maddy closed the barn door and secured the latch. "Assault with a deadly weapon, she tried to hit me with her shoe." She thought she was maintaining the perfect straight face.

Jack froze, "No! Are you serious?"

Maddy punched him, "Sort of," she laughed. "She tried to nail me with a right hook."

He turned to face her, "Tried? How bad did you nail her Maddy?"

She threw up her hands, "Hey I'm from no touch school remember? Didn't lay a hand on her. One of the guys at the office intercepted it before it made impact. (Not a total lie.) "Anyhow, I am supposed to stay away from you. Funny how women keep telling me to stay away from their men," she laughed. "I am conning you in to my bed."

"Really," he laughed. "I'm the letch, it would be me conning you."

"You are not a letch," she said seriously.

"Yeah I am," he winked. "You just don't know that side of me. I'll tell Stella to back off."

"No need, make her think she has to work for you," she grinned.

Jack turned toward her, "Does she?"

Maddy pretended she didn't hear him. She focused her attention on the two little dogs sitting patiently on the opposite side of the yard fence. Jack began to run the length of the fence, stop momentary and spin in a circle then bark. She called it his dance. Rufus, on the other hand, began to bounce against the fence, with each recoil his little body inched closer to the top. On his fourth try he scaled the fence, did a nosedive and when his body hit the ground it somersaulted. Seconds later he was jumping in to Maddy's arms and began to vigorously lick her face. "Did you let them out of the house?"

"Well, yeah, someone had to keep me company," he reached out and scratched Rufus behind the ears. Maddy rolled her eyes.

She invited Jack in for a cold drink. He took a seat while Maddy grabbed a couple glasses and poured them each a tea and pulled a chair next to him. She squeezed in her lemon, stirred it with her finger then sucked the liquid off her finger. "Anything new on the case?...off record of course."

Jack sat silently with both hands around his glass his thumbs caressing it.

"You're kidding right?" Maddy stared at him in disbelief.

"Maddy this is serious shit here—an on going investigation. You know I can't discuss it with you." He glanced over at her. "You understand don't you?"

"Fuck no! Christ Jack, I was there," Maddy rose from the table, disappeared for a few moments and came back with her laptop. Instead of returning to her chair by Jack, she pulled out a chair on the opposite side of the table. She opened the laptop and powered it up.

"What are you doing?"

"Finding out what you won't tell me." Her fingers flew across the keyboard as she signed on to the Violent Criminal Apprehension Program (ViCAP) website. "Or more than likely, what you don't know." She entered in her security code and pulled up the main menu. First she wanted to know what searches Bryan's team had initiated. She typed in missing persons matching the victimology of this case for the tri-state area.—Search in progress. Cool. Search two—unidentified dead bodies, where the manner of death is known and suspected to be homicide within the parameters of their vics.—Search in progress. She was sure Bryan already initiated these same requests; this would speed up her results. She sat back and waited while the ViCAP search engines did their job.

Jack watched her, the puzzlement was apparent on his face.

"What?" she asked innocently even though she knew different.

"You loved the work, why did you quit?"

Maddy scratched the back of her head and gave a long sigh, then she asked him as a matter of fact, "You ever stared down the face of evil?" She watched as Jack's jaw dropped.

He seemed at a loss for words. "No."

She watched the records count flashing on the bottom of her screen. "I have, and just when I thought I had seen it at its worst, another case would come along and prove me wrong."

"Did Mayland tell you about him...and his partner?"

"No."

"How did you find out?"

She ignored his question and continued to watch the screen.

"He obviously keeps tabs on you and your where a bouts. Do you do the same?"

"No!" Damn, she did her best to forget him. "Where you going with this Jack?"

He shrugged his shoulders, "I don't know. I'm just starting see glimpses of the you I don't know. And I want to."

Maddy looked over the top of the computer screen. "Why? To see what kind of fucked up person I am?"

"No," he gave a quick smile, "You're not fucked up. You're just a lot more complicated than I thought you were. I want to know you, Maddy. I mean really know you, and I can't do that without knowing all of you...the good, the bad, the ugly," he kicked her leg underneath the table with his toe, "and the sexy."

She laughed and kicked him back. "And what if that can't happen?"

He ran his foot up her leg, "You won't be able resist my irresistible charm."

She slapped at his foot. "You arrogant jack ass! No pun intended of course," she laughed.

Her computer beeped. Search one complete. She clicked on the download icon. "DNA on Jane Doe back yet?"

"FEB's put a rush on it, came back this afternoon."

Hmmm...he's talking, a positive development. "They ran it through CO-DIS."

It was a statement as opposed to a question. She happened to glance up at him and he had a weird expression on his face. "Now what?"

"You...I guess I am feeling pretty stupid. All this time, working cases, did you ever feel I was talking down to you? I mean, damn, Maddy, you're fucking FBI."

"Was." A second beep, second search complete. She clicked the download icon. "And no I never felt you talked down to me. And no I didn't dumb down to you or anyone else. A poker player doesn't reveal his cards."

"You were playing a game with me?" he said incredulously.

"Jesus Jack, quit reading more into it than there is. It's done, it's in my past."

"No, it's not Maddy. I saw you today. You were amazing, mechanical but amazing. Behavioral Analysis Unit?"

"Yep BAU. That's what a dual major of abnormal and foreignsic psychology will do for you. Why do you think I'm so weird?"

He laughed, "No, I think that's just a personality defect."

She dipped her finger in her tea and flicked it at him. "See you really do know me after all."

She clicked on the downloaded file and brought it up and then brought up the print menu. "You want copies for yourself?"

"Of what?"

She held her finger above the enter key, "Yes or no? going...going..."

"Yes!"

She grinned and hit enter, "Curiosity killed the cat." The files were being sent to her wireless printer.

She got up from the table and went to retrieve the documents. When she returned she found Jack had turned her computer around and was looking at the screen. She reached in over his shoulder and clicked on the sign out icon. "Don't want to be in there any longer than I have to be. Get in, get out." She gave him a little smack on the side of the face. "Quit looking like that, you act like you're in the lion's den."

"ViCAP? You have access to ViCAP? How? Duh? FBI. But you said you're not active."

"I still have all my clearance codes. Bryan never deactivated them. He could at anytime. Not sure why he didn't. Never have much cause to use them. It's too easy for him to trace me through log in access time," she explained. Maddy handed him a stack of printouts.

"What are these?" Jack fingered through the sheets.

"The first is search results on missing persons fitting our criteria for Iowa, Nebraska and South Dakota for the last year. The second is the search results for recovered bodies in situ like ours."

"Huh?"

"Whose bodies were recovered in graves like our vics. Do I need to start talking down to you?"

"Fuck you." They both laughed. It felt good. The tension was beginning to wane.

Maddy's cell phone went off. She picked it up and looked at the caller ID. Caller ID Blocked. She laughed. "I was expecting this." She put her fingers to her lips. "Shhhhhssssh."

She flipped it open. "You're getting slow in your old age, Bryan."

"Minnie."

"I told you not to call me that."

"I listen about as well as you do. What are you doing Maddy?"

"Sitting here at my kitchen table having a nice glass of tea. What are you doing?"

"Working. Did you find what you were looking for?"

"Plead the 5th."

"If you want in on the investigation I can reactivate you. We can work it together. We always did work well together."

"I don't want to come back, you know that. I'm done."

"We always played well together too, Maddy" Bryan teased.

She smiled, "I'm done with that too."

He laughed and growled into the phone.

"Asshole. Don't do that."

He laughed again. "Still gets to you don't it?'

"Shut up. So are you going to chew my ass or what?"

"I'd like to, and more."

"Jesus, you're relentless. Give it up." She was smiling in the phone.

"I never give up and I always win."

She shook her head, "Yeah, well you'll die trying and I'll die laughing."

"Bitch,"

She feigned an insult; "You are the second person to call me that today. I'm beginning see a pattern here."

"Okay, sexy bitch."

Maddy laughed, "That's more like it. So Bryan, my iced tea is getting warm. What do you want? And before you say it, don't. Are you going to take my *gift* away?"

"You think you know me so well. No, I just wanted you to know that I know what you're up to."

"I figured as much. Just wasn't sure if you were going to cut me off or not."

The phone went quiet for a moment.

"What?"

"Maddy, someone was trying to access your file today. You were having a background check ran on you."

Maddy looked at Jack from the corner of her eye. "Really? How far did they get?"

"Surface only, it got red flagged and denied access."

"Thanks Bryan," she said softly. "Do you know who?"

"Yeah, do you?"

"Yeah, I think so."

"Sorry Minnie, don't be too hard on him." He actually sounded concerned. "Oh and by the way, I thought you said you weren't sleeping with Cowboy."

She held the phone back and looked at it like it was a foreign object. "I'm not."

"His girlfriend says otherwise."

"I can't see even if I were, it's any of your business."

"It's my business. Listen Kido, this old man has to get back to work. Behave yourself."

"I always do."

"Bullshit!...Maddy...I love you."

"Me too, good night Bryan." Damn it, Damn it Damn it! It rolled off her tongue without thought or effort. Damn it!

She set the phone on the table.

"He picked up on it that quick?" Jack asked.

"That's one of the things that makes him a top agent. Eyes and ears out all the time and what he can't do, he has others that do it for him."

"You respect him," he said quietly.

"Yeah, I guess I do. The agent, not the man." She fumbled with the papers in front of her. "You ran me through the system." It was a statement.

"Yeah, I did. I needed to know. He has you very well protected, I learned nothing."

Maddy took a sip of her tea.

"Do you want me to go?"

Maddy reached out across the table for Jack's hand and she guided it to her lips and then squeezed it with her hand. "It's okay, I'm not pissed. I would have done the same."

He brought her hand to the side of his cheek. "Have you?"

"No, I love the joys of discovering you one day at a time," her voice was all syrupy. Then she cracked up, "Man that was bad, even coming from me. No, I've never run you through the system. Never had a reason to. You want me to?"

"Go ahead," he replied in all seriousness. "My life's an open book."

Maddy was looking through the pages of missing women, just scanning the pages. "Yeah, so is mine, just a lot of the pages are glued together." She glanced over at him and frowned. "You know Jack, I miss when you used to look at me and see me. I feel like when you look at me now, you're searching for something, trying to read me, trying to figure me out." She slid her chair back and turned it sideways and told Jack to do the same. "Look at me Jack, really look at me. Who do you see?"

He took the back of his hand and brushed her cheek. "I see a beautiful woman with the face of a woman I thought I knew, but I don't. You're not my Maddy anymore—you're his. And I'm finding out you always were. Things have changed between us and it didn't start with Mayland. I knew when I laid eyes on you last Thursday. You, yourself, said something was different. I don't know what changed, but it did. There's something here, Maddy, something real. But I'm afraid, I'm afraid he's going to steal you away before we even get a chance to find out what it is. I want to know you, all of you. I don't like questioning what you're thinking, what you're feeling. What do you want me say, Maddy? What do you want me to do?"

"Wow, that's more than I expected." She put her hand over his and brought it down and kissed it tenderly and released it. She leaned across to him and put her hands on his knees. "I'm not going to lie to you and tell you I don't have feelings for Bryan, but it's not quite what you think. There are no words to describe what he and I have together. It's not normal, it's not sane, and it's definitely not healthy. It's toxic." She slid down on the floor between his knees. Maddy took her hands and cupped his face. "But, I'm not his Jack, I'm not. You asked me what I wanted you to do. I want you to stand by me. I need you to believe in me even when I don't believe in myself. I need to deal with Bryan, to get through this until he leaves. He is not going to change what is going on between us—we won't let it. Only you can let that happen."

Jack lifted Maddy to him. His mouth found hers and he kissed her with a deep urgency. His fingers intertwined in her hair, his other hand slid down her back and pressed her to him. Her arms crept around his neck. When his tongue parted her lips she let out a little cry. Her fingernails dug into his skin. It wasn't until Jack broke the kiss that Maddy was able to take a breath. They gazed at each other, searching, for what they didn't know.

Maddy felt the heat rush to her face and laughed nervously. "Damn Jack."

"Maddy look at me." She did as he requested. "I won't let Mayland hurt you. You fight whatever battles you need to, but you don't have to do it alone. All you have to do is turn around and I will be there. We will get through it."

She kissed him softly. "Thank you," she whispered.

She pinched him on the leg, "What do you say we get to work?"

Maddy cleared the table so she could spread the missing persons profiles out. "I put in parameters of female, between the ages of 25-35, single, abductors unknown. All with in the Tri-state area, all within the last 12 months. I left race open as well as manner of abduction. We don't know if our unsub has changed MO, or if he's progressed in methodology." There were 12 possibilities.

"Profile one—Shawna Stevens, 27, Yankon, SD. Cocktail waitress. Reported missing April 10, this year. Last seen leaving work with unknown male subject in his vehicle. Nope." She threw that one off to the side. "Profile two—Rachel Collins, 25, Ames, Iowa, X-ray tech, reported missing March 3, last seen leaving the mall at 6:45 PM. Iffy." She put that one in a different pile. She went through five more profiles which she felt didn't fit.

Maddy grew silent. She slid down in one of the chairs. She had three profiles in her hand. She would study one, flip to the next one, flip back to other one and then to the last one. She continued to do this for a couple of minutes. "Check this out." She laid all three profiles down in a row in front of Jack. "Tracy Becker, 31, Omaha, NE, March 2nd, disappeared from her home, Linda Meyer, 33, Bellevue, NE, disappeared from her apartment, June 1. Rita Smit, 30, Council Bluffs, IA disappeared from her apartment on April 21." She waited for a response form Jack.

"Yeah I can see the similarities, but they are vague, Maddy."

"You have to look at the broader picture here Jack." She put the last two profiles in front of him. "Rebecca Mallard, 34, Wayne, NE, Went missing June 10. Last seen leaving church. Tina Whethers, 28, rural Bronson, last seen June 28, last seen pumping gas at local convenience store." She waited again.

She smacked him a long the side the head, "Christ Jack, think like a damn cop. You need to set aside all this personal bullshit and think like a cop!"

Jack swung around and looked at her, his jaw twitching, "Is that how you do it Maddy? You have an off and on switch you can just click it and you quit thinking, quit feeling. Just a little while ago, we were holding each other, sharing deep feelings, and the wham, you're all animated over a bunch of profiles, like it never happened."

Maddy stared at him in disbelief. "What the hell is your problem? This is me, the same damn person you knew before. I dive in, I investigate, I find out what the hell is going on. The only difference is I am letting you in, letting you see me do the work I usually do on my own without you, sharing it with you. That's a pretty damn big step for me, Jack. You want to know about me shutting off my feelings? I do it every single day of my life. I do it to survive. I know you will never understand and it's okay. But the ability to do it doesn't mean I quit feeling."

She picked up his stack of profiles and pulled out the five she had separated from the rest. She jammed them into his chest. "I think you should go, Jack. Take those with you and when you feel like being an investigator look at them. See if you see what I see!"

Jack stood up, "Maddy, I'm sorry."

She picked up the tea glasses and brought them to the sink. She turned and leaned against the counter. "Don't Jack. It's like you said the other day. Don't apologize. You feel the way feel, you think the way think. And right now I can't deal with it. This is why I keep my personal life out of my professional life. Things just get too fucked up."

Jack, with files in hand, stood at the door with his hand on the knob. When he turned back to look at her she was staring down at the floor. He wanted to say more, but knew he had said enough so he left without saying another word.

Maddy heard his car door shut, the engine start and leave. She sat down in her chair, the profiles in front of her. She had actually been excited to go over them and get Jack's input, to be partners like they used to be. Despite Jack's claims that he could put his newfound knowledge of her on the back burner, he couldn't. And right now she couldn't deal with it. Her life was all about focus in order to maintain control and at this moment control was the furthest thing she had. She had two men messing with her head and yet she felt so very lonely.

Fuck it. She grabbed a notebook and rulers and proceeded to draw a timeline. She divided it into months and then jotted the names and dates of disappearance. Let's see, she had Becker in March; Smit in April; Meyer in May; Mallard and Whethers in June; Stewart and Mitchell in July; and Granger in August. Maddy went to her junk drawer and dug around until she found a map. She spread it out, took a red Sharpie and marked dots where each girl was from. The pattern was pretty obvious. The first three were in the Omaha area, the last four in the Sioux City area. Their manner of disappearance was the same, but like Jack said it was pretty vague. If by some outside chance the women's disappearances were related, the unsub relocated to the Sioux City area in June. The disappearances had escalated when he moved to the area. Time frame between them had decreased to approximately two weeks apart. If the pattern was indeed as it seemed to be they had one week until another victim would be abducted. Maddy gave a long sigh. This was all circumstantial. There was nothing tying any of these women together. With the exception of Jane Doe and Mitchell. Based on approximate time of death Jane could be either Mallard or Whethers. With this many disappearances in this close of proximity, why hadn't the authorities made the connection? Why were only Granger and Stewart on the radar? This was northwest Iowa; it wasn't like this kind of thing happens all the time.

She flipped through the search for like burials, there were none even remotely close.

She needed help on this one, answers she couldn't get, even by sneaking in through the back door. She picked up her cell phone and stared at it. Bryan had blocked his number when he called. It was a control thing with him; he would always be the one who initiated contact. She called S.C. Police Headquarters and asked for him there and was told he had already left for the day. They would not give her his phone number or where he was staying, but they would be glad to relay the message for him to call her. That would have to be good enough.

Maddy stood up and stretched. She glanced at the kitchen clock. 9:15. Where had the day gone? That was a stupid question. So much had happened today and she was emotionally drained.

She called the dogs and let them outside. She grabbed another glass of tea and her cell phone and went out and sat on the steps. There was a nice cool breeze coming in from the west. The leaves of walnut tree in the yard rustled in the wind. The sun was a blaze of bright orange as it slowly sank into the horizon. The pups took a couple of laps around the yard then came and lay down at her feet. Both were panting heavily.

Maddy's phone vibrated beside her, she picked it up. "How come you get to hold all the cards, Bryan?"

"What? No hello, glad to hear from you? What's with the anger Maddy?" He sounded annoyed.

"You. I have more anger built up towards you than I want to deal with at the moment. But for now, why is it you always have means of contacting me, but yet I am at your mercy?'

"Christ Maddy, if you want my fucking phone number you've got it. It's the same damn number I've always had."

Maddy took several deep breaths. "Oh...I don't have it anymore."

"For how long?"

"A couple of years."

He was quiet for a couple of moments. "I see...Well guess that explains why I haven't heard from you."

"Heard from me?" she asked incredulously. "You hear from me? I can't believe you just said that. You are just too fucking incredible for words." She bit her lip. She had to stop; this is not where she wanted to go. Focus Maddy, focus. "I want this conversation to stop. It's not why I wanted to talk to you."

"What *do* you want to talk about Maddy? Quiet frankly I am quite surprised."

"I want to talk to you about the case." She crossed her fingers.

"You want to work the case, reactivate," he stated flatly.

"Bryan, I can't do that and you know why," she quietly protested.

"Maddy, we've seen shit nobody should have to see, but we put it behind us and move on. What we do, it matters, and it's the good fight. Believe in that. It's time to come back where you belong."

"And become like you, Bryan? No thanks, I want to keep my soul." She knew she sounded harsh, but as Jack would say, you think what you think, you feel what you feel.

She waited for Bryan to reply but nothing came. She looked at her screen and laughed. He hung up on her. Typical.

She got up and let the dogs in ahead of her. She straightened up her papers, put them in a folder and stuck them in her bag then took a quick shower. As she was brushing her teeth she happened to look up at the medicine cabinet. She took out a bottle and held it in her hand. She hadn't needed these in long time, but she could feel herself slipping. Her doctor might call it self-medicating or he might call it prevention. She liked to think of it as prevention. She opened the bottle and swallowed one of the capsules.

When she came out of the bathroom ready for bed her phone was going off on the table.

She picked it up. She knew what was coming. "Yes?"

"Don't pull that shit with me," Bryan's voice seethed with anger.

Not going to play this game, she thought to herself and shut her phone.

She locked the door, turned off her lights and wandered back to her bedroom. He wasn't done. He had to be in control. He had to be the one to finish it, just like always. Maddy was snuggled down in her covers and the dogs were lying at the foot of the bed when her phone went off again. She reached over and picked it up. "Good night Bryan, I will talk to you tomorrow." She hit the power off button and threw the phone in a sitting chair beside the bed. As she was drifting off to sleep she smiled to herself, "Pissed both men off tonight—I win," she whispered.

6

Maddy approached the new day with what she felt were things more in perspective. She arrived at the paper in a good mood and eager to work. The first item on her agenda was to write up and file a story of the two discovered bodies and the two other reported disappearances. She was careful that it be informative and factual and at the same time not divulging any of the privy information she had been given. Even if it hadn't been for the agreement she wouldn't have done it because it could compromise the case. She wasn't a journalist for the sake of exposing the truth at the cost of blowing an investigation.

Sandy was going to try to get some time off later to bring over Vanessa's laptop and go through it with Maddy. She got in and out of the house with no problem. Such an efficient police force. Maddy had no idea what she hoped to find on the computer. She'd be able to check what chat rooms she frequented and go over her emails hoping something would turn up. It would be nice if the computer could be totally disseminated, but it wasn't something she could do herself.

She had never worked a case of this caliber as a civilian and she felt crippled by it. There were so many little pieces of information she needed to compile a true profile that she didn't have access to them. Bryan wouldn't give it to her unless she went on board. Jack wouldn't give it to her because he's a fine upstanding police detective. The latter she thought sarcastically. She hadn't heard from either one of them yet this morning.

Maddy grabbed her missing persons profiles and dashed off to the Chief's office. She rapped on his door and entered when flagged in. "I need to see that crime packet."

The Chief unlocked one of his drawers, pulled out the packet and threw it across the desk to her. Maddy took out the two profiles of Rebecca Mallard and Tina Whethers and placed them face up in the desk. "I need feedback and a fresh eye," she looked at Chief. "That's you."

"Rebecca Mallard, 34, 135 pounds, 5'6, chestnut brown hair, shoulder length, brown eyes. Identifying marks, birthmark on inner thigh, rose tattoo on right ankle, appendix scar."

She picked up Whethers' sheet. "Tina Whethers, 28, 130 pounds, 5'5", chestnut brown hair, shoulder length, identifying marks, belly button piecing." She threw the sheets off to the side. "Well that narrows down the field."

She pulled out the autopsy report and photos on Jane Doe. She couldn't go by height or weight because in the state of decomp the body was in, it could have been either, hair color, both were the same. Maddy studied the autopsy photos and then threw them on the desk. "Damn it!"

"Give me those," Chief snatched them up off the desk, took out a magnifying glass and looked them over closely. "It's Whethers," he stated flatly.

She looked at him in astonishment, "How do you know?"

He showed the full-length photo of the body and pointed to the shot of the woman's right ankle. "No tat, and something you would never notice in a million years because you are a woman."

She snatched the photo out of his hands and studied it, "What?"

Chief picked up the two sheets on the women and put them side-by-side in front of Maddy. "Do you see it?"

Maddy threw her arms up in the air "No, Damn it Chief I don't, what?"

Chief sat back in his chair and gave a deep chuckle. "The boobs, Maddy, looked at the boobs. Whethers' breasts are substantially larger than Mallards. Even in this state of decomp, you can still tell."

She picked them up and studied them again. "I'll be a son of a bitch," she said in astonishment, "you're right."

Maddy sat back in her chair and observed her boss, shook her head and laughed. "Of course I will not divulge how we came, or give credit where credit is due, you came to your scientific identification of the body."

The Chief just grinned. "Of course our findings are not conclusive and would never stand up in court."

The Chief's intercom buzzed. "Chief, there is a gentleman out her to see Maddy.

Maddy stood up and peered through the blinds. "Shit, it's Bryan."

Chief grabbed his cup of coffee and took a swig and chuckled under his breath. "He's persistent. You have to give him that."

Maddy rolled her eyes, "Yeah, like a damn bulldog."

"Nail him with the silver bullet," he laughed.

Maddy's mouth dropped in disbelief, "Coming from you that is so not funny." Then she smiled, "Although that is an enticing thought."

"Go get 'em, Tiger. Show 'em what you're made of." He stacked up the sheets and the packet info and put them in the packet. "I am assuming you want me to hang on to these for you."

She nodded, "You would be assuming correctly."

She left his office, shutting the door behind her. Bryan was standing outside her office. She eyed him up and down liking what she saw. He was dressed in blue jeans and a light blue button down shirt, sporting his gun holster. As she walked by him she commented, "The holster kind of ruins the GQ effect...if that was what you're going for."

He studied her in return with her straight-legged blue jeans, white cotton t, and a soft pink blouse over top. She was wearing her hair pulled back in a loose ponytail, just a touch of makeup, pale pink lipstick. "When you dress like that you look like the girl next door, but I know the vixen that lurks beneath." He winked at her.

"Shut up," she said as walked past him into her office. He followed her in and sat down.

"Any luck with your pilfered info?"

"Yes, actually. Thanks for asking." From behind her desk she studied him. "What do you want?"

"I want you to go somewhere with me."

"You asking or telling?"

"Which ever gets you to come with me," he flashed a smile.

Maddy leaned back in her chair with her hands behind her head thinking about how last night ended. "That's why things don't work with us Bryan, we never deal with the issues."

"Kiddo, I don't want to spend all our time blaming whoever did what to who," He shifted in his seat. "I'm an asshole, it's my fault. I've never denied it and seems to me I have reminded you of that on numerous occasions." He stood up and held out his hand, "Now Minnie, will you please come with me? I'm asking."

"Don't call me that. Where?"

He reached across and tugged at her hand, "Come on, it's a surprise."

She yanked her hand back. "You're acting like a damn kid," she said as she grabbed her bag off the back of her chair.

"Good," he laughed. "Come out and play with me."

She threw him a sideway glance. "I don't like to play with you. You don't play fair."

"All's fair in love and war," he held the door open for her.

"And which would this be?" She pulled her keys out and locked her door.

He chuckled, "Depends on who you ask, for me—love, for you, I am sure you would say war. One would get the impression, Maddy, you don't like me very much, but we both know better."

She rolled her eyes and didn't even bother to answer. What was the point?

Bryan led Maddy to his standard issue black Chevy Suburban and opened the door for her then proceeded to get in the driver's side. He pulled out on Pavonia Street, then turned west on to 6th. "Figure out who Jane Doe is yet?"

"I have a good guess, but then I can't back it up with facts now can I? If I tell you who I think she is, will you confirm it?" It was a long shot, but what the hell, the worst he could say was no, and after all he brought it up.

"Tell me who and how you came to the conclusion...and I *might* confirm it."

She watched as they drove through the traffic, past car lot row, across the Floyd River, by Mercy Medical. "The disappearance of the two additional missing women, Rebecca Mallard and Tina Whethers, times out in June. Decomp on Jane Doe would could easily be measured to someone who died during that time frame."

He glanced over at her and then focused on the traffic ahead of him. "And?"

"So I inferred it was more than likely one of those two women."

"And the winner is?"

"The winner? You are so crass, but why should that surprise me?" She shook it off. "Whethers."

"Based on?"

"Boobs," she replied flatly.

"What?" Bryan turned sharply, the vehicle swerved as he did, just barely missing a car in the next lane.

Maddy braced herself against the dash. "Christ Bryan, watch where you're going!"

"Boobs? What the hell? I gotta hear this one. Explain." He swung the suburban into the Police Station parking lot.

"What are we doing here? Don't you think for one moment that you are going to take me in there and use me as some form as entertainment for you and your lackeys!" Maddy struck out at him with her fist. "That's bullshit Bryan!"

Bryan grabbed her wrist and held them. "Just like old times. If we were in a different place I would take you right here, right now."

Maddy felt as if someone had shot ice through her veins. Flashes of images flickered before her eyes, images of the past. Fire and ice. "Let me go!" she hissed.

Bryan released her and put his hands on the steering wheel. "I'm sorry Maddy. That was uncalled for."

They sat in silence. Maddy watched as patrol cars pulled in and out of the lot.

"For what its worth, you are right," he spoke in subdued voice.

"About? You? I never had any doubt." she gave him a sideways glance.

"Whethers, we got a dental and DNA match." Bryan pulled the keys out of the ignition. "Can I make a deal with you?"

Oh Lord, this could be anything. "I won't commit 'til I know what it is we're playing *Let's Make a Deal* with."

"Tag along with me for awhile today, as friends and colleges. I will try to be on my best behavior. And, here's the deal breaker, you go out on the town with me tonight. And in turn, I will let you in on details of the case."

She looked at him in disbelief, "Full disclosure?"

He nodded, "Full disclosure."

"What's the catch?"

"Just what I said. Do we have a deal?"

"Let see, spend time with you," she did the scale thing with her hands, "full disclosure on the case." She balanced them back and forth. "And I have to go out with you tonight?"

"Yes, is it a deal?"

Maddy scrunched her face up and squinted her eyes like she was thinking real hard. Actually it was a no-brainer. As long as Bryan wasn't being an ass or got too personal she did like his company. And as far as going out with him tonight, that could be dangerous, but she felt like she could handle it. But the best thing, access to the case, which was awesome! "Okay, but it's not because I want to spend time with you, just so that's understood."

"No, of course it's not." He had a shit-eating grin on his face as he got out of the truck.

Maddy followed Bryan into the station. He handed her a visitor's pass and they proceeded to the room Bryan's team had set up headquarters. There were three agents in the room and a couple detectives. She got a couple of covert glances, some snickers, and one cold glaring stare. Whittmer. Maddy stood on her tiptoes and whispered in Bryan's ear. "Red doesn't like me."

He laughed, "Don't worry about it, he's a toad."

Maddy smiled, "My words exactly."

He shrugged, "What can I say, he's not one of mine." Bryan sat at his desk and began going through messages and some files that had been placed in his box. "Be with you in a minute, Maddy."

Maddy glanced around room and saw her gold mine—the case wall. Pictures of all the missing women (the same as her local her list), autopsy photos, several different angles of the grave sites, photos of their homes, friends, boyfriends, lots of cool stuff. She moved closer to the wall. She hardly got a good look when she was approached by Whittmer who informed her to step away from the wall as she was not authorized personnel. She smiled sweetly at him and flipped him off.

"Maddy!" Bryan snapped at her, "Quit bothering the help." He pointed to a chair in front of him.

She covered her mouth with her hand and laughed then sat in the chair as commanded. She whispered, "Just give me ten minutes, that's all I need."

"Not now," he spoke in a low voice not looking up at her. "Later, when Toad's not around."

Maddy snuck a look at the papers on his desk. She could read upside down as well as she could right side up. There were statements from the victims' friends and neighbors. Bryan was reading notes on interviews having to do with Tina Whethers.

Bryan threw the paper work down. "This is going nowhere. We got five women with virtually nothing connecting them, nothing. They're just gone. We don't know why he selects them."

"We have eight," she corrected him.

"Eight? You lost me."

"The Omaha connection. If this all started there, our unsub was triggered there by some event that set him off. We need to find the stressor. Then something happened to make him relocate. It can't be that he was too close to being caught because OPD has nothing connecting the disappearances either. You know except for the basic dichotomy we have nothing."

"Pretty damn hard to find a stressor if we know nothing about our unsub. We have no crime scenes, only two bodies, no motive...no witnesses." He shook his head.

Maddy was snooping though some of the papers on the desk. "We have a witness."

Bryan looked at her abruptly, "We do? Who?"

"Rufus," she replied without looking up.

"Who the hell is Rufus?"

"Vanessa Granger's dog." She pulled out her cell phone and showed him Rufus's picture.

"A fucking dog?" Bryan was incredulous. "Are you fucking nuts, Maddy? How can a fucking dog be a witness?"

Maddy peered over the top of one of the papers, "Lower your voice. Getting a little melodramatic with the "f" word aren't you?"

Bryan shook his head in disbelief, "A fucking dog for a witness. Hell it's not even a dog—it's damn a rat."

"Hey! I take offense. Rufus is not a rat; he's a Yorkie. We found him hiding behind Granger's dryer when we were checking out her house. He is very sensitive to things he relates to Vanessa's abductor."

"I'm not even going to ask what you were doing at the victim's house or why you have possession of a vic's dog. How do you figure the dog knows?" Bryan leaned back in his chair and cross his arms in front of him.

Maddy tapped her nose. "The nose knows. He reacts to the man's cologne and probably more."

"Yeah like what kind of shoes he wore and what his pant legs looked like, and if he weren't color blind he could probably tell you what color his socks were. Better yet, lets get a sketch artist in here and bring the dog in to describe him." Bryan watch Maddy and began to laugh, "No, no...let's bring the dog in and he can pick the unsub out of a line-up."

Maddy picked up the first thing she could get her hands on, a pencil holder, and threw it at him with some force. "Quit being a smart ass, you asshole. I'm serious."

He caught it in his hand and smiled as he nodded in agreement. "I'm sure you are, and that's what's scaring me. I've always encouraged you to think outside of the box, but this time, Minnie, you are waaaaaaay out of the box."

"Fuck you!"

"No," he laughed, "fuck you."

Her eyes narrowed, "I hate you."

Bryan stood up and leaned across the desk. "No you don't," He touched the tip of her nose, "and there's a fine line between love and hate, Minnie."

Neither Maddy nor Bryan was aware of Jack watching the exchange from the doorway. He crossed the room to Bryan. "Sorry to intrude but wanted to inform you the sweep of Bacon Creek with the cadaver dogs is completed without results. We are in the process of organizing a search of Stone Park tomorrow."

"Thank you, Detective," Bryan replied. "What are we looking at with this Stone Park?"

"You're talking about covering over 1,000 acres of dense, rugged woodlands," Maddy jumped in. "How are you going to do that?" Maddy looked up at Jack. When she caught his eye, she swore she saw hurt in them. Let it go, Maddy, she said to herself, this is work, don't let it get personal.

"With all the volunteers we can get our hands on, on foot, on horse back. I meant to talk to you about that. Can you and your horses join us?" Jack asked her.

"Sure, I'm sure I can get off work. I got three horses and I have a friend that has several horses she and I can bring in."

"Do you ride Parker?" Bryan asked him.

Jack looked from Bryan to Maddy, "Yeah...sure I do, no problem." He didn't sound real confident in his answer.

"You never said you knew how to ride," Maddy said in surprise.

"You never asked," he stated flatly.

"Oookay," she shut her mouth.

"I will give you a call when I firm up on the details."

She nodded.

Jack was about to walk away when Bryan called out to him, "Parker, we were just about to head down to the firing range. Would you like to join us?"

"We are?" Maddy looked at him in surprise.

"Sure, I need to get some shooting time in." Then Jack looked at Maddy and smiled softly, "Just one surprise after another with you isn't it?" He turned and left.

"Cowboy a little on edge with you?" Bryan inquired with a smirk in his face.

"I don't know what he is more annoyed with, the fact he found out he knows very little about me after all, or that I'm smarter than he gave me credit for." She was looking at the door that Jack had just passed through. "And quit calling him cowboy, his name is Jack and he's a damn good cop."

Bryan began to stack up the papers on his desk, "I know that. The man's got a lot of potential which he is wasting being a small town detective. He's green and would need quite a bit of seasoning. Depending on how he performs through this case, I might even suggest he go into the training program—if that is what he aspires to."

Jack would probably jump at the chance, so why didn't Maddy feel glad for him? The FBI changes those who follow its path. Depending on what unit you worked in, it could steal your soul. Take Bryan, for instance, it took away his compassion, his ability to feel joy, and his ability to see the human race can being inherently good. Hell for all that matter it took a piece of her she will never get back. She would really hate to see that happen to Jack. He was too good of a person.

"I don't know," her voice far off, "you'll have to ask him."

"Am I getting in the way of a budding romance?" Bryan unlocked a drawer in the desk and pulled something out and laid it on the desk.

"Of course not," she replied a little too quickly. "You've met his girlfriend, even lusted after her." Maddy tried to laugh it off.

"We should ask Parker and his lovely lady to join us tonight," Bryan watched for her reaction.

Maddy's head shot up and she saw how Bryan was looking at her. He was testing her, feeling her out. "Sure.... If you can guarantee me Barbie won't attack me again."

"Hell you could take her down in a heart beat and you know it," he laughed. "So what do you think? Are you up to an interesting evening?"

"Hey, I'm up to anything that doesn't leave me alone with you," she said over her shoulder. "Let's get this show on the road."

She waited for Bryan outside the door. "Well get going then," he said.

"What makes you think I know how to get there?"

"I don't know, I just assumed you did. Follow me," he sighed mocking annoyance.

Down at the firing range, they signed in, got their ammo and their ear-protectors. Jack was already on the range. He nodded at them as they walked by. Bryan took his shots first firing several rounds from his Glock 22 into the head and chest of his target.

"You're turn," he spoke loudly to be able to be heard over the gunfire.

"No." She had no desire to pick up that gun and fire it.

"Come on Minnie, you agreed to my terms. You used to love target practice," Bryan cajoled.

She stood there with her arms crossed in defiance, "I used love having sex with you too, but that doesn't mean I want to do it again."

Jack peered around the corner from two stalls down, laughing.

Bryan gave her the look, "Maddy..."

She touched the Glock, felt the coldness of the resin, the power she knew it wielded. "Fine." She picked up the gun, locked in a fresh magazine. At first her hands shook as she brought it into the line of fire. She took a deep breath, steadied herself, and pulled the trigger firing off all 15 rounds.

She pushed a button, which brought the target up for examination. Jack came over and stood by them to see how Maddy did. Her shots all centered in the heart area and the groin.

Bryan studied it with his mouth open. "Jesus Christ Maddy, what the hell were you thinking?"

She looked at him and smiled sweetly, "I was pretending it was you!" She set the Glock down, turned and left. She could hear Jack laughing his ass off. That would not make points with Bryan.

Maddy was leaning against the wall by the FBI temporary office when Jack walked down the hall, a big smile still on his face. He looked at her and shook his head as he walked by her.

"Hey! Don't I deserve a hello?" she called after him.

He stopped and pivoted. He shrugged his shoulders, "Don't know, wouldn't want to mix person bullshit with business." He turned back and continued walking.

"Whatever," she muttered under her breath.

Bryan followed up the rear with the target folded in half under his arm. He walked passed her into the office and she followed him in. "You keeping that?"

"Yep," He took out some pushpins and tacked it the wall behind him.

"Why?"

"Because I want reminder of how lethal you can be."

Maddy crossed the space between them and reached up to rip it down. Bryan caught her arm. "It's mine, Minnie, leave it be. I talked to Cowboy, we are going to meet at some bar on 4th Street at 8:00."

"He agreed?" She looked surprised.

"Oh yeah, thought it was a good idea." Bryan locked the extra Glock in his desk.

Maddy was still skeptical. "Why do I get the feeling I'm being set up for one fucked up night?"

Bryan put his finger under her chin and kissed her softly on the lips, "You worry too much. It'll be fun. Come on, I will take you back to the paper so you can get your work done and get home to get all sexy for me."

"What about my full disclose?"

"You'll get it...after you complete your side of deal."

"That's not fair," she protested.

"Kiddo, don't worry about it. Let's see how tomorrow plays out. You want full disclosure now or when we know more?"

"More I guess." She was disappointed, but she didn't really know if it was not getting her prize or because Jack blew her off.

Bryan ran his fingers down the sides of her arms sending shivers up them. She looked around the room. There were a couple agents and a couple of DCI agents in the room, all appeared as if they were absorbed by their projects. "Bryan what do think your agents think when they see you acting like this? It's very unprofessional."

He laughed, "Jealous—they're not making this hot red head quiver with their touch."

She pushed against his chest, she felt the blood rushing to her face. "You are such a pig."

He took her face in his hands and kissed her deeply. "Oink," he whispered in her ear. "You ready to go, Gorgeous?"

She grabbed her bag and poked him in the ribs, "Let's move."

On the way back to the Journal Bryan filled her in on the plan for tomorrow. Her group would meet at the east end of the park where they could unload the horses. Maddy would call her friend when she got back to the office and make arrangements for her help and her horses. A good part of the police force, as well the county law enforcement from area counties and civilians would be helping in the search. Several cadaver dogs on loan would be brought in for the search also.

Bryan pulled into the parking lot of the paper to let Maddy out. When she reached for the door handle, he gently pulled her back and kissed her. He brushed a loose strand of hair away from her face. He searched her eyes with his, "You know how much I love you, don't you Maddy?"

She reached up and brushed his cheek, "In your own warped way, yeah, I know you do."

"And you?"

She looked away. "Bryan what do you want me to say? With everything we've been through, with everything you have done to me. It wasn't bad enough you tore out my heart, but you had have her throw it back in my face." Maddy wiped the tears from her face.

Bryan moved his hand away from her. "I have no answers, no excuses for what happened. My head, I was just so messed up. Between Jeff's addictions, Natalia sucking me dry, Donna's constant nagging and ragging on me about you. When I wasn't working, I was drinking sanity or should I say insanity away. You know how depressed I was. You were the only sane, wonderful part of my life."

"No Bryan, I was this sick, drunken obsession who you used and manipulated. You played games with my emotions. You have always said you loved me for my intelligence, my wit, my sense of humor, my compassion, but those were the same qualities you set out to destroy. First you wanted me there, I couldn't just drop everything and do that, and you knew that. Then you begged and pleaded to let you come and live with me. When I said no, you tortured me, you mind fucked me, Bryan. Finally I broke down and said yes. I destroyed my world for you. And when you left Donna, I thought you really did choose me," her voice cracked. "And then out of the blue, well, you know what happened next." A sob escaped her lips. "You left me dangling in the wind by a thread with no answers, no good-bye. You broke me, Bryan. I told you when you came back what getting involved with you could do to me. You knew and you fucking did it anyway! I lost it. I couldn't function for weeks. I quit my job. Finally when I started to heal, I ran. I started over, again. Seems like I am always starting over, always running away."

Bryan pulled her close and held her. She looked up at him, "I'm tired of running Bryan, and I don't want to do it anymore. I hate you...I love you; you know that, no matter how much I try, I can't stop loving you. But when everything is said and done Bryan, you are going to leave me again. We will never be together. You will never be mine. I can never fit in your world. We just get these stolen moments in time when you decide when it is. The only thing worse than having hope, is having hope you know will never be realized."

He kissed her on the top of her head and buried his face in her hair. She could feel the unsteadiness in his breathing. She tried to look up at him, but he held her in place. She had a feeling he didn't want her to see his face. "I'm so sorry,

Minnie, I'm so very sorry." His voice was raspy and full of emotion. She needed to hear him say it, more than she would ever tell him.

She gently pulled away from him and kissed him on the cheek. "Where do you want to meet tonight?"

Bryan reached out and wiped her tears away with the back of his hand. "You still want to go out with me?"

She gave him a weak smile. "I need to deal with reality, Bryan. And that is if this is all we get, then I will take it."

"What about Cowboy?"

She laughed weakly, "He's got Barbie."

"But he wants you. I can see it when he looks at you." He glanced out the window and then back at her. "Maddy, if he is what you want, and what you need, you have to take the chance. Like you said, I will end up leaving you when this is all done. He will be here for you, love you and not put you through what I do to you."

"We decided not to mix personal life with business."

He laughed, "Well we'll see what happens tonight. I bet he gives me lots wanting to kill me looks, even with Barbie there. But Minnie, when the night is over, it's me you leave with."

She gave him a shaky laugh, "You are a sadist. Where we meeting?"

"I'm at the Regency out by the mall. You care to pick me up? I really don't want to drive this tank."

"I'll be there at 7:30." She squeezed his hand and got out of the truck and watched him pull away.

Wow, talk about an emotional catharsis. She was still a little emotional shaky, yet she felt cleansed. She wanted to be with Bryan, but she knew when the time came for him to leave, she would get hurt again. But this time, it was her choice.

When she arrived at the office Max approached her with a laptop in his hands. "Sandy Morton dropped this off. Said to tell you she was sorry, but couldn't get time off work. She would give you call."

She took it from his hands, "Thanks Max." She unlocked her door and placed the computer on her desk. She wasn't going to take work home with her tonight. She wouldn't have time to work on it anyway.

She picked up her phone and called her friend Jessie, told her about the park search and what she needed from her. She agreed to swing by and pick up Maddy's three horses and bring three of her own. Maddy told her where the tack and feed-bags were because she had a feeling she wouldn't be coming home tonight. If she drank too much she would just get a motel room.

An hour and a half later, horses were fed, hay bags filled, bridals hooked on to saddle horns, and lead ropes draped across the saddles. She let the dogs in the house, filled their water bowls and food bowls, grabbed a sandwich and took a shower.

She packed an overnight bag consisting of a sleep shirt, her riding boots, jeans, a t-shirt, a long sleeve shirt and her favorite cap. Maddy blow-dried her hair, scrunching it up so it was good and curly then pulled it back on the sides. She chose a pair of cream-colored silk pants that hung like a skirt. For a top, she picked an emerald green, silk sleeveless that draped in a loose cowl around her neck. She applied her makeup carefully and then stood back away from the mirror and liked what she saw. The green in her eyes appeared luminous because of the emerald green in her blouse as well as the light dusting of green eye shadow on her lids. Instead of the usual pale pink lipstick she normally wore she had applied wine. One last thing, she went to her bedroom and dug through her jewelry box and pulled out a matching emerald teardrop necklace and earrings. They had been a gift from Bryan the first time they were together. She slipped them on and sized herself up in the mirror again and smiled brightly. Perfect.

Maddy felt giddy with excitement, she felt like a schoolgirl going on her first date. This was silly, it was just Bryan. And Jack...and Stella. She kind of hated the fact they were going to be with them. She still wasn't quite sure why Bryan had suggested they double. It was not like Jack and he were buddies and he knew damn well she and Stella didn't get along. As much as she hated to admit it, this was the old Bryan in action, setting up conflict for his own amusement. This was one of the games he liked to play, to set up a situation where tension and conflict were likely to happen and he would orchestrate how things were played out. It was one of his control games. He would watch how Jack reacted to he and Maddy, how she would react to Jack and Stella, how she and Stella would react to each other. It would be awkward, but she had to admit, she wanted to see how this played out too.

An hour later she was knocking on the door of room 204 at the Regency. Bryan opened the door and motioned her in; he was talking on his cell. She took a seat in a chair under the window and scoped out her surroundings. It was a nice room with deep green carpets, floral bedding on a king sized bed, your run of mill the bed stands, bureau, microwave, mini bar—a motel room. The room smelt of cologne and cigarette smoke. Bryan was rubbing his hair with a white towel while he was talking. He was wearing charcoal grey slacks and so far—no shirt. His hard life had not been kind to him, he had the body of a man years beyond him. She could see the star shaped scar on his back where a bullet had gone through and through.

She wouldn't be Maddy if she didn't strain to listen to his conversation. "I don't know when I will be home, when we close the case we close the case. You're getting yourself all worked up over nothing. No, I won't be here; I'm going out with some colleges. Yes, I'm going to be drinking. Don't worry about it. Who gives a fuck about the damn dogs? Go and do something at the clubhouse or something instead of sitting there worrying about what I'm doing. I told you not to call me."

He was talking to Donna. An evil smile crept across her lips. What she wouldn't do to grab that phone and tell Donna Bryan was with her, here alone in his motel room and she was going to fuck his brains out. Sweet revenge, so sweet she could taste it. But of course, she couldn't. Damn.

Bryan told Donna goodnight and powered down his cell. "She'll be calling me all damn night if I left it on. Parker will have his if someone needs to get a hold of us."

Maddy smiled and made a little motion back and forth with her wrist.

"What's that suppose to mean?" he asked.

"Just wiggling your leash," she laughed like she was kidding but actually she really meant it.

He crossed the room with a couple of quick strides and pulled her to her feet and yanked her into his arms, "You are one mean bitch, Maddy."

She was smiling, her eyes fixed on his lips. "I had a good teacher." Her gazed moved to his eyes, they were smoldering. She wound her arms up around his neck, her fingers caressing the back of his neck.

"You always were an excellent student." His hands slid from her hips up the curves of her body. The feel of his touch on the silk sent shivers through her.

She kissed his chest at the base of his neck, his skin and hair still damp from his shower.

"Whoa Minnie," he pulled her arms from around his neck and took a step away from her. "Do you want to end up spending all night right here? It's not that I wouldn't love for that to happened, but I don't want you to think all I am after is your body," he winked.

"Maybe that's all I am after you for?" she laughed.

Bryan went to the dressing bureau and pulled out a white and lavender pin striped shirt and slipped it on. "You don't want this tired old body." His eyes traveled over hers, "Time has been good to you Minnie. You are just as beautiful as the day I first laid eyes on you."

"I bet you say that to all the girls," she laughed and sat back down.

"All the girls, there weren't all the girls," he said in all seriousness.

"Okay, if you say so, but I know better, I know you better. You have had more than your share of trysts. Once a player always a player." Maddy picked up a magazine and thumbed through it.

He didn't reply to the accusation, just continued to button up his shirt and slipped on his shoes. "You ready?"

She followed him out the door and down to her car. Bryan eyed the car and laughed. "You call this a car? I've seen coaster wagons bigger than this,"

She slid in the drivers seat. "Fuck you, this car is a deadly weapon."

"To what? Squirrels?"

"I take offense to that statement, she has been the cause of demise of many other creatures."

Bryan got in and slid the seat as far back as it would go, which still didn't give him much leg room. "Whatever you do, don't get in a wreck, they would have to cut me out of here like a sardine."

Maddy threw her head back and laughed, "Quit your whining, we could have taken a cab."

Bryan seemed content looking at the city as they drove across town to 4th Street. She knew Sioux City was far from what he was used to. He was all big city, bright lights and lots of action. They used to joke around about their differences in life style. She was country mouse. He was city mouse. Minnie and Mickey.

Maddy pulled up in front of the bar on what was referred to as Historic 4th Street. This part of town had once been the home of prostitutes, porno shops, and XXX movie theatres, the underbelly of the city. Now it was home to nice restaurants, trendy bars, a cinema, a promenade, and a civic center. The bar they entered had windows that reached the two-story height of the building. Inside there was a wrap around bar with pillars that reached to the ceiling. There were ample tables, pool tables and a small dance floor.

Jack and Stella had already arrived and were seated at a table close to a window near the dance floor. Jack was nursing a beer and Stella had what appeared to be a martini with an olive. Figures. Jack stood to greet them and shook Bryan's hand and nodded a greeting to Maddy. Not even a smile. He was really taking this business/personal thing to an extreme, probably to teach her a lesson. Sounded like something Bryan would have stooped to. She hated it. Stella smiled sweetly at Bryan and held out her hand to which he brought to his lips. "And you are the lovely Barbie."

Maddy started laughing, "No, her name is Stella." She looked at Jack, "You know...like in a Street Car Named Desire." He was glaring at her.

"Oh, my apologies."

Maddy sat down and when Bryan sat beside her she whispered, "Nice lip job—I think I am going to puke." For his reply he leaned over, took her hand and gave her a soft kiss on the lips, then winked at her. She gave him a beaming smile.

The waiter arrived to take their drink order. Bryan ordered a pitcher of beer and Maddy ordered a vodka sour.

Jack's eyebrows rose up.

"What?" she asked him.

"Is your memory that short?"

"No one asked you," she hissed.

Bryan looked from one to the other, "Problem?"

Stella piped up. "She can't handle her booze. She got shit faced by herself Friday night and Jack had to drive her home."

Maddy reached over and patted Jack's hand, "And Jack here was such a sweetheart and spent the weekend with me nursing my hangover."

Stella stabbed at her olive with a toothpick. Maddy thought she probably wished she that olive was her face.

The waiter returned and set their drinks down in front of them. Maddy quickly picked hers up and downed it. She handed the glass back to the waiter, "I'll take another, make it a double."

Jack had been taking a drink of his beer and choked. He quickly took his napkin and wiped up his spill. "So, Maddy, how's your investigation going?" he spoke quickly.

"Just swimmingly," she replied tersely.

Stella reached across the table and put her hand on Bryan's arm. "It's so exciting, we have an FBI agent with us, Bryan, I am so impressed. You must lead a fascinating life."

"Maddy is FBI, too," Jack said flatly as took another swig of beer.

Stella couldn't hide her surprise, "You're kidding, and I thought she was just a reporter."

The waiter returned with her double. Maddy took her straw and stirred her drink and then took a sip through the straw. "Was. I quit. I wish you would just get over it and move on Jack."

"That's not quite true," Bryan piped in. "She is in inactive status. I am trying like hell to get her to reactivate and take her back with me."

Maddy's head came up, "What do you mean in inactive status?" she asked quietly. She looked passed the "take her back with me" part. She would discuss that with him later.

Bryan leaned over and whispered in her ear, "Just go with it Minnie," and his kissed her on her cheek.

Jack locked eyes with her daring her, but she didn't look away. This game of his was getting real old and she felt very uncomfortable.

Bryan tugged on Maddy's hand. "Come dance with me, they're playing our song." They rose from the table and Bryan guided her to the dance floor. As Phil Collins' *You'll be in my heart* filled the bar, Bryan held Maddy close and sang the song in her ear. She had given him a CD of this song that night they celebrated his birthday a decade ago. He took her arms and put them up around his neck and he held his at the small of her back and they swayed to the music.

"You remembered," she whispered.

His eyes studied her face. "Did you think I could ever forget?" He gave her a long slow kiss and then guided her head to his chest. "Never Minnie, not in a million years."

Maddy's heart was pounding, and she felt all warm and fuzzy. Was it Bryan or the booze? It didn't matter, at this moment in time she was where she wanted to be—in his arms.

Maddy was unaware that Jack couldn't take his eyes off her, that his face was like stone except for the vein in his temples was twitching. There was no mistaking the couple swaying on the dance floor had a very deep connection that no one could break, least of all him. Maddy was lost to him forever.

Maddy hadn't realized Jack and Stella had joined them on dance floor. Her eyes had been closed as Bryan held her close and they swayed to music. When she opened them the first things she saw was the hurt in Jack's eyes. Her heart gave a little pang. This double date thing had been a bad idea.

She wasn't the only one who noticed, "Cowboy's jealous. Did you tell him about us? Our history?"

"Some of it," she whispered.

"The two of you need to talk."

"And tell him what? That even though I love you, just wait a while and you'll leave me and maybe then he and I might have a chance? I don't want to deal with you leaving, not yet. It hurts too much."

When the song finished he took her hand and led her back to their seats. He took a long draw off his beer and set it down. He took her hand and held it in his. "I'm selfish when it comes to you, I have never made any bones about it—selfish to the point where you're the one who suffers. You could have been happy if it weren't for me."

She picked up her glass and downed half of it. "It's done and over with, let it go."

"You say that now because you are making excuses for what I did to you. What you said earlier today, you are right, Maddy. What I did to you was so wrong on so many levels. I knew what you've been through. I knew how fragile you could be. At that time I was so blinded by, like you said, with my obsession to have you back I didn't care. I want you with me for as long as I can have you, but not at the cost of your happiness. Do you understand what I am saying?"

Maddy finished off her drink and held the glass up for the waiter to see and the set it down. "There's something you have a tendency to do and it's for you to cut me off emotionally because you think you are doing what's best for me. Everytime I beg you not to. Please, Bryan, don't do it to me again. I know you are leaving. I will deal with it when the time comes. You keep telling me I belong to you. Well damn it, right now, until you do leave, you belong to me! Don't you dare take that away from me. Promise me," she pleaded.

He touched her cheeks and kissed her, "I promise, but you need to fix things with Cowboy, at least put things back to where you two are friends. Now you promise me."

She nodded.

Bryan took his thumb and softly brushed beneath her eyes. "Don't want to mess up those beautiful eyes with tears."

The waiter returned with her drink and she took a sip from it. "This is not turning out to be a very fun evening. I wish it had just been the two of us." She poked at the ice cubes with her straw.

Bryan downed the rest of his beer. "You and I both know if it were just the two of us we be back at the motel." He filled his glass from the picture. "Now when Cowboy comes back, I am going to take Barbie for a spin on the dance floor and keep her busy so you can have a little private time with him. Two things are going to happen here. It's going to give me a feel how much he cares about her, and will give him a feel how much you care about me."

"What do you mean?"

"I'm going to give her a run for her money. I'm just playing, so I don't want you getting all bent out of shape, okay?"

"You lay one lip on the lipo bitch I swear to God I will scratch your eyes out. And if Jack comes after you?"

Bryan held his glass up, "To foreplay!" Then he dipped his finger in his beer and flicked it at her, "Jack won't lift a finger, trust me."

Maddy threw an ice cube back at him. "Trust you my ass," she laughed.

Jack pulled out Stella's chair for her and then sat down in his chair to her right. She had to secretly smile, funny how the men knew better than to sit the women together. Stella planted a big kiss on Jack and he smiled back at her. Maddy felt a twinge in her stomach. This was insane, here she was with Bryan and she was feeling jealous over Jack. Damn men.

"You two make such a darling couple," Stella said to Bryan, "How long have you two been together?"

"An eternity. We've known each other a long time. Maddy's my soul mate. We don't get to see each other often so when we do, we make the best of it." Bryan squeezed her hand.

"Oh," was all Stella said. Wow, the bitch was at a loss for words.

Maddy felt Stella's eyes bearing down on her. The woman just grated on her nerves. "Is there something specific you're staring at? Perhaps you're just not used to seeing a real woman, obviously you don't see it when you look in the mirror," she snapped.

"Maddy!" that came from both Jack and Bryan simultaneously.

Stella sat there with her mouth gaping open. Bryan grabbed her hand, "Come and show me what your moves are." He looked over at Jack, "Do you mind?"

"No, go ahead." As soon as they were out of earshot, he shot Maddy a look. "Do you ever stop and think before you open your mouth?"

"I call it like I see it." Her chin jetted out in defiance. She downed half of her drink.

"You're getting drunk," he said bitterly.

"Do you have any idea how hard getting through this is?"

Jack slammed his empty glass down on the table, "Yeah Maddy, I do."

Maddy took Bryan's pitcher and filled Jack's glass. They sat silently watching Bryan and Stella on the dance floor. Santana's *Smooth* was playing and the two were getting into some fancy Latin dancing. Maddy studied Stella. She was wearing a skintight white dress with a slit cut up to her thigh that really showed off her long slender legs and of course stiletto shoes, white this time. She had to admit the woman could move and she was all over Bryan. True to his word Bryan gave what he got. Too bad he seemed to be enjoying it so much.

"Does it bother you?" Jack asked quietly.

She shrugged her shoulders. It did but she would never admit it...to anyone. "Not really, that's just Bryan. She's right up his alley, more his type than me. Does it bother you?"

For the first time a while, he smiled, "Funny, not really." He reached in his jacket pocket and pulled out his cigarettes. "I could really use a smoke, you want to come out and keep me company?"

"Sure," she stood up but turned to take a large gulp of her drink.

Maddy and Jack walked toward the door. He held up his pack of cigarettes. Stella waved at him. Apparently she was having more fun dancing with Bryan than she cared Jack was leaving with Maddy.

Outside each bar there were ample benches for smokers since Iowa had passed a law that called for no smoking in public places, which included bars. Maddy sat down and Jack sat next to her and lit up. He took a deep drag off the cigarette, held it briefly and then exhaled it slowly. "Damn I needed that." He held the pack out for Maddy.

She put her hands up and shook her head, "No thank you."

He laughed thinking of her that day on the curbside. She knew what he was thinking and laughed too. "Running with the big dogs, you called it."

He took another drag, "Little did I know you were a big dog. I wish we could turn back time, when things between us were so much simpler."

Maddy had grabbed her straw and was chewing on it. "You mean before we started...feeling things."

"That's not what I meant...at least I don't think that's what I meant. Hell, Maddy, I don't know what the fuck I mean anymore. I'm so damn confused about all this shit. I see you with Mayland and its not what you described—how terrible things were between you, how bad he hurt you. I would think you would stay the hell away from him as possible. What I see is two people who are so fused together, you feed off each other. Its like I said before, you two are like a chemical reaction."

"Fire and ice," Maddy said softly.

"What?"

"We describe each other as fire and ice. When things are good, it's like fire and we melt each other, when things are bad its bitter, cold and ugly."

"I'm surprised he's not out here throwing you over his shoulder and dragging you back in there." Jack put out his cigarette and lit another one.

Maddy pulled her feet up under her. "Actually he is in there keeping Barbie busy so we could have a chance to talk things out."

Jack gave her a strange look, "He wants us to talk?" He was doubtful.

Maddy nodded. "He feels like he has come between us and doesn't want to destroy our friendship. He thinks there is something going on with us."

Jack watched as people walked by them into the bar. "Well he's right on all counts," he paused. "Nothing can happen between us while he's in the picture. I can't compete with the hold he has over you."

Maddy leaned her head back against the wall. "When this is all over, he'll leave, again. Be out of my life...again. But I'm not asking you to wait. That would be selfish."

Jack put his hand on her knee. "I'm sorry Maddy. I don't want to see you get hurt again. But I watch you with him...and you're so alive. When he is holding you, kissing you..." he shook his head.

"Jesus, Jack, what do you want me to do?"

"I have one question for you. If he hurt you the way you said he did, and I do believe he did, how can you just forget that and be with him the way you are?"

"I can't answer, Jack."

"Can't or won't?"

"Can't. Its inexplicable."

"I see."

"Can I check something out, Jack?"

"I guess."

Maddy leaned over and kissed him on the lips, slow and gentle. Jack cupped his hand around her face and returned the kiss, letting it become more intense. When they stopped they let their foreheads rested against each other. Maddy laughed nervously and sat up.

"Did you find what you were looking for?" Jack asked, his voice husky.

"Yeah," she replied softly.

"And what was that?" He stood up and offered her a hand up.

She allowed him to help her to her feet. "That it is real." Before they walked into the bar, she turned to Jack. "Does this make me a slut?"

Jack laughed, "No, just makes you one fucked up chick!"

"Fuck you!"

As they were walking through the door Jack put Maddy in a headlock, she squealed and twisted out of it.

Bryan and Stella had already taken a seat. Bryan had bought another round of drinks. Both looked at the two as they came back to the table. Bryan stood up and kissed Maddy and pulled her chair out for her.

Maddy smoothed out a few loose strands of her hair, "Jack, you asshole, you messed up my hair."

Jack sat down and slid his chair in, "That's our Maddy," he laughed, "forever the lady."

"Isn't she now?" Bryan held his glass up and he and Jack clicked glasses.

Stella eyes darted back and forth between the three of them. "What was going on out there?" she asked Jack suspiciously.

Maddy stirred her drink with her finger, licked it, and then drank the remainder. She would have loved to watch the encounter that was about to take place, but thought it best if she down played her role. She tried not looking, but it was killing her.

"What were you doing out there with her?"

"Christ Stella, I was smoking a cigarette. I showed you when we were walking out the door."

"Why did she have to go? What happened? You two sure came back all chummy chummy."

Jack sighed and ran his fingers through his hair. Uh-oh. "You sound like you are accusing me of something. Stella, I think we need to clear the air here. Maddy is my friend, my good friend. I have known her far longer than I have known you. You either back the fuck off and accept it or go the fuck home!"

Bryan kicked Maddy under the table just as Maddy kicked Jack. Maddy and Jack jumped, both looked at Bryan. Bryan just smiled, held his glass up and made a toast, "To friends!"

Maddy spoke up, "Since we are all friends now, can I make a suggestion, at least when the two of you are off duty, can you call each other by your first names?"

Bryan held his beer up, "To Jack."

Jack held his up, "To Bryan."

The guys looked back and forth at the girls. Maddy downed her drink, "Not a chance in hell!" Bryan and Jack both kicked her under the table. "What?"

Stella was pouting, sipping quietly on her martini. It made things a little awkward at the table. Good old Bryan came to the rescue. "Stella, what do you do?"

Stella perked up at the attention. "I'm a paralegal for the county attorney."

That explains how she and Jack met.

"A respectable profession." He raised his glass to her. She smiled and raised hers to him.

Maddy looked over at Jack and rolled her eyes.

"Since we're among friends here, do you two care if I ask you guys a few questions about what you do?" Jack was referring to Maddy and Bryan.

Maddy glanced over at Bryan when he said, "Fire away."

"Explain the profiling to me."

Bryan took another swig of beer. "You do the honors Minnie."

"Minnie?" Stella asked.

Bryan chuckled and shook his head, "Its just a pet name I have for her." He turned to Maddy, "Go a head and explain profiling to Jack. You fuck up," he laughed, "I'll correct you."

Maddy leaned over and said quietly "You are getting all fucked up, slow down on the drinking. Order something to eat."

She turned to Jack, "What I said yesterday about our unsub, quite frankly it was and abstract psychological profile based on the victimology of our missing women and the bodies that were recovered. You can learn a lot about the unsub by what he does to the bodies."

"What's an unsub?" Stella asked like she was sincerely interested.

"We refer to the person perpetrating the crimes as the unknown subject, the unsub," Maddy explained.

"Why not just call him a suspect?"

"He's not a suspect until we know who we're looking for. Anyhow based on the conditions of the bodies and the cause of death, the body placement gives us clues as to the unsubs frame of mind and the type of personality the unsub has. Crime scenes, manner of abduction, type of weapon, there are so many things that factor into a profile."

"How did you learn how to do this?" It was Stella who was asking the questions instead of Jack. Jack was sitting back taking it all in. Bryan was munching on popcorn.

"By studying criminal psychology, abnormal psychology, and forensic psychology, then vigorous training at Quantico. Takes a lot of practice and you're not always right."

"Sounds really exciting. Why did you quit?"

Maddy's head shot up and she looked at Bryan.

"She was running away from me, let's just leave it at that." Bryan said as he took a sip of his beer.

"You guys ready to get saddle sore tomorrow?" Maddy asked the guys changing the subject. "Good chance we are going to be spending hours on horseback tomorrow. We have a lot of ground to cover."

"We've got several riders coming to cover the trails. The rest of the volunteers and dogs will be on foot," Jack told her.

"You need volunteers?" Stella asked. "I can help."

Maddy kind of felt sorry for her, she was trying so hard to join in. "Do you know how to ride a horse?"

"No, but I can learn," she said enthusiastically.

"Sorry sweetie, we don't have time to mess with a green rider, Stone Park has some pretty vigorous trails not for the inexperience rider and we won't have time to babysit you," Maddy explained trying not to sound too much like a bitch.

Jack chimed in, "But if you still want to help we still need volunteers on foot."

"But you're riding," she protested.

"Christ, Stella, it's not like this going to be a joy ride, we are looking for dead bodies. Is that something you really want you delicate senses to encounter?" Jack asked as he reached out and took a handful of popcorn.

Stella was starting to tear up. Oh God now what? "Stella, I will tell you what, if you really want to help out, and maybe this isn't up your alley, but I am sure they need help at the base stations with getting water to the volunteers and food if they need it."

She smiled weakly, "Yes...yes I could do that." She turned to Jack, "Could I do that?"

"Sure I will tell you where to go before I drop you off."

Maddy looked at her watch. It was almost 11:00 and they needed to be in the saddle at close to daybreak. "I hate to be a party pooper, but I think it's time to call it a night."

"You two have both had plenty to drink, I don't think you should be driving," Jack finished the last of his beer. "Especially you Maddy." Forever the cop.

"I'm not driving home, I got a room at the Regency," she lied. Bryan squeezed her leg under the table and she pinched him back.

"Tell you what, I will drive the two of you back and Stella can follow me, Maddy, your keys please." He held out his hand.

Maddy dug them out of her bag and handed them to him.

"I am NOT riding in the back seat of that sardine can," Bryan protested.

"Of course, not," Maddy shot back at him, "you're riding in the trunk. It's spacious."

"Fuck you, Minnie!"

"Not tonight your not," she smirked.

Jack and Stella were standing waiting for them. "Kids, lets go."

Jack and Bryan chatted amicably all the way back to the motel. Maddy laid her head back and closed her eyes. Her head was spinning, but she didn't feel like she had this past weekend even though she had had the equivalent of seven mixed drinks over a three-hour period. This bar must not have mixed them as strong as Randy at the Country Club did. When Jack pulled into the parking area, Stella pulled in right behind him. Guess she wasn't going to take a chance on loosing him this time.

Jack got out and shook Bryan's hand then turned to Maddy and gave her a peck on the cheek and handed her her keys. Bryan went ahead into the motel. "You want me to walk you to your room."

"Actually no I need to check in yet." She popped the trunk and took out her overnight bag.

Jack raised his eyebrow questioning, "Are you sure you're getting your own room?"

"Jack, I may be playing with fire, but I'm not stupid enough to jump into the flames." She slammed the trunk shut. She was such liar. She had every intentions of spending the night with Bryan, not to have sex with him, but just be with him. Right? At least that's what she told herself.

"Okay...sorry for doubting you." He backed away from her and turned to his car. "See you at the crack of dawn." And he was gone.

She walked into the entryway of the motel lobby. Bryan was waiting there for her. He was dangling the passkey. "You coming up with me?"

"No, I'm getting a room."

He leaned against the wall, probably because he could hardly stand up. "Bullshit, like you had any plans to. If you did, you would have made arrangements before we left, knowing you, you would have made them from home." He grabbed her bag. "Lets go Minnie, I promise I won't bite."

"Cuz you're probably wearing dentures, old man."

He reached behind her and tugged her by hair. "Only one way to show you."

Bryan let them into the room and threw her bag on the bed. "Did you bring something to sleep in?"

She opened her bag and pulled out her nightshirt. He took it from her hands and held up and laughed, "ooooooh so sexy."

Maddy snatched it out of his hands, went into the bathroom and slammed the door. She washed the makeup off her face, brushed her teeth, and brushed her hair.

When she came out of the bathroom she was surprised to find Bryan already in bed...with his eyes closed. She didn't know whether to feel insulted or relieved. He had turned the lamp out on his side of the bed.

She turned the lamp off and slid between the covers, but before her head could hit the pillow Bryan had slipped his arm under her and pulled her to him. When she was snuggled up in the crook of his arm and her head resting on his chest, he kissed the top of her head. "Goodnight Minnie."

She twisted in his arms, "I don't get it. You pissed at me?" She felt hurt he wasn't even going to make an attempt to seduce her.

He stroked her hair and then wrapped his body around hers. "I'm not going to push you into something you're not ready for. As much as I would love to take you in my arms and make love to you, it wouldn't be fair. We have time." He kissed her neck...a lot, nuzzling her. His breathing became soft and steady.

Bullshit, he was too fucking drunk. She smiled and fell asleep in his arms.

7

When Maddy awoke it took her a few moments to realize she wasn't in her own bed but in a motel room with Bryan. She subtly felt around for him with her toe. She was in bed alone. She opened one eye and saw his shadowy figure coming from the bathroom. He left the light on making the room light up however dim. She looked at the clock beside the bed. 3:00 AM. Too early to get up. She held very still to give the appearance she was still asleep.

Bryan lit up a cigarette and stood at the window with his fingers prying apart the blinds looking out over the parking lot. He appeared deep in thought. Despite his constant razzing of her, he had a deep dark side. One she was all too familiar with. Was he in one of his dark moods? She heard him moving across the room and slid back into bed beside her. He didn't snuggle up to her. She was facing in his direction, and was careful to keep still. He stroked her cheek softly, just watching her. He brushed the hair away from her forehead and kissed it.

Maddy sought him out with her hand. He slid down in the bed so they were face to face yet kept some distance between them. She opened her eyes and found him watching her. His eyes were sad.

"Bryan...what's wrong?"

"This was a mistake. I was wrong to come here. Once again you had your life back together and I came and fucked it all up," he spoke softly.

Maddy slid up and braced her head with her arm. "Bryan, don't do this again. You promised. I made the choice to be here with you. If it's a mistake, its my mistake." She brushed a wisp of hair that had fallen across his face. "This isn't a mistake. Lord knows if I will ever get this chance again. It could be couple months, couple years, a decade, maybe never. Like I told you last night," she leaned into him and gave him a deep kiss and said in a husky voice, "you're mine."

He pulled her over so she was on top of him and they continued to kiss. His hands roamed up her legs, over her hips and under her nightshirt caressing her breasts. She pushed herself up and pulled it over her head and threw it off to the side. She lowered herself down onto his chest. Their skin touching felt like fire. In the small hours before the sun rose, fire and ice melted into one.

Two hours later, in the FBI suburban, with Maddy in the front seat next to Bryan, they swung by and picked up the three agents that were in his unit. They all greeted Maddy with a nod and didn't ask any questions although she was sure they had a few. The agents were dressed for the field search in jeans and t-shirt and sporting a cap. Maddy asked if any of them had riding experience, only one had. He would ride with them. It took them a little over half an hour to get to the unloading point a Stone Park.

Maddy explained to the gentlemen the uniqueness of the park. "Stone Park is near the northernmost point of the Loess Hills. The Loess Hills range is one of two sand hill ranges in the world, the other is in China. At Stone Park the hills make the transition from clay bluffs and prairie to sedimentary rock hills and oak forest along the Iowa side of the Big Sioux River. It's located in two Iowa counties of Woodbury and Plymouth. It has steep slopes and ridges, prairie lands, and bluffs. The park contains many miles of hiking and equestrian trails, and is a popular destination for day visitors, overnight campers, mountain bike enthusiasts, and picnickers. It's one of the most beautiful and coolest places in the state."

Bryan laughed, "What are you tour guide in your spare time?"

"I've spent a lot of time there. It's got some of the best trails in the area."

When they arrived at the east unloading area, there were several cars, pickups and a few horse trailers.

One of those trailers was her friend Jessie's with their horses tied to the side of the trailer. She jumped out of the Suburban and hugged her friend. Jessie was her oldest and dearest friend of 20 years. Even though at times they spent years apart, they always remained close. Jessie was 15 years her senior, she was her friend, mentor, and sometimes her surrogate mother, but importantly, her stable buddy.

Jack, Bryan and Michael, a detective from Jack's squad, ambled over to the trailer. "Why don't you guys haul the tack out of the back of the pickup?" They did as they were ordered. Maddy and Jessie dropped the tack by each horse it belonged to.

Maddy's three horses, Buddy, a big muscled sorrel quarter horse, Lily a finer boned solid black paint mare, and Honey, a smaller, but muscled buckskin mare were tied together. In her head, she already assigned who would ride what horse. Bryan would ride Lilly, Jack, Buddy and she would ride Honey. Honey was a firebrand, she may have been small, but she was extremely agile, and could outrun probably any horse here. She was also very temperamental.

Maddyhad a sneaking suspicion Jack really didn't know how to ride, not well anyhow, and to prove it she was going to teach him a lesson. She would start him out on Honey.

"Get moving guys, the horses won't saddle themselves. Bryan, you got the black, Michael, the chestnut (one of Jessie's horses), Jack, you're on the buckskin.

Jack raised a skeptical eye, "You've got to be kidding right?"

"Nope," she threw the saddle pad on Buddy, "She probably the best trail pony out here."

"Pony? Come on Maddy...don't do this to me," he protested.

Maddy patted Honey on the rump, the horse turned around with her ears pinned down. "Give her a try, if it doesn't work we'll find you a different mount. Have faith Jack," she smiled, "you'll do just fine. Now saddle up."

Maddy finished saddling up Buddy and was watching Jack over the top of her horse's back. Bryan, who was done saddling Lily, came and stood by her. "You're mean. You know he isn't experienced enough to ride her."

Maddy smiled mischievously, "I know, and this is what he gets for lying."

"And if he gets hurt?"

"I won't let it get that far."

Jack managed to get the saddle on but he didn't have it tied right. He had to wrestle with Honey's head to get the bridle on her head, but before he could get it over her ears, the horse spit the bit out. "Son of bitch, damn it...Maddy!" his voice boomed over the commotion.

"Be nice," Bryan whispered in her ear.

"Aren't I always?" she asked innocently.

"No," he swapped her on the ass.

"Neeeehhhheeee," she flipped him off over her shoulder as she went to help Jack.

Maddy scratched Honey on the neck, then put her hand gently on the top of her head behind her ears. The horse dropped her head and picked up the bit from her hand. Maddy slipped the bridle easily over her head and secured it. She pulled back and forth on the saddle. It was snug for now but it would come loose. Honey was what is known in horse lingo as a wind sucker. She needs to be led around and have it retightened. Mr. I Know How to ride should know to look for that. "Okay she's ready to go, get on," she commanded Jack.

She held Honey while Jack mounted. The saddle was already loosening up. "Now take her over in that corral area and try her out."

Jack gently nudged the horse forward and then pulled on her reins, "Whoa." He adjusted his butt in the saddle. He heard Bryan laughing, glanced and saw he was looking at him. "Maddy, come on I look stupid."

She led Buddy out away from the trailer, "That's not Honey's fault."

Bryan laughed, "Maddy you are pure evil." She winked at him.

Maddy grabbed Honey's reins and led her to the corral area and gave a little tap on the butt. She took off in a fast walk around the arena area. Maddy could see the panic on Jack's face. He was holding on to the reins too tight. Big mistake, that was Honey's cue to move out and she began to trot. Jack was bouncing all over in the saddle and with each bounce he held the rein even tighter. "Loosen on up the reins," she hollered. He didn't and Honey began to trot faster. The saddle began to slide sideways with Jack's body and eventually sent Jack to the ground with a thud. Honey being the well-trained horse that she was stopped in her tracks. She looked down at Jack as if she were thinking "Dumb ass."

Maddy dropped Buddy's reins knowing he would stand still and ran over to Jack. He was flat on his back looking up at her; his face was kind of white. "What are you doing down there?" she asked trying hard not to laugh.

"What the hell does it look like?" he snapped. He took the hand up that she offered him and got to his feet.

She whistled and Buddy walked to her. She put the reins in Jack's hand. "He's more your speed." She went to Honey, stripped her saddle off and redid it, tying it with the correct knot then swung up in the saddle. "Mount up cowboy," she said as she rode past him.

Jack put his foot in the stirrup and hoisted himself up on the big horse. His legs were still shaky from the fall. He shifted his weight in the saddle making sure it was going to stay in place. He started to relax. This horse was calm. That other one felt like a stick of dynamite from the second he got on her.

Maddy reined Honey around to face Jack. "Ride him around the corral. Cue him with your legs, squeeze with your thighs when you want him to move out, use leg pressure on the side you want him to turn, and neck rein him," she instructed.

"Neck rein?"

"Lay the rein on the side of his neck you want him to turn. When you want him to stop, use a one rein stop." She demonstrated all these moves on Honey. "Got it?"

"Yes," he answered with less than an enthusiastic voice. She watched as he turned Buddy back into the corral area. Buddy was kid broke and bomb proof. If Jack couldn't ride him, he had no business in the saddle. Jack was shaky at first, but with Buddy's familiarity with green riders he did just fine.

Maddy and Jessie took off on their horses down the road to get them loosened up for the ride. Jack rode Buddy up to where Bryan was seated on Lily's back. The two of them watched the women running the horses. "She did that on purpose didn't she?" he said as he admired two women riding.

Bryan was watching too, and smiling, "Uhhuh."

"Bitch."

"Uhhuh." They both laughed.

The search party was gathered together so they could receive their instructions. The coordinator explained what to look for. He handed out at flyer of the second gravesite from Bacon Creek before it had been disturbed. He told them to look for any unusual ground disturbances, whether it be disturbed plant life, soil, look for unusual insect activity, or foul smells. The ground search will comb the prairie fields, walking trails, and the areas in and around those areas. The seven cadaver dogs were being spread out throughout the park. They had one, a German Shepard that would be working the grounds with them. Horse riders would be combing the horse trails and the areas next to it. They would ride spread out, many not using trails. As soon as anyone spotted anything remotely out of the ordinary, the information should be radioed in. Cells phone might not receive reception in some areas. Each group would have their own leaders. Maddy and Jessie would each lead up a team since they were familiar with the area. The team leaders gathered to go over a map of the equestrian trails in their area.

Maddy's group consisted of Jack, Bryan, and two experienced riders. They all mounted up. Maddy rode up next to Bryan and Jack. "Jack do you have any experience riding on trails?"

"No, just pasture riding," he looked away.

"Now listen to me," she said sharply. "This is not a game. A horse in the hands of an inexperienced rider can be dangerous and deadly. I gave you Buddy because he knows what he's doing. Give him his head, in other words, you just ride him, let him do the work. When you ride down steep slopes lean back, when you ride up hills, lean forward. Your horse is going to want to take a run at the steep hills, give him his head and let him do it. Hang on to the saddle horn if you have to, just stay in the saddle. Someone will be with in sight of you, if you have any problems, give a shout out. Understood?"

"Yes ma'am," he answered sternly and he wasn't being a smart ass. He was surprised and impressed with Maddy's ability to take charge of this situation. This was one of those sides of her he had never seen.

Maddy turned to all of them. "The trail we're going to be covering is down the road here a spell. When we get there, Jack, you will be riding the trail itself; it will be safer for you and Buddy. Gene, (one of the civilians) you will ride off trail to his right, Shelia, off to Gene's right. Jack, I will be on your left, Bryan off to my left. Any questions?"

No one had any. Maddy dismounted and checked the tack on her three horses, the other two checked their own. All checked their radios and their water supply. They were ready to ride.

Maddy was riding up next to Jessie catching up on news until they would have to turn off on their assigned trails.

Bryan and Jack lingered back behind them. "I would yell nice ass, but which would they think I was talking about?" Bryan grinned.

Jack smiled at him but said nothing.

"Listen Cowboy, don't let her scare you. She's still the Maddy you know and love, this is just who she becomes when she's working, when she's really working, not that paper bullshit." Bryan spoke to him in a conversational tone.

He nodded and rode a few moments in silence and then asked, "She seems like she's in her element. Why did she really leave the Bureau, and I know it wasn't just because of you?"

"If she wants you to know, she will have to tell you herself. I won't betray her trust. She holds the reason sacred. We all have our demons and we chose how we have to deal with them." And that was all he would say.

"And you want her to go back to it...back with you." It was a statement not a question.

"If it were up to me, yes, to both questions. But she won't because of the same reason." Then it was Bryan's turn for questions. "How is it you have known her for a couple of years and you really don't know that much about her?"

"A couple of years ago she started covering the crime beat for the Journal. She started dogging me about the cases I was working on." Jack smiled. "She was such a pain in the ass, but she was smart, clever, funny, and she had a good eye for evidence. I used to tease how she should have been a cop," He looked directly at Bryan, "Ironic huh? Anyhow I didn't mind having her tagging around with me.

Sometimes I would smuggle her into crime scenes, make her privy to information about cases. She never once betrayed the trust I had in her. She did manage to get us both into hot water a few times with her doggedness." He laughed, "She would come up with these really off the wall theories. We became friends, but the only time we really talked was when she was working the story. Sometimes a couple of months would go by and I wouldn't hear a word from her. We never socialized together, actually didn't really know anything about each other's personal lives. She chose to keep her distance and I didn't push it."

"She trusts you, you must have earned that somewhere. What changed between you two?" Bryan looked over at him.

"What do you mean?" Jack looked ahead of him so he didn't have to look at Bryan.

"Something changed to move the two of you to a higher level, what was it?"

Jack stopped Buddy, "Please don't take offense by this, and I mean no disrespect, but under the circumstances with things being the way they are between you and Maddy, I really don't think you are the right person for me to be talking to about this."

Bryan nodded, "Point taken. I just need to know that no matter what happens, I can trust she will be in good hands."

They rode in silence for a while. "Hey Bryan?" He nudged Buddy up so he was shoulder to shoulder with Lily. "What is Maddy short for? Madaline?"

Bryan smiled smugly. "Maude, and if you repeat that to her, I will have to kill you...and if you think I'm kidding—I'm not, cuz she will kill me and I'm not going down alone."

Maddy turned her head in the direction of the sound of familiar laughter and saw Jack and Bryan chatting away. It gave her a queer feeling. How strange that these two should become friends. She prayed it wasn't one of Bryan's games to get inside Jack's head to find out his weakness and then use it against him. He would break him and destroy him. No, she didn't want to believe it. Bryan was different this time, not like the old ruthless Bryan. Lord, please say she was wrong.

Jessie turned off with her group so Maddy waited for her group to catch up to her. Honey fell into step with the other two. "You two seem to be doing a lot laughing back here. What's so funny?"

"Guy talk," replied Bryan. "We were making fun of you, you give us some pretty good material to work with."

Maddy rolled her eyes, "You guys are such dicks."

Jack and Bryan exchanged looks. Jack laughed, "And your point is?

"No point, just a simple observation about some simple minded men." She nudged Honey forward; she could hear the two men laughing behind her back. Assholes.

"Okay Team listen up," Maddy had pulled Honey up to a stop. "This is where we separate. Remember the instructions I gave you. Don't stray too far apart, it's easy to get lost in the dense woods and it will be a bitch to find you."

Maddy entered the trail first followed by Jack, Bryan, Gene and Shelia. When they had traveled a short ways they broke off into the given paths. Bryan and Maddy were cross traversing. Maddy was silent, watching the footing around her.

"You okay Minnie?" Bryan asked her.

"I'm fine, why shouldn't I be?"

"You seem a little nervous about me chatting with Cowboy."

"We're back to that again are we?"

He laughed, "Not for what you're thinking, I was referring to his riding skills."

"Oh." She paused. "Don't fuck with him please? And you know what mean."

"No worries Minnie. He's a good guy."

Their horses were stepping over forest debris and they had to duck under low-lying branches. "Are you okay...about what happened this morning?" he asked hesitantly.

Maddy felt her cheeks heat up. She looked straight ahead and smiled, "I am very okay, Mickey."

"Ouch! Son of a bitch!" In his surprise of hearing Maddy call him by her once pet name for him, Bryan missed ducking a branch and it whipped him across the face.

Maddy threw her head back and laughed. "Watch where you're going G-man, now let's get to work."

Bryan drifted off further to her left until she could just hear him moving through the timber and catch glimpses of him here and there. She could do the same with Jack on her right. She spurned Honey to move a little faster. The horse was skilled for this environment and she felt because of this, she could cover more ground faster, breaking her own rule.

She had chosen to wear a long sleeved cotton shirt over her t-shirt because of the mosquitoes and the nettles. She felt bad she hadn't told the guys to do so. She smiled secretly to herself...nah, not really sorry. The woods smelled of a mixture of decaying wood, wild flowers, and plant life. If she had been the only one riding the trail she was sure she would hear wild birds, squirrels, maybe even see a deer or two, but with this many people invading their homes they were keeping tight to cover.

They had been riding around 45 minutes when Maddy gave a radio status check. So far nobody had seen anything out of the regular. Maddy took out her cell. She could still get a good signal. She punched the number 3 and Jack answered right away. "How you hanging in hon?"

"My ass hurts," he groaned. "Come and massage it."

Maddy laughed. "That's not in my job description. Are you going to be able to make it? We could be doing this for a few more hours."

"If I hadn't had to pick my sorry ass off the ground, I would probably be in better shape."

Maddy smiled sheepishly, “Yeah, well sorry about that, seemed like a good idea at the time.”

“I bet it did. You owe me Maddy, big time.”

“Time to get back to work. Call if you need anything. Later Jack.” And she ended the call.

A little over an hour later and two radio checks no one had seen anything. Maddy had seen some ground disturbances but they were animal related, deer beds, newly dug borrows, signs of deer ruts. Maddy dismounted to give Honey a break and to stretch her legs. Her legs were starting to cramp up. It had been a long time since she had spent this much time in the saddle. She felt sorry for those riders like Jack and probably Bryan who were not used to riding at all. She slipped her hand in her pocket and pulled out a couple of peppermints. Honey was much more patient than Buddy when it came to getting treats. The horse lipped the candy out of her hand and munched on it making loud crunchy sounds. She took a pocketknife out of her pocket and carefully lifted each of Honey’s feet and cleaned the mud and rocks out her hooves.

Maddy saddled up and forged forward. The air was getting oppressive as the heat of the day wore on. The humidity was high and the damp and density of the woods multiplied it. The deer flyers were biting away at Honey’s ears and she was constantly trying to brush them off by twitching her ears or rubbing them against her legs. The horse had come to a stop to give herself a thorough rub-down when suddenly her head popped up. Her ears were pinned back, her mouth opened making biting like motions and began to throw her head back. The horse began to bulk. Maddy pulled the rein around to keep her in a tight circle hoping she would come out of it, but she began to come up on her hind legs. Maddy did an emergency dismount, but Honey continued to act up. Something was setting her off. Finally she was able to calm the horse somewhat. She looked around the area for whatever was spooking Honey but found nothing. Then she smelt it. The scent of decaying wood gave way to decaying flesh. Oh sweet Jesus. It was then it hit her that horses react to the smell of death whether it be animal or human. This definitely was not animal. She took her lead rope, which she had tied around her saddle horn, and attached it to Honey’s halter under the bridle and secured her to a tree branch.

Maddy timidly began to walk the area trying to follow her nose. As the scent became stronger she began to hear the sound of flies swarming. The point of origin centered a round a pile of downed branches. Something was under that mass of twisted tree limbs. She wrapped her hands around one of the branches and pulled on it, the pile gave way and collapsed. A whiff of the odor came out in a blast.

Maddy backed away covering her face. Her stomach began to lurch the smell was so intense. Her skin felt clammy and her head woozy. There was definitely something under that brush pile and someone put a lot of work into concealing it.

Maddy returned to Honey and removed her riding gloves and some latex gloves from her saddlebag. She took a swig from canteen, swished it around her mouth and spit it out. What she wouldn't do for a jar of vapor rub. She knew she should probably call this in, but she wanted to be sure of her find just in case it was a deer carcass. She returned to the brush pile and took out her cell phone and took several photos at different angles of the scene to preserve the way it looked when she discovered it. She slipped on her riding gloves and began to pull away the branches until she revealed a bare spot of ground beneath where they had been. Flies were buzzing in mass swarms around the soil working their way into the soil itself. The area was approximately 7 feet in length and 3 feet in width, just the right size for a grave. A little voice kept telling her to make the call, but she pushed the voices back. She knelt down on the loam and began to probe the soil with a stick. The stick was only about 8 inches long and it penetrated to its hilt. She grabbed a thicker, longer stick and probed again. This time it came to a halt approximately 10 inches below the surface. At one end of the site she began to scrape away the soil with her hands. She took her time and gently removed it in layers. Make the call Maddy, the voices continued. She had scrapped down an area about a foot in circumference and at a grade of 11 inches when she struck something. She took off her riding gloves and slipped on the latex gloves. She gently brushed the dirt way from the object. The dirt gave way to cloth, gauzy cloth. Make the call damn it, her mind screamed. She brushed in upward direction until she saw the faint hint of blonde hair under the dirty gauze. Body fluids were seeping through the material.

Maddy reeled backward and landed on her butt. She felt the bile rising in her throat. Quickly and recklessly scooted backwards in a fast crab walk until she came in contact with a tree trunk and hit her head. She rolled over on her stomach and began to heave. She half crawled, half ran back to Honey. She peeled the latex gloves off her hands and stuck them in her pocket then pulled out her canteen and splashed water on her face and rinsed her mouth out.

Her hands were shaking violently as she pulled out her cell phone. Her legs were so weak she leaned against a tree and sunk down to the ground. She pulled down Bryan's name from her contact list and hit send.

He answered right away, "What's new Minnie? Need a butt rub yet? I know I could use one," he laughed.

"I...I...gotta body," she stammered.

Silence. "Where are you? Did you radio it in?" he asked quickly.

Maddy looked around at her surroundings. It looked like every other place in these woods and she didn't know how far off the trail she had gotten. "No I haven't called it in, you would have heard me if I did. Bryan, I don't know where I am exactly."

"I thought you knew you're way around this place."

"I know how to get out, I just don't know exactly where I'm am."

"I don't suppose you have GPS on your phone."

"No."

She heard Bryan get on the radio and informed base a body had been located, exact whereabouts unknown and that he would be discharging his fire arm.

"Maddy, I going to fire my gun, see if you can calculate how close I am."

A few seconds later the sound of gunfire echoed through the timber. It was off to her left and behind her.

"Can you figure out where I am from you?" he asked.

She told him.

"I'm going to ride forward calling out to you. Radio or call me when you can hear me." When she didn't answer, he asked her, "Do you understand me, Maddy?"

"Yes, please hurry." Maddy remained sitting on the ground, shaking. She had seen plenty of bodies during her stint with the FBI, worked with them even, but apparently her thick skin had worn off.

Five or so minutes went by before she faintly heard Bryan calling out to her. She screamed out to him repeatedly. The sound of his voice was closing in on her and finally she saw him on foot leading Lily toward her. She stood up and brushed the dirt from her body. "Over here," she called.

When he got within a 100 yards of her she called out for him to tie Lily up and come toward her. She walked around the perimeter to meet him. When she reached him she fell into his arms for comfort. Her body was still shaking.

"Maddy..." he held her away from him. "Come on kiddo, pull it together, you can do this. Take a deep breath."

She shook her head, "I'm okay...the body," she pointed behind her to the area where she cleared the brush. She explained to him how she came up on it.

Bryan and she walked the perimeter. "Maddy what have you done? You compromised the scene," he said sharply. "You know better!"

She felt like a child who was being severely scolded. "Do you know how many deer carcasses are found in these woods? Hundreds. I wasn't going to call it in if it was just a stupid damn deer!" she said defending her reasoning.

"You can't tell me you've been away from this shit so long you can't tell the difference in the smell of a dead human over a fucking deer. Damn it Maddy!" He grabbed a small branch and slammed it against a tree too close to Honey and she reared up.

A coldness settled over Maddy with each angry breath Bryan took. She pulled the emergency slipknot releasing Honey from the branch and began to lead her away.

"Where the hell do you think you are going?" He yelled at her, his voice still filled with anger.

She watched her footing as she led Honey through a patch of twisted low ground brush. She got her foot caught twisting her ankle and she fell in to the patch. "Son of a bitch!"

"Get your ass back over here!"

Her ankle hurt, she was angry, shook up, and hurt. She felt tears stinging her eyes, but she'd be damn if she would let that bastard see her cry. "You're the big fucking FBI agent, you take care of it!" she hissed.

It only took him a couple of strides and he was on top of her, grabbing her by the wrist and pulling her to her feet, literally dragging her back to the small clearing. "*You* are not going anywhere," he said coldly.

She thrashed out at him trying to free herself, but he held tight until she quit struggling. Her expression was but a mask, her breathing fast and deep. She looked at him straight in the eye. "Take you fucking hands off me...NOW!" He released his grip and she fell to the ground.

Bryan grabbed his radio, gave them his GPS co-ordinance, and told them to stay back away from the scene until they could get the parameter taped off. He gave the order to call in CSU, the corner, and to bring a cadaver dog to search for other sites.

"You are going to stay here and help me work this scene, you're not running away from this one. You run Maddy, you always run, that's your answer to everything."

She glared at him through narrow eyes, "I hate you," she hissed.

"Right now, I am sure you do, but you know what? I don't fucking care. You want to poke around like an agent, you're going work like one." He pointed to the gravesite, "You made that mess, you're going to help clean it up."

Maddy looked away and shook her head, "What the hell was I thinking, that things were different this time...."

"This is work Maddy, not personal. Aren't you the queen of that phrase?" When she didn't answer he left it at that. "Now is not the time to get into this. I need your help. You got tape in your saddlebag?"

She got to her feet and made her way to Honey who was patiently standing where she left her. Every step sent excruciating pain through her ankle and she winced each time her foot made contact with the ground. She was feeding off her anger to rise above it. She made it to Honey and removed the crime scene tape from her bag and hobbled back to Bryan and threw it at him.

"Oh grow up," he snapped her.

"Fuck you!"

"Get over here and hold this," he ordered her.

She held the tape while he made a very large circle around the gravesite tying off the tape at different intervals until he made the circle complete coming back to her.

He left her standing there while he went and examined the grave. He could see the sticks in the ground where she probed the earth, where she had removed the soil in layers and stopped as soon as she located the body. Yes, she had disrupted the scene, but she did within protocol measures.

Maddy limped over to him. She pulled out her cell phone and removed the memory card and handed it to him.

He held it in the palm of his hand and studied it. "What is this?"

"Pictures of the scene, from discovery through what you see here. I'm not stupid, Bryan, I do know what I'm doing. I didn't do anything that a," she held her fingers up for quote marks, "professional' wouldn't do." She turned on her foot forgetting about her ankle, pain shooting through, she gasped and collapsed to the ground.

Byran took a plastic bag out of his pocket and quickly dropped the card inside and stuck it back in his pocket. He knelt down and scooped Maddy up in his arms and carried her to a large fallen tree trunk outside the taped zone and gently sat her down on it. Without saying a word, he knelt at her feet and began to loosen the strings of her right boot. He tugged on her boot and she cried out in pain. He stopped abruptly, "I'm sorry, I'm sorry...we need to get your boot off and take a look. Okay, I'm going to try it again...you ready?" She nodded. He pulled as gently as he could and watched as she bit her lip to keep from crying out. With the boot off, his fingers gently grabbed her sock and rolled it off her foot. The tenderness he was showing with her now was by far different from the rage she felt coming from him minutes ago. Her ankle was already bruising and swollen. He turned her ankle gently and she winced.

He stood up and shifted her body so she was sitting sideways on the trunk so her legs were propped up. He sat on the edge of the trunk facing her. He reached up and tugged at her cap until it came off. He placed his hand on the side of her face and stroked her cheek with his thumb. "Maddy, I'm sorry I was such a bastard to you. I was just so angry you could be so careless."

"I wasn't..." she began to protest and he put his finger on her lips to silence her.

"I know, I see that." He kissed here forehead. "We need to get you back to base and have your ankle looked at." They could hear movement in the woods and voices calling out. Bryan called out their location.

Maddy turned to Bryan, "Please let me stay, it's Vanessa," she pointed to the grave.

Bryan looked back at the grave and back to Maddy. "I can't let you, Maddy. And it's not because you're a civilian, or that you would get in the way, but I can't take a chance on putting you back there." He held her face by her chin, looking into her eyes. "I can't risk it for you. Do you understand what I'm saying?"

Maddy looked past him at the grave thinking about the body in it. This wasn't like the body at Bacon Creek. This body was just barley a week into decomp and it was the only one of these women she felt she had any insight into, it would be hard. But she knew this was not what Bryan was worried about. She closed her eyes and the brief image of other bodies in another time flashed before her. She felt the color draining from her. She nodded, "I understand."

"Do you want me to have Jack bring you back?" he asked softly, hesitating slightly.

She put her hand on his cheek. "No, he needs to be here with you working the case. Help me get on Honey and have Jessie meet me here and we'll ride back to base and I will wait for you there." She looked over her shoulder; the searchers were about on them. She leaned forward and kissed him tenderly, "I love you Mickey."

He kissed her back, "I love you too, Minney."

"Is that what you two call working a scene?" It was Jack, of all the people to have to get there first. Maddy looked away.

"Miss Sheridan here decided to tiptoe through the timber and sprained her ankle. We need to get her back to base," Bryan explained as he gently slipped her sock back on.

"And I suppose you want me to take her back?" Jack asked indignantly.

Bryan laughed, "No, Parker, you're my lead. You're staying here with me working the scene. All we have to do is get her pretty little ass back on your favorite jackass and she'll ride back to base with her friend."

"Hey!" Maddy protested, "It was that jackass that found that!" She pointed to the sight.

Bryan put his head in his hands, "Oh God, here we go with the animal detectives again."

Jack laughed, "She told you about Rufus, I take it."

"Yes, our star witnesses. Okay Miss Maddy, how did Detective Jackass discover the body?"

Maddy backhanded him. "Quit calling her that. The only jackass around here is you! Horses can smell death and it freaks them out. It creates intense fear in them and their flight instinct kicks in. She damn near threw me."

Jack shook his head, "Who knew, and we wasted our time and resources on cadaver dogs."

"You're an ass too. It's fact, look it up if you don't believe me."

Bryan stood up. "Well it makes more sense than an eyewitness dog." He bent down and picked up Maddy and threw her over his shoulder.

"Damn it Bryan, show a little respect," she pounded on his back as he carried her to Honey and turned so she could crawl on her back without hurting her foot.

"Parker, throw me her shoe." Jack tossed it to him and Bryan tied it to her saddle horn. He then got on the radio to locate Jessie. "Your friend will meet you at the trail go straight north, you'll see the crews coming in on your way. Don't do anything stupid on your way."

"My hat." It came sailing through the air. Bryan caught and handed it to her.

"This could get pretty late kiddo." Bryan reached in his back pocket and pulled out his wallet. "Here is my passkey. If it gets too late, will you wait for me there...stay with me?" He put his hand on her leg. "Please...I need you."

"I don't have any clothes here," she whispered looking around to make sure no one was listening.

He touched her on the tip of her nose, "You won't need any," he grinned. "Go buy some, I'll pay for them. Will you stay?"

Maddy smiled and squeezed Honey with her legs for her to move out, "What can I say, you're the boss."

"About damn time you learned that," she heard him mutter as he went back to the site. She had to smile.

It seemed like it took forever to get back to the trail. It was amazing how fast crime scene crews were moving in. There were service roads in around the park hidden from most of the trails. It was real apparent where they were now with the emergency lights flashing throughout the foliage of the woods. She thought how it was really sad how this demon could come into its sanctity and destroy its peacefulness.

Jessie was waiting at the trail for her. She thought she would see Buddy and the other horses there too, but Jessie said volunteers were already on their way taking them back to the base camp. They rode in silence for a while until Jessie spoke. "The FBI agent, Bryan, he's your Bryan isn't he?" When she didn't answer, Jessie continued, "Girl, what are you thinking, after all he has put you through?"

Maddy watched the trail in front of her. She hated to disappoint her friend, but she of all people would be the one to understand. "I'm sorry."

"Hey don't apologize to me, you are the one that has to look at yourself in the mirror."

Maddy glanced over at her, "You in friend mode or mother mode?"

Jessie smiled, "Both, so you better listen twice as much."

"If you had the chance to be with the one person who knows you to your soul, that loves you and you love him so intensely it seers your soul, but you knew it was going to be like a flash of lightning, beautiful, but gone as fast as it was there, would you take it?"

"Are you forgetting what happened the last time? You got too close to that fire, he burned you and you lost yourself, you lost your soul. Is it worth it to loose yourself again, Maddy?"

"It's different this time," she protested. "No major depression, no alcoholic binge, no wife, no Donna. We have been brutally honest with each other."

"Have you now? And you're so sure he has been with you? I bet you can't count the numerous times he's lied to you. And he will stay this time?"

"To answer all these questions and the ones I know you're going to ask I will answer in this order. Do I trust him—no. Will he hurt me—not on purpose. Will he mind fuck me—I pray he won't. Will he leave me—yes, that's a given. And will I be crushed when he leaves—probably."

"Friend, what happens if you loose yourself again, what if you don't come back out on the other side? I know you can be strong, very strong, but I have also seen you...gone. I can't bear to see it happen to you again. You've worked so hard to get where you are. Is he worth putting that all on the line for?"

Maddy reined Honey to a stop and she turned to her friend. "My life has been fucked up for so long. It feels like I walk on eggshells all the time; stay to far away from the edge in case I fall. I have to keep this constant wall up around me. I can't let anybody in; I can't let anyone know who I really am. And it sucks, Jessie, it really sucks. With the exception of you, Bryan is the only person who knows me, knows all about me. I don't have to pretend. I just want that, I need that, if only for a few weeks. Can you understand that?"

"What about your detective friend? Where does he fit in all this?"

They cued their horses forward. "Jack? Jessie, he is really having a hard time dealing with what little he has learned about me these past few days. He has trouble seeing that I am still me. He thinks I deceived him because I never let him know I was with the FBI. Can you imagine what he would think of me if he knew everything? I care about the man, very much and I know he feels the same, but what if its not enough?"

"You'll never know if you don't trust him enough to share it with him. Does he know about your Bryan?"

"Yes," she muttered.

"And he is willing to stand back and watch the craziness going on between you and Bryan?" Jessie asked.

"He says he will be there."

"And you believe him? You are willing to risk something that could be real with this Jack to spend an undetermined time with Bryan, that you know is going to end up in disaster for you?"

Maddy looked at her friend, "Call me insane. Bryan makes me feel alive, whether it's him pissing me off so bad I can't see straight, or making love to him. No matter what, Jessie, I feel."

Jessie stopped her horse. "You slept with him already?"

Maddy felt her cheeks burning, "Yes, and I want to do it every chance the opportunity arises. Does that make me a bad person?"

"No not bad, just insane. Okay, so I don't agree with what you're doing, but because I love you dear friend, I will allow you this lapse in sanity. I won't judge. I will even go as far to say, hell with it, go for it and live."

Maddy smiled at her friend and reached across and they squeezed hands. "Thank you, it means a lot coming from you." She paused. "Now I have a really big, huge favor. Bryan has asked or should I say is allowing me to sit in on this case within reason, but I get full disclosure, that and the fact we want to spend our free time together, would you mind taking care of my critters and bring me some clothes in the next couple of days?" Maddy gave her the pleading puppy dog look, "Pretty please?"

Jessie laughed, "You owe me big time girl, race you back to base." They kicked the horse into gear and ran them the rest of the way back to camp.

When they approached the base camp, their horses were tied to the side of Jessie's trailer. She swung her body around on the saddle and lowered herself off Honey landing on her good foot. Whittmer was standing next Buddy running his hand along his whithers.

"You like horses," she asked him.

"They're beautiful creatures, but I don't know anything about them," he replied as continued petting Buddy.

"Would you like ride him in the corral?"

"Can I." His eyes lit up.

She hobbled over and untied Buddy from the trailer. "Stick your left foot in the stirrup, grab his mane, and pull yourself up."

He did as he was instructed and almost overshot the saddle. He settled into the saddle and she gave him the reins. She gave him the same instructions she gave Jack about controlling the horse. He caught on quickly and made his way to the corral. Buddy moved around the parameter of the corral. Whittmer looked comfortable and as happy as a clam.

Maddy returned to the trailer, still stocking footed. Jessie was unsaddling the horses. She told Maddy to stay put and stay off her ankle.

Maddy was leaning against the trailer when who should show up, but Stella. Oh God, Barbie. "What do you want Stella?"

She handed Maddy a water. "Where's Jack?" She looked around the area for 'her man'.

"Where he should be, working the scene. Now if you don't mind, I hurt like a bitch and am not up to idle chit-chat." She dismissed Stella who left in a huff.

She wanted so baldy call Jack or Bryan and ask what was happening at the site, but she knew they were busy and didn't want to bother them. She was hurting and emotionally drained. Jessie had been given the okay to leave so Maddy could get medical attention.

Whittmer rode Buddy up to the trailer. "How do I get off?"

Maddy smiled, "Same way you got on but just the opposite."

He slipped off the horse and handed the reins to Jessie. "Thank you for giving me the opportunity to ride your horse, it was a pleasure."

"You're welcome. You're a natural, you should do it more often."

Whittmer smiled weakly, "Maybe I should."

Maddy looked at him, "Can I give you a little advice?"

"Maybe."

"Loosen up, you're so uptight."

"Yeah, maybe. Thanks again." He turned and left.

Jessie helped her into the cab of her pickup then loaded the horses up in the trailer and they left. Instead of hauling the horses around the city, they drove to the Regency. Jessie parked the trailer off to the side of the parking lot and they took Maddy's car to Mercy.

Maddy was diagnosed with a mild sprain; it would be fine in a few of days. She left the emergency room with a wrapped ankle, a pair of crutches and some painkillers. She threw the crutches in the backseat knowing that's where they were going to stay.

They swung by Wal-Mart where they picked up some clothing and a large bottle of Advil. She snuck off and bought a satin nighty. They swung by McDonalds and picked up some food then returned to the motel. Jessie went with her into the room carrying Maddy's bag of new clothing.

Jessie told her she would take the dogs home with her and would do chores for her. She would bring her some clothing tomorrow after work. Maddy gave her friend a hug and a thanks then Jessie left.

Maddy stood and looked around the empty room. It felt so lonely without Bryan. Her ankle was throbbing from all the running around they had done. She slipped into the bathroom and took a quick shower. She needed to wash the smell of death off her. She finished up, toweled off and slipped on the sweat suit. She grabbed the pain pills out of her purse, took two and washed it down with her diet coke she got at McDonalds. She lay down on the bed and propped her foot up with a pillow. She thought about texting one of the guys—she thought about it. But before she acted on that thought, the painkillers took effect and she drifted off to sleep.

8

Maddy was still asleep when Bryan returned around 7:30. The blinds had been pulled; the room was lit up by the soft hue of what sunlight seeped through. He saw where she had had her foot propped up by a pillow, but she rolled over on her side and was sleeping in a fetal position. Her body looked so small and fragile on the king sized bed. Her hands were tucked up under her face; her copper hair sprawled across the pillow.

On the nightstand he saw a McDonalds bag, a drink and a bottle of pills. He peeked in the sack, the food was untouched, she hadn't eaten anything all day. All he wanted to do was to lie down on the bed and hold her, but he had just come from the gravesite and he knew he reeked of sweat, musty dirt, and death. He grabbed a change of clothing from the bureau, quietly went into the bathroom and closed the door.

The throbbing in Maddy's ankle awoke her as she moved her leg. She adjusted her eyes to the light. She rolled over to see the clock. How long had she slept? 7:45. Wow a little over three hours. Then she noticed a thin stream of light from beneath the bathroom door and the sound of water running and she smiled to herself. He was back.

When Bryan stepped out of the bathroom, his hair was damp, he was clean-shaven, and was wearing a white t-shirt and pajama pants. When he saw that she was awake, he gave her a big smile like he was really glad to see her. "Hey kiddo," He sat on the edge of the bed next to her. "What'd the doc say?"

Maddy flinched as she slid up into a sitting position. "Mild sprain. I'll be back to tap dancing in a few of days.

Bryan grabbed a couple of pillows and slid them in behind Maddy.

He looked so tired and weary despite him having just taken a shower to freshen up. She patted his side of the bed. "Come here and join me," she said softly. She pulled his pillows up against the headboard.

He crawled across the bed and leaned back against the pillows and put his forearm across his eyes. "What a day from hell," he sighed.

Maddy really wanted to know how everything went, but she would respect it if he didn't want to talk about it. She remembered how she felt at the end of a day like this. She would just want to block it out and think of anything but what she had witnessed that day. She reached around him and guided his head to lie against her chest. He slid down and got comfortable wrapping his arm around her waist. She stroked his hair and kissed the top of his head.

"You have no idea how nice it is to come back from a day like this and receive this kind of tenderness and support, instead of bitching and nagging. Normally the first thing I'd do would be either hit the bar first, or suck down a few when I walked through the door. I don't feel that need with you." His fingers caressed her skin where her shirt had ridden up. "This is nice...so nice."

She wanted to tell him she wasn't his wife or his mistress, she was Maddy, the one he left behind, but she didn't. He was relaxing, finally, and she didn't want to irritate him, or put him on a guilt trip.

He looked up at her as if he were trying to read her thoughts. "You're awfully quiet, you feel alright?"

She rubbed her cheek against the top of his head, "I'm fine, just listening to you."

Bryan kissed her collarbone. "Sometimes I think and wonder how our lives would have been different if I hadn't made the choices I did ten years ago. If I had stayed with you and made a life with you...do you ever wonder?" He looked up at her.

She leaned back and rested her head against the headboard. "I can't Bryan. I had to live with the choices you made. I can't go there, I'm sorry."

"No, I'm sorry, that was unfair of me." He sat up, so much for the tender moment. "You've got to be hungry, I noticed you didn't eat your lunch. Would you mind if we called in?"

"No, not at all, you pick, I really don't care." She slid off the bed and hobbled to the bathroom. Maddy studied herself in the mirror. She looked pale in the artificial light, her green eyes were puffy with sleep, and her hair was all over the place. She turned the water on and splashed water on her face and ran a brush through her hair.

When she returned Bryan was on the motel phone ordering supper. "Pizza okay?"

"Yeah," She stepped down wrong on her foot and winced.

"Shouldn't you be on crutches or something?" He came to her, swept her off her feet and laid her gently on the bed.

"They're in the back of the car, and that's where they are going to stay." She leaned back against the headboard and closed her eyes.

"You want a painkiller?" he asked getting up.

She shook her head, "No, I don't want to spend all my time with you sleeping, sleeping with you..." she smiled, "that's a different story. There's some Advil in the Wal-Mart sack."

Bryan started pulling out the items in the bag and came across the satin nighty. He was unaware of her watching him when he brought it to his face feeling its softness. He discreetly put it down and grabbed the bottle of Advil and brought it to her with a glass of water. He waited for her to the take the pills then took the glass from her and put it on the bed stand.

She reached out with her hand and pulled him to her and kissed him softly. He slid onto the bed beside her and returned her kiss. He lips were soft, gentle, tender and yet demanding. He pushed her down in the bed and covered her body with his; caressing her with his hands...and then his phone went off.

He groaned and rolled off her. He had laid his phone on the bed stand. He rolled over and picked it up and looked at the caller ID. He flipped it open and then hung it up without answering it and tossed it across the room. "Fuck that." It went off again.

Maddy giggled, "Maybe you should have turned it off." Just then Maddy's phone went off. It was across the room in her bag. Bryan grabbed her bag and pulled it out. "Who is it?"

He looked at the caller ID. "It's Jack."

She didn't know what to do. He just hung up on Donna, should she do the same to Jack?

Bryan smiled. "Take it, he's just calling to check on you. You have to remember Maddy this was his first time. He's seen and done things he's never experienced today. He might need a friend to lean on. Be that friend."

She flipped it open, "Hey Jack, how's your ass holding out?"

"To be quite honest I'm so damn tired I forgot about it." He sounded as bad as Bryan, maybe worse. "Point is, how are you doing?"

"Drugged up on pain pills, doc says I will be okay in a few days." She paused, "How are you doing...after today?"

She could hear him taking a deep breath on the other end. "I don't know how you guys do it."

"I couldn't. That's why I am where I am. It's okay if it's not your thing, Jack. Not everyone is cut out for it. It doesn't make you a bad cop."

"I don't know, it's just new to me. Above the realm of my experience, I guess you could say. I have to say I've come to respect Bryan a great deal. A guy can learn a great deal from him," Jack's admiration of Bryan was apparent. Maddy didn't know if that was such a good thing.

"Don't tell him, he'd get a big head over the deal," she smiled.

"Well, I don't want to keep you, I am sure you guys have plans, I just wanted to check on you." He sounded so tired.

"How do you know we're together?" she asked out of curiosity.

"It's okay Maddy, I'm cool with it."

"So what are you saying? Things have changed?" she felt panicky.

"Calm down Mads, nothing's changed. I care just as much as I always have." He gave a little laugh, "As you put it...it's still real. It's just not our time...yet. We'll know. Hopefully I will see you tomorrow. Tell Bryan hi and have a good night." And he hung up.

Bryan was sitting on the bed, he legs stretched out and smoking a cigarette. "How is he holding out? He was a real trooper today, I have to give him that. Between me and him, I must say Minnie, you have good taste."

She laughed, "Glad you approve. You got a new fan in him. He thinks you're God," she teased.

He pulled her over so she was laying across his lap, looking up at him and he said with a smile "I am, thought you knew that."

She smacked him, "You are such an arrogant ass."

He snuffed out his cigarette.

"Not going to argue with you. Come up here." He pulled her so she was sitting on his lap, wrapped his arms around her, kissing her deeply. His hand slipped under her shirt, caressing her.

Maddy responded by parting his lips with her tongue, her arms slipped up around his neck, pulling him closer. She felt the heat and the fire burning from within her.

His mouth traveled down her neck then up to her ear. Her head fell back and she arched her back to him. She could feel his breathing quicken, his breath hot on her skin. His hands became more urgent. He whispered in her ear, "God I love you so much." His voice was deep and husky, sending shivers down her spine.

There was a knock on the door. "Damn it...interruptions," he sighed.

"Food's here," she mumbled kissing his neck, nipping at it gently. "We got all night, Mickey..." She slid off his lap.

Bryan slid off the bed and took money out of his wallet, went to the door, paid the guy, and brought the pizza in and placed it on the table. "I got combo, hope that's okay?"

"I'm easy," she smiled.

He laughed, "I wouldn't go that far. Do you want me to carry you over to a chair?"

"No, I can make it." She crawled to the far side of the bed so she was closer to the table and limped over and sat in a chair.

Bryan ripped the top of the pizza box off and then tore it in half and put one in front of her. "Make shift plate," he stated. He took a couple of pieces of pizza and set them on her piece of cardboard. He did the same for himself.

She picked up a piece and took a bite, chewing on it silently.

"You haven't asked about today. I would thought you would hit me with that as soon as I walked in the door." He got up and walked to the mini bar, grabbed her a diet coke and him a beer. He opened her coke and popped the top on his beer.

She looked at the beer and looked at him. "Thought you didn't need that."

"Just to wash down the pizza. Does it bother you that much?" He took a swig of beer and set the can down.

"It's okay, I guess you deserve it after the day you've had," she said quietly. She was remembering earlier times when he drank heavily and he how acted and then last night when he drank over two pitchers.

"No worries, I will keep it down to a minimum. So do you want to hear about today?"

"I wasn't sure if you wanted to talk about it. I know how tough it is and you just want to get away from it." She took a small bite of the pizza. She wasn't really hungry.

"They discovered one more grave back a ways behind a nature center. Too much decomp to identify on the scene. You're pretty sure your find is Vanessa Granger?"

"Unless we have a blonde missing person we don't know about, I'm pretty sure. I didn't get a look at her face. Probably a good thing I guess." She started picking toppings off the pizza and popped them in her mouth. "How is he getting the bodies to where they are? That's a hell of a ways to carry a body."

"The service roads we're figuring. Hell we had to ride a couple of hours to get there on horseback and the service road is around 500 feet from the location. Our unsbub isn't consisent with his burial locations though. We have one older grave and a fresher grave in the same areas so it not like he's established a pattern where he places two and moves on. He's all over the place. We will be searching again tomorrow, hell of a lot of ground to cover. We will work back from the service roads on foot with the dogs first." Bryan took a cigarette, lit it and blew out the smoke.

"And cause of death?" She looked up from her pizza that she was playing with.

"Their throats were slit, that was obvious. We didn't touch the rest, leaving that up to the coroner. Should get prelims tomorrow. Dressed in the same manner right down to the rosary." He flicked his ash.

"I think we need to look at the religious angle more, ministers, priests, deacons, whatever, one that's had a psychotic break. If you have noticed the escalation between the disappearances and if he stays to pattern, we're looking at another abduction within the next week."

"Maybe he is choosing these women as brides, then sacrifices them," he guessed.

"But why?"

Maddy pushed the pizza away and took a sip of soda. "I don't know. This would be so much easier if he were targeting prostitutes, like he's cleansing. But the women he is targeting are your average everyday, common women. They aren't remarkable in appearance, just average. They have average jobs with average incomes, all single, all live alone. I think he chooses them and stalks them, gets to know their patterns. He's has to know them. There's never been any signs of forced entry, no signs of a struggle. Either they go with him willingly, or threatens them with a weapon. There are so many ifs."

"You said the rat reacted to cologne. Some kind of struggle must have happened with Granger." Bryan kicked back in his chair and crossed his arms. "So what do you suggest we do? Pull all our religious leaders in and interview?"

"Don't be silly, do you know how many churches there are in the city let alone in the surrounding communities? I say we need to make up a new profile factoring religion in. I hate to attack one faith, especially since I am catholic, but the symbolism of the rosary leads me in that direction."

"Are these women catholic?"

"How the hell would I know?" She scratched her head. "I'm just trying to find a starting point."

Bryan put his hands behind his head and studied her. "Profile him."

"Now?" She looked surprised.

"You can bypass what we already know, just give me your feel."

"Okay." She looked off toward the window, thinking. "Like I said, I think he has a religious connection, between the ages of 35-45, I'm thinking more into his 40's."

"Why?"

"He's jaded against women. Not young women, ones that are established in character, so that cuts out our younger twenties. I say older because he has had enough life experience to develop his attitude and his disdain. He doesn't keep them long, I would say less than 24 hours from the time of abduction, so he doesn't spend much time with them establishing whatever it is he thinks he wants to know. He knows it already by the time he has chosen them or has an idea and then stalks them, studies them before he makes his decision."

"Okay if we follow this line of thinking, how do you explain how he disposes the body and how he prepares them?" He drank the rest of his beer and tossed the can in the trash and lit a cigarette.

"It's just kind of a paradox. He tortures these women, the sexual sadist in him. At what point does he decide to slit their throats? What provokes him to end it? I don't see his burial rituals as him showing remorse. I think in his mind, he's justified."

Bryan got up and went back to the mini bar, but this time he pulled out a bottle of water, came back and sat down. "You still haven't explained the burial ritual."

Maddy bit at her nails. She honestly didn't know. "Saving their souls?"

"A logical conclusion I guess." He looked at her plate with most of her pizza still on it. "You didn't each much, and I know you didn't eat all day."

"I'm just not hungry, is that okay with you?" her voice was a little edgy. "You don't have to father me."

He looked at her puzzled. "Maddy, where's this attitude coming from? If you think I disapprove of your profile, not at all. You brought some very interesting outlooks to the table, ones that have never entered the equation. So what if you don't know all the answers, I didn't expect you to." He stood up and walked toward the bed, stopping to kiss her on the head. "You did good, okay?"

"I guess so," She stood up and headed for the bathroom to wash her hands and face. While she was in there the door opened slightly and the satin nighty came flying in. She laughed and called out, "Is that a hint?"

"I sure hope so!" he called back.

When she came out, Bryan looked her up and down. The red nighty clung to her curves leaving nothing to the imagination. Bryan gave a low whistle. He had slipped off his shirt and was lying on his side.

For some reason Jack's face flashed before her. What the hell? She shook it off, limped over and crawled in bed beside him. She lay on her side so she was facing him. Bryan reached out and traced the neckline of her nighty. She shivered. He ran his hands over her shoulder, down her body and over her hips. He was just about to caress her legs when his phone went off.

Maddy felt irritated, "Can't you turn that damn thing off?" She showed him her phone—it was off.

"I can't, I'm on call." Bryan picked it up and looked at the caller ID. It was her. "Jesus fucking Christ!"

"Oh just answer the damn thing and get it over with. Take it in the bathroom, I don't want to hear it." She was angry. Even a thousand miles away that bitch could spoil things.

Bryan respected her wishes and took the call in the bathroom. Maddy felt a chill from the air conditioner and crawled beneath the sheets. She was staring at her phone on the nightstand and she thought of Jack. She wondered if it was because she was thinking of him or because she was angry that Bryan was in there having a cozy little conversation with Donna. Fuck it. She wanted to hear Jack's voice. She picked the phone up and hit speed dial.

When Jack answered the phone he sounded as if he had been asleep. "Maddy...what a surprise."

She spoke softly, "I'm sorry I woke you up. I will call you tomorrow, you go back to sleep."

"No, no, its okay," sounding groggy but a little more alert. "What's wrong hon?"

"I'm lonely," she whispered, realizing it was true.

"I thought you were with Mayland."

"I am...I guess. But the crazy thing is, Jack, it's you I'm thinking about." She waited for his reaction.

The phone was silent for what seemed like forever. "I don't understand, Maddy. I thought that was where you wanted to be, with him."

"Me too, but at this moment, I'm not so sure. If it was, I wouldn't be thinking about you." She felt like crying and didn't really know why.

"I'm confused Maddy." His voice was soft and soothed her nerves.

"You and me both. Hey, I will talk to you tomorrow. Would you have time to go to lunch?"

"Don't know hon, we're still working Stone Park. You going to be okay?" The concern in his voice was apparent.

"I'm fine, Jack, I always am. Good night Jack," and she hung up the phone and turned it off.

Bryan was still talking in the bathroom. It had been 20 minutes. She wasn't so pissed anymore, just hurt. This was actually a reality check. Nothing had changed. She looked over on the nightstand and saw the painkillers and wondered if it would kill the pain she was feeling in her heart. She felt hot tears slide down her cheek. She buried her head in her pillow and cried softly.

It was at least another ten minutes before Bryan came out and crawled in bed next to her. She was turned away from him and when he touched her shoulder she flinched. "What? You mad?"

"No," she whispered.

He stroked her bare arm with the back of his fingers. "Then what's wrong?"

"What do you think?" she snapped.

"You told me to take it!"

"I didn't know you would be on with her for half an hour. But that's okay, it brought things back into perspective."

"What's that suppose to mean?"

"Its all the same, Bryan. No matter what we say, or try to pretend, it's all the same. You're still not mine. You never were, you never will be." The tears kept coming.

She felt the bed move as Bryan rolled over. She rolled on to her back to see him picking up his phone. He dialed a number and put it on speakerphone so she could hear the conversation. "Donna."

"I thought you were calling it a night," the familiar voice on the other end said. Maddy still remembered it quite well.

"Listen, I don't want you calling me anymore while I'm gone." His voice sounded cold.

"Why, I miss you so much, I want you to come home," she whined.

"I'm here with Maddy Sheridan. I'm going to be spending a great deal of time with her while I am working this case."

"You're doing all this because of her, you knew she was there, that's why you volunteered. What'd she do, track you down? Why can't she leave us alone?" Donna accused him.

He sighed, "I hunted her down. I came here for her and you are going to keep your nose out of it this time."

She started crying, "Are you coming back?"

"I don't know what I'm going to do, but I want to be left alone to figure it out," his voice was stern and cold. She almost felt sorry for Donna, almost.

"You do this and you're not welcome back here," now she was angry.

"You do whatever it is you need to do Donna, bye." And he hung up. He rolled over on his back. His eyes were staring at the ceiling, his breathing heavy. He said nothing.

She didn't know what to say. Was this a trick? Was he fucking with her head again? She reached across the distance of the bed and took his hand. They intertwined fingers and he squeezed her hand.

"You didn't have to do that. You might have fucked up your life royal," she spoke softly.

"No, Maddy. I know you don't trust me. I am sorry, but I'm tired of you being the one that gets hurt all the time. It's not right. I keep telling you I love you but I'm going to leave you, like this is nothing and go back to my life like it never happened. After everything that has happened, you have no real reason to believe me. But I need you to, Maddy; I need you to believe I love you. That this isn't a game." He was insistent.

"You were so sure a couple years ago, too. You said back then you didn't love her, but when it all came down to it, you still went back to her."

"You know how messed up I was back then. I was desperate; I had nowhere to go. I couldn't go home, not to Natalia."

"You could have come to me. You dogged me until I gave in. I changed my life around so you could and you slammed the door in my face. You walked away from me, and didn't even have the balls to tell me. No sorry, no goodbye, no explanation, for two fucking years, not a word. Now you come back in my life and expect me to trust you? To believe in you? I love you Bryan, I never stopped, but it doesn't make what happened go away. What's changed, why should I believe in you now?" She wiped the tears from her face with the back of her hand.

"Because a few months a go, I spent 30 days in rehab with some intense therapy and got my head on straight." he declared.

She was speechless. He had been so adamant about not getting help before. "What changed to make you go?"

"My job, they said go or get out. It was impairing my ability to do my job, but it was the best thing that could have happened to me. The last couple of months, I thought more and more about you, couldn't get you off my mind. But I was afraid, Maddy—afraid you would slam the door in my face. I felt you were better off without me and I didn't have the right to contact you," he explained.

"Yet you did?" she inquired.

"This case came up. I had kept tabs on you so I knew where you were. It seemed like fate, a message that it was the right thing to do. I took a chance and here I am. Was I wrong?"

It was a question Maddy wasn't sure she could answer, but really it was moot point. He was here now. She had allowed him back into her life; she had shared a bed with him. She didn't have to, could have refused to see him and walked away, but she didn't. "I don't know...but you are planning on leaving again. You made it perfectly clear. You are going back."

"I still have to deal with my job. I got twenty years into the Bureau; I just can't walk away. I don't know what I'm going to do. Eventually I will have to go back, but we can figure out some way to make this work. Will you try with me?" he pleaded.

He slid down in the bed and wrapped his arms around her and pulled her close. "Don't shut me out Maddy, please..."

She buried her head in his chest and let go, all the hurt and confusion coming to the surface.

Bryan stroked her hair and kissed her on the top of her head. "Are we okay, Minnie?"

She nodded her head without speaking a word. She didn't want to fight, as she no longer had the strength. She wouldn't surrender to her fears. They would never know unless they tried.

Bryan released her long enough to slip between the sheets, their bodies met in the middle. He cupped her face in his hands and kissed away her tears then sought out her lips. His lips crushed hers with a fierce passion, unyielding, demanding a response from her.

Maddy yielded to his demands, clinging to him to as if her life depended on it. His hands traveled over her body, searing her skin with every touch. He tugged at the nighty and slipped it off over her head. He rolled her over on her back. His lips burned a path where gown had been. Her nails grazed his back, her teething biting into the flesh of his shoulder. He covered her body with his, his mouth covering hers; kissing her so deep she thought he would suck the breath right out of her. He raised his head, searching her eyes. She looked deep into his, dark and smoldering. "Make me yours, Minnie. I'm surrendering to you, make me yours...."

She aggressively wrapped her fingers in his hair and pulled him to her kissing him with the same passion he had shared with her. The fire rose through her as they united, she screamed out. Her voice trembled as she said in a throaty voice, "You're mine, Mickey. All mine...for now..."

He rolled off her and scooped her up in his arms, holding her close as she cried. He didn't ask her any questions, he knew. You can only be hurt by someone so many times before their faith in you is shaken to the core. He whispered in her ear, "I do love you Maddy, forever and always." He held her while they both surrendered to sleep.

"Maddy..." Bryan was sitting on the side of bed, his hand brushing the hair out of her face. "I'm taking off for work." He kissed her softly. "I will call you as soon as I get chance. Don't over do it on that ankle. Love you Minnie."

"Bossy," she mumbled. "Love you too." She rolled over and went back to sleep.

Maddy woke a couple of hours later, vaguely remembering Bryan leaving. She needed to get going and go back to work at the Journal. She needed some semblance of normalcy and work was like home to her.

Twenty minutes later she was hobbling out to her car and took off for work. When she arrived at the Journal, she decided to use the crutches after all. She would rather look like a klutzy fool than be in pain all day. Needless to say she got lots of looks when she entered the bullpen, but she gave them the look and nobody said a word.

She eased herself into her chair and picked up the phone. She was dreading making this call, but she felt she owed it to Sandy. "Hi Sandy, this is Maddy Sheridan."

"Hey Maddy! Did you get the laptop?" Her voice was cheerful, especially for this time in the morning.

"Yeah, yeah I did, thank you," she paused. "Listen Sandy, I would be doing this in person, but I sprained my ankle and am not getting around to good, but I need to tell you this before you hear it from the press."

Sandy was quiet and then said, "She's gone isn't she?"

"I'm so sorry, Sandy. We recovered her body yesterday. I'm sorry I can't tell you more, I hope you understand." She felt like dirt, especially doing this over the phone.

"Yes...yes...I understand," her voice cracked. "Thank you Maddy, I need some time alone. I will talk to you soon." The line went dead.

Maddy's eyes were tearing up. "God damn it!" she screamed as she threw a book across the room. It was too much. This was all too much. She couldn't do it. Bryan, Jack, these murders, the bodies, Bryan...too much emotion invested. She couldn't do it. She put her head down on the desk, covered her head, and cried.

There was a knock at the door, and Chief popped his head in. He quickly noticed her red swollen eyes. "You okay kid?"

She wiped her eyes. "I'm fine...I'm always fine. I just told Sandy Morton her best friend is dead. That's how fine I am," she spat.

Chief shut the door and sat down in front of her. "Maybe I need to pull you off this story, Maddy."

Her head shot up. "No! I need to find this killer!"

"Now wait a minute, kid. You don't need to do anything. It's not your responsibility. That's law enforcement, and as you have so kindly put so many times, you are a reporter, not a cop. You are getting way too invested in this," he spoke calmly but sternly.

Maddy picked up a pen repeatedly flipped it end for end on her desk. "I am fine...I will be fine. I just need to recoup and get a grip." Tap...Tap...Tap..."I found the body," she said flatly.

"I see," was all he said.

"I sprained my fucking ankle getting tangled up in underbrush, then I get my ass chewed for disrupting the scene, I did everything by procedure, I swear I did." Her words came tumbling out.

"Seems to me, Maddy, your worlds are starting to co-mingle. You're on the fence. How long are you going to be able to balance it?"

Maddy set the pen down. "What are you saying?"

Chief made a face. "How do I put this—you've been put into a situation where your past life is interfering with your present life. There might come a point when you are going to have to choose."

She looked at him in dismay shaking her head. "I can't and I won't. I just need to get things into perspective and get back to me. I am an investigative reporter, a damn good one," she assured him. Or was it herself she was reassuring? "I will do my job, get my story, whatever it takes, and if I have to do that by getting inside the investigation, that is what I'll do. Do you understand?"

Chief stood up. "You're walking a fine line Maddy. It could get dangerous, and I'm not talking physically so much. Now do you understand?"

She picked up the pen and rolled it between her fingers. "Yes Sir."

"Good." Then he left.

She took in a deep breath and blew it out slowly. She closed her eyes and counted to ten, then twenty...thirty. Okay, everything's cool, I can do this, she thought. She needed to call Bryan to see if he could get a contact list for the victims. She really did not want to talk to him. She was feeling too vulnerable. Last night had left her feeling raw and on edge. She reluctantly pulled out her cell phone and dialed his number.

He answered on the third ring, "Good morning kiddo, did you sleep well?"

She didn't answer; this was business, not personal. "Any chance I get a contact list of the vics so I can start researching to see if there is a religious angle?"

"Yeah, of course, I will have them email you one." He paused, "Are you okay Maddy?"

"Damn it! If one more person asks me if I'm okay, I swear to God I will shoot them!"

"Calm down kiddo. Talk to me."

"Its just been really stressful the past couple of days. I need to work and I'll be fine." She started flipping her pen again.

"And I'm sure last night didn't do anything to help with that. I'm afraid...it's shaken up your confidence...in us. I'm sorry Maddy," he said tentatively.

Maddy pondered what he was saying. He was right. It really unnerved her and brought out all her fears about their relationship. "No, it didn't," she responded. "Bryan I just need to work through this okay? I can't promise I can forgive and forget. It's just not that easy. I just got to believe and hold on. I'm doing my best. I just need time. I need you, Bryan."

"You've got me Maddy. I promise. I'm not sure how my day is going to go. We got guys out at the park doing searches. I got my guys and Jack compiling what we have. Hopefully I will get off at a decent time. Will you stay with me tonight?"

She was quiet as she contemplated if she dare let go. Each night she spent with him the more danger she put her stability in, but if she left him, she knew she couldn't go back.

Bryan picked up on her hesitation. "Do you need me to stay away Maddy? If that is what you need, I will do whatever you want."

"No...No, I don't think, hell I don't know." She paused. "In all honesty, Bryan, I'm afraid if we don't, I mean I don't face this, I'll end up running, I know me."

"Okay, maybe we just need to slow down. We'll do whatever it is you need, Maddy. It's all about what you need honey. If you get done before me, I will meet you there."

"Do you have the prelims back yet?"

"Yeah, we ID'd the Jane Doe as Cynthia Steward, our 3rd missing person. We got the tox screens back on the first two. They were pumped full Ketamine."

"Horse tranquilizer? What would that do?"

"It's a dissociative anesthetic. It can separate perception from sensation. At lower doses it has a mild, dreamy feeling similar to laughing gas. The person may experience feeling floaty and slightly outside their body. Numbness in the extremities is also common. In higher doses it can produce a hallucinogenic effect. During this phase it is very difficult to move. In other words in this state, the body is sedated while the mind is still conscious. Depending on dose it can speed up your heart rate or higher doses suppresses the respiratory system."

"So for what purpose do you suppose our unsub used this?"

"You tell me what you think based on your vision of our unsub?"

"Well first I would think he would use it as means to control the vic, however I honestly think he used it as part of his torture regime. He pumps her full of it so she is powerless to do anything to protect herself, yet he makes sure she is aware of what's happening to her. What a sick fuck." Maddy shook her head in disgust.

"Wouldn't it be so much easier for you to work over here where you have everything at your disposal?" he asked.

"Ha! You just want me there so you can keep tabs on me and sneak kisses," she smiled.

"And what would be wrong with that?" he laughed.

"Do you think your supervisor would approve of 1) you bringing in a civilian to work the case and 2) having your lover there and making no bones about your affection for her?" She raised an eyebrow.

"Well we could take care of number one by reactivating you and two—we could hide out in a broom closet...No really, I can bring you on as a consultant, you do have the credentials and as far as the making out, I will do my best to keep my hands to myself. So what do you say?"

"I don't know...do you really thinks this is a good idea?" she asked.

"Full disclosure...what better way to get it then to be in the hot spot?" he asked.

She thought about it. It would be easier to access and compile information. Isn't that what she did...as a reporter? "Would I be able to work alone?"

Bryan laughed, "What? You don't want to be a team player?"

"No," she replied in all seriousness.

"Ooookay..." he was puzzled. "Well, what's it going to be Ace?"

"I'll think about it," she flipped her pen in the air.

"Want me to send a car?"

"Christ! I think I can take care of myself. Why can't you see that? I don't need to be watched over, I don't need taken care of, I don't need to be fathered," she responded angrily.

"Maddy, you really need to mellow out, see you in a while," and he hung up.

"Asshole!" She threw the pen.

Maddy picked up her laptop and Vanessa's and slipped it in her bag. She still needed to go through it and see if she could glean anything from what was on it. Twenty minutes later she was pulling in to a parking lot at 601Douglas Street, in other words, the cop shop.

How was she going to carry her things and use her crutches? She would probably fall and break her neck. There was no way in hell she would call Bryan and ask him to help, not after her little tirade and Jack—anymore he was like an appendage of Bryan.

Whittmer. He owed her. She called the general desk and asked for him. "Agent Whittmer," came his stoic voice.

Then she realized she didn't have a clue what his first name was. She was sure he told her that day he picked her up, but she'd be damned if she could recall it now. "Hi, this is Maddy Sheridan. I need a favor."

"What?" He sounded suspicious. Sheesh after she let him ride her horse.

"I know this might be beneath you, but would you mind helping me get up there. I can't carry my stuff and use my crutches at the same time."

He paused. "I guess so, but only this one time. I won't kiss your ass like Mayland does." And he hung up.

Maddy's mouth dropped as she stared at her phone and then she laughed. Damn, so much for animal bonding.

It took him a few minutes to get to her. He nodded at her, took her bag. He didn't even bother to wait for her. How rude. They must be teaching the new agents how to be dicks.

She made her way across the lobby, signed in and was given a visitors pass. Normally she took the stairs for extra exercise, but needless to say that was out of the question. She took the elevator. This sprained ankle was getting to be a pain in the ass.

Whittmer had laid her bag outside the door. When he saw her, he popped his head out the door. "I didn't think you would want them to see me helping you, would be tough to explain why you didn't ask one of them." He was referring to Bryan and Jack.

She gave him a soft smile, "Thank you, I appreciate it." Maybe he wasn't such a dick after all.

She waited a few moments to let Whittmer go back in and look busy and then went in. Jack saw her come in and quickly went to her aid.

"Need a hand Cripple?" He grabbed her bag.

"Fuck you," she snapped.

"Such gratitude," he laughed.

"I repeat, fuck you."

She hobbled to Bryan's desk. He had a laptop in front of him and was deeply absorbed in his work. She stood before his desk and cleared her throat. He looked up, and then removed his glasses. "Hey kiddo. Glad to see you made it. Also glad to see you using those." He pointed to the crutches.

He stood and came around the desk and leaned over to kiss her. She put her hand up, "We made a deal. I'm here to work."

"We did? I don't recall that." He shrugged his shoulders, "Okay, anything Maddy wants, Maddy gets," he said sarcastically.

"Fuck you, too." She stood there looking at him. "Where do you want me?"

A devilish smile crossed his face.

Maddy felt the heat rise to her face. "To work, Bryan, to work."

He reached out and touched her nose. "All work and no play makes Maddy a dull girl."

She lowered her voice, "Work now, play later."

He grinned, "Now we have a deal. I got a desk for you on the other side of me."

"Do you think that's wise?" she inquired.

"Why not? Unless you don't think you can keep your hands off me?" he grinned in amusement.

She smiled and shook her head, "I'm not going to win this am I?

"Nope, so get your sexy ass over there and get to work." He leaned over and whispered in her ear. "If you weren't being such a proper bitch, I would spank your ass, and I don't care who sees."

"Pervert," she smirked under her breath as she moved toward the desk.

Jack brought her bag over and set it on her desk. "Damn Maddy, what do you have in here? It weighs a ton."

"Stuff," was all she said.

Jack turned to Bryan. "We've gone back through Granger's house combing for evidence. CSU is there now dusting for prints. Her computer is missing though."

"How do you know she had one?"

"Well its like this, she had a router hooked up for wireless and I could have sworn when we searched her house the fist time, there was one in her bedroom." He was leaning against the desk where Maddy was seated. He rubbed his hand on his chin as if he were pondering the wonders of the world. He turned to her, his eyes searing into her.

"What?" she asked innocently.

Bryan watched the exchange between the two of them with amusement.

"You know what, Maddy." Jack refused to take his eyes off her face. He was watching her expression. This was one time Jack knew her better than Bryan. He knew what she was capable of doing and the extreme measures she would take to achieve her goals.

"I don't have a clue what you're talking about, Jack." Come on Maddy, she coached herself, you can do this, don't flinch.

"Bullshit." Jack crossed his arms, still not taking his eyes off her. She would crack, she couldn't hold out forever and he knew, damn it, he knew.

"I have no idea what you're getting at, Jack."

"Damn it, Maddy. You know I know when you're lying and you are lying now. Give me your bag."

She grabbed it and pulled it to her chest. "A lady does not allow men to go through her bag."

"Maddy, you are no lady!" He snatched the bag from her clutches. He slid two laptops out onto her desk. Shit! He picked up her ibook and handed it to her. "I believe this one is yours..." and then he pulled out a black Dell. "and this one belongs to our vic."

"Do you think I would be stupid enough to bring it here?" she snapped.

"Not stupid, sneaky. Did you breach the crime scene?"

"*I* did not breach the crime scene and take the computer." It was the truth. Yes, she breached the crime scene, but not to take the computer. "And I'm not lying."

Jack held the computer in his hand and studied her. She felt like a fly that had had its wings pulled off and was being looked at through a microscope to watch her squirm. "Half truths are as bad as lies, Maddy."

She regarded him closely and remarked, "You are so full of shit, Jack."

"Maddy!" Bryan said abruptly and she jumped. "Did you take the computer?"

"I told you, *I* didn't take the computer."

He sat back in his chair and studied her.

Maddy looked at Jack and looked back at Bryan. "Honest I didn't take the computer from the house. I would never breach a crime scene."

Jack's head came up and he laughed, "Now who's full of shit? How can you sit there and feed me this line of bull? Fact, the computer is in your possession. Fact it disappeared from the house some time prior to our second search, but had been there at the time of the first search. How do you explain just exactly how it came into your possession?"

Damn, there was no squirming out of this one. "Someone gave it to me." She looked away. She couldn't take much more of Jack's interrogation without cracking.

"Who?" Bryan asked.

Maddy sighed and confessed, "Sandy Morton picked it up for me."

"When?"

"Tuesday."

"How'd she get in?"

"She had a key."

"You asked her to get it?"

"Yes."

"Why?"

"What is this? Twenty questions?" she replied blatantly.

"Answer the question." Bryan held steady.

"I think I am in the wrong room. Shouldn't I be in the interrogation room?"

"Maddy, quit stalling, just answer the damn question. What did you hope to find on the computer? I know for fact you don't know how to disseminate a computer."

Maddy sat back in her chair, crossed her arms and sighed. "Okay, I give up. Sandy told me Vanessa spent a lot of time frequenting chat rooms. I want to check the URL's, and check out her emails. I wanted to see if I could find out if there were some chance she met up with someone she met on the net."

"So you interviewed the vic's contacts?"

Jack was booting up the computer and added, "She sure did, even before the police could get to her."

Bryan continued to stare at Maddy.

"What now?"

"I'm beginning to see why Jack says you are such a pain in the ass," he laughed.

Maddy reached out and flicked Jack with the back of her hand, "You told him that?"

Jack chuckled as he played with the computer, "Well it's true isn't it? Now this is interesting. I pulled down the history. Last URL—Verizon Wireless, dated last Friday. Quite an amazing feat considering our vic disappeared earlier in the week," Jack was looking at Maddy again.

Shit, why didn't she dump the history? It was getting hot in here. She pulled her collar away from her neck. Bringing that computer here was one of the dumbest things she had ever done. What good did it do to be so sneaky if she practically brought in her kill and turned it over to the cops? Lousy reporter work, lousy FBI work. She decided silence was her best line of defense.

"You told me Saturday morning that you were able to verify Granger disappeared was Tuesday night. I asked you how and you said phone records."

"Luuucy...you got some splainin to do," Bryan chuckled imitating Ricky Ricardo.

Maddy picked up a pen and threw it at him, "Shut the fuck up!"

"Eeewww, such language for a *lady*..."he snickered. Then he spoke to Jack, "So what is it you're getting at?"

"Maddy said Morton brought her the computer on Tuesday, yet these phone records were pulled Friday morning. Either she is lying about when she got the computer or she indeed breeched the crime scene by breaking and entering on Friday. Which is it Maddy?" Jack asked.

Maddy looked at her watch, "Gee I think I need to get back to the paper. I have a story to file before press time."

"Bullshit," Bryan said.

"Cows do to but they don't brag about it," she stuck her tongue out at him.

"Christ Parker, how do you manage to work with her without strangling her?" Then he turned to Maddy. "Quit being so evasive and just tell us what the hell is going on? Full disclosure...it works both ways, Maddy."

Maddy sighed, "Fine. I went back to the house, found a key hidden under a paver rock in the back and let myself in. I wore gloves, didn't touch anything but the computer" she looked at Jack with her hands in the air waving her fingers, "No touchy rule." Then she continued, "I counted on her access passwords to be stored in memory, which they were. I downloaded her phone bill and printed it off and then left the house—just as I found it. I took the records back to the office and studied them. The last call was an outgoing call Tuesday evening." She looked at Bryan. "Full disclosure, you happy now?"

"You are sure that's everything?"

"Yes, I'm sure. Are we done now, please, I don't need this shit."

"You brought it on yourself Maddy," Jack snapped.

"Jack back off." Bryan ordered. "She's had enough."

"I'm fine, Bryan. You don't need to protect me from Jack. He's been meaner to me." She looked at Jack and wrinkled up her nose.

"Can I make one request, in regards to the computer?" she asked.

"You're not in any position to be asking for requests," Jack stated.

Bryan threw Jack a look and Jack closed his mouth. Then he turned to Maddy, "What do you need kiddo?"

"Can I look for the info I told you about before you take the computer for dissemination?"

He looked at his watch 11:10. "You have until noon."

"That's less than an hour!"

"I guess you better get busy then, shouldn't you?"

Bryan stood up. "I need a smoke. Jack would you like to join me?" Was that a request or an order? Maddy wasn't sure.

"Sure, I will be down in a minute. I need to take care of something quick."

Jack sat on Maddy's desk. "Do you really think it's necessary to have Mayland protect you from me? Telling me to back off? It really makes me feel like shit, Maddy."

"I'm sorry, Jack. What do you want me to do? Bryan can get...very protective when he thinks I am being pushed to far." She looked down. "He doesn't feel I am strong enough to handle it."

"He doesn't feel you are strong enough to handle it..." Jack shook his head. "Mads, I've seen him go off on you far worse than anything I have ever done. And why would he feel you are not strong?"

She was still looking down, running her finger along the edge of her laptop. "I have my moments of weakness. With some of the things that have happened lately...I have been on shaky ground."

"Him being one of them," he said flatly.

"That's not fair Jack," she protested. When she looked at him her eyes were glistening.

Jack pulled over Bryan's chair to her and sat in it. "Maddy, what's happening to you? I've never seen you doubt yourself so much. Its like he's consuming you, turning you into someone else. I should be protecting you from him." He smiled weakly, "this...what just happened, this is us, this is how we do our thing. I didn't like it when he pulled me back. He is keeping us from being us." He put his finger under her chin. "Don't worry about us, Mads, we promised each other we'd get through this, and we will." He stroked her cheek with the back of his hand as he searched her eyes. "I wish I could kiss you, but that really wouldn't help things. Just know that I want too...and I miss you."

He stood up and pushed Bryan's chair back in place. "Better get out there before he comes looking and you better get busy on that computer. Tick Tock." He left to join Bryan for a smoke.

Maddy watched him go, her heart aching. This was so hard. At that moment she actually wished Bryan had stayed away so she and Jack could explore their feelings for each other. Bryan was making her afraid of her feelings. Jack was right; Bryan was making doubt herself, her power over herself. She felt helpless and didn't like feeling that way.

She pushed the thoughts out of her mind; she had work to do. She slid her computer to the side and pulled Vanessa's to her. She had to do this quick; she was running out of time. She stuck in a flash drive and opened a Word document. She pulled down the history and cut and pasted it on to the documents. She saved the file to the flash drive. She opened Entourage and quickly started forwarding all her emails to her computer. There were about 50 of them so it took most of the remaining time Bryan had given her to do it. She finished up with five minutes to spare.

When Bryan and Jack returned Vanessa's computer was shut down and on the corner of her desk. She smiled up at them. "All done."

"Did you find anything?" Bryan asked.

"Don't know yet, I just extracted the info. I haven't had time to examine it yet." She shut down her computer and slipped the flash drive into her pocket. "Any one for lunch?"

9

"Why don't you two go ahead," Jack said as he picked up some files from the desk. Maddy watched his body language. He was rigid and tense. Had something happened out there?

Maddy gave Bryan a questioning glance. Bryan shook his head and shrugged his shoulders. Yeah right, like he was so innocent. "I said we should go to lunch, I didn't say we were going to quit working," she said. "I need you both for some brainstorming. Unless you guys got a problem with that?"

The two men looked at each other. Both said neither had a problem with it. "You want us to bring anything with us?" Jack asked.

"The autopsy reports and photos," she replied, sitting on the corner of her desk, crutches at her side.

Both men shot her a look of disbelief.

"You're kidding right? We are going go eat and you want to look at dead bodies?" Jack shook his head. Why should this not surprise him? This was so Maddy. He turned to Bryan, "What do you think Mayland?"

Bryan went to his desk and grabbed a large packet from his desk. "Well Parker, its like this, it has been my experience she won't quit bitching until she gets what she wants, so we might as well humor her. If she gets sick at the restaurant, we are not held accountable."

Jack laughed, "Oh you find she's like that too, do you?"

Maddy bristled at their words, but then she thought about it if they were picking on her they weren't attacking each other. It's okay, let them play their games between the two of them, she had work to do.

Twenty minutes later they were seated at Applebee's. The waitress had taken and delivered their drink orders and was waiting for their meal orders. Bryan ordered a bacon burger and fries, and Jack something with chicken in it. Maddy looked at the menu and set it down, "Just tea for me."

"Maddy, you need to eat something. You've hardly eaten in two days." The concern in Bryan's voice was apparent. He reached out for her hand.

"Stop!" She pulled her hand away. She turned to the waitress, "I'll have a salad with thousand island." She turned to Bryan and Jack, "You two talk, I don't give a damn about what, just keep yourselves busy while I take a look at these."

"Maddy, quit being a bitch," Bryan said quietly.

Maddy pulled out the autopsy files. She appeared deeply absorbed in them but in reality she was listening to Jack and Bryan's conversation.

"So Parker, what peaked your interest in law enforce?" Bryan asked. He was leaning back against the corner of the booth totally relaxed.

"Went to college, spent some time in the military, went to academy in Omaha, did my patrol time in at the OPD, worked my way up the ranks, got my detective shield while I was there, got offered a good position up here heading up this department and went for it. Needless to say it substantially quieter than Omaha, but I guess that's okay," Jack explained like he was reciting it from memory.

"Do you aspire to something greater than this?"

Jack smiled, "Wouldn't anyone with any kind of ambition? I would like to get on with the DCI. With any kind of luck after working this case successfully I can apply and have a chance."

"Have you considered..." Bryan started to say before Maddy kicked him.

"No Bryan! Not now...please." Maddy pleaded with him. Bryan had mentioned that Jack would make a good FBI candidate, but Maddy didn't want that, didn't want Jack to consider it, for now.

Jack watched the two exchange looks, "What's up? Obviously something."

Her plea fell on deaf ears. "Depending how you do on this case, I would be willing to make a recommendation for entrance to the FBI academy. Would that be something you would be interested in?"

Jack gazed at Maddy, watching her reaction. Although she refused to look up at him, he could tell she was visibly upset about Bryan's offer and wondered why. "Sure I would be interested, but I would still need to take it under some serious consideration." Jack brushed Maddy's leg with his foot. She smiled weakly from behind the reports. "What about you Bryan, how did you get into this?"

"Born into it," Bryan replied like it was a matter of fact. "My Dad was in law enforcement but on an international level. We were constantly moving all over the world. My brother and I both went into the FBI, my sister married into it. Been in the Bureau just a little over twenty years."

The waitress brought their food. Maddy squeezed her lemon into her tea and stirred it with her straw and took a sip. She pushed her salad off to the side.

"Maddy, eat," Bryan commanded. It wasn't a request; it was an order.

"I will later," she said to appease him. She honestly wasn't hungry. She tended to loose her appetite when she was under intense stress that working a case could bring. She studied Vanessa Granger's autopsy report. It was just a prelim, no toxicology report. Granger died from exsanguation. She had been cut from sternum to just below where her throat had been slit. She also had several hesitation wounds in her lower abdomen. This was new. At the point of intersection she noticed a puncture wound. Was this also new or was it not apparent on the older bodies? She pulled out her file and removed the photos. If she hadn't had an appetite before, she surely didn't have one now. Vanessa's face was gaunt, her eyes sunken in. She had a pale pollar, her lips were blue. On her throat was the gaping wound where it had been slit. The injury extended just below her jaw line, but not ear to ear. She had not been cut from behind as most receiving these kinds of injuries. She flipped to Cynthia's photos. With the state of decomp of this body it was hard to tell the antemortem injuries, there appeared to be no hesitation wounds, but here again the throat had been slit in the same location. She flipped back to Granger's photos, to the ligature marks on her ankles, wrists, and at the base of her neck. She had been bound tightly. The marks were angry and red, ranging from an inch to an inch and a half in length. There were deep gouges penetrating the area of the marks. She pulled the photo closer studying the gouges. She had strong suspicion what made these injuries and how the unsub committed the murders. She placed the photos and the autopsy report and laid it off to the side.

She slid her salad over, tossed the dressing in, took a couple of bites and pushed it aside. Bryan watched her and shook his head but didn't say anything to her.

"I need to see the bodies," she requested as she took a large draw of tea from her glass.

Bryan looked at in concern. "Maddy, do you really think it's a good idea under the circumstances?"

"I can't make a proper analysis unless I can study the bodies." Her eyes held his, steady and unflinching. Yes, she was putting an already rocky emotional stability at risk, but she needed to do this.

Jack glanced between the Bryan and Maddy, "Are you two ever going to let me in on to what the hell is going on here? You know Maddy is my friend too. I can't help her if I don't know what's going on."

"I don't need any help," she snapped, "and I don't need protected." She turned to Bryan, "I did just fine before you came—you don't need you to pretend to be my knight in shining armor. Now are you going to let me examine the bodies?"

Bryan still doubted the wisdom of letting her. Despite what she said, he felt she was fragile. But she was insistent, what could he do? He could pull rank on her, but that would just make her angrier. He decided he would let her, but if things even looked the remotest bit shaky, she was out of there.

The guys finished up their meals in silence, Maddy finished her tea. Bryan paid the tab while she and Jack waited by the entrance. Maddy stepped outside. A warm summer rain had just begun to fall. She could smell the scent of dust being disturbed by each drop that hammered the ground.

Bryan took Maddy's bag and her crutches. "What are you doing?" she asked.

"I'm going to get the Suburban, Jack, you grab her in put her in." He left to get the SUV.

"Christ," Maddy shook her head. "This is getting to be pretty damn old."

Jack eyed Maddy skeptically. "We're just trying make things easier for you, you know, be gentlemanly." He nudged her playfully. Then he said, "I wish you would let me in Maddy. I'm not the enemy."

She leaned against a pillar by the door of the building. "I never said you were Jack. There are just some things that belong to me and me alone. Don't take it personal."

"Mayland knows so it's both your secret."

"He only knows because he was there." She reached out for his hand and squeezed it. "Really don't worry about it. I am fine and will get through this without repercussions. Trust me on this okay?"

Jack checked to see where Bryan was. He was still walking toward the truck. He leaned over quickly and kissed her. "Maddy I want to spend some time with you, alone. I haven't had that chance since Monday night, and we all know how that went, which by the way I am sorry. Mayland either keeps me near him or has you so well guarded I can't get near you without him watching."

Maddy smiled faintly, "Do I detect a note of jealousy?"

Jack watched the raindrops as they pelted the cement, "Yeah, I guess you do."

"I miss you too, Jack, really. I will have to see if I can figure out something, even if I have just come out and tell him I want to spend sometime with you. I just don't want to make things difficult for you. He likes and respects you Jack, otherwise he wouldn't have offered to recommend you for the academy. I don't want to compromise that opportunity for you. I'm not worth it ,Jack."

"Listen to yourself, Maddy. Damn it, you are surrendering to him. That's not the Maddy I know," he replied angrily.

"You seem to be forgetting, you, yourself said you really don't know me at all."

Bryan was pulling up in the truck. "Bullshit," Jack growled. "Get on."

"What?"

"Jump on, ride this horse," he chuckled.

She hopped up on his back, her legs dangling out in front of Jack. She leaned forward and whispered in his ear, "The mighty stallion," and she threw her head back and laughed.

Bryan had stepped out and opened one of the back doors for her so she could stretch her leg out. The guys got in and they drove out of the parking lot on to Singing Hills Boulevard. She poked her head between them. "I need to stop at Bomgaars. I need to get something."

"What's Bomgaars?" Bryan asked.

"It's a farm store. Get on Highway 20 up here then turn on to Gordon, it's right off there." Jack gave him the directions. He turned to Maddy "What do you need in there?"

"Just let me out at the door and wait for me there."

Bryan looked to Jack for an answer and he just shrugged his shoulders. "Don't ask me. I quit trying figure out how her mind works long ago."

As instructed, they dropped her off at the door of the store. She hopped her way into the customer service desk, explained her ankle situation and told them what she wanted. Several minutes later the man returned with her request. She asked them to put it in a large bag so she could keep her package under wraps. The guy was even nice enough to carry it out to the suburban for her.

"Okay now to the morgue," she clicked on her seat belt.

Bryan turned around with his right arm over the back of the seat. "Before we go, I want to know what the hell you are up to."

"I need to test a theory, and I can't do that without the actual body." Maddy's expression was stoic. She was keeping her emotions in check.

Bryan was apprehensive. Since they had left the police station, she had been quiet, preoccupied, and distant. Was she really getting that wrapped up in the case or was there something else going on. His fear was that she was starting to pull away from him and he didn't know how to stop it. Parker was getting edgy with him, and he was sure it had to do something with Maddy. He needed to do something to clear the air and head off a situation that could be explosive.

They pulled into St. Luke's Regional Medical Center where the bodies were being kept. Maddy grabbed her bag and left her crutches in the suburban. The morgue was in the lower level so they made their way there. Bryan met with the coroner, showed him his credentials and they followed him in. He brought Vanessa's body out. Maddy limped over to the body and pulled back the sheet to just above her breast. On the outside she appeared to be in control, calm, cool and very professional. On the inside she felt jittery, uncomfortable, panicky, and felt the need to get the hell out of there as fast as she could. But she wanted to prove to both Bryan and Jack she could handle it. They seemed to be under the impression she was weak and needed taken care of. At least Bryan did.

She put on a pair of latex gloves and closely examined the lacerated throat. The laceration was deepest on the left side, becoming shallow out to right. She had already come to the conclusion it was a frontal attack, but this proved their unsub was right handed.

She pulled the sheet down further to reveal the horizontal and vertical incisions. She ignored the Y cut from the autopsy. Her fingers grazed the lines of the wounds. They appeared even in depth and intersected above the heart. In the center of the incision was a puncture. She was sure this was a new item to the unsub. "What do we have for a depth on this wound?" she asked the coroner.

He pulled out the paper work and looked it up, "Approximately inch from the surface."

"Not enough to penetrate the breast bone," she pulled it apart gently with her fingers, "apparently done by penetration with a rounded object, about the diameter of a pencil." She studied the other hesitation wounds on the abdomen. All were superficial done purely for the purpose of torture.

She glanced up at the coroner, "No signs of sexual assault on any of our victims?"

"No, none."

Maddy nodded and continued her examination. She covered the upper torso, moving down to the feet. She needed to study the ligature marks. She pulled back the sheet and closely examined the ligatures injuries. She touched the gouges. They were shallowest at the bottom and appeared like they were dragged across the skin in an upward position digging into the flesh, just what she thought.

She took her Bomgaars bag and removed two stretches of barbed wire at different gauges. She held one against the gouges and then the other. She nodded in satisfaction and covered the body.

Bryan watched her with keen interest. This was the Maddy he used to work with, back before...She was immersing herself in the investigation. This was Maddy, the agent, not Maddy, the reporter. He was eager to hear her assessment.

Jack watched her in amazement. A week ago, he would never have imagined her doing something like this. She was keen, thorough, totally engross in what she was doing. This woman he thought he knew was so full of mystery. Her words came back to haunt him, he really didn't know her at all.

"What ya got for me, Maddy?" Bryan asked.

She went back to the upper part of the body and pulled the sheet back. Her fingers followed the line of the wound. "The incision does not go from ear to ear. This indicates the strike was made from the front of the victim," she pulled the skin back. "The incision is deeper on the left side, once again reinforces the frontal attack. The dept of the wound on this side also tells me that are unsub is right handed. Each of vics have this vertical and horizontal incision which intersect over the heart. I don't believe this is a coincidence. The depths of the wounds are uniform indicating a steady hand with lots of practice. This here is new," she pointed to the puncture wound. "From the reports and pictures I have seen, I don't recall this being here. It and the rest of the shallow wounds, I believe, were part of the torture procedure. These too are new, so I believe our unsub is escalating, feeling the need for more torture to get off." She took the hand and pointed out the ligature marks. "You can see this more on the feet, but I believe we would find that these ligatures were created by 2-point barb with with 12 3/4 gauge wire." She held a piece of the wire she brought lining it up to the gouges. "If you looked here," she pointed to the tearing and scraping, "the vic was bound then hung in an upright position. The tearing and scraping, to me, indicate that the ligatures were placed on the vic and she was 'hung up'. The tension on the wire is what caused the deep gauges and the scraping." Maddy covered the body and waited.

At first nobody said a word. Maddy looked at the coroner, "Plausible?"

"I concur, are you done with the body." She nodded to him and he took it away.

Jack stood dumbfounded and amazed. Who knew? He thought back about the little spitfire who followed him around, seeming to be so innocent, yet able to pick up of the finest details at a crime scene. He just thought she had a keen sense for her surroundings. This was beyond the realm of what he ever thought she was capable of doing. To say he was impressed was an understatement. He knew he didn't have the talent or the skills to infer what she had just done with the body. He left that information to be supplied by the coroner, which by the way was in none of the reports.

Bryan smiled. He was proud of her and it wasn't just because of the report she had just given him, but because he knew what it took for her to do this. He knew each time she did this kind of examination it took a little piece of her she couldn't get back. "Excellent job kiddo. Now lets get you out of here."

He guided her out the door with Jack following up the rear. He put his hand on her shoulder and she immediately brushed it off. "Don't," she said coldly.

When they were about out the door, she turned to them, "Please excuse me for a minute. If you could bring the sub around by the door, I would greatly appreciate it."

As soon as they were out of sight, Maddy found a little nook where there were vending machines. Her hands were shaking and her legs felt weak. She leaned her back against the wall and slid to the floor. She put her head on her knees, covered her head with her arms and cried. It was so hard. This was one of the reasons she left. She had gotten to the point where contact with the victims tore her apart every time.

Bryan and Jack were waiting several minutes without seeing her come out. Bryan opened the door and got out.

"Where you going?" Jack inquired.

"Something's not right. I'll be right back." Bryan entered the building walking back toward the morgue. He found her crumpled in the corner, doing what he feared would happen. She was falling apart.

He squatted down in front of her and stroked her hair. She batted his hand away. "Maddy, don't. Its okay, let me be here for you. Don't push me away, baby." He pulled her to her feet and wrapped his arms around her and pulled her close, stroking her hair. "Go ahead sweetheart, let it out."

She gave into him and let him hold her. She felt safe again in his arms, like he could protect her from her demons. She loved this man and hated him at the same time—both for the same reasons—he knew her better than any other living soul. This fact, she knew, made her even more vulnerable.

He picked Maddy up in his arms and began to carry her out. "No," she protested. "I don't want to Jack to know."

"Don't worry about Jack. If he cares about you, he has to get to know every aspect about you, even your vulnerable side."

She wiped her eyes on his shoulder then wrapped her arms tight around his neck. "Wait," she asked. She took her head off his shoulder and she kissed him tenderly. He returned the kiss gently and undemanding.

He kissed her on the cheek and then whispered in her ear, "I would go through hell for you Maddy. I won't let anyone or anything hurt you."

Then he heard her whisper, "Except you." He felt a pang in his heart but he let it go. She was right.

Bryan placed her in the back seat. She slid to one side, leaned against the door and closed her eyes. Jack didn't ask any questions and she was glad. He had put down his visor and she saw him take glances at her. She was sure he was full of questions, but once again she couldn't give him any answers.

When they pulled into the SCPD parking lot Bryan turned to her. "What do you want to do Maddy? Do you want to come up or do you feel you need to do something else? Do you need to go rest?"

She was able to regain her composure, "I need to type up the report with the photo references," she replied with her head still against the window. At the moment she felt numb, void of all emotion. She sat up, grabbing her autopsy reports and photos packet. She stepped out of the vehicle, leaving the crutches behind. The numbness made it easier to block out the pain in her ankle. If one didn't know better, one would hardly know she was hurt.

Jack turned to Bryan. "We need to talk."

Bryan parked the suburban in the lot. "Okay, lets talk."

"I know you know how I feel about Maddy and if you hadn't come along who knows where that would have gone. I can deal with it. I only want her happiness and if that's with you so be it. But what I can't deal with is seeing her being ripped apart like she is. I don't know what the hell happened in her past, but it's coming back to bite her in the ass. Is this what you want? To put her through this personal hell? You put her in the middle of this investigation by pulling her in here on Monday by making her profile our guy. That wasn't necessary. You used it to show what kind of control you had over her. I swear to God Mayland, if you break her, I will personally see you burn in hell." The contempt in Jack voice was unmistakable.

At first Bryan said nothing. He stared ahead looking over the parking lot. "I'm not sure how to explain this to you, Parker. Granted I came here for selfish reasons. She's like a part of my soul that I can't let go even though I have tried. I didn't come here to hurt her."

Jack regarded him with a critical eye. "If my understanding of your history with her is correct, you had to know what would happen. You can't keep leaping in and out of her life to satisfy your momentary whims." Jack ran his fingers through his hair pushing it back. "I have the upmost respect for you as an agent..."

"But not personally..." Bryan stated flatly.

"Fuck I don't know, I only know what she told me you did to her in the past."

"Yeah, it's not something I am proud of." He pulled out a cigarette and offered one to Jack. He took it. He lit it and tossed his lighter to Jack. "Maddy has been living a lie for a long time. She does it so she doesn't have to deal with her past. Things start getting too close; she cuts and runs. She builds walls around herself, won't let anyone in, won't let any one care. She thinks it's safer that way. She lets me in Parker. I know it looks bad now, but this is the first time she is trying to deal with it. I know it's tearing her apart, I wish I could take away her pain, but she's not letting me. You saw her push me away. The only thing we can do, and that means you and me, is to be there when she falls, to help her get back up. She needs to work this out for herself. She knows that too, or she never would have gone in to that morgue."

Jack inhaled deeply, held it in and then blew out the smoke. "It would help if I knew what the hell I'm dealing with."

"I can't tell you. As I've said before, they're her demons. I can't betray her trust in me. And she does trust me with it. I'm not going to destroy that trust even for you." Bryan flicked his cigarette out the window. "We need to get back up there. Anything else you need from me?"

"Not you are willing to give answers to," Jack remarked.

"There is one thing, Maddy is not taking care of herself. She's not eating. The most I've seen her eat in the past two days is a couple of bites of pizza. This is going to sound odd coming from me, but after she gets done doing her report, get her out of here, away from this. Do you know of some place?"

Jack pitched his cigarette out the window. "Her sanctuary. Her home."

"Okay, take her home. If she wants to stay there okay, but I don't really think she should be alone. You either stay with her or bring her back to me. Can you do that?"

"What if she won't go?"

"Don't tell her."

Jack agreed. He wanted time alone with her, but this wasn't quite what he was thinking. "Do you trust me with her?"

"No, but one way or the other, she has to follow her heart." Bryan got out of SUV and started to walk toward the station.

Maddy was seated at her desk with the autopsy photos spread in front of her. She was tagging points on the photos to corresponding notes, preparing a formal report. She had made the transition back to agent. Chief had been right. Now she had to let him know. Bryan and Jack were still gone—bet they were giving each other an earful. She didn't care, she didn't want to hear any of it.

Maddy pulled out her cell phone and dialed Chief's direct line. When he answered she blurted it out. "I need to take a leave of absence."

"So you've made your choice, Kid. I'm not surprised. You can't be both—it just wouldn't work. The motivation for the two jobs are different. Now I have to ask you, do you think you will be coming back?"

"Yes, I just have to see this through. And you are right, I can't do this with the objectiveness of a reporter, I'm in too deep." She held back a tear. "I'm sorry, so sorry, I don't want to let you down. You have been so good to me."

"It will be one hell of a story when you get done, Kid. Stay in touch and keep me posted...and Maddy?"

"Yeah?"

"Do you think Mayland's going to let you get away?"

"Ultimately...it's my choice." And she closed her phone.

Maddy leaned back in her chair and covered her eyes. What a fucked up day—what was turning into one of many. Her nerves were raw, her mind numb. She had done what she swore she would never do, come back to the Bureau. She had already gone over Bryan's head and requested the paper work. He had been right, she had only been put on inactive status, Bryan's doing, which kind of pissed her off. He tricked her. She took the time to fill out the forms and have them ready for Bryan's return. She wondered if he would gloat.

Bryan came through the doorway, Jack not far behind him. Neither looked happy. She couldn't help it. He came and sat at the corner of her desk. "What ya doing kiddo?" he tried to make his voice light and cheerful.

She handed her the completed reinstatement forms. "What's this?" He looked through the pages and looked up at her, "Maddy are you sure about this?"

"I thought it's what you wanted." She averted her gaze.

"I never thought you would do it," he laid the papers on his desk. "Maddy, you don't have to do this. Do you know what you're risking?"

"What I'm risking?" she replied incredulously. "What I am risking is the opportunity to find this sick fuck and get him off the streets. This has nothing to with anything that's happened before—you got that? Do you understand, nothing!" she said vehemently.

"Calm down Maddy, I understand and I will support your decision. I just don't know why you are willing to put yourself through it."

She rose from her desk and sat beside Bryan, "Because I have to, but there are some stipulations."

He covered her hand with his, "You're going to leave me?" His touch made her feel comforted.

She smiled weakly, "No, that's not going to happen. I need you—more than ever to help me get through this case."

"Good," he leaned over and kissed her on her forehead. "And your demands Miss Maddy?"

"I have the leeway to investigate in my own way, to be only accountable to you, and when this investigation is done...I'm done." She searched his face for his reaction.

He appeared to be staring off into space, but she knew he was listening and considering her words carefully. "Okay—with the following rules, use common sense, don't do anything illegal that will screw us up for a conviction, you won't have the freedom like you did as a reporter. You do things by the book. Keep me informed as to what you are doing, and that means at all times. I don't need a loose cannon. I need to keep you out of trouble. But most of all Maddy," he put his arm around her pulled her to him, "don't do something stupid or dangerous, I couldn't bear it if anything happened to you over this. Promise me."

She stood up and moved between his legs, putting her arms around his neck and kissed him on the lips. "I promise."

Bryan wrapped his arms around her waist, "Thought you said no hanky panky in the office." He smiled down at her.

She kissed him again. "I changed my mind, it's not what I want. What I want..." she kissed him deeper "...I want to go back to our room, get away from here, into our own little world." She playfully bit his lip. "Can we...please?"

Bryan moaned softly, "Damn you woman..." his breathing was heavy, his hazel eyes like smoke. "Em....Jack wanted to take you for a drive..." She shut him up with her mouth crushing his.

"Not tonight, I want to be with you, no phones...no mistresses...no pizza man...no Jack, just you." Her voice was low and husky, the fire in her emerald eyes sparkled. "Let's go home."

He leaned forward and spoke in her ear. "Jack is going to come over here and ask you to go for a drive. He's been wanting to be alone with you. Can you let him down without hurting him? He's been watching us over here by the way..."

Maddy stood back and searched his eyes and smiled softly, "I appreciate that you appreciate Jack's feelings. You are regaining your ability to feel compassion for others. I'm proud of you, sincerely. What do you want me to do?"

"What do you want to do?"

"What ever you say, but don't expect that answer very often," she laughed.

"I need to get your paperwork faxed in so it can be filed and have Omaha get you your credentials sent up here first thing tomorrow morning. I need to get a briefing from the others. We'll wait until tomorrows to give them yours. I have probably another hour's worth of work before I can really leave. And my sexy little tiger, you need to eat proper. Insist that Jack take you out to get something to eat, and promise me you will eat it, all of it, I will be checking with Jack." He took his finger and put it under her chin, "Promise me you will eat."

She grasped his hand and brought it to her lips. "You know how I get when I'm like this, its hard for me to eat, I just don't have an appetite."

"And you're not going to do me any good if you collapse from starvation. Besides," he brought her hand to his lips, "you'll need the energy." He leaned forward and growled in her ear.

She slapped him playfully, "You're incorrigible. Okay I promise I will eat like a big girl. Happy now?"

"Not until I know the mission is accomplished," he touched the tip of her nose. "Now go look busy so when he comes over and asks you act surprised and pleased."

"What makes you think I won't be?" she scrunched up her nose and smiled.

He rose from her desk, "Shut up and get back to work," he laughed.

Maddy sat down and rubbed her face with both hands. She scanned the photos on her desk and resumed the tedious task of relieving the horror of her day by documenting her conclusions. Except this time...she would not let the horror dictate her. She was busy jotting down notes when Jack came to her desk.

"Hi Maddy, you want to get out of here for awhile?" He tried to sound cheerful, but Maddy could sense his anxiety.

"That would be great," she smiled up at him. "I'm starving, can we go get something to eat?" She glanced over at Bryan who was deep into a conversation on the phone. "Just the two of us?"

A big smile crossed his face, "Yeah, I would really like that. When can you go?"

"Now."

She stacked the files on her desk and walked them to Bryan's desk. "Will you lock these up for me? My desk doesn't have a lock."

He opened the drawer and she dropped them in. He covered the mouthpiece and whispered, "I'll meet you back at the motel."

She whispered back, "You make me feel so cheap."

"Liar," he said out loud.

She laughed, "Fuck you!"

He pointed to the phone and put his fingers to his lips.

Maddy grabbed her bag. "Lets get the hell out of here." She stepped down on her foot and flinched. Shit, pretty dumb thing to forget about.

"Your crutches are in the suburban. But since I know how much you hate to look *crippled*, I can bring my car around front if you can make it there."

"Oh I think I can handle that," she smirked. Jack left to retrieve his car.

As Maddy limped past Bryan he made a motion with his finger for her to come to him to which she complied. He covered the mouthpiece again, "Would you mind not telling Jack about your decision? I need to talk to you about somethings before we announce it."

She looked puzzled but didn't see a problem with it. What was one night? She started to walk away and he caught her hand and brought her back and kissed her lightly. "See you soon tiger."

As she limped off it occurred to her he hadn't called he Minnie all day. She shrugged it off and went on her way.

Jack was waiting as promised in front of the station. Like a gentleman he got out and opened the door for her. "Where do you want to go?"

"Somewhere that serves soup. I don't feel up to anything real solid. Not the most appetizing day, if you know what I mean," she smiled softly.

"I know the perfect place," he smiled.

Maddy leaned her head back and closed her eyes. "Keep talking, I'm just unwinding."

"You go ahead and relax." He popped a CD in, the music was soft classical.

She opened one eye and laughed, "Who knew?"

"Shut up." He cracked his window and lit up a cigarette.

Maddy must have dozed off because the next thing she was conscious of was Jack standing at her open door holding out his hand. She took his hand and got out and looked at her surroundings. They were in residential area, in front of a two-story brick house, with green, shingled awnings over each window. The roof was different, it was kind of like adobe tiles, very unique and attractive. Over the doorway way was an archway with like tiles. The door itself was an ornamental glass door. Well manicured shrubs surrounded the house. It was the kind of home you raise a family in. "Where are we?" she asked.

"Welcome to my humble abode. You were generous enough to share yours, now I am returning the favor." He slid one arm under her legs and the other around her waist and picked her up. "I know you are going to bitch, but don't. Its easier and faster." He brought her to his stoop and set her down gently. He pulled out his house keys and showed her in.

He escorted her to his living room and advised her to take a seat. "I'll be right back." He dashed somewhere to the back of the house.

Maddy took in her surroundings. The ceiling had vaulted beams. The furniture was a brown leather couch with matching love seat, and recliner. The coffee table was square and black, as were the end tables. The lamps were wood based, appeared to be oak, the shades small in stature and beige colored. She looked around. No TV, interesting. Then she saw it, a beautiful big fireplace with a beautiful painting of two wolves in the snow over the mantel. Maddy smiled and nodded; totally masculine and in very good taste.

Jack returned with two glasses of lemonade. "I know you like tea, but I don't have any. I also know you like lemon so I thought lemonade would be as close as I could get."

Maddy laughed and took the glass from him. "Lemonade is fine, thank you."

"I had some homemade chicken soup in the freezer, I stuck it in the microwave to warm."

Maddy had to laugh to herself. She had never seen him behave like this. He was like a schoolboy eager to impress her. He didn't have to do. "You have a nice place here," she looked around the room, "very manly," she grinned.

"Is that a bad thing?"

"No, not at all. It suits you."

Jack had sat on the loveseat opposite of Maddy. They both sipped on their lemonade in silence.

Jack furrowed his brow, "Why does this feel so awkward? Its just us."

"Because we are in new territory. We have begun to cross the line of professional to personal," she responded. She felt a calmness she hadn't felt in a while.

"Is that a bad thing?" he asked tentatively.

"Would you quit saying that," she laughed. "No it's not a bad thing. I guess, Jack, we need to face reality. We can't undo everything we have been through this past week. We are both different people than we were that Thursday at Vanessa's house...and its not just because you know more about some of my past. You have moved on to a whole new phase of your career. You have done things, seen things that will leave a mark on everything you touch from this point forward. When we experience these things, they become part of us, we're stained and we can't wash it off."

Jack leaned forward, took a deep breath and slowly blew it out. "Wow, now that was a loaded answer. You seemed to have reconciled yourself to the situation."

"We do what we have to do to survive," she answered softly.

"Would it be overly out of line if we talk about today?"

Maddy swirled her finger around in her lemonade watching the ice cubes circle. "What do you want to know?"

"Its just that...well when I watch you...work, for lack of a better word...never mind, I don't know what the hell I am talking about."

"You want to know how I do it? I don't have an answer for you Jack. Its just kind of this gut instinct," she shrugged her shoulders, "being able to read what is in front of you. To be able to...able translate what's before you into what happened. That's the best answer I can give you, I'm sorry."

"No need to apologize." The timer on the microwave went off. "Excuse me." He got up and walked to the back of the house.

Maddy stood up and followed her nose to the kitchen. She stood in the doorway and watched Jack as he was trying to remove the microwave bowl with his bare hands. The hot steam from under the lid escaped and burned him. "Son of a bitch!" he cussed as he brought his scorched wrist to his mouth and blew on it.

Maddy laughed and said, "That's what they make potholders for."

Jack looked over at her, his face turning red with embarrassment. "I know that," he said quickly. This was such a different Jack then she was used to. Normally he was strong, confident, and professional. She smiled to herself, he was nervous. It was kind of cute.

As Jack was reaching up into the cupboard to grab some bowls, she came up behind him and wrapped her arms around his waist and laid her head on his back. He slowly lowered the bowls to the counter. He held her arms around him, not speaking, hardly breathing. He slowly twisted his body around to face her, wanting to be careful not to break the moment.

Maddy laid her head against his chest. She was a good five inches shorter than him and standing this way it made it quite obvious. She could hear the beat of his heart, slow and steady, his chest rose and fell in shallow movements. With one arm on her back, he stroked her hair with his other hand. It was almost as if he were afraid she would disappear.

She tilted her head up at him. He was studying her, searching for something. "It's still real," she whispered.

He slowly bent down, his face moving closer to hers, and then he kissed her, slow and tender, tentatively. He pulled back, his hands slid down her shoulders and arms as he gazed into her eyes. He cleared his throat. "Time to eat."

Jack's kitchen had an island bar/counter. He pulled a stool out for her and helped her up on it, then placed a bowl of hot chicken soup in front her. He handed her a spoon. "You need crackers?"

"No thanks."

Jack set another bowl beside her and sat on the stool next to her. He watched her as she stirred the soup around. "I eat in this kitchen, not play with my food," he joked, "but seriously Maddy, eat, you need to."

She blew on a spoonful of soup. "You've been hanging around Bryan too long." She brought the spoon to her mouth and let the liquid slide into her mouth. She looked up at him. "You make this? It's really good."

Jack chuckled, "Oh hell no. Complements of my mother."

Maddy nodded in appreciation. "You're folks live around here?"

"On Grandview, near the park."

They ate in silence. Jack watched her as she finished the bowl. Mission accomplished.

Maddy pushed the bowl back and held her stomach. "I think I ate too much. Thanks Jack, that was great." She smiled at him.

Jack took the bowls, rinsed them and put them in the dishwasher. The remainder of the soup he stuck in the fridge.

He scooped her up and carried her back into the living room and sat down on the couch with her on his lap. "Are you in a hurry to get back?" he asked her.

She traced his lips with her fingertips. "Not that big of hurry. This is nice, being here with you like this."

His fingers brushed the side of her cheeks, their eyes never leaving each other. "I have a confession to make, Bryan set this up."

"I know." She kissed the corner of his mouth.

"Knowing how he feels about you, why would he do that?" He leaned his head back as she kissed his neck.

She tugged at his tie until she freed it from his neck and unbuttoned his shirt partway down planting kisses along his chest.

His fingers were tracing circles on her lower back and her leg. His breathing was becoming more rapid. "He said he didn't trust me with you..."

"Did he..." she kissed up his neck along his jawbone, "what else did he say..."

"He a.... said you need to follow your heart...Oh sweet Jesus, Maddy..." he pushed her down into the couch cradling her head in his arms, taking her mouth with his own, possessing her. His hand tugged at the zipper of her shirt, he caressed her bare skin sending sweet shivers through her.

Maddy rested her head on Jack's chest, trying to catch her breath.

Jack tugged her zipper back up. He nuzzled his face in her hair. "Maddy, Maddy, Maddy..." He turned her face up so he could see her. "There isn't anything more in the world I want right now than to make love to you, but when I do...I want all of you and there would be no turning back."

She stroked his face with her hand. "I know, and when that happens, I want to be able to give you all my heart." She kissed him softly on the lips and laid her head back down on his chest. "Just hold me..."

She had agreed with Bryan not to tell Jack her decision, but she didn't want to lie to him and an omission was as bad as a lie. She wanted what they had to be pure, with no lies, no holding back. She had to tell him. "Jack, there's something I need to tell you..."

He kissed the top of her head, "Okay."

"I reactivated today. After we got back from the morgue. Bryan didn't know I was going to do it. I went over his head while you guys were downstairs. I'm so deep into this investigation, I can't keep perspective as a reporter, and I can't just walk away." Her voice was soft, even timid. She didn't know how he would react.

Jack's head was resting on top of hers. "I don't have a problem with this Maddy. I only have one thing I need to do know. When Bryan leaves, are you going with him?"

"No, it's a conditional reactivation. When this case is over, I'm done. I took a leave of absence from the Journal. I will be returning to work there," she explained. Did she really think it would be that easy? No, but she would cross that bridge when she came to it.

"Hon, we need to get you back before he sends out a search party," Jack pulled them up into a sitting position.

They kissed one more time then Maddy slipped off his lap. When they stood up, they fell into each other's arms and held each other tight. "God only knows when we will get this chance again." Jack whispered.

Jack helped Maddy out to the car and got in himself. "I'm going to take you back to the motel, Maddy. You can ride in with Bryan in the morning. Your car will be fine in the station lot." He put the car in gear.

They rode in silence, the air between them feeling awkward. "Jack is something wrong?"

Jack reached over and squeezed her hand. She slid to his side of the car, laying her head on his shoulder. "It's nothing you did, hon. It's just really hard for me taking you back to him when I want you all to myself." He grimaced, "but Maddy, I have to block it out or it's going to tear me up. I have to work closely with him, and now you." Jack kept rambling, she thought he was talking to himself more so than her. "I can't figure him out. I know he loves you, obsessively, yet he wants us to spend time together? I don't get it. He's highly intelligent, sure as hell knows his job." He glances down at Maddy. She had fallen asleep.

Jack pulled up in front of the Regency. The black suburban was parked in the lot. He looked at the clock on his dash. They had been gone over three hours. He hoped Mayland wouldn't be angry at Maddy. He gently nudged her awake. "Mads, we're here. Do you want me to walk you in?"

Maddy sat up and got her bearings. "No...no, that's okay." She leaned over and kissed Jack. "Good night hon, I had a really nice time." She smiled and kissed his him again. "Don't let on that you know about the reactivation okay."

"I won't." He leaned over and kissed her forehead. "Good night sweet Maddy." He watched her until she disappeared inside the building.

With each step Maddy took, she felt her stomach churning. It had to be nerves. She ran the passkey through the slot and barely making it through the door before she turned and ran into the bathroom.

When Bryan came and stood in the doorway, he found Maddy sitting on the floor retching into the toilet. She spat in to the toilet, grabbed some toilet paper, and wiped her mouth. "I'm sorry." She threw up again. "I tried, I really tried."

Bryan grabbed a washcloth from the rack and ran cold water onto it. He knelt down on the floor and placed the cloth on her forehead. The coolness of the cloth felt good on her clammy skin.

Bryan left for a moment and came back bringing her shorty pajama set. "Jessie dropped off your clothes. Is this okay?"

She leaned her head against the toilet. "Not very sexy."

He chuckled. "That's okay, tonight you rest. You are emotionally and physically exhausted. Get ready for bed kiddo."

Maddy took a quick shower, brushed her teeth, and slipped on the pajamas. Her stomach was settling down now that it was empty. When she left the bathroom Bryan was lying on the bed watching TV. He patted the bed beside him. He had turned down the sheets for her.

She slid under the covers and snuggled up to him, he put his arm around her. From his nightstand he grabbed a can of Sprite Zero. "Sip on this."

She took the can and took a drink and handed it back to him. "You're getting bossy again."

He kissed the top of her head. "As of tomorrow, I will be." Then he laughed, "And you'll be sleeping with the boss."

She poked him in the ribs, "Shut up. You are such an ass."

"Did you have a nice time with Jack," he asked in a regular conversational tone just as if he were asking how her day was.

"Yes, it was nice. He took me to his house and fed me homemade chicken soup. Please don't tell him I threw it all back up." She laughed, "He was so proud he got me to eat a whole bowl."

Bryan chuckled. "Good boy, he completed his mission."

She poked him in the ribs again.

"Would you knock it off? I would hate to have to beat you up in your weakened state."

She squeezed him tight. "Not so weak."

"And you got to spend some quality time with him?"

She looked up at him. "What are you getting at?"

"Nothing, I just felt like the two of you needed some quality time together," he replied nonchalantly.

"Aren't you the least bit jealous?"

Bryan leaned over and kissed her deeply. "Extremely. My only consolation is at the end of the night, it was me you came back to."

"I didn't sleep with him." She watched his face. He didn't even flinch.

"I know."

"How?"

"Jack is a find upstanding gentleman. He won't sleep with you as long as I am the picture. He won't share you and neither will I. You won't sleep with him because that's just the kind of person you are."

"What if I wanted to?" Was nothing going to get a rise out of him? He was so cool and collected. It was weird.

"I am sure you two would like nothing better than to consummate your love, but you won't do it, not as long as I am here."

She threw him a look. "We never ever said we loved each other, just have feelings for each other."

"You do, you guys are only fooling yourselves. Maddy the kind of love we feel for each other, its all consuming, passionate, intense and deep rooted. But we both know how destructive it can be. What you feel for Jack, its sweet, gentle... and safe."

Maddy slid her arm across his stomach and laid her head back down on his chest, contemplating what he just said. "It's wrong of me. I shouldn't be doing this, it's not fair to either one of you."

"No, it's wrong of me. I am the selfish one and it's not fair for the two of you. Something was starting before I came back into your life and I fucked it all up. Like I always do. I pursued you, banking on the intensity of the feelings we shared before. You think I don't know the power I have over you? There was no doubt in my mind I would get you back. Despite the hate and hurt you felt when I came back, here you are." Bryan reached over and grabbed a cigarette and lit it up.

She lifted her head, "You almost sound smug about it, so sure of yourself that I would take you back. I don't know if I like the sound of that."

"I don't really have you back, Maddy. You still don't trust I won't hurt you and with good reason. You don't trust me and you don't trust your heart. You said last night that I will never be yours, in truth, you will never be totally mine because there is nothing I can do or say that will remove the doubts you have. You will never trust my motives and because of that, you never will be mine."

She sat up and looked at him. "So what exactly is it that you are saying?"

"I love you with everything I am capable of giving, everything I have. I can't promise you forever. I can't promise you I will never again be what I was before, cruel, manipulative, as you put it, a mind fuck. I can't promise you I won't start drinking again. Are you willing to risk it Maddy?"

"Bryan, I don't know where this is all coming from, but you should have thought about these things before you made me love you again. I can't go through what I went through before. I won't! I catch one whiff of you acting like that I will be so far gone you won't be able to find me! Do you understand me?" she said angrily.

He sat quietly staring at the television.

"Do you understand me?" she repeated.

"Yes." He looked over at her. "Maddy...you're my savior."

She hit him several times with her fist, "Yeah and you'll be my downfall, damn you!"

He grabbed her wrist and pushed her down in the bed, crushing her with his body. His lips came down on hers hard, rough, passionate, yet without tenderness. His hand slid up her shirt, running over her body urgently.

She struggled beneath him, kicking at him until she made contact where she knew he would stop. He rolled off her groaning. "What the hell do you think you're doing?" she screamed at him.

"Taking you back!" he snapped. "I'm only human Maddy. You think I don't know you layed in his arms? You don't think I know how he kissed you—touched you. You're mine damn it!"

She slid to the side of the bed. "So this is all about Jack. If you don't want things like that to happen, quit pushing us together. You act so fucking cool and calm about the whole damn thing and all this time it's eating you up. You don't make any fucking sense, Bryan. You don't tell someone you love them and send them off to the arms of another man. That's fucked up, Bryan, just fucked up." She picked up a shoe and threw it at him.

"Would you stop with the violence? Jesus Christ, I'm sorry," he yelled at her. "I just didn't want you to loose him because of me."

"Why, so he would be there waiting with open arms when you leave me? So he could pick up the pieces of the mess you leave behind? The fact that he even still cares about me after I just up and leave him to fall into your arms is astounding knowing he's second choice. How the hell do you think that makes him feel—to see us together, the way we are. He won't admit it; he never says a word. He has to work with you, no for you. And now I will be there too, a constant reminder of what he can't have. Jesus Christ why don't you think about someone else but you, you selfish bastard!" Her blood was boiling. She picked up the other shoe and threw at him just as hard as she could.

Bryan let it bounce off him, not looking at her staying silent. He slipped on his own shoes and left the room without telling her anything. She got up and went to the door as quickly as possible and yelled after him, "That's your answer to everything, leave without saying a word." She slammed the door.

She went to the bag Jessie had left her and pulled out a pair of blue jeans and a t-shirt, then threw the rest of her clothes in the bag. She came across the red satin nighty. She grabbed the center of it and ripped it with her teeth repeatedly and threw it on the bed. Maddy then went in the bathroom, grabbed all her stuff and threw it in the bag and zipped it up. She was so done with him.

She pulled up the tow handle and left the room. She left the door ajar just in case Bryan didn't have his passkey on him. She left her passkey on the bureau. She drug her bag down the hall and down the stairs, and out through the lobby. It wasn't until she hit the parking lot that she realized she had no car. Shit! Shit! Shit!

She looked at her watch. It was after 10:00. Damn it. She couldn't really call anyone. Jack would be the last person she would call. She resigned herself to spending one more night. With any luck Bryan would stay gone.

Maddy went back to the room, the room where she had been happier than she had in years, the room she bared her soul, the room she got more pissed off than she thought she had been in her life. She didn't want to be there.

It was after midnight when Bryan came back. Maddy lay quietly on the bed, still dressed in her clothes. He came around to his side of bed and found the nighty. He picked up and sat on the bed holding it. "You didn't leave."

"Only because I don't have my car," she said into her pillow.

Bryan lay down beside her. He put his hand on her shoulder and she shrugged it off. He propped himself up and laid his cheek on hers from behind. She felt dampness on her cheek and it wasn't hers. She leaned over and flipped the lamp on and sat up in the bed and looked at him. His eyes were red. She bent over and sniffed him. No alcohol.

Bryan rolled over so he was facing the opposite side of the bed. He tucked his hands up under his face. Maddy slipped in behind him and wrapped her arms around him, her anger melting away. He took her hands in his and brought them to his face. She could feel the dampness on his cheeks.

"Bryan...despite what happened tonight...I still love you," she said softly to his back.

"For the life of me, I don't know why," he choked.

She brushed her cheek on his shoulder. "Me either."

He rolled over to face her. "I don't know what to say to you Maddy..."

"A sincere apology would go a long ways."

He tentatively touched her hand, "It's not enough. It's not just the argument; it's my warped way of thinking. I went for a long walk, did some serious soul searching. I thought about what you said about me being your downfall. No matter how many angles I look at, you're right. I start out well meaning, but I end of destroying what I love the most...you. I don't want to do that anymore, Maddy. I love you; I mean I really love you. I have gone through my life going without the one thing I hold dearest...you Maddy. I'm the one who runs, not you. You were always willing to be there, I wasn't. I took the easy way out and didn't fight for you. It's no wonder you're afraid of me and can't trust me. Hell I wouldn't trust me either."

She squeezed his hand, "So what are we going to do about that?"

"Ask that you stay with me, believe in me," he half-heartily smiled, "tolerate me while I try to change. Become the man I should have always been with you."

"Bryan, I love the man I know is in here," she put her hand on his heart, "the man I fell in love with ten years ago, before you got so jaded. I know he is still there. I see a little more of him more and more every day. You just need to quit playing games, be honest with me about your feelings, your wants, and desires.

This crap you pulled tonight with me and Jack, that's the old Bryan. You set us up and that's not fair. You can't manipulate people's emotions and think they are going to be okay with it. Jack is a good man; he's never done anything to you but given you respect. I care very deeply for him and that's not going to change. But Bryan, we both agreed that as long as you're in the picture, nothing will happen, out of respect for you and me. Jack and I are putting you and me first. I can't have you thinking that every time he and are together we are going to jump in bed, or that he's going to steal me away from you. Can you deal with that?" Maddy searched his face, looking for honesty.

"You want me to be honest about my feelings. I'm not going to say I will be comfortable when you are alone with him, but I will deal with it okay?"

"Maddy, if it hadn't been for your car not being here, you would have walked out of my life and I know that would have been it, you would have been gone. With everything I have lived through, nothing scares me more than loosing you. I don't take well to fear; it's not in my nature. Thank you for staying."

Maddy smiled softly, "Don't thank me, thank Jack. He was the one who told me to leave my car at the lot. I need you to promise me something."

"Anything." He reached out and stroked her hair.

"Don't punish Jack, don't play head games with him. He doesn't deserve it."

"I promise. I've never denied he is a good man. Are we cool now?"

"I got one more question for you. You haven't once called me Minnie today, why?"

"Mickey and Minnie came to be during a bad time in our lives. I don't want that in our relationship anymore. You said when I first got here that Minnie died when I left you out in the cold two years ago. This is here and now, I don't want them in our lives now."

"And this is something you decided today, before tonight?"

"Yes."

She pulled him close and whispered in his ear, "I love you Bryan."

They held each other close and fell asleep in each other's arms.

10

The lights of the black Lincoln reflected off the window of the motel lobby. Maddy grabbed her bag and met it at the curb. She opened the back door threw her bag in and hopped in the front. "I really appreciate you coming to get me this time of the night."

"No problem Kid," Chief stifled a yawn. He was still dressed in his pajamas with a black coat thrown over them.

She smiled faintly. "Hope you don't get pulled over by a cop dressed like that. I bet you don't have your drivers license on you."

"Beings I'm taking you to the police station, my odds of running into one would be pretty high wouldn't you say?" He kept his concentration on the road.

"I'm sorry," she answered. "I'm sorry about a lot of things."

"Having second thoughts?"

"You have no idea." She leaned her head back.

Twenty minutes later she was in her own car heading out of the city. It was 3:00 AM. The stillness of the night was comforting. The lines on the highway raced under her car like tracks under a train. Her mind was tired, weary and confused to say the least, her body wired with tension. She had made her escape, from what she still wasn't quite sure. Her decision to leave...she could no longer stay. The only thing she wanted now was to be in her own home, in her own bed, her sanctuary. She would only get a couple hours sleep, but she felt those two hours would do her more good than a complete night in that motel room.

She felt no guilt, no remorse, and no regrets. Some things you just have to do because you know it's the right thing for you.

There were no dogs barking excitedly to greet her at the door. Jessie had taken them home with her. She didn't even bother to turn on any lights. She felt her way around in the dark to her bedroom. The room was dimly lit by her alarm clock. She peeled off her clothes down to her bra and panties and crawled between the sheets. The sweet smell of Gain dryer sheets and the silky softness of 800 county Egyptian sheets were like heaven to her. The only thing missing was Bryan's warm body to hold her. This was her choice. From now on that's the way things were going be, of her choosing. She drifted off to sleep.

Maddy was awakened at 6:00 by the sound an early morning serenade of robins, morning doves, red-winged black birds, and meadowlarks. God, it was good to be home. She wished she could hide out here all day, but she had signed on the dotted line. Her ass now belonged to the FBI. If only she had waited one more day.

She rolled out of bed and padded her way to the bathroom and took a quick shower. She toweled herself off, brushed her teeth and dried her hair.

Her overnight bag was by the kitchen door where she left it. She opened it up and dug out a bag containing an ankle brace she picked up at an all night Walgreens. She went back to her room, slipped on her relaxed fit blue jeans and a lightweight, short-sleeved cotton sweater. She slipped on some anklet socks and then slid the ankle brace over the socks. When she put her shoes on it was a snug fit but that would just give her a little extra support. She stood up and tested it. It felt pretty good, no limp, no crutches.

Maddy packed up her 17-inch Mac book Pro and her scanner. She wanted to get into the office to compile a composite PowerPoint demonstration of the unsub profile and victimology analysis. This time she would do a professional job rather than the half-assed surprise Bryan made her do. Bryan made her do...he didn't make her do anything, she let him.

She loaded her up car and hit the road. On the way to the city she stopped off at a convenience store and grabbed a bottle of orange juice. She still had no appetite and the smell of breakfast pizza about made her throw up.

As she pulled into the cop shop parking lot, she looked around for the black suburban. None of the three units were there yet, good. She gathered her bag and her equipment and entered the building. She still had to sign in since she didn't have her credentials yet. When she entered the temporary headquarters, the room was empty. She guessed the early bird did catch the worm. It was 7:30. She was surprised Bryan wasn't here yet; he was an early riser and liked to get to work by 6:00.

It took her about twenty minutes to get her computer set up with the scanner. She brought her home laptop just because it had the large screen and it would be easier for her to study photos. Plus it had all the programs she needed to do the kind of work she was planning on doing. Photoshop can be a real amazing program when it comes to discovering the secrets the photos are keeping.

Whittmer and his fellow minions were the first to arrive. He greeted her with a nod, but didn't ask any questions.

Bryan arrived at 7:45, looking like hell and holding a cup of coffee. He sat at his desk and thumbed through his files. He grabbed his keys, unlocked his desk drawer and pulled out her files and dropped them on her desk. He walked toward the door and then he stopped in his tracks and turned back towards her. "Maddy, can I talk to you in the interrogation room?"

"Sure," she grabbed her OJ and walked toward him.

He cocked his head sideways as he watched her walk. "No limp?"

She pulled up her pant leg revealing the black brace. He nodded his head in approval.

Maddy sat herself down and took a swig of her juice. Bryan had gone back to grab his coffee, came in and sat down across from her.

He sat quietly watching her, unnerving her, exactly what he had planned on doing. Standard interrogation procedure. He leaned back in the chair and crossed ankles under the table. "Why Maddy?" he asked softly. "I thought we were working things out. You left me...in the middle of the night no less."

"Will you listen to me if I tell you?" she asked.

"I told you I am going to make every effort I can to be the man you want me to be, you just have to give me a chance. Are you not interested?"

She leaned forward. "Give me your hand." She took it in hers and kissed it. "I didn't leave because of you. I left because I had to. I have only been allowed to be alone for about 12 hours since last Thursday night. I have spent the majority of the last 7 years, more so the last two years by myself. I isolated myself and I like it that way. It allows me to detach from the rest of the world. It allows me to be me. When I'm around people, any people, all the time, I can't deal with it. It doesn't allow me to put my guard down. It's not that I don't want to be with you, Bryan, I just need my own space to be me."

"And you can't be yourself around me? I thought I was the one person you could be." His face held a look of confusion.

She squeezed his hand. "For the most part, yet there is still part of me that is always watching, always wondering what your motives are. You and I...we are high velocity. Everything with us is intense. Honey, I need down time. If you want me at my best, to do this job and to be with you, I need you to give me some room. I love you Bryan, that hasn't change. But in order for me to keep my stability, I need my time alone. Does any of this make any sense to you?"

A weak smile crept across his lips, "I think so. My bed will be pretty lonely without my tiger though." He tried to laugh it off.

She laughed softly, "I never said I wanted to sleep alone. I just feel our personal life shouldn't be contingent on a motel room."

"But you won't allow me to come to your home?" When she didn't answer he answered for her. "No, because in your line of thinking, with your inability to trust me, you won't let me into you home because when I leave, you don't want that reminder of who hurt you to touch you sanctuary."

Maddy realized she was chewing on the inside of her lower lip. "They don't call you the G-Man for nothing. We agreed in so many words last night, to take things one day at a time. I'm not going to trust you just because you tell me to. That stunt you pulled last night with Jack and me. That was wrong on so many levels. It still pisses me off. You tried to tell me it was so Jack and I would have time together, to make sure I had someone should you leave. Which confirms by the way you are still planning on leaving me. Is that what you wanted me to believe or what you made yourself believed? When every thing was said and done, you were testing us, testing me to see how far I would let it go, whether or not you could trust me. Let me build confidence in you, when I feel the time is right, when we're right, I will let you into every part of my life, even my home."

Bryan stood up and pulled the blinds to the interrogation room. He came to her side of the table and pulled her to her feet. He held both her hands in his and looked down at her. "Honesty, brutal honesty, that is something else I promised you last night. I understand and I accept what you have told me here today. It will take me some adjusting in my line of behavior." He laughed, "I tend to be pushy and controlling."

Maddy laughed, "Gee you think?"

"Shut up, you don't have to agree with me," he bent down and kissed her softly. "Do, I have to control my urges?" He pulled her close.

She wrapped her arms around his neck, "Baby, I want you to be you. Don't change that part of yourself. Just teach the evil in you how to behave, at least when it comes to me."

He cupped her face and kissed her, a soft, tender, lingering kiss. "Well Special Agent Maddy Sheridan, you ready to go in and get sworn in?" He held the door open for her.

"Honestly, I'm kind of scared. Your men aren't going to respect me. They're just going to see me as the big boss's lover and not take me seriously."

He grabbed her by the head and pulled it to him playfully. "No, no, you got at all wrong, you're my bitch," he laughed.

"Fuck you, you're still a jerk," she jabbed him in the ribs.

Bryan mocked a rib injury, "Damn Maddy, what is it with you and physically pain lately? I don't think you're getting enough sex."

She threw her head back and laughed, "You'll have to talk to my boss and tell him he is slacking in that department."

When the two of them arrived back in the squad room, everyone was accounted for. A fed-ex package was lying on Bryan's desk. He reached for an envelope cutter and slit the seam of the box and slid out the contents. Inside were Maddy's badge, credentials, and a brand new Glock 17 complete with side holster.

She took a deep intake breath; her face turned pale looking at the contents. Lord what had she done? This was so not in her plans of things she aspired to. She should have just worked the case from the outside. But she also knew to actually accomplish her goal, and that was to put the psycho away, she had join forces with the devil, the FBI.

"Do you want to do your swearing in private?" Bryan whispered.

She nodded enthusiastically.

"We need two witnesses. I know we agreed not to mention this to Jack, but I also know you well enough to know you told him. I am going to assume he will be one of your witnesses, who do you want for the other?"

Maddy glanced around the room and her eyes came to rest on Whittmer. "I'll take him," she pointed to her redheaded nemesis. Actually he wasn't that bad, just a stick in the mud.

Bryan raised an eyebrow at her choice, but he didn't argue with her. He grabbed Jack and Whittmer and took them into the interrogation room.

The four of them sat at the table while Bryan explained was going on. He wanted to give Whittmer some of Maddy's history with FBI so he didn't think this was a farce. He was sure Jack would learn a thing or two also. Then he thought twice about it decided to kill two birds with one stone. "I changed my mind, we will do it in the squad room."

They all followed him back out. He sat on his desk bringing in the attention of those in the room. "Hey, listen up here. You all have been asked to participate in the swearing in ceremony of Maddy Sheridan. Miss Sheridan has an extensive history working with the FBI several years ago before she decided to become an inactive agent for personal reasons. Sheridan's primary area of expertise is in profiling, she was an instrumental participant in the Behavior Science Unit i.e. the BAU. She has decided to rejoin the ranks to help us solve this case and to get our unsub as quickly as possible."

He turned to Maddy, "Are you ready?"

She lifted her right hand, Bryan began to read the words and she interrupted him. "You don't need to do that, I already know them."

"Proceed."

"I, Maddy Sheridan, will support and defend the Constitution of the United States against all enemies, foreign and domestic; that I will bear true faith and allegiance to the same; that I take this obligation freely, without any mental reservation or purpose of evasion; and that I will well and faithfully discharge the duties of the office on which I am about to enter. So help me God"

Bryan presented her badge; credentials and her gun then presented her to the room. "I would like you to welcome Special Agent Maddy Sheridan." She got the superficial applause, exactly what she was expecting, but then again she wasn't here to impress, she was here to do a job.

Jack came up to her, hugged her, and kissed her on her cheek, "Congratulations, Mads, I proud of you."

She hugged him back and whispered in his ear, "Don't be, I'm scared shitless."

Whittmer came and shook her hand, "It will be an honor working with you."

Maddy slid into her chair and began to thumb through her files. Something was missing. "I am really surprised at you," she declared.

Bryan was sitting at his desk studying some reports. He reared his head up, "What are bitching about now?"

"These files, these reports, they are inconclusive simply because they are done half-assed. These autopsy reports, where are the findings on trace evidence, where are the full tox screens. We don't have measurements; we don't have a comparison analysis. Where's the reports on the crime scenes. You got any reports back yet on the search of Granger's house. Where are any of the reports of searches of our other vic's homes? Where are the interviews with the friends and families? Where are the formal reports at the Bacon Creek finds, where are the reports on the Stone Park search. It's a little hard to compile a true composite when so much information is missing," she criticized.

Bryan rose from his chair and disappeared momentarily. When he returned, he carried in his arms two large file boxes and dropped them on the floor at her feet. "This is what we have. No, they are not up to your standards, but this is what I have been given to work with. The officers didn't work the home scenes because they didn't know they were crime scenes at that moment and enough time has lapsed that it's a moot point now. Parker has the full report on the Bacon Creek search and is in the process of compiling the Stone Park search, which by the way, is still in progress. As for your autopsy reports, the autopsies were done half assed. You can't expect a small town coroner to perform the kind of autopsies we need for this kind of case. What are the odds? The bodies and copies of the current reports were shipped off this morning to Ankeny so the DCI can take a look at them." He stood and looked down on her. "Didn't take you long to settle in and want everything your way again."

"And I can't believe how sloppy you are running this investigation," she quipped meeting his stare.

Maddy was unaware of the attention from the others in the squad room she was drawing. It was never cool to question a superior officer, let alone question his handling an investigation. Bryan's body stiffened and his jaw was twitching, his eyes cold as steel. She had been an agent for less than a half an hour and already she had pissed him off. But damn, she was right. It was no wonder they weren't getting anywhere. There was no system of checks and balances in the investigation, nothing formally that they could use to tie everything together.

Bryan nudged the boxes toward her and said, "Well guess what you are going to be doing for the next few hours, *Agent Sheridan*?" He bent down and leaned on her desk, his eyes boring into her. "Welcome back to the unit," he said coldly to her.

Maddy reached down to grab the boxes, when she lifted them they threw her off balance and a shot of pain shot up through ankle. "Son of bitch," she murmured under breath.

A pair of hands reached down and picked the boxes up for her. She followed them up to discover them belonging to Agent Whittmer. "Where would you like these?" he asked politely.

She pointed to the interrogation room. "In there would be good...thank you."

He smiled weakly at her. "And it's Andy." He took the boxes in and set them on the table. "If you need any help with these I would be glad to assist you." He flipped his head back over his shoulder, "He doesn't let me really do anything anyhow, and I might as well be useful to someone."

Maddy nodded, "I understand where you're coming from. I will see what he says. He's not exactly pleased with me at the moment."

Andy gave a soft chuckle, "And you don't seem to be afraid to rub him the wrong way. I would tell you to be careful, but I don't think I need to say anything about it to you."

Maddy could feel the eyes burning in to her back, Bryan. She moved her eyes for Andy to make a break for it and he left her.

Bryan entered and closed the door behind him and said coldly, "Don't you ever show me the disrespect you just showed me in front of my men again."

Maddy began pulling folders out of one of the boxes. "I'm sorry. I was out of line."

"You damn right you were," he slammed his hand down on the table causing Maddy to jump.

"I said I was sorry, what more do you want from me?" She began to sort the files in to piles.

Bryan spun around to leave, "Not a Goddamn thing, Maddy, not a damn thing!" and he slammed the door behind him.

She thought about going after him, but she couldn't. She couldn't keep running after him every time he got angry with her. Although it was her fault...and she was in the wrong...he had every right to be upset with her. Oh fine damn it, when you're wrong, you're wrong.

Bryan was sitting behind his laptop. He had his glasses on, his hair was a little messed up, his face was stoic. She stood in front of him for several moments while he refused to even look at her.

"Listen Bryan," she started.

"Not now Maddy. I'm busy...doing my job. Might I suggest you go do yours."

"I will, after we talk." She waited. Nothing like playing hard to get.

Bryan pulled off his glasses, "Oh I think you said more than enough. Like how inept I am as a Supervisory Agent. You haven't even been back for an hour and you already know more than I do. It's a shame Maddy, you being so proficient at what you do, that you wasted it all these years as a reporter." He pointed to the chair in front of his desk. "Sit," he commanded.

Ouch—that stung. Maddy slid in to the chair. She couldn't argue with him, she was in the wrong. She would take her medicine.

"How long have I been here? On this case?"

"Since Monday."

"And where did we spend Wednesday?"

"Searching Stone Park."

"And yesterday we spent here and at the morgue. Now I want you to tell me when I have had the damn time to go through and 'organize' the files for presentation. And let's not forget the fact that I haven't worked in the field for several years. I'm still getting my bearings here, Maddy. You could cut me some slack."

"When I said I was sorry, Bryan, I meant it. I spoke without thinking," she kind of half laughed, "It's something I tend to do."

"What are you working on?" He shut the lid on the laptop.

"I just started sorting the files, then I thought I would make a compilation of what we have so I can figure out what we're missing and need. May I submit a list to you of documents I believe are germane to the case that aren't with what we have?" she asked.

"Yes of course, what ever you need." He took a sip of his coffee.

"I have a question for you, since I have been out of this for so long, but would it be possible to get all our crime scene photos, autopsy photos, and x-rays on digital? It would make my job so much easier, saving me the time of scanning them. I believe I can better study them with the use of Photoshop," Maddy explained.

"I will make some phone calls and see what I can come up with. You need help in there?" He tilted his head toward the interrogation room.

"If you don't mind," she asked tentatively, "can I take Whittmer?"

"The toad," he laughed. "One more takes a fall to the fire fox."

Maddy laughed, "God I haven't been called that in a long time. I forgot all about it. And no I wouldn't say that. He's just a kid. You scare him so much I think if you were to yell at him he would piss his pants. Apparently he doesn't feel very useful because you won't use him because he's green." She shrugged. "The kid just needs a break is all."

"Yeah, he's green alright, fresh out of the academy. You're not exactly the best person to expose him to. You are a bad influence."

She stood up. "Don't be mean, I won't challenge his mental psyche. I need a grunt, and he's willing." She smiled, "See, it's a win-win situation."

Maddy scanned the room for Jack. He was nowhere to be found. "Where's Jack? I wanted to get copy of the search scene reports."

Bryan had resumed his work on his laptop, and glanced up. "I do believe that before we descended on his world, he had his own office. You might find him there. And Maddy?"

She turned toward him.

"You're working, no hanky panky."

Maddy took a deep breath. "No shit, Bryan." And she left. It was a lot more fun around here when she was a nobody.

Maddy spotted Jack in his office. She stood back several feet just to watch him through the glass that surrounded his office. He was standing facing an outside window and was talking on the phone. She thought about how the two of them had been last night together, picturing how he looked. His thick brown hair that was normally combed away from his face was tousled but very cute, his rugged features were soften by tenderness, his eyes...deep brown pools, and those lips...wow those lips. She unconsciously brought her fingers to her lips as remembered the heat.

She was brought out of her revere by a tapping on a window. Jack was trying to get her attention and waved her in. She entered his office and sat across from like she had so many times in the past.

"Hey, Mads, heard you caused a hell of seen down in the squad room. Went off on Mayland about what a piss pour job he was doing. Not the smartest things you've ever done."

She looked down at her hands, "Thinking before I speak has never been an attribute of mine."

Jack slid down into his seat and smiled, "I can verify that. What can I do for you?"

"I went home early this morning," she blurted out.

"You left Mayland? I bet that went over well. And you jumped his ass this morning. Living a little dangerously are we? What happened?" He sat back and rocked his chair slightly.

"It got a little ugly earlier in the evening."

"Because of me?"

She tossed her head slightly, "That's not why I left. I just couldn't do it anymore. The constantly being watched over, being taken care of, never having a minute to myself. It felt like I was always on edge. Always being watched to see if I was going to fall apart. If I am going to do this I need to take care of me. If I can't do this and fall apart, I need to be the one to pick up the pieces."

"So where does that put you and Mayland, romantically speaking?"

Maddy laughed, "You mean am I still sleeping with him?"

Jack smiled, "Okay if you want to put it like that, are you still sleeping with him?"

Maddy considered his inquiry. "We hit a major trust element last night, on both parts. I fear it's caused some damage to our relationship." Maddy looked away recalling the pain of last night. Her voice cracked, "I don't know where it leaves us, or if it can be fixed."

Jack grabbed a Kleenex and handed it to her. She smiled, "What no hanky?"

Jack chuckled, "You left the last one in pretty raunchy condition. Disposables for you for now on. Well, Mads, you do what you feel you need to do. You know I will be there for you no matter what. If you decide to stay with him, fine, if you don't so much the better for me." He threw a pencil at her.

"Okay, officially speaking what can I help you with?"

She picked up the pencil and flicked it back at him. "Anything you can give me for reports on the search scenes."

Jack grabbed a file and left the room returning back several minutes later and handed her a file. "Those are the reports for Bacon Creek and what I have so far on Stone Park. That search hasn't concluded yet, I will get you updates as soon as I have them."

"We need to work fast, Jack. He's going be looking for his next target soon," she explained.

"Why do you say that?"

"The time frame between the abductions has shortened. He's escalating. We haven't released any of the details of our finds with the exception of the discovery of the bodies. This could either gear him up or make him slow down. It's hard to tell without knowing more about his profile. I'm trying to compile what we do have to see if it can tell us more about him...and what we have is a mess."

Maddy returned to the interrogation room. Whittmer soon joined her. She instructed him on how she wanted the files sorted. First they sorted by victim, within in those files they sorted by date of execution of each interview or finding, ultimately ending with autopsy reports for those whose bodies had been recovered. They spent the next three hours compiling their information.

Maddy stood up and twisted her body stretching. "Damn...now that was a job. Thanks Andy. You did good."

Whittmer rubbed his temples with his forefingers, "Thank you, Agent Sheridan, for allowing me to help."

Maddy smiled to herself. He was such an innocent, untouched by the evil hands of testosterone. "Kid, if you are going to work with me we gotta set some ground rules. First, my name is Maddy. I will be offended if you call me Agent Sheridan, unless of course its around Mayland, then I will let you squeak. My only other request is, relax, you are in the easiest stage this job gets." She laughed, "It doesn't get much easier than this. You will be jaded and bitter soon enough. Do we have a deal?"

He nodded. "May I ask you some questions?"

Why do men always do this to her? "You can ask, but that doesn't mean I will answer."

"How long have you been with the FBI?" he asked.

"Do you mean that I knew about?" she laughed.

"Huh?"

Maddy shook her head, "Never mind, a little over 7 years."

"Were you always planning to be in the BAU?"

Now she really laughed thinking back to the beginning. Fresh out of college, armed to the gills with psychology degrees and having no idea what being a profiler really entailed, no it wasn't quite what she planned on. "I went through the same training you went through, the only difference was that when I completed training I went into another phase of training. I guess you could say the FBI groomed me for what they needed."

"You don't like doing it?"

Maddy studied this kid asking so many questions, the same questions she knew Jack would love to ask. But she didn't feel threaten or feared of being judged by Andy. She found herself more willing to talk to him about it. He didn't know her, didn't know she had a past—didn't know she was hiding from the past.

Maddy pulled a chair out and sat down. She picked a sticky note and began to tear it into tiny shreds as she spoke. "In theory, it's a fulfilling job in the sense you are the one who plays a major roll in catching the bad guy. Providing everything goes to plan. If you could do everything in the shelter of Quantico it would be livable. You wouldn't have to see the reality of it all. But you don't, you go out in the field to where they need you. You see things..." she paused. "We were the big guns, they only pulled us out for major cases. We had to be invited in by the locals to work the case. Agent Mayland and I worked some very high profile cases. We have seen a lot of things, things no one should see. After a while...well let's just say it's...you need a break."

Maddy was unaware she was being watched from the other side of a two-way mirror. Jack stood watching and listening. It started out he was going to play a joke on her but walked in on the beginning of this conversation. She was sharing with this kid something she wouldn't share with him. He wasn't angry about it. He understood when they talked he put a lot of pressure on her, prying into more than she was willing to share. And it wasn't like she had revealed any deep dark secrets to him. However, the little tid-bits Maddy gave to Whittmer, Jack would keep safe with him.

Jack quietly left that area of the interview room and slipped around to the other door. He knocked and then entered. "Hey you two, a bunch of us are going to walk down to the Wiener Shop. Why don't you take a break and come with us?"

"You go ahead, Andy, I will get things lined up so we can start our boards when you get back," she told Whittmer.

"I don't think so," Jack grabbed her by the hand and pulled her to her feet. "You're one of the guys now."

"But I'm not hungry," she whined.

Whittmer excused himself, telling them he would meet them in the squad room.

Jack closed the door behind him as he left. He shut the blinds, and then led her to the side of the room where the two-ways were. Jack slid down to the floor and pulled Maddy down so she was sitting beside him.

"What are you doing?" she laughed.

He held his finger up to his lips, "ssssssshhhhhh."

He pulled her close, he reached around with his hand and guided her face to his, spreading little kisses on her face.

Maddy giggled, "I repeat, what are you doing? That tickles."

Jack grinned, "I'm sorry, I must not be doing it right." He kissed her gently on the lips murmuring, "bitch, bitch, bitch, bitch, bitch." Then he kissed her deeply.

Her hand slid up around his neck as she responded to him.

Jack chuckled and pulled slowly away from her. "Are you hungry now?"

Maddy laughed and shook her head, "That was cruel dude. Okay that was an appetizer, where's the main course?"

Jack rose to his feet and offered her a hand up. He flashed her that sexy smile she loved so much. "At the wiener shop."

He held the door open for her. "Tease," she laughed as she walked out ahead of him.

They were laughing when they entered the squad room. Bryan looked up from his desk. Thin lines creased his brow as he took his glasses off and smiled at them. "I must be doing something wrong, you two look like you're having too much fun."

"Not hardly!" Maddy sat on the corner of his desk. "Files are organized, got a list for you back in the room. We'll be working on setting up the boards after lunch."

"Meet you downstairs, Mads," Jack touched her on her shoulder and took off.

Maddy looked around the room. It was empty. "The boys are going down to the wiener shop for a bite. Come with us."

"The boys?" Bryan laughed. "Now you're one of the boys." He reached out for her arm and pulled her around to him and she fell across his lap. "You so don't look like one of the boys." He kissed her softly. "It's good to see you smiling, Maddy."

Maddy brushed the hair away from his face. "Are you going to come?"

He kissed her forehead, "No, I'm trying to get some things lined up. But you go ahead kiddo. Go do some male bonding," he laughed. "It will be easier for you if I'm not there. Go have some fun."

She grinned and gave him a sloppy kiss. "I'll bring you back some wieners. This place makes the best Coney's." She slid off his lap and kissed the top of his head and whispered in his ear, "I love you."

Bryan smiled and slid his glasses back on, "Love you too kiddo."

Maddy met Jack downstairs, Whittmer was waiting with him. The two guys were talking pleasantly amongst themselves. It was nice to see Andy making an effort to make friends with the others, or maybe it was Jack reaching out to Andy, she didn't know.

Jack was giving Andy the history of the Milwaukee Wiener Shop. "You're going to love this place if you like hot dogs, there's nothing like it. It's like stepping back into a 1940's joint. They serve hot dogs, Coney's, polish dogs, soda in glass bottles, milk shakes. The joint itself is just like this little cafeteria with a hot dog assembly line. You just have to experience it for yourself."

Maddy's attention was pulled away from the conversation by the sound of a horn honking. She followed the sound and saw a white SUV pulled along the curb. She observed two small children crossing the street to the vehicle. She froze as she watched them dodge the traffic. As they approached the SUV, the children turned and looked at her. The little girl with straight reddish brown hair and dark eyes was tugging on the hand of her little brother, a wavy brown haired little guy who looked to be about three. The little boy was striking out at his sister. A woman, apparently the mother, grabbed the little boy and hoisted him into the SUV and the little girl followed. Maddy felt a rush of anguish wash over her and she cried out.

Jack heard her soft cry and turned toward her. Her complexion had turned ashen and she looked as if she were going to pass out. He reached out and caught her by her arm. "Mads, you okay?"

"Em...yeah...I'm fine. Listen, Jack, I just remembered something I need to do. You guys go ahead. Can you bring us back some Coney's?" A shaking hand reached in her purse to grab some money.

The concern shown on Jack's face, but she refused to let him help her. "Maddy, come on, you don't look so good."

She pushed the money into Jack's hand. "Don't worry about me, I just really need to go." She turned and quickly made her departure.

Maddy found her way back into the building and went straight to the interrogation room and shut the door. She sat down at the table and pulled out her wallet. Tucked away in a secret spot were two photos. She pulled them out and laid them on the table in front of her. The first was of a little girl, the same straight reddish brown hair and dark brown eyes. Her hair was pulled back on the top of her head, her cheeks rosy with rouge and her lips bright red with lipstick. She was wearing a red, white, and blue dance dress and blue sparkly tap shoes. She was smiling from ear to ear. The photo was taken at her last dance recital. The other was a photo of a little boy, wavy brown hair, and big brown eyes. He was proudly standing beside his brand new pony, looking up at the camera with a toothy smile. Maddy's fingers traced these little wonders lovingly with her fingertips. A silent tear slid down her cheek.

Bryan caught sight of Maddy's slight figure as she rushed past the door of the squad room. He thought it odd that she returned and didn't stop in. He followed her down the hall, hanging back far enough to give her some space to see what she was doing. He saw her duck into the interrogation room and close the door. The blinds were closed, so he slipped around to the mirror side. He watched her as she pulled out the photos, caressed them, staring at them without blinking. "Oh Minnie," he whispered.

Bryan slipped out of the viewing room and moved to the side door and knocked. "Maddy?"

"Go away please," she muttered.

"What's wrong, hon?" He remained outside the door.

"Nothing, just leave me alone, please." She wiped her eyes with the back of her hand.

"You know I can't do that. I'm coming in Maddy." He pushed in on the door.

Maddy tried to get the photos back in her wallet, but Bryan put his hand down on top of them to keep her from succeeding. "Don't," she whispered, "Please..."

Bryan slid them out from under her hand and put them back in front of her. He pulled a chair up close to her. "It's okay Baby..." He took the photo of the little girl. "Lexi is a beautiful little girl, Maddy. Tell me about the picture, tell me the story behind it."

Maddy turned away, "No, I can't..."

He held her hand on the photo, "Yes you can..."

Maddy picked up the photo and held it between her hands. "She loved to dance, since she was a baby. I put her in lessons at the age of three...always dancing..." She quickly brushed the tears away.

Bryan handed her the photo of the little boy. "Scotty, tell me about him. Loves the horses, just like his mama."

Her fingers traced the little boy and the pony. "Jessie and I bought him at a horse sale. His name was Simba, like in the Lion King..." her voice was monotoned. "When Scotty came home from visitation with his father, I took him in and had him look in the stall..." her voice cracked. "He...a....said...is he mine?"

She took the photos and tucked them in her secret spot in her wallet and put it back into her purse. "No more..."

Bryan stroked her hair, "Okay, no more. Look at me Maddy..."

Maddy turned her face toward him. Her cheeks were flushed, her green eyes sparkled, no emotion was unveiled by her expression.

"It's okay to remember the good memories, Baby. It's okay. You don't need to go there just because you remember the good." He held her gaze.

Maddy shook her head violently, "No! I can't. I gotta stop...no more." She stood up and turned toward the mirror. She looked at the woman looking back at her, a stranger even in her own eyes.

Bryan stood behind her, putting his hands on her shoulders. "Okay, close your eyes and lean back against me." She did as he asked. "Breathe deep, there you go...focus on something positive." He rubbed her shoulders gently. "...you're on your horse, running free, feel the wind in your hair, it takes your breath away, feel the high Maddy, feel the high."

Maddy listened to the sound of Bryan's voice, gentle, soothing. She let him take her away, to put her somewhere where her thoughts were safe. Yes, riding Buddy, giving into the feelings and sensations. She began to feel as though she could breathe again, the fracture in her psyche closing. It was over.

"Let's go sit outside. I need a smoke, you can keep me company." He guided her out of the room.

They walked out of the building in silence and sat on the steps out front. Bryan pulled out a cigarette and lit it. They wouldn't talk about what just happened. Those memories were back in a safe place, like the photos hidden in her wallet.

Maddy glanced up when she heard the sound of laughter. The guys were coming back from lunch. Jack was amongst them carrying a bag with him. She smiled weakly. He remembered.

"You guys missed out on a good time," Jack remarked handing Bryan the bag, "but we brought some goodies." Jack exchanged looks with Bryan. Bryan looked at Maddy and then back at Jack and shook his head slightly and said silently said no. Jack gave a slight nod of understanding.

Bryan pulled out his wallet and took out a couple of bills and handed them to Maddy. "Hey kiddo, why don't you go grab us a couple of sodas and meet us in the squad room." He gave her a soft smile. "We'll have a picnic." Maddy took the money and left.

"Parker, sit down and have a smoke with me." He nodded a dismissal to the others.

Jack sat down and pulled out a cigarette and lit it. "What's going on?" he asked.

"Maddy was in pretty good spirits when she left here. What happened?" Bryan snuffed out his cigarette.

"She was fine, we were walking along and I heard her make this little cry. When I turned around she was as pale as a ghost and said she had to leave, that she had something to do. I asked her what was wrong, she said she really needed to leave." Jack exhaled, "I don't know, Bryan. Why? What happened?"

"Do you remember what was going on around you when she cried out?"

Jack ran his fingers through his hair trying to remember. He closed his eyes trying to visualize. "I remember a car honking...a white SUV, some little kids bickering, a mother yelling at them..." he shook his head, "That's about it."

"Did you see the kids? Did you see what they looked like?" Bryan pressed.

Jack flung up his hands, "Hell I don't know, I wasn't really paying attention. A boy and a girl, I think, pretty young."

Bryan stood up and brushed his pants off. "Okay, thanks Jack. I need you to do something, and its imperative that you do what I ask. You and Maddy have a tendency take whatever I give for instructions and throw them out the door, but you need to do this. If you don't, we won't be working together anymore, that's how serious I am."

Jack was confused, "oooookay, what do you need?"

"When we go back upstairs, do not ask her how she is or what happened. It never happened, understand? She is just as fine as she was when she first left with you. Do you understand?" Bryan's voice was cold and commanding.

"No, I don't understand, but I will do as you ordered." Jack flicked his cigarette and stood up. "Are you ever going to tell me what this is about?"

"No." Bryan turned and walked away.

Maddy brought the sodas in and set them on Bryan's desk. She went into the bathroom and grabbed some paper towels and laid them out. Surprisingly she was actually hungry for the first time in days. There was so much to do this afternoon.

She wanted to get the wall finished so she could get the most accurate profile on their unsub as possible. The one she had given the team previously was the standard psychological profile, kind of a generic based on what she had at the time. They needed more if they were going to catch this guy, hopefully before he made his next move—the next victim.

Bryan arrived and set the sack on his desk. "Pull up a chair Minnie."

Maddy looked at puzzled, "I thought no more Mickey and Minnie?"

He smiled, "Sorry, I tried, you'll always be my Minnie. Is that okay with you?"

She thought about it for a few seconds, "Yeah, I guess I can live with that." She leaned over and kissed him on the cheek. To hell with whoever saw her, it wasn't like they didn't know anyhow. She grabbed the sack and pulled out four Coneys'. She put one on a napkin for her and the other three on Bryan's. "You have to try these, best in the Midwest."

"You're only eating one?" he raised an eyebrow.

"Hey don't knock it, I'm eating."

"Good point."

Maddy unwrapped hers and pulled it a part to look at it. Mustard, onions, chili and tons of cheese. Jack knew how she liked them and imagined he had them all made that way. Maddy looked in the bag finding ketchup packets and napkins in the bottom. She threw the sack at Bryan. Maddy squeezed hers back together and sunk her teeth into it and closed her eyes. Some of the chili sauce dripped down her chin. "Damn it, tasty but messy."

Bryan reached across and wiped the chili from her chin. "Good food always is, that and be full of fat and cholesterol." It didn't take him long to polish of his dogs. "You're right, very good."

"You really need to visit the shop to get the full experience. We'll go again another day." She wiped her face with her napkin and took a swig from her Coke Zero.

"How we doing on my digital photos?"

"Should be here sometime this afternoon."

Maddy took out her cell phone and typed out a text and hit send.

Seconds later Bryans phone went off. He flipped it open. It read, "LU." A big grinned crossed his face and typed back in, "LU2". It was a code he and Maddy used to use when Donna was around. He glance up at her, she smiled and nodded.

She rose from her chair. Time to get back to work. She asked Andy to retrieve the files from the interrogation room, which he eagerly went to do.

Maddy whispered to Bryan. "You know an 'atta boy' would go along way with this kid, but don't make it so obvious."

Maddy and Whittmer spent the next twenty minutes clearing off all the info that was on the boards before they started from scratch. She had instructed Andy how they would set up the board as a flow chart and how to arrange the material they had. Each would take a separate person and funnel down the material.

At the end of each chart Maddy made empty boxes of the material and information they still needed to retrieve.

The guys at the squad decided since it was Friday night it was time to go blow off some steam by heading down to the bar and Maddy needed to be there since she was now 'one of the guys.' She couldn't see the harm in it and thought it could possibly be fun.

11

Maddy stood in front of the mirror in the ladies restroom. She pulled the hair tie from her hair and ran a brush through it. She looked at her face. She looked weary and had dark circles under eyes. Her mind went back to this afternoon. She had allowed herself to go where she swore she would never go. She didn't want to dwell on what happened, she couldn't take the chance, not again. She splashed water on her face and dabbed it dry. She dug around in her purse and pulled out her makeup bag. She applied an ample layer of foundation, dusted with a touch of blush and applied mascara liberally to her lashes. Good enough.

She crossed paths with Jack on her way back to the squad room. He grabbed her by the arm. "I hope you don't mind, but I called Stella to meet us down there."

Maddy turned away and rolled her eyes. "It's your choice hon," she replied dryly.

"Don't be pissed, Mads. I just need a distraction. I don't want to spend the whole night watching you with him."

Maddy pulled her arm from his grip. "Maybe Bryan and I shouldn't go. I wouldn't want to make anyone feel uncomfortable."

"You're taking this all wrong, Maddy," Jack protested. "I want you guys to be there, but if Stella is there, I won't be so...tempted."

She turned to him, "Tempted how?"

"Maddy, this is getting harder and harder for me every day. I don't want to start something we both may regret." She searched his eyes and saw the hint of pain and doubt there.

She turned away from him and started walking down the hall. She turned her head and said over her shoulder, "Fine, but call her back and tell her to dress like a normal human being. She wears the kind of dress like she has the last two times, I swear I will fucking rip it off her."

Jack rubbed his hands together and laughed, "Cool, a cat fight!"

She stuck her hand up and gave him the finger.

Maddy went straight to her desk, made a few phone calls to some single female friends from the paper and told them to meet her at the bar. If it was going to be a party, might as well make it for the whole crew.

About twenty minutes later she and Bryan pulled up in front of the same bar they and been at Tuesday night. The bar had a section for straight drinking and games. No dancing tonight. Bryan ran around and opened the door for her. They had driven the suburban. She got out and looked him over. "You look like an FBI agent," she laughed. She slipped off his jacket, unbuttoned his sleeves and pushed them up, loosened his tie, slipped it off and threw it in the truck. She reached up and started to unbutton his shirt. Bryan slid his hands up her arms, stroking them gently. For each button she undid, she planted a kiss on his chest. Bryan leaned forward and kissed her on the top of the head.

Maddy stood back and looked at him, watching his face. "What's the matter with you, Bryan? Seems like you have kept me at arms length today."

"After last night," he reached out and touched her cheek, "I don't want to scare you off."

She wrapped her arms around his neck, stood on her tiptoes and kissed him deeply; she kept kissing him until he returned her kiss. She pulled away just inches from his face. "No drama tonight. Just you and me," she threw her head back towards the bar, "and the boys." She smiled. "Let's go in and cut loose and we will see where the night will go okay?" She grabbed his hand and tugged him toward the bar.

Everyone was sitting in the bar area when they got there. Jack flagged them over. Stella was by his side just beaming at the attention she was getting from all the men. Skank, Maddy thought to herself. Stella wore her long honey hair loose, her make-up perfect. She was wearing a loose fitting halter blouse and a pair of high-end blue jeans...and those damn high-heeled shoes. Oh well, Maddy shrugged, two out of three's not bad. Maddy's friends began to arrive before too long and she made her introductions. The beer began to flow—the party had started.

Maddy looked around the room. There was no sign of Whittmer. "Where's Andy?" she asked.

"He had to pick someone up at the airport. He will be here in awhile," Bryan explained.

She threw him a look, "Like you couldn't have sent someone else."

Bryan poured each of them a beer from the pitcher. "You're getting to be quite the protector. He volunteered."

Stella came up to Bryan and wrapped her arms around him, "Bryan, it's so good to see you again. Do you play pool?" She ran her hands over his chest. "I don't know how, come show me." She pulled him toward the pool tables. Bryan looked over his shoulder and shrugged.

Maddy shot a look at Jack. He took a glass and tilted it several times and pointed to Stella. Maddy rolled her eyes. So much for no drama tonight. She took a seat by Jack. She tipped her beer and chugged it down and made a face when she was done.

Jack laughed and poured her another beer. "Not a beer drinker?"

"Tastes like skunk piss," she said picking up the glass and drank half of it in one swallow. "You drink enough of it fast enough, you won't care what it tastes like anymore."

"You want a vodka sour?" he asked.

"No, I'm one of the boys tonight remember?" she downed the rest of it and poured another one.

"You keep up like that and you are going to be drunk off your ass," he laughed.

"Tough shit," she responded. Maddy watched as Bryan bent over Stella, his arms around her guiding her hands around the pool cue. She felt her blood begin to boil and an aching in her chest.

Jack grabbed her hand, "Come on, we can play teams and kick their ass."

Maddy grabbed a full pitcher from the bar and her glass and let Jack lead her to the pool table. Jack put a dollar on the table.

"What's that?" Stella inquired.

"We are challenging you to a game. Maddy and me versus you and Bryan."

Bryan glanced at Maddy. He could see the fire in her eyes. She was pissed. Strangely enough it felt good knowing she was territorial about him. Jack stuck the money in the table and began to rack the balls.

Bryan went to Maddy's side and wrapped his arm around her. She stiffened. He leaned down and whispered in her ear. "She's drunk Maddy, let it go."

Maddy reached for a stick and then rolled it on the table checking it for balance. She turned back and looked at him, "And what's your excuse?" She shook her head, "Don't even bother answering, I don't want to hear it." She walked around the table. "Let's play, I'll break." She took the cue ball and set it down. She bent down and eyed the rack, set the cue ball on the table, pulled her arm back and let it go knocking in two balls, one of each color into the side pockets. "I call solids, are we calling our shots?"

Bryan and Stella both looked at her in surprise. Jack sat back and smiled, he knew she could play, quite ruthlessly in fact.

Maddy called her shots and put three more balls into the pockets before she bounced off the side rail and missed.

"Ladies first," Bryan said to Stella.

"Aren't you going to help me?" she looked up at him with her big doe eyes.

"No he's not," Maddy said coldly. "You're a big girl, you can do it on your own."

When Stella made her shot the cue ball skipped and bounced off the table. "This is not fair," she whined.

Jack chalked up the end of his stick, "Welcome to the real world, Baby."

Maddy laughed as he shot three more balls in.

Maddy tapped Bryan on the shoulder with her stick. "You better get that ass shakin' or we're going whoop your ass before you even get started."

Bryan shot 5 balls in before he finally missed. Maddy knew he missed the last one on purpose. He spent many Friday nights in a sports bar, and he played plenty of pool. He was leaving the table open for her to clean it up.

Maddy called her shots right down to shooting the eight ball into the last pocket. "You shouldn't do me any favors," she mumbled.

"Enough pool for me," Bryan said as he reached for Maddy's hand and led her back to one of the tables by the bar where the group was congregating. Jack and Stella joined them bringing back the full pitcher of beer with them. He topped off all their glasses and set the pitcher down.

Maddy downed half the glass again, and she was still making a face each time she took a drink. She felt her insides grow warm and her head was kind of fuzzy in a nice sort of way. Bryan leaned over and whispered in her ear. "Can we get out of here, just for a few minutes?"

Bryan stood up and helped Maddy to her feet. "We'll be back in a little bit," he told the table.

Bryan led her outside and looked around for a private spot. He led her to an area between two buildings and gently pushed her against the building. The bricks were warm on her back, the heat still radiating from the day's sun.

"My mama told me never to go into places like this with strange men," she laughed feeling the effects of the beer.

Bryan leaned against the building with one arm, "Are you calling me strange?"

"Indubitably." She ran her hand up his side. "She said that was good way for a good girl to get into trouble."

He reached up with his free hand and cupped her face. "You, Minnie, are not a good girl," and he covered her mouth with his taking her hungrily.

She moaned softly, her arms curling up around his neck, letting him take possession of her. After a few moments she pulled back..."Wait, I need to catch my breath." She waited a couple of moments and kissed him again. She slid her hands up under his shirt feeling his chest with her hands.

Bryan groaned and pulled her hands out from under of his shirt. "Miss Minnie, what do you think you are doing?"

"Molesting Mickey," she replied mischievously.

He leaned over and said huskily in her ear, "We belong to each other Minnie, I promise." He kissed her cheek. "We better get back in there and do some bonding."

They held hands as they walked back into the bar, she turned her head towards Bryan, "You do any more bonding with Barbie, and I will use your balls on pool table!"

He squeezed her hand, "No worries, Minnie."

Jack watched them come in the room, noticing Maddy's face was flushed and he was sure it wasn't from the beer. He flinched. Mayland had taken control back.

Bryan pulled Maddy's chair closer to his and she smiled up at him as she sat down. She picked up her glass and took a drink. She thought she had better slow down or they were going to have to carry her out. She didn't want a repeat of last Friday. God was it only a week ago? This had been one of the longest weeks she had had in years.

Maddy looked up to find Whittmer arriving with someone in tow. Her mouth, as well as the other women's, Stella's included, dropped. The guy coming in was one of the finest specimens of manhood she ever laid eyes on. He was a tall, black man—more like mullto, his head was clean shaven, he had chisel facial features, strong features, strong jaw line, narrow nose, lips that were totally kissable. And he had the most provocative blue eyes. His body...Maddy got chills just looking at him...broad shoulders. Rippling biceps, a six-pack that could be seen under a tightly stretched white t-shirt. His stomach was flat. He wore his jeans where a guy should, on his ass, and what a nice ass it was.

"Whoa baby," Maddy said out loud. The other women nodded in agreement.

"You guys are sick," one of the agents said.

"No," Maddy said, "We're in lust." The others laughed.

Michael, the detective that had ridden with them on the Stone Park search, commented, "And they wonder why they get called whores."

"Hey," Maddy bristled. "That's bullshit. You men lust after every woman with big tits that walks in a room. Doesn't matter much what her face looks like, if she's pretty, so much the better. I don't know how many times I have heard the comment 'you can always put a bag over her head.' What a crock of shit! When a man who looks like that," she pointed to the man approaching them, "a man that looks like that...that's like discovering an endangered species—a rare find!" The other women clapped.

Whittmer came to the table, the beautiful creature stood behind.

Bryan poured a beer and handed it to Whittmer. "Sit down, Andy, take a load off. You have had a long day."

Whittmer looked twice to make sure Bryan was talking to him. He looked at Maddy. When she smiled and nodded he sat down on the other side of her.

Bryan stood up, smiled and shook the strangers hand. He turned to the group. " I would like to introduce you all to Special Agent Derek Jamison. He's going to be helping us for a few days."

Jamison did a round of hand shaking until he hit Maddy. He held on to her hand, cocked his head sideways and said, "I'll be damned, if its not the Fire Fox, Maddy Sheridan. Damn if you don't look the same as you did before."

She was confused; she looked to Bryan and then back to Jamison.

"You don't remember me," he laughed. She did happen to notice his voice was sexy too. "1998, we were in training for profiling at Quantico together, same unit."

"Oh.... " she smiled, "Okay, you've....em filled out since then."

Jamison laughed. "Damn woman, where the hell you been? I haven't seen you in years.

Maddy took a drink of her beer then wrapped her hands around her beer. "I left the bureau in 2002," she said quietly.

"Sorry to hear that, but glad to be working with you again." He smiled down at her.

"Only for a while." She downed her beer. "Anyone for darts?"

Jack stood up, "I'm game after I have a smoke. Care to join me?" he asked Maddy.

Maddy regarded Bryan. "You go ahead Minnie. I need to fill Derek in on a few things."

Stella was busy gawking at Jamison to notice where Jack was going.

Maddy quietly followed Jack out to a bench and sat down.

"What's the matter Kitten?" he asked as hit lit up a cigarette.

Maddy threw him a look, "Kitten?" She laughed. "You're drunk."

"So," he snickered. "You've had plenty too. I was watching you in there. When that guy recognized you, you got all quiet, and jumpy. What's with that? Don't deny it and don't lie about it, you know I know when you're lying."

"So you've said." Maddy got up and walked away from him.

"Hey, where you going?" Jack stood up and followed her.

She walked faster. She thought she was well ahead of him until she heard his footsteps running up behind her.

Jack grabbed her by the arm. "Maddy, where're you going? I didn't mean to piss you off."

"Go back in Jack. I just need to be alone right now." She tried pulling away from him.

"Just like this afternoon?" he smirked. "That's my Maddy, always running away when she's trying to hide something."

Before she realized what was happening she slapped Jack across the face, hard enough it whacked. "Don't you dare sit there and judge me. You know nothing about me," she hissed.

Jack rubbed his face where her hand had made contact. He laughed under his breath. "Only because you won't let me. Damn Maddy, you can really pack a wallop."

He reached out to touch her face and she batted his hand away. Her eyes narrowed, "Don't touch me!"

"That's not what you said last night," Jacked leaned against the wall, pinning her body in between him and the wall.

"Jack please..." she pushed against him but he didn't budge. "Don't do this," she pleaded.

Jack's face softened as if he suddenly became aware of how aggressive he was acting toward her. He gently pulled her into his arms and held her to him. "Jesus, Maddy. I'm sorry. I don't know what the hell I was thinking. I'm starting to act just like him. I don't want to be him, Maddy," he spoke softly.

The tension Maddy was feeling began to waiver. This was her Jack, where she felt safe. He had frightened her. She was confused...and drunk. "I don't want you to be like him. I want you for you, can't you understand that?"

He buried his face in her hair, "Sometimes I feel you don't want me enough. I know it's not fair of me, but I can't help what I feel. Whenever you are around I just want to be near you, when you're not, I think about you. I lie in bed at night and wonder what it would be like to have you there with me, to make love to you and then hold you in my arms until we fall asleep. And then I realize that's exactly what he's doing." His voice trailed off.

"He is right you know?" she looked into Jack's dark eyes.

"About what?"

"He said things last night, after I returned from being with you, things about us..."

"Like?"

She shook her head and turned away, "No, never mind, it was ramblings of a angry, jealous man."

He held Maddy's chin up so she had to look at him. "What did he tell you, Maddy? That I'm in love with you? He's right, I am. He's not stupid. And you love me too, Maddy. I feel it when we kiss. It's not lust, it's tenderness, trust, understanding, and it's feelings we can't explain. I love you, Maddy."

"No!" Maddy tried to turn her face away from him.

He held her face so she couldn't look away from him. "Tell me you don't love me Maddy and I swear I will walk away and never bother you again."

She searched his eyes, looking for something, not knowing what. "You know I can't."

"Then tell me Maddy, I need to hear it...from your lips..."

A tear slid down her cheek and he quickly wiped it away with his thumb. She reached up and brushed his cheek with her hand. Her voice was but barely an audible whisper. "I love you, Jack."

His lips caressed hers, tender, loving, ardent. He cradled her in his arms as his kiss intensified. She responded to him in kind. They parted simultaneously and held each other close. "We need to get back," he whispered. "Some day...nothing will keep us apart."

When they returned, they didn't go to the dartboard but returned to their seats. Bryan observed their behavior and noted a red welt on Jack's face. He put his arm around Maddy and kissed her cheek. "What happened?" he whispered in her ear.

She squeezed his hand, "Just let it go okay?"

"Sure Minnie. Don't want to play darts anymore?" he asked. When she looked over at him and shook her head, he noticed her eyes were red. She had been crying. Something had happened and it didn't go well. He didn't want to pry. It had gotten them where they were last night and he didn't want to go there. He promised her no drama, at least not anything he was responsible for.

She placed her hand on his leg and rubbed it gently. "How much longer do we have to stay?"

He studied her closely and decided not to question her motives for wanting to leave. He finished up his beer. "Well folks, I think we're going to hit the road. This old man can't keep up with the rest of you."

Jamison laughed, "That's not the Agent Mayland I know."

"Yeah," he chuckled, "age has a way of catching up with you, and so does a murder investigation.

Andy, who had had a few beers, had become quite talkative. "I have one question before you leave." He looked at Maddy, "Why Fire Fox?"

Jamison spoke up, "I can answer that. The fire, well that's a two-parter, first, look at the color of her hair, second, she's a spitfire. And the fox, this woman has the keenest damn sense when it comes to the powers of observation, more than anyone I have ever seen. She's shrewd, uncanny, smart, clever, and not to mention...."he laughed, "She's hot."

Maddy blushed. "And she is also very tired and burned out." She rose from the table.

Jack rose from the table and came over, hugged her and whispered in her, "I love you, Mads." Then louder, "Get some rest Mads, see you tomorrow." He kissed her on the cheek. "Take care of her, Mayland," he said seriously.

He shook Jack's hand, "You know I will, Parker," he replied just as serious.

Maddy walked out to the truck with Bryan's arm around her. He unlocked the door and let her in. After he had slid into the driver's seat her turned to her. "What do you want to do Maddy? Where do you want to go?"

She looked straight ahead watching people crossing the street, getting in and out of their vehicles. Some ending their nights, some just beginning. "Bryan, I need to go somewhere safe, somewhere away from here."

"You want to go home..." the disappointment was apparent in his voice. "I understand. I will take you back to your car."

"No you don't understand, Bryan," she reached for his hand and held it in hers. "I want you to come with me."

He looked at her in surprise. "Maddy, are you sure? I don't want to tread where you might regret it."

She leaned out of her seat across the console and kissed him tentatively. "Bryan, I want to be with you...away from all this, away from all these people, the agents, Jack, everyone. The past...I want to go where no one can find us. I want the outside world to be gone and the only place I know for sure where that can be is home."

"Okay, if you are sure, Maddy. I will take you to your car. Swing by and pick me up at the motel. I need to grab some fresh clothes. That okay?" She nodded and leaned her head on his shoulder.

He dropped her off at the cop shop and she followed him to the Regency. She waited in her car for him. She didn't ever want to go back in that room. Too much had happened there, emotions too intense for her to face. Once again she hid from that which hurt her.

Bryan came out of the motel lobby carrying a bag. She popped the trunk for him and he threw the bag in and hopped in the car. He slid the seat all the way back and didn't comment about the close quarters in her car.

They were quiet as she left the lights of the city behind them. Bryan chuckled and shook his head.

She glanced at him and then turned her eyes back to the road, "What are you laughing about?"

"Your car," he continued to chuckle.

"What about my car?"

He began to laugh harder, "I am visualizing you running down that poor dog."

She grinned, "Poor dog my ass, he was a vicious attack dog and was ripping up my tires. Its like I told them back at the paper, it was done as a matter of self defense."

He leaned over and kissed her cheek. "Don't bug me," she laughed, "I need to concentrate on the road." She turned on her CD player, the music of Matchbox 20 drifted throughout the car. Bryan laid his head back against the seat and drifted off. She lightly brushed his cheek with her hand.

This was all getting to be too much for both of them. She hadn't really realized this case would be just as hard on him as it was on her. He had retired from the field some seven years ago after his partner got shot. He himself had sustained a gunshot wound that almost killed him. It was enough for him to leave the field and confine his career to training.

When she pulled in her drive she could see the distant flash of lightning. A storm was brewing. She woke Bryan up and he stumbled out of her car. Poor guy was beat. She hit the button to close the garage door and they walked outside. She could hear the thunder rumbling to the west.

As he followed her to the house she turned to him and smiled. "City mouse, welcome to the home of Country Mouse." She took him by the hand and led him in. Then she remembered his bag and ran out quick and got it.

He was leaning against the door watching her as she ran up the steps. He took her in his arms and kissed her deeply. "Thank you," he murmured in her ear.

She cocked her head, "For what?"

"Letting me in, I know what it took for you to do this."

She kissed him lightly and smiled. "The bathroom is to your left, towels in the hutch, go shower."

He laughed, "Me thinks, she's telling me I stink."

She pushed him gently toward the door. "Go."

She waited until she heard the water turn on before she went and grabbed a glass and filled it with tea. She reached for the bottle on the table and shook out two tablets. She hated to have to go back on her meds again, but she couldn't see anyway around it. She needed stability to some how make it through all this craziness. If it had to come by artificial means, it would have to do. She popped them in her mouth and swallowed them with a mouthful of tea.

She was sitting at the table staring off into space when Bryan came out of the bathroom. He was wearing a t-shirt and pajama pants, his favorite attire of relaxation. She messed up his hair as she walked by him. "My turn, raid the fridge for whatever you can find. I don't have any beer." She shut the door behind her.

Bryan took the opportunity to look around her house. The kitchen was homey. The floors were oak, polished to a brilliant shine. The cupboards were a simple style oak; the counter tops appeared to be black granite. Her appliances were newer and white in color. It was an eat-in kitchen; the kitchen table was square with a butcher-block oak top, and the chairs the same color as the top. It was homey and felt nice.

He noticed the pill bottle on the table. He picked up and looked at it—Seroquel XR, an antipsychotic. He looked at the date it was filled. Last night at the all night pharmacy. He felt a knot in his stomach. This was all really taking a toll on her.

He poked his head in the living room and turned on a lamp. It, too, was homey and looked comfortable. He noticed the pictures on her entertainment center. He was surprised and pleased she had pictures of Lexi and Scotty out where she could see them. This meant she wasn't totally shutting off to their memory. Maybe it was fine as long as they were where she considered herself safe. Who knows, maybe she dealt more with her past here than she was able to deal with it on the outside.

He heard the water turn off, he quickly turned the lamp off and went back out to the kitchen. He grabbed a pack of cigarettes and went outside and sat on the steps.

Maddy came out of the bathroom vigorously rubbing her hair with a towel. She looked around for Bryan and found him on the back steps. "Hey baby, what you doing out here?"

He held up his cigarette. She went back in and grabbed her tea, She notice the bottle had been moved. She sat down beside him. "So now you know," she said softly.

"Maddy, I don't think you being anywhere around this case is such a good idea. I wish to God I had never brought you into it."

She brought her fingers to his lips. "One of the rules—no talking about out there." She laid her head against his shoulder and listened as the thunder grew louder, watched as the lightning became brighter and closer. She could smell the rain heavy in the air. The trees, which had been still, began to sway with the wind. It wasn't long before the heavy drops of rain pelted them. Bryan rose to get out of the rain. Maddy stood up with him, but she pulled him down off the steps. She pulled him down to her and embraced his lips with hers. She parted his lips and took him in deeply all while the rain picked up tempo, drenching them. The drops felt warm and refreshing on her skin.

Bryan's arms slid up around her waist, pulling her into him. His hand slid under her shirt and explored her silky wet skin. He paused and held her back away from him. A flash of lightning lit up the air around her. He could see how her wet nightshirt clung to her body revealing the secrets held within. He picked her up in his arms and carried her into the house. She kicked the door shut with her feet.

"Where do I go?" he whispered.

"Down the hall and to your right," she mumbled as she kissed his neck. She had guided him to her guest bedroom. There were just some lines she wasn't willing to cross; him in her bed was one of those.

He put her down at the foot of the bed, taking in her beauty. He reached down and removed the wet nightshirt from her shivering body. He turned down the blankets, lifted her into them. He removed his own wet clothing and crawled in beside her. She met him before he could lie down, wrapping her arms around his neck, kissing him with a fieriness that was so intense it felt as if it would sear their souls together.

"God I love you Maddy," he said with an intense furiousity and claimed her for his own.

Maddy lay quietly in the bed. She could hear Bryan's steady breathing. He was sound asleep. She smiled. They made it though the night without drama, at least between the two of them. She wished she could lock the two of them away here forever.

She was thirsty and a little hungry. She crawled from beneath the sheets and headed toward the kitchen. She slipped in the bathroom and slipped on a fresh nightshirt. She came back out and filled her glass with milk, pulled out the loaf of bread and a jar of peanut butter. She slathered the bread with peanutty smoothness. She stuck her finger in the jar and licked it off her finger.

Maddy looked up when she heard her phone go off. Shit, she hadn't turned it off. She followed its sound to where she had left it in the bathroom. She looked at the caller ID. It was Jack. She went to the kitchen and looked at the clock on the wall. It was only 11:15. She closed the door between the living room and the kitchen.

"Hello?" her voice sounded sleepy even to her own ears.

"Hi Mads, just calling to say good night." His voice was soft and timid.

"The party must be over huh?" she asked.

"I left around 10:30." He laughed softly, "Stella stayed without me. I think she is hoping to get laid by Jamison. Good luck with that. So where you at?"

She was wondering how long it would take for him to get around to asking her. "I am sitting in my kitchen eating a peanut butter sandwich and drinking a glass of milk."

"Did you make it home before the storm hit?"

"Just," she took a bite of her sandwich.

"I'm sorry if what I said made you want to leave early," he stumbled.

"It's not what you told me. Just the things that were said before hand," she explained. "It was just a shame that that's how it all came out."

The line was quiet for a few brief seconds then Jack said with some hesitation, "I love you, Maddy."

How could she do this? She had just gotten out of bed with a man she professed her love to, made love to and then turn around and tell a different man she loved him too? "You know I do too, Jack." That was the best she could do for now. She would not tell Jack she loved him with Bryan in her house.

"Listen Jack, I am really bushed. I will see you tomorrow," she stifled a yawn.

"When are we supposed to go in?"

She laughed, "I don't know, nobody really said."

"I wish I were there with you," Jack said wistfully. "I could be there around midnight.

"No, I just need my space. Another time Jack okay?" She sighed. "Good night hon., sleep well." She hung up the phone and turned it off.

Maddy opened her kitchen door. The storm had passed. She grabbed her kitchen rug and laid it on the steps so she would stay dry and sat down. The sound of crickets filled the air like nature's orchestra. The air still smelled fresh with rain, the soft breeze was cool against her skin. The sky was filled with a smattering of sparkling lights, an endless sea of stars. One of the beauties of being away from the bright lights of the city, the night sky went on forever.

Maddy heard the floor creak from within the house. Bryan must have woken up. He called out, "Maddy?"

"Out here hon," she answered. The door opened. She slid over so he could sit beside her.

Bryan sat down with a groan. "I feel so old." He took out a cigarette and lit it up. He inhaled it deeply and then exhaled the smoke out slowly. "It's nice out here. I can see why you prefer it over the city."

She smiled softly, "You would never last a week out here. Not your style."

He leaned back on his arms, putting one behind her. "I don't know about that. I'm tired Maddy. These past twenty years have taken its toll on me. You said something to me other night that really got me thinking. You said you fell in love with the man I was the first time we were together. I'm not that same man, I don't know if I ever could be. But you're not that same woman either. We're both deeply scarred."

"Scars are a reminder of where we've been but do not dictate where we going," she said under her breath.

"Good quote," he noted. "But where are we going and can we escape the reminder of those scars?"

She shook her head, "I don't know hon."

"I need to make you aware of something Maddy, and I don't know how you will take it, but I want you to know. Okay?" He looked over at her.

"Is it going to hurt me?" she asked nervously.

"It could, but maybe knowing would hurt you less than what you believed transpired," he responded.

"Talk away," her voice had grown distant.

"Ten years ago, you know I was crazy about you. What we had was so unique and special. I lived for you. There was nothing more I wanted then to be with you. Then...what happened...happened. I lost you. The more time went on the further away you distanced yourself from me. I couldn't reach you anymore, couldn't touch you. You were gone from me—you were gone from everyone. You refused any kind of help. The walls went up. You were just a shell, existing. I couldn't do it Maddy. I couldn't live watching the woman I loved die inside. I could no longer have you, so I copped out. It was then I decided to live for my son, and well the rest of that is history.

I never blamed you for shutting me out; you had to do what you had to do to survive. I do blame myself. I felt so much guilt for leaving you out there to fend for yourself while I created a new life for myself. After awhile, you seemed to have pulled yourself together, but it was too late for us. I had already fucked up my life beyond repair, I couldn't put that on you, so I stayed away."

Maddy leaned back so her body touched Bryan's arm. "So what you are telling me is, you left because I had a psychotic break? You felt you needed to save yourself or go down with me?"

"It wasn't quite like that," he refuted. "I'm sorry Maddy, I am sorry I was so weak."

She nodded silently. He cut her out of his life because he couldn't deal with her going crazy. It hurt hearing this, but at least now she knew he didn't leave because he betrayed her, not the way she believed he did.

"And the affair with Donna, how do you justify that?" They never really talked about this, she never knew why.

"At first she was a substitute for you. You two were a lot alike personality wise. I didn't feel the same for her the way I felt for you. I don't think I could ever feel that way about anybody but you. By the time I realized I didn't love her, never had, I had gotten so dependent on her as my escape from my marriage. She knew about you, how I felt. Why do you think she tracked you down? You two became such good friends, stayed friends even after she told you she was involved with me. Lord knows why, maybe you were just as curious about me. I think she made it a point to finally tell me about you, to test us both. When the test blew up in her face...She had to regain control. And it wasn't just that. My head was so fucked up; I was the one falling apart this time. I made another mistake and it cost you."

"I see," was all she said to him. What was she suppose to say, when it came down to it, it changed nothing. The first time she felt she could excuse, but not what happened two years ago. What he did, what the two of them did to her was cruel and heartless and she didn't think she could forget and forgive.

"The antipsychotics your taking, does that mean you are under psychiatric care?"

"I touch base every six months. I have been in therapy for almost eight years."

"You did get help then." It was a statement. "When?"

"After I left the Bureau. I don't go where I don't want go in therapy. I use it as a means to keep control. I worked out my pain caused by you, at least to the point it was manageable, but other things are just best left undisturbed," she clarified.

"I understand." He brushed her arm with his thumb. "What are thinking? What are you feeling?"

She sighed, "I don't know. It's a lot to take in."

She paused, "Okay now I have something to tell you. When Chuck got killed, when you were shot, I came to you."

"I never saw you..."

"I never came near you. I stood in the background, watched and waited until I knew you were going to recover. Then I left and let it go," she explained. "That was the beginning of the end for you. I wasn't there for you either when the bottom fell out of your life. It wasn't revenge, or being vindictive, I just couldn't deal with it either. You had Donna, Natalia, and your son. You didn't need me. I was the last person you needed."

He leaned his head on her shoulder. "I wish I had known you were there."

Maddy stared off into the black hole where her pasture was located. "Honey, it wouldn't have made any difference, any more than if you had tried to stay with me. We had become lost souls."

"Maybe we could have been the light at the end of each other's tunnel."

Maddy shook her head, "No, not with me. You know as well as I do, I won't go down that tunnel let alone be able to see the end of it. Its not something I am willing to do."

"The pictures in the living room...I had hoped that meant you were coming to terms, in your own way." He waited patiently for her response.

"I don't dwell on them. I don't even see them anymore. I just feel not having the photos there...well if I remove the photos, I remove the fact that they were ever there. And I don't want that." She turned to Bryan, "Please don't press this okay, I can't."

He circled her shoulders with his arm and kissed the top of her head. "Okay, no pressing."

"Anyhow," Bryan started, "What I started to tell you, I am thinking about retiring."

"From the field? I already knew that."

"No, Maddy" he paused, "From the FBI."

Maddy whipped her head around, "What are you saying, Bryan?"

"After this case, I am thinking about leaving the FBI. I have twenty years in, I can qualify for early retirement."

Maddy's heart began to pound in her chest. She turned to face him. She couldn't see his expression, just shadows. She was afraid to even go there. "Bryan... what does this all mean? I don't understand."

He smiled weakly, "Always doubting my motives aren't you Maddy? What I am saying is I'm choosing you, Maddy. We aren't getting any younger. I can't afford to wait until fate lets us cross paths again if it ever will. I don't like living everyday feeling like we are on borrowed time and when this is done; it will be time to cash it in. I know you won't come back with me. You couldn't live like that, not with all the history there."

"I know all about you Maddy, I know your history, I know your demons, but I really don't know you, not anymore. I want to be more to you than the protector against your demons, more to you than the ghost that left you behind, more than just your lover based on a passion that never died. I don't want to be the man that you fear, that you can't trust." He looked over at her. "Do you see where I am going with this at all?" His voice was strained and extremely emotional.

Wow. Maddy sat back and took in his words. She never saw this coming, never in a million years. So what did this mean to her? It was never something she contemplated. Bryan stay? The enormity of his words swam around her like sharks in a tank. It all made her feel panicky.

"You're not saying anything Maddy. It concerns me." Bryan spoke softly.

She turned to him and ran her fingers down the side of his face. She leaned into him and kissed him tenderly. "You know how much I love you Bryan. I just quite honestly never thought this was possible." She pulled him to her so their foreheads were touching, her hand resting on the back of his head. "But I'm scared. Hope for me died years ago. I don't dare to dream, I don't allow myself to look forward to anything. I just have this intense fear of getting hurt. If I don't dream, if I don't believe, or have faith, I won't be disappointed and I can't get hurt."

Bryan put his hand behind her head and kissed her tentatively. "I've really fucked you up. I've shaken up your faith so bad, and I'm sorry." He kissed her nose. "What do you need from me Maddy? What can I do to make things right?"

"I feel...I need to try open my heart to you, to try to put all my fears and doubts aside. I need to let you in...without reservation...but I don't know if I can do it—I don't know if I have the capacity to be able to." She hadn't been aware she was crying until Bryan wiped away her tears.

He pulled her over onto his lap and held her tight. "Do you think you could try? Or is it too late? I don't want you to be skittish with me. I don't think we can move forward if you can't let go."

She turned his face toward her and uttered, "I can't promise you I will just let go, I don't know if I can, but baby, I will give it all I have. It's the best I can do."

"I'm only going to ask you to do one thing, Maddy, keep your heart open, not just to me but to everything and everyone around you. Feel again Maddy—just let yourself feel. Before you can really commit to me, you have to learn to trust this," he touched her heart. "If that leads you to me," he smiled, "I will be the happiest man alive."

He took her face in his hand, kissed her, unsure at first then it progressed into a deep tender kiss. Maddy could feel the emotion behind it and it made her feel that much deeper for him. She was so confused, so unprepared. She honestly didn't know what to think. She felt blindsided.

When Maddy woke up Bryan's arms were wrapped tightly around her. When she tried to move they locked up tighter. She nudged him with her elbow. "Bryan, let go. I need to get up."

"No," he mumbled. "Never letting you go..."

"The hell you're not," she laughed and jabbed him in the ribs.

He jumped and rolled over, "Damn Maddy, fucked up way to ruin a good dream!"

"Rise and shine, Babycakes," she kissed him on the cheek. "We gotta job to get to."

He grabbed her and rolled over on top of her, straddling her and smiled down at her, "Not until noon we don't"

She laughed and braced her arms against him, "Did you bother to tell anyone else that?"

"Jamison was in charge of that." He his eyes traveled over her hungrily.

"We're not going there, Bryan," she smiled coyly. "Did he let everyone know?"

He bent down to kiss her and she turned her head and he caught her on the side of the mouth. "You're kidding right?"

"No," she laughed. "We're not going to spend all day in bed."

"How about all morning?" he raised his eyebrows up and down.

Maddy shook her head back and forth smiling. "Not that either. You said you want to get to know me," she laughed, "It's not going to happen in bed, you already know me well enough there."

"Not even a quickie?" he teased.

Maddy burst out laughing, "With you there is no such things as a quickie. You're a perfectionist. If you can't do it right, you won't do it all."

"I can make an exception," he grinned.

"You want some breakfast?" she asked.

"You're not giving in are you?"

She grinned and shook her head, "Nope."

He rolled over taking her with him. "Well hell, forgot how stubborn you can be. Fine, go make me a breakfast fit for a king."

She slid off him and stood up, "You will take what you get!" She ran from the room just as a pillow flew by her head. "Big baby," she yelled as she ran down the hall.

Maddy went to the fridge and pulled out eggs, ham, cheese, onions and peppers. Omelets it will be. She grabbed a pan and a bowl. Within fifteen minutes she had whipped up two western omelets, toast, and orange juice. Bryan came up behind her, wrapping his arms around her from behind and began to kiss her neck. "Damn," she laughed, "for an old man you sure have an insatiable appetite!"

"This time it's for food," he grabbed the plates off the counter and placed them on the table then came back for the orange juice.

Maddy grabbed some silverware and toast then sat down. "I didn't make coffee."

"You're fired," he said as he stuffed a forkful of omelet into his mouth.

She threw a napkin at him.

"Didn't your mama ever you teach not to throw things at people, you'll poke an eye out."

She smeared her toast with strawberry jam and slid the jar across the table to Bryan. "I miss my dogs. Since we don't have to be in until noon, can we drive out and get them?"

"They're at Jessie's?" He took a swig of the orange juice.

"Yeah."

"Sure, why not, even if we're a little late, it won't matter." He leaned back in his chair, "It's good to be the boss."

Maddy shook her hair free, "You are such an arrogant pig."

He finished off his omelet, "Yeah I know. I'm going to change clothes quick."

Maddy smiled to herself and stood by the bathroom, "Don't forget to wear cologne."

He poked his head out of the bathroom. "There you go, saying I stink again."

She gave him a quick kiss, "I just love it when you smell so sexy." She smirked. It was setup and it gave her great satisfaction. She loved it that she was the one manipulating the situation.

Bryan came out of the bathroom dressed in blue jeans and a polo shirt. She nodded her approval. She disappeared into her bedroom and slipped on a pair of jeans and a ruby red button down blouse. She gave herself sprits of Obsession cologne, just so Bryan didn't feel alone. She was still laughing to herself for what she knew was going to happen.

Bryan was standing outside her bedroom. "We slept in your guest room?"

She messed up his hair. "You have to earn the right to sleep in the Queen's chamber."

"You look stunning," he kisses her on the top of the head, "and just to let you know, I will humbly do your bidding until I receive knighthood."

"You ham," she smacked him.

"Nope, had that for breakfast. You ready to go, your highness?"

She resisted the temptation to hit him again, but for now she would apply the no touchy rule.

They had been driving for about five minutes when she asked him, "What's Jamison doing here?"

Bryan rolled down his window and lit up the cigarette. "I requested his help. We are working this case with relatively green agents. This is a hard complicated case, and quite frankly I don't think they have the balls for it. Parker..."

She gave him the look at his referral to Jack.

"Okay, Jack, as I was saying, he's got a better edge on the situation than any of my agents. It doesn't leave us with a lot of manpower to work with. They make good grunts, but not investigators. I wanted a more experience agent I can count on."

Maddy turned off on a gravel road, "In what capacity?"

Bryan grew quiet as he looked forward. She couldn't get a good look at his eyes so she could read him. "I'm waiting."

"He's a profiler," he stated flatly.

Maddy took a deep breath, "Boy, aren't we full of surprises, and you didn't even bother to give me a heads up. What the hell am I here for?"

"Maddy, you said yourself you've been out of the game for eight years. Things have changed, new techniques, advances in the science."

"So I will be working under him not you?" She wasn't too pleased about the situation and she felt like she had been duped.

"There is nothing wrong with your profiling skills, they just need to be brought up to speed. You will still be working for me as is he, and he will be working with you, not you for him. Besides that it gives you a chance to get to that hot body you were lusting after so bad last night."

"You know, I don't know how I couldn't remember a guy that looks like that. My radar must be really off."

Bryan laughed, "I will be watching you. Might have to keep a better eye out for you with Jamison than I do with Jack."

"You are so full shit," she threw her head back and laughed. "Jamison is lust, Jack is sweetness."

He smiled, "I will leave it at that."

Just then Maddy pulled in to Jessie's lane. A giant golden lab ran beside the car. "That's Copper!"

Bryan made the comment, "Are you going to run him down too?"

She tossed him a look, "Fuck you!"

"Touchy," he laughed under his breath.

As she pulled up to the house drive, Jessie came out of the house dressed in boot cut blue jeans, cowboy boots, a cotton button down shirt, and a baseball cap. She went back and opened the house door and yelled, "Come on boys, Mama's come to take you home."

Rufus and Jack came out of the house leaps and bounds. Maddy knelt down to the ground, Jack wagged his tail feroiusly and licked her face and then went over to check out Bryan. Rufus jumped in her arms eagerly smothering he face in doggy kisses. She put him on the ground and observed him moving towards Bryan. His body became rigid, his little stubby tail stuck straight up. Bryan knelt down and called the pup to him. The hair on Rufus's back stuck up like a razor. The closer he got to Bryan the more erratic he became. He snapped out at Bryan's hand and then he laid into his pant leg, trying his best to get to the leg so he could sink his teeth in to fresh skin. "Jesus Christ Maddy, get him hell off me!" he yelled in panic.

Maddy grabbed Rufus and stuck him in a kennel cage smiling as she did. She stood up and wiped her hands in satisfaction.

Bryan brushed off his pant legs. "You framed me, you evil bitch."

"Meet my eye witness. He reacted to your cologne—Polo."

She looked at Jessie and winked.

"You got time for a cup of coffee?" Jess asked.

Bryan's eyes lit up, "I get my coffee!" He gently shoved Maddy. "She wouldn't make me any."

Jessie showed them into a sun porch built just off the side of her house. The room took in the morning light of the sun, yet it could still be cooled by air conditioning. Jessie brought out two cups of coffee and a glass of tea for Maddy. She sat down opposite of Bryan.

"Okay Bryan, I am going to put you in the hot seat. I have a few choice questions, and would like some straight answers," she said as a matter of fact.

"Jess, no, not now," Maddy protested.

Bryan's hands were wrapped around his cup. His demeanor was calm and collected. He had no idea the firing squad he was about to go before. "It's okay, Maddy. Jessie has a right to answers." His gaze met Jessie's, "Fire away."

Jessie didn't blink. "When are you going to stop being so self-centered and stay the hell out of her life?"

Bryan was a little taken aback, "Wow, nothing like going straight for the kill. Obviously you know our history and what I have done in the past is less than honorable, as matter of fact it was damn right cruel. She has no reason to even be with me now. But she is and I am grateful and blessed. I am not planning on a vanishing act this time." He reached out for Maddy's hand. "I hoping she will be willing to trust me enough to make a commitment this time."

Jessie glanced at Maddy and raised an eyebrow then turned back to Bryan. "How do propose to do that?"

"Let's just say we are discussing some alternatives so we can stay together. I decline to discuss it further because it's just something we started talking about. I am sure Maddy will fill you on the details as things progress."

"What about your wife? What about your son? What about your mistress? Where do they all fit into this master plan?" Jessie continued to drill him.

Maddy kicked her under the table and Jessie looked at her, "What? If you had any balls when it comes to this man, you would be asking him yourself."

Bryan answered her quite honestly. "The mistress is out of the picture. I'm not sure where Natalia and Jeff will come into the picture." He paused, "You don't like me very much do you?"

"I don't know you," she said flatly, "Only the hell I have witnessed you have put my friend through. I don't believe she deserves it again."

Maddy picked up on Bryan's answer for his wife and son. Was he planning on staying married to her? He hadn't said anything about that last night. She understood why he couldn't cut ties with his son, but to stay married to Natalia? It would be a deal breaker. She would wait and see what happened. No divorce, no future.

"Anything else you want to know?" Bryan asked as he finished off his coffee.

"Only time will tell if your intentions are what you say they are. I have my doubts, but we shall see." Jessie picked up the empty coffee cups. "If you stay, as you say you are, I imagine we will get to know each other better."

Maddy rose from her chair, "We need to get going." She hugged Jessie. "Thanks for keeping the dogs, if you don't mind, could you keep doing chores. I never know when I'll get home now that I'm working this case full time."

"What you do mean working it full time." A look of horror came across her friend's face. "You didn't? No Maddy, you didn't rejoin?"

She smiled weakly, "Yeah I did, just until this case is over."

"You promise? You will quit when this is all done?"

Maddy hugged her friend again. "I promise."

Jessie turned to Bryan, "You make damn sure she does. You of all people know she shouldn't be doing this at all."

Maddy threw her arms up in the air, "I am so sick of everyone telling me what I can handle. For Christ sake, I'm not a basket case. I'm leaving. Thanks again, Jessie. Bryan let's go."

Maddy sat in her car and waited for Bryan who had lingered to talk with Jessie. She had no idea about what, and at this point she was beyond caring. She was just tired of being viewed as an emotional cripple. She reactivated to prove to herself she could be a whole person again, to prove she was not a hostage to her past experiences.

Bryan slid in the seat beside her. Rufus gave a low growl and scratched at his kennel cage. Bryan looked over his shoulder. "Is he always so aggressive?"

"No, he's a bundle of fun loving, sweetness. I told you he reacts to the cologne...like a mad dog." She looked behind her and backed out the drive and on to the gravel road.

"How do you know the unsub wears this and rat just don't like this cologne?"

Maddy pulled the car off the road and took her wrist and rubbed it vigorously on Bryan's neck just below his ear. He moved his head away from her. "Jesus Christ Maddy, what are you doing?"

"Smell my wrist, does it smell like Polo?"

Bryan sniffed, "Yeah."

She got out of the car and opened the back seat and grabbed the kennel cab. She opened the door and stuck her hand in and scratched him behind his ears. The only reaction she got was Rufus licked where the cologne was, cleaning her skin as if it were dirty. Maddy shut the kennel cage and sat back down in the car and looked at Bryan, her eyebrows raised. "Well?"

"Maybe he just doesn't like men and its got nothing to do with Polo," he remarked.

"No I know it's not that. Jack has been around him a couple of times, with and without the Polo. He only attacked Jack when he was wearing the cologne," she refuted.

"Still doesn't really mean anything," he commented.

Maddy put the car in gear, "Whatever."

They drove in silence for a while before Bryan spoke up. "No comments on the inquisition?"

"Nope."

"You're upset. Why?"

"Nothing," she stated flatly.

He reached for her hand and she pulled it away.

"I love you," he whispered as he watched her.

"I know you think you do," she quipped.

"What do you mean by that?"

She didn't answer. She wasn't sure why she said it. The divorce thing still stuck in her craw. So she told him exactly what she thought previously. "No divorce, no future, at least not with me. We do this, I want it clean."

"The situation is very complicated. You know that," he tried to explain.

"Then uncomplicated it. The way I look at it, it's pure and simple. You want me—unhinge yourself from your past. If I need to let go, so do you."

"You seem to be pretty confident about what you want." Bryan cracked his window and lit up a cigarette.

Maddy glanced over at Bryan and then put her focus back on the road. "Yeah I do. If I let you in, it's by my rules. I have to do what's best for me."

Bryan flicked his ash out the window. "Sounds like we still have some pretty strong trust issues here. I'm disappointed."

Maddy was astonished, "What did you expect from me Bryan? That I could...Oh fuck it. We will just take one day at a time, see if you live up to your promises."

"And your promise to me, Maddy? To open up your heart? To at least try to let go?"

"I promised I would do the best I can, and I will. But it can't be just me, you understand? Do you honestly think just because you said everything you did last night, it fixes everything. If you do, you're wrong." Maddy stared at the road in front of her. She was tired of this conversation. She was tired of talking about all these trust issue. They both needed to move on.

"The remark you made about me just thinking I love you, is that honestly what you feel? That it's all in my head?"

"I know you love me, I just need to see how much. Now let's just drop it okay?"

The two spent the remainder of the ride back to her house without speaking. Maddy turned the pups out into the dog yard. When they walked in the house, Maddy went into the bathroom and tied her hair back. Bryan came in and grabbed his bag. She was kind of pleased he didn't automatically assume he was staying there, yet she felt a pang because he didn't ask. She was undecided whether or not she would allow him to return tonight.

Maddy didn't want the day to start badly. She didn't want to work around him with tension surrounding them; they both needed to be thinking clearly. She stopped him at the door and wrapped her arms around him and hugged him tight. She slid her arms up around his neck and pulled his face down so she could kiss him. When their lips met the tension they were feeling between them ignited.

Bryan picked her up and kicked the door shut with his foot. He carried her back to the bedroom; their lips locked the whole distance. He laid her gently on the bed slid in beside her, kissing her neck and unbuttoning her shirt, burning a trail down her throat. She whimpered and arched her body to him, tangling her fingers in his hair. She leaned forward and whispered, her hot breath against his bare skin, "I love you, Bryan."

His head came up and he cradled her head in his arms. "I love you...at any price," and he hungrily reclaimed her lips. Their arms were a flurry of movement, clothing being stripped and flying off the bed.

Maddy breathlessly whispered in his ear, "We're going to be late..."

Bryan growled sending shivers through her body and replied, "It's good to be the boss..."

12

Maddy sat in the parking lot trying to get the ambition to go into the station. She took out her lipstick and applied a thin coat. Her lips were still tender from this morning. She smiled secretly to herself and thought of their lovemaking. Damn, she had to admit when it came to the bedroom, there were definitely no problems there.

She had dropped Bryan off at the motel. He should be pulling in before too long. She wanted to be up there before he got there. She wasn't sure of her motives, but she didn't want Jack to know Bryan had spent the night with her at her house. She was sure he would make a big deal out of it. She wasn't sure if it was because it was none of his business or didn't she want to hurt him.

She felt uncomfortable he had professed his love for her last night, even worse she had responded in kind. She couldn't keep this up, being torn between these two men. But did she really want to shut Jack off? Maddy rested her head on the steering wheel. She jumped when there was a rap on the window. She looked up; it was Bryan.

"Come on kiddo, you better get that cute ass up there. Heard your boss is a complete asshole," he smiled at her.

She stepped out of car and hit the lock on her keys. "Yeah, that's for damn sure. You don't do what he says and can get real physically with you," she joked. "I was trying to get there before you so it doesn't look so obvious."

Bryan threw his head back and laughed, "Like it's not. Christ Maddy, it's not like we've tried to hide it."

Maddy paused, "Duh, what was I thinking?" She clipped her badge to her waistband and strapped on her holster and slid her Glock in. "Damn, you would think with all this time they could make these things lighter."

Bryan put his hand on her shoulder, "Buck up and quit being such a puss. Let's go tiger."

When Maddy entered the squad room she found Derek Jamison with a chair pulled some distance from the boards she and Andy had compiled yesterday. He had a clipboard on his lap and was making notations. "Any luck?" she asked as she placed her bag by her desk.

"Yeah, lots. Care to guide me through this?" he glanced up at her.

No, not really, she said to herself. "Thought by now you would have had your own profile completed and ready to give it to us."

"Listen Maddy, I'm not hear to criticize your work, you don't have to get hostile with me. I'm here to help," Jamison countered.

Bryan grabbed her by her elbow and guided her away. "Don't be copping an attitude Maddy. It's counterproductive. We really don't need friction between the two of you just because Jamison's pissing on your tree."

Maddy looked up at him cracking a smile. "Pissing on my tree?" She shook her head, "You are so eloquent."

She turned to Jamison. "My apologies. Do you care if we just do this with everyone so I can save us all some time? You can interject with your questions as you see fit."

Jamison gave a light shrug, "Carry on."

Bryan called the guys together and called Jack in from his office. When Jack entered he nodded at Maddy.

"Okay let's get this show on the road. First, victimology. We have a total of five victims, one of which is unaccounted for—our first vic. Our women are all Caucasian, between the ages of 28 and 33. All middle class, single, average white-collar occupations. All five lived alone either in an apartment or a house." Maddy put push pens into a map of the area where each lived. "Three of the five, Whethers, Stewart and Mallard had boyfriends. There is no reason believe any of these men are persons of interest."

"Four of the bodies were recovered from area parks." More push pins. "The graves were shallow, approximately seven feet in length, three feet deep max. Each body had been cleaned, dressed and prepared for burial. MO, each was dressed in a frock, posed with hands crossed at the sternum and a rosary. The rosary was wrapped around their hands like you often see in a Catholic burial. The bodies are covered in a gauze mesh prior completion of the burial. My theory is the burial is the climax of some type of ritual.

Each of the victims were killed by slashing their throats, but only after they were mutilated." She pointed to the autopsy photos. "Antemortem mutilations consist of lacerations from below the neckline to just below the ribcage, and left to right above the breast intersecting just above the heart. The wounds are approximately three-quarters of an inch deep and are consistent in depth."

Maddy pulled a letter opener off Bryan's desk. Bryan was sitting on the corner of his desk. Maddy came up from behind him, pulled his head back by his hair and brought the letter opener to his throat. "If our unsub killed our vics from behind the laceration would go from ear to ear." She demonstrated the action on Bryan letting the opener just graze his skin.

Bryan rubbed his neck where it had welted up. "Jesus Maddy, you didn't have to enjoy it that much."

Everyone laughed.

"Shut up," she said as she faced him. "This is not the case with our vics. Our vics were killed from the front with a right handed lateral move." She grabbed Bryan by the hair again with her left hand and was preparing to make a motion to slit his throat from left to right with her right hand.

He grabbed her hand in mid swipe. "I think we get the picture, why don't you just tell us about it instead of playing show and tell."

Maddy made a mock pouty face. "You always ruin my fun." Which was followed by more guffaws.

"Anyway, I came to this conclusion by studying the wounds on our most current vic, Vanessa Granger, since her body is, for lack a better word, fresher. Her wound is deepest on the left side indicating the point of penetration and tapering off on the right—thus a right-handed kill."

"The ligatures on her wrists and feet were created by a 2-point barb with 12 ¾ guage wire, otherwise known as barbed wire. If you looked here," she pointed to the tearing and scraping on the photos, "the vic was bound then hung in an upright position. The tearing and scraping, to me, indicate the ligatures were placed on the vic and she was 'hung up.' The tension on the wire is what caused the deep gauges and the scraping."

"Granger is also an example that our unsub is escalating, needing more antemortem torture to get off by making these superficial wounds." She pointed to the shallow stabbings on Grangers abdomen. "He has also added a nice little touch by administering a puncture wound at the intersection of the cross section of the lateral and horizontal wounds."

"Another thing that concerns me about his last victim is that our unsub took more time concealing the grave by covering it with brush. What that means, I don't know."

"Onto our unsub," Maddy said as she cracked her knuckles.

"Wait," Jamison interrupted, "What are these blank boxes for?" He pointed to the empty square boxes below each victim's flow chart.

"I will get back to that in a minute," she replied blowing him off just for the fun of it.

"Back to our unsub, he is classified as a sexual sadist. His dichotomy is organized. These abductions are premeditated and carefully planned. He is antisocial but knows right from wrong, is not insane and shows no remorse. He has advanced social skills, plans his crimes, displays control over his victim using social skills, leaves little forensic evidence or clues, and often engages in sexual acts (in this case the torturing) with the victim before the he goes for the kill. It is the suffering that gets him off not the actual torturing. He uses the drug Ketamine to render his victim helpless. This way his victim is forced to watch his torture and is unable to defend herself.

I believe he knows his victims and selects them because they fit with his profile. He gets to know them, their patterns, schedules. He knows when to strike when he's least likely to be noticed."

"In my personal opinion our unsub has a religious connection, someone one connected with the church, I don't know how yet. I also believe he might be a house cleaner." Maddy said as she sat at her desk.

Bryan and Jamison both looked at her questioningly. "A house cleaner?" Jamison asked. "How do you figure? A house cleaner is associated with someone who targets victims from the underbelly such as addicts, prostitutes and the homeless. These women don't figure into that at all."

Maddy leaned back in her chair with her arms crossed. "That's not the way our unsub sees them. Somewhere along the line he met up with a stressor. It warped his perception of who they are. They did something to break his code of right and wrong, something he feels they need punished for. We just don't know what that is yet. Maybe not a house cleaner by definition, but in his eyes, yes."

Bryan dismissed the other officers. Jack lingered and Bryan gave him the nod he could stay. Bryan pointed to the interrogation room and the four of them went in and closed the door.

They all sat at the table and staring at Maddy when Bryan spoke, "Where did you come up with this one?"

"Jesus, Bryan, give me a little credit. We talked about this other night," she explained.

"Not in this direction!"

"What, do you think I am wrong?"

Bryan shook his head in disbelief. "Maddy, Maddy, Maddy..."

"I think she's on to something." It was Jamison that piped in. "Based on the all the notes I have read, studying the case files, and listening to her read, I have to agree with her to some degree."

Maddy met Bryan's stare and scrunched up her nose at him. "See..."

Jamison chuckled. "Some things never change." He glanced at Jack, "These two are worse than a couple of kids fighting over the same piece of candy."

"No," Maddy interjected. "He just doesn't like to admit it when I could be right."

"What imperial proof do you have you are right? Show me the facts, Maddy." Despite the fact that Jamison had backed her, Bryan wasn't accepting her conclusion.

Maddy stood up and leaned over the table to him, getting in his face, "First off all profiling is not imperial, you know it. And second, it's my gut feeling, and *I* am not wrong!"

Bryan reached out and touched her nose and laughed. "Okay, Tiger. We'll go with it."

Maddy beamed at him. "I thought you would see things my way!" She turned and left the room, Bryan right behind her.

Jack looked at Jamison with an uncertain look. "What the hell just happened?"

Jamison just shook his head and laughed. "It's the fire fox in action. Like I said last night, she's clever, observant, she reads things into situations most of us don't see. She connects the dots. She acts on her intuition. Bryan doesn't work that way, he works off of verifiable facts—unless she can persuade him otherwise, and usually she does. But he doesn't just give it to her. She's made good calls, above average, but he still has to challenge her. The more adamant she is, the better the chances are she's right."

"How long did you say you worked with her, you worked with both of them?

"About three years, then she transferred out. It was a shame but totally understandable."

Jack was confused, "Last night you told her you were just in training together. What's up with that?"

Jamison folded his arms on the table. "She experienced a life altering event, one that devastated her. She tried to stay on, but it just didn't work. She lost her perspective and succumbed to the darkness of the job. She doesn't remember because it was part of the life she wanted to forget. I'm not going to awaken those ghosts."

"I don't suppose you would share the event?" Jack questioned.

Jamison stood up, "Nope, FBI code. Why you so interested in Maddy? I sensed some tension between you two last night."

"I guess you could kind of say we were partners before all this." He stood up and pushed in his chair.

"She was a cop?"

Jack laughed, "No a pain in the ass investigative reporter. She kind of grows on you."

"A reporter, who would have guessed, but I can see it. Word of advice?" Jamison asked.

"Sure, what can it hurt?" He answered.

"Bryan and Maddy appear to have taken up where they let off. Those two are like a chemical reaction fusing together to become one. They compliment each other. He keeps her grounded, sort of, and she keeps him alive. She gives him something to live for, to make it all worthwhile. The man has had the life from hell. Them being back together, they are possibly saving each other's lives. He's always been protective of her, tried to keep her away from things that could hurt her. He failed her once, I don't think he would ever do that again."

Jack stood and studied this man, "Just what is it you are telling me?"

"That if you have any designs on Maddy, they're futile. What they have between the two of them, it can't be broken, even by them," Jamison clarified. As he walked out the door, he patted Jack on the shoulder.

Jack stood there for a few moments. Apparently Jamison didn't know their history of the past few years. Maddy confessed her love for him. He knew she couldn't just walk away from it. Could she?"

When Jack left the interrogation room he caught a glimpse of Maddy heading down toward the vending machines so he followed her. "Hey Mads, nice job you did in there. I'm impressed."

She put her first bill in the machine and it spit out a diet coke. She then put another one and it shot out a hard-core coke. "Thanks," she looked up and smiled then she started to walk past him.

He gently grabbed her arm. "Is that all you have to say to me?"

She looked at him innocently, "What do you want me to say?"

"About last night, that was a bid deal, at least I thought it was," Jack felt uncomfortable, as if he were talking to a stranger.

She searched his face, her eyes sparkling, "Yes, Jack, it was a pivotal change in our relationship, but it doesn't change the dynamics of it all. I'm still with Bryan, I love you, but I can't play both sides of the table. I can't be with you; I can't love you the way I want to, not the way you deserve—not while Bryan and I are together. I don't want to hurt you; I don't want to string you along waiting for us to be together. Do you understand?"

Jack wrapped his arms around her pulling her close, his lips closing down on hers. He kissed her with a fiery passion demanding a response from her. Maddy felt her heart quicken and the heat rising from within.

She pushed him back, "No, I can't do this," she protested.

Jack laughed, "As the old cliché says, your words say no, but your body says yes. I'm not giving up Maddy. Every chance I get I am going take it. With or without Mayland."

Maddy stood away from him. "You don't get it do you?"

"Get what?"

"This thing between you and me, then with me and Bryan. What am I suppose to do? Be with Bryan and see you behind his back? I can't do that. It's not fair to either one of you and it's not fair to me. I don't want to loose you, Jack, but I can't let myself be torn in half either." She tried to make it clear.

"So all those promises we made, to not let him come between us, they mean nothing?" he challenged her.

"You are being unfair," she protested. "I just don't know what you want me to do, Jack." She turned on her heels and walked off down the hall.

"This isn't done Maddy, I won't let it be," Jack called out after her.

Maddy stood before Bryan's desk until he looked up from his paper work. "Problem?"

"We need to talk—in private." She was still shaking because of her encounter with Jack. Enough was enough.

Bryan and Maddy went down stairs so Bryan could take a smoke break. Maddy handed him his soda she had brought down with her and opened her own. "We have a problem—with Jack. He won't back off."

Bryan lit his cigarette. "Did you really think he would?" He took a drag off it. "I didn't, I would expect no less from him."

Maddy ran her fingertip around the rim of the can. "What am I suppose to do?"

Bryan popped the top on his can and took a drink. "What do you want to do?"

She kicked his foot, "Don't put me in this situation. For once just tell me how you feel about it."

"I've been sincere about everything we've talked about in the last twenty-four hours. I want us to be together, permanently. But I don't want you wondering what if. I want you to be sure its me you want to be with," Bryan explained.

"I am sure," she looked down watching some ants make a path along a crack in the cement. At least at this moment she was sure, but when she was actually in Jack's company, not so much.

"Jack sees me as an antagonist, his adversary. I came along, just as he was realizing he had feelings for you, same as you. You don't know what would have happened if I hadn't come back into your life. I love you Maddy, I know what loving you can do to a man. I can't fault him for not wanting to give in and let you go, especially to someone he feels is all wrong for you."

She looked over at him, "Is that what you think? That you're all wrong for me?"

Byran put his hand on hers and squeezed it. "No Maddy, I am the man for you. We both know it. No one can know you and love you deeper than I do. We can't refute that fact. Anyone who really knows the two of us would be of the same mind. Jamison knows it."

Maddy tilted her head, "How would he know? He hardly knows me."

Bryan took a deep breath. "He knows you Maddy. He wasn't completely honest with you last night. We're not sure why you don't remember him, but you worked closely with the man for three years, with both of us. He was there Maddy." He watched her to see of she understood what he was insinuating.

"Oh..." She ran what he said through her mind, searching. She just couldn't remember Jamison from before and she didn't know why. Could she really have blanked so much from her mind in order to forget?

"Now is not the time, but some day, Maddy, some day in the not too distant future, you are going to have to face what happened in order to make yourself whole again." Bryan put his arm around her shoulder.

"I can't!" she protested. "I can't, Bryan. Please don't ask me to go there. Do you know how long it took me to be able to function as a human being again after that?"

He took her chin and made her look at him, "I know kiddo. You've been living in a private hell for ten years. When the time comes, I will be with you. I won't let go of you and will be there when you come out on the other side. Put it out of your mind for now. You're not ready. But might I suggest you start getting used to the idea."

Maddy sincerely doubted what he said, that she needed to face her demons. She thought he must be thinking this for her to be really free. He could be right, but she was terrified to find out.

Bryan kissed her softly on the lips. "Now back to Jack. What do you want to do about him?"

"Honestly?" she asked. "I want things to go back the way they used to be, at least to the point when things and feelings weren't left in question."

Bryan put his face in his hands, "Please tell me he didn't."

She looked sharply at him. "What?"

"Last night when you two disappeared...did he tell you he was in love with you?"

Maddy nodded.

"And what did you tell him? And don't panic if you answered him in kind, it's not going to piss me off. I know you love me...more...otherwise there wouldn't be an issue here.

"He cornered me, kept pushing me. Said if I told him I didn't love him he would turn and walk away." Maddy rubbed her temples. "How'd this all get so fucking complicated?" Maddy paused, "And why the hell is all this okay with you? You're not normal. You should be pissed. You should be jealous. Its not normal for a man to be okay with another man telling his woman he loves her."

Bryan leaned his head back and smiled. "You want to know why I'm not running upstairs and bashing Jack's head in for loving my girl? Maddy, I see the way you look at him and I see the way you look at me. There's a hell of a difference. I know how you feel in my arms when you surrender yourself without hesitation. I know you, Maddy. I know it's me you love so completely. And I trust that...no matter how hard Jack tries to steal you away." He kissed her on the tip of her nose. "Minnie, he ain't got nuttin on me!"

Bryan stood up and held his hand out to help her up. "Maddy, handle Jack however you feel comfortable. Just keep in mind, he was your friend first—a good and trusted friend. If you can come out of this and keep that intact, you've won the war. And by the way, unless you are prepared to fill him in on your past, you need to somehow subtly tell him to back off on the probing into your past. He's hit me up several times and today he hit up Jamison."

"Asshole," she mumbled under her breath as they began walk back in.

Bryan laughed, "Who? Him or me?"

Maddy nudged him with her body. "Both, but him at the moment."

Maddy approached Jamison who was studying some photos of the gravesites. "Derek?"

He set the photos down and looked up at her. "Yes, Maddy?"

"I'm sorry I don't remember you..."she said softly.

"It's okay Fox, totally understandable. Don't let it bother you," he smiled reassuringly. "Who told you? Bryan or Parker?"

"Bryan."

Jamison nodded. "Good, I'm glad it was him."

Maddy returned to her desk to find a flash drive sitting on her laptop. She glanced at Bryan.

He smiled as he slipped his glasses back on. "Your digital photos, your Majesty."

Maddy smiled and laughed. "Your Majesty? Are you working on the queen angle?"

He was looking in a folder, "Only if it's working."

"Keep working," she said as she booted up her laptop.

Maddy opened up Photoshop and stuck in the flash drive. She open up Adobe Bridge so she could see the contents of the drive without opening up each individual photos. She zoomed past the autopsy photos, burial sites and the CSU photos of the victims' homes. She went straight for the X-rays of the bodies. She was looking for progression of torture. She opened up the earliest victim, Whethers. She closely examined the bones for any abnormalities. She was studying the skull when something jumped out at her. She zoomed in to the cheekbone. Could it be? Maddy pulled out Whether's autopsy report and read it over again. Skull in tact, no anomalies. Bullshit. The x-ray revealed all, a nasal fracture and hairline fracture of the zygomatic bone aka the cheek bone. This woman was struck across the face with quite some force to cause this damage. The breakage hadn't begun to heal. Maddy deduced the injuries were caused by the unsub. Question was, did it happen during the abduction or was it part of the torture.

"Do we have a tox screen back on Whethers yet?" Maddy asked Bryan.

Bryan pulled a stack of files from a pile on his desk. He thumbed through them and pulled one out and handed it to her. "What are you looking for?"

"You'll be the first to know when I find it." She pulled out the tox screen out of the jacket and skimmed through it. Hot Damn! Negative for Ketamine. Maddy called up Mitchell's x-ray and pulled her autopsy file. Mitchell had a hairline fracture to her carpus on both wrists. She pulled out her tox screen, she however tested positive for Ketamine. "Son of a bitch," she said out loud.

Bryan and Jamison looked up at spontaneously said, "What?"

Maddy was just about to explain when Jack walked into the room. "What you guys having a party without me?" He was trying to sound as of he was joking but Maddy caught the edge in his voice.

"Maddy's on to something and was just about to tell us," Bryan explained. He turned to Maddy. "Let's hear it."

Maddy turned her laptop around so they could see it. She pulled up Whether's x-rays and handed Bryan the autopsy report. "Tell me what you see on one but not the other."

Bryan looked it over and shook his head.

Jamison grabbed the file, his attention jumping back and forth from the report to the x-ray. "This woman has had her face manhandled." He pointed to the nasal and cheek fractures.

"We were also under the assumption that he used Ketamine on all our vics. But not this one. The only thing to determine is at what stage of the game he slapped her around. And we have to face the fact this poor woman suffered the full effects of the torture, unless she was blessed enough to pass out."

Maddy was animated with excitement at her discovery. Her eyes were sparkling like emeralds and her cheeks flushed. Jack had never seen her like this. She was beautiful.

Maddy flipped to Mitchell's x-ray. "Mitchell has fractures on both her wrists. She, however did test positive for Ketamine. Still we have to wonder when the fractures occurred."

"What about the others?" Jamison asked.

Maddy gave a light shrug, "Don't know about them yet, haven't gotten that far."

"How did this all this shit get missed in the autopsy reports?" Jamison was tapping the files on the corner of the desk.

Jack spoke up, "In simple terms the facilities here are not equipped to handle these type of autopsies. The bodies have been shipped to the DCI labs in Ankney where they should have been sent in the first place. We should get results back from there Monday or Tuesday."

"It's no fucking wonder you guys can't move forward with this investigation if you have to rely on shit like this!" Jamison got up and walked out of the room.

Maddy leaned back in her chair. "Wow."

Bryan laughed, "Wasn't that the same damn reaction I got from you yesterday?"

Maddy smiled sheepishly, "Well not quite like that. I blamed you."

Bryan stood up and tapped her on the head with a file folder. "You always do Minnie, you always do." He leaned over and whispered in her "I'm going to leave, talk to him."

"Asshole," she mumbled and when she looked up he was looking at her, grinning, "and yes this time I'm talking to you!"

Bryan threw his head back and laughed as he left the room.

Maddy straightened up the files on her desk, "How's going on your end Jack?" She forced a smile. She hated like hell she had to do that. She never thought she would feel this uncomfortable around him.

"Not as productive as in here obviously," he stated quietly.

"You want to talk?" she inquired.

He raised and eyebrow, "Are we allowed?"

Maddy laughed nervously. "Of course silly. You want to talk here, or go somewhere?"

"Care to go outside or is that where Mayland is?"

Maddy sighed and shook her head. "If you're coming into this with an attitude, I will pass."

"Okay, okay, I will cut the attitude. It's a big building, I'm sure we can find somewhere." He offered her his hand. She took it and allowed him to help her up. "How's the ankle doing?"

She flexed her foot for him. "Livable."

"Good, glad to hear it."

They walked the rest of the way to back entrance of the station in silence.

Maddy sat down on the steps. Jack sat down next to her.

"I hate this...tension between us. It doesn't feel right and I don't like it. I want things back the way they used to be," she uttered.

"You mean before I said I loved you?" Jack was looking down as he was wringing his hands.

"No, Jack, before you started getting all funny on me. The other night we spent together, it was nice, really nice. I felt we were starting get to know each other, the personal side. But ever since then, you're possessive, pushy, prying. We can't just sit and have a nice conversation. You are either forcing the issue of our feelings, or you are playing detective with my past. I don't like it, Jack. If I want you to know what happened to me I will tell you. Maybe I will, maybe I won't. Don't take it so personal. Regardless quit asking. Don't be pushing Bryan or Derek. Can't we just back up and take some of the pressure off? You say you love me, but Jack, how can you honestly say that if you don't know me?"

"Like Bryan does," Jack mumbled.

"Jesus Christ, Jack, get off Bryan's ass. He and I have a long complicated past, and it's not all bad. Not everything that has happened between he and I is bad. There was a lot of good—there is a lot of good. We are taking the time rediscovering that.

He has never said anything bad about you, never said I can't see you or do things with you. He's never forced the issue. He concentrates on what he thinks is important, his and my relationship. So quit blaming him.

I have deep feelings for you Jack, but just as much as you don't know me, I don't know you. We can't base being 'in love' on what we feel at the moment. You can't compare what we have to what Bryan and I have. Bryan and I have been through so much, our feelings are those which have been building for over a decade. And quit comparing yourself to Bryan, you are two totally different men, and that's a good thing. You can't expect our relationship to be like that when we are just beginning to discover each other." She put her hand on his knee. "Is any of this making sense without me sounding like a total bitch?"

Jack put his hand on hers. "Well, Mads, you didn't spare any words. I'm sorry I have been such an ass. The only thing I can say in my defense is that I let fear and insecurity get the best of me." He squeezed her hand. "I've never had feelings like this for a woman. It's new to me, and damn right scary. I'm afraid I am going to fuck everything up. I don't know what to say to you anymore, I don't know how to act...Everything that comes out of my mouth is the wrong thing. Us sitting out here is proof I am fucking everything up."

Maddy nudged him playfully with her knee. "If you fucked everything up, hon, we wouldn't be having this conversation. I just want you to go back to being my Jack. Mellow out, take it easy and enjoy the time we do spend together instead of forcing the issues. Just be yourself, Sweetie."

Maddy slid off the steps and stood on her knees between Jack's legs. She slid her hands up around his neck, leaning forward she kissed him slowly and gently. Jack's arms circled her waist and he pulled her closer. He returned her kiss, being careful not to push her for fear she would pull back. Maddy cautiously let the kiss deepen, feeling frighten of how she was feeling inside. They pulled apart together, letting their foreheads rest on each other both their breathing a little unsteady.

"When we kiss, I get all confused inside," Maddy confessed.

Jack softly ran his hands up and down her back. "Why?"

"Because it doesn't seem right for me to feel this way about two men. It makes me feel...like there is something wrong with me."

"Oh Mads," he pulled her close to him. "There's nothing wrong with you. Just a little screwy is all, but you've always been like that." He kissed the top of her head. "We'll be okay. I will back off and quit acting like a total jackass."

They stood up and turned to walk back in the building. Jack reached for her hand, "I just wanted to let you know, I am getting to know you—watching you working this case. Its fun to watch the way your mind works. You get on to something and your tenacious, like a pit bull," he laughed.

Maddy stepped down on his foot, with a little more force than necessary.

Jack stepped back, "Christ Maddy, it was complement,"

She stood and faced him with her hands on her hips. "Like a pit bull?"

"Oh shit!" He started laughing, "I'm sorry, I wasn't even thinking."

Jack followed Maddy into the squad room. Maddy and Bryan's eyes met and she gave a slight nod to which he nodded back. Maddy sat back down at her desk and flipped up the laptop ready to compare the other victim's skeletal remains.

Jack pulled up a chair. "I'm not real big on how you guys in the FBI going about investigating, but I am curious."

Bryan sat back in his chair and studied him, "And?"

"In my world, as small and insignificant as it is, detectives don't do things the way she does. I mean, I basically know what a profiler does, and what she has been doing doesn't fit that."

Andy came over and joined them. Maddy hadn't talked to him all day, she was glad to see him. "I want to hear this, too," he said.

Maddy sat back, her arms crossed, a smirk on her lips, "yeah I want to hear this, too."

Bryan chuckled, "Derek this is your department."

Derek scratched his chin, "Trying best how to explain this, but I will try. Normally the BAU sends out teams that have three to five profilers working up a profile together. Its kind of a think tank process because each member has the input of his or her perspective. The compilation of these observations go into establishing a profile of both the vic and the unsub. You get a broader vision; which is usually more accurate than what one profiler can do."

"With this case..." Derek shook his head, "Let's not go into that...but anyhow. What Maddy and Andy did yesterday with the file compilation and putting together board is part of her job. Since she didn't have others to give observations, she improvised and did a pretty good job. Things she has done based on what Bryan told me and what I have seen today, are not normally a profilers job. When Maddy gets immersed in a case, everything has to make sense to her. She operates on observation and logic, whether it be physical or psychological. She looks at things and sees holes in them she wants to know why. My understanding is she went to the morgue a couple of days ago because she wasn't satisfied with photos. By her going this extra step she made it possible for us to know enough about the manners of the mutilations she was able to identify things like what hand the unsub favors, direction of infliction, even down to what the unsub used to bind the vics. This goes to methodology. Because of her digging today we discovered that with each kill our unsub is progressing, becoming more polished and more comfortable at what he's doing. Is what Maddy is doing normal work for a profiler? No, but it is normal for Maddy. Does that help explain things?" Derek asked.

Jack smiled, "You don't have to tell me what's normal for Maddy."

Maddy stuck out her tongue, "I'm unique."

Maddy stretched and yawned, "Sorry...something I think that needs to be looked at, we need to find out the religious history of each vic." She turned to Derek, "Those are our blank boxes on the flow charts." She turned to Bryan, "Might I suggest Andy work on that."

"Also," Maddy pulled up a document on her screen and turned it for the others to see, "Based on this timeline, you will notice an escalation of time in between the abductions. As I have ben saying if our unsub holds to pattern we are looking at another woman being abducted this week. We've kept the majority of what we know out of the press so there is not that much info out there. But I'm not sure how the discovery of his dump sights is going to affect him. He doesn't know what we know. It could make him reckless or extremely cautious with the manner of abduction. We already know he is escalating with the need to further torture these women in order to get off. What he has been doing, it's not enough. Lord knows where he will dump a body now. Sure as hell not at a park."

Bryan took off his glasses and rubbed the area where they sat with his fingers. "What do you suggest we do?"

"Ideally catch the bastard, but realistically, based on what we have, he holds us captive too," she sighed.

Maddy closed the lid to her laptop. "Is it time to go home yet? I'm burnt out."

Bryan looked at his watch. It was 5:15. "Yeah, lets call it a day. Unless something comes up, take tomorrow off. We need time to freshen up our minds."

Jack stood up, "Anyone for stopping for a beer?"

The other agents piped up and were all for it. Derek decided to join them.

Jack turned to Maddy and Bryan. Maddy shook her head, "Sorry, not for me, I meant it when I said I was fried. I just want to go home, maybe get some horse therapy in."

"Me either," Bryan said. "I'm just going to grab a bite to eat and go to bed. But thanks for asking Jack. You guys go have fun."

Maddy took her time shutting down her computer and arranging her files. She messed around long enough that everyone but Bryan had left. She went over and stood beside his chair. "Are you really going to go back to the motel and sleep?"

"I would rather spend it with you, but understand if you need some peace and quiet. It won't kill me to spend the night alone," he sounded bummed.

Maddy slid on to his lap, wrapped her arms around him and kissed him softly, "I would rather you came home with me and spend the night alone...with me."

Bryan placed a hand on each side of her face forcing her lips open with his tongue. She moaned softly. "Is that a request or a command from her Highness?" he said in between breaths.

Maddy kissed up the side of his face, along his neck up to his ear and whispered in a husky voice, "It's a command."

Bryan groaned, "Your wish is my command, My Lady." He captured her mouth again with his. He ran his hand under her shirt, caressing her.

She pulled back slightly, "I don't think making love in the squad room is such a good idea," a mischeivious smile graced her lips. She leaned forward and playfulling biting his lips.

Bryan pulled back and took a very deep breath, letting it out slowly. "Damn Maddy, you are pure evil."

She snickered, "You think?"

He slid her off his lap, "I know, you vixen."

Maddy grabbed his hand, "Let's go home, Mickey. Same plan as yesterday?"

"Yep. Meet at the motel...unless you want to come in for an hour or so."

Maddy clammed up.

"What's the matter, Minnie?" He put his arm around her shoulder.

"Bryan, I can't go back to that motel room, not ever. Too much happened there, too much to hold us in the past. I hope you understand." She kissed him on the cheek.

"Perfectly understandable. I would rather wait and be with you...as you so sweetly put it...at home."

Maddy stopped off at a grocery store by the mall and picked up some steaks and a 12 pack of beer. She thought twice about buying him the beer, but it wasn't like he hadn't been drinking anyhow. So far he seemed to be handling it well and didn't get out of control...like he used to. There were those old doubts creeping back in. Would she ever be able to let go of this mistrust? She hoped for the sake of their future.

Maddy pulled into the Regency and parked beside Bryan's Suburban. She rolled down the window, took out her cell phone and called him to let him know she was out there. His phone went over to voice mail. Now that's odd. Wonder what's up with that? Several minutes later Bryan came through the lobby door, the phone still attached to his ear. When he looked up he smiled at her and hung up the phone.

Bryan threw his bag in the back, and slid in the front seat. "Shit, I forgot something. Give me just two minutes." He leaned over and kissed her cheek.

After Bryan had shut the door, Maddy noticed his cell phone had slipped out of his pocket and was lying on the seat. She reached out and touched it. Doubt and mistrust creeping back in. Who was he talking to? It would only take one little peek and she would know. Did she want to know? Yeah, to be quite honest she wanted to know. Was he still talking to Donna behind her back? Was this 'new' committed Bryan just another mind fuck that she was falling hook, line and sinker for? Just one peek...Maddy took a deep breath, her fingers tracing the outside of the phone. She glanced up and saw Bryan heading toward the car. Too late. Thank God.

Bryan had his hand behind his back and when he pulled it out in his hand was this huge bouquet of lilies of assorted colors—ivory, pink, coral, peach and yellow, all with speckles from the center out. Their scent flooded the passenger compartment, better than any car freshener could do. A big smile spread across her face. He remembered lilies were her favorite. She reached across the car and kissed him lovingly on the lips. Now she felt like shit for having doubted him. Yet that was still not saying she was wrong.

Bryan grinned at her, "They're tiger lilies." He leaned over and kissed her, "For my tiger."

He went to hook his seat belt. "What the hell?" He pulled out his cell phone from underneath him. "Must have fallen out," he said quietly and stuck it in his pocket.

Maddy put the car in gear and headed out on Highway 20. She took a deep breath, the scent of the lilies filling her lungs. She didn't know what was sweeter, the flowers themselves, or the way they smelled. They were intoxicating.

"Did you look?"

Bryan's voice pulled her out of her revere. "What?"

"My cell phone, did you look?"

She glanced over at him, "Huh?"

"Come on Maddy. It was lying here on the seat. I know you, you can't help yourself," he said patiently.

Maddy focused on the road ahead of her. "No, but I admit I was tempted."

"Why didn't you?"

Maddy took a deep breath, "Honestly?"

"No Maddy, tell me lie," he answered sarcasticly.

"You don't have to be an ass about it," she snapped. "I didn't look because I was afraid of what I might see."

"So you didn't not look because you trust me, but you didn't look out of fear," Bryan shook his head out of frustration. "Pull over."

"What?"

"Just pull over, please?" he was adament.

Maddy turned her blinker on and pulled off on the shoulder. "Okay, now what?"

Bryan pulled his phone out and pulled up the calls received screen and held it out to her.

"Bryan, no, you don't have to do this." She pushed his hand away.

"Yes, Maddy I do. Now look at it."

She took it in her hand and looked at the screen. There were no calls from Donna, only a couple from his son, and several from work. She unconsciously gave a sigh of relief. She hoped Bryan hadn't picked up on it. When she looked up she saw that he had.

"Now I want to show you something else." He took the phone back from her and pulled up the calls dialed. He handed her the phone.

At the top of the list was a phone call placed to Donna. Maddy felt like she was going to throw up. Why was he doing this to her? This was sick, cruel, and really fucked up. Maddy dropped the phone as of it were a redhot coal. She put her head down on the steering wheel and covered her head with her hands. "I can't believe I fell for this shit again," she cried.

"Maddy, sweetheart," he put his hand on her shoulder. She didn't even have the strength to fight him. "It's not what you're thinking. I wouldn't have shown you it if it were. I shouldn't have done it this way, I wasn't thinking. Please, now listen to me...I called her to make arrangements to pack all my things. Jeff is going over tomorrow to pick them up for me...so I never have to go back there, ever..." He held the phone out to her again, "Maddy, look, look at the call I made just before that one, please."

Maddy raised her head, her eyes stinging from mascara running into her eyes. She reached out, her hands trembling. The second call from the top was one placed to Jeff, his son. Maddy hit the okay button that revealed what the duration of the call was—twenty minutes. She went back up to the call to Donna and did the same thing—eight minutes.

Maddy released her seatbelt and got out of the car, slamming the door behind her. She walked to the far side of the car and leaned against it, crossing her arms across her waist. A hot wind whipped the loose strands of her hair across her face. She reached up with her hand and wiped the tears and mascara from under eyes. She stood there watching the heat radiating off the stocks of corn in the field beside the road. She was trying to clear her mind. Despite everything good that had been happening between them she had found it so easy to believe Bryan would rip her heart out again. What was that saying? He was taking steps to prove to her that he was genuine in his promise to her. Why he chose to tell her that way, she didn't know, but she did believe it wasn't his intent to hurt her.

She heard the car door open and then shut again. Bryan stood beside her leaning up against the car. "Do you forgive me?" he asked in a subdued tone.

She wiped her eyes again. "There's nothing to forgive."

Bryan gave a deep sigh, "Thinking back on it now, given our history, that was a really fucked up thing to do. I...I thought I was doing a good thing, being honest with you about it, showing you that I meant everything I said, and all I did was hurt you...again."

Maddy reached back and pulled the hair tie from her hair, letting the wind play total havoc with her long curls. She ran her fingers along her scalp loosening up her hair. "Its not you, Bryan, its me. I was so quick to judge, and that was so wrong of me." Her voice was unsteady. "Jesus, is this the way I am going to be the rest of my life? Always looking for the worst?"

Bryan moved in front of her and wrapped his arms tight around her. "We can do this Minnie. Things don't change overnight just because we want them to. It takes time and work. This just proves that I am still an insensitive ass doing things without thinking, some how thinking showing you that you were wrong was the right thing to do."

Maddy slid her arms around his waist. She laughed unsteadily, "People are going start looking at us funny." She tightened her hold on him. "Let's go home, Bryan."

He nuzzled his face to her ear, "You have no idea how sweet those words are to me, Maddy. Let's go home." He held her tight for a moment more and then let her go.

Before Maddy got back in the car, she removed her badge from her belt and took off her holster. She gave her gun to Bryan to lock in the glove compartment. She slid into the seat, buckled up and put the car in gear.

They drove in silence for a few minutes before Maddy spoke. "Does Jeff know what is going on?" she asked tentatively.

"Sort of," Bryan answered. "I have a lot of explaining to do. I want to sit down with him, tell him about us—everything about us and why I am doing the things I am."

"How well do you think that will go over, I mean with his mother and all?"

"Well I know he is tickled pink I left Donna. I haven't been with his mother in a very long time, so its not like I am leaving her for you. He's 22 years old. I hope he is mature enough to understand its time for his dad to do what is right for him. Doubt it, but I can only try."

"How was Donna?" Like she really cared.

"Oh we went through tears, the bitching, the accusations and the poor me's, but you know, it does effect me anymore like it used to. It just doesn't matter anymore," he responded flatly.

Maddy just nodded in acknowledgement. She still felt a knot in the pit of her stomach every time she thought about Donna and Bryan together. She shook it off. She reached out for his hand.

He took it and brought it to his lips and then to his cheek. "Maddy..."

"What hon, what's the matter?" she asked with concern.

He shook his head while still holding her hand to his face. "Nothing Minnie, I just love you so much, I can't believe that there's actually a chance you will really be mine." He was all choked up.

Maddy glanced quickly over at him. She thought about how he was when he first got here, cocky, so self-assured, arrogant, conceited, still playing his control games. Then she thought about this man who was sitting beside her. It was almost as if she could smell a hint of desperation. Desperate for what? She had been his constant companion almost since his arrival. She really noticed the change a couple of nights ago when he walked out on her and then came back. Whatever happened or went through his head while he was out made the change. She just prayed that he knew and understood what he was doing. She wished she could ask him, but he seemed to be in his own world at the moment and didn't appear to be too confident in it.

"So what do you think of Derek?" Bryan asked her out of the blue.

"I like him," she smiled softly. "He agrees with almost everything I say."

"I never would have taken you to go for a yes man," he laughed.

"Oh, I would never consider him to be a yes man. I think he would chew my ass in heartbeat if it were called for. He has the one thing you and I no longer have I'm afraid...the edge."

Bryan looked over at her. "Do you really not remember him, Maddy? At all?"

Maddy shook her head. "No, and I've tried. Which got me wondering how much from that time frame have I blocked out. I mean after we talked last night, baby, I really don't remember what went on around me. I'm sorry I hurt you by shutting you out, but try as I might I can't remember even being aware of you around me. It's like during that whole time frame I was surrounded in a shroud."

Bryan was trying to be careful not to press her, but he thought maybe this could help move her in the right direction, bring her to the point of remembering everything, the good, the bad...and her private hell. "If I get to asking you things that are out of bounds, let me know okay? Can you remember when your life... became more focused?"

"It wasn't until after I resigned. Which by the way, how the hell did I get from a resignation to a deactivation?" she demanded.

Bryan smiled smugly. "I intercepted your paper work and let's just say I modified it. I had hoped someday you would come back. How do you think you were able to access records all these years?"

"That I knew you had something to do with. I just figured it was your way of keeping tabs on me."

He smiled, "It helped some, but you used it so seldom and when you did, you were in and out before I could get too much of a trace on you. The longest I clocked you on it was this past week downloading those searches."

"If I were to allow myself to...work through the past...and I am not saying I am, how would I do it?" she asked unsteadily.

Bryan studied her. He could almost smell the fear in her. "I think that is something we would need to discuss with your psychiatrist and your therapist." He put his hand on her leg. "Given the psychological break you experienced, in my honest opinion, Maddy, it would be too dangerous to do it any other way. I can't take the chance of loosing you again, Minnie."

Maddy smiled weakly at him. "I thought I was just fine living the way I have been. It was safe. Ace reporter by day, recluse by night. Guess some might say I have a spilt personality. I believed that if I kept my worlds apart, I could keep myself from being put at risk. With the exception of Jessie, Jack was the closest thing I had to a friend, except Chief, of course. Jack and I were fine for the longest time. I set up the ground rules and he never pushed....until this last time."

Bryan twisted his back in his seat to stretch. "What changed?"

"I don't know. When we were at Vanessa's house it was just like old times. He gave me the info to put together a story and then before I could even get one written its on the damn 6:00 news. I was pissed and didn't wait to let him know. I went off on him and then hung up on him. Which was nothing really out of the ordinary in our relationship. We would usually just let it ride and be fine the next time we saw each other. Except this time he calls me and apologizes, worried that I was pissed at him. It was after that he started acting different." Maddy recalled as she focused on the road.

Bryan chuckled, "And you didn't?"

"Shut up!" She flicked him with her fingers. "He started it. We went to lunch that next day, and he started saying shit, crossing the lines, and then he actually kissed me. He got the call that they found the first body and I talked him in to letting me tag along. He said fine but I had to stay in the car," she laughed. "No, he gave me a direct order to stay in the car."

"And of course you didn't."

She grimaced, "Of course not, I found a clearance pass in his car and I crashed the scene. He was so pissed he had me police escorted back to my car. Man on man was he pissed. I have never had him that angry with me before. Then I had to call him up that night to bring me home because I was too drunk to drive. He was on a date with Stella and she wasn't pleased that he had to drive me home. He breached my line between work and personal life, out of necessity mind you, but the damage was done. He ended staying until Sunday. I set up rules, no conversations about personal stuff and no sex."

"So you spent the whole weekend playing cuddle on the couch?" Bryan joked.

"Hell no! I made him work his ass off helping me muck stalls, moving hay and stuff like that. He got the call early Sunday morning that the FBI was coming in and he left. Little did I know it was you."

Bryan pinched her playfully on her leg. "You going to work my ass off tomorrow?"

She grinned mischeiviously. "In more ways than one," she winked at him.

Maddy pulled into her lane and left the car parked outside. Bryan grabbed her flowers and she carried in the groceries. The dogs darted in between their legs. Rufus gave Bryan a parting gift nipping him on his leg.

"Son of bitch that rat has teeth for such a little dog!"

"He says you stink," Maddy laughed. "Go take a shower and I will run to the car and grab your bag."

Bryan glared at the little Yorkie and snapped at him. Rufus responded in kind by chasing him into the bathroom.

When Maddy returned she opened the bathroom door and slid in his bag. She gathered the laundry that had piled up and stuck it in the washer not thinking about Bryan taking a shower. She heard him shriek and yelled she was sorry, snickering the whole time. A cold shower would never be a bad thing for that man.

Maddy glanced at the wall clock in the kitchen. It was almost 7:15, to late for a ride tonight. She went out and started the grill, and wrapped a couple of baked potatoes and stuck them in the microwave. She pulled a tossed salad mix from the fridge and divided it between two bowls. She seasoned the steaks and dashed out to throw them on the grill.

She sat on the steps for few minutes taking the summer evening. It was still warm, the hot summer breeze was licking the tree leaves. She could hear the buzzing sound of the cicadas reverberating in her walnut tree several feet away. In the distance she saw a cloud of dust rolling through the pasture and heard the sound of thundering hooves. Lily was out in the lead and Buddy bringing up the rear. Her herd. She thought of Socks left to whistfully watch the adult horses running in the wind and thought perhaps in the morning she'd rotate them so he could kick up his heels. Maybe she and Bryan could walk down later and give them some treats.

Maddy rose and turned the steaks. When she sat back down she noticed Bryan watching her through screen. She pretended not to notice just to see what he would do.

When she pulled the steaks off he was waiting at the door for her. He had set the table for them, put out the salad, bottles of dressing, pulled the potatoes out and put the sour cream and butter on the table. "Damn," she remarked, "I could get used to this." She set the steaks on the table. "Medium rare right?"

He wrapped his arms around her from behind, leaning his chin on the top of her head. "mmmhmmm." He turned her in his arms and leaned down to kiss her upturned face. His lips teased hers playfully and until the kiss deepened to the point she couldn't breath. He was getting real good at having the ability to take her breath away.

"The steaks," she murmured between kisses. " I'm hungry."

Bryan kissed a path down her neck and behind her ear, "Me too...."

13

Maddy was resting her head quietly on Bryan's bare chest when the call came in. He reached over, and looked at the caller ID. It was Derek. "Hey, thought I said take the night off," he said with some irritation.

"You need to get in here...now. Maddy there with you?"

Bryan picked up on the urgency of Derek's voice. "Yeah, she's right here. What's going on?"

"We have a failed abduction, and it's not pretty, just get here ASAP," Derek gave him the address and hung up.

Bryan told Maddy what little he knew as they quickly threw on their clothing. Within minutes they were out the door on their way to the city.

Maddy decided to let Bryan drive. "Failed abduction? You mean we could actually have a witness?"

Bryan smiled weakly, "Yeah one that doesn't chew on my leg."

"How could our unsub fuck up like this? He's become so polished at what he does, I just don't get it."

"He must feel we're closing in on him," Bryan turned on the lights as the daylight was quickly waning.

"I don't think so, he thinks he's too smart for us. Something unexpected must have happened. Damn, I wish I knew more details." She was frustrated.

"We will soon enough I guess. When's the last time you worked an active crime scene?"

"You mean one that I was allowed to?" she asked.

He gave her a look.

"Oh, that kind, not in a long time. Jack only let me see the ones after CSU had been through and that wasn't often. Mostly he just gave me pictures."

"You up to it?"

"Oh hell yeah!"

Bryan shook his head. "You seem a little too enthused for my taste."

She smiled, "Don't worry about it. I'll be fine. I still know the procedures."

Although darkness had crept over the city, emergency vehicle lights lit up Summit Street. This was an older part of town with houses ranging from single-family units, apartment building and converted duplexes. The home they pulled up to was an older two-story stucco home. The house was a blaze with lights. Police cars, the coroner's wagon, an ambulance, CSU, Jack's Impala and 2 of the FBI Suburban's blocked off the streets. Uniformed officers kept onlookers at bay. Crime scene tape had already roped off the scene.

Jack met them at the street. "We got two bodies, one male, one female, definite signs of a struggle," Jack reported walking quickly to keep up with them.

Derek met them at the door with his hand held up halting them. "Bryan, it might be best if Maddy sat this one out."

Jack watched as Bryan and Derek exchanged looks, their eyes apparently communicating more than their mouths were.

"Bullshit!" Maddy protested. "I can handle it, besides you damn well know I am better at crime scenes than either one of you. What's the status?"

"Holding back CSU until you guys got here, coroner pronounced but no exam yet."

Maddy pulled out her latex gloves and slipped them on. She stood up against Derek, feeling insignificant next to his towering stature. She met him eye to eye and didn't flinch. "Are you going to let me do my job?" she inquired.

She watched as Derek looked at Bryan, questioning if he should. Maddy turned to Bryan. He nodded his consent. "This is bullshit," Maddy said as pushed Derek aside.

As soon as Maddy entered the room she was struck by acrid metallic smell of blood. Whoa, she stepped back. She took a deep breath. Okay she could do this.

Bryan walked in behind her, put his hand on her shoulder, "Let's do a walk through first." She nodded silently and followed him.

She had entered the foyer coming through the front door. This led into a big open living room, which was in disarray. Maddy scanned the room, looking for details. The room had been originally dimly lit, but blinding lights had been set for the investigation. A couch and a recliner were the center focus. A throw rug, which had lain in front of the couch lay in a twisted state, evidence of a foot peeking out from the end. Just past that she saw an end table smashed against the hard wood floor, a busted lamp close to it. She inched her way over see who the foot belonged to. A man, appearing to be in his early thirties, lay sprawled out face up at the base of the couch. He looked to be about 5'8", 150 pounds, sandy brown hair. She moved closer to look at him. She looked at his face; his glazed eyes stared back at her. Maddy knelt down and put her hand over his lids and closed them.

"Maddy!" Bryan snapped. Her head snapped up to find him staring at her.

"Christ, go back to being a damn FBI agent and still gotta follow the no touchy rule," she grumbled.

Bryan eyed her confused, "Huh?"

Jack smiled and whispered, "I'll fill you in later."

Just because Bryan yelled at her didn't stop her from her examination. She was never one to be a conformist, as long she didn't violate any rules she felt she should be able to do her own thing.

Maddy squatted down by the body again. A large bloodstain appeared just below the man's sternum. She resituated herself so she was able to slightly lift up on the man's shirt to view the wound. Apparent stab wound, approximately an inch in diameter. She continued to study him. Just below his left eye was a reddish abrasion with some light bruising. She looked at his knuckles, no defensive wounds. This was confusing. Was he co-cocked and then stabbed? If so the unsub surprised him, nailed him, then stabbed him, but this didn't make sense. She got on her hands and knees and looked around, nothing but a few dust bunnies.

She got up and looked around the room again, nothing really caught her eye.

Maddy poked her head into the kitchen where Bryan, Derek and Jack were standing around a body. "Why are we assuming this is connected to our unsub?"

Bryan stepped back. "See for yourself."

Maddy stepped in and looked down at the body. Her head pulled back, her eyes flew wide open. "Holy shit!"

A blonde woman, looked to be in her late twenties, 5'6", maybe just shy of 130 lay at her feet was laying face up, pale blue eyes wide open, her lips slightly parted. Her blouse was cut away from her body exposing her torso for full view. And there it was, the signature cross incision, her throat slashed. Clutched in one hand, or maybe she should say wrapped around her left hand was a rosary. She had bled out; the crimson fluid seeped to all angles of the kitchen. Maddy wasn't so eager to closely examine this victim. She would wait for the photos on this one.

"How do you suppose he did this without a struggle? Slit her throat first?" Jack asked.

"No," she studied the body from a distance. "His whole MO revolves around the ritual. He has to follow it with as little of deviation as possible. Let's just say his normal scenario is to show up at the vic's door. She knows him and lets him in. He convinces her to leave with him or somehow makes her leave using little force as possible. He takes her to wherever and does whatever to her and disposes the body by completing the burial."

"This time his planning was faulty. Either he didn't know boyfriend was home or boyfriend arrived prior to departure. What I want to know where was our vic when our unsub was disposing of the boyfriend? Why didn't she run?

"Because he was in the act of butchering her," Jack offered.

Maddy shook her head, "If our unsub had that much access to or vic he would have had her out of here by then. The only reason he did this," she waved her hand across the scene, "was because he was cornered."

"Why not just flea then?"

Maddy knelt down, picked up the victim's hand and examined her fingers and nails, "Because she is one of the chosen ones," her voice sounding distant. "We've got defensive wounds here. Her knuckles are scraped up." She turned the woman palms face up reveal small shallow cuts. "And she got a piece of our unsub, look at her nails." Maddy ran her hand under the victim's head and discovered a nasty contusion on her backside. "He either knocked her out or she hit her head falling. But either way she had to be conscious when he did his thing. She has to be aware for him to feel complete in his ritual. He wouldn't do it otherwise."

Maddy squatted down, but not too close to the body and scanned the room. She ran her hand along the under lip of the dishwasher until her finger hit something. "Come to mama," she said out loud.

She stood up with a syringe neatly pinched between two fingers. "I am guessing Kedamine and if we are lucky" she smiled, "fingerprints!" She asked for an evidence bag and dropped it in then handed it Bryan.

Maddy was so intent on studying the room she hadn't realized she backed into blood spillage. Her foot came down and slid out from underneath her landing her flat on her back in a pool of blood. Her head thumped against the floor. A bright flash of white exploded in her brain. She blinked trying to focus, but the white light remained until it filled with color, the color of burgundy wine—

Maddy was exhausted yet excited she was finally returning home after having been out in the field for two weeks. She pulled her SUV into her driveway. She had expected to see Lexi and Scotty waiting on the steps for her like they always did when they knew she was coming home. But the steps were barren, no children to greet her. As she walked up the steps she could hear Reggie, their border collie howling from somewhere deep in the house. Maddy started to feel a dull ache in the pit of her stomach. Something wasn't as it should be.

She took out her keys and when she went to put them in the door, it creaked open. Out of pure instinct she pulled her Glock from her holster and took on the defensive stance. The thought never entered her mind one of the kids just might have left the door open. They knew better. Maddy entered the house, her senses keen and vigilant. Except for the barking of the dog, the house was ominously quiet. When she called out hello, it echoed throughout. She slipped quietly into the kitchen.

A pair of feet extended out just past the kitchen island. Maddy rushed to her housekeepers aid only to find the elderly woman lying in a large puddle of crimson blood. Blood spatter dotted the cupboard doors like someone had taken a paintbrush and flung it across the room. Her hand trembling, she felt for a pulse. Margie's body was still very warm. She hadn't been gone long. She turned her over to find a butcher knife protruding from her chest. The front her body was drenched in blood. Maddy backed up in horror, her mind racing. Oh my God, where were her babies. As if on cue a bloodcurdling scream resonated from upstairs. Her heart was pounding and felt as if it would burst from her chest. Maddy rose quickly and went to run, but her feet slipped out from under her as they made contact with the pool of blood and fell face first in it. She crawled on her hands and knees until she reached the carpeted area, rose to her feet and took the hardwood steps two at a time. Her wet shoes slipped at the top of the step sending her backwards jarring her elbow and hitting her head on the wall.

Maddy couldn't feel the pain messages her body was sending her, she could only hear the terror filled cries of her daughter. She followed the screams to her children's playroom. Of all the horror she had witnessed in her life, nothing could prepare her for what she would suffer when she stumbled into it.

Scotty's tiny form was slumped over some stuffed toys. A tall man dressed in a black hooded jacket stood over Lexi wielding a large hunting knife. He had her by her hair, shaking her around like she was nothing but a mere ragdoll.

Maddy screamed freeze. The man's eyes made contact with Maddy's. He smiled at her then plunged the knife in to Lexi's little body. Maddy emptied all thirteen rounds into the man's chest.

It only took seconds, but seemed like an eternity for her to reach her children. She turned Scotty's lifeless body over. He was completely immersed in blood. Each time he struggled to take a breath, a gurgling sound accompanied it.

"No! No! No!" Maddy cried out in anguish. She reached for her daughter and covered the gaping in wound in her chest with her hand, tying in vain to stop the bleeding. The blood seeped heavily out between her fingers. Lexi was softly crying, whispering mommy. She held her babies, telling them mommy was there, everything was going to be all right. Maddy could no longer hear Scotty. She shook him. "Come baby, you got to wake up...Scotty, Mommy needs you to wake up." When she looked into his face, she saw it; the light had gone out of his eyes.

"Mommy, " Lexi whispered. "It's okay," every breath was labored.

"Shhhhh Lexi, save your strength," she pleaded, tears spilling down her cheeks.

Lexi coughed, blood spewing from her mouth. "We love you," she rasped and went still.

She cradled them in her arms, cursing God. That day her children died...and Maddy died with them.

Maddy gasped and coughed, the tract lighting above her coming into focus. All these voices. "Maddy...Maddy? Come girl. Jack grab her on that side." She became aware she was being lifted to her feet. What were they doing, don't help me, she cried from within, my babies, save my babies.

Maddy put her hands up to block them from touching her anymore. She didn't speak; she shook her head back and forth muttering, "no...no...no."

"We need to get her out of her before she contaminates the scene. Jack, take her out to the ambulance and have her checked out. She's probably just stunned." Bryan instructed with some concern in his voice. She wasn't looking too good. He had no clue.

Jack scooped her up and carried her outside out of the taped off area. He set her on her feet to see if he could get some help for her. When he turned around, she was gone. "Maddy...Maddy?" he yelled. "Son of bitch, girl, where are you at now?"

Jack ran back in the house, frantically looking around. He popped his head into the kitchen, "Did she come back in here?"

Bryan detected the panic in Jack's voice. "How the hell did you loose her? You just had her."

Maddy wandered around looking for a place to collapse, somewhere away from all these damn lights. She found a large oak tree in a secluded place, not dark enough but would do. She leaned against the tree and sunk down to the ground. She brought her knees up to her chest, wrapped her arms around them and buried her head deep within them. The blood, all that blood. She couldn't save them. She didn't try hard enough. The screaming, her little girl screaming for her life. Maddy tightly closed her eyes and covered her ears to stop the screaming.

When Jack found her, Maddy was sitting below a tree, a curled up tight, her body was rocking back and forth, trembling, and it was like she chanting, she kept repeating no, no, no over and over again, but it was barely a whisper. Jack knelt down by her, "Maddy, honey, what's the matter?" He tried to put his arm around her and was surprised at how rigid her body was. He tried to get her to look up at him, but she kept her face down, muttering no. What was wrong with her, he was scared shitless and didn't know what to do. He got on the radio, "Bryan, you need to get out here."

"Give me a minute," Bryan answered back.

"No not in a God damn minute—NOW!" he screamed into the radio.

"Where the hell are you?" Bryan flew out the front door, Derek on his tail.

"Two houses down, back yard, get here fast!" He was in a panic. He was at a loss. He wanted to help her but he didn't know, was it from hitting her head?

Jack heard footsteps running toward them, "Over here!"

Bryan stopped in his tracks when he saw Maddy. She was covered in blood, rocking back and forth. "Oh sweet Jesus, Maddy..."

Derek slammed his radio to the ground, "God damn it! I knew this was a bad idea, I knew it. She had no business in there."

"Derek, shut the fuck up, it wasn't the crime scene it was the fall in the blood—the blood all over her. Now you going to keep bitching or are you going to help me?" Bryan slid down the tree next to Maddy. He looked up at Derek, "Get the other agents and DCI to secure the crime scene and turn it over to CSU. Make sure DCI stays with it all the way through. I don't want any local fuckups."

If Jack weren't so frightened over Maddy he would have taken offense. "What do you want me to do?"

"We need to get her out of these clothes. See if CSU has an extra jumper, hurry."

Jack did as he was told and went in search of clothing for Maddy. His mind of was in frenzy.

Bryan put his arm around Maddy, trying to hold her, but she wouldn't budge, just continued rocking.

Derek returned. "It's almost like watching the whole thing all over again."

"No, this time we win," Bryan countered frantically. "Help me lift her on to my lap."

Derek had no problem picking her up and sitting her on Bryan's lap. Bryan repeatedly rubbed her shoulders.

Jack returned with a pair of sweat pants and a shirt. "Sorry, no jumpers."

"Its okay," Bryan mumbled as he continued to touch her, touching her back, her arms. She needed to feel the human touch. Bryan buried his face in her hair, "Come on Baby, hang on to me baby, don't let go. I got ya. Come on Maddy, it's safe, it over, it's in the past. Don't leave, God don't leave me again, Maddy, not when I just found you again. Come on sweetheart, come back to me." Tears streamed down Byran's cheeks, his voice choked up in agony in his throat. "Please Lord, I'm begging you, don't take her from again."

Derek and Jack stood back and observed. Jack turned to Derek, "This time I'm not asking, I am demanding you tell me what the fuck is going on," he was angry and fed up. Enough of this bullshit, his Mads, his dear friend Maddy had gone off the deep end and he wanted to know why. This all centered a round the great secret of the past and the past was now.

"Just wait, I will tell you. We need to get her through this, if it's not too late," Derek replied with the urgency in his voice.

Maddy felt like she was locked in her own mind, a broken film reel playing over and over again so that was all she could see, all she could hear, smell, and taste. She was all alone in this prison, again. Somewhere in the distance she heard something, it was calling out to her, begging her to come back, a familiar voice...who was it...calling...Maddy slowly lifted her head. She couldn't focus but the voice...was strong and pulled her to it like a beacon on the lost sea.

Bryan saw her beautiful eyes; they held the faintest hint of recognition. He gently cupped her face in his hands, focusing on her eyes. "That's it Maddy, keep fighting your way back. I am so here for you Minnie. I'm not leaving you."

The face began to take shape with the voice. She blinked her eyes, and shook her head. Her hands trembling, she reached out to touch his face. "Bry.... an, Bryan?..."

Bryan broke down, "Sweet Jesus, thank God." He pulled her close and kissed the top of her head.

Maddy's focus was still not with him, she hadn't totally connected. Her voice quivered to the point it was hard to discern her words. "They're dead, my babies are dead. If I hadn't slipped on the blood, I could have saved them." She broke into sobs, "I killed my babies."

Bryan wrapped his arms around her as she buried her face in his chest. "No sweetie, you didn't kill them. That monster did. Scotty and Lexi, they are safe now sweetie. You are safe."

Jack watched what had just transpired. Maddy had been pushed past the point of oblivion by something that set her off tonight. Bryan had mentioned something about the fall in the blood, then Maddy said something to effect if she hadn't fallen she could have save her babies. She had been gone, and Bryan had pulled her back from it. His love brought her back. Everyone had been telling him and he refused to see it, Bryan and Maddy were ultimately supposed to be together, they were meant to be. Bryan truly was the protector of her soul. Jack knew Maddy cared about him, but he could see what these two had and he couldn't nor wanted to compete with it. He would be there for her, share a moment if she desired, he would never stop loving her, but he would stop pushing her.

Derek grabbed Jack gently by his arm. "Come over here so we are out of ear shot, I don't want either one of them to hear us."

Jack followed and they both sat down on the curb. Jack pulled out a cigarette and offered one to Derek. Derek laughed, "with a body like this you think I would smoke?"

"Anyhow you want to know, and given what you just witnessed I will tell as much as I feel comfortable with. Back about nine years ago Maddy had just come back from being out in the field. She had a live-in lady staying with her two children, Scotty, age 3 and Lexi age 7"

The kids in the white SUV, Jack thought.

"Maddy walked in on a home evasion. We don't know the details because she has never been able to talk about it. Bryan had been planning to stop by to see her and the kids. When he got there he found her in the kids' room, the perp shot dead. She was sitting on the floor rocking her two dead children, all of them soaked in blood. We figured this man bludgeoned her children with a knife before her eyes before she could get close enough to them. She unloaded her Glock on him. What you just saw there, happened to her then, except she didn't come out of it, never totally. Byran couldn't touch her. He lost her to it. Eventually she closed up that part of her life and she moved on, leaving that part buried and Bryan pretty much with it. "

"My God," Jack whispered. No wonder she didn't want to share this with anyone, she didn't want to relive it. She didn't have worry about it with Bryan and apparently with Derek because they knew, and she never had to talk about it.

"Now what? Does she need to go to the hospital?"

"Don't know, that's Bryan's call."

Derek went in knelt down beside Bryan. "What do you want to do here? Do you feel she should be hospitalized?"

"She's no threat to anyone or herself. I just need to ride this out with her. If you don't mind I am going to take her home. Help me slip these bloody clothes off and put these sweats on.

Maddy let the two men change her into blood free clothing. Bryan carried her to her car and slid her into the front seat reclining it back as far as it would go. Derek came over with a blanket and a bottle of pills from the ambulance. "What's that?" Bryan asked.

"Ativan and some ambein. She gets too agitated give her the ativan first. If she just needs to sleep give her the ambien, but she needs to numb out for a little while.

Derek covered her up with the blanket and tucked her in. He touched her shoulder lightly. Maddy was turned to the driver's side, zoned off into space. He felt for her, he really did. He prayed this was finally going to be over for her.

He turned to Bryan, "don't worry about coming in tomorrow, get her better and get her stable. She can't come back the way she is. I will stay in touch. And oh you really should talk to Jack when you got time. That kid is really shaken up. I told him the basics but really didn't give him much for answers, but actually he didn't ask."

"Give me one of the ativan," Bryan held out his hand.

He took it and tapped Maddy on the shoulder. "Take this Maddy, I don't have any water...sorry."

Maddy did as she was ordered, mindlessly put the pill on her tongue and swallowed. She didn't ask what it was—she didn't care. She was trying to numb her mind—trying to slip away again. She felt Bryan tuck the blanket back up around her and then shut the car door.

Bryan turned back to Derek. "Tell Parker he can stop out later unless you need him here. I want to get this all behind us. I need to get her home before she crawls back in her shell. This is not the way I wanted to do this. She and I, we talked about it, we were going to get professional help."

Derek put his hand on his shoulder, "Then maybe that's where she needs to be, Bryan. You are not really qualified to deal with this."

"No!" Bryan said angrily. "I can do this!"

Derek shrugged his shoulders, "And if you can't?"

"I can—I have to. I'm not leaving her out there this time." Bryan slid into the driver's side and slammed the door.

Maddy lay quietly back in the seat. At first Bryan couldn't even tell if she was awake until a hand crept out from beneath the blanket and touched his arm. He glanced over at her face and saw her eyes fixed on his face. He gently touched her fingers, stroking them, and smiled softly.

When she spoke her voice was but a weak whisper, "I love you, Bryan. Don't let me go...please."

He squeezed her fingers, "Never Minnie. I can't"

Maddy closed her eyes and let the drug induced sleep take her.

When they returned back at the house, Bryan scooped her out the car and carried her into the house, took her to her own bed and laid her down. He looked around the room and found a throw blanket draped over an old wooden rocker. He covered it loosely around her body. She stirred. He sat down on the edge of the bed, stroking her hair.

Her eyes opened. "Hold me," she whispered.

Bryan crawled on the bed and held her from behind, his arms wrapped tightly around her, his face nuzzled in her neck.

Maddy intertwined her arms with his hands were positioned over her heart. "It's not over yet, is it?"

He kissed her neck, "No, you need to tell me what happened, all of it and then we go from there. The floodgates are open. We will get through this, Minnie, together."

"You know it will never be over...not for me."

"No, kiddo, it won't, but you will able to grieve, you will be able to heal, no more hiding, no more demons." He listened as her breathing had become steady. Sleep had taken her.

Bryan had lost track of how long he had been holding Maddy. He had dozed off and was awaken by the frantic barking of two little loud-mouthed dogs. He quickly slid off the bed and pulled the door shut. He kept telling the dogs to shut up and he led them to the kitchen. He opened the door to throw their hairy asses out the door when he found Jack standing on the steps. "Hey...Jack, come on in." He held the door open for him.

Jack stepped inside. "Jamison said you said it was okay for me to come. How is she? Can I see her?"

"She's resting, but you can take a peek," Bryan led Jack to Maddy's bedroom and quietly opened the door.

Jack peered in and saw Maddy's small form curled up in the big bed. Bryan put his fingers to his lips and shook his head.

They returned to the living room where Bryan offered Jack a seat. He went to kitchen, then returned with two glasses of water handing one to Jack. "Thanks. You seem pretty comfortable here. How long have you been staying here?"

Bryan took a drink. "Last night was the first time. Is that why you're here, an inquisition?"

Jack set his glass down on a coaster. "No, sorry...Is she going to be okay? What happened?"

"I understand Derek told you what happened with the home invasion, how she walked in on it, saw her children get murdered, how I found her lying in a pool of her children's blood holding them while they died in her arms?" His voice was pained and he made no attempt to make eye contact with Jack.

"Yeah, more or less, but how did she get...to be like she is?"

"When I found her, she was catatonic. She was hospitalized where she came out of it, but she would never talk about. She never gave us the details of what happened. Her coping mechanism was to wipe it out. She held it deep inside. She pushed away anyone who was close to her, me being one of those people. To an outsider, she gave the illusion of being a functional human being and was allowed to return back to work. She wasn't the same Maddy. Maddy was once high-spirited, edgy, clever, on the ball, never afraid to dive right into a case—our fire fox. She became distant, detached; any attempt for someone to reach her or get close to, she shut them down.

As for myself, I couldn't take it anymore and abandoned her, tried to start a new life. I transferred out of the unit. Eventually working the BAU got to be more than she handle and she left.

She made a career change to a reporter, jumping from paper to paper until she landed here. She told me herself, she learned to separate..."

"Career life from personal life and never the two shall meet," Jack finished for him. "But she's not how you describe her. For the duration I have known her, until recently, when I worked with her, she was—I mean is, smart, funny, quirky, keen sense of sniffing out the truth and not afraid to write about it. Everybody loves her...with the exception of the people she exposed. She really is a good investigative reporter."

"And how much did she tell you about herself, personally?"

"Again until recently, nothing. She kept her distance," Jack replied reluctantly.

"Exactly, as long as she had controlled of her personal life, she had control of maintaining her choice of not dealing with the past. Her being able to escape here at her home, she didn't have to fight to keep the wall up. She could be herself," Bryan explained.

"And you always watched out for her, even from a distance?" Jack inquired.

"I tried, I couldn't be a part of her life, I was part of that which she needed block out, and I understood, despite my feelings for her I needed to let her go."

Jack watched the multitude of expressions that crossed Bryan's face, gaining an understanding of this man. Was this why Maddy had feared Bryan like she did? "What about what happened a couple of years ago? You hurt her badly and it didn't sound it like it hand anything to do with her past."

"I imagine what she told you was totally the truth. I was having a major personal crisis, she fell victim to a sick son of bitch, yours truly. It all just reaffirmed in her mind that my goal in life was to control and destroy her."

Maddy's eyes fluttered open. A sharp pain went through her heart. She hadn't forgotten the pain of reliving the nightmare. But she was here, thinking, not lost. Maddy could hear the muffled sound of voices in her living room. She sat up in the bed and rose to stand and then had to sit back because she felt woozy. She faintly remembered Bryan making her take something. She rose again, but this time slowly. She walked out of room slowly, reaching out to objects around her to help steady herself. She could see that the lamps dimly lighting up the living room.

Bryan stood when he saw her standing in the doorway. He rushed to her side to help her. "Maddy you should be lying down."

Maddy allowed him to let her lean on him. "Fine, let me lay on you."

Bryan lifted her up and carried her to the couch where he gently lowered her to the cushion. He sat down beside her. She turned her body so she could rest her head on his chest and he wrapped his arms around her holding her.

She lifted her hand and waved over her shoulder at Jack, "Hi Jack." Her voice was subdued.

"Hey Mad's," he responded softly. He regarded the two of them sitting on the couch. Maddy was clinging to Bryan as if she were holding on for dear life, Bryan's arms had protectively enfolded around her like he would never let anything near her, anything that would hurt her anymore than she had been. He had seen them together at the crime scene, seeing them like this just confirmed what he already knew. These two really did need to be together.

Maddy's face felt good on Bryan's chest. The smell the faint hint of soap and laundry detergent radiated from his body. No Polo, she smiled faintly. She felt the rise and fall of his chest, his arms locked around her body. She felt safe. "What are you guys doing?" Her voice was so faint; it was hardly audible.

Bryan stroked her hair softly. "Talking about you."

"Uhuh, good I hope," she snuggled closer to Bryan. Her body was shivering.

Jack slipped into her room and grabbed the throw blanket and returned, covering her up. Maddy murmured a thank you.

"I was filling Jack in...on everything. He has to know, kiddo, if he is going to help us."

Maddy whimpered, "No...please," she protested.

Bryan took her chin and guided her to look at him. Her eyes were misty with unshed tears, her lips trembled. "Maddy, Jack is an important part of your life, we need him to understand so he can help you work through this. Anyone who touches your life the way he has, you need to let him in." He kissed her forehead. "Understand?"

"I feel raw, exposed, like nothing is my own." A tear slid down her cheek. "Make it go away, Bryan, make it go away..." She buried her face in his chest again.

He rested his chin on the top of her head, "But you are feeling, sweetie. That is what's important."

Jack felt pretty awkward watching the exchange between Maddy and Bryan. He couldn't help but feel tinge of heartache. One because it was perfectly clear he never had Maddy, and two because the woman he loved was so emotionally wounded. He slid to the edge of the love seat. "Maybe I should go."

"No," Maddy uttered. "I might need my two favorite strong men." She tried to laugh but it sounded hollow even to her. "Go ahead and talk...tired..." She fell into a fitful slumber.

"God it's tearing me apart seeing her like this. I just wish we could take her pain away," Jack remarked.

Bryan stroked Maddy's hair, speaking into it, "As cruel as it sounds, we need to make her feel her pain, allow her to learn to cope with it or she will never heal. She needs to grieve for her children, to remember what it felt like to love them and their lives."

Jack stood up and removed one of the frames from the entertainment center. It was the one with the little boy and girl with their arms wrapped around a brown border collie. "I wondered who they were." He looked up, "She kept it inside all these years. Why now?"

Bryan was silent. When Jack looked back at him, he seemed to be lost in thought. "You okay?"

"Yeah, just thinking. It's our fault Jack." Bryan stated flatly.

"Our fault? How do you figure?" Jack sat back down. How could it had been his fault, he didn't know anything about it.

"Actually you started it. You broke through a wall when you made her aware you had feelings for her, even more so when she realized she had feelings for you. Then I came along, taunting her, pursuing her, dragging her deeper into this case.

Without meaning to I made her relive her pain of me destroying her. We weakened her defenses."

"She did seem like she was handing the casework well, almost like she was feeding off it. I saw that as moving in a positive direction".

"The other day when you all were going out for lunch and she fled from you to come back to the squad room. Something triggered her."

Jack nodded, "The two little kids in the SUV."

"Yep. It cracked her armor, she allowed herself a brief moment of remembering them."

"And tonight, she seemed to be so into working the crime scene?"

"Until she slipped in the blood and whacked her head. When she came to..."

"She was in a pool of blood," Jack finished.

Bryan nodded. "She and I had been discussing her working through this, but not like this. What happened tonight changes everything."

Jack rose from the loveseat. "I'm going to head home. This is all a lot to take in. I will give you a call in the morning. Is it okay if I stop in tomorrow?"

Bryan smiled weakly. "You don't have to ask my permission. Jack, I know how you feel about Maddy. I'm sorry. If I had to loose her to another man, none would be better than you."

Jack cocked his head to one side looking at Bryan as if he were speaking a foreign language. "Christ Mayland, you're not still planning on leaving her?"

Bryan chuckled, "You really think I would turn her over to you that easily? No, I won't be leaving her this time. Ten years of our lives have been wasted; I think it's more than enough. Drive careful and we'll see you tomorrow—on one condition."

"What's that?" Jack asked suspiciously.

"Bring food, I can't cook worth a fuck."

Jack chuckled as left the house.

Bryan slid out from underneath Maddy and carried her back to her bed. He carefully slid the sweatpants off her body leaving her to sleep in the t-shirt. He kicked off his shoes, took off his socks and his shirt and jeans then crawled in bed beside and wrapped her in his arms. He felt Maddy's arm move beneath him

Maddy wrapped her hand on around his and brought it to her lips and whispered, "I love you."

He kissed the back of her head, "Not near is much as I love you."

A thin stream of light filtered through Maddy's window blinds. Sometime during the remainder of the night, she had turned to face Bryan's body. She watched him now as he slept. Visually she traced the lines of his face. He wasn't the most handsome guy in the world, nothing like he was when he was younger, but hey none of us are. She adored his strong features, sharp nose, and his soft lips. A dark shadow covered his cheeks and chin where he badly needed a shave. She could detect the faint hint of gray shadowing. There was nothing sweeter to her than the sound of his voice, especially when he told her how much he loved her. He had been her antagonist, now he was her savior. She remembered what he said that one night at the motel that she was his savior and he was her downfall. Amazing how events and time can change your perspective on someone. Maddy felt a hot tear slide down her face.

Bryan's eyes fluttered open and were met by Maddy's tearful gaze. "Hey," he smiled softly at her.

"Hey," she smile timidly back at him.

He reached out and wiped the tear from her cheek. "You okay Minnie?"

"I couldn't bear loosing you again." She held his gaze, never wavering.

He leaned over and kissed her softly. "Honey, you're not go to loose me... ever again. I promise."

"Love me," she whispered, "I need you to love me."

He was puzzled, "I do love you Maddy. Don't ever doubt that."

"No," she slid closer to him, "I need you to show me, love me Bryan..." She gently pushed him on to his back and slid her hands up his chest. She kissed him slowly and tenderly.

He responded by wrapping his fingers in her hair, giving her a warm, tender, emotional response. He rolled her over on her back, cradling her in his arms, covering her face with soft, loving kisses. His hands adoringly caressed her body and felt her come alive under his touch. He covered her mouth with his, undemanding, passionate, yet compassionate.

Maddy felt her heart fill with a love so acutely intense it temporarily detracted from the aching pain she woke up with. For as much sorrows she felt at the recognition of the loss of her children, she felt as much joy in the arms of the man she loved. His touch, his kisses felt so achingly sweet. After their loving, while they held each other cheek to cheek, Maddy cried...and Bryan cried for her...their tears mingling to become one.

The clock said 10:15 when Maddy woke up. Bryan was nowhere around. Maddy ran her fingers through her hair feeling a large contusion on the back of her head. Her hair felt stiff. At the realization what she was touching she shot out of bed. Shit! Blood. She grabbed some clothes out of her drawer and took off to the bathroom. She had to wash the remnants of last night off her.

As she stood in the shower, she let the hot water spray down upon her as she vigorously scrubbed her scalp and the rest of her body. Her skin was rubbed raw before she felt even remotely clean. She turned the shower off and toweled herself dry before dressing in a cotton t and Capri pants.

Maddy slipped on a pair of tennis shoes, grabbed a glass of tea, her pills and went and sat on the steps. The dogs were nowhere in sight. They must be with Bryan, wherever he was.

She sat back and thought about last night. It gave her sick feeling inside to think about it, but now it was out there. But she was okay, not good, but okay. She thought when she finally allowed herself to relive it she would loose herself again, but she didn't. She was still here, still thinking, and not crazy. She felt she owed a good part of it to Bryan. He pulled her through it. She also knew she still had to talk about what happened. Putting the experience into words would be difficult but essential. Officially it didn't matter; it was a closed case. She shot and killed that son of a bitch. An image of her children in her arms physically disturbed. Her glass slipped out her hand and broke into jagged shards. She leaned down on the steps to catch herself, the shards dug into her hand and wrist. "God damn it!" she screamed. More fucking blood, damn it.

She ran into the house to the kitchen sink. She examined her arm. There were deep gashes along her lower arm, wrist and her outer palm. Blood was dripping everywhere. She put her right hand over the cuts but the blood squeezed out around her fingers. More flashes. Lexi. Maddy felt the panic rise in her throat. She felt light-headed, woozy and weak in the knees. She tried to make it to the table but her legs gave out and she sunk to the floor. She held her bleeding wrist across her lap, leaned back against the cupboard and sobbed.

Bryan had taken the dogs out for a run in the pasture. He turned them back in the fenced in yard and headed for the house. As he approached the steps he instantly noticed the broken glass and the blood. "Oh sweet Jesus!" He ran in the house calling out for Maddy. Out of the corner of his eye he saw her sitting on the floor. There were blood smears running down the front of the cupboard. Maddy's head was tilted back resting on the cupboard, her bloody arm resting on her lap. Maddy's eyes were squeeze tightly shut, her breath repeatedly caught in her throat.

Bryan knelt down in front of her. When he reached out to touch her, she recoiled away from him. Damn it, he should never have left her alone. "Maddy? Honey? Hey it's me...Bryan."

She opened her eyes, staring at him but not seeing him. "Maddy?" He snapped his fingers in front of her.

She blinked a few times until his face came into focus, yet she didn't speak. Her head felt as if it had been in a dense fog, a fog with demons. She took several deep breaths and gathered her composure. She held her arm up off her lap. "I...I dropped my glass...."

Bryan rummaged through the drawers until he found the dishtowels. He pulled one out and dabbed the blood away from the cuts. "Shouldn't need stitches, lets get you fixed up here." Before he helped her stand up, he mopped the blood off the floor with the towel. The last thing he needed to happen would be to have her slip. Bryan turned on the cold water and held her wrist under it until the blood was washed away. "You have a first aid kit?" he asked.

"Bathroom, in the hutch," she answered more calmly than she felt. He disappeared and came back with the kit.

Several minutes later, her arm was neatly bandaged. She changed her clothing and put the ones she had been wearing to soak. She grabbed the bathroom trashcan and cleaned up the broken glass up outside. Bryan came out with a bucket of hot sudsy water and washed the blood off the steps. During this whole time frame neither of them spoke.

Maddy grabbed the kitchen rug and put it on the steps and sat down.

Bryan sat down beside her and lit up. "Do you want to talk about it?"

She stared off in the direction of the pasture. "No, not really."

"Maddy look at me," he pleaded, "Please."

She glanced at him then turned away.

"I said look at me!" he demanded.

She spun around and looked at him. "What do you want from me?" she snapped. She examined his face. He looked crushed.

"You're shutting down on me..." he felt defeated.

"I freaked out okay?" She felt shattered like there was no way to put the pieces back together. "I thought I was doing okay, and something stupid happens. I get these flashes and it throws me off. I was just sitting here, thinking about things, which leads to something else, which leads me back to...that."

"Say it Maddy, say what that is. You don't have to do this alone, but you have to be able to deal with it. I know it hurts. Tell me what 'that' is." Bryan pulled out another cigarette and lit it. He had a feeling he was going to be smoking a lot more than usual.

She was silent for a brief moment. "I was thinking how I was going to have to talk about it and how much harder it was going to be to put into words. Then I started thinking....about killing him. I got upset, dropped the glass, accidently leaned on it. When I went to patch up my arm...all that blood. I just lost it again." She turned to Bryan, "I don't think I am strong enough. I don't know how to do this. I know how to shut down, I know how to bury things, but I don't know to put this part of my life to rest. It's been ten damn years, Bryan, how much longer to does it take to go away?"

She looked at him sideways, "and so help me fucking God, if you say as long as it takes, I will kick the shit out of you."

Byran smiled and chuckled. "Now that's what I like to hear."

She eyed him strangely, "What?"

"A threat," he grinned. "Can I touch you or will you pounding the shit out of me for that too?"

Maddy smiled and softly chuckled, "I guess I can let you slide on that one."

He leaned over and kissed her cheek, but before he could pull away she reached for him and kissed him on the lips. "You got your work cut out you buddy."

He returned her kiss, "That's okay, a little bit of hard work never hurt anyone."

Bryan disappeared into the house then returned holding a plastic glass filled with tea, gave it to her and handed her meds. "You didn't get these down before you dropped your glass."

She eyed the plastic glass and looked at him, "Smart ass." She popped the pills in her mouth and swallowed.

"I know you are suppose to take those at night. Will it bother you taking them during the day?" he asked.

"Will probably make me sleepy, but I guess that's okay." She leaned her head on his shoulder.

"Derek gave me some ativan for you, too if things get too edgy for you."

"Sleep today, back to work tomorrow," she held up her glass giving a toast.

"Hold on there a minute Tiger. Do you honestly think you're ready to go back to work?"

Maddy gave a soft sigh. "I need to keep living my life. I can't dwell on this. I will face it and cope with it, but I need to move forward," she explained.

"Derek will more than likely make you get a psych evaluation before he will let you return," Bryan announced.

She looked over at him, "You're kidding? I thought you were the boss."

"Not when it comes to making decision as to whether you are fit for active duty," he held up his hands. "I'm sorry hon, he's over my head on this one, I'm too closely involved."

"Oh for Christ's sake. I will call Dr. Freeman in the morning and get it set up as soon as he can get me in." She touched his hand. "Will you go with me?"

He squeezed her hand, "I will do whatever it is you need me to do."

As they sat on the steps Jack's black Impala pulled down the lane. "What's he doing here?" she questioned.

"Lunch!" Bryan remarked with a smile on his face. "Oh yeah, and to see you."

"Hey whatever happened to our supper last night? You know the one we were suppose to eat?"

Bryan laughed, "Rat dog got on the table and devoured the steak. I don't know if he shared with Jack. But he was kind enough to leave the rest for me to clean up this morning."

Maddy smiled and shook her head. "Damn dog is a mountain goat."

Jack walked up carrying a large sack and a bucket of chicken from KFC. "Hope this is to your liking." He handed it to Bryan.

He leaned over and gave Maddy a soft kiss on her lips, "Good morning Mads. How you feeling?"

She smiled weakly, "Pretty jagged around the edges, but doing okay. Nice of you to bring lunch."

He laughed softly, "Your boyfriend wouldn't let me come and see you unless I brought food. I thought it was a fair trade."

Jack had called Bryan her boyfriend? What the hell went on between them last night? And he kissed her on lips in front of Bryan? She began to wonder if she had gone to an alternative universe. Maddy shrugged it off, grabbed the food and went inside to set the table. The guys sat out on the steps, smoked, and played with the dogs.

When the table was ready she pulled the food out of the containers and set it out. She went to call the guys but then decided to hang back and watch them from behind. Jack was playing with Rufus playing tug-a-war with his grey mouse squeaky toy, while Bryan had Jack, the dog, draped across his lap. She got the impression Bryan didn't care much for Rufus, guess he figured his leg was just too tasty for Rufus to resist.

What happened to the good old days when she could come home on a weekend, kick back, do her own thing in her much revered solitude? Now two men that had turned her world upside down, an extra dog, and her past had invaded her home.

Maddy poked her head out the door and called them in, minus the dogs. The guys sat down at the table and dug into the food. Maddy pulled a couple of beers out of the fridge for the guys and poured herself a glass of milk and sat down. She sat quietly listening to the guys talk about baseball. Yuck, she hated baseball...and football...and basketball...and about any other sport that didn't involve horses.

Bryan looked at her empty plate. "You're not eating."

"No shit!" she snapped. "Are we going to start this again? I'm not hungry and I don't feel well, give me a break." She saw Jack and Bryan exchange glances. "Don't even think about ganging up on me either." She downed her glass of milk and left the room.

Jack started to rise to go after her, but Bryan shook his head stopping him. "Let her be. Give her a few minutes, if she's not back, we'll check on her."

Jack slid down in the chair. "I don't know what I was expecting, but this isn't quite how I thought her frame of mind would be."

"She's dealing with a waterfall of emotions right now, I don't think she knows how she's going to react from one minute to the next." Bryan tore off a bite of chicken, and then wiped his hands. "She wants to go back to work tomorrow."

Jack looked up from his plate, "Do you think that's a good idea?"

Bryan popped the top on his beer and took a swig, "It's not my call, but Derek's. I'm too personally involved to make that call, so it's in his hands. I know he's going to want a psych eval on her before he will let her."

Jack played around with his potatoes with his fork. "What do you think though? Can she do it?"

"I think she should take more time off, but I'm not sure if that would be the best thing for her. She made a valid point saying she needs to keep moving forward, to deal with what she knows she has to, yet live a normal life. Whatever the hell that is for her. I believe she thinks if she isn't allowed to go back to work, she will just dwell on things and she is right, it wouldn't be in her best interests." Bryan soaked up some gravy with a biscuit and popped it in his mouth.

Jack took a sip of his beer. "Maddy the chameleon."

Bryan gave him a strange look, "pardon?"

Jack smiled weakly, "She's like a chameleon, and she can adapt to any situation and conform to what she needs to be. And I will bet you a 12 pack she will walk right into that psych eval and make herself look however she needs to get what she wants."

Bryan carefully thought over this description of one side of Maddy's personality. This was a new one to him, something she had acquired the ability to do since they had been apart. He rose from the table and walked back into the bedroom where Maddy was lying down on the bed and sat down beside her.

"If you've come to nag, go away," she said dully.

Bryan chuckled. "I'm not going to nag you. Jack and I were discussing whether or not you should go back to work tomorrow."

"Gee, how nice of you two to decide what I can and can't do," she replied contemptuously.

Bryan put his hand on Maddy's hip and gave it a gentle squeeze. "Quit being such a bitch and come out here so we can figure out how we are going to get you past this psych eval."

Maddy slid up on her elbow, "You going to let me go back to work?" she said surprised.

"Come on," he tugged on her arm, "We need to get your ass past Derek, let's go figure out how."

Maddy tugged back on his arm throwing him off balance and he slipped down on top of her where she grabbed his head and kissed him.

He raised his head, and brushed the hair away from her face then kissed her tenderly. "I love you," he whispered.

She smiled back at him, "I love you to, now let's go get me back to work!"

Bryan slid off the bed and offered Maddy his hand and they walked back out to the kitchen together. Maddy poured herself another glass of milk and sat down at the table.

Jack dug in the chicken bucket and pulled out a leg and threw it on Maddy's plate. Maddy raised an eyebrow in his direction.

Jack looked away from her laughing, "I'm just throwing the dog a bone."

Maddy picked up the leg and flung it back at him hitting him across the cheek. "Fuck you, I'll dog bone you," she replied in mock annoyance.

"Kids, quit playing with your food," Bryan laughed as he pulled two more beers from the fridge and sat down.

"I'm going to put a call in to Derek, get a feel for what he's thinking about with Maddy. Neither of you is to open your mouth," He turned to Maddy, "Not one word from you no matter what he says, you understand?"

"Where's your duct tape?" Jack asked opening his beer.

"Huh?" Bryan looked at him.

"You might as well as slap a gag on her right now because she doesn't understand when you tell her don't do something no matter how many times you ask her if she understands," Jack shook his head.

Maddy choked on her milk. "You are such a dick! That is so untrue!"

Jack locked eyes with her, unflinching until she finally looked away. "Well, not totally true..."she mumbled. "You know you two should not be allowed to compare notes, you leave me at a high disadvantage to be able to defend myself."

Bryan smiled and shook his head. "Are you going to keep your mouth shut? If not I am going to have to ask you to leave."

Maddy sat back and crossed her arms. "Fine."

Bryan pulled out his cell phone and placed the call. "Hey Derek. How are things going?"

"CSU finally finished up at 3:00 this morning. Bodies have been shipped to the DCI lab as well as what trace we picked up. We actually have a couple of witnesses that got a look at our guy. I'll have a full report for you by the end of the day. Maddy was right about the syringe and we were able to pull a good set of prints off it. Good find on her part. How's she doing, Bryan?"

Bryan looked straight at Maddy giving her a visual reminder to keep silent. "Far better than expected. She's coping quite well. Are you going to let her return to work tomorrow"

Derek's end of the phone was silent. "Bryan, you saw her last night, she lost it, how do you honestly believe she can go through that and then be okay to be back on duty tomorrow?"

"Come on Derek, you know Maddy. She can be quite resilient."

"Yeah and you are forgetting, Bryan, I do know Maddy. I was there ten years ago, remember?"

"You seen the work she can do, she still has her edge," Bryan protested.

"Bryan, I am not trying to supersede you on this. But she triggered last night. You don't know what we are going to come across that is she going to react to. She's a loose cannon."

Maddy started to open her mouth and Jack quickly slapped his hand across it and mouthed 'No'.

"Okay Derek, you know if I thought she would put anyone including herself in danger I would be the first person to keep her out. Her welfare has to come first. I just don't feel keeping her off the job is the answer. I don't believe this is going to be an issue."

"You must have a short memory because the woman I saw last night did not have her shit together. I'm sorry, I don't mean to be cruel Bryan, you are not exactly objective when it comes to Maddy."

"When have I ever let my relationship with her interfere with my job?" This was a little more than Bryan was prepared to have privy to open ears.

"You left her Bryan. You couldn't deal with her and your job, so you left her, Maybe if you hadn't she wouldn't be where she is now," Derek said flatly.

Bryan glanced over at Maddy. She was looking down, nervously chewing on her lips. Bryan took the phone off speaker.

Maddy watched Bryan as he flipped the off speaker. She studied his face. The nerve in his temple was twitching; he was getting upset. Maddy went to her cupboard, grabbed a pen and pad and returned to the table and scratched him a note.

'Don't Bryan; don't risk yourself at my expense. It just doesn't matter.' She tore the sheet off the pad and handed it to Bryan and left the room.

Bryan read the note and wadded it up and threw it, mouthing, "God damn it!" He grabbed the note pad and scribbled a note for Jack 'go to her, don't let her slip'

Jack scribble back 'it should be you, it's you she needs.'

"That was a pretty low blow Derek. What does she need to do?"

"Get a sign off of a Bureau shrink. Have her ass down to the Omaha field office by 8:00 AM tomorrow morning. The appointment is already set up. I knew you would be like this so I went ahead and set it up. But Bryan...what he says goes, do we understand each other?"

"Why do you feel like the SSA here," Bryan tried to laugh it off.

"Nope that's still you, Bud, but we have to do this right. For all of our sakes. And Bryan?"

"Yeah?"

"I'm sorry, what I said was out of line. You know I think the world of Maddy. We all just want her to be well. I will email these reports to Maddy so you can take a look and will see you when you get back from Omaha, hopefully both of you." The phone went silent.

Jack found Maddy in the living room in the sitting area behind the couch. She was curled up in a chair staring out the picture window. He sat in a chair beside her

Maddy glanced up and saw Jack. She reached out and grabbed his hand. "I am sorry to put you all through this. It's my problem, I am the one that needs to fight my own battles."

"You don't have to do this alone, Mads." He smiled weakly. "That's why you have two knights in shining armor."

She gave a soft laugh. "Most women would kill to have even one man like the two of you in their lives, how did I get so lucky?" She leaned across and softly kissed him on the lips.

They sat for a couple of minutes in comfortable silence before Maddy spoke, "Please don't ask me if I'm okay."

Jack laughed, "Okay, I won't. Sounds like Bryan got an earful. That Derek can be a real fuck head."

Maddy shrugged, "He's just doing his job, I'm not holding it against him, at least not the part about him not wanting me to go back to work, but that was a pretty shitty thing to do to Bryan."

"Yeah, but I'm a big boy, I can handle it," Bryan said as he came in and sat down on the couch. "We have to be in Omaha by 8:00 AM to meet with the Bureau shrink. Jack says you're a chameleon, do you do this at will?"

Maddy turned in her chair, "What do you mean?"

"I am assuming from what he described to me, that you can role play into any situation and make it believable? Am I correct?" he asked.

Maddy threw Jack a look, "You told him that? Damn it I hate you two talk about me."

"Christ Maddy, it's nothing to get pissed at. It's a talent you have, why not use it if it gets you back on the job?"

"Yeah I can do it, it's all about absorbing your surroundings and go with the flow."

Bryan kicked his shoes off and put his feet up on table. "Given the state of your emotional...situation, are you able to go up against a shrink and convince him that you are stable enough to return to work?"

"I did it for ten fucking years," she said bitterly, "I think I can do it one more time."

"Jesus Maddy...I just keep getting in this deeper and deeper. Can't open my mouth without shooting off my foot." Bryan slipped his shoes on and stood up. "I need to go for a walk. Also just so you know I'm not doing it behind your back, I am going to call Jeff and see how it went getting my things from Donna."

"Christ Maddy, cut the man some slack, he's doing the best he can to get you what you want," Jack argued.

"Oh? And now you're his best buddy?" She smiled scornfully. "Isn't that just precious? You going to be his protector now?"

Jack's head came back not believing what he was hearing, "What the hell is the matter with you? Why are you acting like this? This is so unlike you."

Maddy turned to stare out the window, her eyes narrowing, "Maybe it is so like me, you wanted to get to know the real me? Well here you go!"

Jack sat and studied her even though she refused to look at him. He grabbed her by the wrist pulling her off the chair to him so they were face to face. She tried to look away but he grabbed her by her hair and made her look into his eyes. Her emerald eyes were afire with he sworn was hatred. "It's not going to work," he breathed into her.

"Fuck off," she hissed with out blinking. She tried to pull her head back but he regained his hold. Her respiration rate shot through the roof.

He didn't know where it came from but his lips crushed hers beneath his, kissing her hard until he could actually feel her respond then slowly became gentler. He pulled back and searched her face. Her breathing remained rapid, but her eyes had softened.

He released Maddy to sit on the floor at his feet. She put her head against his knee looking away from him. He stroked her hair, "I do know you Maddy," he spoke softly. "I know you're tough, I know you can be one wicked ass bitch, but you are not mean. Being mean and hateful isn't going to take away your pain, Mads. It also isn't going to work to push us away. Going back into that little shell of yours isn't working for you anymore."

He was right. Maddy was searching for any means she could to get away from this inscruiating pain she felt in her heart. Anger and hate was so much easier to deal with then the hurt. The chameleon, yeah she could do it, she just did.

Jack stood up and helped Maddy to her feet. "I'm going to take off, but first I am going to say something to you so foreign coming from my mouth. You need to go find Bryan and talk to him. Babe, that man has been through so much for you in the last twenty-four hours, I watched him with you last night when he thought he lost you again. That man was in agony desperately reaching for you to bring you back, he was broken. But he found you Mads, he reached deep inside and he brought you back. That takes a pretty powerful love Babe. Don't punish him because you hurt, he hurts too."

"Maddy, I finally saw with my own eyes what people have been telling me over and over again. Last night, for me, was proof. I don't know everything the two of you have endured, the fact of the matter is, you two are here, together, where you need to be."

Maddy felt like her heart was breaking but couldn't explain why. The tears came and wouldn't stop. She wrapped her arms around Jack's waist. "Everything hurts so bad....I have all this pain and nowhere to put it," she sobbed. "I'm loosing everything."

Jack held her close, "Babe, you're not loosing anything but these demons you've been fighting all these years. You've got two incredible handsome men that love you intensely."

Maddy looked up at him, searching, "You....still love me?"

He put his finger under her chin. "I still love you, more than ever. Nothing is going to change that." Jack smiled, "Bryan has been put on notice, he drops the ball even once, you're mine. I don't give up that easy," he winked.

Maddy and Jack held hands as they walked out to his car then he turned kissed her softly. "Hang in there, Mads. You're not alone." He kissed her again and smiled. "I'll call you guys later. Now go get your man."

Maddy watched him drive off down her lane smiling to herself. She really did love that man. As she did Bryan. She really was fucked up.

Maddy brought her hand to her eyes to block out the sun and searched the grounds for Bryan. He was standing by the pasture gate looking over the pasture while talking on the phone. The temperature was sweltering; the air still, buzzing cicadas were deafening. She was surprised the horses weren't up begging for food. The heat of the midsummer sun drove them into the barn.

She quietly walked up behind Bryan slipping her arms around his waist and hugged him from behind. She heard him tell Jeff he had to go and would check in with him in a day or so. He slipped the phone in his pocket and bent down and kissed her.

She touched his cheek, "I'm sorry I was such a bitch. Jack let me know I was being mean and hateful and it wasn't going to work."

"Jack knows you better than you give him credit for. He's a good man."

Maddy rolled her eyes, "You know you two should be dating each other and leave me out of it."

"Naaah, without you we wouldn't have anything in common." He kissed her deeply, caressing her back with his hands. He grabbed her hand leading her to sit beneath a towering silver maple. Bryan stretched out and had Maddy lay her head on his lap.

He brushed the hair out of her eyes and stroked her hair allowing her to relaxing. "How's Jeff?"

"She wouldn't let him pick up my things. Said I could come and get them myself." He continued to caress her.

Maddy laughed, "Not surprising. So now what?"

"Nothing there that can't be replaced." Maddy felt him take a deep breath.

She opened one eye to look up at him, "What?"

"Jeff wants to fly up here to meet you," he said flatly.

Maddy's head popped, "Why not?"

"Now is not a real good time, Minnie. We've have to work through this and this case is really getting fired up. I don't think we need him up here causing problems," Bryan explained.

Maddy reached up over her head and touched him, "How can you be so sure he will cause problems?"

"I have no delusions about Jeff. Despite numerous stints in treatment, I know he uses. He is a pretty self-center young man thanks to mama."

Maddy snickered, "Like his dear old dad."

He poked her, "Brat. Not to change the subject, but do you honestly think you can fool the shrink?"

"I won't have a plan going in, it's not like following a script. I just have to field his questions and answer what sounds good and logical. I just have to give it a shot."

"So what happens if he asks you touchy questions?"

Maddy frowned, "Fake it 'til you make it."

"I can't go in with you, they won't allow it."

"Honey, it would be a dead giveaway. I can do it," she squeezed his hand, "Trust me."

"I'll trust you. Honey you look beat, I think you need to rest," he said softly.

"You just want to get rid of me," she joked.

Bryan helped her into a sitting position, "Not at all, I am going to lay down with you and hold you while you sleep."

She eyed him skeptically, "Sleep my ass."

Her pulled her to her feet. and smiled weakly, "No seriously, it been a long 24 hours, this old man needs a nap too...and if we feel perky after the nap..."he grinned mischievously.

"Mmmm.... Okay, works for me," they walked back to the house.

"I want you to take one of the ativan. You're emotions and nerves are all over the place, It'll help to rest too," he explained.

After arriving at the house Maddy noticed the table wasn't cleared. She looked in the bucket and saw a couple pieces of chicken ripping into them.

Bryan laughed, "I knew you would come around, No one can resist the Colonel." He handed her a glass of milk and one of the pills. "I'll clean the mess later."

Maddy went to her room and pulled the blinds so the room was dark. She kicked off her shoes and crawled between the sheets. When her head hit the pillow, she realized she was exhausted. She had already dozed off when Bryan crawled in bed beside her. He pulled her in her arms and let her drift off; he wasn't that far behind her.

14

Maddy awoke to the sound of the dogs barking. She slid off the bed and peered through the blinds where she saw Jessie's truck pulling down the lane to do the chores. She glanced over at Bryan who was still sleeping peacefully.

Maddy went and greeted her friend and told her of last night's events. Jessie was concerned, but Maddy reassured her everything would be fine. When Maddy walked back to the house, Bryan was still sleeping. She cleaned up the kitchen, changed the laundry around.

Maddy was walking through the living room when the photos on the entertainment center caught her eye. She pulled one down and sat on the couch looking at it. She picked it up and smiled. Lexi was six and Scotty was two. They had spent a couple of hours raking up leaves. Such a beautiful array for colors—bright oranges, yellows, browns and just a touch of green all heaped up in this huge pile. Maddy remembered swinging Scotty over the top of the pile, threatening to drop him. He squealed in delight, a high-pitched squeal, and then when she did throw him in the pile it erupted, leaves flying everywhere. Lexi, not wanting to miss out on the fun jump it to. It all turned it a big leaf fight between the three of them. By the time it was over they had leaves stuck to their clothing and tangled in their hair. It had been so much fun.

Maddy held the photo to her chest and let the tears fall, her little babies, her sweet little babes. God, how her heart ached for them. Ten years and the hole in her heart was no less than it was when she lost them.

Maddy jumped when she felt the hand on her shoulder. She looked up and saw Bryan standing over her. "Hey," she smiled as she wiped the tears from her eyes.

"Hey."

She patted the seat beside her. "Come sit with me."

Bryan slid down next to her and put his arm over her shoulder. Maddy tucked her feet up under her and leaned into him. She held the photo out in front of her, tracing the figures of her children with her fingers. An endless stream of tears fell from her eyes. "It hurts..." she buried her head in his chest, "it hurts so bad..."

Bryan held her close, resting his face on the top of her head as he brushed his hand slowly up and down her arm. "Kidd, I would give anything to take your pain and put it on myself."

Maddy put the picture back in its spot and returned to Bryan's side. She rested her head in the crook of his arm, her hands on his chest. "When does it start to get easier?"

"I don't know Minnie. I don't think there are any time lines. You want to go for a walk or something?" he asked her softly.

She shook her head, "No...I don't want to do anything, sorry."

"No worries, I'm going out for smoke, be back shortly," he kissed her softly.

Maddy stretched out on the couch and put her arm over her head. She felt as if someone had reached into her body and pulled out her insides. It left her feeling stripped of her emotions yet raw at the same time. She hated feeling like this.

She wished she could turn the clock back twenty-four hours. The last couple of days had been good days for the most part. Somewhere along the line this last week, she and Bryan had transcended their past. Maybe it was coming clean about the reasons they did what they did, maybe it was when Bryan finally understood he had to cut the shit or he would loose her. It didn't matter, she thanked God, he was here.

One week...seven days, her life had been irreparable changed. Maddy heard Bryan's phone go off. She was too drained to be curious.

Bryan sat on the steps as he watched the horses tearing around the pastured. It looked like a great deal of fun and they were truly beautiful creatures. He loved Maddy's life here in the country hoping she would invite him in, permanently.

He was putting out his cigarette when his phone went off. Jack's name came across the caller ID. Funny, he thought he would have called Maddy. "Good evening, Jack. What's new?"

"Derek sent the reports to Maddy's email if you want read them. Honestly I haven't looked at them yet. I've been distracted."

Bryan understood quite well. "Okay, I'll pull it up later, not in the mood either."

There was a moment of silence. "How is she?" Jack finally asked.

"She's kind of in a dark place at the moment. She laid down with me earlier. When I awoke she was out in the living room with a picture in her hand. Tears me apart seeing her hurting and there's not a damn thing I can do about it. Tried to get her to go for a walk, no dice."

"What is she doing?"

"Just lying on the couch. I think she just wants to be alone."

"How do you think she is going to do tomorrow?"

Bryan shook his head in doubt, "I really don't know. Guess it all depends on how bad she wants it. If she had to do it right now, she'd never pass."

"Its like you said, just give her time. If she was looking at the photo, it means she was allowing herself to feel, and you said that was positive thing right?"

"Yes, I guess your right. I'm just strung out. You want to say hi to her? Maybe you can cheer her up." Bryan went into the house.

"I will give it a shot."

Bryan knelt down next to Maddy, "Hey Minnie, someone wants to talk to you."

Maddy uncovered her eyes to see Bryan face to face with her. "Hey Baby," she whispered softly.

Bryan waved the phone so she could see it. She took it from him. "Hello?" she voice was soft and timid.

"Hey Mads, you snoozing out on me?" he tried to laugh.

"Mmmm...just really zapped today I guess. Hey, I wanted to thank you for putting me in my place this afternoon. Now I know I can count on you to be an asshole," she joked half-heartedly.

Jack laughed, "Didn't realize there was ever any doubt."

There was a hushed quiet over the line. "It's okay Jack, you don't need to say anything. I understand. Don't force it," Maddy responded.

"I'm sorry, I just wish there was something I could say to make it all better. Do you know how much I love you, Maddy?"

Maddy spoke softly into the phone, "I'm starting to get a good idea, hon. You guys need to quit worrying so much about me. I'm just kind of down right now. Just give me time to lick my wounds and I'll be back to my old self in no time. I'm going hand you to Bryan now. I will see tomorrow. Love you too." She handed the phone to Bryan.

Bryan told Jack he would call him if anything came up, otherwise they would talk tomorrow.

Maddy slipped in her den and brought out her laptop, sat on the couch and booted it up.

"What are you doing?" Bryan asked sitting down beside her.

"Getting your report for you," she signed on to her email.

"Honey, I really don't feel like dealing with that right now. Do you?"

Maddy half smiled, "No, not really." Maddy scanned down her email and found one that caught her eye. "Well, well, well, what do we have here?" Donna had sent her an email. Now this could be interesting. Maddy grinned, "I think I have some hate mail."

Bryan peered around the screen, "Trash the damn thing, you don't have to put up with her shit."

She clicked on the email, "No, I want see what the cow has to say."

Bryan reached for the computer, "Then let me read it first."

"No!" she laughed, "I will read it out loud. Hon, there isn't anything she can say at this point that's going to upset me. I am so far beyond that."

"Maddy, you would think by now you would have figured out Bryan doesn't care for you," Maddy read. *"We've discussed this before. He just uses you. He gets pissed at me, he runs to you because he's just trying to get back at me. I mean look at our history, it's been me he has been with the past seven years, and it was me who he came back to the last time. I gave him a choice and he chose me, not you. I am sorry if that hurts you but it's a fact. Do you really think after all this time; he is going to give up everything for you? Get over yourself, your not that special,"* Maddy burst out laughing. *"He's only been with you a little over*

a week. It took four months to get bored with you the last time, so don't get too comfortable. I talked to Bryan yesterday and will again soon. Save yourself the humiliation and walk away before he just hurts you again. Donna"

Maddy laughed in disbelief, "What the fuck, oh whatever. This is just too good for words."

Bryan raised one eyebrow. "You sure took that well...I think."

Maddy shut the lid on the laptop. "Oh come on Bryan. She's getting desperate. Now you tell me, does it bother you?"

"Nope." He picked up the laptop setting it on the coffee table. He pushed Maddy down in to the cushions of the couch covering her body with his. "As long as you know the truth, that's all that matters to me."

She wrapped her arms around his neck looking up at him, "And what pray tell is the truth?" Her eyes twinkled mischievously.

"I choose you." He lowered his mouth down on hers, kissing her deeply.

Maddy felt warmth spreading through her. She entwined her fingers in his hair bringing him down to her, hungrily kissing him, and tasting his sweetness. She pushed against him until he was in an upright position. She pushed the coffee table back with her foot and straddled him on his lap.

Bryan ran his hands over her shoulders and up and down her sides. "What are you doing?"

She planted kisses on his forehead and worked her way down, unbuttoning his shirt at the same time. She whispered in his ear, "If I have to explain it to you, I must be doing something wrong." She flicked him with her tongue and growled.

Bryan groaned laying his head back as Maddy burned a trail down his neck. Bryan's phone went off in his pocket. When he reached down to get it Maddy pulled his hand back then slid her hand down in his pocket grabbing it. She looked at the caller ID laughing a wicked laugh. "This just keeps getting better and better." She showed the screen to Bryan. When he reached to take it from her, she grabbed his hand and guided it back to her body. She kissed his lips aggressively then answered the phone. "Hello Donna, how nice of you to call," She kissed him again and nuzzled his head.

"Maddy...why are you answering his phone?"

Bryan gently sucked on her earlobe. She tilted her head back and dug her nails into his flesh. "Em...he's kind of in the middle of something."

"Put him on, I need to speak to him," Donna demanded.

Bryan playfully nibbled at the base of her neck and began to unbutton her blouse. Maddy stroked the back of his head and whimpered softly.

"Maddy!" the other end of line screeched.

"Oh...did you say something? I'm sorry Donna, you can't talk to him," she snickerd, "He's got his hands full."

Bryan ran his tongue between her breasts sending Maddy wild. "Em...listen Donna, he's really busy right now. You want to know what he's busy doing?—Me!" She flipped the phone shut and threw it over her shoulder.

Bryan grabbed her hair, pulling her head down to him, craving the taste of her lips. Maddy pressed into to him, their bare skin igniting. Maddy pulled Bryan down to the floor on top her. His eyes roved over her beauty stopping at her face. Her skin was flushed, her swollen red lips were slightly parted, but it was her eyes that held his fascination. They were bright emerald and smoldering. And then she flashed a wicked smile at him. "You are one diabolical bitch Maddy," he told her in a raspy voice.

"And you love me anyhow."

"I love you no matter what," he growled and released their fury.

Maddy lay on Bryan's chest, both were trying to catch their breath. "Damn girl, you're going to kill me yet," he laughed.

She kissed his chest, "That's funny, because you make me feel so alive." Then she laughed, "Who would have thought that cow would be an aphrodisiac?"

When Maddy finished her shower she found Bryan sitting at the kitchen table reviewing the case report Derek sent him. He automatically handed Maddy a copy over his shoulder. "Just figured you would want you own copy," he said not even looking up from the papers.

Maddy studied Bryan over the top of her report. A deep furrow was set across his brow, his face somber, and he kept adjusting his glasses. "Is it that bad?" she asked.

"Read for yourself then you tell me," was all he said.

Ooookay, she thought. The victim was Vicky Thomas, age 27. Preliminary cause of death exsanguination. Along with the unsub signatures were defensive wounds on her hands and her arms. (There was nothing about the contusion on the back of her head.) She definitely put up a fight. Tox screen and official autopsy report inconclusive at this time. Victim two was Alan Bates, age 33. Cause of death—laceration to the lower thorax. No apparent defensive wounds. What about the abrasion under his left eye? According to eyewitnesses the unsub arrived around 7:00 PM, and was let in. The boyfriend arrived approximately at 7:15. Time unsub left was unknown. Eye witness description of unsub was a white male, between 5'10" and 6', late 30's early 40's, dark hair. He was dressed in black pants and black coat. Witnesses were unable to identify his vehicle.

Possible scenario: Unsub was let into the house by Thomas, Bates interrupted the abduction, was caught unaware by unsub and stabbed, unsub in a panic killed Thomas.

"That's not what happened," Maddy said as she threw aside the report.

Bryan looked up over his glasses. "What do you mean?"

"The way they have it written up, that's not what happened. I want to see the crime scene again," she replied.

"No," Bryan answered flatly.

"What do you mean no?"

"I said no, what part of no don't you understand?" He was looking back down at the report.

"Why?"

Bryan laid down the report, took off his glasses and rubbed his eyes. "Because Maddy, I just don't think it's a good idea for you to go back there. It's not safe."

"That's bullshit," Maddy protested. "That crime scene has nothing to do with what happened. It was falling and hitting my head that triggered me. I need to go back so I can get a good read."

"Use the photos."

Maddy grabbed the report and threw it over her shoulder. "You need to let me do my job. I don't want to use the damn crime scene photos. I can't read off photos. Damn it, Bryan, you go with me and if you think I'm getting shaky, pull me off. You can't keep shielding me. What the hell, like what's going to happen—I remember what I already know? So fucking what? Deal with it, I am."

"No!"

Maddy crossed her arms in defiance. "I'll do it anyhow."

"The hell you will." Bryan's voice was starting to get an edge to it.

She was pushing him, how far was she willing to push...as far as she needed to. Maybe she needed to take another approached. "What's it going to take for you to change your mind?"

"It's not going to happen Maddy, so just get it out of your head."

She glared at him. Bullshit, she was going back to that crime scene with or without him. She never needed anyone's permission before—she'd be damn if needed it now.

"No, you're not. I will put a tail on your ass and you won't be able to make a move without me knowing." Bryan met her glare for glare.

Maddy rolled her eyes. "Did I say anything?"

"You didn't have to. I know how your mind works." He picked up his glasses and put them back on and started making notations on a legal pad. "Let it go and that's an order."

"I hate you," she said coldly.

"Oh grow up. You're acting like a spoiled brat."

"Whatever," she grumbled under her breath. He wasn't as easy to manipulate as Jack. Jack!

"He's not going to help you either. If he does I will throw his ass off this case."

Maddy started to laugh. "Would you get the fuck out of my mind?"

Bryan shook his head and smiled. "No one knows you better than I do, Minnie. But I meant what I said."

"We'll see. Anything about the unsub's description sound familiar?" she asked.

"Fits our profile." He continued making notes.

"And he's dressed like?" she waited.

He just looked out over the top his glasses.

Maddy sighed and shook her head, "Duh, like a minister?"

"Or like a man dressed in black as to not call a lot of attention to himself."

"Are you trying to be ignorant to piss me off or what? Get your head out of your ass and work with me here." This was getting to be so frustrating. "I say black, you say white, damn give me a little credit."

"Now I know why you work alone. You're a pain in the ass."

She kicked him hard underneath the table.

"Ouch! Damn it Maddy. You're so damn physical anymore. If you're not throwing things, you're kicking me or hitting me." He rubbed the spot on his shin where her toe hit.

A soft smile crossed her lips. "You don't seem to mind when I get physical most of the time."

"That's different. Now are you done throwing a fit so we can talk about this?" he asked.

"I already told you what I thought. I can't give you anymore without revisiting the crime scene. I agree that the unsub came to abduct Thomas and something went terribly wrong, but to actually tell you what I think happened I need to get a read. I already told you why he did what he did to her when we were at the crime scene, right down to his administering the ketamine," she spelled it out for him.

Bryan put down his pen and studied her. "You remember all that?"

Maddy gave an exasperated sigh. "What the hell have I been telling you? I remember everything that was said and done last night. I remember looking at the scene in the living room and thinking to myself something wasn't adding up and needed to be studied more extensively. I remember the kitchen, the way Thomas's body was splayed, doing an initial exam of her body, checking her hands for defensive wounds...and what's not on your damn report, she had a contusion on the back of her damn head. She either fell or bumped her head or he knocked her out. Which I would know if I were able see the damn crime scene again!"

He continued to stare at her, blinking a couple of times.

"It was the damn fall, not the crime scene!" she shrieked. She stood up and threw her hands in the air. "I fucking give up, solve your own damn case...without me." And with that she stormed outside.

Bryan sat back and smiled. Damn she was fired up tonight...and sharp as a tack. With everything that she went through last night, she still didn't miss a beat. He hoped she would do well with her psych eval tomorrow because she definitely was ready to get back to work. If she got the okay to return to work, and maybe even if she didn't, he would bring her back to scene to do her 'read' as she put it. Hell, who would know? After all he was lead on this case. Should he tell her now or let her stew about it? Nah, let her sweat it out.

He stood up, took off his glasses and stretched. He looked out the screen door. Maddy was lying on the ground letting the pups attacked her. She was squealing and laughing as the two dogs were licking the hell out of her face. Talk about experiencing a wide array of moods in one day. He grabbed his cigarettes off the table, went out, sat on the steps and lit one up.

Maddy was aware of his eyes on her, she sat up and looked at him. The light was beginning to fade as the sun was starting to set. She joined him on the steps and watched as the orange fireball sunk into the horizon.

"How long does it take to get Omaha from Sioux City?" Bryan asked.

"About an hour and a half. Why can't we just leave from here?" she asked.

"We need to take the Sub. So it takes about 45 minutes to get to the city, and we'll say a little over two hours to get down the field office. We'll need to leave here at 4:45. So I am figuring we need to hit the sack soon. What do you think?"

She nodded, "Yeah I guess so." She leaned her head on his shoulder. "You pissed me off on purpose."

He glanced at her with a smirk on his face. "Why would I do that?"

She nudged his knee, "Because I know you. You provoked me to see how far I was willing to go. So how did I do?"

"Much better than I anticipated. We'll see how good you come out in the morning, and then we'll talk. Fair enough?"

She patted him on the knee, "Fair enough. I'm going to bed." She rose from the steps and kissed him on the top of the head.

When the alarm went off at 3:30 Maddy slapped the snooze button. She nudged Bryan. "Get up."

He mumbled something illegible and rose out of the bed. Maddy laid in bed for few moments more then drug herself out of bed. She put on a pair of black slacks and white blouse. When Bryan got out of the bathroom she went in, put on a touch of make up and pulled her hair back.

Within twenty minutes they were on road. Maddy took the opportunity to catch a little more sleep. They arrived at the Regency and switched out vehicles and hit Highway 29 to Omaha.

They pulled into the FBI field office on Court Street at 7:40. After they signed in Maddy was led to an exam room where she received a physical. It was determined she did receive a mild concussion when her head hit the floor. Other than that she checked out.

Following the physical she was led into an office much like that of her own psychiatrist. A man in his late 40's, dressed in a suit sat on the other side of the desk. His hair was graying at the temples. He had sharp features and dark rimmed glasses hid pale blue eyes. He rose from his desk and stuck his hand out and introduced himself as Dr. Lionel Richards.

Maddy shook his hand making sure she gave him a strong assertive handshake then she sat down. She gave the appearance of being relaxed, although she was extremely nervous. She hoped it would not be apparent during the interview.

Richards had a large file on his desk, which he opened up and appeared to be studying, but she was quite confident he had already been it extensively through it. "Is see you suffered a personal lost in 2001 of a violent nature where your two children and your housekeeper will murdered. I also understand you suffered a psychotic break Saturday evening associated with this loss."

Maddy shook her head. "Let's just cut through the bullshit. You know about what happened so I am not going to reiterate on it. I dealt with it the best I could at the time. I even took myself out of the field when I felt I needed to. That should tell you I have enough clarity to know what I can and can't handle. I have since then been under the care of a psychiatrist who I see every six months to be evaluated. So far I have been deemed fit to live a productive life. I go to a therapist every other week just to talk things out and work through any stressors I might be having. Seems to work fine. What happened Saturday night was an isolated incident. I slipped on some blood, fell and hit my head. When I found my children, I was hindered in getting to them by slipping on blood. I imagine the event of how I slipped coupled with the bang on the head triggered the break, which led me to revisiting the incident. I spent yesterday exploring my feelings regarding that experience, spent sometime grieving in a healthy, however painful manner. I am not saying I won't have periods of feeling the loss, but I believe I am perfectly capable of performing my duties as an agent."

Richards sat back in his chair with his arms crossed studying her from across his desk. "You've been on inactive duty for over seven plus years. Why now"

"It was time." She looked at him straight in the eye without flinching.

"On the surface you appear to have everything under control, as to whether its only superficial it's hard to say. I'll tell you what, give my secretary the names and phone numbers of you psychiatrist and therapist. I want to discuss your history in order to come to my final assessment. Until that time I am releasing you to restricted duty."

"For how long?" she asked.

"We'll see what they have to say," Richards pulled out some paperwork and filled it out. "Give this to the SSA who brought you here. I will be in contact with you within the next couple of days." He stood up and shook hands with Maddy.

Bryan was waiting for her in the outer office. She brushed past him and headed straight for the truck. "Maddy..." he called after. This didn't appear promising.

She was waiting beside her door, the psych release in her hand.

Bryan smiled, "You got it?"

She handed it to him and he opened it up, "Restrictive duty. Hey that's good Maddy."

"Restrictive duty? How am I suppose to do my job from a desk?" she frowned.

He pushed her gently up against the truck and put his hands on her waist. "Just because that's what the paper says, doesn't mean that's what's going to happen. I'm still the SSA on this case. What I say goes. You got the release that's what matters." He leaned forward and kissed her lightly. "Get in."

He unlocked the suburban and she slipped in and put her seatbelt on. She leaned her head back against the headrest. Even when she closed her eyes the bright lights were flashing in her eyes. Her lips tingled and she could smell sulfur. Oh God, a migraine. All this stress triggered a migraine, damn it. She dug in her bag for some Advil.

Bryan got in the truck and watched her digging in her bag. He noticed how pale she was getting. He reached for her hand, "What's the matter kiddo? You don't look so good."

"Major head ache coming on. I need something to cover my eyes; I need to shut out the light and the sound. She popped the Advil in her mouth and washed it down with bottled water. Like it would do any good, Advil, won't even touch this.

Bryan reached behind him and grabbed his jacket and handed it to her. She rolled it up and covered her face. "Is there something I can do?"

"Find an emergency room. I need a shot of Demerol."

Bryan called into the field office and got directions to the nearest hospital. After he explained what was going on they sent him to a near by clinic. Twenty minutes later he was helping Maddy into the backseat of the truck. He tucked his jacket under her head leaving the sleeve free to cover eyes.

"I guess I'll be taking you home," he spoke softly.

"No," she mumbled. "I will just sleep on the way back. I'll be fine in a couple of hours."

Bryan drove back in silence hoping she would feel better soon.

When he arrived back in Sioux City she was still out cold. She needed to go somewhere and get some more rest. He thought about taking her back to his motel room but knew she didn't want to go anywhere near there. He drove to the station, pulled into the parking lot and put a call into Jack to come down to the lot.

Jack arrived at the truck in a few minutes. "What's going on?" He looked in the back seat and saw Maddy passed out. "What's the matter with her?"

"Migraine. She's knocked out on Demerol. She seems to be under the impression she'll be fine in a couple of hours." He smiled weakly. "That was a couple of hours ago. We need to take her somewhere where she can sleep this off and I can't take her to back to my motel room. I really need to get up there and do my job. What I am asking of you is can you take her back to your place? Do you have work you can bring home with you for a couple of hours so you can stay with her?"

"Yeah, I'm sure I can find something. I need to run up and grab it. Do you want to put her in my car?" Jack asked.

"No, I will follow you, no sense on moving her more than we have to."

Jack gathered his material, got in his car and pulled out, Bryan following close behind. When they pulled into Jack's drive, Bryan scooped Maddy up and carried her into the house. Jack went ahead telling Bryan to follow him up the stairs. He led them to the first bedroom at the top of the stairs.

"Bring her in here. This room has wooden shutters, it will block out the light better." He turned the blankets down and Bryan laid her down on the bed, took off her shoes and covered her up. She didn't stir.

The men left the room and softly closed the door behind them. After they descended the stairs Bryan turned to Jack and asked, "I just put her in your bed didn't I?"

Jack stopped and looked at him, "Well, yeah, you got a problem with that?"

The thought of Maddy in Jack's bed didn't sit well with him. It gave him a bad feeling. He shook it off; he was just being stupid. "No...no problem," he answered.

"Listen Bryan, she is safe with me. For crying out loud she's passed out," Jack said incredulously. "It's not like I'm going to jump her bones."

"Good," he answered then to himself, if the shoe were on the other foot, he would do it in a heartbeat. There wasn't anything he wouldn't stoop to to have Maddy. But there was one thing Jack had that he didn't—scruples.

"Listen Bryan, if you don't feel comfortable with her being here with me, maybe this isn't such a good idea," Jack said as he led Bryan to the front door.

"Jack you are about the only person I do trust with her. I shouldn't things being the way they are. Bring her in when she wakes up," he said as he left the house.

Jack shook his head as he spread his files out on the coffee table. That man was one unique individual. Sometimes he still felt uncomfortable about what Bryan's motives were when it came to Maddy. He had a hell of a hold on her probably due to their history. Jack had no doubt Bryan loved Maddy, but it was to the point of obsession. It was obvious by the way he had pursued her until Maddy broke down and gave in to the feelings she had buried. Possessive and obsessive, a dangerous combination. It didn't matter what Jack thought, Bryan and Maddy were bound together by their past. How could he compete? The best he could do was to be there for Maddy when she needed him, but he would never give up. He never said he wouldn't try to win her over, just not overtly anyhow.

Maddy rolled over in the huge bed. Where the hell was she? The last she remembered was falling a sleep in the suburban. How did she get here? She took in her surroundings. It was hard to focus as the room was very dim. This room was in an older home, very rustic. The walls were painted a dark green. There were beautiful wood columns stretched to the 12 foot beamed ceiling. Drawn wood shutters darkened two windows. The bed itself was a four-poster bed of the same dark wood as the columns. The bedspread, pillows and shams were fall earth tones. The room was very manly. Something clicked. She buried her face in the pillow and breathed in the scent. Jack. What the hell was she doing in Jack's bed? She stretched out and brought the comforter to her face and breathed in Jack's scent and her heart began to beat faster. What the hell was she thinking? Maddy heard the wood creak outsdide the door. She rolled over and pretended to be asleep.

Jack quietly opened the door and shut it behind him. Maddy appeared to be slepping soundly. He couldn't resist. He reached out and brushed the hair from her face. God she was beautiful. He leaned in and kissed her forehead.

Maddy felt his lips on her skin; she slowly rolled over so she could see him.

"Hey sleeping beauty," he smiled down at her. "Feeling any better?"

"My head's sore, but I'm better. How did I get here?" she asked, making her voice sound groggy.

"Bryan brought you here. He needed to be at the station and said he knew you wouldn't want to be back at the motel." He shrugged, "plus he wanted someone to be with you."

"Forever the protector," she sighed. "Will you lay down with me?" she asked softly.

Jack kicked off his shoes and slid in beside her, outside the covers, and took her in his arms. She laid her head on his chest, her arms across his stomach. He went to kiss the top of her head when she turned her face to his and kissed him softly on the lips. He slipped his hand under her chin and returned her kiss, slowly and gently."

Maddy's breath quickened as she kissed him deeper. She knew exactly what she was doing. She knew it was wrong, but she needed to be with Jack, she wanted to be with him. She wasn't going to fight her heart anymore.

Jack pulled back and laid his head on the pillow. "Maddy, you don't know how dangerous this is. You here...in my bed. I'm only human."

"I know...so am I." She started unbuttoning his shirt. She pulled it out from where it was tucked in his slacks. Then she ran her hands over his smooth chest, the sinewy muscles of his pecks. She looked up at Jack. He was lying back with his eyes closed. His lips were slightly parted, and he was breathing heavily.

"Maddy," he choked, "Don't do this...I can't...I don't know if I can stop."

Maddy laid her face on his bare skin. "Would you think me a bad person if I told you I wanted you?"

Jack ran his fingers along her arm. "You don't know how much I want you, but I don't think you could live with yourself, with the guilt. I don't want to hurt you...no matter how much I want this."

"But would you think I was a bad person?" She looked up at him, searching his face.

He shifted his body so his face was over hers; he cupped it with his hand and kissed her fervently. His fingers unbuttoned her blouse and cupped her breast as he parted her lips with his tongue. Maddy whimpered as he clung to him, then she ran her hands down his strong muscled back to his waistline. God he was so beautiful. More than she could have ever imagined. She ran her fingers along his waistline and then back up his back, lightly grazing his skin with her fingernails.

Jack's hand slipped around her back and unfastened her bra then he kissed a path down her neck, searing her skin as he went. He pulled back the blankets and covered her body with his, pressing against her so she could feel his hardness. He reached between them and undid her slacks and tugged at them.

She fumbled with his belt and tugged at his zipper. She slid her hands down across his narrow hips, touching him feeling his desire for her.

Jack slipped off her and they both removed what little clothing that they had left on off. He lay there beside her, exploring her body first with his eyes and then with his hands. He barely touched her skin yet she felt electricity coursing through her body. His lips took over where his hands left off, starting low and finishing off by crushing her mouth with his own.

She turned her face and whispered in his ear, "I love you, Jack."

He cradled her in his arms looking down at her. Maddy looked into his beautiful brown eyes and she could see it there, she could see the love he held there for her. He didn't have to say it. "Love me Jack," she whispered softly.

He studied her closely, "Are you sure Maddy? I couldn't bare it if I hurt you in anyway." His voice was deep with passion and emotion.

"Without a shadow of a doubt..." Maddy pulled him down on her kissing him, reaching for him, Jack slowly descended into her. His touch was slow and gentle making her cry out. He covered her mouth silencing her with the sweetness of his lips. She clung to him, kissing his shoulder as he made slow, passionate love to her. The feeling was so sweetly intense she thought she would die. As they reached their crescendo Maddy cried out from her heart, "I love you Jack...God, I love you."

Afterwards Jack held her tight in his arms, kissing her tenderly. Maddy smiled up at him and he asked her, "No regrets?"

She kissed him deeply. "No regrets." She put her head back down on his chest. "Damn, you're hot!" she laughed.

Jack chuckled, "Now I know, you were just lusting after my body."

Maddy smiled, "Honey what just happened between us had nothing to do with lust."

Jack smiled happily, "You feel that way too huh?"

She nodded. "Definitely."

Jack's phone was going off somewhere on the floor. He scrambled around looking for it, "Shit!" Finally he found it under the bed.

Maddy giggled and Jack held his finger up for her to be silent and mouthed Bryan.

Maddy put her hands together on the side of her face to signal him she was sleeping. He nodded in acknowledgment.

He flipped it open, "Hello."

"How's she doing?" Bryan asked.

"Eh...the last I checked she was still out. Just a sec, I'll check on her again." Jack got up and pulled the sheet off the bed and wrapped it around him. Maddy almost burst out laughing until her gave her the look. He went to the door and knocked on it and then opened the door. Maddy smiled and gave him the thumbs up.

"Maddy? Hon?"

She put her head down in the pillow surpressing her laughter and trying so hard to behave. She shook it off "Hmmmm....where am I?"

Jack made a face at her. "You're at my house, sleeping it off, damn girl you need to quit drinking so much. Here she is," he handed her the phone.

"Fuck you," she said to Jack.

Jack quickly grabbed his clothes and left the room so they could have some privacy. After the amazing thing that just happened between he and Maddy, he didn't want to spoil it.

"Hey Mickey," she sounded groggy. Damn she was getting good at this. "Why am I at Jack's?"

"You were still out of it when we got back. I asked Jack to babysit you. How's the headache?"

"Pretty much gone, just feels tender now. What time is it?" she looked around for a clock.

"Almost 3:30," he replied.

She tried to read anything into his voice. She didn't notice anything into his inflection. "Can I come in?"

"If that's what you want. Do you feel up to it?"

"I'm fine. Is Derek going to stay off my ass?" she asked. "Are you going let me go to the scene?"

Bryan was silent momentarily. "Tell you what, have Jack bring you to the crime scene and I will meet you there. That way Derek doesn't have to know. Do not, I repeat, do not go in until I get there. Is that understood?"

Maddy sighed, "Understood. When are you going to stop treating me like a mental case?"

"That's not fair Maddy. I just don't want to put you in harm's way."

"I'm never going to get better if you keep coddling me," she argued.

"I'm like this because I love you, you know that."

"I love you too but Bryan, you got to let me go. Either I sink or swim," she tried to explain to him.

"What do you mean let you go?"

"Quit being so damn over protective of me. That's all I am asking...please?"

"I will try. Meet you at the scene. I love you Maddy..."

"You know I do..." she answered him.

"Are you okay? Did something happen?

Shit, did he know or was she just being paranoid. As long as she didn't act stupid she was okay. "I'm just getting really frustrated. When do I get to be me?"

Bryan sighed, "I'm sorry, we'll talk more about this later and I promise I will do my best to back off."

She smiled softly into the phone, "Thank you. I'll see you there."

Maddy searched around to find all her clothing and then went in search of a bathroom. She found one across the hall. She washed up with warm water. She didn't use any soap, dead giveaway. Bryan would notice in a heartbeat. She pulled out the hair tie and ran a brush though her hair and tied it back up. Maddy studied herself in the mirror. Her cheeks were still flushed; her lips still tender to the touch, and her eyes had softness to them. She smiled as she thought of the way Jack made love to her. She had never felt that way with anyone. He was so giving, so tender, and so sweet. It felt so right and so natural. When Bryan made love to her it was all about ultimately possessing her, taking her and making her his own. She knew she was playing with fire, but given the chance she would do it all over again. As if her life wasn't complicated enough, she had added an affair with Jack. She gave herself the once over again in the mirror making sure everything was in place. Good enough.

When she came down the steps, Jack was stacking files together and putting them in a satchel. He glanced up at her and smiled, she sheepishly smiled back. He stood up and held his arms out to her, which she went into eagerly. She stood back and looked at him and started laughing.

"What?" Jack looked puzzled.

"Who taught you how to dress?" She reached up and starting unbuttoning his shirt. She gave him a kiss on his chest and buttoned it back up, correctly this time. She stood on her tiptoes and kissed him lightly. "You're a damn good cop, but you would make a lousy criminal," she laughed.

He lifted her up and she wrapped her legs around him. He smiled at her and then kissed her deeply. "You are amazing. Making love with you was so much more than I could have imagined."

She ran her fingers through his thick hair and kissed him. "We're amazing together."

"What I wouldn't do to take you back upstairs," he whispered in her ear.

She hugged him tightly. "Me to, but we have orders."

He released her and her feet slid back down to the floor. "Damn work. Where to?"

"The crime scene. Bryan is going to let me walk through so I can get a read," she explained.

"Do you think that's wise?"

Maddy threw him a look. "I get enough of that shit from Bryan, I don't need it from you okay?"

Jack nodded, "Okay, I will respect your wishes unless you look like you're in trouble."

Maddy threw her hands up in the air. "I give up."

Jack held the door open for her, just as she was about to walk through he gently grabbed her arm, pulled her back in and kissed her tenderly. "Don't know when I'll get my next chance," he whispered.

As they were driving to the crime scene Maddy noticed Jack looked pretty deep in thought. "What's on your mind hon?" she asked.

"Do you have any regrets?"

She reached for his hand and squeezed it. "Never."

"Okay back to reality. I am assuming this is not something you want Bryan to know. I am figuring what happened with us today, has nothing to do with the two of you. As fucked up as it sounds, I understand. It doesn't change how I feel about you. I know you'll be going back to him. I wish we didn't have to factor that in, but we do." He furrowed his brow, "Do you have any fucking clue what I am trying to say? Cuz I sure as hell don't"

Maddy laughed, "I think so...maybe. I've never felt the way I felt when I was with you today with anyone, including Bryan. Which tells me something, what I haven't figured out yet. Fuck I don't know what I am talking about anymore than you do. I guess what I am saying is I will be with you whenever I can. I can't promise when but know that I want to okay? I love you and I love Bryan, but it's so different. I don't want to hurt you, if you think it's too much I will understand."

Jack took out a cigarette and lit it. "Maddy when did we ever do anything that wasn't crazy? I love you and I'll take whatever moments we can steal. Now my question for you...how is either one of us going to look him in the eye and not give it away? The man can pick up on body language better than anyone I have ever seen."

"I conned a shrink today, I think I can get past Bryan. As long as he doesn't pick up on any changes between us. He knows I have feelings for you. I don't have to hide that. As far as how I act around you, nothing's changed as far as I'm concerned. Question is, can you?" She watched him.

"And he knows I have feelings for you, like you said we don't have to hide that. As far as the rest, I guess we'll find out. By the way, how did you come out?" he asked.

Maddy scrunched up her face, "Asshole put me on restricted duty."

Jack threw his head back and laughed, "Yeah right, like that's going to happen."

Maddy grinned, "Exactly."

Bryan was already at the crime scene waiting in the suburban. Jack reached over and squeezed her hand. "Showtime."

Maddy stepped out of the car and then turned to him, "Hey you got gloves?"

Jack reached in back and pulled her a set out of a box. He snapped her with them as they walked across the street. "Way to be prepared for working a crime scene," he teased.

"Bite me," she laughed and pulled them out of his hand.

"Anytime, any place," he laughed under his breath. She backhanded him.

Bryan joined them in front of the house and leaned over and kissed Maddy on the cheek. Asserting his claim, Maddy thought to herself.

"You're looking like your old self again," he smiled.

She smiled at him, "Mean and ornery just like always. Let's get this show on the road and don't dare ask me if I'm sure. I swear if either one of you gets protective I will beat the shit out of both of you."

Bryan glanced over at Jack, "Damn what side of the bed did she get out of?"

Jack shrugged, "She was like that when she came downstairs. Must be because she's under the influence of drugs."

Maddy glared at him. "Whatever."

The three of them slipped on their gloves and Bryan unlocked the door. He held it open for Maddy to enter and motioned for Jack to hang back in the foyer with him. "She needs to do this on her own, we're just observers."

Maddy stepped in the living room and stood for a few moments studying the room and getting her bearings. The room was in the state of disarray it was in when she saw it last. The only thing different there was no body. Maddy turned to Bryan and he handed her a packet. She pulled the photos out of the envelope. She compared the photos to the actual scene, stuck them back in the envelope and handed it back to Bryan. Maddy quietly moved around the room, squatted and looked at it from different angles. Then she moved into the kitchen. Bryan and Jack followed close behind watching her carefully for any signs of distress. Maddy saw the dried blood on the floor. She saw where she slipped smearing it back as far as the backdoor. "Well I sure fucked that up," she said to no one in particular.

"What?" Bryan asked.

She didn't answer but continued her observation. Maddy went to the stove and opened up the oven, cookies, well done cookies. Okay that answered that question. Now the object of her desire...something he used to knock her out. It couldn't have been too large or too heavy, her contusion wasn't that big, it needed to be just to enough to render her unconscious for a short time. It was never his intent to kill her, not yet anyhow. Something obvious...on the counter was a carafe containing vegetable oil. It had a beveled surface and had ample enough weight. She picked it up and examined the bottom of it. There was a very minute trace of blood and some blonde hairs. She gripped it tightly and swung it against the palm of her hand. She found her weapon.

Bryan studied her facial expressions. She was deep into her read, not once flinching at the sight of where she fell. She was right; he really needed to start giving her more credit.

"You ready?" he asked. Bryan reached in his pocket and pulled out a tape recorded and handed it to her.

"Yes." She went back into the living room. "Vic meets unsub at door, knows him and lets him in. He talks to her for a while while he's trying to convince her to leave with him. She can't leave just yet, why, is she expecting her boyfriend, if so and she tells him, unsub would leave. So it's not that. She has something going on in kitchen. She leaves him to go there and he follows her there. She's doing something in the kitchen when boyfriend enters. Unsub panics hits vic over the head with something." She demonstrates everything as she moves through the house. "Boyfriend hears commotion moves toward kitchen, before he gets there he is confronted by unsub. Boyfriend wants to know what he's doing there. Calls out for his girlfriend. Unsub stands in his way; boyfriend tries to push past him. Unsub shoves him knocking over table with lamp hits face on corner of couch, gets fabric burn. If you look close on photo of the boyfriend you will notice a small abrasion below his left eye. Boyfriend rises from floor, unsub plunges knife into him.

Unsub returns to kitchen; vic is starting to regain consciousness. He takes out his syringe of ketamine and comes at her, she fights him, scratches him, she grabs at his knife, cuts her hand, he jabs her with syringe as she tries to bat it away, sending it flying. He waits for her to succumb to drug. He's agitated and flustered, he doesn't like getting his plan fucked up, he can't take her out of her home undetected but he is driven to finish the ritual. He has to complete it. While she lies there defenseless, he does whatever he does, but he has to do it quickly, he can't do it properly. If you check her neck laceration you will notice the cut is different than the others because he had to do it while she was lying on the floor rather than hung. He slips out through the back door to avoid being seen." Maddy is standing in the kitchen. She opened the oven door showing them the cookies. "She couldn't leave because she was baking. He struck her with that." She pointed to the carafe. "There's trace on the bottom of it. You might want to bag it." She went and stood by the door. "Here is where I fucked up the crime seen when I slipped. If I hadn't smeared the blood so bad, we would have seen his footprints in the blood where he left via the back door." She opened the door and knelt down on the steps. The steps were heavily moss covered but she could still see traces of blood. She looked up, "Who called this in?"

"The couple was suppose to meet up with some friends and they never showed up. They tried calling both parties, got no answer then stopped by. When both their vehicles were in the drive and no one answered one of them looked in the window and saw the boyfriend on the floor and called 911."

Maddy scratched her head. "What is it with this guy and cell phones? He never leaves them at the scenes. That a really odd thing to keep as a trophy."

Maddy stood up, "Well, I'm done here, let's get the hell out of here. This place is creeping me out." She walked back through the house and out the front door. She went and waited by the vehicles for the guys. She knew they were going to 'confer' over her read. Hell, she was sure they would probably compare notes about how they thought she behaved.

Bryan pulled out a plastic bag and dropped the carafe into it. "Well what do you think? Impressive isn't she?"

Jack stood with a blank expression on his face. "She always been like that?"

"Yep, that's why she was one of the best. She wouldn't do it anymore after her kids were killed. Getting her to go to a crime scene was a major stressor for her." He looked over at Jack. "It kind of concerns me how proficient she is able to do it now. She didn't even flinch, not once."

"Why would it bother you?"

"You saw her yesterday...she was all over the charts. I haven't seen one low swing yet today." He shrugged, "But then again she could be just throwing herself into this case to keep from thinking too much. I guess I'll find out when we go home."

When we go home...Jack inwardly flinched. No, he couldn't think like that. They had to make this work. It was all he had to hang on to. He couldn't think about the future, only the here and now.

Bryan nudged him out of his revere. "What's the matter with you, Parker? You seem like you're somewhere else."

Jack took a deep breath, "I don't know. So much shit has happened in one week, then this thing with Maddy. It's just a lot to take in."

"She say anything to you at your house?"

He's fishing, Jack thought. "I really didn't talk to her much, she was asleep up until you called. We talked on the way over here about her restrictive duty status. She's not happy with that."

Bryan smiled, "No, she's not and you know she won't do it either. I just need to keep Derek off her ass. I don't know how she pulled it off. I didn't have a chance to talk to her about it. She came down with her migraine as soon as we hit the parking lot. Took her to get that shot straight from there. She get those often?"

Jack shrugged, "I don't know, Bryan. I would go weeks without seeing her."

"Well let's get back to the station, see what kind of dick Derek's going to be. I'm beginning to wonder at the wisdom of bringing him in."

While Bryan was securing the house Jack went to his car. Maddy joined him and leaned against his car. "How you holding up?" he asked.

"Oh Christ, first you then its going to be him," she sighed.

Jack laughed, "No not about that. You did just fine. I mean us."

Maddy felt the heat rise to her cheeks. "Oh yes," she smiled, "that. Wish we could go back to your place and do it all over again. This is going to be harder than I thought. Wish we could go back and let things progress the way they were meant to, before Bryan came back into the picture."

Jack brushed her cheek with the back of his hand, "Well we can't. All we can do is move forward and deal with the cards we were dealt. You can't tell me you're still not in love with Bryan."

Maddy looked down at her feet. "I don't know how I feel about anything anymore."

Jack turned his head so he was closer to her level, "And us, was that nothing but an unsure feeling?"

Maddy looked at him sharply, "Don't ever say that. You've known all along deep down I've wanted to be with you. Christ I've never been able to hide it from Bryan, not from day one and you know it."

"Maddy, just two days ago you basically told me to give it up, that you and Bryan...well you know. And then I saw him with you Saturday night. He was the only one who could reach you. Hell, I couldn't, I tried." He argued.

"Two days ago I was someone else. I was captive to my past, alone and afraid. Bryan was the only one who knew my world, knew what I had been through and protected me from myself. This whole thing has really messed up my head, but there are three things I am sure of Jack. First, I know I love you, second, I am going to find the son of a bitch that is killing these women, and last, I am responsible for killing my children," Maddy wiped the tears that had started to fall from her eyes. She turned leaving Jack to watch after her and got into the Suburban.

Jack wanted to run after her but Bryan was walking across the street. Son of a bitch, he needed to go to her after her last that comment. He was too late; the Sub was already leaving.

Jack got in his car and slammed his fist into the steering wheel. "God damn it Maddy!"

Bryan glanced over at Maddy and saw she was crying. He noticed her and Jack arguing by his car. "What's the matter? Lover's spat?" he asked half joking.

"Fuck you Bryan! I am tired of taking this shit off you. All this shit is getting to be real old," she snapped.

"Maddy, are you getting sick of me?" he asked quietly.

"Did I say that? No. I'm just tired of people telling me what I'm thinking, what I'm feeling. I just can't do it anymore. Now more than ever I need to find my own way."

"Do you want to be left alone tonight?" Bryan felt his gut churning. He was loosing her...again.

"Yes. Please take me back to my car. I can't deal with the office right now. I can't deal with anything. I just want to be alone to think and to feel without pressure. I'm not angry with you, Bryan, I just need to examine how I'm feeling and figure out how I am going to cope with the reality of my life." she pleaded.

She took Bryan's hand and squeezed it and then brought it to her lips. "I'm sorry baby, I'm just not holding up to well right now."

Bryan pulled into the Regency parking lot next to her car. He went to Maddy's side and helped her out of the truck. He wrapped his arms around her holding her tight. "I'm sorry Minnie. I do understand. I'm just too selfish to see it. I love you with all my heart. There's nothing I won't do for you." He held her chin up and kissed her tenderly.

Maddy put her head on his chest, "I love you too. I just need to do this for me okay?"

Bryan buried his face in her hair, "Can you promise me one thing Maddy? Promise you won't shut me out. I couldn't bear loosing you again."

Maddy felt an aching in her heart. She touched his lips with her finger tips. "You're not going to loose me."

He watched her drive off leaving him feeling totally useless being unable to help her.

15

Maddy kicked off her shoes as soon as she walked through her door. She let the dogs in. Rufus was bouncing all over the place. She went into the bathroom, pulled her hair loose, washed her face and changed clothes. She grabbed a glass of tea with lemon and headed straight for her couch. This had been the first time in a week she was home by herself and it felt good. She had been honest; she needed to be alone to think.

Since revisiting the horrors from her past, Maddy felt so many conflicting emotions. She felt the loss of her children, a loss she already lived through once. She felt suffocated by everyone's concern for her emotional welfare. She knew these people felt they had her best interest at heart. But they needed to let her feel what she needed to feel and trust that she wasn't going to fall apart.

Then there was Jack. She smiled to herself. What could she say about Jack? He had been her friend for the last two years. He never questioned her need for privacy, not until Bryan came along. He had been so patient though all this, his feelings for her never wavering. He didn't judge her or Bryan for their relationship. Hell, he even liked Bryan. And she believed him with all her heart when he said he loved her. He damn well better or he was one stupid ass man. He swore to her he would be there for as long as it takes. She guessed he was counting Bryan not being here.

Maddy was trying to understand what happened today. She and Jack had essentially agreed they would not sleep together while she was with Bryan—until she could give her heart to him completely. But every time she and Jack kissed, her desire for him grew. And damn, when she found herself in his bed, intoxicated with his scent, she didn't want to fight it anymore. It was like since the events of Saturday night her emotions were open and she just acted upon them. All she knew was she wasn't going to hold back on her feelings for Jack anymore. She did love him, differently than she loved Bryan. No it wasn't right to be sleeping with both of them and she didn't know how she was going to be able to manage it or even if she could but she decided she would cross those bridges as they came to her. She definitely was not giving up Jack.

She felt this indescribable anger with no direction to point it to. She was afraid though Bryan was going to take the brunt of it. It wasn't right, Bryan had gone above and beyond loving her by being there for her. He was right, she was feeling the need to push him away. She hoped she had the strength to keep herself from doing it. She began to wonder if she had done this the first time. Had she punished him?.

Maddy looked out her kitchen door. A storm was moving in at a slow pace. Cool, it fit her mood. Maddy changed the bedding in both bedrooms and threw them in the wash. She wiped down the kitchen, mopped the floor, and then vacuumed her living room.

Maddy was near the hall closet when a thought crossed her mind. She grabbed a stepladder and dug into its upper shelves. She found it way to the back. It was a large box full of photo albums and home movies. She pulled it down and hauled it out to the living room. These were albums and movies of her children's lives. She wasn't going to tackle it tonight. She didn't feel strong enough. Actually she would like to have Bryan around when she went through them because she wasn't sure if she could do it without him.

Maddy picked up her empty glass and carried it to the kitchen then stuck her head out the kitchen door. It was raining, a warm summer rain, steady and straight. She turned her face to the sky letting the gentle drops drizzle down on her. Perfect! Maddy ran into her room and changed into a tank top and slipped on some older shoes then took off down to the barn. She grabbed lead ropes and put each of the horses in separate stall except for Lily. Lily was a beautiful blue-black horse, tall and slender with a long barrel. She was the perfect horse for running as she had a very long stride making for a smooth gait. Maddy gave the horse a couple of mints and then slide off her halter and replaced it with a bridle. She grabbed her mounting block and set it by the back entrance to the barn, mounted it and hoisted herself on to Lily's back. As soon as she left the barn the rain began to soak her skin. She nudged Lily forward in to a slow trot and then into a canter. The warm rain pelted her skin drenching her hair and clothing. It felt like heaven. She nudged Lily in to a gallop and took off across the pasture. Water streamed down her skin getting in her eyes and mouth. With each extended lope the horse took Maddy felt a rush, each greater than the one before. She laughed, kind of like making love to Jack. She gave cry of delight. Now this was feeling alive.

When Jack pulled in Maddy's drive he noticed the lights on down at the barn so he proceeded to drive to it. The rain was coming down steadily and he made a dash for the barn entrance. He noticed three of the four horses were in their stalls and the gate was open to the area of the back entrance. He stepped into the area not watching where he was going. Shit...literally. Damn it. When he went to the back door to scrape his shoe he saw her. A small figure of a woman bare back on top a rather large black horse was tearing across the pasture in the pouring rain. Her long wet hair clung to her skin. The two moved as one. Jack took a sharp intake of air. God she was beautiful, they both were. He stood there mesmerized as he watched them run the length of the pasture.

As Maddy approached the barn entrance she spotted Jack standing there. She was pleasantly surprised to see him. She slowed Lily down to a walk. Jack stepped back away from the door. Maddy ducked down and rode Lily past him. She slid down off her back and was caught unaware when she felt Jack's hands on her hips guiding her down.

When her feet hit the ground his hands were still on her, his body close to hers. She could feel his breath on her neck, warm against the coolness of her skin. Her breath caught in her throat.

Jack stepped back and out of her way and watched her as she removed the bridle from the black mare. She went to the other stalls and turned out the other horses. She then came and stood before him, smiling from ear to ear. His eyes roamed her body. She was wearing grey cotton Capri's, a tank top...and no bra. Her wet translucent top clung to her skin leaving nothing to the imagination. Her wet hair hung in ringlets framing her delicate face. "Wow."

Maddy blushed and averted his gaze. "What?"

Jack shook his head, smiling, "You don't want to know."

"What? This?" She reached for his hand and placed it on her breast. The heat of his hand radiated through the thin material.

Jack's eyes locked on his hand. His fingers gently caressed her. His heart began to quicken in his chest. Oh God, what was she doing to him? His eyes traveled to her face. Her eyes fluttered shut as her tongue over her lips. His hand left her breast. He ran the back of his fingers slowly up her arm. The little beads of wetness that glistened on her skin dispersed as his skin made contact with hers. Maddy looked up at him from beneath black sooty lashes, her green eyes sparked with little flecks of fire.

Maddy studied him. She saw the conflict in his eyes. "Something wrong?" she asked softly.

Jack pulled his hand back slowly. He could see the hurt in her eyes. He took her hand and pulled her to him wrapping his arms around her. He kissed the top of her head. "As hot and desirable as you are at this moment, and I do mean hot, I don't want us to be all about sex. We are so much more. God, you don't know how hard its not to succumb to your beauty. But I want more Maddy. I've always wanted more." He picked her up and stood her on a bale of hay. He smiled, "Now we can see eye to eye, you're so short."

"Don't be a pig," she smiled softly.

He leaned forward and kissed her, gently at first. He parted her lips and explored her mouth, tasting her, kissing her deeper.

Maddy felt as if his kiss was seeking her soul. With a slow easiness his lips sought out her inner fire warming her from the inside out. Her arms crept up around his neck and she pressed her body to him.

Jack felt Maddy shiver in his arms and he slowly pulled away from her. "You're freezing girl. We need to get you out of these clothes."

Maddy grinned, "I'm not shivering because I'm cold, but you can get me out of these clothes pretty easily." She kissed him. "Just kidding. Why don't we go up to the house so I can get changed?"

They dashed out to Jack's car and drove up to the house. Once in the house Jack shook off the rain and Maddy disappeared into the back and reappeared in a light cotton sweat suit.

She grabbed her glass off the counter. "You want something to drink? I have a couple of beers left in here."

Jack shook his head, "No beer for me, thanks, if you have a soda that'd be great."

Maddy held up a diet coke, he nodded and she handed it to him. She filled up her glass and sat down at the table. "So what brings you out to this neck of the woods? Are you checking up on me?"

Jack held his coke in his hand, his thumbs running up and down its edge. "No, I just wanted to be with you. I know Bryan said you wanted to be alone, and it wasn't my plan to come here, but...I was heading for home...and this is where I ended up." He glanced up at her, "I hope it's okay. If not I can leave."

"No, I'm glad you're here," she took a sip of tea. "What did Bryan tell you?"

"Only that you needed time to sort through your emotions. I hope what happened today didn't make things more complicated for you." He opened his pop and took a sip.

Maddy ran her toe up his leg. "Baby what happened today...we made love. I am very clear on my feelings and emotions about that. No doubts, no regrets," she smiled, "just a whole lot of warm fuzzies."

Jack laughed, "Warm fuzzies huh? I would have described it as earth moving." He was smiling, his eyes fixed on his pop can.

Maddy blushed. "That's would be an understatement. It was incredible. Something I highly recommend to happen again. There is only one things I would change about it."

Jack looked up sharply, "What?"

"We could have lingered, stayed in each others arms longer."

Jack smiled, "Yeah, it would have been great." He laughed, "But we got caught. I swear the man has radar."

Maddy stirred her tea with her finger. "You know I really don't care anymore. One of the things I have been thinking about is that I need to do is allow myself to feel. And that means feel what I feel, not trying to bury things. One of those feelings is loving you, Jack."

Jack tilted his head as watched Maddy. "Are you saying you are going to tell him?'

Maddy grew quiet. "No. I can't hurt him like that and I do love him. I'm just confused as to why. I still feel he has the potential to be...evil. He doesn't seem like that...now. But I have seen him at his worse and a leopard doesn't change his spots, even if the leopard believes he has. Don't you think I don't keep my eyes open, watching and waiting?"

Jack shook his head, "I don't understand. I guess I must be missing something. So what happens when this is all over? He told me he would never leave you."

Maddy smiled weakly, "That's what he believes in his heart, but I know better. He can't cut free from his past, not even to be with me. He just doesn't know it yet." Maddy rubbed her fingers on her temples. "I don't want to talk about Bryan. Let's just enjoy the time we have."

Jack sighed and silently stared at his coke.

"Don't go getting all on the defensive with him and feel like you need to protect me from him. He is the man you know and respect—it really is him. He just has different sides, as do you or I. I know him better than anyone, I can take care of myself with him."

"I didn't come here to fight with you Maddy. I came here to be with you and enjoy your company. Let's just drop the subject of Bryan."

Maddy took a big swallow from her glass. "Sounds like a plan to me."

Maddy tapped her fingers on the table, thinking. Finally she looked up at Jack and asked, "Do you sleep with Stella?"

Jack's head shot up in surprise, "Whoa, where did that come from?"

"Just asking. Do you?" She watched his face.

Jack ran his finger through his hair. Maddy had made him uncomfortable with her question. She smiled to herself—good. "Well?"

"You really want to go there?" he asked.

"You know I sleep with Bryan. I'm just asking if you sleep with Stella."

"I'm not real comfortable talking to you about this, but...let's just put it this way Maddy, I have sex with Stella, I have never made love to her." He watched Maddy for her reaction.

Maddy was chewing on her bottom lip. What did she expect? That he was chaste? Not a man like Jack, he had needs. After all he and Stella had been dating for a few months. "When was the last time?"

Jack's jaw dropped. "You really want to talk about this? Because I don't."

"Yes, I want to talk about it. When was the last time you were with her?"

Jack took a deep breath and blew it out. "A week ago." He really wanted to tell her the only reason he did then was because he was going crazing knowing she was back at the motel making loving with Bryan, but he didn't because he didn't want to hurt her.

"Oh."

"Well you asked," he said in his own defense. "If you don't want to know the answer, don't press the question."

"Asked and answered." She looked up. "Was it like being with me?"

Jack sighed and put his head in his hands. "It was just sex Maddy. With us, it was making love. At least I thought so."

She reached for his hand, "It was for me too." Maddy stood up. "Wait here."

Enough of this crap of talking about others—it was their time. Maddy went back to her room and lit several candles on the dressers. She had never done this with Bryan. Their lovemaking was never about romance. She wanted to love Jack, completely.

Maddy went back out to the kitchen and pulled Jack up from his chair.

"What are you doing?"

"You ask too many questions," she said as she led him back to her bedroom.

Jack laughed, "I ask too many questions?"

Maddy and Jack stood at the foot of her bed. Jack looked around the room. The shades had been drawn and the only light in the room was the reflection of flames from the candles flickering off the walls. It gave the room a soft burgundy glow.

Maddy turned to Jack, reached up and began to unbutton his shirt. He reached upward. Maddy caught his hands and put them back at his side. "Uhuh, no touchy rule applies at the moment."

Jack threw his head back and laughed. "That's not going to happen."

She held his hands down and smiled at him, "Just for now, baby, trust me..."

She continued unbuttoning his shirt and slipped it off and threw it aside. Maddy let her eyes and hands rove over his body from his broad shoulders, well muscled chest, to his flat stomach tapering off to narrow hips. She loved it when he held her in his strong arms. In her eyes, he was truly beautiful, inside and out. She looked up at him. His eyes were watching her with keen interest; a slight smile graced his lips. When he started to speak, she touched them softly with one finger and shook her head. Maddy pushed him so he was sitting on the bed. She knelt between his legs and ran her hands up his chest. She entwined her fingers in his hair and brought his face to her, kissing his eyes, his nose, and his cheeks, down the line of his jaw, behind his ears and down his neck.

Jack groaned, he reached up and held her head in her his hands and gazed into her eyes. "Enough. No more no touchy." His lips came down on hers, diving deep into her. His hands slid down her shoulders to her waist where he grasped her shirt and pulled upward. Their lips parted only long enough to slip the shirt over her head. He pulled her up and they fell back on the bed.

Maddy loved the feel of their bare skin touching. Jack rolled her over and ran his hand over her body sending shivers through her.

Jack lifted his head and laughed, "You cold?"

"Shut up and kiss me," she laughed.

"Damn you're bossy." He covered her lips with his. His hand searched out her breast, caressing and stroking her. Maddy squirmed trying to get closer to him. His mouth left hers and burned a trail down her neck and between her breasts. He took one in his mouth, teasing with his lips.

Maddy sunk her fingers into his hair and arched her body to him. "Oh my God," she moaned sotly. His hands ran between her legs and then to her waistband where he easily slipped off her pants. His hand resumed his exploration of her. Her head came up off the bed, her teeth gently biting into his shoulder. "Please..."she gasp.

Jack lifted his head to her as he continued to touch her. A wicked smile graced his lips. "Please what Maddy? I thought I was pleasing you."

Maddy gave an unsteady laugh, "Don't..."

"Don't what?" His hand ran hand up between her legs and taunted her breast, "Don't what Maddy? Don't stop?"

Maddy leaned her head back and closed her eyes. Her breathing was so rapid she could hardly catch it.

Jack released his hold on her and slipped off his slacks. He slid to the back of the headboard, guiding Maddy toward him. He lifted her easily on to him, slowly lowering her down on to him. Maddy cried out. Jack held her in place then reached out with his hands and held her face. "Look at me, Maddy." His voice was raspy.

Maddy tried hard to focus. His stillness inside her was sending her over the edge. She looked into his eyes, searching. His brown eyes were soft, his expression loving.

"I want you to look into my eyes as I make love to you. I want you to see it there and know how much I love you. Can you do that for me?"

Maddy whimpered and nodded. Jack guided her arms up around his neck then his hands slid across her shoulders and down her sides to her hips and he began to move. Maddy gasped and her head tilted back. "No baby, look at me..." he whispered.

His hands moved up and held her head. Their eyes locked as they rode the waves together. Maddy felt like she was dying inside and was going to heaven. Lord, she had never felt anything like this before. Jack's eyes pulled her in, surrounding her. She couldn't breath. His movements inside her intensified to the brink she couldn't hold back any longer. Maddy screamed out when they exploded together. Jack entwined his fingers in her hair and pulled her to him kissing her deeply and then they fell together. Maddy's head rested on his shoulder. They stayed like this until their breathing became more regular.

Jack slid her off of him and then wrapped his body around her and whispered in her ear. "I love you Mads."

Maddy hugged him tight. "I love you too." She kissed his shoulder. "So very, very much." Maddy rolled on to her side and propped her head up with her arm looking at him.

Jack studied her. A soft satisfied smile on her lips and her eyes held a softness that touched his heart. "What are you looking at?" He leaned over and kissed her forehead.

She laughed, "You."

Jack grinned. "You think I'm funny?"

Maddy took a deep breath and blew it out slowly. "No...funny is not what was going through my mind."

He brushed the hair out of her eyes, "Then what?"

She leaned over and kissed him softly. "You are just so fucking amazing."

He leaned his head back and chuckled. "Such language. But its like you said this afternoon...we are amazing...together."

"I feel like a kitten that has just gorged on warm milk. If I could purr I would," Maddy said coyly.

Jack laughed in her ear. "You got so mad at me when I called you kitten last Friday night."

She nudged him playfully. "You were drunk."

"And wanted you so badly. But then again when don't I?" He kissed her behind her ear. He ran his hand down the side of her body and when Maddy gave a soft moaned he asked, "You purr for me now, will you be my kitten?"

She reached up and whispered in his ear, "Meeeeeeeoooow!"

He chuckled and kissed her. "My kitten."

They lay there holding each other for another twenty minutes. When Jack asked, "You do know I didn't come here for a booty call right?"

Maddy couldn't help but laugh. "I was the one that seduced you. And wow... I just can't believe how amazing you are."

"Together," he corrected her. "You bring this out in me, you and you only."

Jack glanced over at Maddy's alarm clock. "Damn, did you know it was almost 11:30?"

"Time flies when your having fun," Maddy smiled. "Do you have to leave?"

Jack held her tight and buried his face in her hair. It still smelled of rain. "I would love to stay here with you, but I really should take off. We both have to work tomorrow and if I stay here, we won't sleep." He kissed her tenderly. "I can promise you that."

Maddy turned in his arms and kissed him deeply. "I understand. I will hold on to tonight and today until we can be together again. Hopefully real soon."

"Me too, my sweet kitten," he kissed her again and then rose from the bed. He looked around for his clothes. "We really need to be better organized when we strip."

Maddy laughed. "I wouldn't change a thing."

Jack finished dressing and he turned and looked at Maddy. She was lying there watching him, not shy about her nakedness. "Damn," he said shaking his head.

"What?"

"You look good enough to start all over again," he smiled softly.

"I'm game," she yawned.

He laughed. "Yeah, that's why you're yawning." He turned back the blankets for her. "Get in," he ordered.

Maddy crawled in in between the sheets. "There you go, getting all bossy on me."

Jack pulled the covers up around her and kissed her softly on the lips. "Good night, Kitten."

As he walked out of her room, he swore he heard a meow. He smiled for the whole drive home.

Maddy felt asleep with a smile on her lips, feeling totally relaxed and at peace for first time since she could remember.

Maddy's alarm clock went off at 7:00. She hit the snooze and rolled over. She caught the scent of Jack's cologne on her pillow and smiled. It wasn't a dream. She found it hard to believe she had made love to Jack—twice. And both times were amazing. Amazing was the only word she could use to describe their exchange. Heaven would be a good word. She felt like a schoolgirl first discovering the art of love. She didn't know where this was going but if this was any taste of what was to come, she couldn't wait.

Maddy turned off the alarm, grabbed some clothes and shuffled off to the bathroom to take a shower. After she popped some bread in the toaster and poured herself a glass of orange juice.

She had turned off her phone. She didn't want to be bothered with phone calls from Bryan or Jack. Having Jack show up was a pleasant surprise. She was so glad he did. She turned it on to find seven missed calls from Bryan. He didn't leave any voice mails nor any text messages.

Maddy didn't feel she had to answer to him. She couldn't explain her change in attitude towards him accept feeling suffocated. He counted on her needing him, using it to control her, to keep her dependent on him. And now she resented it. Yet she felt she owed him her loyalty. Yeah right, loyalty, she thought. That's why she was sleeping with Jack behind his back. She was afraid she wouldn't be able to hide this change from him. She finished her last bite of toast and drank her orange juice. Oh well, she felt how she felt and couldn't predict how that was going to be.

Maddy let the dogs out and hit the road. The 45-minute drive was spent thinking about the night before. Jack had a unique way of making love, of proving his love while making love to her. And he was so damn hot!

Maddy had to laugh to herself. She had been celibate for several years and in the past two weeks...well she had been a regular old horn dog. Making up for lost time she guessed. And with two men. This was so unlike her, but then again she didn't know who she was anymore.

Maddy pulled into the cop shop not knowing what the day had planned for her. She would have Derek to contend with and Bryan to hide from. She strapped her on holster and grabbed her gun out of the glove compartment. She attached her badge to her shirt and headed in.

Maddy briefly thought maybe she should turn in her resignation, tell Bryan good-bye and go back to the paper. Back to her old life—one where she was free to be with Jack. But she felt she an obligation to see this case through. She would help catch this bastard and walk away from the FBI forever. She would go back to having a normal life. Yeah right, like her life had ever been normal.

When Maddy arrived upstairs Bryan was already at his desk. The rest of the squad room was empty. He had his laptop open and was sipping on a cup of coffee. He stood up when he saw her, grabbed her hand and pulled her close. "God I missed you last night."

Maddy laughed softly. "It was just one night, hon."

"I tried calling you several times but it went straight to voice mail. What's the deal?"

Maddy sighed, "I didn't want to be bothered. I went home to be alone—totally alone. I thought you understood."

"I didn't think you would totally blow me off," he complained.

"I didn't blow you off," she snapped. "Jesus, do have to go through all this again? You know Bryan, the only way you are going to loose me is if you don't quit pushing me so hard."

Bryan searched her face. When he looked in her eyes, there was something missing. She was putting up a wall between them, pushing him away. He felt panicky. He couldn't loose her, not with everything they had been through. But like she said, if he pushed too hard, he would loose her. "I'm sorry. I guess I am so used to you wanting me around you and now I feel like you don't need me."

"It's not that I don't need you. I just need to need myself more. I want to be come whole again and I can't do that if I am dependent on you all the time. I can't be with you in the way you want me to until I have myself. I'm sorry if this sounds harsh and uncaring but it's the way it's got to be," she tried desperately tried to explain.

"So were not going to be together anymore..."

Maddy sighed in exasperation. "That's not what I said. I just can't be clinging to you all the time. We're still together, but I don't want to be dependent on you for my emotional stability." She touched his hand. "Let's just be us, the way we have been, but without you watching my every move to see if I'm going to crack okay?"

Bryan turned her face up to him and kissed her deeply. When she kissed him back, she felt like a fraud. Things really had changed.

"So anything new happen here yesterday," she put her bag on the floor and booted up her laptop. She still had Vanessa's emails to go through.

"Latent ran the prints through CODIS. No match so the unsubs not in the system. We had a sketch artist talk with the witnesses to see if we could get something there. I played your tape for Derek." Bryan told her.

"And?"

"He got a little pissed that I brought you back to the scene, but liked your analysis of what happened. We sent CSU back to crime scene to go over the backyard and dust for more prints in the kitchen. We don't have a report back yet."

"Can I see the sketch?"

Bryan pulled it out of the folder and handed it to her. The man in the sketch had dark hair. His eyes were narrow set, dark bushy eyebrows. His nose was sharp, a little on the large side. His face was long and narrow, his lips thin. There were really no distinguishing features. "He looks like a hundred other men in this city."

"Well it's more than we had," he replied none to friendly.

Jack walked into the squad room. She felt the heat rise to her face. She dare not look up at him. He went straight to Bryan's desk and handed him a couple files. "Here are your reports back from Ankeny. We have the autopsy reports on our first four vics and the prelims from Saturday night."

Bryan opened the files one at a time and studied them.

While he was waited, Jack sat down on Maddy's desk. "How you feeling?"

Maddy smiled without looking, "Refreshed."

He laughed, "Must have slept well last night, you seem more relaxed."

He was being a smart ass. "Yes it was an exhilarating evening." She looked up at him, trying not to laugh. "I rode."

"Ah you went riding. It was raining, didn't you get wet?" His eyes were teasing. She knew exactly what he was talking about.

She met his stare. "Very wet, I was soaked. I always get off riding bareback in the rain."

"You must have been shivering."

Maddy laughed and shook her head. "Yeah, but it wasn't anything a good snuggle wouldn't take care. Jack's a good dog to cuddle with. Go away, I have work to do."

Jack laughed and got off her desk. He turned to Bryan. "Anything more you need from me?"

"Not for right now. We're going to have a briefing in half an hour," Bryan answered without looking up.

Jack turned back to Maddy, "See you later, Mads." As he turned away she heard him say under his breath, "Here kitty, kitty, kitty."

Maddy burst out laughing. "You're a dick, Parker."

"You bet your sweet ass I am," he called back to her as he walked out.

Bryan looked up from his file. "What was that all about?"

Maddy signed onto her email. "Nothing, was just an old inside joke."

Bryan sat the file down and studied her without her knowing. He noticed her cheeks were flushed and she had a content smile on her face. What the hell was going on? "What happened last night?" he asked her.

"Huh?" Maddy looked up from her computer.

"What did you do last night?"

"Okay, I will give you a blow by blow of what I did last night. I got home, changed clothes, washed bedding, cleaned my kitchen, vacuumed my living room, rode one of my horses bareback in the rain, came back in, took a shower, drank some more tea, did some thinking and went to bed at around 8:30. Anything else you want to know?" She tilted her head to one side questioning him.

"Parker's right, you do look more relaxed." He looked at her suspiciously.

Maddy sighed. "It's like I told Jack, I really get off riding bareback in the rain. It gives me a total rush. I feel free and wild and last night was great for it, a warm gentle rain. Horse therapy. Its cheaper than professional therapy and a lot more effective." She looked at Bryan. Her eyes were sparkling.

Bryan chuckled. "Hell what do you need me for when you got a horse?"

Maddy got up from her desk. "Follow me."

Maddy led Bryan into the interrogation room and wrapped her arms around him. "Have I told you lately I love you?"

Bryan ran his hands up and down her back, "Not enough," he smiled down at her.

"I do need you Bryan and I want you, nothing is going to change that," she kissed him softly.

Before she could pull away, he pushed her gently against the wall, pinning her with his arms and kissed hard, not rough, but hard. When he pulled back he whispered in her ear, "You're mine Minnie." He had reclaimed her. It left her feeling cold.

Maddy left the room and went straight for the lady's room. What was wrong with her? Why was she feeling this way towards Bryan? What did he do to her, recently, that she be like this? Two days go she didn't want him to leave her side. She still had feelings for him. She felt it when he kissed her. Maddy collected her composure and left the bathroom.

She swung by Jack's office and popped her head in, "Hi Baby," she smiled.

Jack rocked back in his chair and smiled, "Kitten, what brings you to my lair?"

Maddy laughed, "You're so wicked."

"Come in, sit a minute," he kicked a chair in her direction.

Maddy sat down and they stared at each other silently, grinning the whole time. "This is crazy," Maddy finally said.

"I want to kiss you," he said softly.

"Me too."

Jack rose from his chair, shut his door and pulled the blinds of his office window. He reached down and grabbed Maddy's hand and pulled her to the corner. He put one hand behind her head and brought her to him. His lips came down on hers soft and gentle. He parted her lips and explored her mouth with his tongue. Her arms circled his neck and she moved closer, kissing him deeply. When they pulled apart they leaned their foreheads together.

"This is so hard," she whispered. "I don't know if I can do this."

"What do you mean?" he kissed her forehead.

"He knows something. I act different towards him, and I can't stop myself. He kissed me, very possessively and told me I was his. I just wanted to get away from him."

Jack put his finger under her chin and turned her face to him. "Do you think we should cool it and back off?"

Maddy reached up kissed him deeply. "No, Jack, I can't. When I am with you, I am happy, I mean truly happy. Do you know how long it's been since I felt that way?" She kissed him again. "I love you."

He kissed her softly. "I love you too Kitten."

She giggled at her pet name. "Meow."

Jack laughed, "We better look professional now or we're going to get busted."

Maddy had barely sat down when there was a knock at the door and Bryan popped his head in. "Maddy, don't you have work to do?" Then he said to Jack, "Briefing in five."

As Maddy stormed passed him he grabbed her arm jerking her back. "Take your hands off me," she hissed. Maddy saw out of the corner of her eye Jack rising from his chair. She looked at him and begged him with her eyes not to do anything.

"We need to talk," Bryan said coldly.

She jerked her arm away from him. "No we don't." And she left.

Bryan came in and sat down across from Jack. "I wish I knew what the hell was going on in her head. She's like hot and cold. Like she's really pissed at me and I don't know what I did."

Jack took a deep sigh of relief and found it ironic Bryan should be confiding in him. "She's been pretty good to me, actually nicer than she was before. But then again Bryan, I don't know her the way you do."

"What do you mean?" he asked suspiciously.

"Maybe I'm out of line here or maybe I don't know what the fuck I'm talking about, but has it ever occurred to you that because you are so much a part of her past, linked to everything she's dealing with, it might be hard for her to separate the two?" Jack tried to explain.

"Did she tell you that?"

"She hasn't told me anything. For Christ sake if I ask her anything about it she jumps my ass about being overprotective of her," Jack laughed. "She's hell bent on doing this on her own."

Bryan sighed and looked down at his hands, "Yeah, don't I know it. I feel like she's pushing me away, that the sight of me just pisses her off. She told me last night that she felt all this anger and she was afraid she was directing it at me. If she knows this why is she doing it?"

"Maybe because you are the only one she can direct. You are the person closest to her, closest to her pain. I don't know what to tell you man. When it comes to this area, I don't know how her mind works. I think she finds it easier to relax around me because I'm not connected to that part of her life. For once I'm glad." Jack leaned back in his chair. He still couldn't believe he was having this conversation. He liked Bryan, just not with Maddy. He felt bad for the guy. "Are you doing anything to antagonize her?"

Bryan chuckled, "Yeah, breathing. I'm just afraid I'm loosing her."

"Just ride it out. Even if you have to keep your distance until she's ready for you. If what you say is true about these anger issues, you need to get her professional help before she destroys the things she cares about the most—you." Jack stood up. "We better get into that briefing, that guy in charge can be a real prick."

Bryan smiled and shook his head, "So I've heard." He shook Jack's hand, "Thanks for the ear. You've been a good friend to me...and to Maddy."

Jack smiled to himself and thought, 'You have no idea.'

Maddy was fuming. She had started downloading all Vanessa's emails when Jack and Bryan walked in to the squad room. They were laughing and joking and that just pissed her off more. Maddy shut her laptop, picked it up and started to leave the room.

"Where do you think you're going Maddy?" Bryan asked her.

"Somewhere else." Bryan was standing in front of her, she moved to get around him and he blocked her move.

"We are going to have a briefing. You need to sit in on it with the rest of us."

Bryan sighed and said quietly, "Maddy, would you please cut me some slack. I'm not trying to piss you off. No matter what I do, or what I say, I can't do right by you. Christ, honey, I don't know what to do."

Maddy saw the hurt in his eyes and her heart ached. He was right, and this didn't have anything to do with Jack. It was much deeper than that. She felt tears stinging in her eyes. She pushed the laptop into Bryan's hands. "I'm truly sorry. I'll be back in a few minutes." She ran from the room.

Bryan looked at Jack pleading, "Go to her, please. I would just make it worse."

Maddy went and sat on the steps at the back of the station. She let the tears come. What the hell was she doing? She was crushing this man she said she loved, that she had always loved. She was just being a bitch.

Maddy heard footsteps behind her and looked up to see Jack. She smiled softly at him. "Hey."

"Hey Mads." He sat down and pulled out a cigarette. "He sent me out after you."

Maddy laughed and wiped her eyes. "How ironic."

Jack pulled out his hanky and handed it to her.

Maddy took it. "Gee I'm back to getting a real one," she half smiled.

He took a drag on his cigarette. "You can keep it."

They sat quietly for a few moments then Jack asked, "Honey, why are you being so hard on him? After you left my office, he actually sat down and confided in me. He's confused, hurt, and doesn't know what the hell to do."

Maddy put her head in her hands and cried. "I don't know. I'm not trying to be this way. It just comes out. I mean I try to make things right and next thing I know I'm ripping into him."

Jack put his arm around her shoulders. "Mads are you pushing him away on purpose? Do you want to loose him?"

"You would think this is what we would want," she said quietly.

He kissed the top of her head, "You would think, but that's not the kind of people we are." He laughed, "What kind of people that does make us, I don't know. But honey, first of all, quit feeling all this guilt that you are treating Bryan like shit because of us. We have nothing to do with what's going on between the two of you. I don't think you can handle this on your own, love, and I don't think Bryan or I can help you with this part. Would you be upset if I suggest you seek professional help?"

"No, I think you're right. You're always right."

Jack nudged her playfully, "You are so full of shit!"

She nudged him back, "You think you know me so well."

"I'm working on it," he winked. He turned to her and kissed her a sweet and gentle kiss. "Mmmmm...you taste good."

Maddy kissed him and then licked her lips, "Tastes like chicken."

Jack laughed and shook his head. "You're crazy...crazy beautiful."

"So tell me Dr. Jack, what advice did you give to Bryan?"

"To let it ride, give you space if you need it, be there when you ask for it...and that you should get help. Then I billed $200 for my fee," he grinned. "You know he said I was a good friend...his good friend that is sleeping with the love of his life." He kissed her softly. "But you're the love of my life too."

Maddy looked at him with a serious expression on her face. "Jack, every day that goes by, I fall more and more in love with you."

He squeezed her tight, "You don't know what hearing that does to my heart, Mads."

"Good things I hope," she kissed his cheek.

"All good things my sweet kitten."

He stood up and helped her up. "We should be getting back."

Maddy dusted off her pants and then dusted off his and pinched him.

"Hey!"

She laughed. "I would rather sneak away and go hide out in your bedroom."

"Me too but we work for a living and we have a killer to catch." He ruffled up her hair.

"Hey!" Maddy ran her fingers through her hair to get it back into place. "No touchy!"

Jack shook his head and laughed. "You and your no touchy."

She grinned, "You started it, you and all your stupid rules."

"Yeah, the ones you never follow."

Bryan was in the middle of giving the briefing when Jack returned with Maddy. He could tell she had been crying. He wished so much she would reach out to him, but he would follow Jack's advice and let her come to him.

Jack was good for Maddy, probably better for her than him. He also knew the two were growing closer everyday and it was only a matter of time before something happened. Especially since Maddy and himself seemed to be growing apart and there was nothing he could do to stop it. He thought Maddy was his, but now he wasn't sure. Only time would tell.

Bryan waited until Maddy and Jack sat down and brought them up to speed.

"Maddy, Andy has that list for you on the religious backgrounds of our vics. If you could take a look at it and analyze it, that would be great."

Bryan handed out the sketch of the unsub, "This is the sketch our witnesses gave us. I was told it looks like hundreds of other men in this city, but maybe to someone who knows the gentleman would recognize him. It is still Maddy's belief that our unsub has a religious connection to our vic. Maddy, you want to take over?"

Maddy sat back with her arms folded. "Our witnesses described our unsub as being dressed in a black coat and black pants. Giving what we already discussed and this new information it sounds like the man is a minister or at least he thinks he is. Something has happened to this man, something triggers him." Maddy shook her head, "I don't know, some women that fits the victimology did something to him, something that has twisted his way of thinking and make him feel he needs to punish, to torture. His torture has escalated. I think with the discovery of his dumpsites has upset his methodology. His planning had flaws and he messed up big time resulting in two deaths and leaving a shit load of forensics. It's a great break for us, not so good for our vics."

One of Jack's detectives asked, "You called him a sexual sadist. Does that mean he actually gets physical sexual satisfaction from what he does? I mean like does he jack off after he does it?"

Maddy covered her face and shook her head, "No...no...no. Not that kind of sexual gratification. He gets the same...what's the word I'm looking for..."

"Hard on," somebody chimed in. It was Michael O'Brien. The men chuckled.

Jack turned to him, "Shut the fuck up and listen."

Maddy looked at Michael, "Well he obviously is not into necrophilia since there is not trace to say otherwise. Our unsub gets the same high as when you pop one off in the shower, but much more intense. It's a psychological thing, kind of like your wet dreams." More laughs, this time at Michael's expense.

"I don't recommend taking the flyer around to the area churches. If our unsub catches wind of it and that we could be closing in on him, he might flee, or he might de-escalate. Meaning he will go on a killing frenzy. We don't want that. You have your sketches, just scope out the churches first. See if anything one you see fits our profile. Don't underestimate this man. He is highly educated, very smooth, and believes he is smarter than us. Chances are he will see you and identify you long before you do him."

Bryan stood up, "Thank you Maddy. I want you guys to listen to this. Our resident profiler went back to our crime scene and for lack of better words I will use hers, did a read of the crime scene. You have the original reports, which you should have read by now." Bryan pushed the play button.

Maddy listened to herself on tape. She sounded so cold and analytical, but that was her job, that's how she operated when she was doing this part of her job.

When the tape was done Bryan added, "We fucked up, we missed the carafe, we missed the blood on the back steps."

Michael O'Brien piped up, "We wouldn't have missed the back steps if she hadn't fucked up the crime scene."

Bryan looked at Maddy to see how she was reacting to the statement. She sat calmly looking down at her desktop. "Yeah I fucked up, but you guys should have been searching the entire scene, including the backyard. That's your job, not mine. This whole case has been one fuck up after another, really piss poor police work," she stated flatly.

That didn't win any points. "For Christ sakes, I have been out of the law enforcement field for eight years and I still catch more things than you do."

"Yeah but you've been chasing Parker's tail for the past two years. And forgive us all to hell, we don't have the training you do. You walk around here like your God's gift to crime investigation. Nobody asked you to come aboard." Michael was challenging her.

"I asked her," Bryan said, his voice had that edge the Maddy was familiar with.

"Only cuz you're fucking her."

"O'Brien!" Jack snapped. "You have just crossed the line. Get out. You're off the case."

"No," Maddy said. "Let him stay. He has the right to his own opinion." Maddy went over and stood in front of O'Brien. Her eyes grew small. "Think what you want, I really don't give a flying rat's ass," she said with ice in her voice, "But I am going to tell you one thing, my little friend, see that target by Agent Mayland's desk? I did that. Every single shot where I meant it to go. There were no misfires. So let me suggest something to you—don't fuck with me!"

The room was silenced by her words. Maddy turned and looked her fellow law enforcement members. "Any one else want to share their words of wisdom? Take your best shot."

Bryan looked around the room; most of the men would not look him in the face. "Briefing over. Let's get back to work."

Bryan and Jack stood in front of Maddy. She looked up at them and said, "You fuckers ask me if I am okay, I will shoot your balls off, and don't think I won't do it."

Jack threw his had back and laughed. "So much moxy for such a petite woman. I wouldn't want to meet you in a back alley."

Maddy laughed, "You already have."

Derek came and stood with the two men. Okay here it comes, Maddy sighed to herself.

'I'm sorry you had to hear that," Bryan apologized to Maddy.

Maddy shrugged it off, "Hey it's no sweat off my balls."

Jack started laughing. Maddy sure had a way with words. "No really, Maddy, O'Brien was really over the line and should be reprimand. He needs to be taken off the case."

She met him eye to eye, "No seriously, leave him on. I want to watch that little bastard squirm."

It was Derek's turn to laugh. "Damn Maddy, you are definitely ready to be back. You're starting to sound like the fire fox I know. I wasn't too sure of Bryan's wisdom to let you go back in the field. I wanted to keep you desk bound."

"Well that just goes to show you don't know everything doesn't it Derek? This is no joke. Six women and a man are dead—the last two because we have been dragging our ass on this investigation. And I'll tell you something more, there are going to be more dead people before we get up to speed. I am just sick with the way this investigation is being run and that's no offense to Bryan or Jack. You only got what you have to work with, and quite frankly, you have bunch of lazy ass men that are dragging their feet every step of the way. They sit on their asses all day in this office when they should be out the in the field. No, they screw around until something lands on their laps. I'm not the perfect agent, but damn it, I'm better then 99% of them. At least I get out there and I find things, things that should have been caught the first time. You know what I feel like? I feel like my job is to clean up their damn fuck ups. The only person over that's worth a damn is Andy; at least he tries. And given the chance he can do a damn good job." Maddy said angrily.

"Maddy, calm down," Bryan said with that edge still in voice.

"I don't want to calm down," she snapped.

Bryan pointed at Jack and Maddy. "You two downstairs."

They walked in silence to the steps in front of the building and sat down. Both Jack and Bryan pulled out a cigarette and lit it. Maddy grabbed one of Jack's and lit and inhaled it and started choking.

Jack plucked the cigarette out of her mouth and chucked it. "You maybe one of the big dogs, Mads, but you still can't smoke."

"Go to hell."

Jack glanced at Bryan and raised an eyebrow.

"Maddy what the hell is that matter with you? Let it go," Bryan told her quietly. "Maybe you're not ready to be back."

Maddy shot him a look. "Do you really want to go down that road?"

"You've got five minutes to calm your ass down or I'm sending you home."

"Ha, like you can make me," she growled.

Jack moved up a step and sat behind her. He put his hands on her shoulders and began to massage them. "Just breathe deep baby, close your eyes. They're not worth it. They're just a bunch of dumb pricks with O'Brien being on the top of the list. Come on baby, you're so much better than this."

Maddy closed her eyes and dropped her head back feeling Jack's fingers working the tight muscles in her shoulders and neck. She took several deep breaths and let them out slowly.

Bryan watched them noting Jack was helping her relax. That used to be him he thought sadly. But that's not what mattered at the moment. All though she seemed to have a calm composure, she was out of control.

Maddy opened her eyes and reached for Jack's hand. "Thank you. I'm better now."

Jack leaned forward and kissed the top of her head. "Good." He moved back down to the step on the other side of her.

Maddy leaned her head on Bryan's shoulder, "I'm sorry. It just pissed me off when that son of bitch dragged you into it. If he wanted to go after me for emasculating him fine, but he should have left you out of it. I don't give a damn about me, but you need to have the respect of your men."

Bryan put his arm around her and smiled, "The tigress is protecting me, now that's a switch." It made him feel good that she felt she needed to. "As you say so much, you don't have to do that, I can take care of myself." He kissed her forehead. "But thank you."

"I'm afraid I have made things worse, I'm sorry."

Jack put his hand on her knee. "Maddy, I would say you gained the respect of the men by holding your own. O'Brien is an asshole. They all know it. I don't know about Bryan's men or the DCI guys, but O'Brien is the worst out of the bunch. I'm not making excuses for my guys, but they don't have a fucking clue what they're doing. Maybe it's my fault, I'm not giving them direction."

Bryan chuckled, "Jack you don't know half of what you're doing. You're winging it, doing a good job winging it, but nonetheless, you are. It's not your fault, you haven't been trained or exposed to this type of crime."

Jack smiled, "Gee thanks for the vote of confidence"

"Now I am asking you, what do suppose we do about this situation?" Bryan asked.

Jack thought about it for a few moments. "Well Maddy is right about needing to get their asses out in the field. I think if its possible sending one experienced man out with a lesser man."

"I got dibs on Andy," Maddy piped in.

"You and Jack will take Andy out. Maddy, you would eat him alive." Bryan lit another cigarette.

Maddy's jaw dropped. "How can you say that?"

"Maddy, you're not teaching material. It will be good for Andy to observe you. Jack is also going with you to learn. And he's going to be keeping you in line." Bryan flicked his cigarette.

Jack threw his head back and laughed. "God do you know what you're asking Bryan? I have never been able to keep her in line. She doesn't listen to me. I tell her to do something and if she decides she wants to, she'll do it, if not..."Jack shrugged his shoulders.

"Eh hem...Hello, I am here, talk to the wild one," she waved her hands in front of Bryan's eyes. Then she turned to Jack, "What do you mean I don't listen?"

Jack cocked his head, "Maddy, I don't have enough appendages to count up all the times you've gone behind my back and broke the rules. Look how many you broke on this case alone."

Maddy stretched her legs out in front of her. "You guys are just being mean."

Bryan put his hand on Maddy's shoulder and shook her playfully. "Poor, poor Maddy. Don't like hearing her negative traits."

"Fuck you," she said under her breath. "You guys are a bunch of pigs. You know what the biggest problem with task forced is, you're all men."

Bryan's cell phone went off. He looked at the caller Id. "I need to take this. Excuse me." He got up off the steps and walked out toward the parking lot.

Jack nudged her with his knee. "Are you pissed at me now?"

Maddy smiled and nudged him back. "You didn't say anything which wasn't true. Hell I know it, but he doesn't have to know."

"Like he doesn't know," he laughed. "Give the man a little credit. I think I'm suppose to make sure you stay within the bounds of the law when you're snooping."

She kicked him with her toe, "I know the law!"

"Ooooh getting aggressive. I like," he grinned.

She nudged him with her shoulder. "Meeeeeeeeeooooow!"

He burst out laughing. "God, I love you."

When she looked at him, her eyes were twinkling with an undeniable sparkle. "I love you too."

Jack leaned back and stretched his arms on the step behind him. "Sooooo... you going home to your place tonight?"

Maddy copied his pose, "Yeeeeeees...I am."

He looked at her and raised his eyebrows up and down, "Alone?"

"Weeeellll, I'm driving home alone," she winked at him.

He nodded, sporting a big grin across his lips. "I see...do you think you might be having any company a little while after you get home?"

She tapped her head on his shoulder playfully, "God I hope so. I have my heart set on this really sexy guy who I adore."

"You got someone else?" he asked in mock seriousness.

"I'm this man's kitten. He likes to pet me in the right places." She looked at him coyly. "You know anyone like that?"

He stretched his hands behind his head, "You know, I'm pretty sure I know a man who fits that description. What time do you want him there?"

"Whenever he can get there, sooner's better than later," she beamed.

Jack took out his notebook from his chest pocket and took out his pen. He spoke as he wrote, "Sooner." He underlined it three times.

"I'd love to plant my lips on you right now," she said wistfully.

Jack laughed softly, "I would like to do more."

Maddy put her face in her hands, "God we're terrible, but it's so much fun!"

When they heard footsteps approaching they looked up to see Bryan coming at them. Maddy noticed the tense look on his face. She glanced at Jack. He nodded and got up.

"I need to check on something. I'll see you guys up there." He disappeared into the building.

"Problem?" she asked.

Bryan sat down beside her. "It's complicated."

Maddy looked down at her feet and wiggled her toes. "I see."

"You see what?"

Maddy sighed, "I've seen this all before. What is she doing now?"

Bryan glanced at her but wouldn't meet her gaze. "How do you know it's a she?"

Maddy stood up. "Fuck this, Bryan, I'm not playing this game with you again."

He grabbed her hand and pulled her back down. "I meant what I said. I want to be with you."

"Yeah? And I know it's not ever going to happen. You were are so eager for me to let go of my past when you don't have the slightest inclination of how to let go of yours. You're hooked Bryan and you can't let it go," she stated as a matter of fact.

Bryan looked at her incredulously. "How can you say that after I bared my soul to you? After everything we've been through?"

"Look at you? You said you were done with her, but she always finds a way to get back in. You say it's over, then fucking walk away."

"It's lot more complicated than that," he said with his head down.

Maddy stood up again. "Is it?"

She turned to walk away and Bryan caught her arm and pulled her into his lap. He put his hands around her head and brought it down to him kissing her passionately. When the kiss ended Bryan put his head on her shoulder. "Jesus Maddy, what's happening to us? It all seemed so simple."

Maddy stroked his hair. "Life gets in the way hon. Things don't always go the way we want them to. I love you Bryan. I know you are sincere about what you want to happen, but what if it can't? We can't make things go away just because we want it to. I, of all people, know it doesn't work that way. We can ignore the truth and hope it changes, but it doesn't. It stays there and it haunts us."

"Can we be together tonight, Maddy?" he asked her.

Maddy sat up. "Nope. You are going to take the men out and get them shit faced. You are going to get to know them and them get to know you." She kissed him softly. "To know the man I know and love. You need to bond with these men—without me there. I would just hinder it. Do you understand what I'm saying?" She put her hand under his chin.

He searched her eyes, "I need to be with you, Minnie. Please?"

"Tomorrow, I promise. We'll spend a nice quiet night at home, just the two of us okay?"

"What are you going to do?"

"Some emotional homework, and I need to do it alone. You okay with that hon?" she looked into his eyes.

"You promise tomorrow?"

She put up two fingers, "Scouts honor, tomorrow."

He pulled her close and buried his face in her hair. "I just miss you so much. I feel lost without you. But you're right. I need to do something to pull this unit together. And you...you need to do what helps you—so we can be together again and back on track."

They stood up and started walking back to the station when Maddy asked, "Was it Donna?"

Bryan smiled weakly, "No, I haven't heard from her since the three way on Sunday. It was Jeff. He's in trouble with his dealer."

"Oh God, I am so sorry hon," she felt bad for thinking the worst. But isn't that what she always did about Bryan, think the worst?

He leaned over and kissed her on the cheek, "No worries, Minnie. What you said still applies."

Maddy yawned. "Damn it's only morning and I'm shot already."

"Why don't you go on home? Take your laptop and read through Granger's emails. You don't have to do it here and it will get you out of harms way, let things settle down if you know what I mean." He opened the door for her.

"What about going out in the field?"

"We'll start the church search first thing tomorrow morning. Would you mind compiling a list of all churches in the city and out lying areas and split them into five groups?"

"No, not at all." Then she laughed, "You're going to make them go out with hangovers aren't you?"

He swatted her on the bottom, "You bet your sweet ass I am, especially that dumb fuck O'Brien. You don't mess with my Minnie!"

When Maddy and Bryan returned to the squad room the men all watched them and waited. Derek was sitting on the corner of Bryan's desk.

"Maddy is going to work from home for the rest of the day," Bryan told Derek quietly. "Hopefully this will settle things down and we can get something done. Then tonight you and I are going to take the squad out and get them drunk. It is of the opinion of my advisory committee it will give them a good chance to bond with each other and us. Maddy will not be there. Guys only. Maddy is going to run a search of all the surrounding churches in the area. In the morning we will split up into teams. I want the experienced agents taking the inexperienced ones. Whittmer is going out with Jack and Maddy. Can you group up the others?"

"Sounds like a plan. Nothing against Maddy, but I think you are doing the right thing getting her out of here for the rest of the day. Mostly for her, she's really high strung today."

"No shit. I'm going to go invite Jack to go out with us, you take care of the rest.

Bryan knocked on Jack's door. Jack was on the phone but motioned for him to come in.

Bryan sat down. "Well what did you think about what just transpired?"

Jack just shook his head, "It wasn't pretty."

"She's really volatile don't you think?'

Jack just smiled, "No, that's the Maddy I know. Not the angry one she is with you, but that woman up there in the squad room? That's my Maddy. There are lots of uniforms and a couple of detectives who can't stand her. They tolerate her because I make them. This is not the first run in she's had with O'Brien. She's made him look stupid on more than one occasion. What makes it tougher for him right now is she is essentially over him. And the fact he knows now she is FBI and always has been makes him look even more like a dumb fuck. I really think we need to remove him from the case. I have a bad feeling about allowing him to stay on. He's damn lucky I haven't written him up."

Bryan shrugged. "She seems dead set on keeping him on."

"Only cuz she wants to mess with his head. Don't let the coy little innocent demeanor fool you. She's no angel Bryan, she gives just as good as she gets. And she can be damn right nasty when it comes to revenge. She'll set him up for a fall and then let him have it." Jack stated seriously.

"Gee I wonder where she picked that up from?" Bryan rubbed his temples. "Here I thought she's spent all this time hiding out in her shell."

Jack threw his head back and laughed, "I thought you knew her so well?"

"I guess not. Find something else to hang O'Brien with and then let him go. I don't want it to be because of Maddy."

"Insubordination is not a good enough cause for you?" Jack asked.

"Find something else. Anyhow what I came in to tell you is I am sending Maddy home to work for the rest of the day to cool things off. Maddy recommended that I take all the guys out tonight," he coughed, "and let them get to know me. So I guess that includes you."

"Sorry man, I can't. I have a date tonight with my lady and if I make a no show she is going to string me up by the balls," he laughed.

Bryan smiled, "Understood. Well I better get back, check in with you later."

When Bryan returned to the squad room, Maddy had already packed up and left. On his desk was a folded piece of paper. He picked it up and unfolded it. *Mickey, I just want to tell you anger is an easier emotion to deal with. I can deal with anger. I can't deal with the pain. I will try harder not to make you the target of that anger. I love you. Minnie*

He brought the note to his nose. It had the faint scent of her perfume. He smiled to himself. Maybe there was hope yet.

16

Maddy pulled over in the Perkin's parking lot at the edge of Gordon Drive and picked up her cell phone and texted Jack. 'Are you alone?'

An answer came back immediately. 'Yes.'

Maddy hit speed dial 3. "Hey Baby. I was going to stop by and tell you bye, but Bryan was in there. I didn't think that would be too cool."

"Probably not. He was inviting me to go boozing with him and the rest of guys from the squad. He said it was you're idea." She heard him laugh.

"He wanted to come home with me tonight," she softly laughed. "This was a good way to keep him busy and it's a good idea. Are you going?'

"Nope."

"What did you tell him?" she asked.

"I told him I had a date with my lady and I couldn't break it."

Maddy smiled. "And he automatically assumed it was Stella."

"He can assume anything he wants. I didn't lie. The closer you can keep things to the truth, the less you look guilty of lying," he said as a matter of fact.

Maddy nodded, "Good point. Well I am going to head on home. I want to get my work done so when my hot man shows up, I'm free to spend my time with him."

Jack laughed, "Damn he is one lucky man."

Maddy smiled, "Isn't he now? I will see you later Lucky. Get here as soon as it's convenient for you. I love you.

"Love you too Kitten." And they hung up.

When Maddy returned home she spread out her materials on the kitchen table, took out her laptop and booted it up.

The first thing she did was look up the church directory for the Sioux City area. Holy shit, Maddy sighed. There were 108 churches just in the metro area, not including the near by rural towns. She highly doubted their unsub was from one of those, but then again you never know. She resorted the list by location and divided the list into five groupings—21.6 churches to check out per group. Damn that was going to take awhile.

She grabbed her phone and called Bryan. "Hey hon, I didn't realize what kind of undertaking canvassing all these churches was going to be." She told him how many and what it broke down per team.

"Well kiddo, if your gut feeling is right, we have to do this. The one church we don't check out could very well be where he is."

"I think we need to be cool about this, don't make a bid deal of our presence," she offered her opinion.

"You know we still have to identify ourselves when we talk to them," he replied.

"I know, but we are there for observation. If we find someone we need to talk to we tell him or her who we are then. I just don't want this guy see us sniffing around and bolt."

"Okay we will do it your way, but we follow protocol. Is that understood?" he warned her.

"Duh, I know, I do know my job."

"Quit being a smart ass. We both know you don't always play by the rules."

Maddy sighed and stayed silent.

"You still there?"

"Yes, I'm just keeping my mouth shut. I don't want to be accused of being an antagonist."

"No one said you were."

"Listen hon, I got work to do so I will talk to you later. I will call you if I find anything in these emails. Love you, talk to you later. Have fun tonight." She hung up.

Maddy pulled up the emails. She had fifty to go through. She quickly scanned them by sender. Most were benign, but she did come across five that looked promising. The sender went by a user name A Higher Power. She went to the oldest email first so she could read them in order.

July 11- 'My Dearest Vanessa, Thank you for joining our family. You will find us a loving and supporting group of individuals sharing in the joys of God and what he has to offer us. With my personal guidance I will show you a new way to fulfill your obligations to Him. Come share with us and I will teach the ways of the Lord. A Higher Power'

July 22- 'My Dearest Vanessa, your kind heart and willingness to accept the Lord and his power have filled my heart with love and joy. You have shown yourself worthy of my personal attention. I look forward to expanding on this when we meet again. A Higher Power'

August 01- 'My Dearest Vanessa, I must say I am joyfully surprised at how responsive you are to open up to me. It is with great comfort knowing you have accepted God and share in all the gifts he can give you through me. You have become a candle in my offering of love, shedding light for other lost souls. You are truly a golden sheep in my flock. A Higher Power.'

August 15- 'My Dearest Vanessa, I am disappointed you did not keep your obligation to fulfill your duty onto the Lord. It saddens me that you have pulled back on your commitment to me. Please meet with me to discuss how we can bring you back in the cradle of his love and my lessons. A Higher Power.'

August 19- 'My Dearest Vanessa, You have not approached me to have your sins forgiven. Don't you know when you enter my flock and become one with me and the Lord, you are obligated to do his bidding. You are a chosen one. Soon you will see for yourself. A Higher Power.'

Holy Shit! Jack Pot! If only she had the emails Vanessa sent to A Higher Power. Damn, why didn't she think of checking her sent file? Damn, Damn, Damn!

Maddy grabbed her phone and called Bryan. It went straight to voice mail. Shit. "Bryan, this is Maddy, call me ASAP."

Maddy drummed her fingers on the table. This was just too much to sit on. She didn't have the patience to wait for Bryan to call her back. She hit the speed dial.

Jack picked up immediately. "Hello Kitten, got your homework done?"

"You won't believe what I found," she said her voice full of excitement. "Vanessa got emails from our unsub—five of them! He calls himself A Higher Power. Give me your email and I will forward them to you."

She jotted it down and forwarded them to him. "They're on their way."

"Okay, let me check."

She waited while he pulled them up. "Well?"

"Damn, Maddy, give me a chance to read them."

There were a couple of minutes of silence then he came back on. "Wow. Too bad you didn't have the corresponding emails."

"I know, I fucked up. Where's her computer?" she asked.

"In Ankeny. We don't have anything back on that yet. Why?

"The email address comes from a common server, Yahoo. I can't trace back an originating URL without the computer, even if I had access, I don't know how. We need to have DCI to specifically look for that. Plus I need those sent messages. Did any of the other vics have computers? I'm sure they did, everyone and his dog has a computer. We need them," Maddy babbled on.

"Maddy...slow down, take a deep breath. It's already 4:45. There's not a lot we can get done tonight. The lab closes in 15 minutes. Have you talked to Bryan about this yet?" Jack asked.

"No, he didn't pick up his phone. I left a voice mail."

Jack sighed. "I will print these out and take them to him. God, I hope he doesn't make you come back in."

"Oh." Maddy slid back in her chair. "I don't know why he would, like you said it's too late to do anything tonight."

"Like I said, I will make sure he gets these. Don't you have chores or something you need to do? Some reason why you leave your phone in the house and miss the call?"

Maddy laughed, "Are you asking me to hide so I can't come back in?"

Jack shook his head, "Nope, nope. I would never do anything that might hinder an investigation. He will have the emails, but he won't have you." He laughed, "I'm greedy. Are you game?"

Maddy smiled, "I'm game. When you coming?"

"I'm planning on getting out of here at 5:00 if Bryan doesn't corner me. I want to run home, take a quick shower, and head out. How does that sound?"

"Like warm fuzzies," she said softly.

Jack laughed, "I will see you soon Kitten."

"Bye, Jack." She closed her phone and took off to do chores.

Jack printed off the emails and took off for the squad room. When he arrived Bryan was talking on his phone. He looked at Jack and nodded to a chair at his desk. Jack tried not to listen in on Bryan's conversation, however it was kind of hard not to, it was a very heated conversation.

Finally Bryan finished his call and looked over at Jack. "What do you need?"

Edgy, Jack thought to himself, and knew for fact that wasn't Maddy he had been talking to. "Here," he threw the emails on Bryan's desk.

Bryan picked them up, "What are these?"

"Emails Maddy retrieved off Grangers computer, emails she says were sent by our unsub."

"She sent them to you?" Bryan eyed him. "Why you?"

"If you check your voice mail, you will find one from Maddy. She couldn't get a hold of you so she called me. She needed to go do something and wanted to make sure you got these." Sounded good to him.

As if he didn't believe Jack, he checked his voice mail and did indeed find a voice mail from Maddy. It was time stamped twenty minutes ago. He had been on the phone for 45 minutes arguing with Natalia. He tried calling Maddy, but she didn't answer. "Did she say what she was going to do?"

"It's not my turned to be her keeper," Jack mumbled.

Bryan's head shot up, "What the hell is that suppose to mean?"

"It means Bryan, that we don't need to keep her on a leash and know her whereabouts 24-7. Has it ever occurred to you she might have a life that doesn't involve either of us?" Jack countered.

Bryan leaned back and studied Jack—who in turn was sitting back in his chair calmly studying Bryan. He picked up the emails and read them over. "Christ and she's been sitting on these for how long?"

"A week," Jack replied.

Bryan laid the pages down and shook his head. He said nothing.

"Maddy said we need to get DCI to get a trace on the unsub's email. It's through Yahoo, a public provider. She said they should be able to access or go through them to find out where the emails originated. She also said she needs to get her hands on the emails sent from Granger. She didn't think about retrieving them at the time," Jack explained.

"I can't believe she's been sitting on these for week," Bryan shook his head. "Key evidence and it's been in on her laptop the whole time."

"Christ Bryan, it's not like she hasn't been busy working on other parts of the case. She's pretty much compiled this case single handedly. She's given us almost every piece of solid evidence we have." Jack argued.

Bryan sighed, "I know. It's pretty damn bad when our whole case has depended on someone that's been out of the field for eight years." He looked up at

Jack. "Keep this under wraps until she gets in tomorrow. You going to be talking to her tonight?"

"Told you, I've got a date. Wouldn't be too cool if I were chatting up another woman now would it?" he laughed.

"No, I guess not. You go ahead and take off and have a good time. I have to go play kiss ass to a bunch of morons," Bryan grumbled.

Jack threw his head back and laughed, "Nice attitude. Derek will be there with you. Go let your hair down."

Bryan smiled weakly, "Would be more fun if Maddy were there."

Jack stood up, "But she's not, and you will be more effective without her being there. She's a smart woman. Trust her instincts."

When Maddy returned to the house she checked her phone. Bryan had retuned her call. She was so tempted to call him back, but didn't dare, not yet anyhow. She would wait until she knew he was out of the office. Maybe she would give him a call later to see how things were going with the male bonding session. She knew he would hate it.

Maddy cleaned up her mess of paper work and stuck it in her bag. No more work tonight. She felt all giddy and excited because Jack was coming. She thought they could share their lives tonight; really start getting to know each other.

She took a quick shower and slipped on a pair of shorts and a tank top. She thought about getting all fancied up, but that's not really who she was. She knew Jack wanted her to be herself.

Maddy was sitting on the steps playing with Rufus when Jack pulled in the lane. She stood up when he got out of his car. He was dressed in pale blue short-sleeved button down shirt, a pair of blue jeans, and sneakers. She didn't care what he was wearing—he was one sexy dude. As he walked toward her, a kind of shy smile played upon his lips. She couldn't help herself, she walked towards him, the closer she got to him the faster she walked. Jack stopped in his tracks, wearing a big smile, and held his arms out to her. She squealed and jumped up in his arms wrapping her legs around his hips. Maddy pulled his face toward her and kissed him deeply. Then she leaned into to him and whispered, "I love you."

Jack set her down, still holding her. "Damn Kitten," he grinned, "That's one hell of a greeting." His kissed her softly holding her close. "Oh baby, it feels so good to hold you."

Maddy buried her face in his chest taking in his scent. "You too."

They turned to walk back to the house. "How did Bryan take the emails?" she asked.

"I don't want to tell you because it will just piss you off," he squeezed her hand, "and I don't want you pissed off tonight."

Maddy laughed, "It went that well huh?"

"When I brought them in he was on his phone having a very heated conversation with someone so he was already pissed off. Then I gave him the emails, he read them, had a fit about us sitting on them for a week. He whined because you weren't around to answer the phone and wanted to know where you were at." Jack explained as they walked.

"Oh shit, what'd you tell him?" she glanced at him.

Jack chuckled, "Told him it wasn't my turn watch you."

Maddy gave him a playful smack, "You didn't?"

"Sure did, told him you had a life too that didn't revolve around him or me."

"I bet he wasn't pleased hearing that. How was he taking tonight?" she asked.

"Oh he was bitching about that, too. Said he had to play kiss ass to a bunch of morons." They had reached the steps and he held the door open for her.

Maddy shook her head. "He's already set himself up for a bad night." Maddy laughed, "Maybe you should have sent Stella down there."

"Hell no!" Jack blurted out. "He is under the impression I'm out with her tonight. Remember?"

"Is that what you told him?" she asked looking up at him.

"No sweetie, I told him I was going to see my lady...that's you." He kissed her on the tip of her nose.

"Are you hungry?" she asked walking towards the fridge, she pulled two sodas out and handed him one.

He pulled her down on to his lap as he sat down. "Depends." His lips lightly touched hers.

"Food." She kissed him back letting it linger. "We keep this up, we won't make it that far.

He ran his fingers through her hair and parted her lips with his tongue, kissing her deeply. He pulled back and smiled at her. "Just needed to get that out of the way. Okay now that I've had my appetizer, what you got in mind?"

"Lasagna, with garlic toast and me for desert," she kissed his cheek and slid off his lap.

Jack feigned disappointment, "Damn, can't we eat desert first?"

Maddy threw a potholder at him. She opened the oven door and slid out the lasagna she had prepared earlier and kept warm and set it on the stovetop. Then she pulled out a basket of garlic toast.

Jack had gotten up to pull plates down and grabbed the silverware and set the table. He grabbed a dishtowel from the drawer and laid it on the table to put the hot pan on.

Maddy noticed him moving freely around. One weekend with her and he knew his way around the kitchen like he had always been there. She placed the lasagna and the bread on the table and they sat down to eat.

"Bryan thought you were, what's the word he used, volatile, today in the squad room with the guys. I told him you were always that bitchy with cops. Told him the department has a hit out on you," he joked as he took a bite.

Maddy threw a piece of toast at him which he caught in mid-air. "You make me sound like a cop hater."

He held up the toast, "Thanks. No actually, I just told him there are a few you have rubbed the wrong way, O'Brien being one of the worst."

"The man is a total dumb fuck. I don't even know what he's doing on this case. He doesn't do anything," Maddy complained.

"Wasn't my call."

Maddy looked at him, "But you're the chief of detectives, you should have some say."

"He got the originating call on the Bacon Creek discovery so he kind of came with the territory. Please be discrete when you seek your revenge okay? I don't want an all out war between the two of you." He decided to pass on telling her that Bryan had already told him to get rid of him.

"If I were a man, I would piss on his tires," she mumbled.

Jack cracked up, "Oh that would make him pay."

Maddy smiled. "Shut up. You and I both know I am capable of doing much worse."

Jack stuffed the last of his bread in his mouth and took a drink. "I know exactly what you're capable of doing, Maddy, and that's what scares me."

After they had cleaned up the kitchen Maddy led Jack into the living room and they sat on couch. Maddy sat on one end facing Jack who was at the other end facing her.

"You look like you have something planned. What's up?" he asked curiously.

"We are going to play twenty questions," she stated with a grin.

Jack cocked his head to one side, "You're kidding. Explain yourself Miss Maddy."

"I think it's time we got to know about each other. We don't know things like about each others families, where we grew up, where we went to school, you know...stuff."

Jack studied her. She was leaning back against the arm of the couch with her toes touching his. She looked so young and innocent. "How old are you?"

Maddy's mouth dropped. "What kind of question is that? How old do you think I am?"

Jack twisted his jaw kind of funny. "I'm guessing 35-36, but could easily pass for 26."

Maddy laughed, "Good guess, 36."

"And how old am I?"

Maddy looked him over like she was assessing him. Who cared how old he was, he was gorgeous, sexy and built. "I'm saying 36-37, a very well preserved 36-37."

"Touché. Actually I am 38. Not to change the subject, but how old is Bryan?"

Maddy frowned. "He's 47 but he looks older I think. Hard living does that to you. No more questions about him. This is about us. Okay, my turn, where did you grow up?"

Jack rubbed his toes on hers. "Right here in Sioux City, born and bred. You?"

"In a small town about 18 miles from here."

"Are you serious? How the hell did you end up at Quantico?"

She nudged him with her foot, "You're cheating, you can't jump ahead," she laughed. "How many is in your family?"

"Two brothers, a sister and mom and dad. My oldest brother, the one who dropped my car off, is an accountant and lives in the city. Then I have another brother, still older, lives in Sioux Falls, and then my little sister lives in Des Moines. I already told you Mom and Dad live in the city. Okay, your turn."

"Mother and father are deceased. Mom died when I was a teenager, father passed away when I was 26. I have one sister who lives in Houston," she answered.

Jack noticed when she told him about her parents there wasn't a hint of sadness in her voice. But then again after the loss of her children, what could be worst. "Marriage...unless you don't want to talk about it."

Maddy shrugged, "No it's fine. I married my high school sweetheart at the ripe old age of 18. We had two children together. I was going to college working on my degrees. I grew up, he didn't. I got out. Took my maiden name back. You ever been married?"

Jack ran his foot up along her leg as he spoke, "No, never even been close."

"Why? A man like you, you could have your pick of any woman?" She watched his face.

"Don't know...just never found one I wanted to commit to. Always felt that when I found her, she would make me feel this certain way. I wasn't finding it and wouldn't settle for anything less," he told her softly. "I've never even told a woman I loved her...until you." He looked up at her.

She ran her foot up his leg. "I love you."

They sat silently for a few moments. Maddy was taking in what he just told her. She was the only one, she had never been anyone's only one. Wow, she didn't know what to say. She only hoped she was worthy of his love. She prayed she would never let him down. "Okay, schooling and how did you become a cop?"

"Do we have to sit like this? I want you over here with me," he asked. His admission of his love life made him feel awkward.

Maddy moved around. "Spread you legs," she ordered him.

Jack burst out laughing, "Isn't that what I'm suppose to say to you?"

"Ha!" She moved between his legs so she was resting between them with her back against his chest.

He wrapped his arms around her. "Yes, this is much better." He kissed the side of her head. "Okay, schooling. I graduated from North High, graduated from Morningside College, spent four years in the marines, went the police academy in Omaha, did my time on the streets, earned my shield, worked down there for a few years as a detective, two years ago I took the job as chief of detectives up here. I wanted to be closer to Mom and Dad and had hopes of raising a family here. You're up."

"Started out at BV, then after I got divorced, I packed up Lexy and moved down to Texas since that's where the only family I have was. I found out I was pregnant with Scotty when I was there. I got accepted in to Baylor and became a hardcore student. I got degrees in abnormal psychology, forensic psychology, forensics, and English. One of my professors put in a recommendation to enter in to the FBI's special agent program. I figured what hell, on paper it sounded great. I got trained and certified as a profiler, spent seven years in the field, had to get out, worked at a newspaper in Virginia, Houston and then here." She rested her head back and closed her eyes.

He started kissing her behind her ear. "Baylor huh? At Waco?"

Maddy tilted her head to accommodate him. "mmmmhmmmm"

"Beautiful and smart...damn..." He shifted her around until he could find her lips and his mouth came down on hers kissing her with a deep emotion. He finally stopped. He whispered in her ear, "You give me that feeling Maddy...the one I've searched for my whole life for."

Maddy touched his cheek, "I want so much to be that person. I don't ever want to hurt you."

Jack put his chin on the top of her head and entwined their arms together. "You are Maddy. We just have lots of complications to work out. We knew it when entered into this. My heart has never steered me wrong. You are the one."

Maddy moved to get up. "Where are you going?" Jack asked thinking he scared her away.

"I want to share something with you. Something I've never shared with anyone since..." Maddy went to the box by the TV and pulled out a photo album and brought it over and sat back down and snuggled back against him. "I want you to meet my babies. Now if I get emotional...please bear with me."

Jack wrapped his arms around her really tight. "Maddy, sweetheart, you don't have to do this if you're not ready."

"No, I want to. I know with you I am safe. I want to share this part of myself with you..." Her hand ran back and forth over the leather cover. Her fingers trembled as she opened up the book. She found a picture of her daughter at age two. "This is Lexi. She was hell on wheels, precocious some might say. She loved life, always getting into trouble."

"Her mother's daughter," Jack whispered in her ear.

Maddy felt a little shaky, but she went on. She flipped the pages as she talked. "When she was in kindergarten, there was this boy that kept pushing her down and she kept getting hurt. I chewed out her teacher for not watching them close enough, that it had to stop." Maddy laughed nervously, "The next day I get this call from her, Lexi punched out this same kid. When I went into the school, I asked Lexi why she decked him. She told me he spit on her. I just looked at the teacher and told her I would have done the same damn thing."

Jack smiled and squeezed her. Maddy's daughter was the little version of herself. He didn't talk; he just let her go where she wanted to go.

Maddy flipped a few more pages until she found some of her son. "This is Scotty. He was my little daredevil. He was always up for an adventure. We used to go these excursions like in the pasture or the horse yard. One time we played safari. The horse were zebras, the cats were lions and tigers," she laughed, "I can't remember what the dog was." Maddy shut the book and sat in silence.

Jack took the album and set if off to the side and then turned her so her face could lie against his chest. He could feel her tears dampening his shirt, but she never said a word. He didn't pry, he didn't probe, and he just took her in his arms and held her. They sat like that for about fifteen minutes then Maddy kissed his chest.

Jack stroked her hair and whispered, "Thank you Maddy for sharing this with me. It means more to me than you know that you trust me with it."

Maddy got up off the couch and went into the bathroom and closed the door. She ran some cold water and splashed it on her face. When she looked at herself in the mirror her face looked pale, her eyes red. She knew when she decided to look at the album she was putting herself at risk for feeling the pain, but she wanted to share a special part of herself with Jack. She had allowed herself to be vulnerable with him of her own choosing. To her it was the ultimate proof of trust.

Jack stood outside the bathroom door. He wanted to ask her if she were all right, but didn't want her to go ballistic on him. He knocked on the door. "I'm going to sit on the steps and have smoke. Do you want to come out with me?"

"Yes, Babe, I'll be there in second." Maddy grabbed a towel and patted her face and then joined Jack. She leaned her head on his shoulder. "Have I told you how crazy I am about you?" she asked.

Jack gave a soft smile, "No, only that you were crazy." He nudged her.

She nudged him back. "You really suck you know that?"

He looked at her and raised his eyebrows up and down. "Is that an invitation?"

She laughed, "And if it were?"

"I would take you up on it," he said mischievously. He ran his fingers up her bare arm and could feel the goose bumps rising. He loved knowing his touch evoked this reaction from her. He turned to her and with both hands he ran them up her arms, just barley touching her. They traveled over her shoulders to the soft skin of her neckline. He learned over her and kissed the line along her collarbone.

Maddy closed her eyes blocking out everything but the feel of his fingers on her flesh. Her heart rate went up a notch, and her breathing became shallow.

Jack kissed up along the sensitive spot behind her ear and whispered, "What do you want me to do Maddy?"

"I...um...." She couldn't find the words. Her hand dropped between his legs and stroked his inner thigh.

Jack's mouth made a path along her chin until he found her mouth. He covered it with his and gently pride it part with his tongue. He was surprised when Maddy slipped hers in his gently sucking his back into her mouth. She was still feeling his inner thigh, high into the danger zone. Jack's breath stop when her hands grazed across him, barely touching him. But he was definately aware she was there.

Maddy strayed from their kiss and looked deep into his dark eyes. She could see the fire brewing there; the same fire she knew was burning in hers. "The question is, love, what do you want me to do?"

He stood up and took her by the hand, led her into the house and into her bedroom. He had her sit on the bed while he closed the blinds and lit the candles. He took her hand and had her stand up. His finger brushed across her shoulder pushing the straps of her tank top down so the top fell to her waist. He decided that wasn't good enough so he pulled it over the top of her head. He then grasped both side of her shorts and slowly pulled them down, kneeling as he went and help her step out of them. Then he whispered in her ear, "your turn."

The first thing she did was untuck his shirt. She took her hands and ran them up underneath his shirt, feeling the lines of his chest. She had him sit on the bed so she could reach all of him and unbuttoned his shirt with her teeth. After each one she gave him a lingering kiss. When she reached the bottom she ran her hands up his ribcage, over his chest and pushed the shirt off over his shoulders and let it drop to the floor. She then had him stand back up and she dropped to her knees in front of him. With shaky hands she unbuckled his belt and fumbled around until she got them unbuttoned. She leaned in grabbing the zipper with her teeth. She looked up to see Jack. He had a content smile on his face, his eyes very dark and beautiful. He brushed the back of her hair with his hand. She slid his jeans down over his hips. She kept her eyes closed as she kissed along his waistline. She looked up at his face and said with a husky voice, "What do you want me to do Jack?"

A soft moan escaped his lips, his hands gently guiding her downward. Her lips nipped gently on his soft skin, her tongue exploring. She took the tip of her tongue and ran it on all sides of him being careful not to touch the point of his desire. She looked up at him again from her position on the floor. "What do you want me to do baby? Tell me..."

Jack's head fell back, his eyes half closed; his lips were parted and was breathing heavily. "Sweet Jesus Maddy...please...."

She gave an evil laugh, "Please what Jack, I thought I was pleasing you."

Jack moaned, "You bitch, don't torture me so...Please Maddy—Kitten don't make me beg..."

Maddy took her tongue and ran it up along his desire and flicked the end with her tongue. Jack grabbed her hair but didn't push her one way or the other. She put her hands on his hips and guided him to her where she took him in; slow at first, painfully slow. She could feel his breath at a rapid rate. Before she could go much farther he pulled her up to him, his mouth hungrily taking hers, their bodies meshed together.

He scooped her up and laid her in the center of the bed. He lay down beside her, his eyes exploring her body. He reached out and brushed the hair from her face and then kissed her gently. "You are such a beautiful creature. Do I dare hope you could ever be mine?"

Her eyes bore into his, the emerald fire burning there once again. "I love you, Jack Parker, with all my heart. With all the craziness still ahead of us, don't ever doubt it." She pushed the hair away from his eyes, and then pulled him down to her. Her mouth pressed into the softness of his lips, searching, exploring. She squirmed until she felt his body covering hers, his hands roving all over her body. He gently pulled her knees apart, entering her with slow and deliberate penetration.

Maddy squirmed more under him, pushing against him wanting more, but he continued, this sweet torture, finally she gasped, "Please, Jack, please.... "

"What Kitten...just tell me what you want and it's yours," he said huskily. He himself needed release, but wouldn't give in until she was ready.

Maddy was to the point of panting, "Please....Jack...give me all of you."

Jack thrust all of him inside her and began a slow rocking motion. He watched her face, her eyes were half closed, and a content smile graced her lips. Her breathing was heavy and erratic. When he increased his tempo, she dug her nails deep into his shoulders. Her head tossed side to side, she was whimpering and biting her lip to keep from crying out.

"It's ok Kitten, let yourself feel it, don't hold back, don't ever hold back on me." He was so close.

Maddy reached up and grabbed his hair. She arched her back against him and literally screamed out.

Jack collapsed on her. "Oh, sweet Jesus." He sought out her lips and kissed her passionately and then lay beside her, holding her.

"How would you feel about meeting my parents?" Jack asked as he kissed her neck.

Maddy looked at him in surprise, "Are you serious?"

"Dead serious. I want to introduce them to the woman I've been waiting all my life for."

Maddy thought about his request. She guessed it would be okay. She was beginning to feel she was leading a double life. As Jack put it, things were complicated, very complicated. "I suppose it would be okay."

"You don't sound very thrilled. You don't have to do it." The disappointment in his voice was apparent.

"No, baby, it's not that. It's just something I've never done. When would you want to?"

"Tomorrow night, would that work?"

Wow, nothing like rushing it. "Tomorrow won't work. I had to promise Bryan I would see him tomorrow night to get him off my back. I'm sorry baby. How about Thursday? I'm sure your mom would appreciate a little more warning."

"Okay." Jack became quiet, running his finger up and down her arms.

Maddy rolled over to face him, "Talk to me."

"It's just hard Kitten. I knew it was going to be this way, but it doesn't make it easier. I want to be the only one touching you," he kissed her softly. "I want to be the only one who makes you purr."

"What do you want me to say Jack? You are the one I want to be with, but it's just not that simple. Just know you are the only one that makes me feel this way, this wonderful, glorious way. Honey, I don't even know if I can do it.

Things are so different now. I love Bryan, but I don't think I'm in love with him. A week ago I wouldn't have batted an eye about walking away from him. But lately, its like he has this air of desperation. To be honest I miss the cocky, assertive, controlling asshole he was when he first got here. Something happened and it happened before I lost it."

Jack nuzzled her hair. "You didn't loose it, Kitten. You gained your life back, one without fear of the past. Bryan is part of that past. I think he's afraid if you face the past and let go, you'll let go of him too."

Maddy took in what he was saying. Maybe he was right. She was so confused when it came to Bryan. And at the same time she had no doubts about Jack. She just didn't know what to do about it.

Maddy reached up and put her hand on his cheek and kissed him tenderly. "I wish I could tell you how much I love you, but there are no words. This is all so new to me, these beautiful warm feelings instead of feeling like I need to keep to myself, not let anyone touch me. Now all I want to do is be around you."

"Kitten, you don't have to tell me, you show me by the way you look at me, the way you give everything to me when we make love. I know it and I feel it here." He put his hand on his heart. "Do you understand what I am saying?"

She nodded and buried her head in his chest. "Hold me and don't ever let me go, promise me, Jack."

Jack held her so tight he thought he would break her. "I promise, Maddy. But you have to promise, when all is said and done, it's me you choose. I don't think I could bare loosing you."

"Jack, I chose you the moment I decided to make love to you yesterday. I don't take this lightly. I would never do that to you unless I was willing to commit to a relationship with you." She vowed. She guided his face to him, her lips lightly touching his.

He put his hand around her head and crushed her lips with his, kissing her deeply and passionately. He looked deep into her eyes, "I love you Maddy. Nothing is going to change that and if comes down to it I will fight for you."

He glanced over at the clock, "Its getting late, Kitten, I need to hit the road."

Maddy groaned. "I wish you could stay here with me."

Jack got up and started dress. "Me too." He leaned over her and kissed her. "Soon, maybe on the weekend if we can get Bryan to stay away."

Maddy slipped off the bed and pulled a nightshirt out of her drawer and slipped it on. She walked Jack to the door, slipping her arms around him. He pulled her close and kissed her. “Good night Kitten. Get some sleep. And thank you.”

“For what?” she asked.

“For opening up to me and letting me in.” He kissed again. “See you in the morning.”

Maddy leaned against the door and listen to his car drive away. Her heart ached and she missed him already. She went to bed and fell asleep. It was a restless sleep, tossing and turning with fitful dreams.

She was awakened abruptly by the dogs’ warning barks. Someone was here. Maddy peered out her bedroom window and saw the black Suburban. Shit! What the hell was he doing here? She watched as Bryan stumbled out of the truck and headed for the house. He was drunk.

Maddy sat on her bed and waited for him to knock. Thank God she had locked the door. She looked around her room. She couldn’t let him in there, the essence of her and Jack still lingered. Damn it, damn it, damn it! He was breaking the rules.

Maddy heard him pounding on the door. The dogs were going nuts. Maddy sprits the room with some cologne but she still wanted to keep him out of there. She didn’t want him spoiling her memories of Jack’s presence there.

She went to the door and peered out through the blinds. She looked back at the wall clock. 1:15. She opened the door and stood back to let Bryan in. Her displeasure at seeing him shown on her face had he taken the time to look.

Bryan stood before her. He was having a difficult time standing in one place. His eyes were blood shot and his face was red. He was shit faced. She didn’t like being around him like this. It changed him into a totally different person, one she did not like.

“Bryan, what the hell are doing here? You have no business driving in the condition you’re in. You could have killed someone.” Maddy snapped.

He put his arms around her, leaning on her for support. “Minnie, I’m sorry, I couldn’t stay away. I had to be with you.”

Maddy tried to push past him, but he had her locked in. “Bryan, let me go.”

He grabbed her face and kissed her roughly, “I’m never going to let you go. You’re mine.”

He tasted of beer and cigarettes. She felt repulsed and a little frightened. When he was drinking heavily before, she was never with him in person. It had been strictly phone calls. She pushed against his chest, but he was unyielding.

His hands slid up her nightshirt, groping her as his mouth came back down on hers. She twisted her body out of his grasp. “Damn it Bryan, back off! I hate it when you’re drunk. Let’s get you to bed and sleep this off.”

Maddy pushed him to the back of the house. He stopped at her bedroom. “No, I won’t sleep with you when you’re like this. Keep moving.” She got him into the spare room and sat him on the bed. She pulled off his shoes and removed his socks. She unbuttoned his shirt and his pants and took them off his body so he was down to his shorts. She pulled back the blankets. "Now get in," she ordered.

Just as she was about to walk away, Bryan grabbed by her wrist and pulled her down on the bed. He pinned her hands over her head with one hand while he reached under her nightshirt and removed her panties. "Bryan, please...please don't do this," she cried. He removed his shorts. He then pushed her nightshirt above her breast where he took them hungrily in his mouth, his free hand exploring her body.

The hold he had on her wrist was painful, his touch far from gentle. She tried to free herself but it seemed to excite him more. He parted her legs and entered her with a driving need. Maddy cried out but it wasn't from pleasure. When he finished he said harshly in her ear, "Now your mine again." Oh my God, Maddy thought, he knew! He collapsed on her body and passed out.

Maddy had a hard time rolling him off her. She looked down at him, snoring away, out cold.

With tears streaming down her eyes, she ran to the bathroom, stripped off her nightshirt and threw it in the trash. She turned the water on in the shower setting it as hot is she could get it. She let the steaming water wash her body as she scrubbed herself vigorously. She leaned against the back of the shower and slid down into the tub and sobbed. What he did to her tonight...he raped her.

Maddy stayed in the shower until the water began to turn cold. She stepped out and toweled herself off. She wrapped a towel around her and returned to her bedroom and locked the door behind her. She put on a pair of shorty pajamas and crawled between the sheets. Her mind was numb. She wouldn't allow herself to think. She never did fall back asleep that night. Finally she got out of bed around 6:30. As she was pulling out a pair of jeans she noticed the deep bruises in the shape of fingers on her wrist, a reminder of last night. She felt sick. She picked out a light weight long sleeved shirt and put it on.

She was in the kitchen drinking a glass of orange juice when Bryan stumbled in. He looked like hell. He was holding his head. "How did I get here?" he mumbled.

Maddy looked away from him, "You drove."

"Fuck, damn my head hurts."

"Good," Maddy snapped. "There's some Advil in the bathroom."

Bryan came to her and tried to kiss her. She glared up at him, "Don't touch me," she hissed.

Bryan looked confused, "What? You're angry because I got drunk? You were the one who suggested it."

"You don't remember what happened when you got here?" Her voice was cold as ice.

Bryan shook his head, still looking confused.

Maddy rolled up her sleeves exposing the bruised flesh. "This is what happened! So don't you dare lay a hand on me, you son of a bitch."

Bryan slid down into a chair and put his head in his hands. "Jesus Maddy, I am so truly sorry. You know I would never hurt you on purpose. I don't even remember doing it. My God, what have I done?"

Maddy stood up and threw the orange juice in his face. "You want to know what did? You raped me you fucker!"

Maddy grabbed her bag and let the dogs out. "Lock up when you leave." She slammed the door behind her.

She got in her car and laid her head on the steering wheel and burst in to tears. His black side reared its ugly head. The leopard revealed his spots. She looked up to find Bryan walking towards her. She jammed the car into gear and spun her tires as she drove up her lane.

He didn't even remember doing it. She shook her head. How could she deal with him now? How could she ever trust him again? Drunken amnesia was no excuse. She felt crushed. She flipped down her visor and glanced at herself in the mirror. Her skin was paled, her red swollen eyes looked washed out. She hadn't put any makeup on because she figured she would just cry it off anyhow.

When Maddy pulled into the parking lot she didn't know what to do. How was she going to face anyone? How was she going to face Jack? She couldn't tell anyone what happened.

Bryan pulled up in the Suburban parking next to Maddy. He approached her car and she flipped the locks.

"Maddy, please, we need to talk about this, please." When she looked at him she saw pain and fear in his eyes. She would talk...but she wouldn't forgive.

Maddy stepped out of her car. "I will talk, but don't you dare touch me," she said bitterly.

Bryan leaned against the truck. "There is no excuse for what I did to you. I have never ever meant to hurt you. You have to know that. This is one of the reasons I don't drink very much. I black out. I love you Maddy, so very much. Do you think you can find it in your heart to trust me again?"

"Right now Bryan I am too hurt and angry to even begin to think how I am going to feel about you. Until that time, don't you dare lay a hand on me. Don't even think about coming to my home. We have a professional relationship. And until I can sort things out—that's all we have."

Bryan reached out to her and she recoiled. He looked down and then looked up at her, "I'm so sorry. I will leave you be, but please remember Maddy, I do love you with all my heart. I would give anything to undo the damage I have done. I will earn your trust back, I promise."

Maddy left him standing in the parking lot. As she was heading to the squad room she had to pass Jack's office. He was already in. She tried to sneak past but he popped head out and greeted her.

"Come in for a couple of minutes if you have time," he waved her in.

How could she hide this from him? How could she hide anything from him? She wanted to no secrets and no lies between them.

When she entered, Jack grabbed her arms to pull her close and she flinched when he touched the bruises. He picked up on it right away and looked down. He could see the slightest trace of darkness. He slid up her sleeves exposing their ugliness.

"Maddy, what the hell is this?" he asked. He searched her face. "Something happened, something bad. I can see it in your eyes. Did he do this?"

Maddy reached for him and he put his arms around her and pulled him close. "If I tell you, you have to promise you will maintain control and let me deal with it. You have to promise."

He stroked her hair softly, "If he hurt you, I can't let it go."

"I'm not asking you to let it go, I am asking you to let me deal with it. We have to work together, we have a job to do and we can't let this interfere. Promise me," she pleaded.

"For now. Sit down and tell me," he held the chair out for her then went and sat in his. "What happened?"

"He showed up at my house last night around 1:30 or so, totally shit faced. I don't know if I told you, but he used to be a heavy drinker...and his dark side comes out. He hurt me. Now he doesn't even remember doing it. He blacked out, but I can't forgive him. He's very remorseful, but it's not enough. I told him for now, we just have a professional relationship, nothing more." Maddy looked up at Jack. His jaw was twitching, his nostrils flaring. He was pissed. "Let me handle it Jack, please..."

Jack worked on calming down by taking several deep breaths. "For your sake and the case, I will try. I can't promise you Maddy, I'm sorry. If I see him make one out of line move on you..."

"I can handle it Jack." She stood up and leaned over his desk and kissed him lightly on his lips. "I love you."

"I love you too, Kitten. Be careful."

She had decided not to tell him about the rape. Bryan hurt her. Jack didn't need to know how.

Maddy proceeded to the squad room. Bryan was sitting at his desk and didn't look up when she walked by. She noticed he had changed his clothes at least. She sat down at her desk and realized she had forgotten her laptop at home. She took out her phone and called Jack's cell. "Hey, I forgot my laptop at home. Could you print me off those emails?"

"Sure Kitten, I will run them down to you," he replied.

"Remember," she reminded.

"I know. I love you."

She smiled softly, "I know."

"Did you have a chance to look at those emails?" she asked Bryan without looking at him.

"Yep," short and sweet answer but didn't tell her anything.

"And?"

"Pity they sat on your laptop a whole week," he commented.

"Fuck you!" she snapped.

He glanced over at her. His pain was written all over his face. Damn it he was the one that did it. Why should she feel bad for being cold to him?

"I'm sorry. God knows I am sorry," he whispered.

"Bryan, just let it go for now okay? I need to deal with this my own way, and the best chance you have is to give me space, a wide space. Can you do that for me?"

"Can we at least not be enemies?" he asked quietly.

"I don't hate you. I'm pissed, very pissed, and very hurt. It's like two years ago all over again except this time you did it in person," she tried to make him understand where she was coming from.

"Two years ago...I really hurt you that bad?" he asked.

She looked at him in disbelief. "You devastated me Bryan. You totally mind fucked me, shattered any faith I had in you. And with everything that has happened since you've been back, I can never forgive you for what you did to me. I realize you weren't yourself, like you claim you weren't last night. But the fact of the matter is, that same person dwells within you. You still have the capacity to be cruel and selfish to fulfill your own needs."

Bryan was silent for a brief period. "I didn't realize you still harbored so much resentment toward me over that. Again, I am sorry, for both accounts."

"Just give me time and space and we'll see what happens. When and if I can get past this, I will come to you okay?" she asked.

"Can we at least be friends?"

"Hon, that's the best way you have for me to get over this. Can you handle that?"

"Maddy, I will do whatever it takes." He picked up as papers off his desk. "These emails, they're kind of cryptic don't you think?"

"It almost sounds as if he recruits people into a cult like situation. I mean it's like he puts himself right up there with God himself." She felt more comfortable talking about this.

Jack came in the squad room carrying Maddy's copies of the email. Their eyes met, hers pleading. He gave her a slight nod that he understood and would behave. "Hey Mad's, here you go." He kept his voice, light and controlled. Maddy loved him even more.

"Why don't you join us, Jack. We were just starting to discuss the implications these emails could hold." Bryan asked him. Bryan didn't know she had talked to Jack. That was okay.

Jack sat on the corner of Maddy's desk. "What do you guys think?"

"I was just telling Bryan this guy appears to have a God complex. You kind of have to read between the lines. As far as Granger goes, he like sucked her in under the guise what she does for him—she does for God. That the only way she can redeem herself in God's eyes is by doing what he says. But what does he have her do? Is it sexual? It appears she wised up and left the 'flock'. And when she wouldn't come back in, she became the chosen one—victim number five."

Maddy drummed rolled her fingers on her desk. "It would be easier to get a read on the significance of these emails if I could have her replies. I fucked up. Downloading those emails never crossed my mind."

Bryan sat back in his chair, "Don't knock yourself out, kiddo. We can get them yet."

Jack looked back and forth between the two, puzzled by their behavior. Then he realized Maddy was pulling her chameleon to get by. He had to admire her for that.

"We confiscated a computer at the Thomas scene. DCI has it. Do you suppose it's to late to see if we can retrieve the others' computers?" Jack asked Bryan.

He shrugged, "We can sure give it one hell of a try. Maddy, why don't you make a list of the items you want DCI to look for and we'll get it sent down to them right away."

Maddy nodded. "Oh, another thing, I hate to do this midstream, but I feel the profile has changed. I don't believe our unsub is a mainstream minister. He would have no way of maintaining his control over his flock if it had any kind of size."

"You know we probably should have Derek over here on this." Bryan got up to go find him.

Jack turned to Maddy, "Hey Kitten."

Maddy smiled softly, "Hey, sweetheart."

He reached for her hand and squeezed it. "You're doing good. I really admire you."

She laughed, "For what?"

"Being able to maintain a civil relationship when I know you're hurt and angry with him." He kept a hold of her hand.

"Baby, we do what we have to do to make things work," she laughed weakly. "I'm an old pro at faking it, remember."

Bryan returned with Derek. He noticed Jack holding Maddy's hand. Derek noticed too and glanced over at Bryan but didn't comment.

Bryan brought Derek up to speed of what they had discussed so far.

"So what are you saying? We don't need to do the church canvass?" Derek asked.

Maddy rocked back in her chair. "I don't know Derek. What do you think?"

Derek crossed his arms. "I'm not sure. He has to get to them some how. Do you suppose maybe he could be operating under a minister and putting together his own followers? He has to be able to recruit them from somewhere."

"So is that a yes?" Jack asked.

"Maddy, go a head and get your list ready for DCI. I'm going down for a smoke. When I get back we'll get it called in." He turned to Jack. "Come down with me please, I want to go over some things with you."

Jack and Maddy exchanged looks. They communicated though their eyes. Maddy knew he would be cautious.

Jack met Bryan on the steps. He sat down and pulled out a cigarette and lit it. "What do you need?"

"I wanted to talk to you about Maddy," Bryan said as he took a drag.

"What about her?" Jack was going let him talk, see what he said compared to what Maddy told him.

"I fucked up last night. I showed up at Maddy's house last night, drunk beyond all recognition. I don't even remember how I got there. Anyhow, to make a long story short, I hurt her physically, I hurt her bad." Bryan spilled it out.

Jack flicked his cigarette, "I know."

Bryan glanced over at him. "I guess I should have known. What did she tell you?"

"Same thing you just did. I saw the bruises," Jack felt himself tensing up. "What the hell were you thinking? What the hell did you do to her exactly?"

Maddy didn't tell Jack about the rape? Bryan wondered why? To keep peace? "I don't know. I don't remember it. I have a drinking problem, Jack. I can handle it in small does, but when I drink too much, I have blackouts. It was one of the major contributors to what happened two years ago. I was on a drunken binge for several months. Maddy caught the worst of it."

"Why are you telling me this, Bryan? I'm not going to help you get back into her good graces. Damn, man, look what you did to her? You of all people know how vulnerable she is right now. I told you right off the bat, you hurt her you would have me to contend with," Jack replied coldly. "She wants to handle this in her own way, and I'm going to let her, but I will put you on notice, I will be watching."

Both men said nothing for a couple of minutes when Bryan turned to Jack, "How long?"

Jack was puzzled, "How long what?"

Bryan looked straight at him. "How long have you and Maddy been sleeping together?"

Jack felt his stomach rise to his throat. He did know, but he wasn't going to give him the satisfaction of having it confirmed. "Don't be throwing your insecurities back on us, Bryan. What Maddy and I have together is between us, always has been. I'm there for her whenever she needs me and I always will be. Do I love her? You're fucking right I do. I won't deny it and never have. But my feelings for her are not what's important, it's her feelings, her needs, she comes first with me, and what she wants." He turned to Bryan, "How about you Bryan? Can you say the same? Or do your needs ultimately come first?"

Bryan pondered his question. "I thought I had her best interest in mind. I thought I proved it over the last few days, but now I'm not to sure. I'm a control freak. I will be the first to admit it. Before she had her break though, she needed me. She depended on me. Since then she doesn't need me anymore. She wants to be independent. I should be happy for her. But I have lost control of her and maybe that is why last night happened. She doesn't need me anymore."

"Oh quit feeling sorry for yourself. Buck up and be man. Support her decision to become stronger, to heal herself, don't sabotage her." Jack said angrily.

Bryan laughed, "Damn Jack, don't hold back. Maddy asked me to back off and give her some space and I will because I don't have any choice if she's ever going to forgive me. I will be her friend if she needs me and not cause friction while we are working. As for you and me, Jack, where does this put us?"

Jack kind of half smiled, "Gee Bryan, I didn't think you cared. Listen guy, other than what happened last night, I don't have a problem with you. If you respect Maddy's choice, you and I are fine. If I feel Maddy needs you when it comes to her dealing with her issues, I will let you know."

"Will you let me know how's she doing?"

"Yeah Bryan, I know what she means to you. I promise I will keep you in the loop." Jack held out his hand to Bryan. "Deal?"

"Deal." Bryan shook his hand. "Thank you."

They stood up and headed back for the squad room.

When they returned Jack went to his office and Bryan went back to the squad room. Maddy handed Bryan her list and excused herself.

She found Jack in his office. He was leaning back in his chair smiling.

She wondered what he found so amusing. "What?"

"I was wondering how long it would take for you to get here. So I take it you came for the lowdown huh?"

She sat down. "Well?"

"He told me about last night." Jack took a drink of his cold coffee and made a face.

"What did he tell you?" She was nervous he told Jack everything, but if did, Bryan probably wouldn't have much of a face left.

"Same thing you did, and that he didn't remember it. He told me about his drinking problem and his blackout history. I believe he is truly remorseful, but I told him it doesn't get him off the hook. I told him I would not be helping him get back into your good graces."

"Did it piss him off?"

"Nope, his temper never flared once. But he did pose a unique question." Jack was rocking back in his chair, a grin on his face.

"You asshole," she threw a pen at him. "Tell me!"

"He wanted to know how long we've been sleeping together." Jack said smugly.

Maddy's mouth dropped. "Oh my God. I told you he suspected. What did you tell him?"

"What went on between the two of us is our business." Jack threw the pen back at her.

She caught the pen in midair. "And how did he take it?"

"He dropped the subject. But anyhow, he's is going to give you your personal space as you requested and just be your friend when you need him, or so he says. I still want you to keep your radar up."

"Well duh," she quipped. "I know that better than anybody. I better get back. I don't want to make things rockier than they need to be."

When Maddy returned to the squad room Bryan was reading the Journal and did not appear to be happy with what he was reading.

When Maddy sat down at her desk, Bryan threw the paper at her. "Would you like to explain what the fuck that is?"

Maddy picked it up and looked at it. On the front page was a story of their unsub. The headline read "Serial Killer Preying On Area Women". She skimmed the story. It gave the facts of the story, a good part of everything they had leaving out the MO and the direction the investigation was going. It even had a copy of their sketch of the unsub. "What the fuck? Who released this?"

"Gee Maddy, read the bi-line," Bryan bellowed at her.

Story by Max Sutton with contributions by Maddy Sheridan. Maddy felt the heat rise to her face. "You can't really think I would do something this asinine do you? With all the fucking work I've put on this case, you think I would blow it up like this? I'm the one that said to keep it on the QT. Come on Bryan, you know me better!"

Everyone in the office was staring at them. Maddy stood up and grabbed her bag. "Andy, come on."

"Where the hell you going?" Bryan barked at her.

"To find out who in the hell leaked this to the paper, I am going to the source." She turned to Andy, "Are you coming or what?"

Andy looked at Bryan for the okay. Bryan nodded.

Maddy went back to her desk and snatched the paper and then stopped in front of Bryan's desk. She looked him in the eye. "You know damn well I didn't do this and if you don't, then damn it, you never knew me at all!"

She stopped by Jack's office. "Come on, we got to move."

Jack grabbed his jacket and took off after her, Andy in tow. "Where we going?"

"Field work!"

17

They took Jack's car. She asked that she be allowed to drive as she wanted him to read the article before they got there. She was fuming.

Jack's eyes scanned the article as Maddy whipped around street corners. "Would you watch how the hell you're driving? This is my car." He finished reading paper and set it aside. "I'm confused. How the hell they get a hold of this and why is your name on it?"

"You know I had no part in it don't you?" she asked.

Jack laughed, "Oh hell yeah. First of all you would never risk the integrity of a case and second, you would never share a bi-line with anybody. Who do you think did it?"

"I have a sneaking suspicion, but I'm not going to say until I have proof. Let Andy see the article so he knows what the hell we're talking about."

Jack handed the paper back to Andy. "What you are going to be seeing is not so much standard investigative work, but Maddy on a rampage. However," he laughed, "you will see some interrogating."

Maddy glanced over at Jack, "Why are you find this all so amusing? This is serious shit here. This much exposure could loose us our unsub."

Jack shrugged, "I don't know. It's not all that revealing. It shows the case is still pretty vague with the exception of suspicions of someone of the religious sect. Thank goodness we hadn't discussed the emails with anyone else."

When they arrived at the Journal, Maddy walked several steps ahead of Jack. "We better hurry up or we're going to loose her," Jack chuckled. Why he found this whole thing so funny he didn't know. But he did know he and Andy were in for one hell of show.

When they arrived at the bullpen it felt like home. Maddy hadn't realized how much she missed this place. She walked by her office. The lights were off, the door closed, her name was still on the door. She smiled to herself. Chief knew she would be coming home.

Maddy went straight to Chief's office and knocked on the door. He looked up and saw her, a broad smile crossing his face. He flagged her and came around the desk and hugged her. "God, it's good to see you kid."

He held out his hand to Jack, "Hello, Jack," he smiled, "Who's tagging along with who now?"

Jack shook his hand and smiled, "Well, yeah, she's still a pain in the ass on this end too."

"Bite me," Maddy mumbled.

She turned to Andy, "Chief, this FBI Agent Andrew Whittmer, he's my partner."

Andy looked at her in surprise then turned and shook Chief's hand.

"What can I do for the prodigal child?" he asked referring to Maddy.

She handed him a copy of today's Journal. "I want to know where the information came from for this article."

"Okay before we get to far into this, let's grab Sutton. Actually it's a little crowded in here. Let's move to the interview room." The three of them followed Chief. As they walked by Sutton's desk, Chief said to him, "Sutton, come with us... now."

When they arrived at the interview room everyone took a seat but Maddy who leaned against the wall, one leg raised resting against it. Sutton looked around at everyone who was there. He knew Jack, the kid he recognized as the FBI agent that had picked up Maddy that one Monday, and then he looked at Maddy. He noticed the badge hooked on her belt and she was sporting a gun on her hip. What the hell?

Chief noticed his observation, chuckled and said to him. "Sutton, let me introduce you to FBI Special Agent Maddy Sheridan."

Sutton's mouth dropped, "But how..."

"She's not just an agent," Andy piped in. "She's a profiler."

"She was in inactive status and reactivated to work this case so you see your story has caused a problem here," Chief explained.

"And don't get any designs on my office because I'm coming back," Maddy said coolly.

"Okay let's get down to the facts here," Chief said. "Where did you get your information on this serial killer case."

Sutton looked up at Maddy with a confused look on his face, "From Maddy."

"I personally handed it to you?"

"No, I got a packet with the information. It was in an envelope with your signature," he explained.

"I want to see it," she requested.

Sutton retrieved the envelope and handed it to her. Maddy looked it over. "This is an evidence voucher envelope. Of course it's got my signature on it, as well as six others. How did you get it?"

"It was dropped off at the front desk. I just assumed you sent it over," Sutton explained.

"And you never bothered to check out its validity?" she asked.

"Hell Maddy, it had your signature. You would never give me false information. Despite your cockeyed way of getting info, your information is always accurate," Sutton said in his own defense.

Chief spoke up, "First of all, Maddy never puts anything to print without running it by me first. Second this is the first I have seen this story, it ran without my approval."

"It came in last night, you were already gone. It was a big story, I thought the info came from Maddy and I ran with it. Christ I gave her a bi-line," Sutton threw his hands up in the air. "What was I suppose to do?"

Maddy grabbed the envelope and threw it down in front of him, "Journalistic rule number one—verify your fucking facts! You dumb ass, do you know you could have compromised this case?"

Sutton looked down shaking his head, "What do you want me to do? I can hardly write a retraction."

"No, its pointless now. If anything else comes into this office having anything doing with this case you call me and verify it." Maddy told him. "Oh, yeah, keep your mouth shut about me being FBI."

Sutton's eyes were down cast as he nodded.

Chief stood up, "See that you do." He turned to Maddy. "Get this case wrapped up so you can get you ass back to work," he winked at her.

As they were walking out of the building Maddy said she had to make one more stop. She went to the front desk. "Miranda, were you the one who received the envelope for Sutton late yesterday?"

"Hi Maddy," she smiled. She turned and looked at Andy, blushing, "Hi Andy."

Maddy glanced at Andy. His face was bright red. She laughed, "I'll be damned, I take it you two had a nice time the other night."

Miranda said, "As for your envelope. A guy brought it over."

"What did he look like?" she asked.

Miranda thought back for a few moments, "Oh, I don't know. He was kind of short, maybe 5'8", kind of chunky, dark hair, these stupid sideburns...and a gap between his two front teeth. He was at the party that night."

"O'Brien! I knew it!" Maddy shrieked. "That son of a bitch!" She started to storm out and Jack grabbed her, accidently gripping her wrist. "Ouch, fuck!" She rubbed her wrist.

"Oh, shit, I'm sorry, Babe." He moved his grip to her elbow. "You can't go back there going off half cocked. O'Brien is under my command. It's my job to deal with him. You got that? I'm serious here Maddy. Let me deal with it."

Maddy stood in front of him taking in everything he said. He was correct. It was not her place to confront O'Brien. She had no real say over him. "Okay, but that doesn't mean I don't want to pound the shit out of him."

When they returned back to squad room, Maddy went straight to her desk and began looking over the lists of churches they would canvass. She would let Jack do his job and not sit in on his meeting with Bryan.

"Bryan, we need to talk about this paper situation," Jack stated.

"Just a sec," Bryan signed off on a paper. "Grab your smokes."

When they arrived downstairs, Jack filled Bryan in on what they discovered at the Journal. "So you see, Maddy had nothing to do with it, as she told you.

It was O'Brien getting back at her for yesterday. I told you it was a bad mix and should have been dealt with yesterday like I wanted."

Bryan lit up a cigarette. "Well now you have your rope to hang him."

"Yeah, but it cost Maddy. He discredited her in front of the squad, twice. And you? How could you have ever doubted she would do something so stupid? Damn, Bryan, you keeping bragging how you know her better than anyone and yet you accuse her going behind our back and leaking out info."

Bryan looked at him angrily, "I saw it and I was pissed. For the past couple of days she's been a loose cannon. Who the hell knows what's going on going on in her head."

Jack looked at him in disbelief. "Funny, I don't have any problems knowing what's on her mind. You are the one that needs to get your shit together." Jack stood up. "I just thought I would let you know what really happened before I fire O'Brien's ass. I don't want you having anything to do with it because it will just look like you're doing it for Maddy. And by the way, you owe that girl an apology... again." And with that he turned and walked away.

Bryan sat with his head in hands. To say he was depressed was an understatement. Things were getting so out of control. Natalia was on his ass about Jeff. Jeff was begging him to bail him out with his dealer. He totaled another car. Donna had been calling him even though he hadn't been taking her calls. And worse of all, Maddy was slipping through his fingers right into Jack's arms. Last night could very well be the final nail in his coffin. What did he have left without Maddy? He looses her this time, there will be no next time. No leaving and coming back for another try. He didn't know what to do and he had no one to turn to. Jack had become a good friend he could talk to, but after last night, he would always have Maddy's wellbeing on the forefront. Which he should. Which Bryan should have. Even though he couldn't remember what he did last night, he knew it was all about taking control back, to reclaiming her for his own. Maddy wasn't the same woman she was a week ago. She was stronger and feeling the need for independence. He wished she would talk this out with him, but she wanted him to stay away.

When he went back up stairs though he went straight to Maddy anyhow and sat on the corner of her desk. She wouldn't look at him. "Maddy, can we go somewhere and talk, maybe like lunch or something?"

"Bryan...I don't feel comfortable being alone with you right now," she answered softly.

He put his hand on hers and she jerked it away. "Maddy, please. I won't press you on...us. I just really, really need a friend to talk to."

Maddy studied his face. He was in so much pain it broke her heart. He had been there for her through so much, how could she not be there for him...as a friend. "Okay." She grabbed her bag. "Where do you want to go?"

"To be honest, I'm not hungry, I just need to talk. Somewhere with some privacy. I'm not feeling real strong right now."

"Okay," Maddy nodded. "We'll go to a park and sit and talk alright?"

"Thank you."

Maddy took him to Grand View Park. They didn't speak to each other on the way. She pulled in to a parking area and shut off the car. "Do you want to get out or stay in here?"

He was looking down at his hands. "Here is fine." He turned to Maddy. "First I want to apologize for doubting you this morning. Jack explained to me what really happened. I should have had more faith in you."

Maddy refused to argue with him, she was here to listen. "Yeah, you should have, but you're forgiven."

Bryan bent down and put his head in his hands and lost it. "I can't do this anymore, Maddy. I feel like I am loosing it. I don't know who the fuck I am anymore. I don't know what I was thinking going back out into the field. I'm not equipped for it anymore. The way this case is being run is proof of that. My life is a miserable existence. Living with a woman I can hardly stand, a wife that hates me and just wants me for my money, a spoiled son who steals and lies to get one more fix, and a job that is unfulfilling. When I saw this case on the list and knew you were here, it gave me hope, hope that there might be chance you could forgive me and love me again. When I first saw you again, I saw the fire in you, the hate for me, and I knew you still loved me. You can't have that much hate without the love. And you did Maddy. You still loved me with the same fire you always had. You didn't trust me, but you loved me. That night when you almost left me, I saw my life for what it really was and I wanted more. I wanted a life with you, a real life. Jack said you clung to me and depended on me to be your rock, but Maddy I was doing the same thing with you. You were all I had to hang on to. I don't know what happened, but it's like Monday, something happened to you. I lost you. And just like you said, my old life is coming back to bite me in the ass. I'm not asking you to say anything or do anything, I just needed someone to talk to."

Maddy listened to him and she hurt for him. She got out the car and went around to the passenger side and opened the door. She knelt down beside him and took him in her arms and held him. "Get out of car so I do this right," she laughed between tears.

He got out of the car and she hugged him tight. He stood there with his arms at his side. "Its okay, you can hug me."

He wrapped his arms around and held her tight, burying his face in her hair. She reached up and put her hands on both sides of his face. "I want you to listen to me, Bryan. I don't love you any less than I ever have. I love you, you understand, I do love you. You frightened me last night. You hurt me. I thought that part of you was gone, but it's not. How do I know that part of you won't come out again?"

"You don't. I know now I can't drink. My drinking problem has caused you too much pain. It's no excuse and I'm not asking you to forgive me." His voice was low. She could hardly hear him.

He looked up at her and then down at her wrists. "How...how did I do that?"

Maddy unconsciously touched her wrist. "I was putting you to bed." She hesitated, "You grabbed me and pulled me down on the bed...you ahh...you held me down by my wrist..." she looked away from him. "You forced yourself on me... even after I begged you not to."

Bryan released her and began walking away from her. He found a bench and sat down. He covered his face with his hands and kept shaking his head back and forth. Maddy sat beside him and put her hand on his knee. Her heart was hurting for him. He seemed so lost. She started to wonder if this was how he felt when she hurting.

Bryan took a deep breath, "Why didn't you tell Jack I raped you?"

"I wouldn't have told him the other if he hadn't seen it." That was a lie. "Listen Bryan, we can't go back, but we can move forward. We can start over and try to build things back up. Are you willing?"

Bryan looked up at her; his eyes sparkling with unshed tears. "You would be willing?"

She nodded, "But I want to be honest with you. I am going to start seeing Jack. I owe it to myself to explore my feelings for him. I love Jack, but it doesn't mean I love you less."

"So we are done?"

"That's not what I said. We're not done unless you want us to be. There is no law that I can't see you both. I need to know you can be who you want to be. I can't live with wondering when you're going to snap. Babe, you have to prove it to me. Hon, I jumped into your bed two days after you got here. I went from hating you to being your lover in less than two days. Don't you think we rushed that?" She was trying to explain to him how she felt at the same time she wanted to bring her and Jack out in the open. No more sneaking around.

"No I don't want to be done. If you're saying I have the remotest chance, I will take that gamble. It's more than I deserve after what I did to you. How does Jack feel about this?" Bryan asked.

"I haven't talked to him about it. I haven't talked to him about dating him. So I guess that means I am talking to you about it first. You two are my two best friends. You both have been there for me, and been there to support each other. And you both have known all along about my feelings. The thing is, can you both deal with it and remain friends?" She watched him.

"I have never held Jack's feelings for you against him. You know that." Bryan twisted a ring on his finger nervously.

"Nor him you. So are we okay?" She brushed her hand on his cheek.

Bryan smiled weakly, "I suppose a kiss is out of the question?"

Maddy smiled. "Don't press your luck."

She stood and then she turned back to him, "And Bryan, as far as being able to do your job, you can do it. You just need to pull on your inner strength." She smiled, "and you can lean on me and Jack." She kissed him on the cheek. "I believe in you."

She grabbed him by the hand and pulled him to his feet, "Come on boss, we have a killer to catch."

Maddy went to Jack's office as soon as she returned. She poked her head in, "You got a minute?"

"Always for you Kitten," he motioned for her to sit down, "What's up?"

"I just had a long talk with Bryan," she said as she sat down.

Jack looked up alarmed.

"Don't worry, we just talked. You know with everything that has been going on, I have been so wrapped up in my own shit, I never saw how depressed he was getting. Jack, he broke down in front of me. I felt so helpless. He has all this other shit going on in his life, I didn't have a clue. He feels he's doing his job miserably. He felt he lost me way before what happened last night, and he feels incredibly bad about that." She took a deep breath.

"So you forgave him for everything?" Jack asked quietly.

"What is it? Do I not speak English? Nobody ever fucking listens to what I have to say," Maddy snapped.

"Wait, wait, wait. I'm sorry. I guess I'm just confused as to what you are saying." Jack leaned forward in his chair, resting his head on his arms.

"Do you still consider yourself as his friend?" she asked.

"I told him this morning, other than the fact he hurt you, I didn't have a problem with him, which I would say yes. Why?"

"He needs our support. Jack, you saw what he got me through; it's my turn to be there for him. You too." She didn't seem to be doing a very good job explaining this whole situation.

"Maddy, I am still his friend, I will do whatever he needs me to do, but what I want to know is where does that leaves us?" Jack was getting impatient.

"I told him you and I were going to start dating," she blurted out.

Jack sat back with a blank look on his face.

"That's all you have to say?" she expected so much more.

"I'm stunned. So no more sneaking around?"

She shook her head. "No more sneaking around."

"Wow," Jack said still not believing what he was hearing. "And he was okay with us dating?"

"As long as I don't shut him out. I explained to him, he and I have to rebuild our relationship. That he shot what we did have all to hell last night and he has to prove to me nothing like that will ever happen again," she explained.

"But you still love him?"

Maddy dropped her head to the desk and banged her head up and down. "This shouldn't have to be this hard. There is still a Bryan and Maddy. There is still a Jack and Maddy. But the Bryan and Maddy aren't what how they used to be. He wants the opportunity to win me back knowing full well you and are seeing each other—officially."

"You're going to see us both?" Jack asked.

"I'm not going to be sleeping with him." She waited for his response.

Maddy stood up. "I don't get it. Fuck you both." She turned and she left the room.

Maddy went back to the squad room. She was getting tired of all this male shit. She thought maybe she should go back to being celibate. It wasn't worth it.

She looked around her desk. Damn she wished she had her laptop.

Bryan was sitting outside when Jack saw him. "You mind if I sit down?" he asked Bryan.

Bryan smiled weakly, "Be my guest, pull up a step."

Jack sat down and lit up. "I'm sorry you're having a tough time and I didn't pick up on it."

"Don't knock yourself out, you've been there. I hear congratulations are in order," Bryan flicked his cigarette.

"For?"

"Maddy said you two were going to start dating, congratulations, I'm happy for you," He look Jack straight in the eyes, "sincerely."

Jack laughed, "So that's what she was trying to say. By the time she left I think we both got dumped."

Bryan smiled, "Why do you say that?"

"How would you interpret 'fuck you both'?" Jack shook his head.

"I'm am glad for you, but I'm not going to roll over and play dead. I love Maddy, I will do my best to get her back. I will give it everything I got, and I expect no less from you to do the same thing." He smiled at Jack and stuck out his hand, "May the best man win."

Jack laughed and shook his hand, "I'm younger and faster than you old man."

Bryan chuckled, "And I'm older and wiser."

Maddy looked up from a report she was reviewing and saw Andy standing beside her. "May I help you?"

"You called me your partner earlier. Did you mean it?" he asked shyly.

Maddy smiled, "For the duration of this case, while I'm still here, you have been assigned to me. So, yeah, I guess that makes you my partner."

"Cool. This message came in for you while you were gone." He handed her a slip of paper.

Maddy unfolded it. It was a message from Sutton to give him a call as soon as possible. Maddy took out her phone and dialed the paper. "Sutton, it's Maddy. What do you need?"

"Maddy, a guy called here looking for you. Wanted to talk to you real bad. I asked him if I could take a message. He said no, he would call you back, so I asked him if I could tell you who called. He gave his name as 'A Higher Power'. Does that mean anything to you?"

Maddy's heart dropped.

"Maddy? Maddy? Did you hear me?" Sutton asked.

"Ah...yeah. Did you tell him I wasn't working at the paper right now?"

"No, I got the impression you didn't want that to be public knowledge. I told him you were out on an interview. I didn't want to give him your cell without your permission. Was that okay?"

Maddy breathed a sigh of relief. "No, you did good, Sutton, you did great."

"Who is he Maddy?"

Maddy's voice dropped. "I'm going to tell you because you're going to help me, but if you tell anyone, I will shoot you myself, understand?"

Sutton dropped his voice, as if anyone would be listening to him anyhow, Maddy thought. "I understand."

"He's our unsub," Maddy whispered. Maddy looked up and saw Bryan and Jack come into the room. They were actually joking with each other. Maddy shook her head. Who the hell could understand men? " I have to go, if he calls back, do the same as you did. Stall him. I will get back to as soon as I can. Thanks Sutton."

Maddy stood up. "I need to see you, Jack and Derek in Jack's office ASAP," she said urgently.

Bryan went to get Derek, Jack and Maddy left for Jack's office.

Jack stopped Maddy in hallway, went to kiss her and she turned her cheek. "Sorry I was such an ass."

"I'm sorry you were too, but don't worry about it, I forgive you. Come on, this shit's not going to wait." She continued her way to his office and sat down.

Jack came in and sat at his desk and studied her. She was worried, very worried about something.

Derek and Bryan came in and stood by the wall. "What's the urgency?"

"I just talked to Sutton at the Journal. Someone called looking for me, didn't leave a message, said he would call back. Sutton asked him who was calling." Maddy looked at all of them, "He said his name was 'A Higher Power'."

The three men exchanged looks.

Maddy waited, "Jesus Christ, somebody say something!"

"He read the article," Derek said at last. "He's finally being recognized. He's making contact. But why not the reporter, why Maddy?"

"As far as the readers are concerned Maddy is still an investigative reporter. Her name was on the article too. Our unsub feels he's more in control with women so he wants to use her as a point of contact. Its not uncommon for an unsub to reach out to the press," Bryan explained.

Maddy secretly smiled. Now he's thinking like FBI.

"So now what, what do we do?" Jack asked.

"We let him contact her," Derek said.

"No!" Jack shook his head violently. "I'm not letting Maddy anywhere near that madman!"

Maddy looked sharply at Jack. "Let me? There's no letting any where in the equation, Jack. It's my job. And it's not like I'm going to be talking to him in person."

Jack looked at Bryan, pleading with his eyes and shaking his head.

"I'm sorry Jack, this is the biggest break we've had. We have to go with it." He turned to Maddy, "How are you supposed to make contact?"

"He's supposed to be calling back. I thought maybe we could get a designated cell and have Sutton give him that number. I sure as hell don't want him having my real one."

"Now wait a minute here," Jack stood up, "What's to stop this guy from stalking her?"

"She's not at the paper, so he won't be seeing her go in and out there. She doesn't live in the area. The only one at the paper who knows where she does live is the editor. He's not going to know to look for her here. She is virtually untraceable. I know, I've made sure of that." Bryan spelled out to Jack. "Get on your computer, Google her."

Jack did as he instructed. He pulled up Google and typed in her name, nothing came up. "How can that be, you would at least think something from the newspaper would come up."

Bryan shook his head. "Remember when you tried to do a background check on her?"

"Yeah, I didn't get very far."

"After you did that, we put a full block on her. Anytime someone tries to access any information on her, it gets red flagged and they're going to hit a wall." Bryan explained.

Maddy turned around and asked, "What did you do that for?"

"For your own protection." He put his hand on her shoulder, "Now aren't you glad we did?"

"It's not just you Maddy, if you were to run Bryan or me you would get the same results." Derek told him. "Anyhow, I do have one major concern with Maddy. And Maddy please don't take this as an insult, but do you think you are emotionally stable enough to do this?"

Maddy sought out Bryan, "I don't know kiddo. On the surface I would say yes, but only you really know what's going on inside. The only thing I ask is be honest with yourself, Maddy. Don't put yourself at risk. Think about it hon before you give us an answer. If you can't, we'll figure something else out. No shame in looking out for yourself, Maddy."

"Derek let's go get the cell hookup with a trap and trace." Bryan and Derek left the room.

Jack walked around his desk, closed his door and took a seat beside Maddy. He reached out for her hand. "What's going through your mind?" he asked her softly.

She turned to him, "Honestly?"

He nodded, "Honestly..."

Maddy took a deep breath, "I'm scared shitless. I don't know if I can do this." She sat in silence for a few minutes. "I'm going to tell you something I have never told anyone, Jack."

Jack turned their chairs so they faced each other. He took her hands in his, "Go ahead, whenever you're ready, Maddy."

"I can't look at you while I'm telling you this."

"I understand."

"When I came home that day...I knew something was wrong. I found my housekeeper in the kitchen. She had been stabbed." Maddy paused.

"Take your time Kitten."

"There was blood everywhere, on the cupboards, on the walls, all over the floor. While I was in the kitchen, I heard Lexi screaming. As I took off to run to her, I slipped on the blood. That's why I'm saying the fall Saturday night is what triggered me. Anyway..." Maddy proceeded to share with Jack the event which altered her life forever—the loss of her children. Maddy took a deep intake of air, and ran her fingers through her hair. Her breathing was unsteady. "They were both alive, but they were dying, bleeding out...I couldn't help them. I took them in my arms...." A sob escaped her lips. "Scotty went first...he slipped away..." she looked at the ceiling, tears streaming down her cheeks, "he wouldn't wake up, I begged him and he wouldn't wake up. Then Lexi...she put her little hand on me.... and then she left me too. I held my babies as they died, and I couldn't stop them." Maddy buried her face in her hands and let go of the pain she was feeling inside.

Jack wasn't sure what he should do. He couldn't comprehend the horror she had been living with all these years, it was no wonder her mind had blocked it out. Damn it, Bryan would know what to do to help her. This should be Bryan here, not him. But she chose him.

Jack leaned forward and wrapped himself around her, holding her. He kissed her forehead, but he didn't speak, he didn't know what to say.

After several minutes Maddy sat up and wiped her tears. She nervously laughed, "Where's my hanky?"

Jack pulled it out of his pocket and gave it to her, "Sorry."

"Thank you...for not saying anything. I didn't tell you because I wanted your pity or your coddling." She wiped her eyes. "I don't need that, just your understanding as to why I have conflicted feelings about all this."

He remained in his chair leaning forward. "You speak, I listen."

"I haven't had any contact with an unsub since then. I couldn't do it. I worked scenes, none that had anything to do with children. It just got to be too much. That's why I left. It was just too hard. Working this case, it's been tricky. Most of the time I can detach. But to have contact with a real unsub...." She shook her head, "Jack, I don't know if I can do it." She knelt on the floor and leaned against him.

Jack pulled her to her feet and held her. "Baby, you don't have to do anything you don't want to do. Bryan said you didn't have to if it was too risky to your wellbeing."

"But this could help us catch this bastard, save some lives, put this monster away," she protested.

"Maddy look at me," he turned her face to him, "I don't want you doing this. It scares the hell out of me you having any contact with this man. I can't bare the thought of anything happening to you. I know you're a gutsy broad, but baby, we're small time here. This isn't what we do. Not what you do anymore."

Maddy saw the concern in his eyes, it wasn't just concern, it was fear—fear for her safety. "I can't even go back to the paper, I'm trapped. Until we catch his guy, I can't get away. What am I going to do?"

"I can take you away from here until they catch him," Jack said desparately.

"I can't run—you know that. Let's go hear what our options are. Hopefully we'll have enough time you and I can talk about it tonight. Okay?" She asked. She had to admit, she really was afraid to do this. It sounded so simple, just talk to someone on the phone. But seeing what this monster had done to all these women, how could she keep it together? But how could she not?

As they were leaving Jack's office, he stopped her. "Maddy, when this is all over, will you promise me you will leave the FBI and go back to the paper? This was all kind of cool at first, but it's not funny anymore."

Maddy smiled softly and kissed him on the cheek, "That's one promise I will keep."

Derek made arrangements to set up a cell phone they could record the conversations. As far as a trap and trace a lot would depend on where the unsub called from. If he used a cell, they would have to triangulate off of cell towers. It could get pretty complicated, but hopefully they had enough time to get it set up.

Derek sat down by Bryan's desk. "Got the wheels going. It's going to take up a little time to get everything in place. Do you think she will do it?"

Bryan frowned, "Yes."

"Bud, if you don't think she can do this, don't let her. We could bring in a decoy."

Bryan sighed, "In the end, no matter how she feels about it, she'll do it because she feels she has to. I'm kind of hoping Parker can talk her out of it."

Derek gave him a strange look. "Shouldn't that be you doing the talking?"

"Things have changed. I'm too much a part of the past she needs to leave behind," he said sadly. "At this juncture in time, she doesn't trust me. She trusts Parker, and I trust him to do what he can."

"I sorry man, I didn't think anything could break the two of you."

Bryan smiled weakly, "I never said it was over, she just needs her time to find out who she is. She'll be back. We both need to rediscover each other without the past hanging over us."

"Good luck man, I'll be rooting for you." Derek patted him on the back and left.

Bryan stood up when Jack and Maddy walked in the room. Bryan looked to Jack for an answer. He shrugged his shoulders and shook his head. She didn't know yet what she was going to do. Bryan and Jack communicated well with their body language. Bryan smiled to himself. They should be enemies, but they were friends, and he was glad.

"What you do want me tell Sutton?" Maddy asked.

"We're putting things together. We won't have a number to give him for a while. Hopefully the unsub won't call back in until we can get things in place. Maddy, we can bring in someone else to do this, you don't have to do it." Bryan was trying to dissuade her.

"I don't know what I'm going to do. I need more time to think about it. That is unless time runs out before I have the choice. This might be just the break we've been looking for. I don't want to be the one who blows it." Maddy took a deep breath and blew it out slow. "What I wouldn't give for a nice normal day like I used to have."

"I'm sorry I drug you into this," Bryan told her.

"You didn't. I was already in to it when I pestered Jack into letting me check Granger's house."

"No shit," Jack cracked a smile. "She pissed of the uniform cop I had in the house with me by showing him up on her observations of the scene. The dog discovery was the final straw."

"Rufus, the eyewitness." Bryan chuckled. "Did she tell she sicked that rat on me?"

Jack threw his head back and laughed, "Oh Maddy, you didn't?"

"He wouldn't believe me, so I set him up," she smiled weakly.

"Little shit tore a hole in my leg." Bryan pulled up his pant leg.

Jack pulled up his, "Me too."

Maddy sat in her chair and listened to them. It warmed her how well the three of them were getting along. She didn't think it was possible, but she was pleasantly surprised she was wrong. She laid her head on the desk resting it on her arms.

Jack and Bryan exchanged looks. Bryan scribbled something on a note of paper and handed it to Jack. Jack took it and read it. 'Get her out of here, but don't let her be alone' Jack nodded.

Jack brushed his hand across her hair, "Hey Mads, lets get you out of here."

"I can't I gotta wait to see if Sutton calls." She didn't even raise her head.

Bryan spoke up. "If he calls, we'll call you. Just leave your cell on okay?"

"You sure?"

"I'm sure."

Maddy stood up, "You letting Jack off too?"

"Yep."

Bryan stood up not sure if he should hug her or not, but she took the question out of his hands. She pulled him close and leaned her head on his chest. He whispered in her ear "Don't do it Maddy, let someone else do it. I love you."

She kissed him on the cheek, "I have to think about it. I love you too." She stepped back and smiled weakly. "Call me if anything comes up."

Jack put his arm around Maddy, guiding her out. "Good night Bryan."

"Good night Jack," then he mouthed "Keep her safe."

Jack nodded.

When they got down to the parking lot Maddy stood beside her car. "Can I stay with you tonight. I don't want to go home and I don't want to be alone."

Jack smiled, "You're just trying to get into my bed again."

Maddy laughed, "Well yeah that too."

"I would be glad to have you with me, Kitten. Follow me home, I am going to have you park you're car in the garage, just for my peace of mind okay?"

"Because of Bryan?"

"No, Bryan knows you're going home with me. He's cool with it."

"I don't get you two."

"He and I talked today too. We both decided we were going to give you everything we got without interfering with the other and let the best man win."

Maddy punched him in the arm. "You make me feel like stuffed animal at a carnival."

Jack pulled her to him and kissed her tenderly, "Kitten, you are much better than any prize." He smiled and kissed her on the nose, "You're the one remember?"

Maddy followed Jack to his home. He had opened his garage door, which had two stalls. They pulled their vehicles in and closed the doors.

The garage entrance came in through the kitchen. Maddy remembered the supper they had there and smiled. That was such a sweet night—for them anyhow, it was one of the worst nights for she and Bryan. She shook the image out of her head. She was here with Jack. Maddy stood in the kitchen and waited for him. Maddy had started carrying an overnight bag in her trunk. Jack had grabbed it for her and set in on the counter.

He stood before her and brushed the hair out of her eyes, "You look beat, Kitten. Why don't you go lay down for awhile?"

"Will you lay down with me?"

"Only if you promise to rest. Last time you asked me that look what happened," he grinned mischievously. "Then if you are in the mood, later...well see. We have the whole night, Kitten." He kissed tenderly. "You go lay down, I will be with you in a minute."

Maddy went into the living room. The big overstuffed couch looked so inviting. She was so tired, between the lack of sleep last night and the emotional drain she had today, it had done her in. She grabbed one of the pillows and curled up on the couch. She was asleep within minutes.

Jack snooped through her purse and found her cell phone. He found Jessie's phone number under her contact list and asked her to do chores and let the dogs in for Maddy. Jessie asked him who he was and when he told her she laughed and said she was looking forward to meeting him. Jack thought it was kind of a strange reaction.

Then he called his mother and told her he might be bringing Maddy over later, it all depended how she felt. His mother told her that would be great, if not tonight, maybe tomorrow.

His last call he put into Bryan. Jack glanced into the living room and saw Maddy was sound asleep on the couch. "Hey Bryan, got her here a safe and sound. Her car's is shut in the garage. She's already asleep on the couch."

"Thank you Jack. I'm glad you are there to watch over her. Like I've said, you are the only man I trust with her."

Jack gave the phone a puzzled look. "Even now?"

Bryan chucked, "Even now. Do your best to talk her out of doing this phone thing. I really don't want her doing it either. Evening if it hinders the case. Her safety and sanity are worth more."

"Bryan," Jack said slowly, "She told me...about what happened when she found her children. It was horrific. I can understand why she had a mental break. I don't know anyone who wouldn't."

Bryan was silent before he spoke. "She must really trust you. She has never talked about it with me."

"It's like I told you before, dude, you are too close to the pain. It should have really been you there with her though. I didn't know what to say or do, not like you do. But her experience is what is holding her back. If this is what will do it, then let it happen. I don't want her anywhere near this guy, even if it's by phone. I'm going to go check on her. I will keep you posted. Later." And he signed off.

Jack changed clothes in to something more comfortable. He sat on the edge of the couch. He scooted her over and curled up around her body and folded his arms around her. She stirred in her sleep and wrapped her arms around his. He dozed off holding her.

Maddy woke up an hour later with Jack's body surrounding her. She smiled softly. He felt so good holding her.

When she tried moving Jack woke up. "Hey Kitten," he whispered. She had turned so they were facing each other. He kissed her softly on her lips.

"Hey, Babe."

"Feeling rested?"

"For the most part. I need to stretch." Jack sat up so she could move. Maddy stood up and stretched her limbs and then sat back down.

Jack put his arm around her and squeezed her shoulder. "Honey, this job is taking so much out of you. I wish we could make it go away."

Maddy leaned her head on his shoulder. "Me too, but we can't. And now I can't even back out and go back to the paper. I'm afraid he will stalk me. I don't want to live in fear. I have to do something."

"You're going to take the calls aren't you?" he asked.

Maddy nodded. "I have to. I want this over."

"I know you want to be independent and not be protected all the time, but Bryan and I both feel it's best someone is with you at all times. This guy is cunning and we don't want to take any chances. Do you understand where we're coming from?"

"Yeah," Maddy acknowledged. "To be honest I would feel better about it too. If someone is with me he isn't going to try anything. Listen I need to shake off this doom and gloom. I will do what I have to do. I just need to detach from it again."

"Come on, we're going to go for a ride." Jack nudged Maddy to get up.

"Where are we going?" she asked.

"It's a surprise," he said smiling.

Maddy went up stairs, freshened up and met Jack at the back door. They got in Impala and took off. Maddy watched the scenery as they drove wondering where they going. They were in the older part of town and she recognized immediately the large historical homes in the Grand View Park area. Maddy turned to Jack, "No, your not?"

Jack smiled, "Yes my love, I am taking you to meet my family."

She smacked him on his arm, "You could have warned me. I look like hell. I could have done something with my hair, put on some makeup or something." Now she was going to feel self-conscious.

Jack squeezed her hand, "You look beautiful just the way you are."

"Yeah but you're blinded by love," she grumbled. "They'll be there with their eyes wide open."

Jack pulled into a gated driveway hidden by tall, lush, manicured shrubs. It opened up it an expansive front yard. The landscaping was immaculate accenting the drive and around the tree bases. The house itself was a sprawling brick home with pinkish tinted stonework. Tall pillars marked the entrance of the two-story home. The stoop was rounded brick leading to a double ornamental door. It was a beautiful home obviously owned by people of wealth.

"Damn, you never told me you came from money," Maddy said softly.

Jack threw his head back and laughed. "I don't. They worked all their lives for this home. This is not where I grew up."

"Yeah and I believe you too—not!" There was so much about this man she didn't know. He was just full of surprises. Most were pleasant ones...she hoped.

After Jack pulled into the parking area, he came around to her side of the car and opened the door for her and led her to the house. Maddy quickly ran her fingers through her hair trying to look presentable.

Jack squeezed her hand and kissed her on the cheek, "Quit freaking out, you look fine." Before they walked in the side door, Jack took her in his arms and kissed her slowly and gently on the lips. Maddy responded, her arms crept up around his neck pulling him closer returning his kiss. She felt warmth spreading through her making her feel more alive. "Ready?" he whispered in her ear.

Maddy smiled softly, "As ready as I'm ever going to be. I'm nervous."

Jack laughed and led her inside. The door opened into a hallway that they followed in to a huge living area. The room had a bright airiness to it. Along one side tall, expansive windows opened up to a view of an extensive courtyard with a tennis court and swimming pool off to the side. No money, my ass, thought Maddy. The furniture in the room was a couple of couches of soft tan leather. The center focus to the sitting area was and expansive modern fireplace. Oak end tables and other accent pieces were scattered tastefully throughout the room. The floors were a soft tanned marble that brought out the color of the furniture. Large pieces of modern art adorned the walls. It was beautiful, but not what Maddy would call homey. This place was just the opposite of Jack's home. She liked his better.

A small woman entered the room, if she weighed 110 pounds wet would be pushing it. She was a lovely lady, with brownish gray hair; her features were soft and delicate. Maddy figured she was somewhere in her early 60's. She was dressed in blue jeans and a nice blouse. The woman's eyes lit up when she saw Jack.

She rushed to Jack's side, hugged him and kissed him on the cheek. "It's so good to see you honey. Seems like it's been ages. Here we live in the same town, but we don't see you nearly enough."

She turned her attention to Maddy, and then looked Jack, "Well Jack," she smiled sheepishly, "Make your introductions." Then she just bypassed Jack. She took Maddy's hands in hers and patted them. A warm smiled graced her lips. "I'm Alisha Parker, Jack's mother. And I did raise him better than this." She smiled over at Jack. "And you must be Maddy. I've read your articles often. I love your work."

Maddy blushed. "Thank you. You'll have to excuse my appearance. Jack kind of surprised me with this," she apologized.

"Nonsense, you look beautiful. Let me go get us some drinks." She disappeared into another part of the house.

"You asshole," Maddy smacked his arm. "You blindsided me."

Jack guided her to one of the couches and they sat down together. Alisha returned with a tray of glasses. She handed Maddy a tall glass. "Black tea with a twist of lemon right."

Maddy smiled, "Yes, thank you, Jack must have been filling you in I take it.

"I've talked to him more in the past couple of days, than I have in months, and most of it has been about you," she grinned. "All good, honey. So Maddy, how do you like living a double life?" Alisha asked as if it was the most natural thing in the world.

Maddy's mouth dropped and she looked at Jack. Damn what all did he tell her? She turned back to Jack's mother. "In all honesty, it sucks. I will be glad to get back to a normal life."

A silence fell over the room. It made Maddy edgy.

Alisha laughed. "You must be nervous hon. From what I have heard you are normally are very outgoing and outspoken."

Maddy turned to Jack, "Jesus Jack!"

Jack threw his head back and laughed. "We are a pretty open family. Relax Maddy, no one's going to bite you." He leaned over and kissed her on the cheek.

"You are the first woman Jack has ever brought home to meet us. He told me you are the one he's been waiting for. Maddy, you don't know how happy that makes us. He's always been so picky. Now maybe he can settle down and have a family." Alisha was beaming.

A family? Whoa, this was getting the cart way before the horse. She glanced over at Jack questioning him with her eyes.

Jack picked up on her confusion. He wished his mother had never said anything about starting a family. Especially after what Maddy had shared with him today about the loss of her children. "Mom, let's not get carried away okay. We just started formally dating."

"I know, but in away you've been together for a couple of years. Sometimes it just takes us awhile to see what was in front of us all along." Alisha took a sip of her tea and set it down.

"May I use your restroom?" Maddy asked. She had to get out of here for moment to compose herself. She was kind of pissed at Jack for putting her in this situation.

Jack showed her the restroom and returned to the living room. "Mom, knock it off with the family crap. Maddy had two children from a previous marriage who were murdered in a home invasion. Needless to say, she never got over it. Don't be pushing so hard, please. I don't want to scare her off."

"I'm sorry, Jack, you should have said something. I guessed by the way you were talking about her, you were further along in you relationship than you seem to be," she apologized.

"It's complicated Mom. The feelings, the trust, the love, it's all there, but we are just getting to know each other on a personal level. Maddy is a hard person to get to open up given everything she's been through. I let her share what she feels comfortable sharing. She has opened up to me so much in the last couple of days. It's going very well. But I also want you to know; she is under immense pressure with this case. A good part of it rides on her shoulders, which is a lot for anyone to carry. Can you understand and not judge her by her shyness today?"

"I'm not judging her at all, honey. I know the pressure you're under. If she has more involvement than you do, I can't imagine what she must be feeling. I will back off and let her get to know us at her own speed," his mother told him.

"If you don't mind, I'm going to take her back home. Today has been an extremely hard day for her. Maybe it would have been a better time to spring this on her later. I thought maybe it would get her mind off things. Did you have a chance to get what I asked you to?"

"Yes, it should be at your house now. I had them put it in your back foyer. Don't keep the little thing back there too long. It's too hot out there."

Maddy was silent on the drive back to Jack's. She felt the first meeting with Jack's mom was a bust. What must she think of her? She acted like a total idiot. And his mother, Jesus, talk about speaking her mind. Maddy smiled to herself. Under other circumstances Maddy would respect that in a woman, just not today.

Jack glanced over at her. "Are you pissed at me?"

Maddy looked forward, "Yes."

"I'm sorry. I rushed things and I shouldn't have. I thought it would be a nice deversion. And I'm sorry about my mom. She is a lot like you, she speaks before she thinks." The words spilled out of his mouth.

"Don't worry about it hon, it's just my mood. It's been shit day since early this morning. It has nothing to do with you." She took a deep sigh.

"What?"

"I have more days anymore feeling like this than I don't. I'm tired of it. I want to go home to where I used to find piece. I can't go home. I can't take the remotest chance some fucking sicko might be following me. I want my world back, before all this started, before Bryan, before I was forced to relive something I didn't want to and now I have to put all the pieces back together...again." Maddy leaned her head back against the headrest.

"Before us?" Jack asked quietly

"No baby, not before us, there would have been an us anyway, it just wouldn't have gotten this complicated. Jack, I don't know if you know this, but I am not a stable person. I take antipsychotics to help me keep my shit together. And still I'm not doing a very good job of it. I think I need up my dose." She was exasperated.

"How long you have been taking these...antipsychotics?"

"Since Bryan got here, which is also the same time I got dragged into this mess. Sometimes I just feel I have been forced to deal with all my past crap, that if it hadn't been for Bryan being a reminder of it all, and this fucking case pushing me to my limits everything would have been fine."

"Facing your past is not a bad thing. Yes, it's painful but you are getting stronger, I can see it." Jack pulled into his drive way and hit the garage door opener.

Maddy turned to look at him, "Am I really? Or is it the chameleon?" She got out of the car and went into the house.

Jack got out his phone and looked at it. He needed help; he needed to get her settled down. He began having doubts if he were strong enough to help Maddy get through this. He wasn't Bryan.

He dialed the phone. "Help me..."

"Jack? What's the matter?" Bryan asked.

"I can't calm her down. I feel likes she's on the edge and the slightest tap and she'll be over. How can she go from being a hell fire to this second guessing, self-doubting mess? And how can I get her out of it." Jack asked in a panic.

Bryan chuckled, "You ride out Bud, it comes with the territory. Being with Maddy in her current state is no walk in the park. You just have to be there for her, let her say what she needs to say, let her do what she needs to do, and feel what she needs to feel. Just be there. And I will warn you, her moods change with the breeze. She'll be this dark person, like she sounds she acting like now, and twenty minutes later, she'll be our Maddy again. Loving her takes work Jack, but it's all worth it."

"What about these meds she's taking, aren't they suppose to help? She said something about upping the dose," Jack asked.

"Not without an okay from her Doctor. You don't mess with psych meds and she knows it. Have her call him. It's really not such a bad idea. She really does need to get stabilized and it doest sound like she is." Bryan explained.

"Okay...thanks Bryan," Jack sounded defeated.

"Hey kid...it will be okay. She dealt with some pretty rough shit today. Peace, quiet, and rest are what she needs. Get her mind off things...and I hate to say this...but do whatever it takes. Surround her with love, that you'll be there and not run out on her. That's what she needs at a time like this. She gets scared."

Jack gave a weak laugh. "It's pretty damn bad when a guy has to call his girl's other boyfriend and ask how to handle her."

"Hey," Bryan said, "That's what friends are for. Good luck Jack, hang in there, and I'll call if anything arises. Give Maddy a kiss for me, you don't have to tell it's from me though," he laughed. "Check in with me later if you need to."

Jack hung up the phone and got out of his car. The three of them really did have a weird relationship. It was one he was sure no one would understand. He popped his head into the back foyer. As promised there was a little carrier—his gift for Maddy.

When he opened the kitchen door he found Maddy sitting at his counter dipping a spoon into a carton of chocolate ice cream. Jack started laughing, "You should see your face. You look like a little kid who got caught with his fingers in the cookie jar."

She licked the spoon and dipped it back in. "Chocolate is good for you, makes the endorphins rise giving you a natural high. Besides they say chocolate is an aphrodisiac," she smiled as she sucked the ice cream off the spoon.

Just like Bryan had said, she had flipped moods.

Maddy heard a strange sound coming from behind Jack's back. She tried to peer behind him, but he turned so she couldn't see. "What is that?"

"I got something for you." He put the kennel on the counter.

Maddy looked inside, "Oh my God! For me?" She pulled the kennel to her and popped open the door. Inside was this adorable, longhaired, white kitten with green eyes. She reached inside and gently pulled it out. She was grinning as she brought the kitten to her face and brushed it against her cheek.

Jack stood beside her. He turned her face to him and covered her mouth with his, kissing her tenderly and deeply. He could still taste the chocolate on her. He pulled back and smiled. "A kitten for my kitten."

Maddy gently placed the kitten on the counter and wrapped her arms around Jack's neck and kissed him deeply, exploring him with her tongue. From her position on the stool, she wrapped her legs around him, pulled his body close and pressed her body into his. With the feel of her body pressed into his, she felt an aching need for him, to be as close to him as she could be.

Jack felt the fires stirring within him. He slid her off the stool, her legs still wrapped around him and carried her upstairs and laid her down on the bed. He pulled off his shirt and lay down next to her. Maddy propped herself up on her elbow. She traced the lines of his chest with her finger.

He laughed, "You seem to have this strange fascination with my chest."

Maddy grinned, "It's just so damn sexy." She leaned into him kissing the hollows between his pecks. She ran her tongue across one of his nipples. When he groaned a shiver ran through her.

Jack unbuttoned her blouse and slid it off her shoulders. He reached around and unclasped her bra. He ran his finger along her collarbone, down the center of her chest. He watched Maddy's face as he touched her. She was watching him with keen interest, a soft smile touching her lips. His finger circled her breast finding its way to her nipple. He rubbed it between his thumb and forefinger. He leaned over her and took it in his mouth, teasing her. His free hand found her other breast and massaged it.

Maddy threw her head back and closed her eyes. The fire in her was slowly building. With each touch he laid on her sent sparks through her. She ran her fingers through his hair, softly moaning.

Jack reached down and undid Maddy's pants and removed them without his mouth ever leaving her. He ran his hand up her thigh and explored her, taunting and teasing her.

He backed away from her and removed his pants. He gently parted her legs and moved between them but didn't touch her. He lingered over top of her, their bodies barely touching her.

Maddy felt his skin barely sliding over her and his mouth descended down on hers, kissing her hungrily, and taking possessing of her mouth. She arched her body to be closer to his. Jack moved away from her so she couldn't.

"You don't want me do you, Maddy?" his deep throaty voice whispered in her ear.

"Mmmhhmmm," she whimpered. Her body was crying out of him. She could feel him brushing against her inner thigh. She pressed down on his shoulders with her fingers.

"I want to hear you tell me," he was searching her eyes, seeing the desire burning in there.

"I want you," she choked. Damn why did he torture her so?

"Do you just want me or do you want me to make love to you?"

She wanted to scream at him 'Who gives a shit, just give it to me' but she knew that wasn't what he wanted to hear from her. "Love me Jack, please...just love me."

He slowly entered her, taking his time as he made love to her. He slid his hands up under her hips and raised her from the bed. He moved his knees underneath him and pulled her up to him so they were facing each other. Maddy wrapped her legs around him meeting him move for move. Their bodies clung to each other as they were locked in a passionate kiss that seemed to go on and on. As their tempo increased the kiss deepened until their bodies shuttered together. Jack laid her back in the bed without leaving her. He continued to kiss her face and her neck. "I love you my kitten."

Maddy started laughing.

Jack gave her a strange look and laughed, "That's the reaction I get for making love to you?"

"No, no," she kissed him tenderly, "We left the kitten on the counter."

Jack chuckled and rolled off her. "He's a cat, he can take care of himself," he said as his hands slid over her body.

She brushed his face with her hand, "You're greedy." She was grinning at him then she kissed him softly. "I love you."

Jack turned on his side, studying her face. He brushed the hair away from her eyes. "You really do love me don't you?"

"Is that a question or a statement?" Maddy asked. "Do you doubt my love?"

"No, Kitten," he said, "I just can't believe we are finally together. Free to be together."

"Well believe it." She grabbed his shirt, slipped it on and buttoned it up then slipped her panties on. She stood up and struck a pose. "What do you think?" she grinned.

Jack chuckled. "You look better in it than I do."

She picked up her shirt and threw it at him. "Your turn."

He held it up to his chest and shook his head, "I don't think so."

He went to his dresser and pulled out a pair of sweat pants and put them on.

They entered the kitchen together.

Maddy looked around for the kitten. When she found him she burst into laughter. She pointed to the ice cream carton. The kitten poked his head out. His beautiful white fur was matted down with chocolate ice cream. She scooped him up. "My poor baby!" She took the kitten to the sink and ran warm water over him, lightly scrubbing off the ice cream. Jack stood behind her and handed her a towel when she finished. She wrapped the kitten up in the towel.

"What's your middle name?" she asked as she toweled off the kitten.

"Why?"

"His name. What's your middle name?" she laughed.

"Edward," Jack said flatly.

Maddy snickered, "Jackson Edward Parker."

"Shut up Maude," Jack slipped. Shit. He and Bryan were both dead meat now.

Maddy whipped her head around. "That son of a bitch! He is so dead. Where's my phone?"

Jack grabbed it off the counter, "No! You can't tell him. He said if I ever repeated it he would have kill me. I'm sorry..." he darted around the other side of the counter, "I'm so sorry. That name will never cross my lips again." He crossed his chest with his fingers, "Cross my heart, never again. Just don't tell him. Pleeeeeeeeeease!"

Maddy laughed, "Okay, but I'm putting you on notice. You ever call me that again, I will castrate you."

"Ouch, no worries, it won't happen again." Jack was looking down at her phone. "Babe, you got a missed called on here." He threw her the phone.

She looked at it. It was from Bryan from about ten minutes ago. She called him back. "Hey hon, what's up?" She started feel her nerves kicking in.

"Sutton called. The unsub left a number for you to call." Bryan said softly.

Maddy sunk down onto a stool. "Oh shit. Did you run the number?"

"Prepaid cell."

Maddy looked up at Jack and then said into the phone, "What do you want me to do, Bryan?"

"You know how I feel about this, you know how Jack feels about it, but ultimately Kiddo, it's your call."

Maddy was silent for a few moments. "Do you want me to come in?"

She could hear Bryan giving a deep sigh on the other end. She needed him at this moment. He was her strength. Only he could give it to her. "Your phone is ready, it's your choice."

"I will be there shortly," she finally said.

"Okay kiddo, let me talk to Jack." She handed the phone to Jack while she went upstairs to get dressed.

"Hello," Jack said into the phone, "What's up?"

"Our unsub called for her again. He left a number for her to call. No luck on talking her out of it, I take it?"

Jack looked up at the ceiling, "She said she wanted to do it so we can push this to an end. She wants to take her life back."

"Bring her down I guess. See you in a few." Bryan disconnected.

Jack popped upstairs and pulled on a t-shirt and some jeans and met Maddy in the kitchen. She was putting the kitten back in the kennel.

She poked her fingers through the wires and was playing with him. "We need to stop on the way back and get some food and a litter box. Eddie can't stay in here forever."

"Eddie?" Jack smiled.

She kissed him on his cheek. "Yep, named him after his daddy. We already have a Jack."

Jack pulled her in his arms and kissed her deeply. He loved the way she said 'we'. He finally had his family, he laughed to himself, even if it were animals.

She hugged him tight. "Let's get this show on the road so we can get back home."

18

Derek and Bryan were the only two in the squad room when she and Jack arrived. Bryan asked he be able to talk to Maddy alone. Bryan grabbed something from his desk and a bottle of water and carried it back to the interview room.

As soon as the door was shut, Maddy threw herself into Bryan's arms. "I need you. I can't do this without you. You are my strength, Bryan."

Bryan held her close, running his hands up and down her back. He kissed the top of her head. "I'm here for you Minnie, always. Kiddo you're shaking like a leaf."

She pulled away and sat down. Bryan took out a pill bottle, opened it up and gave her a little green pill and the bottled water.

She looked up at him, "What's this?"

"Klonopin. It's for your nerves. I take it everyday. It will help you relax," he explained.

Maddy popped the pill and took a swig of water. "How long does it take?"

"Around 15 minutes. I want you to wait until it kicks in before you make that call okay?"

Maddy nodded and stood up. She kissed Bryan softly on the lips. "Don't leave me okay?"

He squeezed her hand, "I'm not going anywhere."

They returned to the squad room where Derek and Jack were waiting.

Derek handed her a cell phone. "This phone has a transmitter which will be received by this," he pointed to a recorder. "We will be taping the entire conversation. Don't give up anything personal and don't antagonize him. Just feel him out. Find out what he wants from you."

Jack stood behind Maddy and massaged her shoulders. He leaned into her. "You don't have to do this Mads. It's not too late to back out."

Maddy shook her head, "No, I can do this. Just let me handle it. I just need some quiet time so everyone just shut up for a few minutes okay?"

Maddy sat quietly at her desk until she felt herself calming to some degree. She picked up the cell phone. Her hands were shaking so badly she couldn't dial the phone. Bryan took it from her and punched in the number. When it started ringing he handed it back to Maddy.

On the third ring a man picked up and said hello.

"This is Maddy Sheridan. I was given this number to call. Whom am I speaking with?" Jack and Bryan looked at each other. Her voice was surprisingly calm. "Chameleon," Jack whispered.

"I'm the person you wrote the story about, the one you referred to as a serial killer. I don't care much for your choice of words." The voice was deep, very calm, almost sounding pleasant. A narcissist, Maddy thought.

"What would you call a person that snuffed out the lives of six innocent women and a man?" she asked.

"I didn't murder them, I saved them. The gentleman was an unfortunate incident."

"I see, collateral damage. How do I know you are who you say you are?"

"What do you want to know?"

"Tell me where you dumped the first body," Maddy said flatly

"Not so fast Ms. Sheridan. I don't have to prove myself to anyone but God," the man said.

"What do you want from me?" she asked.

"For you to set the record straight. I am hanging up on you now. I am sure you are not alone. I will contact you sometime in the near future and we will discuss this further." And with that the phone went dead.

Maddy stared at the phone for a few seconds, flipped it shut and tossed it on the desk. "Well that was fruitful. You son of a bitch."

Maddy picked the phone back up and hit redial before anyone could stop her. When the man answered, she went off on him, "Listen, Mr. Holier than thou, you want my help *setting the record straight* you don't get to call all the shots. I'm not one for letting someone try to play me like a puppet on a string. You want my help, you give me answers, and until you decide you're going to play by those rules, don't contact me!" She slammed the phone shut.

"Jesus Christ Maddy!" Derek shrieked. "I told you not to antagonize him. Don't you ever do anything you're told?"

Jack and Bryan exchanged looks, both hiding a smile.

Just then the phone went off. They all stared down at it. Maddy reached down and picked it up. "What?" she snapped.

"There's a small roadside park off Interstate 29 leading down to the Big Sioux River. You will find your answer there." And he hung up.

Maddy sat back in her chair with a smug look on her face. She glared at Derek. "Well don't you think you need to be making some phone calls?"

Derek stormed off to call in some of the agents, line up a dog, and CSU.

"Make sure you call Andy. I want my partner with me," she called after him. She was just being a bitch.

Maddy was aware of two sets of eyes on her. She regarded them skeptically. "What are you looking at?

"Do you think that was the smartest thing to do, Maddy?" Bryan asked her.

"It got us results didn't it? I'm not pissing around with this guy. I'm not one of these kiss ass women he gets under his spell and he needs to know it right from the start. He's not going to be using me—I'm using him," she replied defiantly.

Maddy got up and walked out to the hallway. She was shaking her fingers and breathing deeply trying to release the tension she was feeling.

"What did you say to her to get her like that?" Jack asked Bryan.

"I gave her one more chance to back out, then I gave her my little green friend," Bryan held up the bottle.

Jack laughed, "You drugged her?"

Bryan smiled and shook his head, "It's Klonopin. It's an anti-anxiety pill. A good one. It helps me get through the day."

"Why do you take them?"

"Not something I want to get into. I'm just glad they came through for her, but most of that was Maddy. I'm going to go check on her." Bryan left in search of Maddy.

He found her out pacing the hallway. "You okay Kiddo?"

"It's just starting to hit me what happened. I talked to our unsub, no I bitched out our unsub. Am I fucking crazy or what?"

Bryan chuckled, "Well the jury is still out on that one." He hugged her. "You did good kid. You have the upper hand. Now do you think you can keep it?"

Jack joined them in the hallway and saw Maddy in Bryan's arms. He felt a tinge of jealousy but told himself to stay in check. This was going to happen.

Maddy pulled back and leaned against the wall. "He just pissed me off. He just has this air of self-righteousness about him. He's an arrogant narcissist. He's a dom and one thing I am not is submissive. There was so much I wanted to say to him. If I hadn't been scared shitless, I would have."

"Thank your fear for keeping you in check, Maddy," Bryan said. "Don't push him too far, you don't know what he could do."

They all turned when they heard footsteps coming down the hall. Maddy smiled when she saw Andy Whittmer. "Hey partner, ready to go dig up a body?"

Andy stopped in his tracks. "For real?"

"For real." Bryan put his hand on Andy's shoulder and steered in to the squad room. "I'll bring you up to speed."

Jack leaned against the wall next to Maddy. For some reason, he didn't know what to say.

Maddy leaned over and kissed him on the cheek. "I'm okay, really." Then she smiled weakly. "This isn't how I thought our first night together would be spent."

Jack nudged her and smiled, "At least we got to spend some time together."

Maddy grinned and nodded. "Yep....that we did. How long do you think we are going to have spend out there?"

"At least until we unearth her, providing he's not sending us on a wild goose chase." He looked at his watch 7:45. "We'll if we could get moving and find it soon we might make it home by midnight."

Maddy peered around the corner into the squad room. "What the hell's taking so long?"

He grabbed her by the hand and led her back in with the others to find out what the status was.

As they were waiting two DCI's walked in and one other FBI agent. They decided to have Jack be the only local on the scene. His department was still stinging over the O'Brien fiasco. However if one were to look at it, if O'Brien hadn't set Maddy up, they never would have made contact with the unsub.

Derek joined the rest of them and informed them that a cadaver dog and CSU would meet them at the scene. The only thing they were waiting for was to find out where that was.

Jack went to the wall map. "I'm pretty sure he's talking about a roadside park located here." He pointed to an area on the map. "It right off of Interstate 29 near the Riverside exit. There's a road that goes under the bridge and leads back into a river access. Could be anywhere in there."

Derek called in the location. "You guys ready?"

"Let's do it," Bryan ordered.

Maddy, Jack and Andy rode together in Jack's car and Bryan, Derek and others went in one of the SUV's. It took them less than twenty minutes to get to the park Jack was hoping was the dumpsite. CSU and the K-9 unit arrived shortly after their arrival.

The daylight was winding down when the cadaver dog let out a yowl. His discovery was several hundred feet away from the frontage road. To the naked eye, they never would have found it. Because of the length of time that had passed, the ground had settled and the forest had reclaimed the area where the body was put to rest. Remote lighting had to be brought in before they were ready to dig.

The agents stood by as CSU was allowed to turn the earth. It was hard for Maddy to sit back and just be an observer. It wasn't in her nature. There were a couple if times when Bryan had to hold her back from jumping into the scene.

After about half an hour of fine sifting the body was located. The river loam consisted of fine sand, river mud and decaying foliage. The body had been in this location for over two months. It had decomposed much faster than it normally would have in drier soil. The flesh had been eaten away by insects and all that remained were black oily bones. This body had no shroud protecting it. If there had been a gown it had long since rotted away. The only telltale sign it was one of their vics was the rosary wrapped around the skeletal remains of her hands.

Maddy peered down into the grave and shook her head. Miss Mallard was definitely no more. DNA and dental records were all they were going to get for IDing this body.

Bryan guided Maddy away from the site by her elbow. He handed her the cell phone that was being used for contact by the unsub. "You need to keep this with you at all times. The receiver is supposed to be able to pick up any calls that go in and out of this phone. Now listen to me for once in your life—do not, I repeat, do not initiate contact with him. I mean it, Maddy. Promise me."

She looked at him, her eyes twinkling in the artificial light. "I image either you or Jack will be with me at all times until this thing is over doing your protective thingy. Why don't you guys hang on to it, then you know I won't be tempted. Which you and I both know the chances of that happening will be high."

"Good point. I will give it to Jack."

The two of them stood in the shadows a couple of feet apart, each looking for something from the other. "I miss you Bryan," Maddy said sadly.

"Even after last night?" he asked.

"It doesn't matter. I just miss you, so very much."

"You got Jack." Bryan looked away.

"He's not you."

"No, he's younger and faster than me," Bryan laughed under his breath.

"Huh? What's that suppose to mean?" What the hell was he talking about?

Bryan shook his head, "Never mind. I miss you too. What are you going to do about it?"

"I don't know. We were suppose to be together tonight, then everything got fucked up."

Bryan looked down, "Yeah, well that's my fault."

"Don't you need to take a shift as my body guard?" she asked with a slight smile on her face.

Bryan smiled, "Let's just see how tomorrow pans out. Seems like when we plan anything all hell breaks loose and it all gets fucked up."

Maddy went to him and kissed him softly on the lips. "I will keep my fingers crossed."

"Lets go find Jack and get you the hell out of here so you can get some sleep. Call your doctor tomorrow on that med adjustment and ask him for a script for the Klonopin."

"Bryan? Why do you take it?" she asked.

"Anxiety disorder." He started walking away from her.

She caught up to him. "Since when?"

"The shooting." She let it go at that.

They found Jack at the scene. Bryan explained to him about the phone and to keep it out of Maddy's hands unless the unsub should call. It was already 1:15; Bryan doubted he would call anymore tonight. He walked them to Jack's car.

Jack stood by the car waiting for Maddy to say goodnight to Bryan. Maddy hugged Bryan and gave him a goodnight kiss and whispered in his ear, "I love you, Mickey."

Bryan held her head in his hands. "I love you too, Minnie. I really hate this time share thing." He kissed her on her forehead. "Goodnight Maddy." He turned and went back to the gravesite.

Maddy slipped into the car. Jack started the ignition and put it in gear. They drove in silence for a while when Maddy couldn't handle the deafening silence any longer. "Say what's on your mind, Jack."

"I'm just wondering if you are having regrets. I see you two together, and it's still there Maddy." Jack kept his attention on the road.

Maddy put her arm against the door and rested her head against it. "No, Jack, I don't have any regrets. I love you. I have told you that, I thought I showed you how much. As far as Bryan and I go..." she looked at him, "who am I going home with?"

Jack didn't answer her. "I asked you, Jack, if you were going to able to deal with this. Hell you guys made jokes about it...let the best man win...I'll be damned if I'm going to let the two of you put guilt trips on me. I'm putting you first. Doesn't that say something?"

Jack seemed to be deep in thought. Maddy decided to just let it drop. There was nothing more she could do. Even she realized this was going to be more complicated and harder than she thought it was going to be. She did love Jack, with all her heart and she loved being with him, loved the way they were together. But Bryan was her soul, how could she ever explain that to him and have him understand?

Jack's hand reached across the seat. He felt Maddy intwine her fingers in his. "I'm sorry Maddy. I know things are the way they are and I shouldn't pressure you. I will deal with it. After all things are better than they were."

Maddy didn't say anything. She leaned her head back and squeezed his hand.

Jack stopped off at Walgreens and picked up some kitty litter, a box and cat food. When he returned to the car Maddy had drifted off to sleep. He let her be until he pulled the car into his garage.

Maddy went straight into the house and disappeared up the steps. Jack fed the kitten and showed it the litter box and joined Maddy upstairs. She had crawled into bed and was asleep already. He looked down at her and smiled. She was wearing his shirt. He stripped down to his shorts and crawled in next to her. He pulled the covers around them, wrapped his arms around her, buried his face in her hair and fell asleep.

Maddy shot up in bed from a dead sleep having a panic attack. Jack had had his arms around her and felt it when she jerked away from him.

Maddy couldn't breath. She was hyperventilating. "Oh my God," she cried out.

Jack sat up putting his arm around her shoulders. "Come on, Mads calm down, breath Baby. Slow down, just breath." He kept repeating it until her breath returned to somewhat normal. "What wrong sweetheart? Bad dream?" After everything that happed during the day, it would be perfectly understandable.

Maddy turned to him. "He was there, Jack, he was there," she whimpered.

"Who, Maddy. Who was where?"

"The unsub, he was there at there tonight, watching us," she said with an uneasiness.

Jack watched her. Her fear was real. "How do you know?"

"I just know. He knows the area well enough, he could have been anywhere there and we didn't even know. He knows I was there. He was banking on it." She put her head in her hands. "He knows where I am."

Jack got a sick feeling in the pit of his stomach. What if she were right?

"Come on. Let's go downstairs. We need to get you calmed down." Jack pulled on his sweatpants then they went down to the living room. Maddy sat down on the couch and Jacked wrapped her in a blanket. He disappeared to parts unknown.

Maddy tried to her best to numb her mind. She could be wrong. She could be just imagining all this. She wasn't positive he was there. But she had a gut feeling, and usually her gut feelings were right. It was the perfect set up. He knew if he told her where Mallard was buried, she would go. She would be the only woman out there and he knew she would be there to watch. He would have seen her leave with Jack and could have very easily followed them back here. But how would he know he couldn't pick up on her at the Journal? Perhaps he had gone there and Miranda said she was on a leave of absence. Who the hell knows?

Jack had slipped into the kitchen to call Bryan. It was obvious he had awaken him, he sounded pretty out of it. He told him what Maddy had said and asked if Bryan would come over so they could talk. Bryan told him would be there as soon as could.

Jack went to his cupboard and took out a bottle of whisky. He didn't know how much of a drinker she was, but he figured a good shot would help calm down. He poured an ample serving in a tumbler and brought into her. "Here, drink this," he handed her the glass.

Maddy took it from him and brought it to her nose and sniffed it. "What the hell is this?"

"Whiskey."

She wrinkled up her nose. "What am I suppose to do with it?

Jack laughed, "Drink it dummy."

"Fuck you! What if I don't want to drink it?"

Jack sighed, "Just drink it. It will help calm your nerves."

Maddy took a swig and started coughing. "Man this stuff tastes like shit," she complained.

"Quit your whining, bite the bullet and drink it." Jack sat down beside her.

Maddy took another swallow. Her body shuttered and her face contorted. She began feeling a warmness spread throughout her body. She put the glass to her lips and took a bigger swallow. This time it went down a little easier. Finally it got to the point she really couldn't taste it and liked the way it was beginning to make her feel. She downed the last of it and handed the glass back to Jack. "More," she said with a giggle.

Jack looked down into the empty glass. "Damn Maddy. You lush." He went back to the kitchen, poured her another glass and brought it back to her. "Slow down, you're getting drunk."

Jack's doorbell echoed throughout the house. Maddy took another gulp and called out, "Who's there?"

Jack walked to the door shaking his head. He had created a monster. He let Bryan in and they walked into the living room where Jack took a seat beside Maddy and Bryan sat across from her on the loveseat."

Maddy held up her half empty glass to Bryan. "Cheers! What are you doing here?"

Bryan turned to Jack, "You got her drunk?"

Jack shook his head, chuckling softly, "It was an accident. It was just supposed to calm her down." He grabbed her foot under the blanket, "Not make her all toasty toes."

Maddy squealed and pulled her foot back. "Hey!" She downed the remainder of the whiskey. She kicked Jack playfully. "Warm fuzzies."

Bryan watched the exchange with some discomfort. He had never seen Maddy openly flirt with Jack. He noticed Maddy's bare legs and when the blanket slipped, that she was wearing one of Jack's shirts. A bare chested Jack didn't go unnoticed either. Seeing Jack's physique made him feel old and inadequate. No wonder Maddy preferred Jack over him.

"She didn't have anything to sleep in."

Bryan came out of his revere. "Huh?"

"She's wearing my shirt because she didn't have anything to sleep in. She wasn't planning being away from home. Just incase you're wondering," Jack clarified. It wasn't a total lie, but he could tell by the shadow that crossed Bryan's face he was feeling it—the same feeling he had earlier in the night.

"You don't have to explain anything to me. It's none of my business," Bryan replied quietly.

"Tell Bryan what you told me," Jack said to Maddy.

"That fucker was out there with us," she said vehemently. "He was watching and waiting. He set me up. He knew I would be there. Here I thought I was playing him and he was playing me all along." She handed the glass to Jack, giving him the doe eyes look. "Please, just one more."

Jack looked at Bryan who just gave a light shrug. He got up and went back into the kitchen.

Maddy nudged Bryan with her toe. "Hey sexy," she giggled.

Bryan shook his head slowly, "No Maddy. Not here. You're Jack's tonight."

"I don't belong to anyone," she countered.

"Let's just leave it at that, okay?" he pleaded with her.

Maddy may have been drunk but she did notice the hurt look on his face. What she was doing to these two men was wrong and if she didn't feel so good she would have felt bad about it. But for now, she didn't. She was an awful person.

Jack came back in carrying her glass and handed it to her. She took a sip, held it away from her looking at it. "What's wrong with it? It tastes different."

"Nothing, it's just your taste buds." He smiled to himself. He watered it down.

"How sure are you that he was there Maddy? Do you have any proof?" Bryan asked her.

"I just know. I was so stupid. I fell right into it. He's a smart son of a bitch—smarter than I gave him credit for. I will never underestimate him again. Give me the phone. I want to talk to him." She took a big swallow of whiskey. She turned to Jack, "You did something to this, I can tell."

"Don't be stupid Maddy," Jack snapped.

"About the drink or the unsub?" she asked innocently.

"Maddy, you are never to initiate contact with that man again, you got that?" Bryan told her sternly.

"Why?"

"Listen to yourself, Maddy. You verbally attack him—you will provoke him. We don't need that. You don't need that. If he did indeed follow you here, we need to guard you even closer." Bryan watched her.

She looked at him straight in the eye. "I want to go home. That's what I want. I don't want to be held captive for my own safety. I want my life back. This fucking case has taken away everything from me—my safety, my sanity, my freedom. What the hell do I have left?" Her eyes were glistening.

Jack reached out and rubbed her calf where the blanket had slipped off. "Maddy you have us. Do you really think Bryan or I would ever let anything happen to you? I'm sorry you can't go home, but do you really want him to know where you live? Think about it, your sanctuary being invaded by him, I don't think you really want to risk it do you?"

"This sucks. If I ever see that son of bitch in person, I swear to God I will shoot him like he was a rabid dog," Maddy hissed.

Bryan leaned forward touching her thigh, "Maddy, please, you need to get control of yourself. I understand this is all very hard for you, like it wasn't hard enough before, but you got to keep perspective."

Maddy cocked her head, "Keep perspective? Gee where have I heard that before?"

Bryan sighed, "Maddy, now is not the time to bring up old shit. You're looped, you're pissed, and you're scared. Now you're trying to deflect. Let's deal with the here and now okay?"

"Whatever..." Maddy tuned away from them and laid her head on the arm of the couch.

Bryan looked at Jack and nodded toward the kitchen. Both of them rose and left the room. They sat at the counter. Jack took down a couple of glasses and the bottle. "One shot okay?"

Bryan nodded, "Just one. What are we going to do with her?"

Jack poured them each a glass. "I don't blame her for feeling like she does. She has everything she held dearly taken away from her because of this case... Sometimes I wonder if the two of us with our arrangement are not making things worse."

Bryan took a sip from his glass. "I can't agree with you. I think we are the only things that's keeping her together. She doesn't trust anyone but us. She needs us both Jack."

"What if we took her out of the equation?" Jack asked.

"What do you mean?"

"We smuggle her out of the city. Take her home. We could take shifts staying with her there until this is all over," Jack said as he took a drink.

Bryan laughed, "Like she's really going to go for it. I'm sure she would love to go home, but if we do that to her, she's going to feel like a caged animal. Jack, you don't want to be around her when she feels trapped—even in her own home. I don't think you have ever experienced the wrath of Maddy. I've felt her hate, and she would grow to hate us. Trust me, it's not something you want to be the object of. Besides...we need her."

Jack let out a long sigh, "Then what?"

"Where ever she sleeps, have a squad car posted out front."

"Are we overreacting?"

"I would rather we overreact, then under react. She's not going to stay at the motel with me, besides I don't think it's the safest place for her, but I do want to be able to spend some private time with her. I've done a lot damage I need to repair." Bryan traced his fingers up and down his glass.

Jack shrugged, "I don't know, from what I've observed she looks like she's forgiven you."

"No she hasn't. She doesn't trust me with her love and it's going to take a lot to gain that trust back. You said many times she and I have a bond, yeah we do. It's me knowing her, her past, essentially everything that makes her who she is, that's what makes her feel safe with me. Does this make any sense?" Bryan tried to explain.

"Yeah, I think so. You are the one she gains emotional strength from. When she was talking to me about her kids, I felt like it was you she should have been telling, and earlier this evening the same thing. I don't know how to help her."

Bryan laughed, "It's too bad we couldn't take the best of both of us and combine them then she would have her perfect man."

Jack smiled weakly, "I don't know about that, but I only know I love her. She's the first woman I have ever been able to say it about. I'm not letting her go. But I also know you love her, and I know she loves us both. Is anything she's been ever involved in not been so complicated?"

"Not for the last ten years it hasn't." Bryan stood up. "I'm going to head back and try to get a couple of hours of sleep. Starting tomorrow put a squad car out front. I'm going to tell her goodnight quick.

Maddy was sleeping when Bryan went in to tell her goodnight. He knelt down and stroked her hair as he watched her sleep. Maddy stirred and open her eyes and smiled softly, "Hey Mickey."

Bryan kissed her softly. "Hey Minnie, I am heading out to get some sleep. Jack's here to keep you safe okay?"

"Okay," she stretched her arms out and hugged him. "I love you."

"I love you too," he gave her a kiss. "I will see you later. Sleep in okay?"

"Okay," she mumbled.

He stayed with her until she fell back asleep, which wasn't long. He popped his head back into the kitchen and told Jack goodnight and not to hurry in in the morning.

Jack went into the living room and lifted Maddy up off the couch. She wrapped her arms around his neck and let him carry her upstairs. He gently laid her on the bed. She slid over to make room for Jack and when he lay down she curled up in the crook of his arm. He stroked her hair and kissed her forehead. "Sleep Kitten." Then he waited for sleep to come to him.

When Maddy woke up a few hours later the sun was streaming through the cracks in the wooden blinds. Jack held her tightly in his arms. She could feel him breathing softly on her neck. She thought their first night staying together would be this romantically exciting night. The night held excitement, but in the wrong way. Life has a way of fucking things up.

She lay there quietly so she wouldn't wake Jack. Scenes from last night went through her mind. Was she being paranoid about the unsub? If he were there why couldn't she feel his presences? Well it wasn't like she had ESP, it was just a feeling she got in the middle of the night when she was sleeping. Maybe she had been dreaming and it triggered the thought. She didn't know. In the light of day it seemed pretty illogical.

She recalled having Jack and Bryan sitting with her last night, both of them planning a way to keep her safe. She also remembered fighting them. How weird was that?

Maddy carefully slipped out of bed. She grabbed her bag and went in and took a shower and dressed for the day. She popped her head in to check on Jack. He was still sound to sleep. Her heart filled with warmth as she watched him.

Maddy went to the kitchen to see what she could rustle up for breakfast. He had everything she would need to make some ham and cheese omelets, her breakfast specialty. She took sometime to play with Eddie before she tackled breakfast.

Maddy ate her breakfast and snooped around and found a tray. She put Jack's breakfast on it and carried upstairs. She set the tray on a nightstand. She sat on the edge of the bed, leaned over and kissed Jack on the cheek. "Wake up sleepy head. I brought you breakfast."

Jack turned to face her, pulled her down to him and kissed her deeply. "I thought you were my breakfast."

Maddy laughed, "What is it about you, food and sex?"

"Kitten, I am shocked," he laughed. "Sex has never been an issue with us."

She poked him in the ribs watching him jump. "Come on Babe, its almost 11:00. We need to get to work."

Jack slid up into a sitting position and Maddy handed him the tray. "Wow, you're going to spoil me," he said as he took a bite of toast.

Maddy sat at the foot of the bed with her legs crossed. "If you guys are going to be holding me hostage I'm going to need clothes. And what about my animals?"

"I talked to Jessie last night. She went in and did chores for you. We don't know how long this is going to be going on. Could she bring your horses out to her place so it she wouldn't have to run over there all the time?"

"I would rather keep them home, that way she can check on the place," Maddy said.

"How about Rufus and Jack? Do you want to bring them up here?" Jack asked as he took a bite of his omelet.

Maddy laughed, "Hell no, we need to give Eddie a chance to get acclimated before we spring those two on him." She squeezed his foot through the blanket. "But it was sweet of you to ask, thank you." She grabbed his orange juice and took a drink. "So you talked to Jessie. What did she say about you calling her?"

Jack chuckled, "She said she was looking forward to getting to know me." Jack looked up at her, "Does she know about our...strange situation between the three of us?"

"Not the latest development, but I would rather she didn't. She was having a bad enough cow over Bryan. I don't think no matter what that man does, she's ever going to like him. Anyhow, I will give her call and make arrangements and beg her once again to bring me clothes and my laptop. I will have her drop them off at the cop shop."

Jack finished up his breakfast. "We're going to leave your car in the garage. I don't want our unsub knowing what your car looks like.

Maddy flopped back on the bed, "I am hating this already."

Maddy was downstairs playing with Eddie when Jack came down looking all nice and coppy. "Hey Mr. Policeman, why don't you frisk me?" she grinned at him.

"Hey you had your chance earlier when I wanted you for breakfast," he grinned back at her. "You ready to go?"

Maddy grabbed her bag. She grabbed her badge, gun and holster out of her car and hopped in Jack's car. "Hi ho, hi ho, its off to the cop shop we go," Maddy sang.

Jack looked over at her, "You are just plain weird."

Maddy was sitting at her desk reading the report on Mallard. There wasn't much to read since she was there when it all took place. They had shipped the body off to Ankeny; they wouldn't have any results back for few days.

The squad room was a buzz with the events that taken place overnight. The locals were bitching because they weren't called in. Bryan explained to them they didn't need everyone on site since access was limited.

Maddy felt like she was under a microscope. Everyone was watching her, wondering and waiting. She wasn't allowed to leave just in case the unsub called. She was restless and bored. She was also having trouble concentrating. Bryan and Jack were both gone. They had gone out to the scene to see if they could find any trace the unsub had actually been there. Good luck with that, Maddy thought.

Maddy was spacing off when a diet coke was set down in front of her. She looked up to find Andy standing in front of her. "Thanks," she smiled up at him.

He leaned up against her desk, "You look like you could use some mental stimulation."

Maddy laughed, "Gee you think? So what did you think of last night?"

"It was cool," he grinned. "I stayed on there until Mayland made us leave. Said there wasn't anything more we could do. So you actually talk to the guy huh?"

"Yeah I guess you could say that." She popped the top on the can and took a drink.

"What was it like?" Andy asked.

"Creepy, really creepy. The man gave no indication of remorse. He actually thought he was justified in killing those women. Now they got me under 24-hour watch because they are worried he will come after me. It really sucks," Maddy complained.

"You live a pretty exciting life."

Maddy looked at him oddly, "What a fucked up thing to say. You think I enjoy all this? Life as I knew it doesn't exist anymore. I would give anything to go back to living the mundane life working at the paper."

Andy looked down at his feet, "I'm sorry, I didn't mean to upset you."

She felt bad for going off on him, "Hey kid, don't worry about it. I'm just in a bitchy mood. It doesn't take much to set me off right now."

"Well better get back to work doing my grunt stuff," he smiled. "Let me know if you need anything."

"Thanks Andy."

Maddy couldn't take it anymore. She needed to get out of the office. She decided to go sit out back on the steps where she and Jack usually went. She didn't think of telling anyone where she was going.

When Bryan and Jack returned Maddy was nowhere to be found. "Where the hell is Maddy?" Bryan asked the squad.

Andy looked up, "She was her ten minutes ago. I thought she just stepped out to go to the bathroom or something."

"Jesus fucking Christ, Whittmer, when we're not here, you are to look after her," Bryan barked at Andy.

"Yes Sir. I didn't know."

"Well you know now." Bryan turned to Jack. He was in a total panic. "Where the hell would she go?"

"I think I know, come on."

Jack led Bryan down to the back of the station. Maddy was sitting on the steps staring off into space. Jack put his hand on Bryan's arm. "Don't jump on her ass. She really doesn't need it."

Bryan looked at him. "She has got to understand she can't be just taking off. I can't stress that enough."

"I know you're worried about her safety, I am too. But don't you think if we keep pushing her, she's going to take off on us? If she wanted to leave, there is nothing we can do to stop her. Don't drive her away," he pleaded with Bryan.

"Okay fine. You handle it, I'll keep my mouth shut." Bryan wasn't happy about it, but what Jack said was true. He knew if he were to speak out about her taking off he would go off on her."

"Hey Mads," Jack sat down beside. Bryan sat on her other side.

Maddy looked from one to the other. "I know and I'm sorry but I had to get out of there, so please don't gang upon me." She put her head down on her knees.

Maddy stood up. "I want you guys to know, I can't be hiding from this guy. I am a trained FBI agent, I'm rusty granted, but I am not like our vics. If you guys want to take turns playing body guard that's fine with me, but I'm not hanging around the station sitting around waiting for him to call. I can't do it."

As the three of returned to the squad room, she turned to them. "Let's make a list of things we want to extract form my conversations with the unsub. You guys give me an outline and I'll make it happed."

They never got the opportunity. As they walked through the squad room door the designated cell phone went off in Bryan's pocket. The three of them exchanged looks and Maddy held out her hand.

"Are you sure?" Bryan asked her.

"Just give me the damn phone and let me do my job." Maddy wiggled her outstretched hand. Bryan handed it to her.

Maddy flipped it open. "Sheridan."

"Good afternoon Ms. Sheridan. Did you get my present?" the voice on the other end said.

"You know I did. You were there to make sure of it," she replied calmly.

"How astute of you, Ms. Sheridan. How did you know? Or did you? If you had, I would think you would have had one of your police watchdogs looking for me." The man's voice was calm, cool, like nothing would faze him.

"Police watchdogs?" Let's see how much he really did know.

"You have some pretty high ranking law enforcement as your bodyguards. A FBI agent and the chief of detectives, I'm impressed. 24-7 protection? You must be pretty special or think I will harm you." There was almost a taunting tone in his voice.

The squad room was standing back, listening to the conversation. Bryan sat at his desk turned toward her and Jack was sitting at the corner of her desk. Derek had initiated the triangulation of the usub's cell phone.

Maddy aimed her focus totally on the phone call blocking out all others in the room. She needed to have total concentration. She couldn't let him get the upper hand. "Let's just say I have friends in high places."

"It's not necessary. I'm not going to harm you."

"I know that. I'm not your type."

The man laughed. It was a pleasant, almost melodic laugh—one that would quickly put a person at ease. "And what is my type?"

"Like your victims."

"I don't have victims. These women are members of my flock."

"Why did you kill them?"

A long sigh came from the other end. "I thought I explained this to you, I didn't kill any of my flock. They were chosen ones. They gave themselves unto the Lord."

"Voluntarily, or because they wised up and pissed you off?" she asked.

There was a hushed quiet on the phone. Then he spoke, not answering her question. "There was no story in the paper about the discovery of your gift."

"Was too late. Deadline is no later than 10:00 PM. What should I call you, your name?"

"I am the Higher Power," he said as if she should be in awe.

Maddy laughed, "Not in my book, give me something else."

"What, Ms. Sheridan, you are not a believer?" he inquired.

"I have danced with the devil on several occasion. Might even say I've slept with him," she said thinking of Bryan. "I told you I'm not your type. If you are, as you say you are, I have nothing to fear from you. You said you slaughter only the chosen sheep of your flock. I can't be saved, so I should have nothing to fear from you. Is that correct?"

"You have nothing to fear from me. Do you believe me?" he asked expectantly.

"Should I?"

The man laughed, "You are not worthy of my time."

Maddy picked up a pen and chewed on the end of it. "So tell me HP, just what is it you want from me? If I am not worthy of your time, why talk to me?

"I want to know what you know," he put it out there.

Maddy smiled, "like you really think it's going to be that easy. Why don't you tell me, and I'll confirm if I know it?"

The man chuckled, "I know you're not stupid enough to think that's how it works."

Maddy leaned back in her chair, still chewing on the end of the pen. "Humor me then. You tell me how it works."

"Just tell me what you know about me."

Maddy laughed out loud, "You're not a poker player are you?"

"Excuse me?"

"Do you really think I am stupid enough to show you my cards?"

"Show me your cards...how charming. Do you think we are playing a game Maddy?" he asked.

Maddy felt a chill run over when he spoke her name. "Only my friends call me by my first name, and you are definitely not my friend."

"Pity, I think we could be great friends, Ms. Sheridan, if that's what you wished to be called so be it." He sounded a little irritated.

"And what makes you think we could be friends?"

"You said you danced with the devil, even slept with him. You think I am evil, so I shouldn't bother you, should I? Come play with me, Maddy."

Jack saw her stiffen and put his hand over hers. Maddy glanced up at him, a worried look on her face. "There is nothing gamey about this situation. I am not your friend, I am nobody to you and I'm sure as hell not going to *play* with you. Just tell me what the fuck you want from me and get this over with."

The man gave a low haunting laugh, "Aaah finally, I got a rise out of you. I knew somewhere in there you would have fire, an intense fire, an all-consuming fire. You can see it in your eyes. Yes, Maddy, you are so much different than my flock. As you said, they are sheep, my followers. I can't see you following anybody."

"You said you could see it in my eyes," she was trying carefully to keep the panic out her voice. "Have we met? How did you get close enough to see my eyes?"

"I am the Higher Power, I see all," he answered amused. He knew he was getting under her skin.

"Oh bullshit. You know as well as I do, I don't believe that crap. In my book, you are just a man, a simple, egotistical, evil man," she said coldly.

He laughed again, but his voice had an edge to it, "Careful, careful, Maddy, you wouldn't want to upset me. You want to know how I know what's in your eyes...I saw you, you saw me...face to face, last night." The phone went dead.

Maddy gasped and dropped the phone, recoiling from it as if were a snake about to strike. Jack reached for her and she held up her hand, "No! Leave me be." She swallowed hard.

She hollered over to Derek, "Did you get anything?"

Derek shook his head. "He's driving around as he's talking to you. The only thing we have is he was in the upper east end of the city. You okay kid?"

She glared at him, "This *kid* is just fine."

She threw her pen across the room. "Damn it, I got nothing," Maddy said out of frustration.

Maddy leaned in on her desk, "I told you he was there. I just didn't know how close." A chill ran over her. "He was close enough to me to look in my eyes." She turned to Jack and Bryan, "Christ one or the other of you guys were right beside be all night....and he knows...he knows who you are." She was looking straight at Bryan and Jack. "He knows exactly who you are!"

"You might not have learned much about him, but he sure made it a point of telling you how close he was able to get to you without you knowing it," Jack said quietly.

Bryan slammed his fist down on his desk, turned and stormed out the door. All eyes followed him. "What the hell?" Maddy asked.

She left to follow him. She found him out on the front steps smoking a cigarette. She placed her hand on his shoulder as she sat down next to him. "What's up Mickey?"

He turned to her, "Why aren't you more upset?"

"About?"

"Jesus Christ Maddy, he was close enough to touch you last night. Despite his claims that he wouldn't harm you, the son of a bitch is stalking you. And it's not just that he got near you last night, he knows who you're with. It would be one thing if he had referred to Jack and me as a couple of cops, but he knows I'm FBI and that Jack is the Chief of Detectives. He's toying with you." Bryan was incredulous.

Maddy sat quietly. She didn't know what to say to him. Yes, she could and maybe should be freaking out the unsub had be literally right in front of her, but what would it achieve? It's not like he could take her in front of all those people, cops nonetheless. "Let's use a little logic here. If he were truly coming after me, why would he make it a point of letting me know he was there and basically that he is watching?"

"Maybe our unsub is also a hunter." Maddy turned to see Jack behind them. He took a seat beside her and lit up.

"What do you mean?"

"He means, " Bryan flicked his cigarette, "it's more entertaining if the prey knows it's being stalked. There's not much sport hunting a sitting duck."

Jack added, "He needs to instill fear into you."

Maddy shrugged, "Well he's not getting it. I'm not afraid of him."

"You should be." Bryan was looking off into the distance.

Maddy pulled her feet up underneath her. "What I want to know is why he contacted me in the first place. He says he wants to set the story straight yet he's given me nothing."

"Maddy come here and sit in front of me," Bryan requested. She moved to the step in front of him. He spread his legs and guided her body back so she was leaning against him. He guided her head back so her body was against his chest. "I want you to close your eyes."

Jack raised an eyebrow, "What the hell are you doing? And right if front me, damn Byran, I thought you had a little more respect for me."

Bryan laughed, "Shut up, Parker." He covered Maddy's ears. "It's called a cognitive interview. It's procedure designed for use in police interviews that involve witnesses and victims. Its goal is to help a victim or witness put herself mentally at the crime scene to gather more information about the crime. It helps trigger memories. First I have to reconstruct the circumstances of the crime or incident. Then I will have the Maddy report all information that she can. Next I will ask the Maddy to recall all the events in a different order. Lastly I will try to get Maddy to change perspectives and report what happened as if from another person's point of view. That's what I would normally do, but in this case...depends on how cooperative our witness is."

Maddy batted his hands away. "Christ Bryan, it's not like I don't know what the hell you're doing. I've used this technique plenty of times. Get Andy down here so he can watch."

"Screw Andy, let's get this done," Bryan told her into her hair.

She looked up at him, "You're such an ass."

"Are you going to do this or what?" He looked down at her.

"I'll try, but I can't make any promises."

Jack laughed, "Maddy, do what you're told."

Maddy started to rise and Bryan pushed her back down. "Sit. Stay.Woof!"

"Smart ass. Now lay back and close your eyes."

Maddy rested against him and closed her eyes. She could smell the light scent of his cologne, feel the heat of his body, and how rigid his muscles were. Man he was really wound up.

Jack watched as Bryan wrapped his arms around her and buried his face in her hair. He was quite sure this wasn't standard procedure. He listened as he told Maddy to breathe deep and let go. Now he was sure this wasn't normal, but Bryan had away about him to get Maddy to let go, he had witnessed time and time again. He was sure it was a trust thing with Maddy.

Bryan felt Maddy's body relax against him. "I want you to clear your mind, kiddo. Quit thinking about our unsub. I want you to go back to last night. Tell me what happened from the time you and Jack pulled down to the site."

"You guys pulled up behind us. We got out of the car. You and Jack were talking. Derek was barking orders to the others. The CSU truck is pulling in followed by the K-9 unit. The K-9 guys are taking the dog out into the woods. The CSU guys are unloading their gear. They're walking passed us. They are walking so close to us we have to keep moving out of their way..."

Maddy sat upright, her jaw dropped her face went pale, "...it was him."

Bryan rested his hands on her shoulders, rubbing them, "tell us about it, put yourself back there, Maddy."

"There was this guy, a CSU guy, he ran into me, dropped his gear. I bent down to help him pick it. We both grabbed it at the same time and rose together. He apologized and then thanked me. He stood there for a few seconds, smiling, looking at me. I remembered feeling kind of awkward and looked away. He apologized again and then went on his way."

"Describe him Maddy."

"Man, I don't know, there was so much going on that night, so much to see."

Bryan pulled her back to him, "Close your eyes, get back to your place. Now tell me Maddy, what did he look like, sound like, smell like, tell me everything your senses picked up on."

Maddy laid her head back and closed her eyes. She sorted images of last night though her mind like she was thumbing through pages of a book until she got to the page she left off on. "He was wearing dark clothing, a jacket and a black ball cap....em...I couldn't see his hair, but he had dark sideburns, em...bushy eyebrows, his teeth, his smile, nice smile, kind of a pointy nose, dark, dark eyes, piercing eyes..."

Bryan continued to rub her shoulders, "use your other senses baby, feel him..."

"His voice...God it was his voice," she started to breathe faster, "his voice... the same voice...He touched my hand before he left, when he said thanks..." Maddy eyes shot open "....and he smelled like Polo."

Maddy moved away from Bryan. She was nervously pacing a few steps down from them, chewing on her nails. "That son of a bitch..."

Jack glanced over at Bryan who seemed to be content studying Maddy's body language but was remaining silent.

"Do you remember seeing this guy at any other time last night?" Jack asked her.

"Hell I don't know...maybe, down at the scene. He was kind of in the background...like the rest of us."

"Do you remember if he looked at you at all during that time?"

"No! I don't know! I need to go throw some water on my face." Maddy left them on the steps.

Jack pulled out another cigarette and lit it. Bryan followed suit. He took a long drag off of it. "He's not following her. He got everything he needed to know from being on the scene last night." Jack said as he blew out the smoke. "He approached her under the guise of someone who was working the scene. He got to talk to her, look into her eyes...touch her. He saw her there with us. All he had to do was ask anyone there who we were. Chances are he doesn't even know your name. He could find out mine easy enough. He just referred to you as FBI. He was checking to see if she would recognize him and to size her up."

Bryan took a drag off his smoke, "Good analysis. So what does he want from her?"

"Initially to dignify and justify what he was doing. Then after he talked to her on the phone and she stood up to him...he wants to fuck with her head, keep her preoccupied to throw her off his scent. She could be a danger to him, and now he knows it." Jack snuffed out his cigarette and stood up.

Bryan rose from the steps. "So she is still in danger. She is going to have modify her behavior when she talks to him. When he talks to her, he feels her out by saying things, picks up on what pushes her buttons and works it, subtly.

He's one cunning son of a bitch. Lets go back and listen to those tapes. See if this matches our theory."

When they returned upstairs they saw Maddy sitting in Jack's office. Jack glanced over at Bryan and nodded. He went into his office and closed the door and the blinds. He took her by the hand, pulled her to her feet and enclosed his arms around. He reached for her face and kissed her lips tenderly. Her arms circled his neck and she returned his kiss.

"Take me to your house and make love to me," she whispered.

"Mmmmm...Kitten I would love to, but we have work to do. Can you wait for just a little while?" He kissed her again hungrily, exploring, running his hands down her back to her hips pulling her body into his.

Maddy felt her body melting into his. No she didn't want to wait. She wanted him to take her home. She wanted him to touch her so completely it would wipe a way the knowledge the unsub had ever touched her. She needed his touch to reclaim her for his own. "No Baby, I want you to make me yours, surround me with your love."

Then he understood her need. They hadn't made love since late yesterday afternoon. The unsub had touched her since then. She wanted a loving touch to wipe it away the evil. He pulled her close and kissed her on the forehead. "Let me go talk to Bryan, see if he'll let us slip away for a while if we come back. We probably won't be able to linger long. He's not going to be happy, he was assuming today was his turn."

Maddy played with the hair on the back of his neck. "I never said anything about taking turns and letting the two of you decide whose night it is. I decide who I feel the need to be with, and Baby, I need you. I love you. I want to be with you." Maddy kissed him on the cheek.

"Okay, wait here," Jack dashed off to talk to Bryan.

Bryan and Derek were playing around with the recorder box when Jack came in. Bryan looked up a Jack, "Where's Maddy?"

"In my office." How was he going to explain to Bryan that Maddy wanted leave with him for a while? He knew Bryan was wanting to spend some 'quality' time with Maddy today, but hell, what was he suppose to do when Maddy wanted to be with him. It wasn't like Jack was going to tell her no. "She wants to get out of here for a little while. Would you mind if I took her out for an hour or so?"

Bryan studied him. "We are kind of in the middle of something at the moment. It's not a good time for her to be taking off right now. I need her here." If she had asked him, now that was a different story.

"So I take it that's a no," Jack held steady.

"You take that correct. Not now. You want to get her, please?" Bryan turned his attention back to the Derek and the recorder.

Jack returned to his office. "Sorry, Kitten, he said no."

"What do you mean he said no?" Maddy asked surprised. Bryan had never refused her getting out of here for a while. Was he being a dick because it wasn't him that she wanted to leave with?

Jack slid his arms around her waist. "He said we have work to do and we needed to be here." He kissed her softly. "But I bet if you asked him to go, he would let you." Jack wanted to see if it really made a difference who she left with, as long as she could get rid of the feeling of the unsub touching her.

Maddy rested her head on his shoulder. "Asshole. I guess we'll have to wait. He can't keep us here forever."

"Then you don't want to be with him?" Jack asked.

Maddy took her hand and turned his face to her. "Did you see me ask him? No—you are the one I want to be with."

He caressed her cheek, "You know you are going to piss him off don't you?"

Maddy turned away from him and shook her head, "Christ Jack, would you rather I went with him?"

Jack reached out to catch her and turned her back to face him. "What the hell do you think, Maddy? It wouldn't break my heart if you never went back to him. It tears me up inside just thinking about you being with him again. But it's not my choice, Babe, it's yours. And I have to be cool with whatever you decide to do."

Maddy's eyes traveled over his face. He loved her enough to give her the opportunity make up her own mind about who she wanted to be with and when. She held his gaze. "Jack, I came to you. I asked you. What does that tell you?"

She watched him as he searched her eyes. A slow smiled crossed his lips. "That it's me you want to be with."

"Exactly. So let's go in there and do our job so we can't get the hell out of here and go home. Just stay cool when we go in there, like it's no big deal." She gave him a quick kiss and turned to leave.

When Maddy and Jack returned to the squad Bryan and Derek were playing back the tape of the first conversation she had had with the unsub. She froze in her tracks. "You assholes, you could have given me some kind of warning." She turned to Jack with a questioning look on her face. All he did was shrug his shoulders. Then she turned back Bryan. "Why are you doing this?"

"We believe the unsub is picking up on cues you are unconsciously giving him and using them against you," Bryan explained.

"What would be the point?"

"To keep you riled up enough you won't dig any deeper. His initial goal was for you to acknowledge him and to make it known he doesn't consider himself a serial killer. After he discovered you weren't a willing participant and you were smart enough to figure him out, he decided to prey on you mentally. He let you think you were in control when all along he's been playing you," Bryan explained as he listened to the conversation, stopping it and playing it back.

"That's bullshit," she sat at her desk. "We spared, he wasn't playing me."

"Yeah, Maddy he was," he fast -forwarded to today's conversation. "See how he takes the little cutting remarks you make and twists them to get to you. He asks you about his gift. You tell him you knew he was there. He confirms he was there, but wants you to know he knows where you were and who you were with. You try to steer him towards his vics, he twists it around to make it about you. He tells you first you are in no danger from him because he only has his sights on his flock. You tell him more or less you are a sinner, then he tells you since you believe he is evil, then it shouldn't really matter. You brought up the poker; he calls your bluff and wants to play. He knows calling you by name unnerves you, yet he continues to call you by it. He wants you to know he has control by telling you he was close enough to you he could look into your eyes knowing it would really shake you. You loose it on him; he leaves you with a veiled threat. He played you Maddy. He put you right where he wants you, and you let him."

Maddy looked at him with contempt. "I let him? Fuck you Bryan. I didn't let him do anything. You can do so much better, then you fucking talk to him!"

Bryan stopped the recorder, "Oh for Christ's sake Maddy, you want me to play it back for you again? He took every little comment you said that was a put-down on him and twisted it to make it about you. You gave him all the ammo he needed. He left you scared shitless by letting you know he was close enough to look in your eyes. And now we know he wasn't only close enough to look in your eyes, but he talked to you, he touched you."

"Enough Bryan," Jack snapped at him. "None of this is her fault. I thought we agreed he set up that deal last night to see if she could recognize him. He should be satisfied she didn't."

As if on cue the designated cell phone went off. Maddy crossed her arms and stared at it defiantly and let it go.

"Pick it up Maddy," Bryan commanded her.

She continued to stare at it.

He closed the distance between them and shoved the phone in her face. "Answer the God damned phone Maddy!" he said coldly.

Maddy turned her face away from him as the phone continued to ring. Bryan grabbed her hair, put the phone to her face and opened it.

Jack moved forward to protect Maddy. Derek grabbed him to stop him.

Maddy turned to Bryan, her eyes glistening.

"Hello...Hello...Maddy?" called out the voice on the phone.

Maddy took the phone from Bryan with shaking hands, not from fear, but from anger. "What?"

"What? No greeting?" the unsub said lightly.

"What do you want?"

"Why Maddy, you sound as if you're irritated. I just thought it would be nice to chat with you again."

"I thought we had established we are not friends. If you want something from me, it would be nice if you would tell me what that was, otherwise you are wasting my time." She kept her voice calm and cool.

"Edgy aren't we? You don't want to play?"

Maddy held herself in check. She would not let him pull her in. "I'm working here, unless you have something relevant to say to me, this conversation is done."

Bryan nudged her. Maddy flipped him off. There were several moments of silence on the other end of the line.

Finally the unsub spoke again, "What do you want to know?"

"You tell me. You're the one with all the power, isn't that how you want to play it?"

"I expect to see a story about your gift in tomorrow's paper." The line went dead.

Bryan grabbed Maddy by the wrist disregarding her flinching and pulled her out of the office and into the interrogation room and slammed the door. "What the fuck do you think you are doing?"

Maddy focused on a bent blind in the window. "I was just following orders," she replied flatly.

"Would you quit acting like a stubborn bitch, Maddy? I wasn't criticizing; I just gave you an analysis of what he was doing to you. You're handling of that last call...what the fuck was that? You're suppose to be pumping, not cutting him short and telling him to get lost."

"It's good to see you back, Bryan, the real you. Must feel good to let him back out of his cage." She kept her voice calm and steady.

Bryan was towering over her. Amazing how fast someone can revert to their old selves. This was the same Bryan who arrived in town almost two weeks ago. This was the Bryan she knew, the one she knew was still there just below the surface.

Maddy took a deep breath, "You know you really need to make up you're mind as to what you want me to do. You either let me handle it my way, or I play it your way, which is what I just did. You're the boss, you make the call."

Bryan sat down across from her. "Is that how you see it?"

"There's nothing to see, it is what it is. I knew it was only a matter of time. You can't keep pretending to be something you're not."

"All that time we spent together, everything we've been through these past couple of weeks, and this is still how you see me?" he asked sadly.

Maddy looked at him, her eyes emotionless. "I wanted to believe, I begged to be true, but look at you, Bryan. You're the same bulling prick you always were. What's you're excuse this time? You don't have alcohol to blame."

Bryan sat quietly across from her. He was afraid to say anything to her. What happened to put them so far back that things had digressed to this point. "I'm sorry, Maddy."

"Not as sorry as I am. You know something, Bryan, it doesn't really matter anymore. I spent all these years running from pain, going out of my way at all cost to keep from hurting. I'm done hurting. I'm done running. I don't give a fuck anymore. I can't be hurt anymore—you have to be able to feel to get hurt."

Bryan looked into her eyes. He couldn't see her anymore. Was the transformation complete? Had he just pushed her into her new protective persona?

Jack stood just outside the interrogation room. Derek had his hand on his shoulder. "You need to leave them alone and let them work it out in there own way."

Jack turned to Derek, "The fuck I am. The way he pushed her around and bullied her, that was totally uncalled for."

"Don't let the obvious fool you. She got exactly the response from him she was asking for. You always look at things of how he affects Maddy. Have you ever looked at it from the other side of the mirror? How she affects him? She knows how to push his buttons to get certain reactions out of him. She went into that room with a chip on her shoulder because she didn't get her way. She defies him, pushes him, and taunts him. She's not stupid and she sure as hell is not the victim."

He brought Jack to the mirror side of the room. "Look, you look at her, cold, calm, self assured. Look at him. He looks to me like he is ready to break. She has the power to crush him. You saw the way those two were this weekend. They were clinging to each other for dear life. He helped her escape from her past. But she hasn't escaped it; she just found a new way not to deal with it. What better way to remove the past than to destroy it? Let's see how complete her transformation has become."

Jack watched the couple in silence. This was part of Maddy he had never seen before. Now thinking back on it, what Derek said, it explained a lot of the change in Maddy's behavior towards Bryan, the lashing out at him. She had been the cruel one. Did this same behavior have anything to do with Maddy allowing herself to love him? As he watched, he prayed Maddy would back down. If she didn't how would he ever know if her feelings for him were even true.

Maddy sat quietly with Bryan. He sat there looking at her, looking for something within her. She saw the awful pain she was inflicting on him. At first she felt no remorse. After all isn't this what he had done to her? Was this really what she wanted? To exact revenge on him, to break him as he had broken her? What was it Jack said, not being able to separate the past from Bryan? Was she blaming him for bringing out the pain she had been experiencing since the break? He hadn't caused it; he had saved her from it.

Maddy got up from her chair. Bryan remained seated, staring off into space, not blinking. Maddy caught the faintest hint he was shaking. She walked around to his side of the table and stood behind him. She stood for a moment and then pulled a chair up beside him. She reached out to him with a shaky hand and took his. "I'm sorry. I have no right to go off you on like this."

Bryan turned to her and wrapped his arms around her holding her tight. "No, I'm sorry. You're right...about everything."

Jack and Derek watched. Jack gave a deep sigh of relief. She didn't do it. She came back. Derek tapped Jack on the shoulder. "Come on, let's give them some privacy." They returned to the squad room.

Maddy felt the hot tears slide down her cheeks as she felt Bryan's body shake around her. God what had she done. She was no better than him—maybe even worse. "I'm so sorry," she whispered into his hair. "I can't even say that I didn't mean to hurt you, because I did. I wanted to hurt you. I don't know what the fuck is wrong with me anymore, baby."

Bryan sat up. "Maddy...you need help. Sweetheart, you are trying to do this on your own and it's not working." He kissed her softly on the cheek. "I can't help you, you won't let me. Jack can't help you, he doesn't know how. We can do our best, but honey, it's not enough." He held her head in his hands. "Baby, I don't want to loose you, and that's what's happening. I can help you fight your demons, but I can't fight you. You won't let me near you anymore, and it's not because of what happened a couple of nights ago, it's been since Sunday night." He put his forehead against hers, "I'm not your enemy, baby, I'm not."

Maddy collapsed into his arms. "What do you want me to do? This fucking case has got my head so filled with crap, I can't think straight. I can't deal with the past and maintain control with this at the same time. I shouldn't have come back yet, but it's too late. I can't back out now. I'm trapped."

Bryan held her close, "Yes, baby you are and I don't know how to help you. I can't pull you off the case as long as you are our only point of contact. Who the hell knew things were going to get this fucked up. Christ this is small town Iowa."

Maddy laughed softly, "Just goes to show you, fucked up people know no boundaries."

Bryan smiled weakly, "It's all your fault, trouble follows you wherever you go."

Maddy jabbed him, "Quit being a pig."

Maddy looked up at him, her eyes sparkling, "I know I have been a total bitch, my behavior irrational, and I have no excuse. But please know this, I do love you; don't ever doubt that. I just don't know how to deal with all these mixed up emotions that are getting in the way. You're right, I need help, but how am I going to do that and do this job at the same time? I don't think I can wait."

"As soon as we get back to the squad room, I want you to call your doctor and make some arrangements. If you need me to go with you, or if you need Jack, you do what you need to do."

"How can you be okay with me and Jack? I don't understand."

Bryan hugged her tight. "I'm not okay with it. It's tearing me up from the inside out. He has a part of you I can't touch anymore. And it hurts, Maddy, it hurts like hell. You won't let me be there anymore, but as long as he is there, I know you are safe."

He released her. "Let's go back, you make your phone calls and then I'm going to have Jack take to you back to his house. Take the phone with you, if he calls, I want you to apologize to him and then explain to him that you have some family problems you need to deal with and you need to be gone for a few days. See how he takes it. Maybe it's the wrong thing to do, but we need to get you fixed. You can't be much help to the case in the condition you're in. You're too volatile. I'm not saying this to be mean, you know that don't you."

Maddy nodded, "I know, you're right. I need to file that story though for tomorrow's paper."

"I'm sure Jack has a computer you can write and file it from there. Would you send it to me before you do though?"

"Yeah, no problem. Are you saying you want me to stay away?" she asked as they began walking back to the squad room.

"Yes, I think you need to. I'm going to have Jack stay with you, he can do some of his work from home."

Maddy stopped. Bryan turned to her, "What's the matter?"

"Will you come and spend time with me? Maybe go for a drive or something?"

Bryan pulled her close and kissed her tenderly. After they separated Bryan said, "Try keeping me away, kiddo. And if you should need me all you have to do is whistle. You know how to whistle don't you?" he winked.

Maddy laughed half-heartedly. "Pucker up and blow. You're a sap."

19

Jack looked over at Maddy as he pulled out of the parking lot. She hadn't spoken a word to him since Bryan asked him to take her home with him. She was very subdued when she and Bryan returned to the squad room, but they were not at odds with each other anymore. Maddy had made a few phone calls and then they left.

"You want to talk about it?" he asked her.

Maddy reached for his hand, "A little later okay, Babe?"

Jack smiled weakly, "Sure Kitten." It least she wasn't shutting him out.

Maddy watched all the people and traffic go by as Jack drove through the heart of the city. She would talk to Jack, just not now. She just needed a little time to examine her behavior as of late. Bryan said she was volatile. She would have called her behavior erratic with severe mood swings, out of control and yes, volatile. She was going fucking nuts. She had an early morning appointment with her psychiatrist and had asked Bryan to take her. She wanted him to come in with her to help explain what had been happening to her that was influencing her mental state and to better to explain her behavioral patterns as she was not an objective observer.

It wasn't as if she were excluding Jack, he just didn't know or understand her state of mind and she didn't want him thinking it had anything to do with her feelings for him. What she felt for Jack was up and beyond any of this bullshit. It was still the one thing she felt to be pure at heart, untainted by the rest of this nightmare. Maddy asked him to stop at the pharmacy so she could pick up some prescriptions her doctor had called in.

Maddy waited until Jack opened the door to his house and slipped in around him. She went to the sink and began to down the pills.

"Care if I ask what those are for?"

"Mood stabilizers and anti-anxiety pills. I guess now is as good as time tell you as any. Pull up a stool sweetie." Maddy patted the stool next to her. Jack took a seat beside her.

She turned to face him, "First of all none of this has anything to do with us and how I feel about you, okay?"

"Sure sweetheart."

"I am sure you noticed how quickly my moods change. One minute I'm quiet and reserved, next I'm obsessively frighten, I can be aggressive, outspoken, easily angered and out of control. I never know how I am going to be from one minute to the next...and I can be damn right mean."

Jack smiled, "I just thought that was you."

Maddy laughed, "Yeah that is me, but not to the extremes I have been. Poor Bryan takes the worst of it. One minute I love him dearly, the next minute I hate the ground he walks on. My moods with him change more dramatically than anyone and I can't keep doing this to him anymore. It's not right; he and I have been through hell together and apart. All he wants to do is be there for me. I lead him in and then I shit on him, try to crush him. I said things to him today were...well that were just wrong. We decided I'm not facing the real issues in my life. I need help and I need to take the time to get it or I am to going loose him forever and jeopardize everything around me. That includes this case and my future. I start treatment tomorrow morning. Bryan is going to take me to my first visit to help me explain my issues to the psych doctor."

Jack understood what she was saying and agreed her getting help couldn't hurt. "So you're taking time off?"

Maddy nodded. "For a few days, until I can get things under control. And guess who gets to be my bodyguard?"

Jack reached for her and pulled her toward him. "It will be my honor. But what about the case, Kitten? We can't just put it on hold."

"The next time he calls Bryan wants me to tell him I have a family emergency I need to take care of and need to be gone for a few days hoping to stall him. I don't know, just because he's talking to me doesn't mean it's not business as usual for him. He might be gearing up for his next kill. I have to write up a quick story for our unsub and then can we just forget about all this and just enjoy each other? I really need that." She kissed him softly.

Jack brushed her cheek lightly. "Would love to." He took her into his den and showed her where his computer was. "I will leave you to your writing muse." He left her alone.

Maddy observed her surroundings. She had little knowledge of his house. She knew it was rather large, especially for a single man, and it was beautiful. The den, like the rest of house was heavily adorned with dark wood trim. The walls were soft beige with several Terry Redlin prints accenting the walls. This room, too, had a fireplace but on a smaller scale as the living room. The center focal point of the room was a large mahogany desk with a big oversized desk chair behind it. Ferns were placed sporadically around the room on accent furniture which matched the design of the desk. An iMac computer was on one corner of the desk. Good, he had good taste in computers. She was partial to Mac computers, but then again coming from the newspaper world, it was only natural.

The room had a wide, tall bay window that opened up into his backyard. Huge maple trees lined the edges of a very large yard, with a couple of ash trees in the perimeter. Brick pavers circled each of the interior trees with hostus within the pavers next to the tree trunks. An eight-foot brick fence separated his yard from his neighbors.

Maddy booted up his computer and composed her story:

Final Body Recovered At Local Park

Thanks to an anonymous tip the body of the last missing woman was recovered late Wednesday evening in a rural park near Riverside. An anonymous call to officials was received late Wednesday evening revealing the location of a body of a young woman who has been missing since the middle of June. Although a positive identification has not been made yet, the source stated the body is that of Rebecca Mallard, 34, Wayne, NE, who went missing June 10.

It is believed the unknown source is the perpetrator responsible for the deaths of six-area woman and one man. The caller made contact with a reporter at the Journal after a story ran in Wednesday's paper about the murders. The murders are believed to be a part of a religious sacrifice ritual although this has not been confirmed.

The Sioux City Police Department is investigating these crimes in a joint task force with the Federal Bureau of Investigation and the Department of Criminal Investigation. There has been no official release made by members leading the investigation.

She called Chief and apprised him of the recent events concerning the unsub and the need to run this story. She would email it to him but to wait until she got the confirmation from Bryan.

Maddy called Bryan to let him know the story was coming, to look it over and let her know as soon as possible so the story could be filed.

"Get this off your mind sweetheart and I will see you in the morning," Bryan told her.

"I will do my best. TV is starting to sound good. See you tomorrow. Love you Mickey."

"I love you, Maddy, bye." He hung up.

Maddy heard the sound of Jack's doorbell echoing throughout the house. There was no missing it even from this far back in the house. Maddy made her way to the front of the house deciding to hang back to see who was at the door. When she peered out into the living room she saw the guest was Stella and she had her arms wrapped around Jack kissing him deeply.

Maddy felt sick to her stomach. What was even more disturbing was that Jack appeared to be returning her affection. It hadn't occurred to her that Jack would continue to see Stella after they started dating. She had no right to ask him not to since she was planning on resuming her relationship with Bryan. Her morbid curiosity got the best of her. She continued to watch.

The couple finally separated, but continued holding hands. Stella was looking up at Jack, her eyes sparkling. "Baby, you haven't called. I was beginning to worry about you."

Jack released her hand, "Sorry Babe, I've been really busy. How did you know I was home?"

Stella ran her hands up Jack's chest. "Work told me. I thought you were never too busy for me," she smiled up at him. Maddy saw Stella take Jack's hand and lead him to the stairs. She had seen enough. She turned and sought out the back of the house.

Jack stopped Stella and the bottom of the staircase. "Stella what are you doing?"

Stella continued to tug on his hand, "We have some loss time to make up for, come on let's go to your bedroom and burn the midnight oil."

Jack peeled her grip off of him. "Stella stop. I can't do this."

"Yes you can Baby. I need you," she pleaded with her big doe eyes.

Jack moved away from her. "I can't see you anymore," he told her flatly.

Stella stepped down and stood in front of him, "Excuse me, I must have misheard you. Did you say you can't see me anymore?"

Jack turned away from her then leaned against the wall. "That's what I said. I think, no, I know it's time to call it quits."

Stella crossed her arms and looked at him. "You better have one damn good reason."

Jack heard a door slammed at the back of the house. Shit, had Maddy witnesses what had just transpired?

Stella heard it too, "What was that? Who's back there?" She took off down the hall. Before Jack could stop her she opened the den door and saw Maddy sitting by the bay window looking out over the yard.

Stella stood in the doorway. "Maddy...what are you doing here?"

Maddy didn't even bother to turn and look at her. "I'm under house arrest and it's Jack's turn to guard me. Don't let me stand in your way. You and Jack carry on as if I weren't even here."

Jack pushed past Stella. "Maddy, it's not what it looked like."

A confused Stella looked back and forth between the two. "Like what it looked like, Jack?" she asked him.

Jack took a seat beside Maddy. He reached out and touched her face. She wouldn't look at him, she couldn't. "Don't worry about it Jack. You go do whatever it is you need to do."

"What I was just doing was telling Stella I couldn't see her anymore," he told her.

Maddy turned to him, searching his eyes, "You were?"

He nodded and leaned in and kissed her softly.

"Excuse me," Stella screeched. "What the hell is going on here?" She stood for a moment, and then she looked like a light bulb came on. "Ooooooh I get it. You're screwing Maddy. That's why you haven't called me. Does Bryan know? Because if he don't I am sure as hell going to tell him!"

"Relax Stella. Bryan knows all about it. I'm sorry Stella, it just isn't working out between you and me," Jack stood up to face Stella.

"Well Maddy, I guess since you're fucking Jack, it leaves the field wide open on Bryan don't it?" Stella said snidely.

Maddy flew off her position under the window. "You stay the fuck away from Bryan, or I swear to hell I will scratch your eyes out!" she hissed.

Stella studied Maddy. "Dear God, you're doing them both. What a whore!"

"Stella!" Jack snapped. "Get the hell out of my house, NOW!"

Stella stormed out of the room. They heard the front door slam and seconds later the sound of squealing tires.

Maddy sat back down at the window and focused her attention on the backyard. Stella was right. Sleeping with both men just proved what she was accused of being. She was a whore. Even if she hadn't been with Bryan since she became involved with Jack. (Except that awful night of the rape.) It didn't mean it wasn't going to happen.

Jack put his hand on her shoulder. "Come on Maddy, don't even go there. All three of us know the ground rules. None of us are going into this blind, so you are not doing anything wrong. Who gives a fuck what Stella thinks. She's just pissed because she lost out to you."

Maddy looked up at him. "Okay, lets look at it from this angle. You just broke up with your girlfriend because you're seeing me. You did it to be loyal to me. And I can't even do the same for you. Don't you see anything wrong here?"

"No, I don't. You want to know why? Because it's my choice. I told you before the relationship I had with Stella wasn't real and as far as me sleeping with her—it was just sex. So you see there really wasn't much to leave. I love you. I believe you love me. I also believe that ultimately when the dust settles, it's going to be me you end up with. I think you do too or you never would have started this."

"And what about Bryan? Where does that leave him?" Maddy asked.

"As the man you will forever love, but could never commit to because the two of you have too much history. You can't build a solid future based on your rocky past. You two just haven't come to terms with it." Jack sat down beside her. "I know it's not what you want to hear or even believe and that's okay. I could be wrong, but I don't think so. I guess only time will tell and I won't stand in the way of whatever does happen. But Maddy, you do belong with me, not to me, but with me."

Maddy leaned back against the windowsill and smiled, "You know that is the first time I have heard if phrased like that."

Jack looked at her puzzled, "What?"

"You said I belong with you, not to you. I like that, you don't look at me as a possession. Bryan does, he has to possess me, to feel he owns me and controls me." She smiled again and repeated. "I belong with you." Maddy reached out to him pulling him close.

Jack cupped her face in his hand and kissed her deeply. When she responded in kind, his fingertips slid down her neck and traced the line of her collarbone. Maddy tilted her head back as Jack's lips traveled along her jaw line and back behind her ear then down her neck. The feel of his hot breath on her skin felt like a hot summer breeze on a glass of ice and she melted into it.

Her fingers fumbled with the buttons on his shirt until she was able to free him from it. Her lips hungrily traveled over his chest, nipping and teasing as she went.

Jack's hand went up around the back of her head, barely touching her hair. A soft moan escaped his lips. He entwined his fingers in her hair and brought her head back up to him taking her mouth and exploring her deeply with his tongue. His fingers quickly unbuttoned her blouse, sliding it off her. He unclasped her bra freeing her for his touch and touch he did. Every inch of her.

Maddy flipped her leg over top of his and squirmed into his lap. One of his hands slid down between her legs, caressing her through her blue jeans. He could feel her body quivering under his touch. His hands unsnapped her pants and he tugged at her jeans to free her from them. She was in his arms; naked to his touch, even though the room was chilled from the air conditioning, her skin was on fire.

Jack laid her down on the bench of the windowsill, burning trails a long her body. His hands left no part of her body untouched. She cried out in need for him, she begged him. "Jack, please..."

Jack put one knee between Maddy's knees while he undid his belt and unzipped his slacks. He pushed them down. He grabbed Maddy by her hips and guided her to him entering in her slowly. He wanted to take her swiftly, but this wasn't about his desires, but her needs, and she needed to be loved. He moved into her as he watched her face. She watched him, a languid expression on her face, a deep glowing in her eyes. He smiled at her, a slow tender smile. He leaned forward to kiss her lips, nipping at them playfully. Maddy pushed her body into his, forcing the rate of penetration. Her fingers wrapped around his head, bringing his mouth down harder on hers. Their lovemaking became frenzy and until they both cried out in ecstasy.

Jack collapsed on Maddy's naked body. She kissed the top of his head, her breathing still labored. She looked out past the two of them into the backyard and laughed. "I hope you don't have voyeuristic neighbors."

"Baby, I have an eight foot fence with a wrought iron rail around the top all around the perimeter of my entire yard. We could go out there and make love until the cows come home. And unless you're a screamer," he laughed, "no one would know the difference.

Maddy threw her head back and laughed, "I don't know, am I?

Jack grinned, "Yeah a little."

Jack's doorbell resounded throughout the house again. "Shit, now what?" He grabbed his pants and quickly slipped them back on. He gathered Maddy's and tossed them to her then left.

Maddy quickly dressed and ran her fingers through her hair trying to get some kind of control over her wild curls. When she finally decided she was presentable she traveled to the living room.

She found Bryan sitting on the couch. Jack was sitting on the loveseat. "Hey Bryan!" She bent over and gave him a soft kiss. "What brings you out into the boondocks?" She sat beside him.

He nodded toward the door. "Jessie dropped off your bag. Thought you might need it. That woman still doesn't like me," he laughed.

Maddy smiled, "You're both territorial. Don't take it personal. Did you read the story?"

"Yes. Do you really think it is what the unsub is looking for you to report?" Bryan asked. He turned to Jack, "Did you read it?"

Jack shook his head, "No, haven't had a chance. Stella decided to make an unannounced visit."

Bryan raised an eyebrow and chuckled as he turned to Maddy, "And you're still alive?"

"Yeah, I can hold my own," she smiled weakly. "But I will put you I notice, she pretty much implied she's going to be going after you."

Bryan laughed, "Good luck with that, I have my hands full as it is. Maddy, will you go print off your story so Jack can take a look at it."

Maddy left to retrieve the story.

Bryan turned to Jack. "Don't you ever wear a shirt?" he laughed. "How do you think she's doing?"

Jack shrugged, "Okay, I think. She's been relatively calm, even when Stella was here. She has conflicting emotions about seeing both of us and Stella calling her a whore didn't help. She took her meds as soon as she got home. I don't know if that has anything to do with it."

"The only one she's probably taken that would, would be the anti-anxiety med. The others take time to start working, a couple of days even. It's gradual process."

Maddy returned to the room and handed Jack the story. "I wish you guys would stop talking about me behind my back."

Neither man commented on her request. Jack quickly read the story. "There's not much to it."

"Damn guys, there is only so much I can print without revealing too much of the case. I'm not going jeopardize the case or my journalistic integrity. If I report bullshit, that's what's going to happen. Besides he has never given me what I want to know—what exactly he wants from me," Maddy explained.

Bryan stood up, "Okay, let's see where it takes us. Jack has the phone. If the unsub calls you, it will still be picked up by the remote. Jack, you need to call me or Derek to make sure it's being monitored." He turned to Maddy. "I'll pick you up in the morning.

Maddy stood up and walked him out to the Sub. They stood there leaning against it for a few moments. "He suits you, Maddy. He has a calming effect on you." Bryan said softly.

"Don't. I don't want to do this. We can't recover from all the damage that has been done if the two relationships keep getting mixed together and constantly compared to one another," Maddy sighed.

Bryan turned to her. "Okay, new ground rule. I'm just not real sure what the rules are, hon." He took her hands in his. "I love you and I will do whatever it is you need me to do, you know that."

"I know, Sweetie." She stood on her tiptoes and kissed him softly. "It's new ground, we'll explore it together." She wrapped her arms around his neck and pulled him down to her and kissed him deeply.

Bryan ran his arms up her back and held her head in his hands. He parted her lips and took her all in then he pulled her to him. "I wish I had known Sunday it was going to be the last time I made love to you, I never would have let you go."

Maddy felt sadness between them. "We just have some issues to work through." She kissed his lips, "Are you willing to do the work?"

"I have told you before, I will walk through fire for you. I didn't wait ten years just to walk away from you." He kissed her on her forehead. "I need to take off. See you in the morning, Minnie. Call if you need me."

She watched him climb in the Sub and drive away.

Maddy put in a quick call to Chief giving him the okay to run the story.

When Maddy returned to the house, Jack had taken her bag up to his bedroom. "I cleared some closet space and a drawer for you if you want to put things away. I think things will be easier if you don't feel you are living out of a bag. The laundry room is just off the kitchen if you need to wash your clothing."

She had never given much thought as to how long this exile was going to last. She felt grateful Jack was trying to make her feel at home, but this wasn't home. She had her own home, and she wished she were there.

Jack wrapped his arms around her and pulled her close. "What's the matter Kitten?"

"I want to go home." She rested her head on his bare chest. She loved the feel of his skin on her cheek, loved the feel of the rise and fall of chest as he breathed.

He kissed the top of her head, "I'm sorry." It was the only thing he could think of to say to her.

There was knock on Jack's door followed by it creaking open. Maddy froze until Jack's mother popped her head in.

"Hey kids," she came in, in her hands she held a casserole dish. "I figured you guys were up to you heads in police work so I brought you some supper."

Jack stepped away from Maddy and kissed his mother's cheek. "Hey Mom, you didn't have to do that. I am perfectly capable of feeding us."

Maddy watched the exchange feeling a little awkward. Observing family behavior was something so foreign to her. For some odd reason she always found it to be contrived and forced. Maddy knew what was coming next. The proverbial peck on her cheek with the 'how are you dear?' She wanted to barf.

And as predicted Alisha Parker grabbed Maddy's hands and kissed her on her cheek. Maddy felt herself stiffen involuntarily.

"Good evening, Maddy, so good to see you again. Is my son taking good care of you?"

Maddy peered over the top of her head meeting Jack's gaze. "I take care of myself, but he is a gracious host."

Jack picked up on Maddy's discomfort. He didn't understand why she would distance herself from his mother. Most people found Alisha charming and very likable.

Alisha stood back from Maddy and studied her. She too had sensed something in Maddy. "What is it you don't like about me, Maddy?"

Maddy looked between mother and son. Oh, hell, how as she going to explain this? Honesty was the best policy, as long as it didn't hurt anyone. "Mrs. Parker..."

"Alisha, please."

"Alisha," Maddy continued. "I don't...I know how to be an FBI agent, I know how to be a reporter, I know how to pretend to be anyone but who I am." She smiled weakly. "But I don't know how to be me because I don't know who that is." She moved away from them and sat on the couch. "I don't have a lot of experience with...for lack of a better word—family skills. Affection is foreign to me. With the exception of very few people, your son being one of those people, I don't know how to relate on that level."

Jack and Alisha exchanged looks. Jack shrugged his shoulders. Hell this was new to him. But then again with Maddy, there was so much to her he didn't know. "Mom," he steered her to the couch. He took the casserole dish to the kitchen and came back. If he could have given his mother a history of Maddy and she would understand, but it wasn't his place. Bryan had always made in perfectly clear, never betray Maddy's trust.

Maddy tucked her feet up underneath her and nervously chewed on her fingernails.

Alisha sat on the edge of a loveseat cushion as she waited for Jack to return. This girl of Jack's, she held a great depth to her and had built a very high wall around herself. She was amazed Jack had been able to penetrate it. Perhaps that's why it took two years.

Just as Jack returned to the living room, the unsub phone went off. Maddy and Jack exchanged quick looks. It was too late to get Alisha out of the room.

"Mom, this is very important, do not say anything during this phone call, understand?"

Alisha nodded.

The phone continued to ring. Jack sent a text to Bryan as Maddy answered the line.

"Hello" She flipped it on speakerphone.

"Good evening, Maddy. Are we in a better mood?" Once again his voice was smooth, smooth as ice and just as cold.

"I'm fine, is there something I can do for you?" Maddy glanced over at Alisha who was watching her intently even if she didn't have a clue what was transpiring.

"Did you write the story?"

"As per your instructions."

"Good girl, you follow orders well." His voice was patronizing. She was having trouble restraining her urges.

"I did as you requested, I didn't take an order from you. I did my part, now you do yours," she said keeping her tone steady.

"I gave you mine first, I gave you a body."

Maddy sat back on the couch. "So tell me, what are your plans?"

"For?"

"Your next victim."

Jack shot her a look, damn it Maddy.

"I don't have victims, I have told you this before. These ladies are chosen," The unsub's voice went up an octave.

"Victim, chosen one, no matter how you look at it they are dead—at your hands. I just want to know what are your plans now?"

"You are starting to irritate me, Maddy," he said coolly.

Maddy laughed, "Really? I am getting under your skin now? Funny, I didn't get to look into your eyes to see the fire. But then again, you're going to hell so I imagine you will see plenty of fire."

Jack waved his hands in front of Maddy and shook his head violently mouthing, "Don't!"

The man on the other end of the line gave a long drawn out sigh. "Do you really want to do this Maddy? Can't we just talk as friends?"

Maddy laughed again, "Fuck no! We are not friends; I thought I made myself clear. However, I do have something to discuss with you. I have a family situation that has come up and I won't be available for a few days, I won't be working. I won't be available to do your bidding. Do you understand what I am saying?"

"And what if something arises that I feel you need to attend to?" he asked.

"Can't do it. This is something I need to take care of, a matter of life or death," she said softly trying to tame things down.

"And if I have something that is a matter of life and death?"

"Leave a message at the paper and I will contact you."

"As you wish Maddy, but just because you're gone does not mean life goes on." The line went dead.

Jack sat down beside Maddy, took the phone from her hand and set it on the coffee table. He wrapped his arms around her and pulled her close.

"He's going to kill again," she said into his chest.

Jack's cell phone went off as was expected. Jack put it on speakerphone.

"She there?" Bryan's voice boomed over the speaker.

"She's right here beside me."

Maddy lifted her head, "I didn't antagonize him, Bryan. If I'm meek he thinks something is wrong. He's going to kill again, soon. You know that don't you? How can I be gone if we know this is coming?"

"He's going to kill again with or without you, Maddy. You will be reachable, but we need to take care of you first. Don't beat yourself up, Kiddo. Nothing has changed. Take me off speaker phone."

Jack pushed the button and handed the phone to Maddy.

"Hang in there tight, Minnie. I know you hate hearing this, but humor this old man, are you okay?" Bryan asked.

She smiled weakly. "I'm okay. I just freaks me out knowing I am talking to a ruthless killer and there is nothing I can do to stop him. Why me?"

"You're just so sexy he can't stop himself," he joked.

Maddy laughed, "This is so not funny and you know it."

Bryan chuckled, "Yeah, I know Baby, but I got you to laugh didn't I?"

Maddy smiled into the phone, "Yeah, you did, thank you."

"Any time, Minnie, you know I love you right?"

"I love you too, Mickey, you want to talk to Jack?'

"Yeah, I'll see you in the morning, love you."

Maddy handed the phone to Jack.

Maddy glanced up and notice Alisha sitting opposite of them. Shit, she forgot she was even there. Lord knows what must be going through her mind. She knew Jack talked a lot to his folks but surely he would not have filled them in on case information. It would be very unprofessional. Alisha was studying her with keen interest. Maddy decided to stay silent until Jack got off the phone with Bryan. Let him do the explaining.

Jack closed his phone and threw it on the coffee table. He looked over at Maddy, "Are you sure you're okay?"

Maddy rolled her eyes. "Yes, just like I told Bryan, I am fine."

Alisha kicked Jack's leg.

"Ouch! Damn it Mom." Maddy laughed as he rubbed his leg. "What did you kick me for?"

"You didn't make me leave, does that mean you can tell me what just happen?" she asked expectantly. Her eyes were sparkling with anticipation.

Maddy smiled to herself, this woman was more like her than she thought.

Maddy and Jack looked at each other like Jack was expecting her to say something. "Hey, she's your mother," Maddy smiled weakly.

"Were you really talking to the killer?" Alisha asked, her gaze shifting back and forth between Maddy and Jack.

"Mom, what you saw and heard or will hear goes no further than this door. You can't even tell Dad. Promise me." Jack was adamant.

Alisha held up two fingers, "Scouts honor."

Jack took Maddy's hand in his and looked at her for some kind of answer. Maddy nodded that it would be okay.

"A couple of nights ago our unsub contacted Maddy because of the story that ran in the Journal. Even though she didn't write it, the guy who did put her bi-line as co-author on it. Anyhow Maddy got him to give up where the last body was buried. He's been playing cat and mouse with her ever since." Jack was careful not to go into detail about her contact with the unsub. Maddy was relieved.

"Is that safe?" Alisha asked.

"No Mom, it's not safe. Why do you thinks we have someone on her 24-7. Damn she can't even go to her own home," Jack snapped at her.

Maddy put her hand on Jack's arm, "Babe, don't be like that to her. She doesn't know." She turned to Alisha. "We don't have anyway of knowing if the unsub is stalking me, it's not likely, but the guys want to be sure."

"God, no wonder you're under so much stress." Alisha sat back on the love-seat and stared at Maddy in awe. "I'm sorry sweetie, you don't need me putting on all this pressure and putting you on the spot. However, I am impressed with the way you handled yourself when talking to that...that man. I don't think I could have done it. You are a strong woman."

Maddy smiled faint-heartedly, "I told you, I can be anyone I need to be, just not myself. I don't mean to be standoffish to you. I don't have any family except one sister who lives thousands of miles away. I'm just uncomfortable with affection when it's thrust up on me. I'm sorry. It's got nothing to do with you and I am sure in time, it will be okay."

Jack leaned over and kissed her softly, "You don't seem to have any problem with affection coming from me," he smiled.

Maddy looked at him and laughed, "And how long did that take?"

Jack's forehead wrinkled up as if he were deep in thought, "Two years."

She nudged him playfully, "Exactly."

Jack grabbed her pulled her up on to his lap smothering her face in kisses. Maddy pushed against him laughing, "Jack, not in front of your mom!"

Jack cupped her face and kissed her deeply. He smiled mischievously at her. "I'm desensitizing you."

Maddy stared into his sparkling brown eyes and brushed the side of his face with the back of her hand, "I will never be immune to you," and she kissed him tenderly.

Alisha watched the couple and smiled, her doubts about Maddy beginning to fade. Maddy was obviously a very complex woman, one with a dramatic history. And her son was crazy in love with her. She saw the way Maddy was looking at Jack and knew without a doubt, she was equally in love with her son. She didn't doubt Maddy was his intellectual equal, but she was more than sure Maddy's life experience by far superseded that of Jack's. Jack seemed to be aware it and as long as he knew it going in, she was sure they would be fine.

Alisha stood up. "I'm going to leave you kids alone." She laughed, "I think at the moment you would prefer it that way." She leaned over and kissed Jack on the top of his head and smiled at Maddy. "Good night and stay safe."

Jack pushed Maddy down into the cushions and covered her body with his. She ran her hands over his bare chest and laughed, "You just chased your mother away."

Jack started kissing her behind her ear and whispered, "She takes hints very well."

She pushed against him in a playful manner, "You're a mean son."

He raised his head up and looked down at her, a half smile playing on his lips, "You want to make war or you want to make love?"

"War," she grinned watching his reaction.

"Bullshit." His mouth came down on hers demanding a response to which she gave to him two-fold. His hand slid under her shirt seeking her breast. He teased and taunted her feeling her melt underneath him.

Maddy could feel the urgency in him. This was new and sexy at the same. Making slow sweet love with him was incredible but a little hot sex never hurt anyone. Maddy reached between them and tugged at his belt until she unloosened it, unfastened the snap and slid down the zipper. When her hand touched him, he let out a deep groan, his tongue slid down deeper in her throat. His kiss took away her ability to breathe. She felt him fumbling with her pants and was amazed at how easily they slid off her. He was very skilled at stripping women it seemed. She wrapped her legs around his hips and guided herself to him.

He cupped her head in his hands as he slowly moved inside her, looking soulfully into her eyes. "I love you," he told her in an emotional voice. "God I love you." When he looked into her eyes they were glistening.

She entwined her fingers in his thick hair. "I love you," she choked and she pulled him down to her kissing him deeply. He took his time with her, loving her with each stroke. It was so sweet she thought her heart would break. She clung to him, begging him silently for release. He wouldn't give it to her. She took him in until she couldn't stand it anymore. "Please..."she whispered hoarsely. He pulled her head back by her hair and made her look into his eyes as their bodies shuttered together. When Jack collapsed on her, the sweat on their bodies mingled.

Jack pushed himself up so he could see her face. He was surprised to see a tear sliding down the side of her face. "Kitten, what's wrong?" he asked in concern.

She smiled and said while trying to catch her breath, "Nothing's wrong, baby. I just love you so much."

He sat up and gathered their clothes giving her hers. "New rule around here. When we are home *relaxing* you can't wear so many damn clothes."

Maddy slid on her panties and laughed, "You never warned me we were going to make love at the drop of a hat."

Jack stood up and pulled on his pants and smiled, "Are you complaining?"

She flicked him with her finger. "You are a virile man." Maddy pushed her damp hair away from her face. "Damn, I don't know if I can keep up with you. I'm not used to this."

Jack sat down next to her, studying her.

She felt his eyes bearing down on her. "What?"

"How many times with Bryan?"

Maddy felt her cheeks burning, "Jack...I really don't feel comfortable talking about this."

"How many?"

Maddy tilted her head back and took a deep breath. "I don't know, five maybe six times."

"And before he came back, you dated?"

Maddy shook her head. "No."

"Not even to get your needs met?" Jack looked at her in wonderment.

Maddy blushed, "No...not even for that."

Jack crossed his arms still watching her, "So we're talking about how many years?"

"Jack, please, do we have to do this?" she pleaded. When she looked at him he was still looking at her expectantly. "Let's put it this way, the only man I have been with since getting divorced was Bryan."

Jack sat back and shook his head. "Wow. So you're talking lots of years."

"Christ Jack," Maddy stood up, "What's the big fucking deal?" She snapped her jeans.

Jack pulled her back down onto his lap. "Honey, you're getting this all wrong. I'm not criticizing. It's just amazing, I didn't know women like you existed." He put his finger under her chin so she looked at him, "And Kitten, it's not a bad thing."

"Okay, you now know my sexual history, let's see about yours?" she stared at him defiantly.

Jack chuckled, "Kitten, you are looking at one of the original he-whores. Getting a woman into bed has never been a problem. Getting one I actually wanted to keep there, that's never happened." He kissed on her nose, "And now after you, I never want another."

Maddy grinned, "A he-whore. I guess that explains why you're so damn good in bed."

Jack smacked her on the ass. "No, that's just for you!" he laughed.

"Now I know why they call cops pigs, cuz you are!" Maddy slipped off his lap. "I'm going to go take a shower." And she took off upstairs.

After Maddy finished her shower, she dressed in her cotton t and shorts that she often slept in and laid back on Jack's bed thinking about the day. Just one more fucked up day to add to all the others. She was actually looking forward to having a few days away from all it, even if it meant going under some intense psychotherapy. Hell it couldn't be anymore fucked up than the life she had been living. Who would have ever thought facing the demons of her past would be more preferable to dealing with the present?

Maddy grabbed her cell phone and called Bryan. "Hey Mickey," she smiled into the phone.

"Hi Minnie, this is a nice surprise. How you feeling?" Bryan sounded pleased to hear from her.

"Just got out of the shower, going to go down and eat here shortly. Was missing you so I thought I would give you a call."

"Glad you did." She could almost hear him smile. "You made my night."

"You still at the office?"

"Nope, laying back on the bed watching TV. I just need to vegetate for a while, forget about that damn place."

"Hear you there, hon. Heard from Jeff?" she asked.

Bryan gave a deep sigh, "I sent him the money. Once again I saved his ass. One of these days I just need to let him suffer the consequences of his actions."

"You won't cuz you love him too much. It's not in you. If it was, you would have done it years ago and saved yourself a lot of heartache," she replied sympathetically.

"I miss you, Maddy. You are safer with Jack, but I still miss you."

"I miss you too, Bryan. I'm sorry."

"Minnie, listen to me. You have nothing to be sorry for, you did nothing wrong. I'm the one that fucked things up." Bryan said quietly.

"No, I was the one that changed. Who would have thought I was better off staying in the dark? At least I would still have you."

"You haven't lost me kiddo. Besides, you have Jack now."

The silence between them was deafening. "Maddy?"

"I'm here. It just saddens me if I have him, I don't have you." She laughed weakly. "I was supposed to have both of you. You know, have my cake and eat it too?"

Bryan was quiet for a few moments. "Can I ask you a question?

"You can ask, but I can't promise I will answer," she replied.

Bryan laughed, "Minnie, you don't have to be so evasive anymore. The past is out."

She smiled, "Okay ask away."

"If I were to change motels, would you be willing to spend some private time with me."

"Yes," she answered without hesitation.

"Not to spend the night, you are safer with Jack, but I would love to have some time just to be alone with you, away from the squad room."

"Bryan, I said yes, what more do you need?"

"Thanks Minnie," Bryan's voice was lighter than she had heard it quite a while. "Go eat your supper and say hi to Jack for me. Enjoy. I will see you in the morning. Love you."

"I love you, too." She shut the phone and threw it on the dresser.

Maddy padded down to the kitchen where Jack had set the island up for supper. He placed the casserole on the center of the island. A tossed salad was beside each plate. Maddy picked up Eddie and was playing with him as Jack poured them each a glass of milk. Maddy set the kitten down and washed her hands. "Bryan said to tell you hi."

Jack set the glasses down on the counter. "You talk to him? How's he doing?" Jack asked in a purely conversational tone.

Maddy picked up the glass and took a sip. "Back at the motel watching TV. Trying to get away from all this shit. Gee I wonder why?"

Jack pulled up a stool next to her. "This is all taking its toll on him too. Too bad he couldn't take a few days off."

Maddy studied Jack closely, "You really do like him, don't you?"

Jack looked up and laughed, "Yeah, of course I do, he's a good guy. Kind of messed up, but hey so are you and I love you. Seriously we all have our reasons for doing things the way we do. Sometimes we make bad choices; sometimes those choices are taken out of our hands. I'm not going to judge him based on what he's done in his past. I look at him for the man I know today, and he's not a bad guy. Just one tired man."

Jack turned to her, "I'm going to tell you something, Maddy. Sometimes when you get into...one of your moods...I don't know what to do to help you. I am at a loss. I talk to Bryan, he helps me understand, helps me to be able to help you. That is pretty unselfish of him don't you think?"

Maddy thought about it. She never knew. Maddy played with her salad. "Yeah, I guess it is."

He leaned over and kissed her on the forehead, "He is putting you first for once, Maddy, and sets aside his own feelings. Don't blame him for it."

Maddy smiled weakly. "You two are so weird."

Jack laughed as he put a spoonful of casserole on their dishes. "Yep, that's why you love us both."

"And it wouldn't bother you if I spent time with him?" she looked up at him.

Jack was bringing a fork full of food to his mouth and stopped mid-air. "Maddy, I would be lying to you if I said it wouldn't. Just as much as I am sure it bothers Bryan you spending all this time alone with me. But that's the rules. I will live with it."

"I'm not going to sleep with him, Jack. I can't and won't do that to you."

Jack didn't comment on her declaration. He wasn't sure if he believed her. He wanted to, with all his heart. He just didn't know if he could.

Maddy returned her attention to her supper. She took a bite of the casserole, some kind of hamburger casserole with tater tots on it. Duh, tatertot casserole. "Did your mom teach you to cook?"

Jack smiled, "Baby, I've be on my own for 20 years, I think I have learned a few things along the way."

Maddy smiled. "Yeah, like being a he-whore," she smirked.

"Fuck you," he laughed. "A man has needs, evidently more than a woman. You, my sweet Maddy, when it comes to sex, you are just a babe in the woods."

Maddy kicked him hard.

"Ouch, Jesus Chirst, what is it with you women and kicking?" He rubbed his ankle.

Maddy laughed, "I'm barefoot, it couldn't have hurt that much. Besides, you don't seem to be...unsatisfied."

Jack took another bite of food and washed it down with his milk. "Kitten, you are by far more than enough woman for me." He looked over at her grinning, "And I don't think I could ever get enough of you, if I haven't proved that already."

After they cleaned up after supper, Jack led Maddy in the living room where she sat down on the couch. Jack walked over to a large armoire and opened it revealing a large TV and a stereo system. He had the best of everything. No money my ass, she thought once again.

He kissed her softly. "I need to go take a shower." He handed her the remote. "You find something to watch and I'll join you shortly."

Maddy sat back and flipped the TV on. She channel surfed without really paying much attention to what was on. She was thinking back on last night. She focused on the unsub's face. How could she have missed him studying her, those dark penetrating eyes? Then he looked at her, as if he were looking right into her. She remembered he made her feel uncomfortable, but at the time she never really gave it much thought. Maddy grabbed her bag and pulled out a file she had slipped in there before she left the station. She removed the sketch of the unsub and studied it. It really didn't look like the man she had seen. His face was rounder, eyes bigger, and was clean-shaven. She was sure she would recognize the face if she ever saw it again.

Maddy glanced down and saw the designated cell phone sitting on the coffee table. She glanced at the stairs and listened. Nothing. Maddy picked up the phone, went under calls received, pulled up the number and hit send.

The phone rung several times before the unsub picked up. "Maddy, this is a surprise. I thought you were going to be out of contact."

Maddy took a deep silent breath. "I thought maybe we could talk, without all the bullshit, no games, are you willing?"

"Maybe, I can't guarantee you will get the answers you're looking for."

"I will decide."

"Can you tell me how one becomes a member of your flock?"

The unsub was silent briefly. "They come to me, if I deem them worthy, I welcome them into the flock."

"You don't recruit them?" she asked tentatively.

"No, they come to me."

"Without revealing your whereabouts, how do they find you?"

"Through my connections with the church."

"Protestant, Catholic, or Baptist?"

"Beings there are over a hundred churches and I would be in no danger of being linked to any of them, I will tell you Protestant." The man seemed completely at ease talking to her.

Maddy was also surprised at how calm she was being. This was the reporter in her kicking in. Perhaps not having the pressure of having others around she was better able to do her job. "Are you a real minister?" she asked.

The unsub laughed, "Yes, I am an ordained minister."

"But aren't you suppose to be the keeper of souls? Why would you...sacrifice a member of your flock?" she chose her words carefully.

"When a member of my flock has deviated from the decrees of my congregation, we do our best to enclose them and bring them back to our ways. If the sheep has wandered too far, it is my job to bring them on to the lord. They must give of themselves to become complete with him."

"They're a sacrificed." She stated flatly.

"No, it's an offering."

"Why do you do what you do to them?"

The unsub lost his voice then finally came back, "That is something I do not wish to discuss with you."

"Fair enough," Maddy replied calmly.

"What about the way you prepare them for burial?"

"Pass on that one too."

"Okay." She paused.

"I think this enough for you this time Maddy. Hope you enjoy your visit with your family and all is well. Good evening." He hung up.

Maddy sat the phone down on the coffee table. Any minute now all hell would be breaking loose.

Jack's phone was also on the coffee table and immediately went off. Maddy picked it up and answered it. It was Derek.

She knew he would be angry and she didn't really care. She got more out of the unsub in this one conversation than she had in any previous one.

"Where's Jack?" Derek asked her coldly.

"In the shower."

"I am going to go grab Bryan. Don't you move a hair...and stay off that damn phone!" he yelled at her and hung up.

Jack came down the stairs dressed in a t-shirt and sweat pants. She couldn't meet his gaze. "Was that my phone?"

"Yes," she continued flipping through channels.

"Who was it?" he asked sitting down beside her.

"Derek," she was giving as little information as possible. He would be jumping down her ass soon enough.

"What did he want?"

Maddy started chewing on her nails. "Said something about him and Bryan coming over to discuss something with you."

Jack looked at her with a puzzled face, "About what?"

Maddy coughed, "Em.... He really didn't go into detail." Well he didn't.

"Oooookay. You want something to drink?" he asked getting up.

Yeah, arsenic. "No, I'm good."

She could feel herself under Jack's scrutiny. "What's up with you? You're acting weird."

Maddy smiled weakly. "You will find out soon enough, I'm afraid."

It took a little under twenty minutes for the doorbell to ring. Maddy slid off the couch and crept up the stairs while Jack was opening the door. She hid at the top of the landing. Hell she knew it wasn't going to do her any good to hide, but what the hell, she wasn't going to surrender to them, right?

She could hear muffled voices talking below. Five...four...three...two... "Maddy get your ass down here NOW!" Jack yelled up the steps.

Maddy rolled her eyes and mumbled, "Oh fine..."

Jack was standing at the bottom of the steps. She could see the anger in his eye. She hadn't seen him look at her like that since the Bacon Creek fiasco. Derek and Bryan were standing by the couch, both looked unhappy.

"God damn it, Maddy! What the hell were you thinking? No better yet, do you ever think before you do?" Jack bellowed at her.

"Christ, Jack, I'm right here, you don't have to yell!" She refused to meet his gaze.

Derek and Bryan stared at her. "Sit." Bryan ordered. His voice wasn't as cold as she thought it would be. He knew her well enough that he wasn't all that surprised.

Maddy plopped down on the couch. "Give it your best shot," she told them all.

"Maddy," Bryan spoke to her in a low subdued voice. "You were told not to initiate contact with the unsub. But you had to go and do it anyway."

Maddy turned to him defiantly, "Have you listened to the recording?"

"No not yet."

"Then before you start ripping in to me, listen to it. I got more out of him tonight than ever before—just listen to it before you judge me."

Derek set the recorder down on the coffee table and hit the play button. It played her conversation back for all to hear. Maddy listened to it and was actually quite pleased with herself.

Jack took a seat beside Maddy. "Why did you go it alone, Babe? Christ what if something would have happened?"

"Like what? He attack me over the phone? Nothing happened except he actually talked to me for once," she said defending herself.

"So calm, so cool..." Bryan shook his head as he listened.

"Chameleon," Jack sad flatly, "reporter mode."

Maddy looked at Jack, "Damn you act like it's a bad thing."

"Why this? Why now?" Derek grilled her.

"What the hell are you talking about?"

"How come you can do this," he pointed to the recorder, "and every other time you're all over the place, being a smart ass, egging him on. Why couldn't you have done this all along?"

"You guys were breathing down my neck!" she snapped.

They sat quietly as the tape finished playing. Derek hit the control. "We're going to need a full report, Maddy."

"She's on leave for a few days," Bryan told him.

"Why?"

Jack and Bryan exchanged looks, "She has a medical issue that needs immediate attention. She can still be reached, but I want her ass staying out of the station." Bryan told him.

Derek turned to Jack, "And you're the babysitter for this mission?"

"Hey!" Maddy snapped.

Jack nodded, "I guess you can call it that."

Derek grabbed the recorder and moved to leave. "Better get a tighter leash on her, even if you have to use a choke chain to do it," he said is he slammed the door behind him.

Maddy ran to the door and yelled after, "Fuck you, Derek!"

Jack sighed, "Maddy, I do have neighbors. Come over here and sit down."

Neighbors? Oh yeah, now she felt stupid as hell. "I'm sorry, I wasn't thinking."

Bryan shook his head, "Like this is a new thing."

Maddy propped her feet up on the coffee table. "You know what? You guys can say any damn thing you want to me, because I don't care. I did good, damn good and you can't deny it."

Bryan stood up and rubbed his temples, "I am tired, I have a headache, think it was stupider than fuck to be called out here. I am going back to the motel and pass out." He leaned down and kissed Maddy on the cheek. "See you guys in the morning. I don't want to hear from you or about you anymore tonight. Good night, Maddy."

Maddy looked after him, "You know if I didn't know he had such a fucked up day, I would be offended by that."

Jack chuckled. He slid down far enough in the couch that he could rest his head on Maddy's shoulder. "This is a perfectly typical Maddy stunt. Like in the early days, before all this shit started."

Maddy kissed the top of his head, "I bet you miss those days and regret the way things are now."

He looked up at her, "Kitten, I would love to have our old life back, but if living through all this drama is what it took to finally get you, I would do it all again in a heartbeat."

"Do you remember back to that day at Perkins a couple of weeks ago? Did you know what you wanted already then?" She leaned her head against his.

"I didn't know what was happening back then. I saw you that day at Granger's house. I hadn't seen you in a couple of months." He smiled softly, "It was like

I was seeing you for the first time. Something stirred in me. Then when I saw you at Perkins, touched you, I knew it was something and I wanted to find out." He laughed, "But you didn't seem to interested."

"Subconsciously I was interested, but my wall was still intact full force." She laughed, "I warned you remember?"

Jack turned and kissed her cheek, "But I pulled a Maddy, I never listened. You up for tomorrow?" Jack asked her.

Maddy shrugged, "Guess so. My mind has been so full of this case, I haven't dwelled on it that much."

"It's been sneaking in hon, you just aren't so aware of it. That little show you put on Bryan today, that's your demon poking its head in." Jack put his arm across her waist.

Maddy sat quietly thinking about what happened. She had set out to crush Bryan and she damn near did it. No, that wasn't her; that was something fucked up from her past. Maddy shifted her body so she was laying her head across Jack's lap. "I don't want to think or deal with it anymore tonight. I am sure I will be getting my fill over the next couple of days."

Jack bent and kissed her softly, then stroked her hair with his fingers. "I love you, Kitten."

Maddy snuggled down into the couch, turning her head to watch TV. "I love you, too, Babe."

Jack took the remote and flipped through a few channels and then came to a stop.

Maddy started laughing hysterically, "You've got to be kidding right?"

Jack looked down at her innocently, "What?"

"Law and Order???"

20

Bryan sat with Maddy in the waiting room waiting for her name to be called. To say she was nervous was an understatement. Even with Bryan at her side she was apprehensive about this visit. She had already been in to see her psychiatrist. All he did was reviewed her meds and felt comfortable with what he had prescribed her yesterday. He told her she just needed to give them time to take effect. She was waiting now to talk to her therapist, Lonnie McKenzie. She was totally comfortable talking to Lonnie but having Bryan go in with her was going to prove somewhat more than a challenge. Lonnie knew all about Bryan and their history. It was Lonnie that pulled her out of the depression Bryan had put her into two years ago. Lonnie will surely have her mind made up about Bryan before she ever met him. Maddy hadn't been in to see Lonnie since Bryan had arrived.

"Maddy?" Lonnie popped her head around the corner. "You want to come in now?"

Bryan stood to go with her and Lonnie stopped him. "I would like to talk to Maddy one on one first Mr. Mayland. I'll come and get you when we're ready."

Maddy looked back at Bryan and then followed Lonnie back to her office. She made her way to the familiar loveseat where she had spent many an hour. She picked up a small throw pillow and held it in her lap.

Lonnie pulled up a chair in front of Maddy, kicked off her shoes, and tucked her feet underneath her on the chair. "So how you been, Maddy?"

Maddy smiled weakly and shrugged. "I have had better days."

"Well hon, we have two hours cleared, we got plenty of time. I understand you finally had your breakthrough. How do you feel about this, Maddy?"

She squeezed the pillow to her chest. "It was very painful reliving it. I wasn't sure I could live through it."

"But you did."

Maddy met her eyes, "Only because Bryan pulled me out of it. I don't know what would have happened if he hadn't been there."

"I'm going to be asking you some tough questions, Maddy. Don't over think them, just give me your gut reaction, give me the first emotional response you feel, okay?" Lonnie asked her taking a drink of her Mt. Dew.

"Okay."

"The last time we talked, you were pretty comfortable with the way your life was going. Granted you had your life compartmentalized, but you felt strong. You weren't in any danger of letting in the past, which you didn't want to relive anyhow. What changed that?"

Maddy leaned back to think.

"Maddy don't think, answer."

"Jack, no Bryan, fuck I don't know, both of them."

Lonnie laughed, "Leave it up to a man to fuck up your life and you got a double whammy. Why Jack? I thought you were comfortable with him."

"He let me in on a crime scene. Everything was cool, just like it always had been. Then he started acting all weird on me," Maddy explained.

"Like how?"

Maddy smiled as she thought about that day at Perkins, "Like he wanted more. Kept asking me questions like if I was attracted to him at all, stuff like that."

"And you told him or better yet, how did you feel?"

"He caught me off guard...made me nervous. But honestly I liked the way he was making feel," Maddy confessed. "But I told him on no uncertain terms that all we could be was friends."

Lonnie studied her, "Did he believe you? Did you believe you?"

Maddy laughed, "He didn't, I did."

"I sense warm feelings when you talk about Jack. Your eyes light up. How are things between you and Jack now?"

Maddy looked away, her cheeks growing hot. "Things are good, very good."

Lonnie smiled, "Are you in love with him?"

Maddy nodded.

"So in a two week period you went from wanting to just be friends to falling in love with him. Wow, Maddy, that's a hell of stretch for you. How do you explain it?"

Maddy ran her fingers through her hair. "We tried to fight it, we really did. Even with Bryan in the picture, it couldn't be stopped. Falling in love with Jack just all felt so natural."

"That's the way it should feel. Hang on to that thought. Now let's turn back to Bryan, who I am assuming is waiting out there. I remember what a hard time you went through because of him. So what is he doing back in your life?"

Maddy took a deep breath, "This case we're working on. He more or less hunted me down, sucked me into it."

"Sucked you into it?"

"He showed up, he pursued me until I gave in. The next think I know I am being reactivated into the FBI. Now I am shit deep into something and I am in way over my head."

Lonnie took another drink, "Let me ask you this, way over your head with this case, or way over your head with Bryan? Are you thinking clearly about him, what he is to you, about your feelings for him?"

Maddy hugged the pillow tighter, "I don't know."

"Do you love him?"

"Yes."

"Okay I want you to think about when we talked about Jack, how you felt when you told me you loved him. Do you feel that same feeling when you say you love Bryan?"

"No, it's different."

"How?"

Maddy felt her eyes cloud over, "Loving him doesn't make me feel happy. I mean...damn, I have always loved him. I mean he has been there for me though all this, he pulled me though my break. How could I not love him?"

"Maddy listen to yourself. You don't owe him your love. Just because he demands it, you don't have to give it to him. Where has he been for ten years? Even two years ago hon, he made you love him again, get it, he made you. Then he took that love and used it against you. Did he make you love him again this time?"

Maddy shrugged, "Maybe. It didn't feel like it at the time."

"How did the two of you get over your rocky past?"

"We didn't."

"So you are telling me with everything he put you through you can say you love him with a free conscious?"

"He said he was sorry and I believe he meant it."

"Just because he said he was sorry, did it make all the pain and mistrust go away?"

"No."

"Do you still feel it?"

"Yes, deep down, no matter how hard I try to push it away, ultimately it's still there."

"Then why?"

"I felt weakened. I needed him," she looked at Lonnie, a tear sliding down her cheek. "He knows everything, everything about me. I felt safe, like he could protect me from everything and everyone. We have such a bond; everyone kept saying it was unbreakable. He told me he was going to leave the FBI and stay with me. He wanted us to have a real life together."

Lonnie was quiet for a few moments. "Who's going to protect you from him, Maddy?"

"Lonnie why are we doing this? I thought we were going to work on other stuff?"

Lonnie shifted in her chair. "We have to figure out how you got to the state of mind you are in now. Maddy, Bryan has always been a weakness for you. He may have the best of intentions with you, but when you get down to bare facts, he still has the power to control you, to take away your conscious free will."

"Since he's been back, he has never gone out of his way to hurt me. Only once, when he was heavily under the influence of alcohol," she protested.

"What happened?" she asked.

Maddy looked away, "I really don't want to talk about it."

"Maddy, alcohol was a major contributor to what happened two years ago. At least be honest with yourself. What happened?"

Maddy's fingers nervously played with the strands of a tassel on the pillow. "He arrived at my home uninvited and forced himself on me." There, she said it.

"He raped you." When she said it it felt far worse than it was, even though it was fact.

"It wasn't like that," Maddy refuted.

"Did you say no?"

"Yes."

"Then it was rape."

"But he doesn't remember doing it. It was the booze, he blacked out."

Lonnie sighed, "Maddy, you are making excuses for his bad behavior. You are enabling him." Lonnie handed her a box of tissues.

Maddy set the pillow off to the side. "I don't know why you are doing this, Lonnie. Why aren't we working on my feelings after the break, or what this cases is doing to my state of mind?"

"Because Maddy, chances are high you wouldn't be in this weakened state if it weren't for the influence Bryan has had on you emotionally." Lonnie stood up.

"What are you doing?" Maddy asked.

"Bringing in your nemisis." Lonnie left the room and returned with Bryan in tow.

Lonnie introduced herself to Bryan. She didn't appear to show any animosity toward Bryan despite the conversation she had been having with Maddy.

Bryan sat down next to Maddy, smiling weakly. He looked as if he were the lamb being brought in for slaughter. He wasn't far from it.

Lonnie took her place back in her chair and turned to Bryan. "Mr. Mayland, I am quite familiar with your past with Maddy and what an effect you have had on her life. Tell me how you feel about it?"

"Please, call me Bryan," Bryan did seem to be jilted off kilter with Lonnie's direct approach. "I love Maddy, I have always loved her. I know I have done some undefensable things to her, for which I am very sorry. I came here to see if I could make up for those things, make things right by her. I want us to be together, for real this time." Bryan tried to explain.

"What about what Maddy feels?"

Bryan glanced at Maddy, but Lonnie cut him off. "Don't look to her for the answers to these questions. You look at me. I want them from you. What do you think Maddy feels?"

Bryan met Lonnie's gaze, "I don't knows how she feels. I don't think she trusts that it could happened."

"Now why would she think that?" Lonnie held steady.

"Because I have never really ever given her a reason to trust me," Bryan turned away.

"How many times since you have been here have you put her trust in you in question?"

"Without meaning to, several."

"How many times have you failed her trust in you by actions?"

Bryan looked sharply at Maddy. Maddy couldn't look at him, but why should she feel the shame over what he did. Maybe Lonnie was right, she made excuses for his behavior at every move.

Bryan gave a deep sigh, "Once, while I was under the influence."

Lonnie picked up her soda and took a sip. "Do you think that excuses you—that it justifies what you did, what you ever did to her? It's not your fault, there were mitigating circumstances?"

"Damn, you don't mince words do you? So what are you getting at? That I'm bad for Maddy? That I'll always going to be hurting her in some way or another, even when I am trying my hardest not to?"

"Are you?"

"You seem to know everything, you tell me," he countered.

"Lonnie, please," Maddy pleaded.

"Maddy, you are not to make any excuses for him. Quit trying to protect him. This part is for him, not for you," Lonnie gave reason to her method of questioning.

Bryan leaned back on the couch. "I have tried my best to be there for her, be what she needs me to be. I have gone out of my way to be honest about the other parts of my life. I love Maddy, I would do anything for her."

Lonnie raised her eyebrow, "Yet you keep putting her in harms way."

"What the hell is that suppose to mean?" Bryan snapped.

"When you decided to come here, it was because of her. You knew her need to keep the past in the past. You had to know your coming here would just remind her of that and endanger the possibility she would break. You also knew she was angry and hurt over the way you left her two years ago, yet you came and threw it in her face. You pretty much forced her into a dangerous situation by pulling her into this case. You knew she would do it because of her need to feel like she was doing something. You pressured her into rejoining the FBI, a major part of a life she needed to leave behind. Being put back in that atmosphere is ultimately what led to her breakdown. Now, Bryan, what would you call it?" Lonnie watched for his reaction. She could see he was beginning to anger. He didn't like what he was being told.

Bryan averted his gaze away from the therapist, taking in everything she just said. There wasn't anything she said that was untrue. So where does that leave him? What does that make him?

Lonnie turned her head to one side to see his face, "Bryan?"

Bryan cleared his throat. "I can't argue with you, you're right. The only thing I can say is that even though what I did...it was not something I set out to do. I make myself sick with guilt every second of every day lately wishing I could undo this mess I have created. I don't know how to undo it. The only thing I know to do is to protect her until it's over." His voice was filled with emotion.

"You're not her protector, Bryan. Maddy needs to be that for herself. She's been protecting herself for years, maybe not in the best way, but the only way she knew how. Your actions have left her vunerable."

"Now wait a minute," Maddy interjected, "you can't be putting this all on him. I had my hand in it. Nobody forced me to do anything. Bryan and I have done a lot of talking, learning truths about each other, coming to terms with our history. How can that be so wrong?"

"I didn't say it was wrong. I just needed for the two of you to see what really is. In the past, Maddy, you told me Bryan is toxic to you."

Bryan whipped his head around, "You said that? Is that how you really feel?"

Maddy looked at him, "Did you not here the words *in the past*? You've changed. You're not even the same man you were when you got here. If anything it almost seems you have lost your fire. Is that because of me?" Lonnie had them questioning their entire relationship, their motives, their feelings toward each other. What was the point of this?

"The road to hell is paved with good intentions, Maddy, I feel like I have led you down that road. Don't get me wrong, Maddy, I love you with all my heart, but if I had to do it again, I wouldn't." Bryan told her somberly.

Maddy searched his eyes, "So what are you saying, you would have let me keep believing the worst of you?"

"Would that be worse than the danger I have put you in?" he asked her.

Lonnie watched them with keen interest. She wanted to see how they interacted with each other—to see if Maddy was truly emotionally dependent on him.

"Yes, it would be to me. Yes, I know things are fucked up...with this case... with me and you, but I wouldn't trade what we have learned about each other, what we've shared for anything." Maddy wiped a tear from her eye.

Lonnie leaned forward in her chair, "Let's take a 15 minute break."

Maddy and Bryan went around to the loading dock where people were allowed to smoke. Maddy sat on the top of picnic table that was set there for people to use. Bryan sat down beside her.

He pulled a cigarette out and lit it. "Man, she's brutal," he smiled weakly.

"I'm sorry," Maddy whispered. "I had no idea this was going to happen."

Bryan put his hand on her knee, "Kiddo, if this is what needs to be dealt with to help you, we will do what we have to."

"You know, I really don't blame you for any of this, I never have."

Bryan leaned over and kissed her on the cheek, "Well you should. So what do you think, Minnie, are we doomed?"

She leaned her head on his shoulder. "I don't know what the future has in store for us. I just want to take things one day at a time. No demands, no expectations, just to be. Does that make sense?"

Bryan slipped his arm around her back. "Yes. We are kind of in unchartered waters with each other. We are both cautious, afraid, confused. We need to put the past behind us if we are ever going to maintain any kind of relationship." He laughed weakly, "Do we even know how to act with each other?"

"I miss how we used to tease and taunt each other. With the way I am now, I just antagonize you and make you feel bad. I don't want to be that person."

Bryan kissed the top of her head, "We'll get back to that; we just need time."

Lonnie was on her way out to tell Maddy she needed to cut their session short due to an emergency when she saw the couple sitting on the picnic table. She observed a sadness about them. She noticed it when they were both in the room. Something had happened which snuffed the fire that had once been there between the two of them. Maddy was lost and confused, Bryan defeated. She didn't know how to help them, wasn't even sure she wanted to. Despite the love that had lasted years apart, it wasn't sustainable in a full time relationship. Eventually in some way, they would destroy each other.

"Hey guys," she smiled at them. "I'm sorry Maddy, but I got an emergency call. We'll take up again tomorrow. Bryan you're off the hook. Listen, it wasn't my intent to totally trash you. But for Maddy's sake, I think you both need to really take a look at what you do to each other...and to yourselves. Take care."

Maddy was sitting in the front of the Suburban as Bryan got in. "Listen Bryan, I know you wanted to spend some time together, but can we do it later today? I just kind of want to be alone right now."

"No problem, kiddo. I understand. Kind of feel that way myself. I'll call Jack and have him meet us back at the house." Bryan took out his cell phone.

"I don't really want to be around him either. I just want to be alone. I want to go home." Maddy leaned her head back against the seat.

"Hon, you know we can't do that. I don't care if he does think you're gone. We can't take the chance."

Maddy looked at him with tears in her eyes and pleaded, "I need to go home, can't you understand? I need my sactuary...please..."

Bryan leaned back and took a deep breath. How could he keep her in the city against her will? He was trying to do right by her and give her what she needed and she needed to be in her own home. "Okay, but only if Jack is with you. Is that a deal?"

Maddy threw her arms around him and kissed him. "Oh thank you!"

He looked at her, "With Jack..."

"Yeah, yeah, whatever," she sat up in her seat like an excited child. "I get to go home!" She clapped her hands together.

Bryan laughed. Such a small thing was making her happier than he had seen her in a long time. He called Jack to meet them at the house.

Jack had been given instructions to take Maddy home by using gravel roads and make sure no one was following them. He was to bring her back tomorrow for her next therapy session.

Maddy was so excited. Home. Glorious home. A pity she couldn't stay there longer than overnight, but hey, at this point she was thankful for whatever she got. She watched Jack out of the corner of her eye. She was admiring his features. She loved all of his face, but it was his eyes she loved the most. Those deep brown eyes, the way those eyes looked into hers when they were making love so she could see how much he loved her.

Jack felt her eyes on him. He looked at her and smiled shyly, "What?"

She smiled at him. "I was just thinking how much I love you."

He leaned his head back and laughed, "You're just saying that because I'm bringing you home."

"Naah, I really do love you. We talked about you in therapy—me and Lonnie. She asked me how loving you felt," Maddy grinned.

"And you said?"

"Warm and really, really good. She kind of laughed how I went from just wanting to keeping it friends and within two weeks I was head over heels in love you."

When he looked at her smiling up at him her eyes were sparkling, God he loved her. He turned his attention back to the road. "Warm fuzzies...What did she say?"

"She said it was only natural and that that was the way it should be." She leaned over and kissed his cheek.

Just as they were driving by a rolling pasture, Jack pulled over. "Come on," he said as he got out of the car.

"What the hell?" she laughed as she opened her door.

Jack came around to her side of the car and pulled her by her hand down into the ditch. He lifted her over the barbed wire and then crawled over it himself. Her brought her to the edge of a gently rolling creek. "Take your shoes off."

"We're trespassing." She slipped her shoes off and threw them off to the side.

"So, I'm a cop. You are FBI, what are they going to do? Arrest us?" He took off his shoes and socks off and rolled up his pant legs. He tentatively stepped down into the water.

Maddy watched as he made a face when his feet hit the bottom. She followed him in. "Eeeeeew...this mud feels so gross," she said as the slimy creek bottom mud squished between her toes. "Honey, just because I love living in the country doesn't mean I like to get," she picked a black foot, "...dirty."

Jack flicked water on her, "Oh you puss." He picked her up and carried her toward the shore. Just as he was stepping up, his foot slipped and they both landed in the water.

Maddy screamed when she landed on her ass in the water. "You are like so fucking dead." She struggled to get up finding it hard to get her footing.

Jack laughed as he grabbed her and pulled her back down into his arms. He held her head in his hands and kissed her deeply. "Okay," he smiled mischeiviously, "I'm ready to die."

She relaxed in his arms and kissed him back. "You get reprieve this time. Just cuz you're so sexy."

Jack found his footing, scooped her up and tossed her onto the bank. Maddy gave out a little yelp. "Damn Jack, I knew you were a hard ass, but I'm not!" She rubbed her backside.

Jack chuckled as he sat down beside her. "I would have suggested we go skinny dipping, but I'm afraid those cows would freak out."

Maddy smiled at him, "The water is just a tad bit shallow."

He grinned at her, "So what's your point?"

She flicked him with the back of her hand. She pushed him down into the tall grass and climbed on top of him, smiling down at him.

Jack smiled and laughed. "I don't think this is the best place to molest me."

Maddy poked him in the ribs then bent down and kissed him softly. "You couldn't get so lucky."

In one swooping motion, Jack had her flipped on her back. "Kitten, I'm already lucky.

Maddy pulled him down and kissed him tenderly then brushed the hair from his eyes. "We're both lucky. I really do love you, you know."

He kissed her on her nose. "Yeah I do, and that's what makes it so much sweeter. Ready to go?"

He helped Maddy to her feet. They grabbed their shoes and headed for the car. Jack grabbed a blanket from his trunk and spread it over the seat. "Good thing they're leather," he laughed. "You're helping clean it up."

Maddy slid into the car, "Bullshit. You made this mess, you clean it up!"

Jack started up the car and put it into gear, "Bullshit," he laughed, "This is a partnership." Jack reached down and looked at his cell phone. "Shit, missed a call from Bryan."

"Hey Buddy, what can I do you for?" Jack asked him when he called back.

"Where you been? I was starting to worry about you guys." Bryan sounded concerned. He hadn't been himself when he returned from therapy with Maddy. Jack was the one concerned about Bryan.

"I'm sorry. We stopped off on a gravel road to look at cows," Jack said in all seriousness.

Bryan was silent for a few moments, "At cows...no more fucking around Jack. Get her home okay?"

"You okay, Bry?"

"I don't know. Just need to do some soul searching. Give me a call when you get her home okay?"

"Sure, of course. Maybe you could stop by later?" Jack asked hoping it would put some spark into his friend.

"No, I think it's best if Maddy and I spent some time apart. It will give us both time to think." Bryan's voice was soft and quiet.

"What happened? Anything I can help with?"

"No, we each have to do this on our own. But I appreciate the offer, thanks Jack. I'll talk to you later." He rang off.

As soon as they arrived at Maddy's, she grabbed the blanket out of the car, they went in changed clothes and she threw them all into the washing machine. Jack went out and cleaned the rest of his car.

Jack had called Bryan to let them know they had arrived safely. Jack was concerned at Bryan's demeanor. He was quiet, subdued and asked very little about Maddy. For all the matter Maddy had said very little about Bryan. Something happened this morning at therapy and it was affecting them both.

Maddy was sitting on her steps with a fresh glass of brewed tea and a Dr. Pepper for Jack. He sat down beside her and took the soda she offered him. "Maddy is everything okay between you and Bryan?"

Maddy looked into the distance at the pasture. "I don't know."

"Do you want to talk about it?" he asked.

She took a sip of her tea. "No, not really. It's just something he and I need to deal with together and separately."

Jack pulled out a cigarette and lit it. "Okay, I respect that."

Lonnie felt Bryan was responsible for her downfall. Had he done it again without knowing it? She knew he didn't do it on purpose. She loved the man but was discovering not the way she thought she did. Her feelings for him were no longer all consuming. She no longer lived for being held in his arms. He was her safety net, her security without her feeling very secure. She thought Lonnie had been implying that she loved him because she felt she had to. Maddy couldn't see them having a long- term future together anymore. They really didn't have anything to base it on, surely not their history. Maddy felt a great sense of gratitude towards Bryan, yet just below the surface she still had a great deal of resentment towards him. Why? Because he was so intertwined in her past and he would always be a constant reminder? And Lonnie was right, if it hadn't been for him, she wouldn't be where she was.

Would Jack's pursuit of her have made her vunerable if Bryan hadn't come along? She doubted it. He never would have pushed her about her past if Bryan had not been so protective and possessive. Then the realization came to her. Bryan used her fear of the past to keep her with him. When she did have her break, she no longer clung to him, she wanted to deal with her feelings on her own terms and that's when things fell apart, that's when her attitude towards him changed. She no longer wanted to depend on him for her strength.

So what was her motivation for deciding to sleep with Jack? Was it to get away from Bryan? Was it to find someone else to cling to? She didn't want to believe that. She loved being with Jack. He was funny, smart, sweet, sensitive, and so damn sexy it made her tingle when she thought about him. The love she felt with

Bryan was never like her love for Jack. Jack had been her good friend, and it had evolved into something more. Like Lonnie said, a natural progression had taken place, a little rushed, but when it happened, it wasn't forced. She thought it was destine to happen. Deep down they both knew it, and that was the reason neither would let go even after Bryan showed up. Although Bryan didn't try to come between them it had been he who kept them apart. Ultimately Jack and Maddy both sensed what they felt was real.

Maddy came to the realization when everything was said and done, if not for Bryan, these past two weeks would never have happened. Her life would not have been altered so dramatically and in many ways destroyed the life she had known before. He did it to her again. Bryan would never know she felt this way.

Jack slipped his arm around her and scooted closer to her then kissed the top of her head. "I can hear all that heavy duty thinking going around in your head, Kitten and it's making you sad. I am sorry."

Maddy leaned into him and rested her head in the crook of his arm. "I guess sometimes when you look at reality in the light of day, you find out it's not what you perceived it to be, and it can be really sad."

Jack squeeze her shoulder, "You know I'm here for you if you need me."

At that moment she loved him even more. He wasn't pressing her but let her know he was there for her. She reached over and turned his face toward her and kissed him tenderly. "How did I get so lucky to have you?"

"Goes both ways, Babe. It's early, do you want to do something?" he asked.

Maddy stood up and stretched. "If you don't mind giving me some alone time, I want go tackle some more photo albums. Oddly enough, I feel more comfortable doing that than thinking about our unsub."

Jack stood up, hugged her and kissed softly. "Go ahead, just don't push yourself too far okay? I'm going to go take a walk."

Maddy sat on her living room floor and pulled the photo albums and movies out of the box. She thought she could handle photos, but definitely not the movies. Seeing her children in still life was one thing, but seeing them in action and hearing the voices—it was just more than she could bear. Maddy spent the next 45 minutes thumbing through an album that was designated for Lexi. It contained all her baby pictures though the time just before her passing, right down to the sonagram she had when she was pregnant with Lexi. Maddy let her mind wander and absorbed herself in the memories. Although she found it painful, she also found it comforting.

Maddy had just closed the book up when she heard a cell phone ring. It wasn't her personal phone, it was the unsub's. She followed the ringing until she found it in Jack's bag. She picked it up and wondered whether or not she should answer it. Jack was nowhere around and she didn't know if the recorder would pick up this far out. She took a deep breath and answered it.

"Hello?"

"Good afternoon Maddy," his calming, smooth voice came across the line.

"Hi," she answered him quietly.

"How are things going with you and your family? You sound a little on the fragile side."

Maddy removed the phone from her mouth and took a deep breath. She sure as hell wasn't going to confide in him. "What does it matter to you?"

"I didn't call to antagonize you, Maddy. Just to check on your wellbeing."

"I told you I needed to be away to deal with some family matters. This is what I am doing. It's difficult enough without having to deal with you. Don't take offense, it's just the way it is," she explained quietly. This was her time to heal herself, not to contend with a serial killer. Call it selfish if you want, she thought.

"I understand. My prayers are with you. Good night Maddy." The phone went dead.

Maddy set the phone down and took a deep breath. That was harmless enough. Their unsub was a very complicated man. He actually sounded genuinely concerned.

It wasn't even a minute later her cell phone went off. There was no reason for Derek or Bryan to chew her ass as she didn't do anything wrong. She just didn't do anything at all. As far as she was concerned, she was off duty. Her time was her own.

"Hello?" she answered for the second time in the last five minutes.

"Hey Maddy." It was Bryan. His voice sounded distant and impersonal. What was happening to them?

"Hey Bryan, I take it the recorder picked up on the call?"

"Yes it did, you kept it short and sweet."

"I'm off duty, I was going through photo albums making use of my time alone. Is there something wrong with that?" she replied a little irritated.

"No, Maddy, not at all. I'm proud of you. Your courage is building. Glad to see it."

Maddy stood at her kitchen door and looked out over her property, "But?"

"No buts. The unsub didn't seem to be put off by the cool response from you, so I see no harm. You said you are alone, where's Jack?" She couldn't quite pinpoint Bryan's mood. She never talked to him like this.

"He's outside, giving me my space." Maddy searched the area and saw no sign of him.

"Can you see him? He's not answering his phone."

"He's down by the barn," she lied. "He might have left it in his car, I don't know. Do you want me to have him call you?"

"Yes, please. He needs to keep his phone on him at all times. If I don't talk you later, have a restful evening and I will talk to you tomorrow."

"You're not going with me to therapy tomorrow?" she asked confused.

"No, I don't think you really need me," Bryan said distantly.

"What are you saying—that I don't need you at therapy, or I don't need you at all?"

"I don't know what you need from me anymore, Maddy. I created this problem, perhaps it's best if I just stay away."

"What's wrong with you?" she questioned his attitude towards her. It was almost cold. "You're just giving up on me? You're not responsible for what's going on."

"That's not the impression I got from your therapist, and I think she has a better perspective on things than either you or I do."

"I don't agree, and I'm kind of pissed you are just going to roll over and play dead and not fight for us," she argued.

"You've got Jack," Bryan said flatly.

"Fuck you, Bryan," she snapped the phone shut.

Maddy felt exhausted by the whole exchange. She left a note for Jack to call Bryan and went back and layed down on her bed. She grabbed a pillow and wrapped her arms around it. She felt dead inside and yet at the same time her heart ached. Therapy always had the potential to be draining. The most beneficial ones often were the most painful. This one must have been a doozey. She buried her head in the pillow and let the tears fall eventually crying herself to sleep.

When Jack entered the house, it was quiet. He noticed the note on the table, as well as her cell phone and the unsub phone. Shit, what did she do now? He read the note to call Bryan, but before he did he searched the house for her. In the living room Maddy had stacked the albums into piles and the tapes were set off to the side. One album was left off to the side. He then stood in the doorway to her bedroom. She was curled up in a ball with her arms wrapped tightly around a pillow, sound asleep.

He should have been here with her, but he didn't want her to feel he didn't trust she could handle things on her own. She needed to gain her own inner strength and if someone was always there to pick up the pieces, she never would get that. He hoped she understood. Bryan would have been hovering over her, arms outstretched to catch her when she fell. But he wasn't Bryan.

Jack went to his car and retrieved his cell phone and called Bryan. "Hey, got your message. What do you need?"

"You left her all alone?" Bryan asked irritated.

"She asked to be left alone to give her some space to go through her children's things. I gave her what she needed. I wasn't far from her. What's your problem?"

"You left her alone to do something you knew would put her in a fragile state and then the unsub calls her. I trusted you to keep her safe. This not what I call fulfilling that duty," Bryan chewed his ass.

Jack felt the anger rising in him. "First of all, I don't consider what I am doing here with Maddy a duty. Maddy is by far stronger than you give her credit for and if you would get off your knight in shining armor soap box you would see that. She is not weak. Every day that goes by she gets stronger and more independent.

For the first time in her life she is coming into her own. It's the way it should be. Now what's the deal with the phone call? What happened?"

Bryan remained silent for a few moments. "You haven't asked her?"

"She's asleep and I'm not waking her."

"He called her to see how she was doing. He was concerned for her. Ironic don't you think?" Bryan asked coolly.

"Listen Bryan, I don't know what bug crawled up your ass, but get off mine. Something happened between you and Maddy this morning that left you two somehow at odds, but it's got nothing to do with me. What is happening between the two of you is your problem. The only thing that matters to me is how it affects Maddy. She doesn't want my help with this, and I respect her decision. But just because things might not be going to your master plan, don't punish Maddy for it. She doesn't deserve it."

"You're right Jack," Bryan told him darkly. "Maddy doesn't need me. It's been me that's fucked up everything for her, as always. I'm done...I'm finished with her. She is free to live her life on her own. Congratulations Jack, she's all yours." The line went dead.

Jack slid his phone in his pocket. What the hell was going on? How could he just walk away from her? How can one day you say you love someone more than life it's self and the next cut them off? Was Maddy aware of this turn of events? Yes, he wanted Maddy to himself, but not like this.

Jack quietly crept into Maddy's bedroom, slipped off his shoes in laid down on the bed with her. She was facing him, her breathing shallow and steady. Oh, Maddy, how many more dragons do you have to slay before you're free? He wanted to reach out and brush the hair from her face but he knew that would awaken her and he want her to stay asleep. At least she was a peace this way. He decided to leave her to rest.

"Where are you going?" Maddy asked him softly as he rose from the bed.

Jack sat back down on the bed. "I was leaving you so you could get some more rest."

"Don't" she stretched out her arms to him.

He slid next to her and wrapped his arms around her. "Anything you say Kitten." He held her close.

Maddy picked up on a strange vibe from him. "You going to tell me what's up?"

"I don't want to hurt you." He kissed the top of her head.

She smiled weakly at him. "Partners remember? No secrets."

Jack took a deep breath. "I called Bryan back. He was acting strangely and I still don't understand why, but you do." Jack looked away from her.

She took her hand and made him look at her. "Go ahead, you can tell me. What did he say?"

"He said that he fucked up your life like he always has and that he wouldn't be doing it anymore, that he was done. That he wouldn't be part of your life anymore. I'm sorry Kitten. I'm sure he didn't mean it." He searched her face expecting to seen pain there, but saw none. She just averted his gaze.

Maddy lie back on the bed. "No, I'm sure he meant it. Lonnie more or less told him he was the one who initiated the chain of events that ultimately led to my breakdown and put me at risk with this investigation...and he and I can't dispute the facts she put in front of us. I know he feels this overwhelming sense of guilt and believes the best thing he can do for me is cut himself out of my life. Just like he has in the past." He did it again, made this decision on his own without discussing what she wanted, always thinking he knows what's best for her. And once again, didn't have the balls to tell her.

"Just like that? How can you have what you two have and just end it like that?" Jack asked.

Maddy rolled away from him. "I don't care anymore. I'm done."

Jack watched her feeling helpless as to what to do. He was so confused as to what was going on with these two. "Maddy look at me...please?"

Maddy turned to him, propping her head up with her elbow. She studied his face seeing the confusion and worry crease his brow. She reached out and stroked his face with the back of her hand. "Things happen in life that changes the course of our lives. Because of Bryan's selfishness, he changed the course of mine, like he has so many times before. He does it under the guise of love. Life was a game to him, a conquest. I was his favorite one. However things changed this time, he realized his own mortality, realized you can't go back and repair the damage just by saying you're sorry. Does he love me? Yeah, I believe he does, with all his heart... still. Do I love him, yes with all my heart...but I can't forget and forgive the past. I know that now. He unconsciously used my fear of the past to bring me back to him. I don't know that when this is all over I won't hate him for doing what he did. I believe he knows it too, a major indicator by the way his behavior has changed, the cockiness gone, his fire...it's all gone. In his desparation and alcoholic influence he raped me to try to gain control back. It failed."

Jack sat up in the bed, angry, "He raped you? When? No, don't tell me. The same damn night he put those bruises on your arms. Son of bitch! Damn it, Maddy, why didn't you tell me?"

"I told you he hurt me. It was all you really needed to know. He didn't even know what the hell he did," Maddy tried to explain her reasoning for not telling him.

"Are you fucking making excuses for him Maddy? And you forgave him so easily, wanted to start all over, make things right..." Jack got up off the bed. "Your therapist is right. You two have one fucking sick relationship!" He stormed out of the room. Maddy heard the kitchen door slam.

Maddy sat on the edge of her bed fear sinking in. Jesus what did Jack really think of her? Maybe now he was realizing she wasn't the woman he thought she was. Loosing Bryan...that didn't seem to matter anymore, but loosing Jack, she didn't think she could live with that. An omission is as bad as a lie, Jack always says to her and she was sure this is how he would see this.

Maddy went to the kitchen and saw Jack sitting on the steps smoking a cigarette. She could tell by the rigidity of his body he was still very angry. God what had she done? She quietly opened the door and sat down beside him. He refused to look at her.

"I'm sorry I'm not the woman you thought I was," she said shakily. "I'm sorry I'm not the one...my love for you is real, but maybe it's not enough."

Jack glanced at her and turned away. "I'm just pissed right now, Maddy. Me being pissed at you doesn't lessen my feelings for you okay? I just don't understand why you didn't trust me enough to tell me. I don't understand your warped way of thinking—that everything could all be made better, to still want to be with him after what he did to you. It's not normal Maddy. But why should that not surprise me? Nothing about your relationship with that man has ever been normal."

Maddy pondered what he was telling her, trying to formulate answers for him, but really didn't know quite what to say. "I haven't been able to be with him. I've tried to fix things because I didn't want to admit they couldn't be fixed. At the time, emotionally, I still needed him. It wasn't until today, until it was put in front of me in black and white I finally saw what reality is." Her voice was but a whisper. "And he saw it too..."

Jack flicked his cigarette, put his head in his hands and shook it.

A tear slid down Maddy's cheek, "Have I lost you, Jack?"

Jack turned to her, saw her tears. "Oh Maddy," he put his arms around her and pulled her close. "You haven't lost me. Christ, if you think our love is so weak you got a lot to learn. We're together because we want to be. I didn't manipulate you into being with me. I didn't lie to you. I'm not your protector, Maddy...I'm your partner. We share things, we don't hold out on one another. You understand? This is how it's got to be. Promise me."

Maddy buried her face in his chest, "I promise. No more secrets."

21

Maddy returned to work Friday afternoon after her last therapy session. The last couple of days had been an eye opener for her. It was time to take her life back. No more running, no more protectors. Despite Jack's insistence she ride with him, she took her own car.

She hadn't spoken to Bryan in two days. They were done. She didn't know how she would react when she finally saw him face to face. She was angry with him, very angry. Deep down she knew things would end when this was all over, but this wasn't how she thought it would be. At least the last time he did this to her she didn't have to see him again.

She poked her head into Jack's office on her way to the squad room. "Hey, hon," she smiled at him nervously.

"Hey Kitten," he smiled and stood up. When she came in he hugged her and gave her a kiss. "You sure you want to do this? It could wait until Monday."

Maddy pulled away from him and shut his door. "We need to talk." She sat in the chair in front of his desk.

Jack took his place behind his desk. "Okay hon. This sounds pretty serious."

Maddy smiled weakly, "Yeah, it is. I am telling you this just because I want you to be the first to hear it and hear from me. I didn't come here to return to work. I came to turn in my badge and gun."

Jack sat back in his chair and stared at her. "How come we haven't discussed this? I'm not saying its good or bad, I'm just wondering why you didn't talk to me about it first."

Maddy met his gaze. "Because I didn't know it until after I finished therapy today. You, as well as anybody, know my joy in working stems from my natural curiosity of why things are they way they are and if they're not, then why not. This case is an obsession, but not for me, it has become me. I don't want it anymore."

Jack pressed his fingers together, openly studying her. "Okay, I'm following. What are you going to do? Return to the Journal?"

"No, net yet. I'm going to Houston. I can't stay here where the unsub can make contact with me. I'm not going to be his puppet anymore, and I am not staying in protective custody anymore." She reached across the desk for his hand, "Not that I don't love being with you because I do, I just don't want to do it this way. Do you understand?"

He brought her hand to his lips, "Yes I understand, but can I ask you something?"

"Sure."

"Are you doing this to run away from Bryan?"

"Maybe a little. But mostly it's for me. I have to find me, away from all this. I can't do it with this case hanging over my head. If I stay here, even going back to the paper, it will still be there. If you want to say I am running away from this case, that would be a fair assumption."

"When will you leave for Houston?"

"First flight I can catch out of here."

"Part of me wishes you could wait until tomorrow so we could spend one more night together, but I do understand, Maddy." He rubbed his chin, "But you know something Maddy, as much as I am going to miss you, I think I will feel more comfortable having you away from this, knowing you are safe."

Maddy stood up and Jack came around the desk, pulled her into his arms and kissed her, exploring her deeply. She ran her fingers through his hair pulling his head closer to her. "I am going to miss you to baby, so very, very much. I promise I will call you at a minimum of once a day. If things string out too long, can you fly down for a couple of days?"

He kissed her softly on the lips, "In a heart beat, Kitten. You want me to go in there with you?"

She shook her head, "No, I need to do this alone." She turned and she left.

When she arrived in the squad room, Bryan was nowhere to be found. Good, it made it even easier yet. She took her badge, her gun and holster, and its clip and laid it on his desk. He would know what it meant.

Maddy went to her desk, emptied what personal belongings that were there into her bag, and grabbed her laptop. As she got up to leave, Vanessa's photo on the board caught her attention. Vanessa, the one vic she had any connection with. How long would it go before her killer would be behind bars? She felt a pang of sadness and an overwhelming sense of guilt. She couldn't do it. She couldn't leave Vanessa's killer to walk free when she could possibly be the only chance of finding him.

Maddy turned from the board just as Bryan was walking in, Jack right behind him. Maddy reached for her badge and hooked it on her belt. Then reached for her gun.

"Maddy? What are you doing?" Bryan asked in surprise.

"I was going to quit, but I changed my mind, not because of you or anyone in this squad, but because of her." She threw her head back back in the direction of Vanessa's photo.

"You're still going to be working with me, you do realize that don't you? Even after everything that has transpired. Aren't you concerned?" Bryan asked her in all seriousness.

Jack stood back, watching to see how Maddy would react. Was she truly giving up on Bryan?

Maddy picked up her holster and ran it through her belt. She picked her gun up and the clip. Her eyes met Bryan's. There was a moment of sadness in them and then it was as if a wall went up around her. "You have fucked me so many times.

Your answer to fixing things is just to cut me off. But do your best to break me, Bryan. You can't break what has already been broken. Our relationship has been like a baseball game—we've had some good innings, we've had some bad, but when it all come down the ninth inning..." Maddy locked the clip into her gun making a metallic click, "three strikes and you're out!" She turned and left the room.

Jack was suppressing a laugh when Bryan turned to him.

"Where was she going? Was she really going to quit?" he asked Jack.

"She was going to Houston until this was all over. She didn't want to be part of it anymore. She said she needed to save herself and this was the only way she could do it. But evidently something changed her mind," Jack told him.

"Pity, it probably would have been the best thing for her," Bryan said as he picked up a file and thumbed through it.

Jack raised his eyebrow. "Best for her or best for you?"

Bryan met Jack's gaze. "I only want what's best for Maddy, I always have."

"And that's why you chose just to shut her down without a second thought right? Because *you* felt it was what was best for her? I would have thought after what you two meant to each other she deserved so much more from you."

"I would have thought you would be happy about all this. It gives you an unhindered shot at Maddy," Bryan said nonchalantly.

"First of all, I've never had to scheme to get Maddy. I honestly waited for her to make that decision on her own. Maddy is not with me by default. I was more than willing to let her make her own choices. Now if you will excuse me, I have work to do." Jack turned on his heal and left the room.

Maddy had gone into Jack's office, sat in a chair and grabbed a couple of newspapers. She was scanning the obits when she noticed a couple of their vics' obits were in a couple of different issues. She scanned through them learning little tid-bits of their lives. She looked for any reoccurring information. It was there in black and white. Trinity 1st Reform Church. Then it dawned on her, the last call Vanessa Granger had made on that fateful Tuesday was indeed, Trinity 1st Reform Church. She had found her unsub.

When Jack eventually came back to his office he was fuming. She assumed he had words with Bryan. She didn't want to know the details. She jumped when he came in and kicked his chair. "Fucking son of a bitch," he growled.

Maddy laughed, "You don't have to say a word." She looked up at him. "What do you say, you, me and Andy go do a little surveillance?"

Jack sat down and looked at her, "What do ya got?"

"A sneaking hunch. We need a vehicle that we can go unnoticed in. The unsub knows your car, we sure as hell are not going to take mine, and how could you miss one of the FBI vehicles? Might as well be waving a red flag on that one." Maddy was excited. She really felt like she was onto something.

Jack smiled at her enthusiasm. He loved it when she got animated about what she was doing. "Are we going to fill Bryan in on this? He is after all our CO."

"Fuck him," she said with a wave of her hand. "He doesn't know how to run the show anyhow. Besides given his attitude towards me at the moment he would probably shoot any idea I have down. Besides it's nothing concrete, just a hunch, like I said."

Jack rocked back on his chair watching her. "We still have to tell him something. We can't just disappear. Work with me here Kitten, by the book remember?"

Maddy chewed on her lip, "Well hell, help me think of something. I don't want to tell him what we're really doing."

"Why?" Jack grinned. This sounded like something she would pull on him.

"Cuz I don't want to, isn't that a good enough reason?" She batted her eyelashes at him. "Pleeeeeeease?"

Jack laughed, "That shit don't work on me and you know it. Give me a minute. Let me see what kind of rabbit I can pull out of my hat."

As he stood up to walk by her, Maddy grabbed his hand. "You do this and I will show you a trick or two," she winked.

He laughed and gave her hair a tug, "I am going to hold you to that." He turned and left the room.

Jack found Bryan sitting at his desk talking on his cell phone. It was obviously a personal call, and from what Jack could infer, it was a woman. The last words he said into the phone were "I love you too, I will see you soon."

Christ, Jack thought, that didn't take him long to move on. Anyhow, that's not what he was there for.

Bryan looked up at Jack expectantly. "Something I can help you with?"

"I need to grab Andy and go check out some possible leads," Jack said quickly hoping he could pass it by him while he was still preoccupied.

"What leads?"

Shit. "I want to go check out a few protestant churches taking Maddy with us so she might be able to make an ID." It wasn't a lie was it?

"Do you think it's wise taking her with you?" Bryan asked, not blinking as he looked at Jack from behind his desk.

"Maddy is the key to this whole case. She is the only one who has ever seen this guy. For Christ sake Mayland, let her do her fucking job!" he snapped.

"So we are back to this now?"

"What?"

"Last names."

Jack gave a deep sigh and ran his fingers through his hair, "When you do right by Maddy, things will be cool with us, but until that happens, I just work under you. Now are you going to let us do our job or what?"

"Keep me posted, none of this going off half cocked shit of Maddy's. Do you understand?" This whole thing reeked of Maddy, Bryan thought. He wished he knew what she was thinking. He was half tempted to tail them just to see what they were really up to.

"Will do. Thank you." Jack went to retrieve Andy.

Jack went to the motor pool and signed out an unmarked police car. With Jack driving, Maddy riding shotgun and Andy in the back, Maddy gave Jack an address.

The church was on the west side of town in a lower end neighborhood. It was an older brick building, not so churchy looking. It looked more like it had been a store in its previous life. The only real defining churchlike quality was a wooden cross above its threshold. They parked across the street. The place seemed pretty quiet.

"What are we hoping to see here?" Andy asked.

"Okay, I will let you both in on what I know. Stewart and Mitchell both belonged to this church," Maddy started to say.

"How do you know? We didn't get that from the families." Jack asked. It still baffled him where in the hell she came up with some of her information. Her sources were less than orthodox.

"Best source in town, I read it in the paper," she tossed two newspapers at him opened to the obit page with the churches circled in red. "And I happened to know for fact the last call Vanessa Granger made was to this church."

"When did you figure this out?" Jack said as he scanned the papers.

"While I was sitting in your office a little while ago," she replied smugly.

"So shouldn't we go in there and check it out?" asked Andy.

"Can't. He knows what Jack and I look like from the other night, and possibly you too," she explained to Andy. "And even if he didn't notice you, you reek of FBI."

"So now what?" Andy stretched his arms.

"We sit and we wait," Jack was reading an article in one of the papers. "Welcome to the joys of police work."

And so they sat, watched, and waited. Andy was sprawled out in the back seat. After reading the papers from cover to cover Jack mused his time making phone calls. Maddy had pulled her hair up on top of her head and was sporting a pair of sunglasses. The ultimate undercover agent, Maddy laughed to herself. Minutes turned to hours.

Maddy caught movement out of the corner of her eye. People were starting to filter into the church. She looked at her watch. 5:15. Damn they had been here for a while. Maddy perked up in her seat and watched as folks entered the church. One guy in particular caught her eye. He was dark haired, built the same as the guy she saw at the scene, but she couldn't see his face. She had to see his eyes to make sure; the eyes...there would be no mistaking the eyes.

Maddy backhandedly smacked Jack's arm. "Look...look, that guy there." She pointed to the man dressed in black slacks and a light blue shirt.

Andy shot up in the backseat, "What...where?"

"Is it him?" Jack leaned over to get a better view.

"I think so, but I can't be sure without seeing his eyes," Maddy had her hand on the door handle.

Jack grabbed her and pulled her back. "Oh no you don't. You're not stepping one foot in that church, especially with him in it."

"How we going to know then?" she asked.

"I could go in," Andy offered.

Maddy frowned, "You would stick out like a sore thumb. Besides, if those people happen to be his flock, he would know you're not one of them. Damn it. I need my camera." She turned to Jack. "How fast can you get me to the paper and get back here?"

Jack laughed as he started the car, "Let's play cops and robbers!" Jack waited until they were at least a block away from the church, flipped on the lights. He gunned the vehicle through the traffic until they made it to the Journal. He pulled up front and let Maddy out to retrieve her camera.

"Holy shit, Jack," Andy was laughing. "I feel like a damn pinball!"

Jack turned to him and chuckled, "That's why we always wear seatbelts."

"Yeah right. Now this is the best police work I've gotten to do since I got here," Andy's eyes were aglow with excitement.

Maddy came flying out of the building with a large camera bag in tow. "Okay, let's blow this joint and get back to the church before they let out."

As Jack drove back through the city Maddy pulled out her Nikon camera and changed the lens to a zoom lens. "Let's just hope they get out before dark, I don't have a night lens."

Jack pulled the car across from the church but in a few parking spaces down. Not only would it not look so obvious, but it would also give Maddy a better angle for pictures.

They had to wait 45 minutes before the group began to break up. Maddy rolled her window up leaving just enough room to get the camera lens out.

"Why are you doing that?" Andy asked.

"It won't be so obvious she's taking pictures," Jack explained. "Roll yours up, too."

"Here he comes," Andy said excitedly.

Maddy zoomed the lens in on the man's face. When she focused the camera in on him, she involuntarily gasped. It was him, it was definitely him. She took several shots of the unsub. "Okay, lets get the hell out of here."

Jack put the car in gear. "Well?"

"It's him," she said quietly.

"Shouldn't we go pick him up?" Andy asked from the backseat.

"On what grounds?" Jack asked. He reached across the seat and took Maddy's hand and squeezed it. She looked over at him and weakly smiled.

"Maddy ID'd him."

"It's not enough. She ID's him based on someone she saw at the gravesite the other night. For all she knows he could have been a CSU guy. Now is where our investigative work comes in, Andy. We got to find out who this guy is, get a background on him. We need to get just cause to bring him in for questioning."

Maddy turned back to Andy, "Right now we have no probable cause. We have absolutely nothing linking him to these crimes. No witnesses, no forensics, nothing."

"When do you get the film developed?" Andy asked.

Jack and Maddy looked at each other and smiled. "Andy, sweetie, nobody uses cameras with film. It's all digital." Maddy move her view screen back a few frames and then zoomed in. She handed the camera back to Andy. "That Agent Whittmer, is our unsub."

"Give me that," Jack grabbed at the camera and looked at the face on the screen. "I remember him...I'll be damn the son of a bitch was right in front of us on more than one occasion that night."

Maddy took the camera back from him and stuck it in her camera bag. "Okay, now how much of this are we turning over to Bryan?"

Andy looked confused. "I don't understand, don't we have to report all this back to him."

"Andy, let me ask you this...do you want to go back doing grunt work like Mayland always makes you do or do you want to work this case?" Jack asked him over his shoulder as he drove.

"Work the case of course, but what's that got to do with reporting?"

"Sometimes investigating is more productive if those investigating are kept to a minimum..."

"And you don't have to answer to anyone," Maddy added.

Jack raised his eyebrow, "Anyone Maddy?"

She grinned sheepishly, "Well you know what I mean." She looked back at Andy, "First we get our ducks in a row, get our facts straight and know for sure what the hell we're talking about and then we go to the *boss*. The question for you Andy, can you look into Mayland's eyes and lie to him?"

"Maddy!" Jack jumped her. He turned to Andy, "You don't lie, you just don't exactly tell the whole truth. The closer you can keep to the truth the safer you will be."

Maddy threw her head back and laughed. "Mr. An Omission is as bad as Lie. You are so full of shit."

"Okay," Jack said to the kid in the back seat, "Can you keep a straight face with Mayland without giving up the gig?"

"Gig?" Maddy snickered.

Jack reached across and smacked her arm, "Shut the fuck up, I'm trying to prep him here or we're busted."

Maddy rubbed her arm still laughing, "Listen to you, you're sinking to my level."

Jack threw his head back and laughed, "It's kind of fun."

Maddy wrinkled her nose up, "Aint it now?"

Andy leaned forward poking his head between the two of them. "I can do this. He thinks I'm stupid anyhow so he really won't notice me playing dumb."

Maddy high-fived him over the back of the seat, "That's my partner!"

"Okay now, here's the game plan," Maddy laid it out for them. "We went to two churches, actually one, but we went there twice, but that's beside the point. We parked in front of a church twice. We spent several boring hours waiting and watching. What we saw was people coming and going. We saw nothing remarkable, all and all it was a bust." She looked at Andy, "You got that?"

"What if he asks which churches?"

Maddy and Jack exchanged looks. Smart kid, they didn't think of that. "Andy, flip through the newspaper back there. There should be a church directory in there. Find two protestant churches somewhat close together." Andy named two off. "Okay now we all have to commit them to memory. Everyone got it?"

It was after 8:30 before they returned back to the cop shop. Jack signed the car back in and the three of them went up stairs. Andy went ahead to the squad room and Maddy lingered in Jack's office. She didn't want to risk seeing Bryan. Despite her vow she was done with him it still hurt like hell seeing him and the way he looked at her with no feeling.

Jack picked up on Maddy's pain and took her in his arms. "I know it hurts, Kitten. And it's so wrong for him to do this to you. I'm sorry." He kissed the top of her head.

Maddy buried her face in his chest, "I love the way you sense my feelings... you always seem to know." She then looked up at him and traced his lips with her fingers.

Jack kissed each of her fingertips and then sucked one inside his mouth. He then kissed her wrist and worked his way up to her face. By the time his mouth reached her lips she felt like she had been waiting an eternity. His mouth covered hers, his tongue deeply exploring her. Maddy's arms went up around his neck and she pressed her body into his. Jack's hand slid up to cup Maddy's breast and caressed her. Her heart stopped for a brief second. She involuntarily made a purring sound.

Jack pulled his head back slightly and whispered in her ear, "That's my Kitten," and then took her mouth hungrily. Maddy ran her hand up his inner thigh and stifled a laugh when Jack jumped. She continued to touch him inching closer and closer to him until he let out a deep groan.

She moved her lips to his ear, "We need to go home...and fast," her voice was deep and husky with desire.

Maddy grabbed her bag and the camera bag and waited for Jack to lock up his office. He grabbed her by the hand and led her out of the station.

He led her to her car, ran his hand through her hair and kissed her slowly and tenderly. "Hurry and get home, no tickets." He kissed her again and then went to his car.

Bryan stood back away from Jack's door and witnessed the very heated, passionate exchange between Maddy and Jack. She had melted into his arms like butter. Bryan had lost her. She was Jack's 100%. But wasn't that what he had wanted?

Maddy pulled into the open garage a couple of minutes behind Jack. He was waiting just inside the door, swooped her up and threw her over his shoulder. Maddy squealed and laughed. He took her upstairs and threw her down on the bed. Their hands were in a flurry unbuttoning each other's shirts. Maddy slid off her blue jeans and as Jack removed his slacks. Maddy stared at him and smiled. "Damn, you held on to that that long?"

"Shut up," he laughed and lowered himself down on her and took her mouth hungrily. Maddy wrapped her legs around his hips and arched her body into his. There was no foreplay—they had done plenty of that at the station. Maddy groaned softly as he pushed himself into her lighting the fires within her. Her body rocked with him as he moved within her. Her arms clung to his neck. His mouth left hers and kissed a trail down to her breast. Maddy screamed out as he took one into his mouth and bit gently on it. She laced her fingers in his hair, whimpering as he made love to her. As his rhythm increased he returned his mouth to hers taking her so completely she couldn't breathe. With a driving force he pushed her beyond what she could endure and they exploded together.

He lowered himself down beside her and pulled her into his arms. Their damp bodies felt cool against each other. He kissed her behind the ear as he nuzzled her. "Sorry, I couldn't stand it anymore."

Maddy took his hand and held it to her heart and still trying to catch her breath. "Don't be sorry, just because it's hot sex doesn't mean we're still not making love."

He rolled her over on top of him and kissed her, his tongue once again seeking her. His hands slid up and down her naked body sending shivers through her. He rolled her on to her back, his lips never leaving her. His hand slipped between her legs and ran up her inner thigh, touching her, exploring her. He shifted his body so one hand could tease her while the other cupped her breast massaging them. Maddy's body was quivering beneath his touch. She could feel his hardness against her leg. Her hand sought him out, touching the velvety hardness. She heard a deep groan within him and smiled to herself. Jack pulled her up and lifted her on top of him, slowly guiding her onto him. This time when they made love, it was slow and easy as they gazed into each other's eyes. Maddy controlled the rhythm. She let it linger as long as they could stand it before Jack took over pushing her until they climaxed together.

Maddy slumped against him breathing heavily, "Damn.... I love you..."

Jack chucked, also trying to catch his breath. "I love you, Kitten."

Jack's phone went off in his pants pocket. "Damn it, why is it every time we make love that damn phone goes off." Jack leaned off the side of the bed and snatched his pants from the floor. When he dug out his phone he looked at his caller ID. It was a phone number he didn't recognize. "Parker."

"Hi Jack, this is Andy. Since it's Friday night a bunch of us are going down to the bar. We were wondering if you and Maddy would like to come down for a little while."

Jack glanced over at Maddy who was giving him a questioning look. "Did you guys invite Mayland?"

"Not that I'm aware of," Andy said.

"Tell you what Andy, let me talk it over with Maddy and I will call you back. I'm not sure how safe it would be for her to go." He shut his phone and threw it on the bed beside him.

"Andy wants us to come down to the bar far awhile. He said he didn't think anyone invited Bryan. He's not the most popular guy in the bunch," Jack laughed. "Anyhow, what do you think? Do you feel safe enough to be out in public?"

Maddy thought for few moments. It had been awhile since they had been out, before her break, and she had been under lock and key for so long getting out would do her good. "It wouldn't hurt for a little while, I guess. I need to take a quick shower."

"You don't want to go home tonight?" Jack asked as he brushed the hair from her eyes.

Maddy caressed his cheek, "Home is where you are, baby."

Jack leaned in and kissed her tenderly. "That's a sweet thing to say Kitten."

Maddy slipped off the bed and took her shower. Clothed in just a towel she ran out to her car and grabbed two of her suitcases that she had planned on taking to Houston.

Jack was in the kitchen and took them from her to carry them up to the bedroom. "Does this mean you're moving in?" he said half joking, half serious."

She cocked her head slightly, "Would you want me to? We've only really been together a week."

Jack considered the possibility. He never had anyone live with him, never had the desire to. "If I were to say yes, would you be willing to make that kind of commitment?"

Maddy searched his face, "Maybe. It would take a lot of consideration."

Jack smiled weakly, "You would have to consider whether or not you could make thay kind of commitment to me?"

Maddy laughed, "No idiot. What would I do with my place? My horses? It's not just something we could do at a drop of a hat."

Jack set down her bags and took her hands in his, "But are you ready to commit to me?"

Maddy leaned in and kissed him softly, "Yes, I believe I already am."

Jack surprised her by picking her up and swinging her around letting out a holler. He finally set her down and kissed her deeply.

Maddy's towel had started to slip. "Hold on there, cowboy, I'm loosing it here," she laughed. She looked at how he was dressed. He stood before her in nothing on but boxer shorts. She cracked a smile. "You going dressed like that?"

Jack struck a model pose, "Don't you think I'm sexy?"

She pushed her body into his, "Very sexy, but I'm not sharing you with the world." She ran her hands over his naked chest kissing it down the center. "Go take your shower before we end up in bed again."

Jack chuckled, "It would only take one phone call and we could make it happen."

Maddy gave him a look. "Okay, okay," he laughed. "Give me 15 minutes." He grabbed her bags, dropped them off into the bedroom and left to take a shower.

Maddy opened her bag and decided to hang up her clothing and put them in drawers. Moving in with Jack...wow. They had come a long way in two weeks. Were they rushing things? Well it wasn't like she was really moving in, kind of like part time.

Maddy slipped on a pair of black leggings and a cream-colored long tunic, low cut, very low cut. She brushed her hair out and scrunched it up with her fingers give her curls the most volume. She took out her makeup bag, dusted her face lightly with mineral powder, applied just a whisper of blush, copper colored eye shadow, mascara, and just a hint of lipstick. She studied herself in the mirror and was pleased with the results.

Jack slipped in behind and pulled out a pair of blue jeans and a polo shirt and slipped them on.

He looked at Maddy studying herself in the mirror. He kissed her on the top of her hair. "You look beautiful, but you are missing something. Wait here." He disappeared briefly and came in with a blue jewelry box. "Close your eyes."

Maddy closed her eyes. She felt Jack's hand go over the top of her head then felt the feel of a fine chain around her neck. Jack fumbled with the clasp then kissed her hair. "Okay, open them."

Maddy opened her eyes to find a beautiful emerald pendent surround by a cluster of diamonds. The chain was a very fine thread of silver. "On my God," Maddy gasped as she brought her hand to her throat. "Jack, it's beautiful. When? Why?"

Jack placed his hands on her shoulders and kissed the side of her face from behind. "This morning, and just because. I don't need a reason to buy you gifts."

Maddy turned in his arms, "Do you realize this is the first time we have gone out as a couple?"

"Are you worried about what the others will think?"

"Not your men. I think they know this has been coming for a while. However, the others...not so much. They are used to seeing me with Bryan. They will probably think I'm a slut." Maddy said quietly.

"Kitten, you are not a slut. Don't even go there. We belong together, no matter what others think about it. Just let it go and let's have some fun. You ready to go?" he asked.

When Maddy and Jack arrived at the bar it was almost 9:30 and the party was well underway in the dance area of the bar. Maddy had to laugh when she saw several of the girls from the office there as well. What she didn't expect was seeing Bryan seated among them, at his side was a dark haired woman. Maddy stood back for a moment so she could study the woman. There was something oddly familiar about her. Then Maddy heard her speak. She knew that voice...Donna. What the hell was she doing here? Damn it, it sure didn't take Bryan long to hightail it back to his old life. And to bring her up here? What the fuck? She had never met Donna in real life and had only seen pictures of her. The pictures must have been old because this woman looked considerably older than she remembered. Donna had never seen what Maddy looked like, not even a photo.

Maddy pulled Jack over and whispered in his ear, "That's the mistress, Bryan's mistress, from Virginia."

Jack looked at the woman and then looked at Maddy. "You okay with this, Kitten? If not we can go, it's no big deal."

Maddy shrugged her shoulders, "No, I'm okay with it. It's his life. Besides, she's the outcast." She waved her arm in the direction of the other woman, "These women are my friends, my co-workers." Maddy smiled up at him. "I have the power to make her feel uncomfortable, not the other way around."

Andy caught a glimpse of them and called them over. Jack led her over to a couple of chairs near Andy and Miranda. Maddy smiled a greeting to Miranda as she sat down in the chair Jack held for her. Jack disappeared for a moment and returned with a beer for him and vodka sour for her.

"Man you should see Maddy," Andy was telling Miranda. He was all animated, his eyes gleaming. "She's amazing." He was pretty well on his way to being drunk.

At the mention of her name, Donna looked in her direction. Maddy could feel her eyes on her.

Maddy kept her focus on Andy and Miranda. "Andy, you're exaggerating."

"No, I'm not. She profiled our unsub, found evidence forensics missed, she even got to talk..."

"Andy!" Jack cut him short and shook his head, "No more. Some things need to be left in the office."

"Yes, yes of course. I'm sorry," Andy apologized to Maddy. "She's just so cool to work with," he told Miranda.

Miranda laughed, "Andy, I have worked with Maddy for the last two years. I could tell you stories about her that would make your toes curl. But then you could ask Jack about all them since he was involved in them." She turned to Maddy nodding toward Jack, "So are you two finally a couple?"

Maddy looked up at Jack, smiled proudly and nodded, "Yep."

Jack leaned over, kissed her and squeezed her hand, "Definitely."

Miranda clinked a fork against her glass to get everyone's attention. "To Jack and Maddy, together at last. About fucking time!" The girls from the paper cheered and the Jack's guys rose their glasses.

Maddy glanced covertly at Bryan. His eyes were on her, watching. She couldn't tell what was running through his mind because it was almost as if he were wearing a mask hiding all that could be revealed from beneath it. Donna was watching her with great curiosity. It took everything that Maddy had not to flip her off.

Andy asked Miranda if she wanted to dance. Maddy had to smile. She never would have taken him for dancer material. But between being smitten with Miranda and having consumed several drinks, he was up for anything.

Jack left the table momentarily and then returned and whispered, "The next song is for us."

When the last song was winding down, Jack pulled Maddy to her feet and led her to the dance floor just as Pink's song *Glitter in the Wind* came on. Maddy smiled brightly up at him. Jack ran his hands down her arms and guided them up around his neck. He pulled her as close to him as he could and wrapped his arms tightly around her waist. Maddy rested her head on his chest as they swayed to the music. When the refrain of song played, Maddy pulled his head down and sang the words into his ear. Jack cupped her face in his hands; his mouth came down on hers possessively kissing her. When he was finished it left her breathless. She laid her head back down on his chest and he rested his head on the top of hers, burying his face in her hair.

Bryan watched them as he downed one of many beers. That used to be them, except they had never quite been like the couple on the dance floor. Maddy responded to Jack in ways she never responded to him. Bryan always had the need to possess her, to make everyone know she belong to him. With Jack, Maddy was there of her own free will, just like Jack had told Bryan that afternoon. Jack knew who Maddy really is, intimately. He only knew who she was.

Donna leaned over and said softly to Bryan, "So that's the notorious Maddy. She's prettier than I thought she would be...and younger. Too young for you."

Bryan looked at her. "She's beautiful, smart, funny, witty and not too young for me."

"And belongs to that guy," Donna said scornfully.

"Only because I allow it," Bryan sneered as he poured himself another beer and downed it.

The song that was playing was just getting over. Bryan stood up and stumbled to the dance floor. He held his hand out to Maddy for the next dance.

Maddy was surprised and looked nervously at Jack.

"It's your choice Kitten, I will be right here."

Maddy shrugged her shoulders and turned to Bryan. Bryan pulled her aggressively to him, his hands running over her body. "Bryan stop, you want to dance, we'll dance. But that's it. For Christ's sake, Donna is sitting right over there. How do you think you are making her feel?" She felt uncomfortable in his arms. He was drunk, the possessive, the controlling Bryan in charge.

"She knows I'm still in love with you, I will always be in love with you. Can you say the same?" he growled in her ear.

Jack watched from the table. He could clearly see Maddy's discomfort, felt his temper rising at the way Bryan was touching Maddy. He would give her a chance to handle him, but if he got out of line, he swore he would pound Mayland.

Maddy could smell then intense odor of beer and cigarettes coming from his breath when his mouth was just inches from her. "You're not kissing me," she said softly.

"You know you want me to, you want me to take you back to the motel and make you mine again, Minnie" he held her face in his hands.

Maddy tried pulling back, "Bryan, don't do this. Haven't you done enough already?"

He put his mouth next to her ear, kissed her neck, feeling Maddy flinch under his touch. He became angry. She was fighting him. "Does Jack make you scream, Maddy, does he touch you until your body sings to him..."Then a low tone he asked her, "When Jack fucks you, do you scream when you cum?"

Maddy pulled back sharply, doubled up her fist and let him have it right across his nose. "You sick fuck! Get the fuck away from me!"

The next thing she knew Jack was holding her back. Maddy was holding her hand close to her with her other hand, "Damn it, son of a bitch...fuck that hurts!"

Jack was caught between laughing his ass off and the desire to go finish what Maddy started. Bryan's girlfriend was leading him back to the table, blood spewing from his nose. Way to go Maddy! Jack led her back to their seats.

The waiter brought two bar towels filled with crushed ice. He handed one to Donna, which she held to Bryan's nose. He brought the other to Maddy. He bent down between Jack and her and said softly, "Nice right hook." Jack burst out laughing.

"You've always been such a bitch, Maddy," Donna hissed from across the table.

Maddy looked at her coolly. "If you would learn to keep him on a shorter leash, maybe he wouldn't get into so much trouble."

Donna turned to Bryan, "Can't you have her arrested for assaulting a peace officer?"

Bryan chuckled from beneath his bright red spotted towel. "She is a peace officer."

"Jesus Christ, Bryan, can't you do something?" she screeched.

Bryan turned to Donna, lowering the towel. "Would you shut the fuck up? I got everything I deserved." He looked up to Maddy and Jack, "My apologies to the two of you. I was completely out of line."

"No shit!" Maddy snapped practically coming up out of her chair. Jack pulled her back down by her waist. "You're not suppose to be drinking like that, you dumb shit. What the hell do you think you're doing?" she screamed at Bryan.

"What do you care?" he asked her point blank.

Maddy stared at him incredulously and then shook her head. "Whatever...I am not going to dignify that with an answer. All of this...all this is by your own hand. No one told you you had to turn into this self-defeating moron, forever playing the great protector, deciding what is right for me, deciding what's best for me. Who the hell do you think you are? I told you before, I'm big girl, and I can damn well take care of myself. Do I need you anymore? No I don't need you. The only person I need is myself, and you can't handle it. But you know something Bryan, it is your problem not mine so own it!" Wow, that was a lot more than she had planned on saying. She was shaking she was so angry.

She felt Jack's hand rubbing her arm gently. "Kitten, you need to calm down. You are letting him get to you. Don't let him bait you. Remember with him it's all about the power."

Maddy leaned back into his arms taking several deep breaths to get herself to relax.

"Bryan, let it go. We came here to enjoy ourselves, not for you two to have a brawl. Don't you think Maddy at least deserves a little reprieve?" Jack asked quietly.

Bryan gave a silent nod, "Yes, of course."

"Come out with me so I can have smoke," Jack said in her ear.

Maddy rose up with him and he took her by the hand and led her out of the building. They took a seat on one of the benches and Jack took out a cigarette and lit it.

Maddy moved the bar towel from her knuckles. "Damn it, look I broke the skin."

Jack chuckled. "No one can say you can't hold your own, Kitten. What the hell did he say to you that pissed you off enough to deck him?"

Maddy turned to him and said in all seriousness, "He wanted to know if I scream when you make me cum."

Jack coughed on his cigarette. He threw his head back and laughed. "What did you tell him?"

Maddy smiled, "You saw what I told him."

"Maddy, Maddy, Maddy," Jack smiled. "You are definitely not an ordinary woman." He kissed her on the cheek, "One of the things I love about you."

Maddy leaned back against the wall. "The conversations we've had on these benches in the last few weeks. God has it only been weeks? Seems like months."

Jack leaned his head on her shoulder as he took a drag off his cigarette. "No shit, the last time we were here you were telling me to back off and stay in line."

Maddy kissed him on the top of his head, "Now you are in the front of the line, as a matter of fact the only one in line." She smiled, "My one and only."

"I overheard Bryan telling his chick that you are only mine because he allowed it to be. Am I?"

Maddy laughed, "His chick? And no, I chose to be with you before everything went to hell, remember? You're bedroom...me seducing you...sneaking around his back? This all coming back to you?"

Andy and Miranda came out of the bar and took a seat by them. "Jesus Maddy, I know the guys in the bullpen call you hell on wheels, but I didn't exactly know what they meant," Miranda laughed.

Jack put his hand on Maddy's shoulders and shook her gently. "They have no idea how much," he smiled. "I do."

"Am I really that bad?" Maddy asked looking at him.

"Hon, you are smart, funny, crazy and totally unpredictable," Jack told her smiling.

"But is that a bad thing?"

Jack grabbed her by her head and put her in a headlock. "No, Mads, that's what makes you who are and I wouldn't want you any other way."

Miranda sat holding a quiet Andy's hand. "I think it's so cool you two are finally together. We used to have bets around the office how long it would take."

Maddy and Jack glanced at each other and looked at Miranda, "Who won?"

"Well for one, no one knows yet that you are, and I think we all gave up," she laughed.

Miranda leaned back against Andy. He shyly kissed her on her cheek. "Jack, do you think, that when this case is completed, if I resigned from the FBI, could I get on with your squad? I have really gotten to like being here. And you two know how badly I suck at being an agent."

Maddy and Jack laughed. "Sweetie, you haven't even given yourself a chance," Maddy told him.

"I've watched you and I've watched Mayland. I've seen what it can do to a person. I don't think it's for me. Besides," he turned to Miranda, "there are other considerations."

Jack grinned, "I think we could probably work something out. I'm a man short since O'Brien got demoted. I will see if we can hold off on hiring or promoting until we can free you up."

Jack turned to Maddy, "You want to spar some more or are you ready go home?"

"Oh you can't go home yet," Miranda pleaded.

Maddy flexed her fingers—her knuckles were bruised, bloody and swollen. "Next time I haul off and punch someone, remind me to wear gloves. Anyhow, I know Donna's going to want to have it out with me yet. It's been a few years coming."

"And this is something you want to contend with?" Jack remarked.

"Babe, she was one of people responsible for that shit that happened to me two years ago. Don't you think I would love to get a piece of that bitch and tell her exactly what I think of her?"

Jack raised his eyebrow, "Are you going to come to blows?"

Maddy grinned, "No, I will handle it with much dignity and class. Best way to fight a woman is not stooping to her level."

The two couples returned to the bar. Maddy gave Jack a kiss, telling him she was going to go freshen up.

He looked at her and grinned, "Are setting your bait?"

She touched him on the tip of his nose, "You bet your sweet ass I am."

Miranda had gone ahead so she could hide out in one of the stalls. She didn't want to miss out on this and Maddy found it hilarious.

Maddy was standing in front of the mirror touching up her lipstick when Donna walked in. Right on cue, Maddy smiled to herself.

Donna leaned up against the wall and sized Maddy up. She was small 5'5" to 5'6", maybe 125 pounds, but well proportioned, long copper curly hair, green eyes. She looked to be in her early to mid-thirties. As she had commented to Bryan much younger than she thought Maddy would be. What the hell was Bryan doing chasing someone like this? She was too young for him, at least ten years. And she was, as Bryan so blatantly put it, beautiful. She was way out of his league. What the hell was he thinking?

Maddy, in turn, was assessing Donna by her reflection in the mirror. Donna's shoulder length black hair framed a fuller face, with brown eyes, pug nose and thin lips. Laugh lines and crows feet etched in her face. She appeared closer to Bryan's age of 47. She was a little on the heavier side and a couple of inches taller than her. Maddy thought at one time she had been a pretty woman with a warm smile. Maybe all those years with Bryan did her in.

Maddy closed her lipstick and popped it in her purse, "Well have you seen everything you need to see?" Maddy turned to her with one eyebrow raised.

"It's just nice to put a face with the voice. You are not at all like I pictured," Donna said calmly.

Maddy shrugged. "Sorry can't help you. What you see is what I am."

Maddy leaned back against the counter, "Is there something specific you want to say to me? I am really not in the mood for a cat fight."

"We used to be such good friends, Maddy."

"Well you were the one who chose to end that, not me."

"You were screwing around with my boyfriend," Donna said in disbelief.

Maddy smiled weakly, "How can I screw around with someone from 1,000 miles away?"

"It was an emotional affair and you know it."

Maddy shook her head, "No it was a total mind fuck. What the two of you did to me was unforgivable. But it's over with and I've moved on. I've already dealt with all this shit with Bryan and I'm not much into reruns. Say what you have to say to me and get on with it. I want to get back to my boyfriend."

"I told you how this would all end," Donna said smugly.

Maddy threw her head back and laughed. "How it ended, dear Donna, was that Bryan came up here to take up where he left off. It didn't quite work out like he had planned. I'm not into the submissive/domination thing the two of you are. I don't know how to explain this to you or even if I want to. I love Bryan, I always will, but we can't be together. I can't to be what he wants me to be. When he came here, I was already falling in love with Jack. Bryan thought he derailed that," Maddy shrugged lightly, "but it didn't work. I am happy with Jack. I love him very much. Anything else you need to know?"

"I told you Bryan would come back to me," Donna said smugly.

Maddy furrowed her brow. Did she not hear a damn thing she said? "Okay honey, if you want to hear it like this, then this is how you are going to get it. Bryan and I split cuz it was the right thing to do. As for him coming back to you? Baby, you are the booby prize." Maddy walked out of the room.

Maddy slid in beside Jack and took a long sip of her drink. He reached out and grabbed her hand and held it tightly.

A couple of moments later Miranda came out and joined them. "She's in there bawling," she snickered.

Jack looked down at Maddy, "Were you mean to her?"

Maddy looked shocked, "No, I thought I was very well in control."

Maddy stood up, "Come on, Sexy, dance with me."

One Republic's *Stop and Stare* was playing. Maddy wound her arms around Jack's neck as he ran his hands up and down her body. Maddy felt all tingly at his touch. She pulled him down a little so she could reach his neck, kissing behind his ear and down his neck. She took her tongue and flicked his earlobe. Her lips then traveled along his jaw line until she found his mouth. She gently parted his lips with her tongue tasting him. He pressed his mouth down on hers taunting her tongue with his. His hands held her head, his fingers getting tangled in her hair. Their bodies were pressed about as close together as could be under the circumstances.

When they finally came up for air, they were both breathing heavily and laughing. Jack bent down and whispered in her ear, "I think it's time to go..."

Maddy kissed him again, "Uhuh."

Jack surprised Maddy by picking her up and throwing her over his shoulder. He walked over to the table, grabbed her purse, "See ya guys later," he grinned. As he turned and left the bar, Maddy waved from her position on his shoulder.

Donna watched Bryan's face as his eyes never left Maddy and her boyfriend on the dance floor. She was surprised when she didn't see jealousy, but a great sadness. Donna reached out for Bryan's hand. She held it limp in her hand. "I'm not saying this to piss you off, but they seem really happy together."

Bryan glanced at Donna. "Jack's a good guy. I couldn't ask for anyone better for her."

"What happened? I know you didn't just let go of her. I know your obsession with her, and after seeing her I can understand why."

Bryan leaned back and put his arm over the back of Donna's chair. "I love Maddy, more than life it's self. But loving her that much, I have to know that she's the happiest she can be and it's not with me. You know how fucked up I am. She's been through too much in her life for me destroy her again and again. She has a chance of happiness and a life with Jack."

Jack finally set Maddy back down on her feet and unlocked his car. He opened the door for her and she slid in. Jack got in on his side. "Take your shirt off," Maddy commanded.

Jack looked at her puzzled, "Huh?"

Maddy grinned, "Take your shirt off, please."

"You're kinky." Jack pulled his shirt off over his head and tossed it into the back. Maddy lay sideways on the seat so her upper body was across his lap facing his chest. She pressed her hands on his beautiful chest and kissed him along his collarbone.

"Home Jack," she ordered him with a laugh.

Jack leaned back his head and closed his eyes enjoying the searing of her lips on his skin. "How am I supposed to drive while you are doing this? We'll get pulled over."

Maddy whispered in his ear, "You are the chief of detectives, love. I am sure you could talk them out of a ticket." She nipped playfully at his neck.

"Mmmm....Maddy, I don't know..." He started the car and put it into gear.

Maddy took her time with her mouth tasting his skin. She kissed along the side of his neck, tracing his collarbone with her tongue. She took her tongue and slid it down between his pecks. She sucked in one of his nipples and gave it the gentlest nip, the car swerved.

"Jesus Maddy," he moaned.

Maddy smiled to herself. Her mouth traveled lower across his tight belly to just above his waistband. She fumbled with his snap.

Jack gently grabbed her hair, "No Kitten, please...you...have to wait..." Jesus what the hell was she doing to him? He could hardly breath let a lone try to concentrate on the road.

Finally he turned off into the residential area where the traffic was near dead. Maddy had resumed her oral exploration of his chest. Jack slid his hand down to her hip and tugged at the tunic until it was above her waistline. He easily slipped his hand down her leggings touching her gently. He smiled when her heard her gasp as his finger rubbed just the right spot. Her head froze in mid-air, her fingers dug into his skin.

Maddy's hand slid between his legs and she rubbed his hardness through the heavy material. She dropped her head down kissing along his zipper, caressing him with her thumb. She pulled on the button until it gave and frantically tugged at the zipper. She could only free part of him. She rubbed the expose shaft gently across her cheek and then flicked her tongue over the head making Jack groan loudly.

He removed his hand from her leggings and groped around the visor for the garage door opener and pulled the car in shutting the door behind him. He reached on the side of his seat and reclined his seat all the way back.

Maddy tugged his jeans down lower on his hips exposing the full length of him. One thing Jack wasn't was lacking in any department. She took her tongue down to the base of his shaft swirling circles around it. Maddy felt Jack place his hand on her head but he didn't push, instead he softly stroked her hair. She could hardly hear him breathing. She ran her tongue up one side and down the other. She peeked up at his face. His head was tilted back and he was panting softly from his mouth, licking his lips occasionally. It gave her great pleasure knowing she was pleasing him. She put a hand on each side of him and lowered her mouth slowly down on him, tasting a sweet saltiness, smelling the musky scent of his maleness. She bobbed her head slowly up and down on him and increased with each upward stroke. Jack's fingers tightened in her hair and she felt the pressure of his hand.

"Maddy..." she barely heard him, his voice was but a whisper. "Maddy...you have...to stop..."

Maddy removed her lips but she continued to caress him with her cheek. "Why..."

"Want to..." he was breathing so heavy "...want...together...both..."

Maddy gave him a parting kiss and sat up in the seat. Jack was still trying to get control over his body. Maddy was satisfied with the reaction she got out of him.

Jack reached down and pulled up his jeans but he didn't bother to zip up. Maddy smiled to herself. He probably couldn't. He sat his seat upright and reached over and pulled Maddy across the seat devouring her lips. When he finally released her he held her face in his hands, "You are pure evil. Now come on, or I'm going explode, literally."

Jack took Maddy by the hand and led her straight to the bedroom. "Clothes off," he said with urgency. They quickly stripped off all their clothing. Maddy laid out on the bed in her nakedness. Jack's eyes roved over her hungrily. Thanks to Maddy, the urgency to take her was immense. He spread her legs and ran his hand between them, caressing her. His finger rubbed her slowly at first. He watched as her legs dropped to the side of her body. She struggled to take full advantage of his hand touching her. Her arms were over her head, her fingers squeezing the pillows. He applied a little more pressure and gradually increased his speed. Maddy's pelvis began to move with the rhythm of his touch. She was whimpering and moaning, flinging her head back and forth. She was ready.

Jack stood off the edge of the bed and slid her body to the edge. He lifted her legs onto his shoulders and entered her with one swift deep thrust. Maddy screamed. Jack leaned forward, "Did I hurt you?" he asked frantically.

"No..no...don't stop..." Maddy mumbled.

Jack resumed his thrusting into her, her position allowing deep penetration. Maddy squirmed and writhed beneath him. Just when Maddy thought she could take no more, he slowed down to a slow gentle rocking, dropping her legs down to his side, and slid her back on the bed without leaving her. Maddy locked her legs around him, grinding herself into him. Jack crushed her lips with his, eagerly seeking her out, his arms on both sides of her head. "Are you ready Kitten?" he whispered huskily into her ear.

"Mmmmhhmmm....yes.... oh God...yes." Her fingernails dug into his flesh as he moved faster inside her. Maddy felt her fires building with each stroke until her body felt like a volcano about to erupt. When Jack finally gave her one deep explosive thrust Maddy cried out.

Jack slid off the bed and turned down the sheets, "Come on baby," he requested softly, "bedtime."

Maddy climbed in beside him and cuddled up next to him. "Damn Jack. You're killing me," she laughed still a little breathless.

Jack wrapped his arms around her and nuzzled her ear, "This was all your damn fault, you tease...but I loved it. Thank you."

Maddy woke up in the early hours of the morning, tears streaming down her face. She tried to slide off the bed but Jack's arms tighten around her. She carefully pried his hands from around her and got out of bed. She went to her drawer grabbed a pair of panties and a nightshirt.

She went to the garage, grabbed her bag and went back into the kitchen. She rummaged through it and found her cell phone. She held it in her hands, staring at it. Did she dare call him at this time of the night? Donna would freak out, but she needed to talk to him, to make things right. She couldn't keep going like this. She hit the speed dial for Bryan.

It rang several times before he finally picked up. "Hello," he had been asleep. Then she began to wonder if he were still drunk. She couldn't talk to him when he was drunk.

"Hey," she spoke softly into the phone.

After hearing her voice, Bryan sat up in his bed, "Maddy...what's wrong? You okay?"

"I'm okay...can we talk?" She listened the deafening silence on the other end.

"I can't see we have a lot to talk about Maddy. It is what it is." His voice was distant.

"I don't understand," her voice quivered, "how can you be like this...after everything we've been through..."

She heard Bryan sigh deeply, "It's because of everything we've been through. You just need to let it go, Maddy."

"I can't let it go. Can we please meet somewhere and talk...please, Bryan."

He gave in to her, "You can come to my motel...if you trust me," he said quietly.

"What about Donna?"

"She has her own room. I don't want her staying with me. I switched motels by the way." He gave her the name and the address of the new motel. She remembered he had asked her if he got a different room, would she spend some time with him. It must have been before he decided to cut her off.

She told him she would be there in about twenty minutes. She slipped up to the bedroom and put on a pair of blue jeans.

Jack was still sleeping soundly, or so she thought until he grabbed her hand as she walked by the bed. "Going somewhere, Maddy?"

She sat on the bed beside him and leaned her head on his body. "I am going to meet Bryan. I need to get this settled once and for all. Jack, I need to do something. I don't like things being this way."

Jack ran his hand over her hair and sat up in the bed. "Give me a couple of minutes to get dressed."

"Why?"

"You're not driving across this city in the middle of the night by yourself. I'm going to take you." He went to his dresser and pulled out a pair of sweatpants and a t-shirt.

"That's sweet baby, but you don't have to do this," she argued lightly with him.

He slipped the shirt over his head. "Kitten, it's not open for discussion. I understand your need to fix things with Bryan. I think he is being a jackass and he is wrong. Where you suppose to meet him?"

"At the Sheffield."

"Thought he was at the Regency."

"Guess he moved."

"What's his girlfriend going to say when you show up at his door in the middle of the night?" Jack pulled on his tennis shoes.

Maddy smiled, "She is in a different room."

Jack chuckled, "Guess there is trouble in that paradise." He gave her the once over, "Please finished getting dressed."

Maddy slipped on a t-shirt and her shoes and met him in the car. "What are you going to do while I am talking to him?"

Jack yawned, "Sleep. He gonna come down and let you in?"

"I guess so."

"Call him when we get there so I know for sure."

Maddy smiled, "Damn you're protective."

He brought her hand to his lips, "Yes, and I'm not going to change so get used to it."

Jack pulled into the motel parking lot so Maddy called Bryan to come out and get her.

"Now if he gets stupid on you, you get the hell out of there, understand?" Jack warned her.

"I will," she kissed him on the cheek.

When she saw Bryan walking across the parking lot she started to open her door, but Bryan walked to Jack's side of the car.

Jack rolled down his window. "Bryan," he nodded.

Bryan bent down and rested his arms on Jack's window. "Thanks for bringing her, Jack. Do you want to come in?"

Jack shook his head. "No, this is something the two of you need to work out. I'm just going to recline back and catch a couple of z's. Call me when she is getting ready to leave."

Maddy followed Bryan to his room, he slid the pass key card through the lock and stood back while she entered. This room wasn't that much different than his last one.

They stood just inside the doorway looking at each other awkwardly. Maddy noticed his nose was black and blue. She reached out tentatively to touch it.

Bryan gently grabbed her hand, "Don't, it still hurts like a bitch. I can't believe such a small woman could pack such an unbelievable punch."

Maddy smiled weakly, "Well...yeah. Sorry about that. Sometimes I just react."

Bryan chuckled, "No shit."

"You looked beautiful tonight, Maddy. Not just your appearance, but with Jack. You two look...like you belong together," Bryan told her as he looked down at her. "You looked happy."

Maddy reached out hesitantly, moved towards him and gently put her arms around him to hug him. At first he was stiff and unresponsive. Then it was as if the contact with her his resolve weakened. His arms slowly went around her and he pulled her close and buried his face in her hair.

After a couple of minutes he pulled away from her, went and sat on the bed and lit up a cigarette. "Maddy, what do you want from me?"

"I don't want things to be the way they are between us." She sat on the bed next to him.

"You need to cut me out of your life, Maddy. I have brought nothing but misery to you in one way or another. I want you to stay away from me."

Maddy's voice caught in her throat, "I don't believe you when you say you don't want to see me or when you say you don't need me. Damn it, don't try to pretend to not love me anymore." Maddy stood up and wiped the tears from her eyes. She moved toward the door.

"Maddy wait." Bryan couldn't let her walk out of his life like this, not when it wasn't anything she wanted, but what he thought she needed. Once again he was controlling the outcome.

Maddy stood in place where he told her to wait. She didn't dare look at him or she knew she would loose it. How could she let go of this man she had loved for so long? Why did she have to?

Bryan came up behind her and turned her to face him. When she looked up at him, his eyes were glistening. "I can't keep hurting you, Maddy, I can't."

"Jesus, Bryan, what do you think you are doing to me now? I know things can't be like we dreamed, but why does it have to be an all or nothing? We have the opportunity to be a part of each other's lives, for the rest of our lives. Why do you want to throw it all away?" she sobbed. "I just don't understand—make me understand, Bryan. Why don't you love me anymore?"

He held her chin up, "I will never stop loving you, Maddy. Never!"

"Our time together before you have to leave is so precious and damn it, you are wasting it all away. So what we are not lovers, it doesn't mean I don't love you with all my heart, it doesn't mean I don't cherish any time I can get with you. We maintained this bond of ours through a hell of a lot—a lot of wasted time. We don't have to do that. When this is all done Baby, we don't have to say goodbye."

Bryan cupped her face in his hands and brought her lips to his. He could feel her lips quivering beneath his as he gently kissed her.

She pulled back slightly, "Please don't make me say goodbye, Bryan...don't make me say goodbye..." She burst into tears.

Bryan bent down and pulled her close. "We won't say goodbye, Minnie, I promise. I will take your lead on this; trust you that this is the right way to do it. I don't want to loose you either, but I thought it was the only way to keep from hurting you. Do you understand?"

Maddy looked up at him searching his eyes, "This is hurting me—being like we are. We don't have to be this way. I love you, I don't want to loose you—not forever, not at all."

They held each other tight. Bryan kissed her on the top of her head. "We need to get you back to Jack, Minnie. It's late, my face hurts, I have a drunk headache and I have a bitch to put up with in a few hours."

Maddy stood back, "Didn't you invite her here?"

Bryan chuckled, "Hell no, she ran into Jeff when he was high and he told her where I was at. The bitch did use my credit card for the plane ticket though."

Maddy laughed, "And separate rooms."

Bryan smiled, "She really flipped when she saw you. Said you were way too pretty and young for me."

Maddy nudged him gently, "Well, she doesn't know my tastes does she?"

Bryan threw his head back and laughed, "Oh yeah, she took one look at Jack. She trap you in the bathroom?"

Maddy nodded, "And didn't get the satisfaction she thought she was going to get. I pissed her off when I told her I still loved you and you were not running back to her because you chose her over me."

Bryan raised an eyebrow, "Even though you didn't know that for sure?"

She stood on her tiptoes and kissed him softly, "I know you."

Bryan walked her out to Jack's car. They forgot to call ahead. Maddy peered in Jack's window. He was reclined back in his seat sleeping. The thought of him reclined back earlier in the evening made Maddy's cheeks burn. She quickly shook the vision from her head. Maddy tapped on the glass. Jack jumped and blinked the sleep away then rolled down window.

Bryan smiled, "I am returning your beautiful lady to you."

Jack yawned, "I take it you two worked things out?"

"Yes, Maddy knocked some sense into me, literally."

Jack laughed, "From what I heard you asked for it."

Bryan put his arm around Maddy, "That I did." He kissed Maddy on the cheek. "Give me a call tomorrow. Maybe the four of us can get together."

Maddy gave him a look, "Are you fucking serious?"

"Dead serious. If I have to put up with this bitch, you two can help me. After all what are friends for if they are not there for you when you need them?"

Bryan waved at them as they drove off.

"So you and Bryan...things okay?" Jack asked as he turned on to the bypass.

"I believe so," Maddy said as she rubbed her temples.

"Does that mean we are back on timeshare?" Jack asked softly looking straight ahead.

Maddy turned and looked at him, "I thought we made a commitment tonight?"

"I thought so too, but that was before you two made up. Thought maybe you have changed your mind."

Maddy shook her head in disbelief. Damn men. Why did they have to be so damn stupid? "Jack, I don't take lightly what we say to each other when it comes to how we feel. You asked me to commit to you on a deeper level and I said yes. I wouldn't have said it, if I weren't in it 100%. Are you that unsure of me? If you are, Babe, we need to do some serious talking before I even consider moving in with you, even on a part time basis."

He glanced over at her, "You were really serious about moving in with me?"

Maddy shot him a look.

"Kitten, I'm sorry. I'm really tired and yes, I feel a little insecure about your feelings for Bryan."

"We are just going to be friends Babe. No sex, no romance—just soul mates without benefits. We agreed it's you and me that belong together, not him and me. There is no disputing it. Okay?" She reached across for his hand.

He grasped her hand and brought it to his lips. He smiled over at her, "You are really going to move in with me?"

Maddy nodded and laughed, "We have to work out some serious details, but yes. I hope you realize how much of a commitment this is for me. I haven't lived with a man since I was married which has been over 14 years ago."

"You never lived with Bryan?"

"No we just dated. He was married remember, and I had my kids."

Jack stopped for a red light and leaned over and kissed her. "I love you."

"I love you too, very much, so don't ever doubt it."

Jack pulled into the garage and turned off the car. "Don't you ever get the wild ass idea of driving off alone in the middle of the night. The thought of it scares the hell out of me."

"I won't." She got out of the car and went into the kitchen. She pulled out a carton of milk and poured herself and Jack a glass and offered it to him when he came in.

Maddy had her meds that she had forgotten to take earlier spread out on the counter, taking one of them at a time popping them in her mouth a swallowing.

"You been taking them on a regular basis?" Jack asked as he watched her.

"For the most part."

"Bryan said you are not suppose to deviate from taking them. Said psych meds are not to be messed with."

"I know," she replied as matter of fact.

Jack studied her carefully. "Do you have a mental disorder?"

Maddy looked up at him and laughed, "Are you calling me crazy?" When he didn't answer she asked, "Would it matter if I did?"

"No, not to me, but I would make sure you stuck to your meds so you feel your best." He continued to watch her.

"When you tell people you have a mental disorder, which I don't, I have a mood disorder, they attach a stigma to you and they can't see past it. They treat you like you're crazy and don't take you seriously," Maddy tried to explain.

"You know I won't judge you."

"You won't freak out on me?"

He shook his head, "Huhuh. You're still the same girl I have always known. Putting a label on you is not going to change who you are."

Maddy really debated on telling him. It wasn't something she told people. Only her psych doctor and her therapist knew. She suspected Bryan did, but he never said a word about it. "I have bipolar disorder which was triggered by the death of my children. I stay stable for the most part, but when I am under intense stress it can trigger break through episodes."

"Are there things I should look for? I mean I want to help you with this the best I can," Jack inquired honestly.

"Read a book. Like I said I have mine, for the most part, under control. I have for years. It was because of my bipolar I went off the deep end over what happened with Bryan and Donna a couple of years ago. Do you think you can live with this, baby?"

Jack took her into his arms, "Of course I can, Kitten. I love every part of you, and this is part of who you are. I love you, Babe, all of you."

Maddy leaned her head against his shoulder. "Let's go to bed, love. I am so tired."

Jack led Maddy up to bed. They changed into nightclothes and settle down to bed together. Jack wrapped his arms around her and they drifted off to sleep.

22

Sunlight was creeping between the slats of the wooden blinds when Maddy woke up. She felt around in the bed for Jack but found herself alone. She smiled to herself. This was nice. She spent some really amazing time with Jack yesterday and last night. She, Jack and Andy made some real progress on the case, and she and Bryan had finally come to a peaceful understanding...she hoped.

After running into the bathroom, brushing her teeth and slipping on a pair of shorts and a tank top, she went in search of Jack. She found him sitting at the kitchen bar reading the newspaper and having a cup of coffee. "Morning, Babe," she kissed him on the cheek.

"Morning," he took a sip of his coffee, "Want some breakfast?"

"Nothing too heavy, toast or something."

"Got bagels in the fridge, juice too. You want me to make it for you?"

Maddy laughed, "I can do it." She opened the fridge, pulled out the bagels, butter and the juice and put them on the bar. She pulled up a stool next to him.

Jack got off the stool, grabbed a glass out of the cupboard and put it in front of her. "You're going to need that."

"Duh, no I am going to drink it out of the bottle." She poured the juice and grabbed her pills, took out what she needed and downed them with the juice.

Jack pinched her on the butt, "Don't be such a smart ass. Hey, I've been thinking about what Bryan said, about us getting together with them today, what do you say we have a cookout later this afternoon?"

Maddy had torn off a chunk of bagel, had it half way to her mouth and stopped. "Are you fucking serious?"

He looked at her totally innocent, "Sure, why not? Thought you and Bryan had patched things up?"

Maddy set down the bagel, "Well, yeah...but with Donna?"

"He asked us...how could you say no?"

She turned to him and put her hand on his arm. "Look at me," He turned to her. "NO! See how easy that was?"

Jack chuckled, leaned forward and kissed her forehead. Then he leaned back, batted his eyelashes and said, "Pleeeeease?"

Maddy cracked up and smacked him, "That shit don't work anymore on me than it does you. Why do you want to do this so bad?"

"Curiosity, I want to watch them interact," Jack grabbed his coffee and took another sip.

"Bullshit, you want to watch how she and I interact. What are you hoping for? A cat fight?"

His eyes were smiling when he looked at her, "Every man's fantasy. No seriously, we would be helping him out, you could fuck with her head, everyone's happy."

A crease crept across Maddy's brow, "You really are serious...okay, say I agree to this, which by the way is just a supposition, if we do this, it's under the condition that we invite Andy and Miranda. I would feel more comfortable if Miranda were here, too."

"Oh I see, so you and Miranda can gang up on her," he stood up and refilled his coffee and sat back down.

"So," she popped the bagel in her mouth. "What's your point?"

"Okay, you win. But don't be thinking this is the way it's always going to be, you getting your way," he blew on his coffee before taking a sip.

Maddy's mouth dropped, "Getting my way...hey, Babe, you got this all wrong...we compromised."

Jack laughed and leaned over and kissed her, "I know, I just like getting a rise out of you. You want me to do the inviting or do you?"

Maddy washed the last of her bagel down, "It's your party, you invite...and you cook."

"What happened to compromising?"

"You won," she smirked.

"Fine, I'll call Mom to make the salads for me."

Maddy glared at him. "You better nip that shit right in the bud, mister. You think you're going to run to mommy every time I don't do things your way; you're full of shit. I'll make you a damn list of things. You pick them up and I'll make your damn salads."

Jack looked at her blinking, "Damn, Maddy. I would never have expected that kind of reaction from you. I'm sorry. I was only kidding. You don't have to do this. I can pick up salads from the deli. I was planning on doing steaks, maybe some sweet corn, throw in some bake potatoes."

Maddy slid off the stool and placed her hand on his arm, "No, I'm sorry. I don't know where that came from. That crack about your mom was uncalled for. I'm used to living on my own, being alone, not dealing with family or entertaining. This couples thing...that too is new. I'm sorry."

Jack put one arm around her and stroked her hair with his other hand. "It's okay, Kitten. No big deal. I forget you have lived a solitary life for such a long time that you might feel uncomfortable around most things I just take for granted. But I do have to ask you, something that concerns me. I am close with my family, are you going to be able to adjust to it? To become part of it?"

"I'm going to try...really hard. It just doesn't come naturally to me."

Jack held her back so he could see her face, "Honey, you are a naturally warm, funny, smart woman. You just need to let your wall down and let more people into that world of yours. Damn, Maddy, with me you are this amazing person, and yeah you are natural, one of the most natural people I know." He put his fingers under her chin, "Just be your self, Kitten." He kissed her softly.

She smiled weakly, "It's easy with you."

"Let down the wall, Kitten, let people get to know the real you, like I know you."

"Do you have a note pad?" Maddy asked as she cleaned up her breakfast mess.

Jack went to one of his kitchen drawers and pulled out a pad and a pencil. "What do you need this for?"

"A grocery list. I want you to pick ingredients for a salad," she told him quietly.

"Hon, I told you, you don't have to."

She smiled weakly at him, "No, I want to. Being it's our first *dinner* party and all, I need to make something."

Jack took out his cell phone and placed calls to Bryan and Andy extending the invitations to their lady friends. He got Maddy's list, gave her a kiss and left to get the groceries.

Maddy decided to explore the house while Jack was gone. If this were going to be her home/part-time home, it would be kind of nice to actually see what it looked like. Just off the kitchen before entering the living room was a set of pocket doors. Maddy slid them open to reveal a lovely formal dinning room. Jack must really be into the dark woods, but maybe that's because there was dark wood trim throughout the house. In the center of the room was an expansive formal dining room table, in what appeared to be cherry. A white lace tablecloth adorned it. Eight cloth chairs circled the table and a matching hutch was off to the side. The room had the same vaulted dark wood beams. The walls were painted rust and were accented by high quality framed prints. Maddy backed out of the room and closed the pocket doors.

The main floor consisted of the kitchen, laundry room, coatroom, dining room, living room, a long hallway, the den, and another bathroom. It seemed as if there should have been another room, but if there was, she didn't know how to get to it.

The upstairs consisted of Jack's bedroom at the head of the stairs, a huge walk in closet, a linen closet, the bathroom, and three other large bedrooms. In the other bedrooms, it was obvious they weren't being used as they lacked the character Jack's room had. Each were painted a soft beige, had earth-tone bedding, matching curtains, brownish colored carpet. All had queen size beds. The wall prints, depending on the bedroom had themes ranging from floral, wildlife, and Tuscan. The rooms were pretty, but she still loved Jack's best.

As she was descending the stairs something occurred to her that she found peculiar. Despite Jack's declaration he was from a very tight knit family, there were absolutely no family photos in any part of the house she had seen. She found that very odd.

Maddy went into the garage and retrieved her camera bag and took it into Jack's den. She booted up the computer and then downloaded the photos onto the hard drive. She wanted to run the photo through the FBI facial recognition software. Bryan should be back at the motel with the little woman so he shouldn't be able to flag her access.

Maddy entered in her access code, uploaded the photo into Technical Support Working Group (TSWG) database and requested a recognition search. The FBI isn't allowed direct access to the database because of privacy issues. The search will be analyzed to determine the statistical variation in the geometry of facial landmarks including the relative spacing between the mouth and nose, width of the eyes, as well as other markers with her unsub. The odds of them getting any hits on him at all would depend if he were in the system for any reason. If not, as with the fingerprints and DNA, the results would turn up nothing. Which she kind of thought would be the case, but hey, it was worth a shot.

She grabbed a phone book and looked up the phone number for the church and dialed the number. An answering machine picked up. The office was closed until Monday, no Saturday services until the middle of September, Sunday services are at 9:30 AM. Strike one.

She pulled down a new tab on the browser and googled the church—Trinity First Reform Church and hit enter. Damn it. Name, address, phone number, times of services. Strike two.

Her search screen beeped, so she flipped back to the FBI site—no matches found. Strike three. She was out.

Maddy sat back in the desk chair and propped her bare feet up on the desk. Damn, now what? Short of going back to the church, she had nothing. And no, she wasn't venturing there, she wasn't stupid.

Maddy was pulled out of her revere by the sound of the doorbell. Shit, who the hell could that be and do she dare answer it? She ventured to the front of the house as the doorbell chimed again. She looked at the door and peered through the peephole. She couldn't see anyone. What the hell? The doorbell chimed again.

"Who is it?" she asked timidly.

"Its Alisha dear." Jack's mom. Thank God, she gave a sigh of relief.

Maddy opened the door. "Good morning Mrs. Par...Alisha," she smiled.

Alisha laughed, "Nice catch Maddy. We'll get you broke in yet. Hope you don't mind, I just thought I would stop in for a cup of coffee."

"No, no come on in. Jack went to the store, but he should be back any minute. I think he has some coffee on." Maddy led Alisha into the kitchen. Alisha made herself comfortable while Maddy poured her a cup of coffee.

"How did you manage to get Jack to leave you unguarded?" Alisha smiled as she took a sip of her coffee.

"He's got this hair-brained idea we are having a cookout with some other couples this afternoon." Maddy smiled, "And guess who's cooking?"

"It's grilling," Alisha, laughed, "that's a man's domain. This ought to be fun. Are you comfortable with this? I mean..."

"You mean with him cooking, or me socializing?" she asked teasing.

"The socializing I guess. I got the impression you were pretty much a loner when it came to your own personal time." Alisha blew on her coffee.

Maddy cocked her head as she looked Jack's mom, "Interesting you picked up on that. It went right over Jack's head."

Alisha smiled, "Just because he's a detective, doesn't make him the most perceptive man in the world. Sometimes he fails to understand not everyone sees the world the way he does. Please don't be offended by what I am about to say, but you and Jack, you have both seen a lot, but not from the same perspectives. Yes, he's seen some wartime, yes he's been a cop for a long time, but he has never been exposed to the horrors you have seen. I did some reading up on profilers and the top profilers get sent to the most horrific cases, and Maddy, I know you were a top profiler.

I can really understand why you left and why you chose to live the way you did. Too much exposure to the evils of the world, hell, who wouldn't hide from it and shield themselves from it. Am I overstepping my bounds, hon?"

Maddy pulled up a stool, "No, not all. Keep going."

"This case you two are working on, this is pretty much run of the mill for you isn't it?

Maddy nodded, "Except for my personal involvement, yeah. I've worked a lot worse. Not as frustrating, but worse. Usually as a profiler, you don't have to do so much of the investigating yourself as we have here. This police force lacks the experience to work this level of crime."

"And you lost your two little children to violence?"

Maddy looked up panic-stricken. No, he didn't.

Alisha took her hand, "No sweetie, he just told me to back off on the starting the family bit because you lost your little ones. He didn't tell me anymore than that. Trust him, hon, he won't betray you, even to me."

Maddy nodded.

"Anyhow, I guess what I am saying is this case is the first of anything like it Jack has ever been exposed to. It bothers him although he will never show it. The things that bother him, he bottles up inside. He can only guess what you've lived through. I don't know if he understands how jaded you might be and might not be so open to letting people into your life....like me."

Maddy laughed, "You're quickly getting closer."

Maddy thought quietly to herself for a few moments. "You know Alisha... you are right he doesn't understand me in those areas, but it's not his fault because I never let him. For the last two years, I wouldn't let him in. I kept him at arms length and outside my personal space."

Alisha looked up from her coffee, "But he loved you anyhow."

"No," Maddy corrected her, "that didn't happen until recently."

Alisha shook her head, "No dear, he's loved you for a long time. He just couldn't reach you and he didn't want to push."

Maddy studied the woman beside her, "How do you know?"

"A couple years ago he came home talking about this crazy reporter that was constantly pestering him, and then went from that to how smart she is, what a good investigator she is, how funny she is...to eventually how beautiful she is... His dad kept telling him to ask you out. He said he couldn't because he didn't want you to tell him no and ruin what you two did have. He was right wasn't he? You would have bolted?"

Maddy thought about it, "Yeah, more than likely. So this didn't just come out of the blue then? I couldn't figure out why this last time...I thought he changed on me with trying to get personal. Wonder why he changed his mind."

"Maybe he just got tired of not knowing what he was missing out on and decided to take a chance." Alisha watched her. "You do love him don't you?"

Maddy smiled and looked down feeling her cheeks burning, "I do...more than I thought it was possible to love anyone. He's a beautiful, amazing man."

Alisha grinned, "It's great to see the feelings are mutual. I thought they were, but I can really see that now."

Both women looked up when the door from the garage opened.

Jack came in, setting a couple of bags of groceries on the bar. He looked from one woman to the other. "Should I be concerned?"

Alisha laughed, "Be afraid, my son, be very afraid."

Jack came around and kissed his mother on the cheek. Then he went to Maddy and whispered in her ear, "Everything thing okay, Kitten?" When Maddy smiled up at him and nodded he gave her a soft kiss on the lips.

He returned to the sacks and started putting things away. "What you have you two been talking about?"

Maddy went to the cupboard, pulled out a glass and filled it with water. She turned and leaned against the counter. "You."

"Me? What about me?"

Alisha laughed, "Nothing bad dear, don't be so paranoid. Maddy was just telling me how much she loves you."

"She did?"

Maddy laughed, "Damn, don't sound so shocked. It's not like you don't know it."

Jack slipped his arms around her, "Can we tell her?"

Maddy looked up at him confused, "About?"

"You...me...us?" He was like a little boy with a big secret he couldn't stand keeping.

Maddy laughed, "Go ahead."

"Maddy's moving in with me!" he told his mom with a big smile on his face.

"Part-time...at first," Maddy corrected him. She waited for Alisha's reaction.

She looked at Maddy, "Why just part-time? Full-time makes more sense."

"Alisha, I live on an acreage about 45 miles east of here. I own four horses and have two dogs. He doesn't seem to understand you just can't pack them in a suitcase and move them to the city," Maddy explained.

"No wouldn't exactly work to well putting them in the backyard. And I am guessing with Jack's job he has to live within certain city limits, so living at your place is out of the question." Alisha looked thoughtful. "Jack, build a new place where you two can live and keep Maddy's horses."

"Okay...wait," Maddy put up her hands, "Let's not get a head of ourselves here. We just decided on this last night. Let's just step back and weigh our options here. You guys are pushing me just a little to fast. Please, don't get pissed, but just back off a little...for now, okay?"

Alisha laughed, "I'm sorry Maddy, especially in light of what we just talked about. No worries, you kids take your time. You'll know what to do when the time is right. I need to get going."

Alisha hugged Maddy and Maddy willingly hugged her back. She then went over, hugged and kissed Jack and whispered in his ear, "Take it easy on her, Sweetie, it's all new to her."

After Alisha let herself out, Jack turned to Maddy. "Well that was quite the transformation between the two of you. I take it this visit went very well?"

Maddy took a gulp of water. "Yep," she smiled. "I gotta ask you something."

"What?"

Maddy set her glass down then slid her arms around his waist. "How long have you loved me?"

Jack took a deep breath and slowly let it out, "Does it really make a difference?"

Maddy placed a hand on each side of his face, "No, Babe, what matters is what you feel now." She reached up and kissed him tenderly. "I'd just kind of like to know is all."

Jack wrapped his arms around her, "What did Mom tell you, Kitten?"

Maddy just looked up at him, smiling. "How long have you loved me?"

"When did I fall in love with you or when did I admit it to myself?"

"Both."

Jack laughed, "You like making me squirm don't you? I just don't want to feel stupid telling you."

Maddy kissed him softly, "You don't ever have feel stupid about what you feel."

He looked upward like he was thinking. "I think I fell in love with you about the second case we worked together. I wasn't conscious of it until my dad pointed it out to me quite sometime later."

Maddy shook her head, "And you never ever let on."

He did his best to put it into words. "It wasn't worth the risk. I knew a relationship wasn't something you wanted...with anyone. I was probably the best male relationship you had and that had to be enough."

Maddy leaned back against the counter and starting biting at her nails.

"I'm sorry."

Maddy looked up, "Oh Babe, don't be sorry. I just can't believe how stupid I was. I mean, Jesus, after hearing they had a pool going at the paper, the guys on your squad...you...your family...For someone that is supposed to be known for her powers of observation...I totally missed it. Everybody knew but me. I'm the one who's sorry."

Jack sat back on a stool. "Kitten, you weren't at any place where you would have known. You kept your private life away from everyone and you really didn't care about anyone else's because you wouldn't let yourself. We never talked about each other's personal life. So why would you think you would have picked up on it? "

"You make me sound like a monster."

Jack took a deep breath and sighed. "Maddy, you weren't even receptive to me when I did start engaging you. You know that. I think you were finally realizing you had some feelings for me, but you didn't want them. Honey, emotionally, you are now a totally different person. With me you are very open, very loving. I don't feel like you're holding back. I don't know if Bryan is the one that helped you gain that gift back, but I am so glad it happened. We wouldn't be here today if it hadn't."

"Well, hon, if it counts for anything, I have always loved working with you, I loved being around you. I admired you, respected you. I trusted you more than any other person...and have always been extremely attracted to you." She grinned and wrinkled her nose, "I've always thought you were so hot."

Jack jumped down off his stool and lifted Maddy up on the counter. "Kitten, beings it was probably the most you were capable of at the time, I am honored." He leaned forward kissed her tenderly. Maddy put her hand around his head, parted his lips and kissed him deeply. He slid his hands down her shoulders to her waist. "I would take you upstairs, Kitten, but we have lots to do today."

She kissed him on the nose and jumped off the counter. "Speaking of doing a lot, I uploaded the photo of our unsub into the FBI facial recognition database, no matches. I tried calling the church to see if I could get a list of the ministers that work out of that church, but the offices are closed until Monday. I tried googling it and got nothing. Anyhow back to the TSWG database, we're only allowed access to searches that have had mug shot records. It's against the privacy act for them to access like driver's license photos or any non-crime related photos in the database. So we are SOL on that avenue."

"Well, you gave it a shot. You're off for the rest of the day."

Maddy walked around the kitchen opening drawers and looking in cupboard doors.

Jack watched her, "What are you doing?"

"Familiarizing myself with your kitchen," she told him.

Jack went back the grocery sacks. He pulled out the ingredients for Maddy's salad, a box of black tea bags and three lemons. He disappeared into the garage and brought in a 12 pack of Coke Zero, a case of beer and slid it into the fridge.

Maddy eyed the beer, "Do you think having beer around Bryan is the smartest thing to do?"

"He said if he kept it to the minimum, he would be okay," Jack said as he slid in her coke into the bottom of the fridge. "You got a problem with it?"

"Given the recent behavior I have received from him because of his abuse of alcohol, yeah, I kind of do."

"Don't worry, Kitten, all will be fine. He will behave." Jack took the steaks out and put them in a cake pan and poured a bottle of marinade over them and then flipped them over. He took six potatoes, wrapped them in foil and set them off to the side.

Maddy took her ingredients, of peas, shredded lettuce, shredded cheese, mayo, bacon bits, celery, and onions. She grabbed a cutting board from one of the drawers and diced the onions and celery, then layered the vegetables in a cake pan. She placed plastic wrap over it and stuck it in the fridge. "There, my part is done."

Maddy hopped up on to the stool. "Where we having this little get-together?"

Jack grabbed her by the hand and led her to the back of the house. Just off to right of the den was a door. She had missed it in her house snooping. It opened up into a huge screened in sunroom. The whole front of the room had huge windows that slid aside to make it screened instead of glass. The room housed a large gas grill that could be pushed outside into a patio area. She couldn't see this room from the den window. There were a couple of glass tables with padded chairs placed around them. A wet bar was off to one corner. A few lounge chairs were folded in the corner. The floor was a stucco tile. Maddy was drawn to a waterfall feature in the center of the room. It was a layering of several flat slate rocks, reaching approximately 5 feet high. Water gurgled out of the top of the structured and flowed down the several layers of stone into a pool. "Wow, this is nice," Maddy commented.

Maddy helped Jack pull out the grill and place the lounge chairs around the patio area. They decided to place one of the table sets out on the patio area incase they wanted to sit outside.

Maddy laughed, "I'm surprised you don't have a pool."

Jack pointed to the far back corner of the room, "No, but got a hot tub."

Maddy had visions of Jack taking different women into the tub for romantic trysts. The thought of being somewhere where he had been with other woman bothered her, but then again she was sleeping in his bed. What was the difference?

Jack watched her face as range of emotions crossed it. "What's up?"

"I want a new bed," she replied flatly.

"What?"

Maddy shook her head softly, "Nothing." She definitely didn't want to discuss this with him.

"Is this all going to be too much for you?" he asked quietly. "Hell, Maddy, it's not like you don't know everyone. Unless you are afraid of dealing with Donna."

"I'm not afraid of Donna!" she snapped.

"Ooookay, you don't have to get so snarkey about it. It'll be fun, you'll see." Jack held the door for her as they left the sunroom. "You want some lunch?"

"No thank you," she plopped down on the couch.

Jack sat down beside her and rubbed her leg, "What's the matter with you? You're acting a little off."

"Just a little overwhelmed is all," she answered him as she laid her head back. "I need to ask you a couple of questions, Jack. Where do you see us going?"

Jack ran his finger through his hair. "Wow, Maddy, you've been asking some pretty tough questions today. Are you having second thoughts about us?"

Maddy leaned her head against his shoulder. "No, Baby, not all. It's just you Parkers, you decide to do something and then you go for it. Like your mom, right off the bat, she sees the problem we are having with the moving in issue, and she wants to solve it by just building a new home to accommodate those issues. We aren't just talking about selling my place, moving up here and everything is all better. It's just not that simple. We are talking about my way of life, the life I have been living for years. You can't expect me to be able to just let go and change over night."

Jack leaned his head on hers. "I'm sorry, Kitten. I didn't mean to push you. Do you want to hold off on moving in with me?"

"No, Jack, it's all cool, but I just asked that you look at this from my point of view and look at the emotional issues this can have for me. Work with me and we will get through it just fine. Just don't push. Now back to the question. We are in a committed relationship, we both agree on that. Soon we will be sharing a home, completely. But just tell me, in your perfect world, what would you like to happen with us? I mean today I find out you've loved me for such a long time and I didn't have a clue. You have to have dreams. Tell me them." Maddy said as she held his hand on her lap.

"You really want to know?"

Maddy smacked him, "No, lie to me. Yes I want to know."

"First you tell me where you see us going?" he asked her.

"That's not a fair question for me and you know it."

"Okay...where would I like us to go...moving in together, I think that is a big step...for both of us. I've never lived with anyone either. In time I would hope you would marry me, be my mate for life." Jacked waited for her response. The silence was deafening. "No comment?"

"Just taking it all in, is all."

"What do you think?" Jack nervously searched her face. "Did I cross the line?"

"If all works out like we hope it will, I think that would be the natural path to follow," she said carefully.

"Geez Maddy, you make it sound so clinical."

Maddy laughed, "I'm sorry hon. Let me word it like this, if we continue to keep growing closer and our loving building, then yes I would probably marry you."

"Probably?"

"I would. Does that make you feel better?" she leaned over and kissed him on the cheek. "Okay, how do you feel about children?"

"Do we have to go into this now? Given the circumstances of everything you have been through as of late I don't think its fair on you to discuss it at this point in time," Jack inferred.

"Thank you, Jack. I appreciate your taking that into consideration. Baby, I can't promise you where my mind set will be in the future when it comes to children. I just can't. Not right now. I have to deal with the past when it comes to this issue before I can even begin to think about the future. Can you understand?" Maddy leaned over and kissed him softly. "I'm not saying no, just I don't know."

Jack put his arm around her and pulled her over to him. He cupped her face with his hand and lightly kissed her several times. When she returned his kiss, his mouth came down harder on hers, parting her lips and kissing her deeply. Maddy's arms crept up around his neck, letting her tongue explore his mouth, their kiss growing deeper. His fingers lightly caressed her arms giving her goose bumps. Jack felt her quivering under his touch. His hand slid under she tank top and sought out her breast.

Maddy moaned softly as he stroked her. "Thought you said no time," she said breathlessly.

"Then don't waste it," he said as he reclaimed her mouth. He lowered her down into the cushions. With his body pressed against hers she could feel his desire for her. He raised up long enough to pull his shirt off and to slip her tank top over her head and then pressed their bodies together.

Maddy loved it when their naked skin touched. It sent little electric shocks through her body. She leaned her head back as his lips lightly grazed her skin down her neck to her breast. She entwined her fingers in his hair, holding his head as he taunted her with his lips. Maddy ran her nails down the smooth flesh of his back down to his belt line of his blue jeans. He reached between them and unsnapped his jeans. Maddy pushed them downwards with her hands as he reached down and slipped her shorts off. He lowered himself down on her entering her slowly as his lips came down on hers. He lifted his head, looking into her eyes. His reflected only love and tenderness, hers longing for what she had missed out on for years. "I love you..." she brushed his cheek with her fingertips.

His slid his arm under her head cradling it and kissed her tenderly as he continued to make slow love to her. Each movement within her felt like a wave ebbing away on an ocean shore.

"My sweet Maddy," he whispered as he looked down at her, "I have been waiting all my life for you..." He kissed her eyelids then pulled her body up to meet his. He felt her legs wrap around his back pushing her body into him, meeting his rhythm. He continued entering her slowly, rocking her within his arms.

She clung to him as he loved her to her core wanting release. "Love me, Jack," she pleaded, "make me complete." Jack granted her request as he covered her mouth with his suppressing her scream as they climaxed together. He continued kissing her as their bodies wound down and then held her in his arms there on the couch.

Jack brushed the lose tendrils of hair out of her face. He watched her, searching. "What's the matter, Maddy? Something just isn't right."

She softly kissed him. "I just feel...like I wasted so much time we could have been sharing...because I was too stupid to see what was in front of me."

He laid his head on her chest. "You are feeling guilty because you didn't pick up on my feelings for you?"

Maddy nodded. "How could I not see it? Everyone else could. Was I so cold and uncaring?"

"Honey, you were where you needed to be for you. I could never blame you for that. Besides Maddy, it's not like I wore my feelings on my sleeve. I blocked it out. I didn't allow myself to feel it. There was no way I could maintain the relationship I did have with you if I didn't bury it. Shit, sometimes we didn't even see or hear from each other for a couple of months. People saw our chemistry, Maddy. That's what they based their *bets* on. Not the feelings that were there hon. You didn't waste time, we couldn't have been together, it wasn't our time yet. Now is our time. This way I have you when you are free to give yourself to me—that you want to. This, here and now, this is what is suppose to be."

Maddy kissed the top of his head. "You are right...I guess sometimes I just over think things. We are here, together, and I am free to love you the way you deserved to be loved."

"Exactly," Jack sat up. "Now promise me you will wipe these doubts out of your mind. You're nervous about this afternoon aren't you? With Donna coming? Are you feeling insecure, is that it?"

"I've dealt with the pain Bryan caused me over that ordeal. But not with her, she was supposed to be my friend. I don't care if she used the excuse I was having an affair with her boyfriend, which really wasn't true. But she was the one who set me up. Bryan was fucked up in the head, what's her excuse?" Maddy slid off the couch grabbing her clothes.

Jack grabbed his jeans and slipped them on. "Normally I wouldn't say this, but Maddy, turn your pain into anger and use it. Anger doesn't leave you vulnerable, pain does. I will not let her hurt you again." Then he laughed, "Like you would even let it get to the point where I would need to step forward. You would probably deck her before I could."

He pulled his shirt over his head. "Does it bother you seeing Bryan with her?"

Maddy shrugged, "No, not really. I guess for the most part because I know he truly does despise her. Even when he was living with her, he didn't like her. It was just some place for him to escape to."

"He used her?" Jack chuckled.

Maddy slipped her shorts back on. "Yep. Fucked up way to waste your life living with someone you can't stand, but hey, it was always his choice." Maddy stood on her toes and kissed him. "I'm going to go take a shower and change. And thanks," she smiled up at him.

He looked puzzled, "For?"

"For being you. We communicate so well together and I really think that's awesome." She turned and ran up the steps.

A half an hour later Maddy returned downstairs to hear voices in the kitchen. She stood outside the door and listened. The unmistakable banter between Jack and Bryan was apparent. Damn, she was hoping to be down here before they got here. She wanted to smuggle a couple of shots of whiskey to calm her nerves and loosen her up. She quickly examined her appearance in the hall mirror. She had dressed in white Capri's, a red satiny halter blouse, and had pulled her hair back into a high ponytail. She decided to go natural on the make-up. What the hell, who was she trying to impress? Damn, she really didn't want to go in there.

The front door bell chimed. Thank God! Andy and Miranda. Maddy answered the door and greeted her friends with a hug. She had to laugh when Andy turned bright red when she hugged him. She could intimidate him so easily if she chose to.

Miranda had a bag in her hand, which she shook at Maddy, "Guess what I got?" She pulled out a large bottle of Tuscan Lemonade. Vodka! Hot damn!

Maddy let out a whoop, "Damn girl, I knew there was a reason I call you my friend."

Miranda whispered, "Is she in there?"

"Yeah, but I haven't been in there. I just finished getting ready. Thank God you guys came when you did. Open the bottle. I need a shot bad," Maddy laughed. She took the bottle from Miranda and downed several swigs.

"Christ Maddy, that's pure vodka," Miranda shrieked.

Maddy gasped and sputtered as she swallowed the fiery liquid. "Damn, that shit is strong." She took three more big swallows and replaced the lid. "Okay I have my shot of courage." She held her fingers to her lips and looked at the couple, "Ssssshhhhhh, this is just between the three of us. Actually I don't care if Jack knows, but hell, you know what I mean."

Maddy gently pushed open the kitchen door and held it open for Andy and Miranda. "Look who's here, Babe?"

Jack shook Andy's hand and gave Miranda a hug and offered them a seat. He then reached for Maddy pulling her close and kissed her. He his head came back looking at her face and licked his lips. Maddy grinned up at him. He shook his head and laughed at her. He kissed her again and whispered, "Behave yourself, your flirting with disaster."

She feigned innocence, "Who me?" She smiled up at him.

He touched her on the end of her nose, "Yeah you."

Maddy went to Bryan and gave his a soft kiss and they hugged. "Hi Mickey."

Bryan smiled at her, "You look ravishing, Minnie."

Maddy glanced over at Donna noticing she was being glared at. "Hi Donna, glad you could come." She went out of her way to make that scene with Bryan just for her benefit. This was her night.

Maddy went to the cupboard and pulled a couple of glasses down for her and Miranda. She filled the glasses with ice and set them on the bar. Jack had given Andy a beer. Bryan and Jack already had one while Donna was sipping on a wine cooler. Light weight.

"Em...Jack, do you have some frozen lemonade? I forgot to pick some up to mix with the Tuscan. That stuff is much too strong to be drinking straight," she was subtly nodding toward Maddy.

"In the freezer in the door," he grabbed a pitcher from cupboard and a whisk. He slid it across to Miranda.

"Chief's been whining for you to come back to work," Miranda told Maddy as she mixed the lemonade. "Wants you to quit playing FBI and get back to being a reporter."

"Christ Miranda, not everyone knows do they?" Maddy asked in horror. She had wanted this to be on the hush.

"Not everyone, but it wasn't too hard to figure out when you came storming in sporting a badge and a gun. Most of it is just speculation."

Donna turned to Bryan, "Maddy is FBI? You never told me that."

Bryan took a drink of his beer, "That's how we met. We were in the same unit, she was in the BAU."

"BAU?" she looked lost.

"Behavior Analysis Unit. She's a profiler," Andy interjected. Andy seemed to take great pride in telling people.

"Maddy, all the talking we did, and you didn't bother to tell me?" Donna stated.

Maddy felt irritated. She grabbed a glass of the mixed lemonade and took a rather large sip. "I don't know why my past has to be the topic of conversation all the time." She turned and left the room.

Jack and Bryan exchanged glances. One or the other could go after her, or leave her alone and let her settle down on her own. "Just leave her be," Jack told him. "She's got a lot going on right now."

Maddy had made her way back to the den. Jack's computer was in sleep mode. She moved the mouse around and her unsub's image popped up. She flipped through the shots. On one of the photos she notice a little gold bar on his blue shirt. She tried to zoom in but the photo became so pixely she couldn't distinguish anything. Jack's computer didn't have Photoshop. She dashed up to the bedroom and pulled her laptop out of the bag Jessie had dropped off. She took it back to the den and downloaded all the photos from the camera. She went into Adobe Bridge and looked through the photos. She found the one she was looking for and clicked on it to bring up in Photoshop. She jacked up the dpi and then zoomed in on the gold bar. She could make out the trace of print on it, but not enough for it to be legible. She went under the filters menu and sharpened the edges by several degrees. She sat back in the chair staring at the screen. Awesome! She felt a rush of excitement and a sense of dread all at the same time. Her unsub had a name, and she was the only one who knew who he was. The Reverend Justin Parsons. Parsons—Parsonage, how ironic. Was he for real?

Maddy leaned back in the chair. This was what she was comfortable doing...working alone. She was just all around comfortable being alone. She could do the bar scene every once in awhile, but as a whole she wasn't a social animal. She picked up her glass and noticed a water ring. Shit, not on Jack fancy desk. She wiped the ring off with the bottom of her blouse. The ring disappeared. She grabbed a piece of paper and folded it into a square. She took a sip of her drink and placed on the makeshift coaster.

Now what to do with this little jewel of information? She couldn't keep it to herself...she couldn't sit on it. She put her head down on the desk. Just because she had a name on the man she thought she saw at the gravesite, didn't mean they had enough to bring him in, and if they did it prematurely all could be lost.

She hadn't heard from him for a couple of days, which didn't break her heart and she wasn't about to initiate contact with him. She couldn't let him know she knew who he was. She felt that really would put her life in danger.

Maddy went back to Jack's computer and googled Justin Parsons. It came up blank. Which basically all this told her is had no landline to match the name. He wasn't listed in any of the minster registries. What was the deal with this guy? Was he really a minister?

Maddy grabbed a pen and scratched his name on a piece of paper and then put both computers on sleep mode.

She downed the rest of her drink. Her head was fuzzy and she felt emotionally high strung. She knew she needed to mellow out or someone was going to get decked and as far as she was concerned it was open season. This cookout thing was a really bad idea.

Maddy found her way back to the kitchen where everyone was sitting around talking and joking around. The room grew quiet when she walked in. She just brushed it off and poured herself another drink and stood by Jack. She took a sip from her drink, "Hey don't stop in my account." She smiled weakly.

Jack slid his arm around her waist and kissed the top of her head. Maddy slipped him the scrap of paper. Jack unfolded the paper and read it, then looked up at her questioning. "What's this?"

She smiled, "You're the detective, you figure it out."

"Maddy," he eyed her, "don't be fucking with me. What is this?"

"It's a name," her eyes pierced into his hoping he would pick up on her meaning.

Jack furtively looked around the room. Everyone was looking at them. "Excuse us a minute." Jack grabbed Maddy by the hand and led her into the living room. "Nice way for you to relax, Maddy. You been back there working this whole time?"

"It's what I do, Jack, it's in my comfort zone. Screw what I was doing, what do you think?" She watched him.

"How did you come up with this?"

"I told you it's what I do," she stated flatly. The alcohol was making her insolent.

Jack shook his head in despair. "Don't do this Maddy. It's you and me here, not you and Bryan. Please tell me how discovered this tid-bit of information.

"In one of the photos, I noticed a little gold bar on his chest. I was guessing it was a nametag so pulled the photo into Photoshop and was able to sharpen it enough to get clarification. And that," she pointed to the paper, "is the result."

"Jesus, Maddy," Jack sat down on the couch and ran his fingers through his hair. "So what are we going to do with this information? We really should take this to Bryan."

"I thought we agreed we were going to sit on this until we had enough to have a reason to bring him in for questioning. We still don't and if we bring him in too early we could blow everything. Especially if he figures out I am the one that tracked him down. I don't want to go back into hiding, Jack. I can't"

Jack put his head in his hands, "I just don't feel comfortable holding out pertinent information. It just doesn't sit well with me. It goes against everything I have been trained to do."

Maddy stripped the paper out of his hand. "I don't have one qualm about it. My training tells me you sit on the info until you can make a case. Get your facts then react."

"That's not your FBI training talking, that's you reporter training. At the current time, Maddy, you are FBI."

Maddy laughed, "Symantec's, that's all it is. You trust my instincts don't you?"

"Yes."

Maddy turned his face up to her and she kissed him. "Then trust me okay?"

Jack sat quietly thinking. "Maddy, I can't. If this gets out that I am withholding critical information on a case, I could get fired. You don't have to worry about it; you're going to be leaving anyway. Can you see things from my perspective?"

Maddy slumped down in the couch. "I should have kept my mouth shut to everyone."

"God damn it, Maddy!" Jack snapped at her. "Don't you ever do that to me. I know you've done it plenty in the past and I excused it. Things we have worked on before have been relatively minor compared to this. We are partners here, baby. You got to stay clean with me. Promise me, Maddy."

Maddy rolled her eyes. "I don't know why everyone is so hell bent on making me change."

Jack turned to Maddy, "Do you want to stay in the past or do you want to have a future...with me?"

"You know what I want," she glared at him. "But why can't I keep the good parts of me. Why do I have to be someone totally different?"

Jack pulled her to him. "Baby, just be yourself. We will deal with the bad issues and how you want to handle them okay? Now can we fill Bryan in?"

"He's going to yell at me. And what if he makes us go in?"

"What good would it do? Like you said we have nothing more to go on."

"I don't want Bryan to know everything. I will take the fall on this. I don't want you and Andy to be reprimanded. Let me do the talking and you play stupid okay?" Maddy insisted.

"You don't want me to know what, Maddy?" Bryan was standing behind them.

Jack stood up. "Maddy has something she needs to show you."

They led Bryan back to the den. Maddy took her computer out of sleep mode and brought up the photo and zoomed back out.

"What are we looking at here?" Bryan asked as he looked down over Maddy's shoulder.

Maddy took a deep breath. "Meet Justin Parsons, our possible unsub."

"How did you get this?"

"I found a common denominator for two of our vics in their obituaries. I remembered the last call Vanessa Granger made was to the same church these women attended. So I staked it out, took some photos and ran some searches on those photos," Maddy explained.

"This is what the three of you were doing yesterday?" he asked.

"Yes," Jack answered before Maddy could. He would not let her go down alone. "Maddy thought this guy looked like the one she saw at the last burial site. I recognized him, too, but just in passing."

Maddy smiled weakly at Jack and then looked back at Bryan. "I didn't look at them until a little while ago. I tried to run a facial recognition search, but it came up empty. There is no common trace on him. I hit a deadend everywhere I turned. We got nothing to bring him in on. Nothing."

"But she did get a name on him," Jack added.

Maddy zoomed in on the nametag revealing the man's name.

"If that really is his name," Bryan said as he put a hand on her shoulder. "Good job. We'll deal with it on Monday. Let's get back to the party." He turned and left the room.

Maddy exchanged looks with Jack, "What's up with that?"

Jack shrugged. "I don't know. Maybe he just doesn't care anymore."

Maddy couldn't let it go. As soon as they returned to the kitchen, Maddy grabbed her drink and pulled up a stool beside Bryan. Jack went to get the steaks ready to grill.

Maddy leaned her head on her hand, which was propped up by her elbow on the bar. "Soooooo how's it going?"

Bryan looked at her and chuckled, "You're drunk."

"Am not."

"You know you're not suppose to be drinking while you're on your meds," he did a mirror image of Maddy's pose.

"Yeah and you're not going to tell Jack either."

"You know I will," he smiled at her.

"Yeah, you have a big fucking mouth. You guys take all the fun out of everything," she continued to stare at him noticing his black and blue nose but chose not to comment. "How come you didn't jump my ass in there?"

"I'm saving it for Monday, so I can humiliate you in front of the whole squad."

Maddy had gone to take a sip of her drink and choked. "You ass! You would too!"

Bryan watched her, a soft smile playing upon his lips. He didn't respond to her last comment.

Maddy was pulled into his eyes, the way he was looking at her. She felt a little tinge in her stomach. "What's going through your mind?"

He took his hand off his beer and ran his fingers along her cheek. "You don't want to know, Minnie."

"Yeah I do."

"It would do nothing but cause problems. And you know I can't do that. Not and hang on to what part of you I have left," he told her softly.

Maddy slid off her seat and put her arms around him and held him tight. Bryan did the same and buried his face in her hair. "Oh Minnie, it's so hard, so very, very hard."

"I know, Mickey," she whispered, "but you have to know how much I love you." She felt her eyes starting to tear up.

He kissed the top of her head, "I know you do, and it's what keeps me going. I love you, too...forever and always."

She nodded, her face buried in his chest.

Donna watched the two of them, not believing what she was seeing. She glanced at Jack, who was placing the steaks on a platter. "Surely you see them."

"Yeah so?"

"And it's okay with you?" she said in disbelief.

"Perfectly okay. They love each other, very deeply. Nothing or no one is ever going to change that. They are a part of each other."

"I don't get it, or you. The woman you claim you love is in the arms of another man, right in front of you and you do nothing." Donna waited for his response.

Jack set down the tray of meat with a thud. "That I claim to love? Let's get something perfectly straight here. I love Maddy more than life itself and I know she loves me just as much. I also know the history she and Bryan have. I know everything he has done for her. He pulled her out of the jaws of a demon not that long ago with the love he has for her. Only that love saved her. It wasn't me, it was him. I will be forever grateful to him. Bryan will do whatever it takes for Maddy to find happiness. The three of us know her happiness lies with me." Jack said in a low cold voice.

"Donna," Bryan said as he brushed the tears away from Maddy's eyes. "You really need to keep your nose out of other's business. The complexity of our situation is so far above your understanding it's not worth trying to dignify it to you. Jack is one of the best damn friends I have had since Chuck was killed. He and Maddy belong together. I know he will take care of her and give her the love and happiness she deserves. If I didn't, they wouldn't be together, I can guarantee that."

"How unselfish and noble of you," Donna sneered.

"Everyone just shut the fuck up!" Maddy screamed. "Damn it, Donna, you came up here uninvited. Why the hell do you always try to make his life miserable? You just can't let go. But you know something? I don't give a fuck. If Bryan wants to put up with your shit for whatever reason, that's his choice. Now you were invited here for a nice afternoon of socializing. You have your choice, sit here and criticize something you don't know shit about, or you can make the effort to have a good time." Maddy left the room and ran up the stairs.

Maddy looked at herself in the bathroom mirror. Her eyes were red with unshed tears. Damn it! She pounded her fist on the sink. She turned the water on and splashed it on her face. A towel appeared in front of her. When she looked back, Jack was standing behind her. She smiled weakly at him. "Well I guess it had to happen sometime right?"

"Come here," he turned her to face him and wrapped his arms around her. "I'm sorry. This is not very much fun for you."

"It's okay. The air needed to be cleared. People will never understand the relationship the three of us have. But that's okay, we know." Maddy braced her hands on his chest and searched his eyes. "I love you Jack, I love you so much."

Jack held her face in his hands and kissed her deeply. "I love you Maddy, God you have to know that."

She nodded, "I do. I'm sorry this whole thing is turning into a fiasco. You put so much work into it and I am fucking everything up."

Jack laughed, "No, you did what you always do, you make life more interesting."

She poked him in the ribs. "Okay, no more drama."

Jack took her hand and led her back downstairs. Maddy stopped, "Where are Miranda and Andy?"

Jack chuckled, "Out in the sunroom getting drunk."

Maddy smiled, "A bunch of cops sitting around getting drunk, nice image we're projecting here."

They went to the kitchen and gathered the food to bring out. Bryan had taken the steaks out and put them on the grill.

Miranda was sitting on Andy's lap. They were joking and laughing having a good time oblivious to the tension that had played out while they were absent. Probably a good thing. At least someone was having a good time.

Maddy looked around to find Donna sitting off by herself. She poured herself a fresh drink and grabbed a wine cooler for Donna. Maddy pulled up a chair next to her and offered her to cooler. "Listen Donna, I'm not sure why you decided to come here. I am guessing in effort to get Bryan back. It doesn't really matter to me. It's up to Bryan whatever he decides to do. Whatever that is, he has my support. I'm not going to spend all my time sparing with you. We will never be friends again, but we can at least get along, so can we just call it a truce?"

Donna took the cooler from her and thanked her. "You know when we were friends, you were one of the best friends I ever had."

"You were too. Hell, Donna, we could talk about anything and everything. You were so much fun to talk to. Why did you have to bring Bryan into it? I begged you not to and then you blindsided me. You could have saved us all so much pain."

Donna shrugged, "I don't know. I guess it thought it would be nice if you two could rekindle an old friendship. Maddy, I didn't know you two had been so deeply involved. Once he found out, you became an obsession."

Maddy put her hand up, "That's all the further you need to go. I know quite well how the story ends and I really don't want to go down that road."

Donna took a drink from the bottle, "Did you two stay in contact the whole time?"

Maddy took a deep breath and then took a big gulp from her glass. "No. I never heard from him again until about three weeks ago. When he showed up here to lead this case."

"And took up where he wanted to be."

"I don't feel comfortable talking about this with you," Maddy took another sip.

"Jack seems like a pretty nice guy," Donna said changing the subject.

Maddy smiled warmly, "He's a wonderful man."

"And he adores you," Donna said longingly. "I wish I had a man look at me the way he looks at you."

"Forgive me for saying so, but Donna, you will never find it if you keep clinging to something that just isn't there," Maddy said softly.

"It used to be."

"Did it? That's not quite the way I heard it, it least it hasn't been in a very long time."

"So what do I do?" Donna looked up at her with tears in her eyes.

"I can't answer that. You and Bryan both deserve to be happy, but it doesn't necessarily mean it's together. Love has to be a two way street, hon."

"You and Bryan love each other. Why isn't it working for you?"

"Because Donna, somewhere a long the line, there comes a time for honesty. Bryan and I can't have a future, not in that way, because there is too much to our past. I know that doesn't make much sense, but it does to us. We still love each other, we always will, but it doesn't mean...I don't want to talk about this anymore." Maddy stood up and started to turn away.

"Maddy? Thank you," Donna said.

The steaks were almost done so Maddy went in to grab the potatoes. She felt her talk with Donna went well. Maybe that was one more ghost laid to rest. Maddy grabbed the oven mitts and removed the spuds from the oven. She placed them in a bowl and headed to the back of the house. As she was walking past the corner the sound of a cell phone startled her. When she glanced at the kitchen counter it was the unsub cell vibrating across the tile. She dropped the bowl.

Maddy grabbed the phone and ran to the sunroom. She stood in the doorway holding the ringing phone up for all to see.

"Fuck!" Jack groaned.

"You better answer it, Maddy," Bryan said sadly.

Maddy's eyes darted back and forth between Bryan and Jack, shaking her head.

Jack sat her down, "It's okay, Kitten, take a deep breath, you ready?"

"Hello?" she answered, her voice but a whisper.

Bryan stepped out and called the squad room confirming Derek was picking up on the call.

"Good evening, Maddy. It's nice to hear your voice again."

"Wish I could say the same," Maddy answered flatly.

Jack nudged her and shook his head. Maddy nodded her acknowledgment.

Andy whispered for the others not to say a word. Miranda and Donna both nodded.

"You didn't miss me?"

"I was pretty busy dealing with my own problems. Sorry if I didn't give you the response you would have liked."

"Did you get everything taken care of?"

"Why do you care? Why do you want to talk to me? What do I matter to you?" Maddy was becoming irritated, maybe it was the alcohol, maybe it was because she knew he was close enough should could snap his neck.

Bryan stood behind her and rubbed her shoulders trying to get her to relax.

"You intrigue me. A smart, beautiful woman as yourself, a self-proclaimed sinner. You are fearless aren't you Maddy?" His voice was so calm, so self-confident.

Bryan felt Maddy tensing up more. He picked up her drink and handed it to her. Maddy took it and downed it. "Don't be silly. We all have our demons...even you. What are you afraid of?"

"I fear only the Lord. He is my Master."

"And you are the Master of those that fear you...your flock." Maddy said her voice steady. She needed another drink. She lifted her glass. Miranda started to pour her a glass and she shook her head and pointed to the bottle. Miranda went to pour her a drink; Maddy grabbed it and poured her glass to the rim. She took a big gulp almost choking on it.

"My flock has nothing to fear from me." His voice had gone flat. Apparently he didn't like the direction this conversation was turning.

Maddy didn't want to push him into anger so she decided to take a different direction. "I would think you would be busy preparing your sermon for tomorrow."

The unsub laughed, "I bet you would just love to come and listen to me spread the word of the Lord."

"Like I think you would be stupid enough to invite me," Maddy forced a laugh.

"I don't preach on Sundays."

"That's an odd thing for a preacher to say. It's the Sabbath, is that not the day to rejoice in the Lord?" she asked.

"So much to learn, sweet Maddy, so much to teach you," his voice had taken on an air of seduction.

Jack reached across and took Maddy's hand and squeezed it. Bryan's hands still rested on her shoulders. "What do you mean by that?"

"In due time. We have much to talk about, many more conversations to have."

Maddy took another drink, feeling the warm fluid spread through her giving her false courage. "Do I have reason to fear you?"

"Do you feel you need to?"

"So we're playing games again. I asked you a simple, honest question. Do I have cause to fear you?"

The sound of laughter rang through the phone, "Maddy, Maddy, Maddy. You have two of the best body guards in the city whom I am sure are standing with you now as we speak. How can I harm you with such noble protection?"

"You didn't answer my question."

He laughed again and then said, "Only in your mind sweet Maddy." The line went dead.

Maddy screamed and threw the phone sending it sliding across the table. "I hate him, I hate him, I hate him!" Maddy collapsed in Jack's arms, clinging to him for strength.

"Who was that?" Miranda whispered to Andy.

Andy looked to Jack who just shrugged his shoulders as he held Maddy.

"That's our unsub," Andy told her quietly.

"Unsub?"

"The killer we've been tracking. He made contact after the stupid article Sutton wrote and put Maddy's name on."

Miranda stared at Maddy, "Isn't that dangerous for her to be talking to him?" she asked.

"No shit!" Andy snapped.

"Andy!" Maddy sat up, "don't get bitchy with her. She doesn't know what the hell is going on."

Bryan knelt down beside her while Jack had his hands placed on her knees.

"You did good kiddo. He's taunting you again, trying to throw you off your game. Don't let him do it. We got a face now and a name. It's only a matter of time," Bryan reassured her.

Andy looked up, "We got a name?"

Bryan laughed nervously, "Oh yes, I forgot, you were one of the wayward agents, too. Yeah, Maddy got us a name now, but that is not open for discussion at this time for reasons I am sure you are aware of."

"I dropped the potatoes," Maddy said softly.

"I'll go get them," Donna rose from her chair and left for the kitchen.

Bryan followed her in, "You mustn't repeat anything you saw here."

"Bryan, have I ever told anyone the things you've let me be privy to? No. How can you put Maddy in that kind of danger?" she asked.

"It's a means to an end," he stated flatly.

"That sounds pretty damn cold to me, especially from someone who claims they care," she snarled at him.

"That's not quite what I mean. She is our only link to this guy. It is because of her we have any kind of information on him at all. Her profiling skills, her powers of observation and her gut instincts are what has put this case together. She has virtually no personal life until we catch this guy."

"What did he mean by body guards?"

"Either Jack or myself is to be with her at all times, Andy in a pinch. Jack does most of the watch. She wants to quit but she can't go back to her job until we catch him. We still aren't so sure he is not going to make a grab for her," Bryan explained to her.

Donna picked up the foil wrapped potatoes and placed them back in the bowl. "You know from talking to her a couple of years ago, when we were friends, I never would have had a clue this was who she was."

"Was is the key word, she never wanted to be it again. Now let's just let it drop." Bryan grabbed some more beer out of the fridge.

Maddy reached for her glass. Jack took it out of her hands and placed it back on the table. "You've had more than enough to drink. I'm surprised you can even stand."

Maddy sighed and looked away, "Whatever."

Jack frowned. The phone called had forced her to shut down and she had been doing so well. "I'm going to ignore that remark."

"Why not? Seems like a plan to me. If we ignore everything, it will make it all go away right?"

"You know damn well that's not what I meant. You need to stop yourself on this path before it gets out of hand and you say something we both might regret," Jack told her coldly.

Maddy laughed, "Are you threatening me? Get in line."

Jack knew it was the booze and the fear talking be she was really starting to piss him off. He pushed her glass across the table. "Go ahead drink yourself into oblivion. I don't give a fuck if that's how little you care. Hide in your booze. You've seen where hiding will get you." He stood up and went to grill to check the steaks.

Maddy pulled her feet up under her. She had succeeded at ticking Jack off. What the hell was going through her head? She knew, piss them off, drive them away. Is that what she really wanted? No, she was just reverting back to her old games. She was dealing with issues she had no business addressing at this point in time—making at commitment, moving in with Jack, trying to come to terms with her losses from the past, destroying the dream that she and Bryan would ever be together, wanting so badly to quit the FBI...just too much shit. And she was drowning it in alcohol mixed with antipsychotics. Not a good mix. God what she wouldn't do to be at home, take one of her horses out and ride until she couldn't breath anymore.

Maddy looked around her surroundings. Miranda and Andy were talking, Donna and Bryan had just returned with her spilt potatoes. Jack was standing at the grill ignoring her. Good.

Maddy quietly left the sunroom. She grabbed her purse and dug out her keys. As she walked through the kitchen she banged into several of the stools. Damn, her coordination sucked. Only few more steps to the garage and her escape. She was going home...at least in her mind.

Jack glanced over his shoulder and saw Maddy was missing. Then he heard the garage door going up. "Fuck! Bryan, take over here!" He tore through the house and out the garage door. He found Maddy sitting in her car, her head leaning against the steering wheel and arms wrapped around her head. When he opened the door, she reached out with one hand and dropped the keys.

"Maddy, what the hell are you doing?" he asked kneeling by the car.

"Going home...but I don't know the way," she mumbled.

He helped her out of the car, "We need to get you sobered up." He pulled her to her feet, which she could hardly stand on. He scooped her up in his arms and carried her into the house.

Bryan had popped in to see what was going on as Jack was carrying her into living room. Maddy's head was resting on his shoulder. "I'm going to take her up and throw her in the shower. There is some black tea made up in the fridge. We may not be able to sober her up much, but we can at least wake her up enough to get her to eat. You guys go ahead."

Jack laid her on the bed while he went in and started the shower. When he came back she was sitting up staring off into space. He shook his head in disbelief. She allowed him to strip her down to her bra and panties. He decided he was just going to throw her in like that.

When Maddy's body hit the cold water she screamed out. "Jesus fucking Christ that's cold!" When Jack reached in to adjust the water she yanked on his arm catching him off balance and pulled him into the shower. Maddy pinned him up against the side, pressed her body against his and crushed his lips with hers. Her kiss was firm, demanding...passionate. She ran her hands underneath his shirt and pushed it up over his head. Her fingertips taunted his chest, her lips burned a path down it and flicked her tongue over his nipple.

Jack groaned, "Maddy, Kitten..." he said breathlessly, "we have company."

"For me...right now...you are the only person in the world," her lips found his again, her tongue sliding deeply into his mouth.

"Oh what the fuck," he mumbled as he stepped back slightly. He reached around her head and pulled out her hair tie and then his hand slid down her back and unhooked her bra. His mouth crushed down on hers as he pulled her body to his. The cool shower of water made their skin highly sensitive to each other's touch.

Maddy reached between them and unfastened his jeans. Jack slipped them off and flipped them out of the shower and then stripped Maddy of her panties. He pinned her up against the shower wall, lifting her up, wrapping her legs around him. Maddy let out a cry of delight as he thrust himself into her. He held her up by her hips as he urgently pushed himself into her. It was crazy, hot sex with the cold water spraying down on them. Jack forced her mouth open with his tongue and shoved it deep into her mouth. He loved the sound of Maddy whimpering softly with each thrust he gave her. He felt her nails digging into his shoulders, her whimpering turning into moans. He knew she was close and he was ready to explode. With one hard thrust she screamed out but his mouth covering hers muffled the sound. He held her against the wall staying in her until the spiral slowly came down then let her feet down to the floor.

Maddy kissed him deeply then stood back a little. She was smiling ear to ear. "Damn," she grinned. "I like."

Jack chuckled, "As a rule, quickies are not are not the way I want you, but we will make an exception."

They suds each other up, dried off, and slipped across to the bedroom to get dressed.

Jack had his arms possessively around her as they returned to the sunroom. They got some unique stares when everyone noticed Jack's hair wet and the change of clothing.

Jack pulled out at chair for Maddy and helped her into it. She was still pretty tipsy, but she was languid and happy. He slid his chair close to her putting one arm around her shoulder.

Bryan set a glass of tea in front of Maddy. He turned to Jack and laughed, "Okay, not necessarily the way to sober her up, but it got her smiling."

Jack turned red, "Shut up. It was her fault."

Bryan smiled and nodded, "I'm sure it was."

Jack got Maddy to eat a little bit, but she never did eat well when she was high strung.

Afterwards they sprawled out on a lounge, Jack lying back, Maddy lying between his legs, her head resting on his chest. Everyone else was partaking in idle chitchat while Maddy just sat back and somewhat listened. She didn't participate; her mind was still too fuzzy. She just took comfort in the feel of Jack's arms around her holding her tight.

Bryan asked Andy and Miranda to drop Donna off at the motel while he stayed behind to talk to Jack about the case.

Jack sat on one end of the couch with Maddy lying down, her head resting on his lap. She was out to the world.

Bryan came in and stopped to brush his hand against Maddy's cheek then sat down across from them on the loveseat. "I'm going to tell you something I know I should have earlier, but by the time I got to her it was too late. She is not supposed to be drinking with her meds. It intensifies the alcohol."

"Hell with as much as she drank, how the hell would you know if it was intensified?" Jack laughed. "I really shouldn't have sprung this on her. She wasn't comfortable with Donna being here. I think she handled it well, especially for her, but just the same it wasn't fair of me to force the issue. And of course the little phone call didn't help."

Jack softly brushed Maddy's hair with his fingers. "She looks so innocent when she sleeps."

Bryan threw his head back and laughed, "So does a tiger."

"My kitten," Jack whispered. Then he looked up at Bryan. "So what are we going to do with Parsons?"

"I gave his name to Derek to run it through the FBI's system. If he has a social security number we will find something on him." Bryan leaned back and stretched.

"Why didn't Maddy do that?"

"You can't do it with an offsite computer and she wasn't willing to give up her prize just yet to turn it over to the squad. I believe she still wouldn't have done it yet if she hadn't been prodded by you."

"It's the reporter thing in her. Whenever she worked a case with me, she always kept things tight to the vest until she could get everything she could on it and then spring it on me. I told her she needed to think FBI not reporter. She still didn't want to but hey..." he shrugged and smiled.

"We'll see what Derek turns up on him, and then I suggest we put a tail on him for a couple days. I know Maddy will want to be in on that so I will assign you three musketeers on that detail. I have to say Whitmer has really stood up with Maddy's guidance. Might make a agent out of him yet."

Jack smiled, "Don't count on it. He doesn't have the stomach for it. He wants to resign after this case and join the force here."

Bryan smiled weakly, "Here I was trying to get you to join the Bureau instead I am loosing an agent."

"I couldn't join, I can't do that to Maddy. We just want to get our lives back to some kind of normalcy so we can start a life," Jack said as he looked down at her sleeping face and traced her lips with his fingers.

Bryan raised an eyebrow, "Things have gotten this serious this fast? Damn it has only been two weeks."

"This part of it yes, but not for the rest. She's free thanks to you and we have made amazing progress. But we both want this."

Bryan felt the now familiar pang of heartache hearing Jack talk this way about he and Maddy. Just a short time ago he thought that could have been them. But the reality of the whole, he could never have given Maddy a normal life. Too many ghosts. "Well I am happy for you, for you both. I know you will do right by her."

Jack looked up to meet Bryan's gaze. "You know I feel like shit that my happiness is your pain. I hate it like hell."

Bryan looked at him, "The better man won."

"There are no winners here. Maddy is still torn. You're hurting. I hurt for both of you. No, nobody wins."

Bryan stood up, "Maddy is happy with you, I can see it when she looks at you. I see joy in her eyes, not pain and mistrust. I just want to be able to be in her life, even if it is in some small way. Better get her up to bed. She's going to have one bitching headache in the morning."

Jack started to get up, but Bryan stopped him. "No, I can show myself out. I will give you a call tomorrow to tell you if Derek turns up anything." Bryan brushed Maddy's cheek as he walked by. "Good night. Thanks for the cookout today." He laughed, "It was interesting to say the least."

23

When Maddy rolled over agonizing pain shot through her head. She put her hands over her eyes, "Oh fuck man....this is so not cool." She heard a snicker from the other side of the bed. "Fuck...you..." she said with slow deliberation.

Jack slowly rolled over then propped up his head with his arm. "You would think by now you would learn," he chuckled. "Vodka is not a friend to you. Besides you're not supposed to be drinking anyhow."

"Shut the fuck up," she groaned. "Big mouth opened up his trap I see."

Maddy lifted her head slightly to look at the alarm clock. 10:40. She laid back down.

"Mom called, wanted to know if we could come over for brunch," Jack smiled down at her.

Maddy opened one eye and glared at him, "Are you fucking nuts?"

Jack lay back down on his pillow unable to contain his amusement. "Damn you got a mouth on you when you're hung-over. You make for one nasty drunk, Kitten. Why don't you get up and take a shower and take some aspirin?"

"Go to hell."

Jack got up from the bed, "No seriously, you need to go get ready. I've already showered while you were snoozing."

Maddy slowly sat up in bed. Her head was pounding, her mouth felt like she had swallowed a pillow. "Baby, are you really serious or you just giving me shit?"

Jack leaned over and kissed on her forehead. "Very serious, Kitten. Get moving." As he walked out of the bedroom door he was hit in the back of the head with a pillow. "Mush, mush baby cakes," he laughed.

Maddy dragged herself out of bed and across the hall to the bathroom. She stumbled on a piece of clothing. When she looked down and saw a damp, crumpled up pair of blue jeans she felt the heat rise to her cheeks. Oh yeah, she smiled, she remembered now. That was hot...like most things were when it came to Jack. She nudged them with her foot into the bathroom.

After her shower she picked up the discarded clothing and stuck them in a clothesbasket. She still felt like crap but at least now she could function. She couldn't believe Jack would accept his mom's invitation knowing full well she was going to feel like death warmed over.

She slipped on her cotton-t sweat suit and a pair of tennis shoes. She decided against pulling her hair back, no mess...less stress...on her head that was.

Maddy entered the kitchen just as Jack came in through the garage door. He held a drugstore sack in his hand. "What's that?"

"Your little fizzy friend," he said as he threw it across the bar. He grabbed a glass from the cupboard, filled it full of water and set it in front of her.

"Thanks," she ripped into one of the packets with her teeth and dropped the two tablets into the water. "Are we really going to your folks? Why do to you keep forcing me into...situations? Especially when I feel like hell."

"You were getting along so good with Mom yesterday, I thought you would like it. Do you want me call and cancel? I will if you really want me to." Jack pulled up a stool next to her.

Maddy eyed him over her glass as she drank the bubbling liquid. Jack was so high energy. He was constantly doing something, always on the move, always planning. She never really realized it before, but then again they had never spent this much time together. Was she going to be able to keep up with him? He was exhausting. She shook the thought out of her head. She just wasn't used to his life-style. Hers was laid back, relaxing, doing things at her own pace...and doing them alone. Food for thought.

"Who else is going to be there?" she asked as she drank the last of the selt-zer.

"Just Dad." He looked at her hopeful.

"No surprises?"

He held up two fingers, "Scouts honor."

Maddy sighed, "Okay, but don't expect Little Miss Sunshine. Man, I can't believe the conditions you make me meet your parents under."

Maddy sat quietly running her fingers around the rim of her glass. They needed to talk. "Jack..."

"What's up Kitten?" he picked up the tone in her voice and it didn't sound good.

"I don't want you to take this the wrong way. But after today...could you please slow down on the social situations? I need down time. I need space....not from you, but from people."

Jack picked up his cell phone and flipped it open and hit a number on speed dial. "Hey Mom, do you care if we take a rain check on brunch? I want to take Maddy to her home. She needs to get out of the city and recoup." There was a pause. "Okay, sounds good. Tell Dad maybe I will bring her over sometime this week depending on how work goes. Love you too. Yeah I will tell her." He flipped the phone shut. "Mom said to tell she hopes you feel better soon."

Maddy slipped off her stool and hugged him tight. "I love you," she said tearfully.

Jack held her back, looking at her, "What's with the tears? I thought you would be happy."

She wiped the tears away, "I am happy. You, your love, I just can't believe how incredibly thoughtful and caring you are."

Jack laughed, "I just got the impression I wasn't being very thoughtful by pushing you into things you're not ready for. Let me go pack a bag. Why don't you put Eddie in his kennel and grab his supplies so he can check out his other home. Don't forget your meds." And with that he was off.

Damn that man could make her head spin. Maddy took her dose of meds and then put the bottles in her bag. She dashed back to the den and grabbed her laptop and camera bag. By the time Jack had returned she had her stuff in his car and was holding Eddie in his kennel sitting on the bar.

"I need to call Bryan quick, tell him what's going on," Jack said as he flipped his phone open.

"Hey Bryan, how you feeling this morning?"

Bryan laughed, "I'm sure a lot better than someone else is."

"Yeah, she is really bitchy when she's hung-over—bitchier than normal."

"Hey!" Maddy howled.

Jack covered the phone with his hand. "Will you grab Eddie and I will be out in a sec?"

"You just want to bad mouth me, I know," she growled as she grabbed the kennel and went out to the car.

"Okay, she's gone. She's kind of stressing today so I am going to take her to her place, get her out of the city. I will take a back route. We'll be staying there tonight and coming to work from there in the morning. I don't know how you feel about this, I will have the unsub phone with me, but I'm not turning it on."

It was almost as if he could hear Bryan thinking on the other end of line. "No, go ahead and do that. He doesn't need to think she is going to be at his beck and call anyhow. If this guy is Parsons, we can quit kissing his ass real soon. I will give you a call when I hear anything on him. Give Maddy a kiss for me and I will see you two tomorrow."

"Good enough take care."

Jack grabbed the unsub cell, powered it down and threw it in his bag. Maddy needed to get away and he was sure as hell going to make sure she got away from him.

When Jack got in his car, Maddy had put on her sunglasses and had reclined the seat back. He laughed under his breath. "You're pathetic."

Maddy laughed, "Shut up and drive."

Maddy hadn't realized she had drifted off to sleep until she felt the car come to a stop.

Jack nudged her gently, "Sleeping beauty, you're home."

Maddy put her seat in the upright position, "No, we're home. If I'm living with you, you're living with me, that makes this your home, too."

Jack smiled, "Okay, when you put it like that. You grab Eddie and I will grab everything else."

Maddy didn't argue with him. She unlocked the door, let Eddie out of his kennel and went straight for the couch. She laid down letting the couch engulf her. Damn she loved being home.

She used to think living out here was a self-imposed exile, but she was really beginning to realize she had been happy with her life. Granted there was always this shadow hanging over her head, but that aside she was happy here. How was she ever going to deal with living in the city? She hated the city. The only thing good about it was Jack was there. Would she be able to hide her misery or would she be able to accept it in order to be with Jack?

The longer she laid there the more her thoughts turned to how good it would feel to be alone, all by herself, no one watching over her—even if it were just for 24 hours. But she knew that wasn't going to happen. There was no way in hell Jack or Bryan would let her stay home alone. She blew that thought off as a pipe dream. No sense longing for something that wasn't going to happen in the near future.

Maddy's eyes were drawn to the box on the floor—her memory box. Jack wanted children. She honestly didn't know if she could give him any. She didn't know if she was capable of giving a child love, or risking loving a child. Her children had been everything to her. They were ripped away from her leaving a hole in her soul that haunted her to this day. Unconsciously she went to the box. The tapes were placed in date order. She picked out the most recent, turned on the VCR and TV and popped the tape in. She grabbed the remote and a box of tissue and settle back down on the couch preparing herself to have her heart torn out... again.

Jack had set the bags and Maddy's laptop on the step and decided to take a walk around the acreage. It was kind of lonely without the Rufus and Jack being underfoot. He found himself down at the pasture gate watching the horses out in the distance at the far end. It was so peaceful out here. He remembered that first weekend they spent together. He laughed to himself...after her first hangover. Coming out here getting away from the city and all the crime, it had been just what he needed. And then all hell broke loose changing their lives forever. Who would have ever known?

How could he ask Maddy to give this all up, her sanctuary? She loved this place. She was as different person when she was here. She was relaxed. She was open to her feelings, even the worst ones. Was it a no-win situation? If he built her a new home on the outskirts of the city, would it be enough for her? She was right; they were pushing her too hard, too fast. It was just the Parker way. They saw a problem; they did something about it. Maddy sat back and thought about things, looked at things from all perspectives, looked for things that could be problematic. The same as she did when she was investigating for the most part. He took a deep breath and sighed. He needed to back off and quit pushing.

When he returned to the house he heard the sound of tiny voices, little children talking and laughing. He peered into the living room. Maddy was scrunched up on the corner of her couch, a pillow clutched to her chest, a tissue squeezed tightly in one hand. He could see tears glistening off her cheeks, but every so often she would laugh softly. What should he do? This is where Bryan would instinctively know. He slipped quietly out of the house and called Bryan.

"Hey sorry to bother you. I need some advice," he said in a low voice.

"What's the matter, Jack?" Bryan asked.

"I went for a walk and when I came back into the house she is in the living room watching home movies of her kids. What do I do? Do I go in there? Do I leave her alone?"

Bryan gave a soft laugh, "Just relax. What does your first instinct tell you?"

"I don't know! That's why I called you."

"Bring her a glass of tea. If she wants you there she will let you know. Just pick up on her cue, she will let you know what she wants," Bryan explained. "Now quit panicking and do it. Talk to you later."

Jack did as Bryan instructed. He had to brew some fresh tea, poured it over ice, cut up a lemon and brought it to her.

Maddy smiled weakly at him, took the glass and said thanks. She slid down further on the couch and patted the place where her body had been. Jack sat down at an angle, Maddy cuddled up to him, resting her body against him. Jack enveloped her in his arms. He wished he had Bryan's intuition when it came to these kinds of Maddy's emotional needs.

Maddy was glad Jack was there. Having his arms around her made her feel safe and secure. The movie she was watching was one of the last one's she filmed before...they passed. She and Bryan had driven them to the beach for the day. Bryan was chasing Scotty a long the shoreline. His little legs carried him as fast as they could with the waves crashing against them. He laughed and squealed when Bryan caught him and threw him up on his shoulders. They waded further into the depths of the pale gray waters. Lexi snuck up behind them, pushing them. All three tumbled into the waters. Bryan looked so young. He was 37, his hair was still dark, his face smoother, his eyes sparkled brighter. This was the man she fell in love with, the man she should have had a future with. With one earth-shattering event, fate had taken everything away from her—her children, the love of her life, her sanity. Maddy took the remote and clicked off the movie. She wasn't hurting so much as she was filled with anger, resentment and hate.

"Who was that guy?" Jack asked softly.

Maddy gave a bitter laugh, "That's Bryan. You would never know it would you?"

"No," he lightly rubbed her arms with his fingertips.

"He loved those kids and they adored him. And you know what's really sad? I have no idea how he dealt with their loss. I wasn't there." Maddy dabbed the tears from her eyes.

Jack kissed the top of her head, "Maybe this is something the two of you need to talk about."

"Why?" she asked bitterly. "We're trying to let go of the past, not keep stirring it up."

"No, baby, you are trying to deal with the past, then you can let go. But you can't do one without the other."

Maddy shook her head, "No, it could do nothing but cause him more pain. I can't do that for my own selfish reasons."

Jack gave a soft sigh. "I think you are wrong. It would be extremely painful for both of you, but have you ever stopped to figure he can't heal without sharing it with you?"

"Yeah, well he's not here is he? And by the time he would get here, I won't be able to do it. I can't hang on to the pain that long."

Jack slipped his phone out of his pocket and handed it to her. "You want me to leave you alone?"

She took his hand and kissed it. "No I need you here." Maddy's fingers shook as she tried to dial the phone.

Jack took it from her, dialed the number then handed it to her. He kissed her cheek and whispered in her ear, "I'm here, Kitten."

Bryan answered on the third ring, "Jack, what's up?"

"It's not Jack, it's me. How did you do it?" Maddy jumped right in before she lost her nerve.

"Do what Minnie?" he asked puzzled.

Maddy's voice caught in her throat, "Morn them, say good bye. You loved them too..."

"Oh Maddy, sweetheart," he said sadly. "Don't worry about me, you concentrate on you."

"I need to know. What happened didn't just effect me, it did you too, drastically."

"You need to say it Maddy. Say what happened," he commanded her in a soft tone. He wished he could be there in person to do this. He would have been able to read her, her reactions, to be able to know when to pull back if he needed to.

"When Lexi and Scotty were taken away from us, yeah us, not just me. I know what I did. I shut down. What did you do?" Maddy wiped her eyes again and took a drink of her tea when Jack offered it to her.

There was a prolonged silence before Bryan finally spoke, "Those first few days are kind of a blur. You were really out of it. They kept you heavily sedated. I helped you make the funeral arrangements...I hurt Maddy, I hurt like hell. I have never felt something so painful and to feel so helpless at the same time. Can we just leave it at that?"

Maddy shook her head lightly, "No, I need to know it all. If it hurts you, I am so very sorry, and if it hurts me...I don't care. Please Bryan, tell me."

Maddy swore she heard him sniff and his voice quivered when he came back on the line. "All I wanted to do was for us to hold each other and cry, to let it all out all hurt together, heal together. I don't want to hurt you, Maddy, God you know I don't. But you never cried. Not after the attack, not since I found you in that room. Not at the rosary, not at the mass, not at the funeral. You never cried. I couldn't help you. I couldn't help me. I tried to get you to remember, I tried so hard to trigger you back into reality. I moved you out of that house. I made up a box, one for Lexi, one for Scotty. There were photos, drawings, toys, stories they wrote. I tried to make you sit down with me and go through them. You wouldn't do it. You wanted no part of it. I took you to the cemetery. I would cry... you couldn't. At some point it just hurt too much. Loosing them, loosing you. You know what happened after that."

Maddy wiped her cheeks with the palm of her hands, but tears just kept coming. Her chest hurt, she felt like she couldn't breathe. God this hurt so much. Her heart was breaking, but it wasn't for herself it was for Bryan. She had her coping mechanism. She shut down, her answer to everything. But Bryan...he was left out there in cold, to deal with his loss by himself. Maddy broke down, "I'm so sorry...I'm sorry..." She hung up the phone, got up off the couch and ran out of the house.

Jack cell went off and he picked it up. "Maddy..." a tortured voice came across the line.

"Bryan, it's Jack. You okay, man?" He could tell he wasn't. What the hell did he do by encouraging Maddy to talk to Bryan about this?

"No, I'm not alright. Whose bright idea was this? It's supposed to be about her, not me. She doesn't need to be put on a guilt trip about what I went through. She couldn't help it. I never blamed her, never!" Bryan's voice was mixed with anger and pain.

Jack ran his fingers through his hair, trying to figure out how best to handle this. "She was watching a movie with you and the kids on the beach. She brought it up telling me she never knew how you dealt with it, that she couldn't remember. She wanted to know. How was she going to know if she didn't talk to you about it?"

"And you had to do it over the phone?"

"She said she couldn't wait for you to get here, she had to do it now," Jack tried to explain.

"Where in the hell is she now?"

"She tore off outside."

"Christ Jack, get out there with her, don't let her shut down. Make her cry it out. Now move! Call me later."

Jack found Maddy in the hayloft, sitting in the open door way looking over the pasture. She was sobbing into her hands. He put his hand on her shoulder and she brushed him away. "Okay...sorry...I will leave you alone."

"No! Just give me a minute," she said without turning. "Do you have your phone on you?"

He handed it to her. Maddy placed a call, "Bryan?"

"Oh Maddy, I am so sorry, you know I didn't want to hurt you," she could hear the pain in his voice. She wished they could hold each other, but he was there and she was here.

"It's okay Mickey, I am glad I know, and it's me who's sorry. I can't change what happened or make excuses for what I did, but I am sorry. I love you for doing what you did to try to help me. I just wish I could have been there for you like you tried to be there for me...Bryan...whatever happened to those boxes?" she asked softly.

The line was quiet and then he spoke, "I still have them. I hope you don't mind. I kept them for me."

Maddy smiled as the tears welled up in her eyes. "No...no, that's good. Where are they?"

"They are locked away at my house where no one can touch them."

"I'm glad...you keep them safe with you...always. I need some time to recover here so I will talk to you later. I love you, Bryan."

"I love you too, Maddy. Talk to you later."

Maddy handed Jack his phone over her shoulder. She scooted over in the window to make room for him.

Jack maneuvered his body in beside her. "I'm sorry. I didn't realize..." The speaker on Jack's phone had been loud enough he could hear both sides of the conversation for both calls. He felt sick inside. The hell these two had endured. Life had really dealt them a fucked up hand. They never stood a chance. That one horrific moment had set into motion a domino effect that took ten years to conclude. It took two people whose love seem destine to be and made it impossible to be realized. That was a part of Maddy he would never ever have. But he knew it coming in and he felt he could live with it.

"I'm sorry Jack, but I don't want to talk anymore about it. Going through this...history. It's difficult. Sometimes, like today, it feels like someone is taking a razor blade to my heart and then pouring salt on it. It's just too much. I'm sorry," she said as she looked out over the pasture.

"I understand. Just know that I am here when you need me," he lightly touched her hand. She didn't pull hers away.

Maddy watched the horses grazing, their noses pointed to the ground, the hair of their manes and tails swooshing in the wind. "I can't give this place up, Jack. Not yet. I'm not saying we aren't still moving in together. I just need this place, even if it's only a couple days a week. I need this place to heal."

"Yeah, I figured that out earlier when I was out here taking a walk. So what do you say we have two homes? We come here when I'm not bound to the city. If you need to get away after this case is over, and I can't, hey, I can live one night without you." He leaned over and kissed her cheek, "but only one night. I would miss your body next to mine when I sleep."

Maddy laughed, "Okay, I can live with that. We're going to have to figure something out for the care of these horses. I can't expect Jessie to keep doing it indefinitely. It's not so bad in the summer; they have the pasture. But in the winter, it does take work. Jessie should be stopping over later to do chores. We can talk it over with her."

"Is it safe to put my arm around you?" he asked tentatively.

Maddy nudged him with her body. "Always."

He nudged her back, "You wanna get frisky in the hayloft?"

She raised her eyebrow and looked at him. "Seriously?"

Jack threw his head back and laughed, "Hell no. I don't want to get itchy."

Maddy smiled, "You puss. Can sure tell you're a city boy."

He slid back away from the door, "Guilty as charged, and this city boy is dying of thirst." He offered his hand to her, "Will you join me?"

Maddy took his hand and he pulled her up, "As long as it doesn't have alcohol in it."

They spent the remainder of the afternoon curled up on the couch watching TV. It reminded Maddy of that first weekend together. Who knew then they actually would end up together? Jack did.

Maddy ended up calling Jessie and told her they would take care of chores themselves so she wouldn't have to make the trip over. They would talk to her another time about the horse care.

Jack and Maddy had just finished cleaning up supper dishes when they heard someone pulling up the lane. She peered out the door to see Bryan pulling into her drive. And he was not alone. Maddy felt a knot in her stomach. How could he bring her out here?

He got out the Suburban and walked towards the house leaving Donna in the Sub. Maddy stepped outside and met him at the door. He didn't say a word to her but pulled her into his arms, held her tight and buried his face in her hair. He was still shaking.

Maddy looked up at him watching his face. His eyes were red and puffy, his skin pale. The hazel in his eyes almost appeared to be washed out. She touched his cheek with her hand, "Baby?"

"I'm sorry. We were just out for a ride...I needed to see you. I'm sorry I brought her out here."

Maddy kissed him softly, "It's okay, Baby. Don't worry about her. She's not important, you are. Why are you here, hon? What can I do to make it better?"

Jack poked his head out the door, "Bryan," he nodded a greeting. "You want me to go keep Donna busy so you guys can talk?"

"I don't want to keep you," Bryan said. "I just needed to see her for a minute."

"Nonsense Bryan, there's something you need, I can tell," Jack told him.

Maddy turned to Jack. "Bring her in here into the kitchen. I will take Bryan in the living room and shut the door so we can talk in private."

Jack opened the door and let them step inside and he went out to fetch Donna.

Maddy led Bryan into the living room and shut the door behind them. Bryan sat on the couch and Maddy took a seat beside him. She put her hand on his knee. "Honey, you don't look well at all. You're scaring me."

Bryan smiled weakly, "Kiddo, don't worry, I'm not having a heart attack, heart break yeah, but not a heart attack."

Maddy sat back and leaned on his shoulder, holding his hands in hers. "Talk to me Bryan."

Bryan wouldn't look at her, but looked down at their hands intertwined. When he spoke, his words came out slow and steady. "When you had your break... I guess I thought we would go through this together. We would morn together." He swallowed hard. "I just assumed I would be the one you would tell what happened that awful day. I know you told Jack, and that's okay."

"Do you want me to tell you?" she asked him nervously. She really didn't think she could relive it one more time, but if he needed it, she would.

"No, if you want me to know, just give Jack permission to tell me. I don't want you to go back there." He hesitated. "He said you had a movie you were watching this afternoon—with me and the kids...May I borrow it? I swear I will return it."

Maddy chewed nervously on her lip. God this was hard. "Would you like me to watch it with you?"

"I can't ask you to watch it again."

She leaned forward and studied his face. She could see the pain in his eyes. There was no way she would let him do this alone. Any more then he would let her if he had anything to say about it. "I think we need to do this together. It's our loss. We should have been there for each other when it happened. We weren't, we can now."

She told Bryan to sit on the end of the couch where Jack had been earlier. The tape was still in the VCR. She flipped on the TV. She sat beside Bryan and he wrapped his arms around her. "Are you ready?" she looked up at him.

He nodded silently.

She hit the play button. They watched the movie in silence, but Bryan's arms were hanging on to her for dear life. Once again her eyes filled with tears. She could feel Bryan's damp face against her skin while his face was buried in her hair. She could feel the unsteadiness in his chest and his breathing became erratic.

In the kitchen, Jack had given Donna a soda and they sat in awkward silence.

"I know you don't know me, probably have heard plenty of bad about me, but I really don't mean Maddy any ill will," Donna said as she sipped on her soda.

"I don't judge. If I did, Bryan and I wouldn't be such good friends," Jack told her calmly.

"So you have no preconceived notions about me?"

Jack smiled, "Now I didn't say that. I know what you and Bryan did to Maddy. And in a way you did it to Bryan. You set them both up to take a fall. The only difference between Bryan and Maddy—Maddy was the one that got hurt. Do you have any idea how badly you hurt her by what you did?"

Donna shook her head. "No, we cut off all contact."

"No you cut off all contact. It's done. It's over with. They got passed it, that's all that really matters, don't you think?" He looked up at her, "You smoke?"

They moved out to the steps. Jack lit Donna's cigarette for her. "Do you really even know anything about them?"

Donna took a long drag off her cigarette, "Apparently not. I lived with the man for over eight years. I thought I knew everything. I didn't know they worked together at the FBI, that that was how they met. There was a lot more between them than either one let on."

"Do you know why they split up?"

"Bryan went back to his wife."

"Maddy walked in on a home invasion and witness her two children being murdered. Bryan was the one who found them. Maddy went off the deep end and no matter how hard Bryan tried; he couldn't save her from her demons. He left her." Jack looked off into the distance as took a puff and blew it out. "How's that for answers?" he said coldly. Jack glanced over at her, "Nothing to say?"

Donna's hand was shaking as she brought her cigarette to her mouth. "I didn't know. My God, no one ever said anything, never."

"Maddy never spoke about it for the last ten years. When Bryan came here...things happened and it triggered her memory. He almost lost her again, but he pulled her through it. His love pulled her through it. I saw it with my own eyes. They sat beneath a tree. She was lost to everyone. The man held her, crying his heart out begging God to bring her back to him." Jack watched her for her reaction. He didn't know why he was telling her this. It was really none of her business and he was sure Bryan and Maddy wouldn't approve. But he wanted Donna to know. He had no idea why. "Maddy deals with her loss one step at time. Right now, the two of them are dealing with it together. You say nothing to Bryan of what I have told you, and you damn well better not say anything to Maddy. You got that?"

Donna nodded and put out her cigarette. "Can I ask you...why aren't they still together?"

"Because both of them know their demons of the past will always haunt them and keep them from having a future." Jack stood up. "I meant what I said. You really don't want to have me on your bad side."

The VCR had long since quit playing. Maddy and Bryan held each other tightly, feeling all the pain of the past. Bryan cupped her face and kissed her, at first tenderly, tasting the salt of their tears as they mingled. Maddy returned his kiss, which deepened more the longer it lasted. Maddy's arms went up around his neck pulling him closer. It was a kiss of desperation and pain.

When the kiss finally ended Bryan took her face in his hands searching her eyes. "If I had one wish, it would be to love you one last time. But I know it can't happen because if I did Maddy..." a tear ran down his cheek, "I could never let you go." He kissed her again and then held her.

Maddy cried into his chest, "God I love you so much. It hurts, it hurts like hell—to come all this way...and to know we can never be together."

"I know, baby, I know." He stroked her hair over and over again. "But we both know in our hearts, even our love for each other is not enough. It's heart-breaking and it's tragic, but it is what it is." He kissed the top of her head. "But we still have each other. We will always have each other. That's so much more than we had in the past."

Bryan stood up and helped Maddy to her feet. He held her hand as they walked out to the kitchen.

Jack watched as they came out. Bryan's eyes were red, he was breathing shallowly through his mouth. Tears were still running down Maddy's cheeks. She was sniffing and her breath intake uneven.

"Jack," Maddy averted his gaze. "Sometime...not now, and if he wants it," a sob escaped her lips, "tell him.... tell him what happened." She wiped her eyes.

Bryan took a deep breath trying to compose himself. "Thanks Jack." He held out his hand.

Jack surprised him by giving him a hug and a couple of pats on the back. "Hang in there, Bud, you know I got your back."

Bryan hugged Maddy and gave her a kiss. "Thank you, Maddy, it meant more to me than you could ever know."

Maddy brushed his cheek and smiled weakly, "I love you."

Bryan pulled her close, "I love you, too, Maddy. I will see tomorrow."

Jack glanced over at Donna and she nodded. "Good night Donna, maybe we will get the chance to visit again."

"Yes, that would be nice." She turned to Maddy. "Good night Maddy."

Maddy sat on the steps and watched Bryan leave. Jack brought her a glass of water and sat down beside her. She glanced over at him. "I love you."

"Hey," he smiled, "I love you too, you know that."

She brushed her eyes with the back of her hand and took a deep breath. "That was one of the most painful experiences I have ever had."

Jack kissed her on the cheek, "I can't imagine, Kitten. You have to be pretty raw by now. It was a very emotional day for you."

Maddy gave a nervous laugh, "Maybe I should have just settled for brunch huh?"

Jack put his arm around her and squeezed her. "You did good today, Kitten. It was hard...for both of you. But it was a step in the right direction for healing."

They sat quietly until Maddy asked, "What did you talk to Donna about?"

"I told her the truth," he waited for her reaction. What the hell, he couldn't lie to Maddy.

Maddy just nodded. "It doesn't matter anymore. It happened, it's out there. Can't keep pretending it never happened."

"I threatened her though."

Maddy looked at him, "With what?"

He smiled, "I told her if she said anything to you or Bryan I would come after her."

Maddy laughed, "Playing tough cop huh?"

"Gotta throw my weight around somewhere."

Maddy stood up. "Can we just go to bed? I don't have anything strength left."

Jack hugged her and kissed her, "Sure Kitten, and I won't even molest you tonight."

Maddy smiled and kissed him back, "Just hold me and don't let go...that's all I ask."

Maddy and Jack sat waiting in Jack's office for Bryan. When he finally arrived he shut the door behind him. Maddy went to him and hugged him tight, "You okay?"

Bryan smiled, "Now the shoe is on the other foot. I'm okay. Thank you again for last night. You too," he nodded at Jack.

"No problem. We just thought this would be better handled in private," Jack said from behind his desk.

Maddy and Bryan took seats across from him.

"Derek ran the background check on Parsons." He pulled out a file. "It's actually his real name. He is originally from Seattle, Washington. Age 43, was a minister at several churches out there. He disappeared from radar a year ago. We have no record of his existence until he popped up here. Funny thing about it, there are no records linking him here."

"Do you have a photo with that file," Maddy asked.

"Nope," he closed the file. "Physical description fits, but that doesn't necessarily mean anything. We can't even be sure if he is Parsons and didn't just steal his identity."

"Not even a driver's license photo?" Jack asked.

Bryan shook his head, "No record of ever having had a license."

"We have the unsub's finger prints and DNA. Can't we bring him in, print him and get a swab?" Jack asked.

"We can't get a swab without consent or a court order," Maddy said looking through the file.

"If we could get him in here, we could get a print. But I still don't want to bring him in prematurely. If he is a fraud he'd be in the wind the second he caught a sniff of us." Bryan shook his head. "We're so damn close I can taste it."

"Maybe I could lure him in," Maddy said without looking up from the file.

"Fuck no!" Bryan and Jack said in unison.

"You think I am going to put you out there for bait, you're fucking crazy, Maddy," Bryan barked.

Maddy put up her hands, "Okay, okay. I think I get the drift. No Maddy bait."

"So now what?" Jack said tapping a pencil.

"Stakeout," Bryan said flatly.

"Hey isn't there some way we could get someone in the church office to ask questions about him? Like his schedule, what he does there....junk like that?" Maddy closed the file and looked at both Jack and Bryan.

"Not you," Jack flipped his pencil in the air.

She shot him a look, "Duh. Can't be one of you guys. He's seen both of you. If he happens to be there when you get there...nope can't be you. Can't be one of your agents. You guys look too much like agents. It needs to be a woman. And not a cop."

"We can't send a civilian in there," Bryan scratched his head. "Not good policy."

"I know the perfect person," Maddy smiled.

"Not Miranda."

"No, Sandy Morton, Vanessa Granger's friend. She won't have to know exactly why she is going in there. She could go in under the ruse of finding out about the church and what they offer. Just an innocent person checking out churches to affiliate with."

Bryan sighed, "She's a civilian. We can't do that."

"But we're not putting her in any danger. If she doesn't know what she's doing or doing it for, how can she be put in danger? She has virtually no connection with this case," Maddy argued.

Jack looked at her horrified, "Maddy, she's the best friend of one of our vics. What part of connected does that not sit with you?"

"She would do anything to help me out. She went in a nabbed Vanessa's computer for me."

"Heisting a computer is not doing undercover work," Jack leaned back in his chair.

"Fine, I don't see you guys coming up with any solutions," Maddy snapped.

Bryan and Jack exchanged glances. Bryan took a deep breath. "Okay, fine. This stays between us and I suppose Andy since he is your sidekick. You three go out and talk to this woman and feel her out. See how receptive she is. Then call me and fill me in before we send this woman out."

"The woman's name is Sandy. I think we need to take an unmarked car like we did on Friday. I don't want to draw attention to ourselves with our vehicles."

Jack laughed, "You just like playing secret agent."

Maddy stuck her tongue out at him.

"Jack, you go sign out a car from the motor pool. Maddy, you wait here for Andy and meet Jack out front. Remember, no moves without me knowing," Bryan ordered.

Maddy sat up in her chair, "You know, Bryan, this was a lot more fun going behind your back."

Bryan threw her look. "Behave, Jack's in charge."

Maddy stood up, "But I outrank him!"

"Do you want to stay here sitting at your desk all day?"

"No, but why is he in charge?"

Bryan stood at the door, "Because he has common sense, something you are sadly lacking in the field. You act on impulse, and at this stage of the game, Maddy, I'm not going to gamble on you. He keeps you in line." He turned and left the room.

Maddy poked her head out the door, "That's bullshit and you know it, Bryan."

He raised his hand up and flipped her off as he walked back to the squad room.

Maddy's mouth drop as she turned to Jack. "He just gave me the finger."

Jack laughed, "Isn't it great to be working as a team again?"

Maddy smiled, "You go to hell, too. And yeah...it is."

Maddy, Jack and Andy were on their way to Tyler Construction when Maddy said, "I want to go in there first and talk to Sandy. She doesn't know you, and I don't want to make her feel uncomfortable. I'm not quite sure how to present this to her though. Any suggestions? I mean I don't want to send her in there to see if Vanessa's killer is there. Hell that would freak me out."

"Why can't you just tell her we are checking out this minister angle and we need information on the ministers and anyone that works in the capacity of administering council or acts as a member of the clergy?" Andy asked. "We could go to two or three churches and get the same information. She wouldn't have a clue what she was really doing."

As Jack pulled into the parking lot, both Maddy and Jack turned around and looked at Andy with a surprised expression on their face. Maddy smiled at Jack. She didn't want to belittle Andy by telling him that was a great idea.

"Excellent approach, thanks, Andy," Jack spoke up.

Maddy entered the office to find Sandy sitting behind her computer.

Sandy looked up, saw Maddy and smiled. "Hi Maddy! What brings you out to these parts?" Sandy came to the counter. Her mouth dropped when she did a visual scan of Maddy noticing the badge and the gun. "Since when do reporters carry hardware?"

Maddy smiled, "I was an FBI agent in a previous life and got reactivated to work this case."

"So you are honestly trying to find the man that killed Vanessa?" Sandy asked.

Maddy nodded, "Quite frankly she is the only reason I am still on this case. But I came here to ask you a favor. You might have read in the paper that we suspect someone who works closely with a church to be involved. I need someone I can trust to gather information about the clergy and support staff of different churches. In light of the bad press they are receiving, I don't feel sending a law enforcement to get the information would be the most productive. I think sending someone they didn't feel threatened by would be best. I would like that someone to be you. Are you game?"

"Why can't you do it?"

"I'm too well known as the press."

Sandy looked like she was thinking it over. "Do I have to give you an answer now?"

"It would be nice. We need to move on this guy and until we find out who he is we can't," Maddy explained.

"When would it need to be done?"

"Now."

"Wow," Sandy took a deep breath. "I don't know if I could get off work."

"Can you get a hold of your boss, and I could have Detective Parker talk to him?"

Sandy stood quietly deep in thought. "I'm sorry Maddy. I can't, I won't."

Maddy felt the air deflate from her plan. "You're sure?"

"I really don't want anything to do with this. I want you to catch the guy that murdered Vanessa, but I just can't do it. I hope you understand."

Maddy nodded, "Okay. Well thanks anyhow, Sandy. You take care."

Sandy waved as Maddy left the office.

She slid into the passenger seat. "It's a no dice. She won't do it."

"Now what?" Jack asked as he lit up a cigarette.

"I don't know. We have to rethink this. Go to the church. I got to sort through this."

Jack parked the unmarked car katty corner across from the church so they could observe anyone entering the church.

Maddy pulled out at slip of paper from her purse and her cell phone. She dialed the number.

"Trinity First Reform Church, how may I help you?"

"Hi, my name is Shelia Walker. I just relocated to the city and I am trying to find a church that fits my needs. Can you tell me something about your church?" Maddy changed the inflection in her voice.

"Why yes," the voice replied on the other end. "Trinity is a nod-denominational church that promotes spiritual growth. We offer a wide variety of services ranging from traditional, contemporary, and alternative."

"Alternative? What's that?"

"It is a small congregation led by a very progressive minister. He likes to keep his congregation small so he has more individual contact with each member. Is this something you might be interested in Ms. Walker?" the woman asked.

"When are the services?"

"On Thursday evenings."

"This might be what I am looking for. Can I get the name and number of the minister and give him a call so I can talk him more about his beliefs?"

"His name is Pastor Justin Parsons. I would be glad to take your name and number and have him return your call. He prefers direct contact. I am sure he would be glad to set up an appointment to meet with you."

Damn. Now what? "When is he there? Maybe I could just stop in and see him?"

Jack smacked Maddy across the arm. She turned and glared at him.

"He actually doesn't have an office here. He's not really an associate of our parish. We allow him the use of our facility for a nominal fee," the woman explained. "He checks in with us for his messages and occasionally stops in when he has an appointment."

"I'll tell you what," Maddy glanced at Jack, "let me check out some other churches and I'll get back to you if I want to set up an appointment. Thank you for your time."

Maddy clicked her phone shut. "Fits our unsub to a T don't you think? Based on everything he, himself has told me."

Andy leaned over the front seat, "Why didn't we just do this in the first place?"

Maddy flashed him a look, "I didn't hear either of you suggest it." She turned to Jack. "We need an excuse to bring Parsons in. We know it's him. There has to be something we can do."

"Hell Maddy, we don't even know where he is. We would have to sit around here and wait until he pops up." Jack laid his head back against the headrest. Stakeouts really sucked.

Maddy kicked off her shoes and propped her feet on the dash. "You know, she said his services were on Thursdays. What was he doing here Friday night?"

"If this were my car, I would slap your feet."

Maddy smiled, "Well it's not, so get over it. Back to my question, what was he doing on Friday? Do you suppose he holds additional sermons at odd times?"

"What the hell you looking at me for? How would I know?" Jack pulled out a cigarette and lit it up.

"Damn, you're on the cranky side. What do you think Andy?" She looked back at him. She really didn't expect an answer from him either. Jack was right, how the hell would they know?

Andy made a face and slightly shrugged his shoulders. "I don't have a clue."

They sat silent for several minutes. The heat in the car was getting intolerable. "Turn the a/c on for a few minutes."

Jack started the car, "Damn, you're getting bossy."

"What the hell's the matter with you? You're snappy." Maddy looked at him.

"I hate sitting around doing nothing. It drives me fucking nuts," he growled.

"Well you don't have to get bitchy about it," Maddy snapped back.

"Kids! Mellow out!" Andy barked from the back seat.

Maddy and Jack started laughing and looking back at Andy. He was stretched out in the back seat reading a book. "You suck," Maddy said shaking her head.

More time lapsed. "We are wasting our time here," Jack growled.

Maddy looked up. "Give me the unsub phone."

Jack looked at her sharply, "Hell no, I'm not giving you the phone. Is your memory that bad, you are not to initiate contact with him."

Maddy shrugged, "I just want to chit chat with him. I get more info from him by doing that then I do when he calls me. Who knows, I might get a good lead. Hand it over."

Jack glared at her. "I said no."

Maddy propped her elbow on the edge of the window and rested her head against her arm.

"Quit pouting."

"Would you shut the hell up? Damn." Maddy starting biting on her lower lip.

Maddy dug out her phone and hit the speed dial. "Hey Bryan."

She could feel Jack's eyes bearing into her.

She heard Bryan sigh on the other end of the line, "What do you want, Maddy?"

"Jesus, is everybody on the rag or what?"

"What do you want? I'm in the middle of something."

"I want to call Parsons," she stated flatly.

"Where's Jack?"

"Sitting here beside me."

"Did you ask him?"

"Yeah, he said no." Maddy chewed on her fingernail.

"So what the hell you asking me for?" Bryan asked crossly.

"Cuz you're over him."

"Give the damn phone to Jack." Damn what the hell was wrong with everyone today?

She held the phone out to Jack and he snatched it out of her hands. "Hey Bryan." Jack's voice sounded very annoyed.

"Can you step out of the car with out being obvious to your surroundings?" Bryan asked.

"Not really, but I can drive around the block."

"Do that, then call me back."

Jack shut Maddy's phone and tossed it back to her. "Thanks a fucking lot, Maddy."

"What?" she looked at him innocently.

"Going over my head. Is this what you're stooping to to get your way? Not cool, Maddy, not cool at all." He was pissed. What the hell was her problem? Why would she do something like this?

"Christ, all we are doing is sitting on our asses getting nothing done. I want to get things moving and that's the only way I know how. I am sorry if you feel I stepped on your toes."

"That I feel? You don't think what you just did isn't going over my head? Start acting like a damn cop instead of a spoiled brat!"

Jack put the car in gear and took off. Maddy looked into the back seat. Andy was calmly reading his book. "Don't look at me," he said. "I'm staying out of this one."

"Coward," she mumbled under her breath.

Jack drove to a supermarket a block up from the church. He opened the door and got out. He leaned against the car and called Bryan and lit in to him. "What the fuck? What the hell does she think she's doing? I thought you said I was in charge and then she goes behind my back and calls you. I told her no, God damn it. Now if you let her do it, I'm telling you, Bryan, I will not work with her again!"

He heard Bryan chuckle on the other end. "No, I'm not going to let her. She is not calling the shots here and she needs to know it. Who put the burr under her saddle?"

"Morton wouldn't do the interview so Maddy did it over the phone, which went well. She got the details on Parson's connection with the church. So we're sitting here, sweating our balls off, everyone except Andy, who is all nice and calm and laid back. We're getting bitchy and annoyed and she lays this on me. Says she wants him to somehow slip up and give her some info so she can bring him in. Fuck, we don't even know where the hell he is. He has no office here and the only way you can contact him is to give him your name and number and he will call you. And damn it, Bryan, quit laughing I can hear you, you know."

Bryan burst out laughing, "Temper, temper. Remember this is the woman you want to spend the rest of your life with."

"There is a hell of difference between living with her and working with her. She is driving me fucking nuts!"

"You've worked with her before," he couldn't stop laughing.

"Fuck you! I only had to be around her for a couple of hours at a time. Not sitting in an oven for hours with her. She can't sit still, gotta always be doing something, always asking questions, never shuts up. Christ her mind never stops! She's like a God damn dog with a bone!" Jack was on a tirade. He couldn't help it.

"Do you think you can bring her in without killing her?"

"With pleasure. I just won't talk to her. That really pisses her off then she will know how I feel."

Maddy watched Jack through the driver's side window. She could hear his raised voice and he was really animated. She smiled to herself. She had really pissed him off, but she knew it wasn't anything he wouldn't get over. She had to admit she was being obnoxious and was wrong to go over his head calling Bryan, but as usual, she acted before she thought.

Jack got back in the car and slammed the door. He put the car in gear. When he pulled out onto the street and accelerated the tires squealed. Damn, he was pissed. She was almost afraid to ask him, "Where are we going?"

He just turned and looked at her, the muscles in his jaw twitching, a frown creasing his brow. Oooookay. Not a good time to talk to him.

Maddy slipped her shoes back on, put her seatbelt on, leaned back in her seat and kept her eyes focus out the window. She didn't want to annoy him anymore than he was. She peeked back at Andy, who was sitting there quietly watching out the window.

When they arrived back at the cop shop, Jack got out of the car, slammed the door and left Maddy standing in his wake.

Maddy turned to Andy, "Christ, was I really that bad?"

"You were pushing him, Maddy. Calling Mayland after he told you no was the last straw. You surpassed his authority. That shows you don't respect him. Yes, you were that bad," Andy told her as they walked into the building.

Maddy stopped and studied him then shook her head, "You are really starting to scare me."

Andy laughed as he held the door open for her.

Jack went straight to his office and slammed the door shut behind him. He pulled the blinds and sat down at his desk. Damn it, Maddy. His blood was still boiling. He loved her dearly, but she was such a pain in the ass to work with. How quickly he had forgotten this little detail. Tenacious, that what she was, tenacious. Damn reporter. It was a damn good thing this was not a permanent arrangement. He really would hate to have to kill her.

Maddy stood outside Jack's office debating whether or not to knock on his closed door. She looked up to see Bryan standing over her.

"I wouldn't. Just leave him alone and let him cool down. Come on missy, we have to talk." Bryan led her into the interrogation room and shut the door. "The only thing I am going to jump your ass about it the fact that Jack gave you an order and you thought you could count on me to override that order. Do not play us against each other Maddy. It's not fair."

Maddy sat down, "Is that what you thought I was doing?"

Bryan raised his eyebrow, "Wasn't it?"

"No! I wanted to call Parsons. He wouldn't let me. I thought you would understand and let me," she tried to explain.

"So you did it because you wanted to get your way?" he asked as he sat on the corner of the table.

Maddy looked away from him. "Yeah more or less."

"And you really expected me to say yes?"

"No," she said quietly.

"Then why'd you do it?"

"I don't know..."

Bryan leaned over and tapped Maddy on the top of her head, "You need to start using this before you act. You're going to get yourself in some deep shit one of these days, Maddy, if you don't learn to get a handle on your impulsiveness." He turned and left the room.

Maddy sat quietly and thought about what Bryan had just said. What she had pulled with Bryan and Jack reminded her of what a child would do with its parents, play one off the other. It wasn't what she set out to do, but ultimately that was what had transpired. And yes she wanted to have her way, she always did. Wasn't that only natural, to want to have your way?

So now what? She had to make amends to Jack, but if he were really, really pissed at her he wouldn't be receptive to her. Maddy took out her phone and texted him. 'I know you don't want to hear from me, but I just wanted to say I am sorry. I acted like a spoiled brat and it was wrong of me. I love you. Just wanted you to know that.' She hit the send button. She didn't expect an answer. She grabbed her purse and went to the squad room.

This was the first time she had been with the men since the great brawl of Friday night. Maddy was surprised that no one gave her a second look.

Bryan was at his desk sorting though some stacks of papers. He turned to Maddy. "Could you print off ten copies of the best front head shot of Parsons for me?"

"Sure." She pulled out her laptop, opened up the file and sent the photos to the printer. "What are we doing?"

"Give me a minute to get these sheets together. What exactly did you find out at the church this morning?" He continued collating papers.

Maddy reiterated what she learned from the phone call this morning. "So you see, in my opinion, what that lady at the church said coincides with what the unsub has been telling me on the phone. Parsons is our unsub."

Bryan called Jack to come to the squad room then called everyone to a briefing. Bryan handed one of the packets including Maddy's photo to each one of the squad members.

"This gentleman is the man we believe is our unsub. His name is Justin Parsons, 43, originally from Seattle, WA. The enclosed photo was taken Friday afternoon of Parsons in front of Trinity First Reform Church where he is believed to be a minister of an alternative ministry. According to sources at the church, his functions at this church tie into the information he has given Maddy through her conversations with him."

"Why don't we bring him in?" One of the detectives asked.

"We don't have sufficient cause. For one thing, we don't have a fix on him yet. We have no home address, and he is not at the church as specific times. We don't have anything to tie him to the crimes. I don't want to move to prematurely on him or he could slip through our fingers. We need more firm answers before I am willing to take a chance. What we are going to do for now is stakeout the church. We will do it in three-hour shifts until this guy shows up. I want him tailed—find out where he goes, where he lives. Then we start asking questions and bring his ass in for questioning. We have the unsub's DNA and prints. We get him in here we got something to work with. I will be posting a your surveillance schedule on the board in a few minutes. Remember, this is strictly an observational surveillance. Do not approach Parsons. We do not want him to know we are on to him." Bryan finished up and returned to his desk.

Maddy smiled to herself. She was glad Bryan down played how the information was obtained, that she was the one that got it all. She didn't want to be super cop.

Maddy sought out Jack with her eyes. He hadn't come and sat at her desk like he normally did. He was sitting on Andy's desk talking to the other guys. She felt hurt and left out. She shrugged it off and went to grab a soda.

Maddy was feeding the machine her dollar when her phone text message alert went off. She flipped open her phone and smiled. It was a text from Jack. 'I love you too. Turn around.'

Maddy whirled around to find Jack leaning up against the wall. She wanted to run to him, but she decided to hang back. "Hi baby..."

"Kitten." A soft smiled played upon his lips.

She slowly moved toward him. "You forgive me?"

Jack shook his head, "No...but I will. I just wanted you to know, like I've said before, just because I get pissed at you, and I am sure I will again and again, it doesn't mean I love you any less. You understand?"

She nodded. "Can I hug you now?"

Jack opened his arms to her and held her tight. He kissed her and whispered, "I love you, Kitten."

"Me too," she whispered back.

He stood her back away from him, "But we do have to talk. I can't have you undermining my authority. Do you remember your little saying of keeping work life and personal life separate? We need to apply those rules here, hon. I don't mean that on the strictest level, but you need to respect me for who I am at work. I have my title as Chief of Detectives for a reason, Maddy. I earned it. Quit bulldozing me and disregarding what I say. Can you do this?"

Maddy brushed his cheek, "I will try very, very hard. You let me know when I start getting out of hand, because you know I do that and don't even know that I am..."

Jack silenced her with a deep kiss. "Shut up. You talk too much. Think before you do, it's all I ask."

She smiled up at him. "Yeah, I got that lecture from Bryan, too."

Jack chuckled, "Okay so you heard it from two wise men. We both can't be wrong."

Maddy and Jack returned to the squad room where Bryan was waiting for them. "Are the two of you going to be able to do your surveillance shift without killing each other?"

Maddy smiled, "I think so."

Bryan looked at Jack. Jack threw his head back and laughed, "If not I will stick her in the trunk."

Maddy smacked him.

Bryan smiled and shook his head. "If you can't behave Maddy, you will be in the back seat and Andy will sit up front with Jack."

24

"Maddy quit fidgeting," Jack said from across the car. "For Christ sake, it's just my dad."

Jack was taking Maddy over to meet his dad. He asked her before he made the arrangements because he did want to just spring it on her. She felt after all the bullshit she put him through earlier it was the least she could do. She asked that they meet up after supper and it be totally informal. Less stress—she hoped.

"So what's he like? Is he like your Mom?" she asked nervously.

Jack threw his head back and laughed. "Would you please relax? No, he's not at all like my mother. He is very down to earth, laid back, just lets things roll off his back. How do you think he can handle my mom?"

"I was beginning to wonder that about you," she said softly.

Jack studied her from across the car. "What do you mean? Wonder what about me?"

"Haven't you noticed how different our personalities are?"

"Yes of course. So what?"

Maddy turned to him, "And it doesn't bother you? You are this smart, professional, very outgoing, very organized, high energy, incredibly sexy, slightly anal man...and I am...just simple me?"

Jack chuckled and shook his head, "Slightly anal...I like that. Simple you huh? Maddy, Kitten, there is nothing simple about you. You are one of the most complex people I have ever had the misfortune of meeting. You are moody; you can go from quiet and reserved to ballistic in a matter of seconds—angel to bitch. You can be vulnerable and yet at the same time be tough as nails. You are so damn smart you put others to shame. You are such a contradiction of terms I can't begin to describe you. But Kitten, the things you do that drive me nuts are the very same things I love so much about you."

His mood shifted, "But I don't think this is the issue here, is it Maddy? Can you deal with my personality? Do things I do bother you that much?"

Maddy leaned her head on his shoulder, "I love you, all of you. And you have to remember I am used to being a loner. I'm passive, you're aggressive."

Jack choked on a laugh, "Whoa baby, you got that all backwards. You are so not passive when it comes to anything! And Kitten, with the aggression you demonstrate when we make love...damn Maddy, there isn't anything I can..." he shook his head smiling. "Let's just say, you are on fire and I love it!"

He leaned over and kissed the top of her head, "But you still didn't answer my question. Do you think our personalities are not a compatible match?"

"I never said that. We've known each other for a couple of years. I knew you but really didn't know you...Jesus Jack, this is all coming out wrong." She laughed nervously. "This relationship thing, its all so confusing. I get scared; I get nervous. It's like I don't know how things are supposed to be. I learn new things about you everyday, and its wonderful; sometime intimidating, but it's not a bad thing. Am I making any sense at all?"

"Kitten, this is what having a relationship is all about, the learning, the loving. Quit panicking and just let it happen. I am going to annoy the hell out of you, a lot, just like you do me. But it's okay. We're not clones. What would be the fun in that? When you see my folks together, watch them, unless of course they are on their best behavior," he laughed. "They are opposites, like you and me and they have been together for over forty years. Being different is not a bad thing."

Alisha met them at the garage entrance giving Jack a kiss on the cheek and Maddy a quick hug. She pulled Maddy off to the side. "Honey, you'll be fine, Ed's a sweetie. Just relax and be yourself."

"I know, I know, Jack has already given me this talk," she smiled.

As soon as Maddy laid eyes on Edward Parker she knew she would love him. He was a mirror image of her beloved Jack thirty something years older. He had Jack's stature, same facial features; the fine lines of age etched his skin. The same dark brown eyes smiled back at her when he spoke. He didn't overwhelm her by attempting to hug her but held out his hand. He offered her a seat by the patio table then sat down to her left. Jack pulled up a chair to Maddy's right.

"It's a pleasure to finally meet you, Maddy. I hope Alisha hasn't been talking your ear off. She can be quite overbearing at times," he smiled over at his wife.

"I am not overbearing," Alisha defended herself good-naturedly. "I'm just nosey. Besides she figured that out for herself."

Maddy laughed. As the evening progressed she enjoyed the banter between the couple. They constantly insulted each other but in a good-natured way.

Maddy was surprised how little Edward asked her about herself. For whatever the reason he didn't push her and for that she was grateful. When Alisha and Jack disappeared into the house Maddy turned to him. "Either you have been warned against it, or you really don't give a shit, but I noticed you have no questions for me."

Edward took a sip from his drink. "I don't need to ask you any questions about yourself. I know all I need to know. Jack has been waiting for his chance with you for a long time. Now he has you and I've can see the way you interact with each other, I am satisfied. As far as getting to know you, sweetie, it will happen in its own time, naturally. Does that answer your question?"

Maddy sat back and nodded. "I knew from the moment I saw you, I'd like your style," she laughed.

A couple of hours later Maddy and Jack were lying on the couch, Jack with his arms wrapped around Maddy's waist. Soft music played in the background. Jack kissed her on the top of her head. "You are awfully quiet this evening. What's up?"

Maddy shrugged, "Nothing to say I guess."

Jack raised one eyebrow, "Bullshit. There is always something going on in that head of yours."

"Just wondering what it would feel like to have a normal life again I guess."

"Soon, Kitten, soon. We are close, it's only a matter of time." His fingers were softly stroking her arm.

"But the worst is yet to come. I can feel it. It's not going just be a simple arrest. Something bad is going to happen, something really bad." Her voice was soft and very controlled.

"You honestly believe that? Like what?

"I don't know. Wish I did. And yes I do believe it."

They both turned their heads when they heard the sound of phone ringing in the kitchen. Maddy sat up while Jack went in to retrieve the phone. He handed it to her, "Here is your chance," he said guardedly. He hated it every time she talked to the unsub.

Maddy took the phone. Instead of feeling dread and fear she felt eerily calm. "Hello?"

"Maddy, so sweet to hear your voice. Would you like to talk for awhile?"

"Are we actually going to talk, or are you just going to fuck with me?

"We can talk. You alone?"

"It's 9:30 at night, what do you think?" Evasiveness never hurt anyone.

"Doesn't mean a thing. I am sure you have at least one of your bodyguards there." Once again his voice was smooth, reeking of confidence.

"Well a girl needs her personal time sometimes don't you think?"

"I still think you have someone there with you," he cajoled.

"The only one in this house with me is my lover," she answered in complete honesty.

"And which bodyguard is that? Let me guess, our own chief of detectives. Puts a different twist on bodyguard doesn't it?" he teased.

Maddy found herself laughing, "Why would you say it's him?"

"Wasn't real hard to pick up on watching you two together."

Maddy looked sharply at Jack, a chill running down her spine. "You're watching me?"

"Occasionally."

"Where?"

"Not telling you. Then you would know where to look and to look for me. I can't allow that."

"How do you know I don't know where you are already?" He could play the mind fuck so could she.

Jack grabbed the phone out of her hand and covered the mouthpiece. "You are playing with fire Maddy. Stop!" He handed her back the phone.

The unsub laughed deeply. "If you knew where I was I would have the police force and the FBI knocking down my door."

"Once again you are right." God she hated playing down to him. "What do you want to talk about? We are still playing cat and mouse here, and I don't want to play."

"What denomination are you Maddy?"

"I was raised Catholic."

"But you are not a practicing Catholic? Where does the Lord fit into your life Maddy?" he asked. She swore she could hear traffic in the background, truck traffic.

"I put God out of my life a long time ago. You are putting everything back on me again. I don't see what the point of our conversations are if I am the one giving up all the information." Her voice had taken on an edge. She was annoyed, restless.

There was a pause on the other end of the line. More traffic noise...and voices. Where the hell was he?

"If you are not with the Lord, Maddy, how can you be saved?"

"I'm not looking to be saved. What, do you think you are so gifted you can save the most jaded sinner?" Ha, let's see where he would take that.

"My flock is hand selected, Maddy. They must be pure at heart. Your heart is to full of bitterness and mistrust. You would never be open to let the full extent of our love into your life."

"Pure of heart, but not virgins. At least three of your victims...sorry, let me rephrase that, chosen ones had boyfriends. How do you know if they are pure of heart before you allow them into your flock?" Now this had potential to go somewhere.

"I interview them before they are allowed to attend one of my sermons. My members are a select few."

Maddy laughed cynically, "You interview them? Like they are applying for a position?"

The unsub chuckled, "Yes so to speak. They must fit a profile. No one enters my flock unless I feel they can meet my expectations.

"Humor me. What expectations?"

"They must be accepting of my ways, give onto themselves and the Lord." The unsub seemed relaxed, laid back. The background sounds had changed, a train moving across the tracks, warning bells ringing. He was driving around to keep from getting tracked.

"To the Lord or to you?"

"One and the same."

"Do you have relations with them?"

Pause..."I am not sure what you are getting at Maddy. Would you like to clarify?"

"Is having sex with you a requirement to be in your flock? I mean it's not like you are priest and have to be celibate. There is no shame for a minister to lust after a woman; after all you are a red-blooded man are you not? You must have needs"

The man smirked, "Now who is getting personal? Do I ask you about your sex life, Maddy? Do I ask you what tasks you perform for your detective?"

"You tell me yours, I'll tell you mine," she quipped. Jack smacked her arm. She held her hand up and mouthed "just wait..."

"Let me just say whatever relations I have with women are all consensual. Your turn."

Maddy looked straight at Jack and smiled as she said, "We fuck like rabbits, every chance we get, any place we want. You would be amazed."

"Okay, a little more detail than I was prepared for you to supply," he stammered obviously being caught off guard. "I don't desecrate the souls I share my body with."

"No you just kill them when you're done," Maddy replied flatly. "You're like a black widow in reverse."

The unsub gave a deep sigh. "Maddy, Maddy, Maddy. What's it going to take to make a believer out of you?"

"That's quite easy, seeing you burn in hell, but then again, you are an arm of the Lord, so I imagine in your eyes, that's not going to happen."

"I think we are done talking tonight, Maddy. Pleasant dreams." The line went dead.

Jack snatched the phone out of her hand. "God damn it, Maddy! What the hell do you think you are doing? You always do this!"

Maddy pinched him in the leg and laughed, "Oh just relax, I just told it like it is."

Jack cell phone went off. He looked down at it. "Guess who? Now I have to listen to him bitch about your behavior...again." He flipped the phone open, "Hey Bryan."

"Do I really need to say anything?" Bryan asked sounding very annoyed.

"Nothing I haven't said already. But what do you want me to do? It's not like we can write her a script," Jack argued.

"He is watching her...and you. And you don't know where. How do we know he didn't watch you while you were on your stakeout?"

Jack leaned back on the couch. "Because we were in an unmarked car. Not only that he would know we were close to him and I don't believe he does. I would say he watches the parking lot."

"Do you suppose he has seen her with her badge and gun?"

"Naaah," Jack shook his head, "He's too smug not to let on."

"I think we need to move quicker on this. We have to find Parsons, and fast." The urgency in his voice was apparent.

"I'm not going to argue with you. So what do you want me to tell her?"

Bryan chuckled, "Fuck like rabbits huh?"

Jack put his hand over his face. "Shut the fuck up. Those were her words not mine. She was just trying to get to him."

"Uuhuh, and she did. But I bet it has a ring of truth to it." Jack could almost hear him grinning on the other end.

"What...you want details?"

"No, no, no...I don't even watch to imagine it. It's okay bud, I would do the same in your shoes," Bryan answered softly.

"Hey, listen Bryan, I'm sorry man. I didn't mean to..."

"Don't worry about Jack. I know it happens. It's as it should be. Goodnight."

Jack slid down into the cushions, leaned his head back and closed his eyes. He wanted this over with. He wanted Maddy safe—back working at the paper. He wanted to be back working robberies, stabbings...whatever, just not trying to catch a serial killer. He wanted to come home every night to Maddy's waiting arms to comfort him, to love him. So many wants, so many doubts.

Maddy watch the range of emotions washing over Jack's face. He was upset and she knew it had nothing to do with the phone call. It was one of the first times she had seen a hint of depression in him. Maddy lie across the couch and laid her body across his chest facing him. She circled her arms around his waist and rested her cheek on him. "I love you," she whispered.

He enclosed her in his arms and buried his face in her hair, "I love you, too. More than life itself, baby. I don't want to do this anymore, Maddy. I don't want to play his games. I hate knowing he's out there, watching you...thinking he could snatch you away from me, hurt you...and there is not a damn thing I can do about it." He softly stroked her hair. "Maddy, I want you away from here. I want you to go to Houston until this is over."

Maddy sat up and studied his face. His face was stoic. The light in his eyes dim with worry, his stare distant. Maddy cupped his face in her hands. "Baby, please don't say that. I don't want to go."

He turned to her, "Is this case so damn important we have put your life on the line?"

She searched his eyes, "Don't you know, Jack? It's not this case...it's you. I don't want to be without you. I don't want to leave you." She leaned in and softly grazed his lips with hers. "Don't make me leave you."

Jack took Maddy's head in his hands, kissing her tenderly. Her lips felt soft and yielding. He parted them with his tongue tasting her sweetness wanting to explore her further. He pushed tongue further, his kiss deepening. He felt her responding to him, her body softly melting into his.

He pulled back looking at her face. Her eyes were sparkling with unshed tears. His heart was aching, feeling the need for her. "Let's move this upstairs.

I want to love you, Maddy..." He reached over turned the lamp off and used the remote to turn stereo off. He took her by the hand and led her to his bedroom.

Maddy stood silently at the edge of the bed as he slowly removed her clothing. Without taking his eyes off her he removed his own. His eyes traveled over her body and back to her face, tenderly caressing her face with them. He guided her face to him kissing her forehead, then her eyes, moving down to her lips.

Maddy kept her eyes on him, feeling his lips on hers, tender, loving, and softly demanding. She pressed her hands against his naked chest, softly stroking his smooth skin.

Jack gently lifted her up and laid her down on the bed. He knelt over her, his knees on the bed. He lowered himself down beside her. His lips kissed her behind her ear, his tongue gently stroking her skin as he did. Maddy's body felt a slow burning rise within her as he continued to brush her skin with his mouth. Her fingers gently caressed his back not wanting to push the sweetness of the moment.

His fingers barely brushed against her silky skin as they wandered over her body. One hand cupped her breast, tenderly kneading it, caressing her nipple with his thumb. His lips found her mouth, gently forcing her mouth open, his tongue entering, sucking hers into his mouth.

Maddy moaned softly as she ran his fingers down his sinewy back and across his hips. She was afraid to breathe; afraid to break the magic she was feeling. She felt his body shift. His mouth left hers and migrated downward to her breast. His hand reached down to her thigh. His fingers made a circular motion as they made their way upwards. He gently parted her legs, caressing her, touching her. She felt fire shoot through her as his fingers connected with her.

Jack could feel Maddy yielding to him so completely it made him want to savor her even more, to taste her skin, to feel her body quiver under his touch. He wanted to be inside her, to feel her heat and her softness as she surrendered to him. He spread her legs and moved between them slowly entering her and at the same time covering her mouth with his kissing her deeply.

Maddy's hands ran over his hips as him moved painstaking slow inside her. She could feel the length of him each time he descended on her. He placed his elbows on each side of her head and held it with his hands. He brought his head up and gazed into her eyes. When she searched his face she could see the intensity of his love through his eyes. It made her heart want to burst.

As he stared into her sparkling eyes, his heartbeats quickened. He leaned in and kissed her forehead as he continued to make love to her. "I love you," he told her, his voice a hoarse whisper.

Maddy's fingers were entwined in his hair. "I love you, Jack Parker, with all my heart." She brought his head down to hers and kissed him deeply. "Love me, Jack. Make me complete..."

He held her as his thrusting increased in tempo. Maddy pushed against him thrust per thrust. When she thought she could take no more, he didn't stop. She pressed her face into his shoulder, whimpering...begging for release.

Jack heard her pleas, but he wasn't ready to let her go. He wished for an endless night, where he could hold her and love her. Finally he got to the point where his body betrayed his desire. He thrust deep inside and shuttered. He smiled to himself as he felt her dig her nails into his back, her body arch and she in turn quaked followed by several little aftershocks. He lowered his body on to her being careful not to crush her. He covered her face with soft kisses before he finally gently rolled off her. He took her in his arms and pulled her close to him. "You are my world, Maddy. Please think about getting out of here. I can't loose you, I just can't."

Maddy turned on her side. She brushed the hair from his eyes. "You're not going to loose me, baby. I promise I won't leave your side. Please don't make me go away. I can't be away from you."

"I need to know you are safe and the only way that is going to happen is if you are nowhere near here, away from him." He brushed his fingers along her cheek. "Please, Maddy, please think about it...for me."

She kissed him lightly several times and laid her head down facing him. "Okay, I will think about it. I don't want to leave, but I will think about. That's the only thing I can promise." She snuggled up to him laying her head in the crook of his arm.

Jack circled her with his arms and held her tight. No, a promise wasn't good enough. She would go, he would make sure of it. He never thought he would force her to do anything, but this was one case he would do what he had to do—get her to safety.

Jack had asked Bryan to meet him in his office—without Maddy. When he arrived he sat down across from Jack. He noticed the strained look on Jack's face. Something was not right. "What's up Jack?"

"I want Maddy out of here," he said with sternness in his voice Bryan rarely if ever heard coming from Jack.

"I'm confused. You mean you don't want to work with her? I'm not sure what you're asking."

"You heard Parsons last night. He is watching her. You know as well as I do he is waiting for us to fuck up and leave her alone, even for one second. He doesn't want anything from her—he wants her. And I will be damned if I am going to give him the opportunity to snatch her. I can't do it, Bryan. We need to get her out of here...make her go to Texas until this is over."

Bryan took a deep breath and let it out slowly. "I agree it would be the smartest thing to do, but you know as well as I do, we can't make her do anything. Did you talk to her about this?"

Jack leaned back in his chair, his gaze shifting to a window in his office. "Yeah, I did. I even pleaded with her."

"And she said?"

"She would think about it. I don't want her to think about it, I want her to do it, as soon as possible. If I had my way she would be on the first plane out of here. I think we could both concentrate better on this case if we didn't have her safety in the back of our minds all the time."

"Yeah, like I carry any clout with her anymore," Bryan shook his head, "She's not going to listen to me. What do you want me to do, take her off the case?"

"That's not what's keeping her here," Jack replied.

"You, you're what's keep her here aren't you?" Bryan looked up at him. "You can take her."

"I can't. There is no way in hell the department is going to let me take off in the middle of the biggest case this precinct has ever had. Christ Bryan, I am the Chief of Detectives."

"Call her in here."

Maddy was in the squad room studying the tape from the previous night. She was looking for something in the background noise, something that might give him away. Her phone went off and she picked it up she saw it was Jack ordering her to his office. Okay here we go. She was going to get hit from both sides.

She rose from her desk and made her way to Jack's office. She didn't bother to knock. As predicted Bryan was sitting across from Jack's desk, both their expressions reflecting major concern. She turned to Jack. "Damn it, I said I would think about it. Now you're both going to gang up on me? That's not fair."

Bryan turned to her, "What's it going to take to get you to go, Maddy?"

"You don't even know he is after to me, that he's not just fucking with me," she protested.

"Do you honestly believe that, Maddy?" Jack asked.

Maddy shrugged lightly, "I don't know. I don't know about anything any more. Tell you what; you guys bring him in for questioning. The minute that interview is over, I will go. I want to at least be here for it. Can we do that?"

"And where are we suppose to find him?" Bryan inquired.

"Force the issue. Send a couple of your best guys, not my team, to the church to question the secretary. They have to have a home address on him—they have to. Get the official info on him. Make them aware he is under investigation, not necessarily for this case. Maybe you can present it as fraud. The man is definitely not a real minister. Just bring him in, give him water or coffee. You will get a set of prints and DNA from his cup." Maddy was adamant about her request.

"Okay, say we get him in here to question him. What are we going to hold him on?"

"Duh, you have the call tapes, you will have his prints and DNA from the last crime scene. Get your eyes witnesses in here from the Thomas case; see if they can ID him. Christ Bryan, we've got convictions on less and you know it."

"And if he disappears in the wind?"

"We have 48 hours to hold him. Do you honestly think he is going lawyer up? And tell them what?" Maddy argued.

"We do this and you will be on the first flight out of here?" Jack asked her, meeting her gaze.

"I don't want to leave you, Jack, but if this is what it takes for you to have peace of mind I will. But only after I see him interrogated. I wish I could do it myself, which you know if I am going to be leaving right afterwards, I don't know why I can't." She was trying hard to convince them and she would keep her promise. She would leave town until he was being held over for trial.

"Okay, it's a big risk, but we will do it your way. We'll send Andy and Martin. Andy is most familiar with the case. Martin is good at info gathering. Until that time, Maddy, you are not going out in the field." Bryan stood up. "You got that Maddy. No leaving."

"So, I'm locked up in the cage again? Man this really fucking sucks." She got up and left the office.

Maddy was pissed. They were forcing her hand and she didn't like it. She had wanted to see the investigation through, but it wasn't worth watching Jack go crazy wondering when Parsons would make a move on her, and yes it was inevitable he would. Even she knew it, but she had just hoped the guys would be there to keep it from happening.

Three hours later Maddy got the word. They were bringing Parsons in for questioning. Twenty minutes later he was sitting in the interrogation room. Maddy pleaded to let her sit in on it. She told them she had the best advantage since she knew more about him then anyone else.

"Maddy, I don't think you interrogating him is a good idea. What if we can't hold him? Our only hope is getting prints on him."

Maddy turned to Bryan, "You know I am the best one for the job."

Bryan shook his head and said no, a firm on unrelenting no. "You can watch through the glass."

Bryan and Jack decided to do the interrogation themselves. Andy would stand behind the glass with Maddy.

Parsons had been led into the room and offered a chair. He stood beside it until Bryan pulled it out for him then he sat down. Bryan excused himself for a moment letting Parsons alone. He used this as a psych tool to make Parson's edgy and nervous. Which was unsuccessful, he was as cool as a cucumber.

Bryan joined Jack, Maddy and Andy behind the mirror. The four of them were silent as they studied the man behind the glass. Maddy focused intently on his face...his eyes. Seeing him this close in person unnerved her. She wanted to hear him speak, to match the voice with the face. "He looks so calm," she remarked softly.

"Narcissist." Bryan commented. "I bet he doesn't flinch at one question we ask him."

"I bet he would if I asked him." Maddy knew she could get to him. She knew how to push his buttons.

"Maddy...no." Jack turned her towards him. "Please, for once don't let your ego get in the way making you do something stupid."

"He doesn't look like a monster does he?

"It's what he banks on." Bryan observed the man as he sat there. Parsons sat straight in his chair with his arms folded across his chest. He was noticing the man was careful not to touch anything with his hands—not the door, not the chair, not the table. Bryan would offer him a bottle of water which he knew the unsub would refuse. This guy was no dummy. He would leave them nothing for which to pull prints off from and definitely no DNA. "You ready?" he asked Jack.

Jack leaned over and kissed Maddy lightly. "For once in your life, please, stay put."

Bryan and Jack entered and sat down one across from Parsons, the other at the end of the table. Bryan held in his hand a file, a pretty much empty file, but Parsons didn't need to know that.

Bryan introduced himself and Jack. Maddy watched Parsons face and picked up how he gave Jack more than a fleeting glance. He was sizing him up. It made the hair on the back of her neck stand up.

"Do you know why we brought you here Mr. Parsons?" Bryan started off.

"Reverend Parsons," the man corrected him. "I think you are under some misguided perception that I have something to do with the recent demise of several young women." Parson voice was very well controlled, not a hint of anxiety.

Jack slid over a piece of paper listing the disappearance dates of their victims. "Can you tell us you're where you were at on these dates?"

Parsons was careful not to touch the paper as he peered down at it. "Sorry gentlemen, without looking at my calendar I couldn't be sure. I image I was either at home or performing my churchly duties."

"Could I get you something to drink?" Bryan asked.

The minister smiled as if it were a private joke. "No thank you. What I would like is for you to finish this inquest so I may return to my work. Ask me anything you wish, I have nothing to hide."

"What church do you minister to?"

The man smiled, "Come now, Detective. You already know the answers to those questions. You knew that before you ever sought me out. Let me just give you everything in a nutshell. If I have left anything out, please feel free to ask. My name is Justin Parsons; I am a minister at Trinity First Reform Church. I have been at my post for eight months. I help out at the church on a regular basis, but I hold a private alternative service on Thursday evenings for those who wish to participate. I am a quiet man, I keep to myself, and I live modestly."

Bryan sat back, crossing his legs under the table and folding his arms across his chest. "How do you account for at least three of the women were members of your congregation?"

"They were members of Trinity, not members of mine," Parsons replied without blinking an eye.

Jack spread headshots of each of the women in front of Parsons. "You don't recognize any of these women?"

Parsons looked them over and shook his head. "Might have seen them around the church, but I can't be sure."

"How about when they looked like this," he spread the photos of each of the women as they were found in the burial sites plus the body of Thomas.

Parsons leaned over and studied these a little closer. Maddy watched his face. She saw the glimmer of excitement in his eyes, and the slightest trace of a smug smile playing upon his lips.

"My, My...such rage this person had towards these women. But no," Parson shook his head, "Not these either."

The three men sat in silence. It took everything Maddy had not to storm into the room and start hurling questions at him, but Andy was keeping a tight leash on her. Jack and Bryan were teaching him well.

Parsons took a deep breath, "So unless you are going to charge me with something I believe I am free to go."

No, no, no! They weren't done with him yet. Maddy felt the panic rise up in her. They had nothing to hold him on, absolutely nothing. Bryan was right; this interview was premature. Now this son of a bitch was going to walk without so much as leaving a print they could use. She had to do something.

Maddy ran from the room to Jack's office and grabbed a bunch of file folders. She moved to the stair well and waited. She knew he would take the stairs because he wouldn't want to leave a print on the elevator button. She knew what she had to do.

Parsons stood up and waited in front of the door until Jack opened the door for him. He smiled at them and told them good day and left.

As soon as he was out of earshot Andy stormed in the room, "Maddy took off!"

"God damn it!" Jack and Bryan took off after her.

Maddy peered around the corner and saw Parsons coming towards her. She was on the second level of stairs and could hear his footsteps approaching her. She quickly took off up the stairs with her head down ramming right into him. The files flew everywhere.

Parsons unconsciously bent down and helped her pick them up. As the two of them rose together they made eye contact.

Maddy acted all flustered, "I am so sorry," she laughed nervously. "I guess I should pay more attention to what I am doing. Thank you so much for helping me."

Parsons continued to stare at her, watching her, looking to see if she showed any signs of recognition. "No worries, my child." He then began to continue his decent down the stairs. As he was leaving she heard him say, "You should slow down, life ends before you know it...sweet Maddy."

Jack witnessed the encounter and heard what Parsons said as he left. He felt sick to his stomach. He grabbed Maddy by the arm and hauled her ass into his office where Bryan met up with them. "What the fuck? Damn it, Maddy! I can't believe you would be so fucking stupid to pull such a stupid stunt like that. You heard what he said. He knows you know. For Christ sake he just as much as said you're next!" Jack bellowed at her.

Maddy slunk into a chair. Her face ashen, her hands trembling, her heart felt like it was going to explode in her chest. She held on tightly to the files in her hand. She saw it in his eyes; she heard it in his voice. She would be his next target. She was oblivious to Jack's ranting. She heard none of it.

Bryan watched her. He had seen this look before. He turned her chair and knelt down in front of her. "Maddy...Maddy...look at me. Come on honey, just look at me."

Maddy slowly raised her head. Her shut down mechanism in place, she calmly looked at him. She raised the stack of files up and handed them to him by the edges. "Finger prints...on the files."

Jack continued going off on Maddy until he realized she was just sitting there, staring off into space. He looked at Bryan. "What's going on?"

Bryan held up his hand. "Maddy, look at me kiddo. Please? Now is not the time for this. You need your wits about you now more than ever. Come on. Don't do this."

Jack came around the corner of his desk, watching them, confused as to what was transpiring. "Bryan?"

Jack motioned for Bryan to step aside and he knelt down by Maddy. "Kitten? Honey? You okay?"

Maddy slowly turned to him and said without emotion, "I got what you couldn't. I got his fingerprints. Now you have something to arrest him with." She turned away from him.

Bryan grabbed Jack by the arm and took him out into the hallway.

"What the hell is going on?" Jack asked looking back at Maddy in the room.

"She's shut down. We need to shock her out of it. She could be dangerous in this mood. She will act without thinking, do whatever it is she feels needs to be done."

"He threatened her Bryan. His exact words were: 'You should slow down, life ends before you know it...sweet Maddy. He knows and told her as much."

"That explains why she is where she is. Come on, we have to snap her out of this." They returned to the office and shut the door behind them.

Parsons words echoed in her head over and over again. How could someone's voice be soothing and menacing at the same time? Jack was right. It was really stupid thing to do. She thought they had forced the interview, by her prodding of course. But what she did was throw fuel on the fire. They couldn't arrest him on her say so. But if she got good prints on any of those files and matched them up to Thomas's house, then they had him. But what in the mean time? He knew she knew, therefore it wasn't like he was going to be sitting around waiting for them to come and get him. He would go underground. If she hadn't set him up, he would have left here and been none the wiser and they could have continued to investigate to find more leads to link him to the crimes. But because she did what she did, if they could find him they could put him away. And now Parsons was going to put her away, forever.

Maddy put her head in her hands and leaned forward. Bryan was all freaking out because she had momentarily put up her wall. She was okay. When was he going to learn to trust she could handle herself now? She wasn't weak, not anymore. She could feel them standing behind her. "Don't have a cow. I'm fine. No more wall. You going to get those files down to trace or what? Time's wasting. Every minute that passes that's that much farther away he is getting from us. He's not stupid enough to wait around knowing I can ID him."

Bryan left with the folders and Jack sat down across from Maddy. "Why did you do it? You had to know what you were risking."

Maddy looked up at him. "He was getting away. Just walking right out that door and everyone including him knew he was going to get away with it. He was so careful. Said nothing, gave nothing away, never touched anything, had an answer to everything. I am getting sent away until he is behind bars. I don't want that to be forever, Jack. I want this over with. Yes, I did it without thinking, but somebody had to do something and do it fast. Do you understand? I had to do it... for us."

Jack reached down and pulled her to her feet wrapping his arms around her. "Kitten, you forced his hand. You never should have done it." He pulled her close resting his head on hers. "We need to get you a flight booked and get you the hell out of here as soon as possible. You're not leaving my sight until you get on that plane. Understood?"

Maddy nodded. She would not argue this point with him. She needed to leave town to be safe. She wasn't stupid and she wasn't a martyr. "God, I am going to miss you."

"I would rather have you miss me then let him get his hands on you." He turned her face up to him and kissed her tenderly. "It could be just a few days, hon."

"Or weeks," she sighed. "You don't know where he is going to take off to."

Jack released her, sat at his desk and got on his computer. He booked a flight leaving at 6:30 this evening.

Maddy called her sister informing her of her impromptu visit. They would leave shortly for her to go back to Jack's to repack her bags.

Forty-five minutes later the fingerprint results came back. Bryan had made the lab drop everything to run them. Three sets of prints on the folders were at least a nine-point match—enough to arrest Parsons. A squad car had been sent out to pick him up, but it was no surprise to anyone one Parsons had packed up most of his personal belongings and fled. CSU had been sent out to go through his home and hoped to secure items they could pull DNA from.

It felt like they were on a deathwatch. A gambit of emotion ran through Maddy. She felt the excitement of the chase, which was finally heading in the right direction. She felt fear every time Parsons voice echoed in her mind. She felt sadness at having to leave things she felt were unfinished. Her heart ached already at having to leave Jack. Then she looked up and saw Bryan watching her. Something she hadn't thought of, when this case was over, Bryan would be leaving.

Maddy stood up and took him by the hand. "Come on, let's go talk."

They decided to go down to the back entrance instead of the front steps for obvious reasons. They sat down on the steps and Bryan lit up a cigarette. "This could be the last time we get to do this Minnie," he said sadly.

She leaned her head on his arm. "I know. We never did get to spend that private time together did we?" she laughed shakily.

Bryan slipped his arm around her. "Nope. It was like you said, life just gets fucked up and gets in the way."

Maddy wiped her eyes, "I know we can never be together as a couple, but I don't want you to go away. I want you here, with me, always. I haven't had enough of you yet."

Bryan smiled weakly, "If I asked you that a few weeks ago, you would have said you had more than enough. It will be okay, Maddy. We are in each other's lives now. I'm not letting it go now. We will still see each other. There is nothing to say we can't fly out to see each other."

"Do you really think that is going to happen?"

He kissed the top of her head, "Yes, because I am going to make it happen. I didn't come this far to walk away from you. We still need each other, Maddy. Nothing is going to change that. Not time, not distance. We don't have to be like we were before. I promise."

Maddy moved to the step below him and in front of him. She took his face in her hands and kissed him slowly and deeply. "Promise me you will wait for me, wait for me to get back. Promise me you will stay long enough that we can spend a couple of days together."

"I promise." Bryan pulled her into his arms taking her possessively. But this time she didn't mind, she yearned for it. This was her Bryan, forever and always her Bryan.

"I love you, Mickey," she whispered softly.

Bryan kissed her again, "I love you Minnie. We need to get you back in there. You have a flight to catch." He pulled her to feet.

Jack was waiting for them in the squad room. He noticed a sadness about them and totally understood. This was going to be tough on them too. "We need to go, Kitten."

Maddy turned to Bryan. They hugged and kissed one last time. "Just think Minnie, the next time I see you, you will be a free woman," he smiled down at her, but she could see the sadness in his eyes.

"Yeah, we can go raise some hell then okay?" Maddy smiled up at him. "Good bye Bryan..."

He put his finger under her chin, "It's not good-bye, Maddy. Good-bye is forever...this is an 'until I see you again'." he kissed her softly. "Have a safe trip, and there is nothing saying you can't call me...often."

She laughed weakly, "Okay, until we see each other again. And I will call you. It works both ways though."

Jack put his hand on Bryan's shoulder, "Okay you two, hate to break up this long 'until I see you again', Maddy's going to miss her flight if we don't get going."

"Jack, sign out a car and take Maddy out the back way. Just in case Parson's is watching the lot." He turned to Maddy, "Please call me when you get there so I know you're safe okay?"

"Yes boss," she smiled.

Maddy and Jack drove to his house in silence which sort of disturbed Maddy. They had so much to say to each other and nothing was getting said. "Are you still pissed at me?"

Jack grabbed her hand and brought to his lips. "I'm not pissed at you, Kitten. I'm just thinking how badly I am going to miss you. I've gotten pretty attached to you and love having you around. The house is going to be damn lonely without you. And what really sucks, is we don't even have time to make love before you go."

Maddy smiled, "Just keep last night in your memory for awhile baby. I know I am. Remember you said you could fly down if things dragged out too long."

Jack laughed, "You think your sister will mind me molesting you non-stop over the weekend?"

"The guest room is upstairs. We just can't howl...and she has a swimming pool. Maybe we can get that skinny-dip in," she grinned.

"We're going to catch this son of bitch fast so I can get you back home where you belong?"

"The sooner the better."

Maddy went upstairs and packed her bags and met Jack in the kitchen. "You'll take care of Eddie for me won't you?"

Jack pulled her close. "Kitten, you know I will. I will even let him sleep upstairs with me. You ready?"

Maddy looked around the house. "I've really come to see this place as home, but only with you in it."

Jack threw her bags in the car and they left for the airport. Conversation was light as they tried to stay away from subjects that were too emotional. When they arrived at the airport they checked Maddy in and checked her luggage. They didn't have a lot of time before she had to board the plane. She would layover in Minneapolis and then fly into Houston where her sister would meet her.

They had to part outside the gate. They held each other tightly giving each other a long tender kiss. Jack smiled down at her, "Until I see you again."

Maddy held him tight, "Which better be soon. I will call you when I get there, and probably a hundred times after that."

Maddy grabbed her carryon, kissed him quickly and went through the gate. She didn't look back at him as she thought of an old Irish saying. If you look back, you will never see them again. Once she got situated on the plane, she broke down and cried. She was leaving two men, two men she loved. One she didn't want to live without, the other she couldn't live without.

Jack stayed at the airport until he watched her plane take off. It was breaking his heart to see her go, but he knew she had to. It was the right thing to do and the safest thing to do.

When he returned back to the precinct he went straight to the squad room. "Well she's safe. On her way to Minneapolis as we speak."

Bryan sat back in his chair. "It's going to be real quiet and a lot less exciting without her around here."

"Well, we'll just need to nail Parson's ass that much quicker. What are we doing?"

"We have an APB out on him. I sent his picture to the papers and the networks with a description and what he is wanted for so people are going to be on the lookout for him. That is if he hasn't left town."

Jack sat down at Maddy's desk. "He won't leave town, not without Maddy. Maddy says when he chooses someone he can't let it go. It's obsession with him."

"Well this is one he is going to have to. He can't get to her now."

Jack sat back with his feet up on her desk, "Why do you call her Minnie?"

Bryan smiled, "Do you really want to know?"

"We're big boys here...yeah I want to know."

Bryan laughed, "Well it's a two part story. First of all it was code between she and I when Donna was around. We called each other Mickey and Minnie. The other thing is when she gets real excited; her voice gets high pitched, like Minnie Mouse. Okay you're turn, why Kitten?"

Jack grinned with a devilish gleam in his eye, "Because I can make her purr."

Bryan shook his head. "We are terrible."

"Say do we have someone watching the parking lot?"

Bryan stacked some files up on his desk, "Yep, across the street at the library lot."

"How long do you think he will wait for her before he gives up?"

"Until he is caught."

"You know as much as it pissed me off, what she did this afternoon was quick thinking on her part. She took a gamble he would stop and help her pick up those files." Jack started snooping through her drawers. He found her badge and her gun. It only made sense; she couldn't take them with her.

"Nobody said she wasn't resourceful. She is a hell of an agent, but quite honestly, her time spent as a reporter has ruined her for the field." Bryan sat back and put his feet up on his desk.

Jack looked over at him. "I thought she was doing a hell of a job. Look at everything she gave us."

"She's reckless, too impulsive. She never used to be that way. She used to think everything though. Of course she wasn't an active investigator, but she never took careless risks like she does now. That kind of behavior would get her killed in the field. So I guess I am glad she won't be staying on as an agent. Don't ever tell her I said this, but I think she is best as an investigative reporter."

The unsub cell phone was still sitting on Bryan's desk when it went off. Jack and Bryan looked at each other. Jack picked it up, "Hello?"

"Where's Maddy?" the man's voice was agitated.

"She won't be talking to you anymore," he told the unsub coldly.

"This must be her lover, the detective. You can pass on a message to her. She betrayed my trust and for that she must pay. All the watching you can do will not keep her from her destiny."

"Good luck with that," Jack said as he hung up the phone. Jack shook his head, "Damn that felt good. Brazen mother fucker aint he?"

25

Maddy lay stretched out on a lounge chair by the pool sipping an ice tea. She was alone at the house because her sister was working. She couldn't take time off just because Maddy was there. For weeks she longed to be alone, to have her personal space. Now she hated it. She missed Jack and she missed Bryan. She was lonely. She had plenty of books to read. She had even written the story up of the case, which she would submit when it reached its conclusion.

When she had talked to Jack in the evenings their conversations was strained. They wanted to be together, but couldn't. It was much harder than she thought it would be. Nothing had happened with the case. He had filled her in on what little he did know. Parsons had disappeared in to thin air. They were sure he was still around waiting on her. This wondering and waiting was driving her crazy.

Her conversations with Bryan weren't much better. She longed for the comfort he gave her and doing it over the phone just wasn't cutting it.

Sixteen days into it and they were no closer to getting Parsons than when she left. This was pointless she wanted to go home.

Jack was going crazy without Maddy. He was constantly on edge, snappy at everyone who came his way. He spent many of his evenings at his parent's house not liking being in his home without her.

"Jack, just get on a plane and go see her," his mother told him.

"I can't get off work. We're working seven days a week looking for this guy. When we talk at night, there's nothing to say except how much we miss each other. We don't talk much about the case because there is really nothing to tell. This is really put some strain on our relationship," Jack explained.

"Honey, if you can't pass this test, you two are really in trouble."

"I didn't mean like that. I need her—here with me. But I can't have her. I know this and it's so damn frustrating."

Bryan wasn't much better. He missed having Maddy around. He missed her irritating ways. He missed seeing her face. So much time they had wasted. He thought it would be easier with her gone, that they could concentrate more on the case. But it was at a stand still. Almost two and a half weeks had gone by. When he talked to Maddy each night she had such a longing in her voice. How long would it be before she jumped ship and came back even though her life was still endanger? He didn't voice his concerns to Jack. It would be just one more thing to contend with and he was already on the edge.

Donna had left on the Tuesday after the weekend at Jack's. She finally realized the facts of the situation. She told him he would always be welcome in her home, but she would no longer push him to love her. Maybe she should have stayed. At least she would have been a distraction.

Maddy's plane had just departed Minneapolis. She could no longer do it. She told no one what she was doing. Jack and Bryan would both have a fit and she didn't want to contend with it until she saw them. She would sneak in, see Jack, and then head home. Parsons didn't know where she lived. She should be safe in her own home. She would rent a car from the airport, park in the back of the station and sneak in and surprise Jack.

An hour later Maddy was pulling into a parking spot just off the police parking lot. She pulled her hair back and stuffed it up under a baseball cap. She was dressed in painter's pants and jacket. She thought maybe she could pass off as a boy, but with her delicate features if someone were to really look close you could definitely tell she was female. The early October sun had turned cool. Amazing how much could change in just a little over two weeks.

Maddy did enter through the front entrance because she really didn't feel like walking all the way around to the back of the station. She took the elevator up, keeping her head down. She waited in the hallway, kind of back out of the way. She peered around the corner and saw Jack's office was empty. She quietly snuck in and stood back in the corner. She pulled out her cell phone and text Jack. 'Hey baby, where are you?' and hit send.

Jack was sitting at Maddy's desk chatting with Bryan when he cell phone went off. He pulled it out and was surprised to see a text message from Maddy. How odd, she hadn't text him since she had left and only called in the evenings. He hit the reply option. 'Just sitting in the squad room talking to Bryan.'

'How is he doing?'

'Same as me, pouting.'

Maddy smiled. She wasn't sure what his reaction to her arrival would be. She only knew she was more than excited to see him. 'There is something in your office you need to go see.'

'Huh?'

'Just go, it's something special.'

Jack flipped his phone shut. "I'll be back, I need to check something out," he told Bryan.

When Jack walked though his office door he saw a kid standing there with his back turned toward him. "Excuse me, is there a reason you're in my office?" he asked.

Maddy turned to him and smiled not saying a word. Jack rushed to her picking her up and swirled her around. He set her down, pulled off her cap, his lips came down on hers crushing them with great intensity.

"Jesus Maddy," he kissed her again, "I have been so lost without you. What the hell are you doing here?"

She put her head against his chest. "I couldn't do it anymore. I couldn't stay away. I need to be with you. I love you so much, baby."

Jack held her face up so he could see it. He hadn't realized how much he missed her sparkling green eyes, her pert little nose, and those ever so soft kissable lips. And there was something new, a light dusting of freckles across her nose the Texas sun had left. He couldn't help but notice her glistening with unshed tears. "It's okay, Kitten. But what are we going to do with you?"

"I rented a car from the airport. I thought I would go home and stay put there. You like my disguise?" she grinned.

"Very tomboyish," he smiled down at her. "You want me to call Bryan in?"

"Not yet, I just want you to hold me."

Jack pulled her close again and buried his face in her hair smelling the sweetness of her mixed in with the scent of shampoo. It felt so good and so right holding her in his arms like this. He leaned her back and kissed her, his tongue parting her lips, letting his kiss linger. "I wish I could scoop you up and take you back to the house and show you how much I missed you."

Maddy smiled up at him. "Me too. I just want to crawl inside your skin and stay there."

Jack laughed, "Well you are definitely under my skin. I'm going to call Bryan." He walked over and shut the door to his office and called Bryan to come to his office.

Maddy could hardly wait to see him either. When he walked through the door, she jumped in his arms hugging him tight.

Bryan stepped back. A big smile crossed his lips. He bent down and kissed her then held her next to him. "I knew it. I just knew you would sneak back. Minnie, what are you doing here?"

"I made a jail break. I'm not staying long. I just wanted to see you guys before I head home."

"You know Parsons could be out there watching, just waiting."

"He won't see me." She put on her baseball cap and stuffed her hair up in it and put on her sunglasses. "See, I'm invisible. I rented a car so he won't know to look for it."

"Just the same I am going to call the Sheriff in your county to see about getting a car placed by your house. I want you to check in...often. Will you do that for us?"

"Don't suppose you would let me sneak off for an hour or so," Jack asked him sheepishly.

Bryan smiled softly, "Wish I could, Jack, but I can't. You know as well as I do we have the brass biting at our ass. However, I will cover for you if you went to spend the night at Maddy's."

Jack turned to Maddy and reached for her, "Sorry Kitten, I tried. You wait up for me?"

She kissed him tenderly, "You know I will, but for now, I have to get the hell out of Dodge."

"I'll walk you out."

Bryan stopped him. "You can't. You would be a dead giveaway."

Jack shook his head. "Damn everything about this sucks." He held Maddy close and kissed her deeply. He was sorry Bryan had to see that, but at this point he really didn't care.

Maddy hated leaving Jack. He made her feel whole again, but he would be with her tonight. They would be shut away in their own little world. "Well I guess I better take off." She kissed Jack on the cheek and hugged him one last time. "Hurry home," she whispered.

She hugged Bryan and gave him a quick kiss. "There is nothing saying you can't come and see me either."

Bryan smiled, "I will, I promise—just not this evening. Cranky over there needs you alone tonight."

Maddy adjusted her baseball hat, pulled up the collar on her jacket, and slipped on her sunglasses. "Later boys!"

She walked discreetly out of the building and across the parking lot. She looked covertly around for anything suspicious, but nothing looked out of the ordinary. She looked both ways and ran across the street to the library parking lot. She dug into her jeans pocket and pulled out the keys to her car and unlocked it. She didn't hear him come up behind her. The only thing she was aware of was the sharp pain as something striking her head. She fell forward into the car then she felt the piercing of something being poked into her neck. A white fog descended over her.

Maddy had been gone a little over an hour and Jack was wondering why she hadn't called yet. She should be home by now. He constantly looked at phone waiting for it to ring. Finally he called her. It rang and rang finally going over to voice mail. Something wasn't right.

As he was walking out of his office two uniforms approached him, one of them being Bobby Russell. "Jack, I got something you need to see." He held out a bag...Maddy's bag.

Jack snatched it from his hands, "Where did you get this?"

"From a car parked across the street. We found the car with the driver's side door open, the bag was in it...It's not the only thing we found in the car..." Bobby said slowly.

"What?" Jack snapped. His heart was racing, panic quickly taking over.

"There's blood on the seat."

Jack didn't wait to hear anymore and took off to find the car. "Get Mayland and send him down," he yelled over his shoulder. It seemed like it took an eternity to reach the bottom of the steps. He scanned the parking lot and spotted a police car in the adjacent parking lot guarding the car. He ran across the lot and crossed the street without looking. Cars came to a screeching halt. Tires squealed as they locked up on the pavement. When Jack finally made his way to the car, two uniforms were standing guard over it. They put their hands up to block him from seeing what was inside. He pushed them aside, "Get the fuck out of my way." They still tried to obstruct his view.

"Let him through." It was Bryan. "Get back out of our way."

The uniforms released Jack and let them through. Jack didn't know what he expected to see, but what he found made him feel sick. There was blood spatter splashed across the doorframe, a smear across the back of the driver's seat and a large pool of blood in the passenger seat. Jack punched the side of the car, "God damn it! The son of bitch has her!"

Bryan kept his cool as he examined the blood. Someone had to stay calm in the face of reason; it sure as hell wasn't going to be Jack. "Looks like he hit her on the head with a blunt object resulting in this splatter. She either fell into the car or he pushed her into to it, making this," he pointed to the smear across the back of the seat. "Her head came to rest on the passenger side. There are copious amounts of blood here, but that wouldn't be uncommon with a head injury. My guess is he left her here, retrieved his car and came back and got her."

Jack looked at him in disbelief. Bryan was so calm, so clinical. He sounded like Maddy when she was describing a crime scene. "How the fuck can you be so..."

"Calm?" Bryan raised an eyebrow. "Because we have to be. Loosing it isn't helping Maddy. Does the parking lot have surveillance tapes?"

"Yeah both the police lot and the library do," Bobby, who had joined them, told him.

"Impound the car. I want CSU going through it with a fine-toothed comb. Bring the tapes up to the task force squad room." He turned to Jack, "Come on, Jack. What's done is done here. We need to get on this ASAP." He turned and left.

Jack watched after him. How could he be so FBIish, for lack of a better word? Maddy was in the hands of a madman. She could be already dead. He felt tightness in his chest and weak in the knees. He had never experience fear to the degree he felt at that moment.

He felt a hand on his shoulder and turned to see Bobby, "Go ahead Jack, I'll see that this gets taken care of properly. We'll get her back."

By the time Jack made his way to the squad room, Bryan had a VCR set up.

"You better sit down before you collapse, Jack. Kid, you got to keep your wits about you. You aren't going to do Maddy any good by falling apart." Bryan grabbed a pill bottle form his desk, opened up and handed Jack one of his pills. "Take it."

Jack shook his head, "No...No, I'm okay."

"God damn it, take it! I need you. I can't do this on my own, and if you think this is easy on me you are full of shit. My insides are tearing apart as we speak, but I know if Maddy has any chance in hell on making it out alive it's going to be up to us, so pull your shit together and help me!" The anger in his voice raised to a new pitch with every word he breathed.

Jack popped the pill and took several deep breaths trying to get his emotions under check. Bryan was right. They needed to concentrate on finding Maddy before it was too late.

Andy entered the room followed by a man pushing a cart with a LED monitor and a tape machine. "I have the surveillance tapes. This Carter," he pointed to the guy behind him. "He's the station's video tech. I think he can help us better than you can fake it," he told Bryan.

Bryan raised an eyebrow. This kid was taking more initative everyday. He was sure it was thanks to Maddy's guidance. Maybe she wasn't such a bad influence after all. He smiled to himself and then felt a wave wash over him sending him back into the present.

The man set up the equipment and popped in the first tape of the station parking lot. "What time did she leave?"

Bryan looked at Jack, "Around 2:30 wouldn't you say?"

Jack nodded. It seemed like an eternity ago.

Carter fast-forwarded the tape to the time stamp of around 2:30. He flipped through different camera views before he stopped on one frame. "Is that her?"

They all gathered around the screen. It revealed a distant shot of Maddy walking across the street to the vehicle, unlocking it, and someone approaching her from behind.

"Can you zoom in on that?" Jack asked as he watched intently.

From this vantage point it was really hard to see anything. The man, wearing a stocking cap, paused behind Maddy. Maddy disappeared from view, and then the guy turned and left. Minutes later a vehicle pulled up next to Maddy's in the parking lot. The man got out, appeared to be opening his passenger side door and her driver's side door. He pulled what was apparently Maddy from her vehicle into his and drove off.

"Okay, give us the video from the library."

The tech popped in the tape and fast-forwarded it to the same time frame. From this shot, they zoomed in at a different perspective than the last. "Zoom in further." They were able to get a close enough shot to see the man actually hitting Maddy in the head with what appeared to be the wrong end of a pistol. Maddy slumped down. The man then took something out of his pocket. "Zoom in more, on his hand." It was a syringe which the man injected something into Maddy's neck. The tech zoom back out slightly revealing him shoving Maddy back into her vehicle. The tape verified pretty much exactly as Bryan said it happened.

Bryan went to his desk and pulled out the unsub cell phone. Jack looked at him. "What are you doing?"

"Going to attempt to make contact." He flipped the phone and looked through the numbers dialed and hit send.

Parsons answered on the third ring. "Now you know I keep my word," he said before Bryan could even get a word out.

"Where is she?" he asked coldly.

"Don't worry. She's not going anywhere for a while. She is safe...for now. Whom am I talking to?"

"FBI Special Agent Bryan Mayland. I want to talk to her."

Parson's laughed, "Ah, the other bodyguard. Missed out on bagging her didn't you? Let her slip away into the arms of the detective. Is he there with you? Be careful how you answer, I am the one calling the shots here."

"I'm here," Jack answered. "What did you do to her?"

"Oh, just a little bump on the head. And you two thought you could hide her from me didn't you? It was only a matter of time before she turned up for her detective. Patience is a virtue."

"Fuck you!" Jack went after the phone. "Let me talk to her. Prove to us that you haven't already killed her."

A sinister laugh echoed over the hollow line. "She isn't in any condition to talk at the moment. She's such a sound sleeper. She said she likes to play games so that is what we are going to do. Cat and mouse I think she said her favorite is. I'm the cat, you two are the mice..." he laughed again, "and sweet Maddy is the bait." The line went dead.

Jack picked up the phone and continuously hit the redial. He let it ring and ring, until finally Bryan couldn't stand it and snatched the phone out of his hands. "He's not going to answer, damn it. Like he said he's calling the shots. We just have to figure out what kind of game he is playing. She's alive and he's using her as the bait. For what I don't fucking know."

Jack put his head in his hands. "What the fuck does he want from us?"

"Amusement," he lit up a cigarette.

Jack looked at him in mild disbelief at his actions.

"They can fucking kick me out of here if the want to," Bryan held out his pack of smokes. When Jack took it he lit it for him.

Maddy groaned feeling the full force of her head exploding. She brought her hand to her head feeling a deep gash. Her hair was sticky and warm. Fuck, what the hell happened? She opened her eyes slowly. The light, it was so bright it hurt. She blinked until things became more in focus. She was in a room, a prison, with cement walls and a concrete floor. The ceiling, she guessed was approximately 12 feet high. She sat up slowly, holding her throbbing head as she did. She was sitting on an old mattress, which had been thrown on the floor. A bucket sat in the corner of the room. Nice accommodations. It sure as hell wasn't the Hilton.

Maddy felt a pinching on the back of her leg. She ran her hand down and felt her cell phone. She was wearing painter's pants and had slipped her phone into her side leg pocket. What a dumb fuck. He didn't bother to even search her. She knew who had her. Parsons couldn't have been that stupid, could he?

Her eyes roved over the room, scanning it from floor to ceiling. In one corner she notice a tiny red dot in the middle of a circle. The son of a bitch had a camera on her. How long had he planning this? Did he take his other victims here? She stopped. No she was not one of his victims. She refused to be.

Maddy laid back down facing the wall opposite of the camera. She slid her hand down to her leg and removed the phone. She carefully reset the ringer on it to silent and opened it up. She didn't dare make a call; she couldn't risk being heard. She curled her arms up by her head so it would look as if she were using them for a pillow. She laid the phone down. It had a full charge on it, but she knew she needed to reserve the power for as long as she could. With one hand she punched in Jack's number 3 and text option. She typed in with one finger 'I'm okay. Don't call.' She hit the send button.

Jack felt his phone go off in his pocket and pulled it out. "Jesus Christ, it's Maddy." Bryan stood over him as he opened it and read her message. "What should I say?" He looked up at Bryan.

"Ask her something only she would know to make sure it really is her."

Jack typed in 'why do I call you Kitten?"

Maddy smiled, her baby. "U make me purr."

A broad smile spread across Jack's face. "Its her!" 'Do you know where you're at?"

Maddy peered over her shoulder. 'Don't know. Locked in a room. Smells like auto grease.'

"A auto garage," Bryan said as he read the post. "Ask her about her injuries."

'How bad are you hurt?'

'Pistol-whipped. Hurts like bitch. Worse than hangover.'

Jack laughed. "I'll be damned she still has a sense of humor. God I love that woman. Now what?"

'Where is he?'

'Haven't seen him yet. Camera on ceiling. Watching me.'

"Make sure she isn't going to get caught doing this."

'Can he see you using phone?'

'No. Turned away from camera. Dumb fuck missed it when searched me. Can't stay long. Need to reserve battery. I luv u...both.'

'We luv U 2. Text when can'

Maddy smiled softly, her heart aching. 'k. til we see each other again'

Jack and Bryan both smiled when they got her last text. "You got yourself one hell of a woman there, Jack. Hearing from her make you feel any better?"

"Doesn't it you?"

"Oh hell yeah. Let's find our girl."

"Can a text message be traced?" Jack asked.

"Will check into. If she hadn't turned her cell off we could track her by locking in on her signal. Next time she contacts you; we'll have to see if we can get a trap and trace. Let me make some phone calls." Bryan left him to follow up.

Jack leaned back in the chair. Thank God she was okay for now.

Maddy closed the phone and powered it down. Her hand crept down feeling the side of the mattress. She found a small fray in the fabric and pulled on it until it gave away. She slid the phone deep into the bedding. It was her lifeline to the world, to Jack.

Maddy heard keys in the door and her body stiffened. He was coming in. She lay still on the mattress to give the appearance of sleep. The door opened with a grating scrape that sent shivers through Maddy's spine.

"Get up, Maddy," Parsons ordered her.

"Fuck you," she hissed.

Maddy felt herself being yanked up off the mattress by her hair. She steadied herself on her feet. "Jesus fucking Christ, do you have to pull my hair? As if my head doesn't hurt enough thanks to you."

"Then don't be insolent. Do what you're told and you will make this more pleasant for both of us." He released her hair and stood back.

Maddy eyed him and laughed, "What the fuck did you did do to your hair?" It was now blonde instead of the dark brown. His eyebrows were still dark. Maddy thought it look ridiculous.

"For someone whose life is in grave danger you sure have a mouth on you. Do you think this is all fun and games?"

Seeing him up close and personal, he didn't seem so intimidating although she knew otherwise. She wasn't going to let him see any fear in her. He would just get off on it. And it's not to say she wasn't afraid, she was scared shitless. The chameleon had kicked in, this time it was a matter of life and death. "I thought that was what you were into—mind fucking. Weren't you the one that said I was fearless?"

Parsons studied her. He was sizing her up. "Your fearlessness could get you killed, Maddy," he said calmly.

Maddy held her chin out defiantly. "Then save us both the time and just do it."

He put his finger under her chin, "Such a hell fire..."

Maddy batted his hand away for which she was reward a solid backhand across her face. She tasted blood in her mouth, but she didn't flinch.

"Fuck, you could have just slapped me. Would have been just as effective." She wiped the blood from her split lip."

Parsons stepped back away from her and laughed ominously. "You really are a paradox, Maddy. I thought you were just blowing smoke when we talked on the phone, but you are the real McCoy. So tell me, when did you figure me out?"

"Can I sit down? My fucking head is pounding like a freight train?"

"Go ahead."

Maddy slid down onto the mattress. Parsons left the room momentarily and came back with a chair. "Now we talk. Answer my question."

Maddy brought her shirt up to her mouth and dabbed off the blood. She could taste it in her mouth and wanted badly to spit, but thought better of it. "I knew what you looked like from the time I saw you at the grave site. You were dressed as a CSU guy."

"How did you know it was me?"

Fuck it. She spit off to the side. "I knew you were there. I sensed it. You were the one who gave yourself away when you told me you looked in my eyes. How long have you been following me?"

Parsons leaned back and put his arms folded behind his head. "I watched you off and on going in and out of the Police Station. It was the one place I knew I could find you. You were the one that tipped the cops off on how to find me."

"Well duh...you don't think they weren't taping all our conversations? I was working with them all along." Maddy leaned back against the wall. The pain she felt was making her nauseous.

"You set me up with that little collision on the steps."

Maddy closed her eyes to block out the blinding light. "Can't you dim these lights, they hurt."

"Answer."

"Somebody had to. You were so clever at making sure you didn't touch anything. When they questioned you, you were very evasive. You would almost think you had it all rehearsed. If they would have let me at you, you would never have left that place without handcuffs." It was out before she thought about it. She better watch what she said. If she let on that she was FBI, lord knows what he would do to her.

"You like to play detective. Does that come from sleeping with one?" Maddy wanted so badly to wipe that smirk off his face.

"He is not open to discussion with you," Maddy replied flatly. Jack was hers and she would be damned if she would let him tarnish anything about him.

Parson grinned, that polished, insincere grin. "I found your Achilles heal. Quite protective of your detective...as he is of you—along with the FBI agent. Did they fight over you and your detective won?"

"Fuck off."

Parson stood up and grabbed his chair. "Enough chit chat. We will have plenty of time for that."

"Can I get some water...and some aspirin?"

"In awhile. I want your sweethearts to see how you look all bloody and beaten," he laughed as he walked out the door.

"You sick fuck!" she yelled at him as she heard the lock click into place. She lay back down on the mattress. She wished so badly she could call Jack just to hear his voice and tell her everything was going to be okay—even if it wasn't.

Derek was helping Bryan set everything up for the next time Maddy made contact. Jack felt useless. Parsons was holding her in a garage somewhere. It could be anywhere.

The unsubs phone vibrated on the desk. "Byran," Jack yelled. Derek and Bryan moved to his side. Jack picked up the phone. "You going to let me talk to her?" he blurted into the phone.

"I'm going to do one better. I am going to let you see her. I'm talking to her detective this time am I not? She's such a sweet little thing."

"Listen you smug son of a bitch, if you lay one hand on her I swear to God I will hunt you down and kill you with my own bare hands." Jacks voice was low and ominous.

"Too late."

The laughter coming from the opposite end of the phone angered him even more.

"Now listen closely super cop. I am going to give you a URL. Sign on to it and you will get a special treat." He gave Jack the addy and he quickly wrote it down. Then the line went silent.

Bryan rushed to his computer and signed on to the Internet. Jack repeated back the URL. After a few seconds the site came up. Jack felt the color drain from his face when he saw the screen. It was Maddy. The camera had a view of the room she was being held captive in. She had told them there was a camera, but who would have dreamed this sick fuck would do this with it. They couldn't see her up close, but she was sitting on a mattress on the floor. She was leaning back against the wall with her eyes closed. Crimson red covered part of her face and the front of her shirt. She kept bringing her shirt to her lips. Jack wished she would look up so he could see her eyes.

Bryan sat dumbfounded. She was hurt, more than she let on. He wished she would move, do something besides sit there so he could tell just how much and how well she was holding on.

Off to the side they saw a door open and a now blonde Parsons entered the room. He told Maddy to stand up. She glared at him from the mattress. Parsons grabbed her by the hair and jerked up, again.

"God damn it, I told you not to do that!" she snapped at him.

Jack smiled. She still had her fire.

"Do what you're told and I won't have to. Somebody wants to see you," he said smiling at her. He pointed upward.

Maddy followed his hand seeing the camera she already knew was there. "What do you mean, somebody wants to see me?"

Parsons threw his head back and laughed. "Your sweethearts. They are getting a birds eye view of all this."

Maddy looked into the camera. No...she didn't want them to see her.... not like this. They would just worry. Maddy turned to Parsons. She hoped Bryan would pick up on what she was about to say. "Listen asshole, you can't just play some Mickey Mouse game with me and think it's okay." She raised her pitch slightly as she said *it's okay.* What are you hoping to achieve? Are you that bored with your life you have to sink to this level?"

"Maddy, shut up," Jack whispered, "Don't antagonize him."

"Shhhssh," Bryan whispered. "She's trying to tell us something."

Parsons laughed. "I enjoy a good match every now and then." He grabbed her by her hair again and drug her closer to the camera so they could see her face, the damage he had done. "You wanted to see the cheese," he said into the camera. "Here you go."

Maddy looked directly into the camera as if she were looking into Jack's eyes. She hoped she would see what she wanted him to see.

Jack looked into her eyes. He saw no fear, a hint of defiance, but otherwise calmness. Chameleon. He saw her bring one hand up to her heart and saw her eyes soften. She was telling him she loved him. He felt himself choke.

Derek reached behind Bryan and hit a couple of keys on the computer.

"What are you doing?" Jack snapped, "We're going to loose her."

"You are about to any second anyhow. I'm did a screen shot. I will explain it later."

Parson shoved her. "Tell your detective good-bye Maddy. He will see you again later."

Maddy looked back up at the screen and said softly, "Until I see you again..." He shoved her onto the mattress and left the room.

Their video feed went blank.

"God damn it!" Bryan kicked a trashcan clear across the room. "That son of a bitch. Did you see what he did to her face? I will kill him!"

Jack sat quietly in front of the computer. "She's okay. You heard her say so herself. I caught the message for you. I'm sure you did too. I also saw it in her eyes. She's in chameleon mode. She won't let him smell any fear in her. She won't give him the satisfaction." He smiled weakly. "She told me she loved me."

Derek sat in front of the computer and pulled up the screen shot. "She's in control, more so than Parsons knows. As long as she keeps him going, makes herself a challenge, she holds the upper hand. He won't kill her as long as she does. If she becomes meek, he will loose interest. Years of profiling assholes like him, she knows exactly what to do. She is not your average captive."

Derek picked up the phone, "Hey Stan, Derek, I'm going to give you an URL. I need you to track down a server for me." He gave the address to the man on the other end of the line. "Put a rush on it. A woman's life is at stake." He hung up.

Bryan watched Jack with a puzzled look on his face. "What's up?"

Jack smiled softly. "You know, just when I think I am beginning to know her, she surprises me. Answer me honestly, after all she has been through recently, would you have expected her to be like that?" He pointed to the screen.

"Honestly, no. As long as she doesn't get triggered." Bryan looked at the screen. Derek had caught her just as she was giving her signal to Jack. It was easy to see to someone who knew her well enough, exactly what she was saying with her eyes.

"We need to start searching every empty auto repair shop in this city. That's where she is being held. The room she is in is an old parts room. Did you notice all the little holes on the wall? Peg boards for hanging gaskets and such. She said she smelt grease. Hopefully she can keep picking up on things and relaying them back to us."

He hollered over to Andy, "Get to work on getting all the address on these garages. Pull someone to give you a hand."

Maddy laid her head back down on the mattress away from the camera. She slipped out the phone and dialed Jack's number. She spoke, her voice but a whisper. "I can't talk but for a couple of seconds. I just wanted to hear your voice. I love you Jack. You are the only thing that keeps me going. I think about our last night together, how you made love to me. Just tell me you love me, that's that all I need to hear and then I have to go."

"I love you, Maddy, more than life it's self."

"Thanks baby." She hung up the phone, turned it off and slid it into its hiding spot.

A couple of minutes later Parsons came in with a glass of water and a couple of Advil. "Take this."

Maddy popped the pills and drank the water. She was so thirsty. He handed her two bottles of water. "You can use one to rinse your hair, drink the other. I need to run some errands so you need to sleep. I made sure of it. He pointed to the glass of water.

"You bastard." She could already feel the drug taking affect. She was so tired. She laid down on the mattress, darkness descended on her.

Alisha Parker looked into Jack's office. Her son was slumped over his desk, his head resting on his arms. Her heart ached for him. He hadn't left the station since Maddy's abduction. It was taking its toll on him both emotionally and physically. She knocked lightly on the doorframe. "Jack...sweetie?" she spoke softly.

Jack slowly raised his head and wiped the sleep from his eyes. "Hey Mom," his exhaustion apparent in his voice.

Alisha sat in the chair across from him. "Honey why don't you go home for a little while. Take a shower, get a little sleep. Are you eating?"

Jack smiled weakly. "Always the mother. I can't Mom. I need to be here when Parsons makes contact. I don't want to be gone when he does."

"How long has it been?

"Three long fucking days," he sighed. "Haven't heard from him, haven't heard from her. For all I know she's dead."

"Don't say that! Don't ever give up hope, Jack." She rose from her chair and moved the back of Jack's chair. She wrapped her arms around him as he sat. She leaned her head on his. "Tell me something, can you still feel her?"

Jack placed his hand over his mother's. "Do I feel like she's dead...no. But God only knows what he is doing to her. Last time we saw her she was covered in blood, a split lip and a large bruise across the side of her face. I don't think he is beyond pounding the shit out of her. And knowing her, she will sit there and take everything he's got and not break. Bryan and Derek said as long as she stays strong, he won't kill her, but I don't know...I just don't know. How long can she keep it up? She has her cell hidden, why hasn't she texted me?"

"I don't know honey. Maybe he found it. I brought you some fresh clothes and your razor." She touched his bristly face. "You can take a shower in the locker room right?" She pushed him out of his chair. "Go do that and you'll feel a little better."

Jack took the bag from her. He picked up his cell phone and looked at the blank screen. "I need her Mom." His voice trembled. "I can't loose her, not now..."

"Have faith Jack," she kissed him on the cheek and hugged him. "And pray."

Maddy stirred on the beat up old mattress. The lights in the room had been dimmed. How long had she been out? She sat up slowly. She was wearing different clothing, a gray sweat suit that was much too large for her. God he had undressed her. She felt a sense of loathing. She reached up and touched her hair. It was clean.

"Did you think I would leave you a mess?"

Her head shot up. He was a dim figure sitting in the corner of her cell. "Thanks...I guess."

He stood up and brought her a sandwich and a bottle of water. "You should be hungry, you haven't eaten in three days."

She took the food from him. She was starving. "Did you drug this too?"

He returned to his chair laughing. "No sweet Maddy. I had things to do and couldn't leave you to your own devices. Go ahead and eat. You need your strength."

She hungrily devoured the sandwich and washed it down with the water. "Have you contacted the guys at all?"

"Nope. Make them squirm."

She crumpled up the paper the sandwich was wrapped in and tossed it in his direction. "For a man of the cloth, you are evil. I don't suppose you would show a little mercy and let me talk to Jack?"

"Your detective. I suppose that could be arranged. I will pull up the feed and let you use my cell so he can talk back to you. See I am not totally without heart. You have three minutes. Don't say anything stupid because I will be watching." He left the room. The lights went up and he returned with his phone. He called into the station.

Bryan picked up on the call.

"She wants to talk to her detective. I am going to open the feed. Is he there?"

"Is she okay?" Bryan asked urgently.

"She's in good health, don't worry about her. Where's her detective? She will only have three minutes from the time the feed goes up." Parsons explain.

"He's not in here at the moment. Can you give me a couple of minutes to find him?"

"I will call back in five minutes." The phone went dead.

Bryan went tearing out of the squad room to find Jack. Jack was walking down the hall, freshly dressed with a clean-shaven face. "He's going to let you talk to Maddy," Bryan told him.

"You heard from him? Where have they been? I get to talk to her?" The questions just tumbled out of his mouth as they practically ran to the squad room.

Jack sat in front of Bryan's computer signed on to the webside, the unsub phone in his hand. He was nervous, scared for Maddy...and himself, and anxious to see her and hear her. The phone vibrated in his hand.

"Super cop, is that you?"

"Yes, let me talk to her...please."

Parsons gave his easy laidback laugh, "You are humbling detective. Just what I want to hear."

Parson handed Maddy the phone. The feed came up on the computer. There was his Maddy. She looked a hundred percent better than she had a three of days ago. She still had bruises on her face and a swollen lip, but she had been cleaned of the blood. "Maddy...baby...are you okay?"

"God baby, it's so good to hear your voice. We only have three minutes before he cuts us off. I wish I could see your sweet face. I'm fine, he is being decent." She looked into the camera.

Jack could see she looked as if she were going to burst into tears. Hold in there, Kitten, he whispered to himself. "Where have you been, why hasn't he contacted us?" He was careful not to mention the cell phone.

"I've been drugged up while he attends to his business I guess. How are you baby, how you holding out? How's Bryan? He doing okay?"

"We're holding in there. We just want you home safe and sound."

It warmed his heart when she smiled softly. "We will get through this, Babe. We didn't come this far not to."

Parson's popped his head in. "One minute." And left again.

"Jack, I love you so much. It's all I am hanging on to." She wiped her hand across her face.

"I love you too, Baby, so very much. What does he want with us? You know what you need to do right?" He had so much to say and no time to say it.

"Don't know, he hasn't said. And yeah I do." Her time was drawing near. She brought her fingers to her lips and blew him a kiss. "Send that to Bryan, too, tell him I miss him and no triggers. I love you, love you both."

Parsons had returned and took the phone and left with it.

The feed went blue, but Parsons was on the phone. "Feel better now?" he asked Jack.

"Thank you. Parsons, what do you want from us? What do you want us to do to get Maddy back?" he asked insistent.

"Who ever said you were going to get her back? You just need to keep her alive," he laughed that sick laugh and hung up.

Jack put his face in his hands. "Jesus this is so hard."

"Jack, he is fucking with you," Derek placed a hand on his shoulder. "It's not only her he wants to break. He wants to break you, too. And you're letting him. He is picking up that you are weakening. Maddy is doing her part, you need to do yours. Stay strong. This is all a game to him."

"Couldn't trace the feed huh?" He knew they told him but his mind was mush.

"It's being routed to a proxy server out of Canada somewhere."

"And the searches of repair shops?"

Bryan sat on the edge of the desk. "Nothing yet. Andy got a list of all the repair shops in existence within the last five years from city hall. We have unis, your detectives and my agents all out searching. Maddy's picture is plastered in the paper and the news with a new composite of Parsons. We're working on it kid. "

Jack looked over at him. "How are you doing this? My brain feels like it's going to explode. I'm edgy, frustrated...going crazy."

Bryan smiled weakly, "This is what I am trained to do, Bud. They engrain it into you until you know nothing else when you are put into situations like this. You learn to just shut down and block out your emotions. I think that's why Maddy wanted you to have no part of it. I just wish I knew what he wanted, make some kind of demands. It's a little hard to play the game if you don't know the rules."

Maddy sat on the mattress trying hard to hold back the tears. She was so glad she was allowed to speak to Jack, but it left her heart aching. She needed to get out of here, but how?

Parsons came back in with his chair. "You're welcome," he said as he sat down.

"Thank you," she replied softly.

"I am beginning to believe it's not all lust with the two of you. Am I right?"

Maddy sat back against the wall. "We have been together more or less for over two years. It's not like it just happened overnight." She glanced over at him, "Why do you care?"

"You're not the sinner you claim to be. I am glad to see it. It means you have a soul."

"You changed my clothes...did you do...anything?" she stammered.

Parsons smiled, "No sweet Maddy. As you so blatantly put it, you're not my type. I have no desire for you."

"You have been toying with me all along. What is your fascination with me? Why are you doing this to me? What did I ever really do to you? I never would have went after you if you hadn't started fucking with me." She watched his reaction.

He was pensive for a few moments, preparing his answer carefully. "What did you ever do to me...you challenged me from the start. You didn't the play the game by the rules. You made demands from the first phone call. What am I going to do with you? I honestly don't know. I want you to understand who I am. That's all I ever wanted."

"And then what? Will you let me go or are you going to kill me?"

Parsons stood up and grabbed his chair. "Can't answer that just yet." He turned to Maddy, "It is good to see you do care about someone." He left.

Maddy heard the keys in the lock. Alone again. And to think she was bitching how she never got to be alone. Be careful what you wish for. She lay down on the mattress and slipped her hand to her hiding place. Her phone was still there. She assumed the same position she had the other day and powered up the cell. It was 4:30 PM. She really had been out for three days. Would he drug her up all the time, every time he had to leave?

Maddy pulled down Bryan's number and texted him. 'Hey Mickey, U ok? How's Jack, really?'

Jack was going over some things with Derek when the text came in. He saw it was Maddy, and figured there was a reason she text him instead of Jack. He decided to keep the text to himself for now. 'Minnie, I am holding up. U know us FBI. Miss U beautiful. Jack's not doing well. He's a wreck. Doing best to help him keep it together. Working hard 2 find U. Don't give up. Keep your cover. If u could leave phone on we can trace u.'

'I can't hon. Don't know how long battery is going to have to last me. Can't trace text?'

'Not origin, so far. Sweetheart I L U. Trying 2 stay strong. Need U'

'Need U 2. U make me strong. Need 2 go. Take care of u both. L U both, Mickey'

'Stay in touch when U can. L U 2'

'Don't panic if u don't hear from me. He drugs me when leaves. Don't tell Jack about this text. Until I see u again. Minnie'

Bryan quietly closed his phone and slipped it in his pocket. Maddy was being held captive by a monster and she was worried about them. He was concerned about how long she could hold out. He caught her code about the no triggers, but then again Parsons wasn't done with her.

Maddy sat up on the mattress. Parsons was messing with the three of them. Was he doing it because he could? She was tired of thinking about him so she thought about the last evening she and Jack spent together. She thought about the tenderness Jack showed her when he made love to her. Thinking about this only made her heart ache more.

She decided to think about her children and what joy they her brought her. Her time with them had been short and their deaths violent, but that aside she decided to cherish the time she had with them. If she ever got home she would look through all the albums and watch the tapes and rejoice in them.

She also decided that if Jack would ask her, she would marry him in a heartbeat. She had never given much thought of being with another man let alone getting married again. She loved him and she wanted to spend the rest of her life with him. He longed for a family and she wanted him to have his dream. She didn't know how she would come to terms with having another child. That was another thing she never, ever gave a thought to. But she was now. If she and Jack would get married it would be like a new beginning to her life. Having his child would be part of that new beginning. A new start. All she wanted to do was to make him happy. She wanted to be happy too, for the first time in a very long time.

Then she thought about Bryan. Sweet Bryan. The love they felt for each other was intense and yet forbidden. Life had really fucked them over. She tried to remember the last time they really made love. It was so different than she and Jack. Fire and ice. She could no longer hold it against him. It's the way he had always been with her, the need to make her his. She hurt for him because he had been living in his own hell for such a long time too, but there was no happy ending for him. Maybe life would bless him with a woman he could start over with and feel the joy she felt with Jack.

Wow, this was a lot of heavy-duty thinking. She wondered if she was just trying to come to terms with her life because deep down she really didn't believe she was going to come out of this alive. That was really fucked...that she should finally find happiness and then having it taken away from her.

She looked up when she heard the key rattling the lock. Parsons came in with two Styrofoam boxes and couple of sodas. He handed her one of the boxes and a soda.

"I don't know what you drink, so I got you a Coke. Also brought a hot meal."

Maddy popped the top on the can, "Diet Coke for future reference. I don't consume sugar, but in this case I will make an exception." She took a long drink from the sweet nectar. "God, that tastes wonderful." She lifted the lid on the box. Roast beef, mashed potatoes, gravy and corn. Okay, she could definitely live with this. "What am I suppose to eat this with? My fingers?"

Parsons threw her a packet of plastic silverware. "I expect every piece returned to me when I leave."

She looked at him with a raised eyebrow, "You're eating with me?"

"Do you find that so offensive?"

Maddy shrugged, "I don't care, do what you want. You make the rules." She tore the plastic off the utensils. She tore the packet of salt and sprinkled it over her food then she looked up at him. "Did you fuck with my food?"

Parsons laughed as he opened his soda. "No I didn't *fuck* with your food. Your mistrust of me runs deep."

"No shit. Can I ask you something?" She tore off a piece of meat and popped it in her mouth.

"Wouldn't matter if I said no, you would ask it anyhow. Its just a matter if I choose to answer." He set his can on the floor and opened up his dinner.

"Yeah, you're right. Do you see anything wrong with what you did to those women? Just level with me, at this point in time what do you have to loose? I mean do you feel any remorse?"

Parsons set down his fork. "When my flock disobeys me, the Lord tells me the chosen ones need to be sacrificed to save their souls. Who am I to deny God's message?"

"You honestly hear God talking to you?" She continued to eat her meal. It tasted like heaven, no pun intended.

"Yes, he speaks to me."

"How do you choose who becomes a member of your flock. I am assuming they are all women. They must have to meet a certain profile." She dug into her mashed potatoes.

"I look for lost souls, the meek, the lonely—the ones that need love and the guiding hand of God."

"What about the ones with boyfriends?"

"They were missing something else in their lives. You see they didn't have what you have with your detective." He watched her.

"And what's that?"

"Fulfilling love, where you heart is full and you are complete with him."

Maddy stopped her fork midway to her mouth. "You know all that from a conversation? I thought you said it was lust."

"Some things you can just tell. The inflection in your voice when you spoke to him, the way he spoke to you. He and you both care more about the others feelings then you do your own." He took another drink of his Coke.

"For an asshole you are pretty perceptive," Maddy said quietly.

Parsons threw his head back and laughed. "An insult and a complement in the same breath." He paused looking at her in puzzlement. "Why aren't you afraid of me when you should be, considering you know what I am capable of?"

Maddy shrugged. "I told you I have stared down the face of the devil on many occasions. Seen a lot of really bad things, worse that what you have done. I figure how much worse can hell be than what I have already experienced?"

"And you honestly believe you are going to hell?" Maddy almost could have sworn there was concern in voice.

"God has forsaken me. He took away the two things that meant the most to me, therefore there is no place for him in my life." Maddy put her tray down. She had lost her appetite.

"Children...only the loss of a child could explain the pain on your face. I am sorry Maddy. Children are the innocent creatures of this great kingdom. How?" His voice was soft, soothing, and sympathetic.

"Murdered, that's all I want say about it. Can we talk about something else?" What the hell was she doing? She was actually having an open, honest conversation with him. But then again her training told her to befriend her captor; it would make it harder for him to hurt her. Unless he went psycho on her.

"Sorry, we won't mention it further. You said you saw worse than what I have done. How is that possible as a reporter?" He set his empty tray aside.

"Pass on that too." She looked past him at the wall with a sea of holes poked in it.

"Okay I won't stir up your demons. Do you want to be alone? You look upset."

"No, it's okay. Gets pretty lonely in here. Where did you grow up?" Get the topic back on him.

"Washington. You?"

"Here in Iowa. How old were you when you got your calling?" She leaned back against the wall.

"Late, I was in my 30's."

"How did you end up here? Washington is a long ways away."

"Like you I met up with some demons and needed to change my environment." He leaned forward in his chair and gazed at the floor.

Hmmm...this could be his trigger. "While you were there...did God speak to you like he does here?"

"It started there. At first I fought it, thought I was just imagining it. But his voice became louder until I had no choice to do his bidding. He chose me to do his work and he would not be refused." His voice sounded saddened. Who was this guy, was he fucking with her? She was kind of seeing where this was all coming from. He was suffering from some kind of psychosis more then likely triggered by what ever happened to him. She wouldn't ask him until she gained his trust which she felt like she was starting to. He was opening up to her, talking to her, not yanking her chain. At least she thought so; he was kind of hard to read.

"You're not going to pursue this subject?" he asked surprised.

"You didn't push me about my demons, I respect you enough not to do the same," she told him softly.

Parsons shook his head. "You are one unique person, Maddy. It's getting late. You've been a good girl. Would you like to tell your detective goodnight?"

Maddy's eyes lit up. "You would let me? I wish I could see his face."

"That I can't help. But we could do like we did earlier if you like." Parsons stood up and held out his hand.

"What?"

"Your utensils."

"Oh, yeah, I forget." She handed him the carton, which had everything in it. She handed him the empty pop can too.

"I'll be right back. Sit tight why I make the connections." He opened the door, pitched the containers out the door and grabbed his chair. He was careful to lock the door behind him.

Jack was picking at a piece of pizza they had ordered in. His mood was dark. He didn't know how to cope anymore. He doubted his ability to keep it together for Maddy.

The unsub's, Parsons, since they had a name for him, cell went off on Bryan's desk. He was alone in the room. He flipped it open. "Detective." The smooth voice came over the line.

"Yeah it's me." Jack's held the phone with a shaking hand. He reached across with his other to steady it.

"Do you have access to a computer where you are alone?"

"In my office, why?"

"I want you to go there, alone. Sign on to the website. I will call you back in a few minutes." And he was gone.

Jack picked up the phone and took off for his office. He went in, locked his door, and pulled the blinds. He signed on to the website to a blue screen and waited.

A couple of minutes went by when the phone finally vibrated in his hand. Jack picked it up, "Hello?"

"Are you alone?"

Jack looked around him, knowing he was, but for some odd reason double-checked. "I am in my office with the door locked."

"Hold on there. I need do something quick. Don't leave." He was gone again.

Parsons unlocked the door. "Come here Maddy. I have a way for you to see your detective while you talk to him. But you have to promise me you won't try anything stupid. I will be in the background and I do have a gun. Understand?"

Maddy nodded. "I promise I will behave. Just let me see and talk to Jack."

He held Maddy's arm and led her into another room. She tried to take in everything around her, but it was dark until they went into the room. He sat her down in a chair in front of a computer. "I'm going to sign on to the site and put you on web cam. If he has one on his, you can see him. That's the best I can do. Now sit still."

Parson's called Jack back. "Do you have a web cam on your computer?" he asked before Jack could say anything.

"Yeah, I think so. It has a little square up above the middle of the screen." Jack was confused. This man sounded so different than the one they had been talking to. Parsons walked him through how to use it.

"Now you are sure there is no one else in there with you?"

"I swear, there is nobody here," Jack replied urgently.

Maddy watched as Parsons punched a bunch of keys. The screen came up showing Jack sitting at his desk. She bought her hands to her face. "Oh my God," she touched the screen, "My baby..."

When Maddy's face appeared before him on his computer screen his heart took an extra beat. He touched the screen where she was touching it.

Parsons was still on the phone with Jack. "You two have five minutes. If you say or do something stupid, the feeds off. If I even sniff someone else being there with you it's off, and you won't get this opportunity again. Do you both understand?"

They both agreed. Parsons hung up the phone and told Maddy he would be back behind her and to remember what he told her. "I will...thank you."

Jack saw Maddy smiling at him, that sweet smile he loved so much.

"Talk to me," she was so excited to see him. "Smile for me, laugh for me," she laughed nervously.

Jack laughed, "God it's so good to see you smile, baby." He wouldn't use her pet name in front of Parsons. "Are you okay, how are you? God I miss you."

"I miss you too...so much. I am fine. He is treating me good. Feeds me, waters me," she smiled. "Damn your face never looked so good. How are you holding up? Don't lie to me," she laughed softly, "you know I know when you're lying."

Jack smiled, "Using my own lines on me are you? Babe, I have been better. I never knew what hell was like until now. He's not hurting you?"

Maddy shook her head, "No...he's been good. We've been doing a lot talking. Everything is fine...except being locked up. But hey," she shrugged her shoulders, "you can't have everything can you? Your folks...how's are they?"

"Worried about you. Mom brings me fresh clothes, stuff, you know her." He loved watching her face, seeing her green eyes sparkling. He knew she was close to tears. He wasn't far from it himself. "God I love you, Maddy."

A tear slid down Maddy's cheek, "I love you, Jack...always. I wish you I could touch you, smell you...taste you. I think about our last night together...it helps."

"Two minutes," they heard Parsons say in the background.

"I don't want to leave you," she said really tearing up. "This is so hard."

"I wish I could hold you and wipe your tears away, baby." Jack touched her face on the screen.

"You can't tell the others we did this," she told him between sniffs. "If you do we won't be able to do it again. Promise me."

"I won't. It's just between us. I wouldn't do anything to risk anything for you, you know that, baby."

"One minute."

Tears streamed down Maddy's cheeks. She felt like her heart was breaking. She didn't want to let go. "You take care of yourself Jack. I need you healthy when I come home. And you remember what we talked about a few of weeks ago...the long term...the answer is yes." She smiled between the tears.

A big smile crossed Jack's lips, "Really? You will?"

She nodded, "And I don't want to wait a long time either."

"Time Maddy."

"Gotta go. I love you. Until we meet again, baby." She kissed her hand and brought it to the screen.

The feed went blue before he could answer her back. He face felt cool. When he brought his hand to his cheek he felt the wetness. Jack shut the lid on his laptop, put his head down on the desk, his hands over his head and lost it.

Maddy sat in front of the computer staring at a blank screen. "Thank you," she whispered to Parsons. "Can I go back to my cell please?"

She stood up and he grabbed her arm and led her back to the room walking her into it. She went straight to the mattress and laid down curling up into a ball. She had sworn she wouldn't let him see her cry, but this was so far beyond her control.

Parsons came in and placed a bottle of water beside the mattress. "I'm sorry Maddy."

She didn't even look up at him. "For?"

"Putting you two through this. But I had to do it. It was an order." He turned and quietly left the room and locked the door behind him. He dimmed the lights down so she could sleep.

Maddy sat up on the mattress. Everything clicked into place. The man she had been talking to was not the same man who killed all those women. He *was* suffering from some kind of psychosis. He heard a voice in his head that commanded him to do the things he did. As he said, he was just following orders. He truly believed it was God talking to him.

Maddy laid back down on the bed and pulled out her cell phone, powered it up and texted Jack. 'Hey baby. Was good 2 see U.'

Jack was still in his office recovering from what had just happened when his cell went off. "U 2 Kitten. Why did he let U?'

'He is like 2 different people. Suffers from psychosis. Believes God commands him 2 do the things he does. Have 2 watch out for other personality. That's the mean one. This was the good side, wanted me 2 have chance to see and talk 2 U.'

'U be careful. Stay on your toes. Hope he lets us talk again soon. I love U Kitten. U mean what u said about marrying me.'

'Most definitely. We just have to get me out of here. I will work on his good side. Will be careful for bad side. Need to go 2 save power. Love U Jack. Remember, tell no one about web cam.'

'I remember. I love U 2 Maddy. Goodnight. Hope 2 hear from U soon.'

'Me 2. Love U'

She powered down her cell and stuffed it back in her hiding spot. She wrapped her arms around herself wishing it was Jack and cried herself to sleep.

Jack hadn't realized someone was banging at his door. He peered through the blinds. It was Bryan. He unlocked to door and let him in. "Hey," he said quietly.

Bryan studied him. Jack's eyes were red and puffy. The man was loosing it. Derek had been pushing. He knew he should make the call to take Jack off the case, but he didn't have the heart. It would tear Jack up more than he already was. "You okay kid?"

"Kid?" Jack smiled weakly. "You're not that much older than me. I'm okay. Just needed time alone is all. I got a text from Maddy. She said this guy is suffering from some kind of psychosis. Hears voices he believes it's God and gives him orders to kill. Says it's like he has a split personality."

"Wow she got that all out of him in one afternoon?" Bryan studied him under close scrutiny. Jack was hiding something, but he didn't push it. It was probably something personal between them.

"I guess. She couldn't really go into detail with the limited time she used on her phone. I told you when she goes into her chameleon mode she can fit in anywhere and get info out of anyone." Jack regarded Bryan carefully. "What?"

Bryan shook his head, "Nothing, just something seems off." He noticed the unsub phone on his desk. "He call?"

"Did you want me to leave it in there without anyone in there?" Jack was getting agitated.

"No, of course not. Why don't you go home tonight? You really need to get your shit together Jack to be able to work this case. That's an order."

Jack grabbed his jacket and his keys. There would be no more contact tonight and if there would be, Maddy would contact him personally. He wasn't going home though. He didn't want to be there without Maddy. He would go sleep at his folks. He waited at the door of his office for Bryan to leave and locked it up behind him.

Bryan watched as Jack left the building. He opened the phone and looked at the calls received. Parsons had called three times, each with duration of less than a minute except for the last one, which lasted just a hair over five minutes. What the hell was going on and why was Jack hiding the fact the Parsons called?

Bryan pulled his keys out of his pocket and ran down to his Suburban. It took him a couple of blocks to catch sight of Jack and then hung back. When Jack should have turned to go to his house, he turned the opposite direction. He kept his distance as he followed Jack into a residential area. This was near the area Maddy had taken him that day they talked. Near a park. He saw Jack pull off on the side of the road and get out of his car. He stood beside it leaning against it with his arms folded. He watched Bryan as he came nearer. He was busted.

Bryan pulled the Sub over. Jack walked over to the driver's side as Bryan rolled down his window. In the pale street light, Bryan saw Jack's jaw was set with a slight twitching, his eyes narrow. Jack was angry.

"Despite my behavior the past few days, I'm still a cop and a damn good one. I know a fucking tail when I see one. What the fucks going on that you feel you need to tail me?"

Bryan pulled out the cell phone and flipped it to the calls received screen. Jack wanted the truth—Bryan wanted it, too. "Three phone calls, two really short, one relatively long. You want to explain?"

Jack looked away. "He let Maddy talk to me. We could only talk personal and private things, not about him. He gave us five minutes." He met Bryan's gaze. "And I fucking took it. I will take whatever I can get. What the hell did you think I was doing?"

"I'm sorry Jack. You could have been honest with me from the start. I thought perhaps you were on to something and was going rogue on me. You left the precinct pretty willingly." Bryan pulled out a cigarette and lit it. He offered one to Jack, but Jack refused.

"Maddy text me after we were done talking and told me what I told you. I wouldn't hold out information on you, Bryan. You should know better." Jack was still pissed Bryan didn't trust him and followed him.

"I said I was sorry. You haven't been yourself, Jack. I don't know what might be going through your head. Derek thinks I should pull you off the case, but I won't. I wouldn't do it to you." He tried to smooth things over with Jack.

"Thanks, I guess." He shook his head in disbelief. "I still can't be you tailed me, and you're not even very good at it."

Bryan chuckled, "Okay, not my specialty. What the hell you doing way out here, or were you leading me on a wild goose chase?"

"See that estate right there?" He pointed to the gated property across the street. "That's where my parents live. I'm going to sleep there tonight. I can't be at my house without Maddy there. It just doesn't feel right."

Bryan reached through his window and patted Jack on the shoulder. "I'm really sorry about not having more faith in you. This bullshit I think is driving us all crazy. Get some sleep, Jack, you really need it. Leave your cell on. If anything comes up I will be sure to call you."

Jack looked sideways at him, "When are you going to sleep?"

"I take cat naps at the station. I don't sleep well anyhow. Goodnight Jack." He rolled up his window and pulled away.

Jack shook his head and pulled in his parents drive. Maybe tonight, after getting to see and talking to Maddy, he could sleep.

26

Maddy was awaken the following morning by Parsons kneeling over her with a syringe in his hand. Maddy quickly scramble to the corner, "What are you doing? I've been good," she screamed frantically.

"It's only a sedative. It's for your own good. It's the only way I can keep you safe. Please trust me. If I don't do this you will be in grave danger," Parsons told her frantically.

Maddy whimpered as she felt the needle pierce her arm sending a stinging sensation as the serum shot through her skin. She immediately became woozy as Parsons helped her lie back down on the mattress. It took less than a minute and she was out.

Jack sat at his parents' kitchen table drinking a cup of coffee looking over the paper. The Journal was doing an excellent job of keeping Maddy's story front page. It only made sense—she was one of their own. Jack did the best he could by keeping Chief posted without giving away any sensitive information. He trusted Chief enough that even if he did, it would stay safe with him.

Alisha came into the kitchen surprised to see her son sitting in her kitchen. She glanced at the clock. 7:15. She kissed him on the cheek. "When did you get here?"

"Last night. I got ordered to go home. I couldn't be in that house so I came here. Is that okay?" he asked as he set the paper down.

Alisha poured herself a cup and sat down next to him. "Of course its okay. You are always welcome here. Any news?"

Jack smiled weakly, "It was the weirdest thing. And this isn't for public knowledge, the task force doesn't even know this, but Parsons arranged for Maddy and I to talk via web cam. He even told me how to use it. He gave us five minutes to talk. But we got to see each other while we talked. It was great but it was also very hard."

Alisha stared at him over her coffee mug. "Your killer allowed and made it possible for you to talk to Maddy? Kind of a bizarre thing to do, don't you think."

"Maddy thinks he has like a split personality, some kind of mental disorder..." Jack set his cup down with a thud. "Fuck..."

"Jackson!" Alisha snapped. She didn't approve of that kind of language in her home.

When Jack said mental disorder he thought of Maddy's illness. What was going to happen without her meds? Bryan said it was important her meds weren't messed with or it could really fuck her up.

"Sorry," he kissed his mom on the cheek, "I gotta go. You're taking care of Eddie right?"

"Yes dear."

Jack started to head out the door then he popped his head back in, "By the way, Maddy said she would marry me." Then he left without another word.

Alisha watched him as he got in his car and drove off down the drive. Maddy agreed to marry him. Normally this would have been reason to celebrate. She prayed Maddy would be allowed to live to fulfill her promise.

Jack went straight to the squad room. Bryan was at his desk as usual. "Maddy's meds. What will happen if she doesn't take them?"

Bryan gave a light shrug, "Depends, maybe nothing, possibly send her manic, possibly put her into a deep depression."

"With that in mind, what could be her behavior towards Parsons?"

Bryan gave a deep sigh, "If she goes manic, she might do something stupid, be braver and push him too far. If she gets depressive, she might become submissive. You just can't tell, Jack. It would take a few days for her meds to get out of her system."

Jack sat at Maddy's desk. "Great. She could possibly turn into a loose cannon."

"Since Maddy is aware of her mood shifts, hopefully, she might be able to control them."

"Heard anything?" he asked Jack.

Jack shook his head. "Kind of early in the day."

"Well she said not to worry if we didn't hear from her for a while. Parsons drugs her when he leaves," Bryan opened a file and studied it.

Jack glanced sideways at him. "When did she say that? I don't remember that coming up in any conversation with her."

Bryan kept his head buried in the folder. "She text me to find out how you were really holding out. She's very worried about you."

"And you never told me," He shook his head. Now Bryan was hiding things from him.

"She asked me not to."

Jack thought about it, feeling mildly betrayed, but how could he? By rights he had no room to talk. He had his own little secret.

Jack and Bryan spent a good part of the day plotting all the repair shops the officers had already checked out. The eastside was completed. The central area and the north side held the majority of the shops.

Maddy felt like she was in a deep fog. She couldn't see or think clearly. She heard someone moving around in her cell. "Parsons?"

"Justin, Parsons is so formal," he said from his spot in the corner.

She blinked a few times. He became a little more in focus. She sat up and squinted her eyes. The room was still dimly lit but she noticed red covering his arms and the front of his shirt. "Christ what have you done?" she whispered.

"I had to do it for you. I had to protect you from him," Parsons replied with a steady voice.

"What do you mean, you did it for me? Protect me from who? What did you do...Justin?" Maddy felt panic rise within her.

"God. He said he needed a sacrifice. He wanted it to be you. I gave him someone else."

"You murdered someone...someone for me?" she asked in horror.

"Would you rather it be you? I need to put you under again. I need to clean up." He stood and approached her with a syringe in his hand.

"Please, Justin, don't. You don't have to do this." She struck out at him.

Parson's grabbed her by the hair, Maddy frantically kicked and swung at him. He dropped the syringe and struck her across the face. Maddy fell back and knocked her head on the wall.

"I don't want to hurt you, Maddy. Don't make me." He picked up the syringe, grabbed her arm and plunged it into her. "Now sleep. I have work to do."

Maddy fought the drug. She had to stay conscious long enough to warn to the guys. Between the rush of the drug and the pain in her head Maddy felt herself sinking into oblivion.

It was 9:45 PM when Parsons' phone vibrated on Bryan's desk. Bryan nodded for Jack to pick it up since Parsons seemed to prefer talking to him. They hadn't heard from Maddy or Parsons in two days.

"Hello?"

"I have a present for you." The voice on the other end was different than the man he talked to the other night. This guy was confident, self-assured, and with an edge to his voice. The bad Parsons.

"What do you mean, you have a present?" Jack looked up at Bryan, a cold feeling washing over him.

"She was such a sweet thing, but she fought me like a wild cat." He laughed coldly.

"Where's Maddy?"

"In safe hands. Latham Park," he laughed and hung up.

"Derek, get your ass over here! Get the team together and some uniforms. I want a dog to Latham Park." Bryan turned to Jack. "Where the hell is Latham Park?"

"Morningside. Come on man, time is wasting!"

The uniform officers made it to the scene before Jack and Bryan arrived. Derek and the others got there moments before also and were already at the dumpsite.

Derek approached them, "I can't allow the two of you down there," he spoke guardedly.

"What the hell you talking about? Move Derek," Jack barked.

"Derek, let us by," Bryan tried pushing past him.

"I said no!" he pushed back.

As Bryan and Derek were in a pissing match, Jack slipped by them and ran quickly down to the scene. The uniforms were taping it off. Jack ducked under the tape. That's when he saw her. A small form lay crumpled in the dirt. His eyes were draw to the blood soaked coppery colored long hair. Her face was beaten beyond recognition, her body drenched in blood. Jack moved slowly closer to the body. It was dressed in a gray sweat suit. "No..." he shook his head violently. "It's not her... it can't be her." He felt the life drain from his body.

Bryan appeared behind him seeing the carnage below him. Maddy. The fucker had savagely beat Maddy and killed her. He felt his stomach lurch as he moved away from the scene.

Derek and Andy escorted Jack and Bryan back to Bryan's Suburban. "I'm sorry," he said softly to them. "I don't feel you two should be here. Let me take care of her." He turned to Andy who also was visible shaken. "Take them back to precinct."

"No!" Jack snapped. How could he leave her...like this? Despite his protest, he let Derek put him into the truck.

As Andy drove them back, Bryan and Jack were both silent, lost in their own grief. Jack kept telling himself it wasn't her. He could feel it. She was still alive.

"COD?" Bryan asked trying to keep from choking up. From the looks of the body, Parsons was in a rage when he killed her.

"Hard to tell. She suffered massive head injuries. Forgive me if I don't go into detail. I think its best you don't know. Her throat was also slit." Andy was shaking. His friend was gone.

Bryan put his head in his hands. His body shuttered as he felt himself fall apart.

"It's not her God damn it!" Jack screamed from the backseat. "It's not Maddy!"

Jack's words barely came through Bryan's consciousness. The kid was in denial. Let him stay that way. At least it would prolong him from feeling her loss.

When the other men returned to the squad room several hours later, Jack was locked up in his office, Bryan sitting at his own desk staring into space.

Jack repeatedly called Maddy's cell only for it to go straight to voice mail. He tried calling Parsons on his phone, but it just rang repeatedly. No contact. He signed on to the website only to be met by a field of blue. Why the hell would he do this? The other night he had been so human. Was Maddy right? This man had a split personality? Did she do or say something to set him off letting the monster out? He had no answers only lots of questions.

He wondered if he should call his parents, but somehow he still had a gut feeling that body in the ravine was not Maddy. There had to be some kind of mistake.

He rose from his desk and went to the squad room straight for Derek. "I want to go see the body," he demanded in a low, cold voice.

"No Jack, I don't believe you should. Not for your own sanity. I don't want you see the condition her body is in. You need to remember her as she was. Do you understand?"

"I don't care. I want to see her. Are you going to take me, or am I going to go by myself?"

"I will go with him." Bryan stood behind Jack.

"Damn it! You both know better. You are too close to this. For Christ sake this is Maddy. He followed through on his threat."

Jack and Bryan looked at each other and nodded. They left the room and made their way to St. Luke's. "You know it's not her," Jack said insistently.

"You need to face up to realty. You saw her hair. How many women have hair like that? She was dressed in the clothing each time we saw her. As much as we pray it's not, it is our Maddy."

"Whatever," Jack replied quietly. Then he turned to Bryan. "For as well as you know her, for as long as you have loved her, can't you feel her?"

Bryan focused on the road ahead of him. "I've been through this all before. I can't base false hope against the reality of what I saw."

They arrived at St. Luke's and went straight to the morgue. "You don't have to do this, Bryan. I can go in on my own.

Bryan shook his head, "No, I will go with you. You shouldn't do this alone."

The coroner pulled the body out of the cooler. It would be shipped to Ankeny in the morning. He left them to do their viewing.

Her small form lay on the gurney, her matted hair fell to the side under the sheet.

Bryan put his hand on Jack's shoulder. "Don't uncover her face...please."

Jack did it anyhow. He removed the sheet from her face. Her eyes sockets had been bashed in, her jaw broke, her nose was mangled and her face was bloody. She had literally been beaten to pulp. Jack felt sick to his stomach. Even seeing her face, he still felt it wasn't her. This face was unrecognizable in this condition. Her throat had been slit in the same fashion as the past victims. As he moved down her body, her arm slipped off the gurney. Jack picked up her hand, the hand he held so many times. Then something caught his eye. This hand...her fingernails were long, finely manicure despite several having been broken off. A light coat of pink mother of pearl covered them.

"I told you it's not her!" Jack remarked happily.

"We need to get you out here of Jack. I think you're loosing it."

"No, look," he showed Bryan the woman's hand. "Have you ever known Maddy to grown her nails long, let alone polish them. Never! They get in the way when she types. And she bites them, remember? This is not her!"

Bryan picked up the hand and studied it. Jack was on to something. Something wasn't right with this body. "Maddy has a small scar on the side of her rib cage on her right side where she was stabbed several years ago." Bryan relocated to the body's right side, pulled the sheet back and lifted the body's right arm. A big smile crossed his face. "No scar."

"I told you! I can feel her. I know she's still alive." He felt joy and great satisfaction proving Bryan wrong. Now Bryan believed what he had been insisting all along. Maddy was still with them.

Bryan grabbed Jack and hugged him. "She still alive," he said, his voice choked up with emotion.

Bryan stood back. Reality setting in. "Why would he want us to think she was dead? Why would he go to all the trouble to find someone who had the same physical traits as her? He went to a lot of trouble, but why?"

"First let's get the hell out of here. I've seen enough." Jack covered the body and turned and left. They kept their mouths shut until they got into the Suburban. Jack turned to Bryan. "Parsons went to a lot of work to make us believe he killed Maddy. I think we should give him the satisfaction of thinking we believe so. The autopsy reports confirming what we already know won't be back for a week. I say we play along with this charade and find out what he really is doing. Which means you and I are going to have to break every rule we are sworn to uphold."

Bryan studied his friend. "You mean not let on that we know the body is not Maddy. Okay, say I play along with this, do you think the people that matter to her need to know the truth. I don't want to cause undo grief of allowing them to think she's dead."

"Who did you have in mind and can we trust them to keep their mouths shut?"

"Chief for one, Jessie, and your parents. Those are the people I think matter. What about you?"

Jack thought about it. "What about Andy?"

Bryan shook his head, "No, he's too transparent. I hate to do it to him, but I don't think we can risk it. Maybe we just need to keep our mouths shut to everyone. I know I can fake my grief because I'm cold and callous so I've been told repeatedly, but how are you going to be able to pull it off? Lately you have been wearing your emotions on your sleeve."

"Fact of the matter is, Maddy is still missing, he still has her. Just because I know she's alive, she isn't safe. I can't be happy about that. I am still scared shitless for her. Don't worry about me. I will do whatever it takes, whatever we have to do." Jack looked out the window at the passing traffic.

Silence fell over them for a few moments before Jack spoke up. "I guess this means we won't be getting anymore live feeds from Parsons."

"If Maddy can get to her phone and she's not kept drugged up, we will hear from her." Even though Maddy was still in grave danger, knowing it wasn't her lying on that slab in morgue did wonders to his peace of mind.

Maddy slowly opened her eyes. The room was still dimly lit so she laid still and listened. Silence. Could that mean Parsons was still gone? If he were present, she didn't want him to pump her full drugs again. She hesitantly turned her head and scanned the room. She was alone.

What had he done? And what did he mean he did it to save her? Who told him to kill her? His God? If so how could he disobey his own God, better yet how could he fool him?

She had no idea how long she had been knocked out. She rolled over to face the wall and reached into the mattress and pulled out her cell phone and powered it up. She went under her text option so she could text Jack and Bryan simultaneously. She typed in 'I'm okay.'

Jack and Bryan had just pulled into the station parking lot when their phones went off at the same time. They pulled them out and read the text from Maddy, turned to each other and smiled. "You go ahead and answer. Let her know I am here with you" Bryan tucked his phone back into his pocket.

'We know Kitten. Bryan is here with me. I knew it wasn't U. I could still feel U alive.' Jack hit the send button.

Maddy read the message confused. 'What do U mean, feel me alive? U thought I was dead?'

Jack looked up at Bryan. "She doesn't know. What should I tell her?"

"The truth. She has to know what exactly is going on."

"Parsons found some who looks kind of like U. Killed her. Destroyed her face so we couldn't tell. Wants us to believe it was U. I knew better.'

'How?'

'Will explain later. Parsons flip personalities?'

'Yes. Said he killed someone to save me. Very confusing. Shot me full of drugs. I have to go soon. Need to reserve power. I love U. Tell Bryan 2.

'Love U 2 Kitten. Mickey says so 2. Text when U can. Probably is our only contact. Until we see U again.'

'Same here, baby'

Maddy turned off her phone and slipped it into its cubbyhole. Parsons killed someone in order to make the people think it was her? Why? How was that protecting her from danger? This was all too confusing.

She rolled over on her back and put her arms behind her head rubbing against the spot where she hit her head on the wall. Ouch. That son of a bitch nailed her again. God she wished he would keep his fucking hands off her. Sure she was striking out against him, but what the hell did he expect?

She must have laid there for an hour or so when she heard the key rattling the lock. Her stomach knotted up instantly. Who would be coming through that door? Dr. Jekyll or Mr. Hyde?

Parsons came in with a sack and a couple of bottles of water. "Hello Maddy. Glad to see you are awake," he commented in a soft even tone.

She remained lying down. "Why so you can shoot me full of drugs again?" she shot at him.

"I told you, I had to do it to keep you safe. Are you hungry?" He took a couple of sandwiches out of the bag and brought her one and one of the waters over to her.

"Not really. I have fucking headache...again...thanks to you. I don't feel good."

"You should eat though. Please?" He continued to hold out the sandwich.

This was obviously Justin. She called this side of him Justin, the asshole was Parsons.

Maddy slid up into a sitting position taking the sandwich and water from him. She opened the water and drank over half of it at one time. "Can I trust you to get me some aspirin with out slipping me a mickey?"

"Yeah, I will after we're done eating," Justin took a bite of his sandwich.

Even though she knew better she thought she would give it a shot. "Are you going to let me talk to Jack tonight."

"Maddy it's 3:00 AM. Besides we are not allowed to let you make contact with them." He looked away from her as he tore off a piece of bread.

"What do you mean, *we* are not allowed? Does this have something to do with whatever went on today?" She watched him for any change in his demeanor.

"I was suppose to kill you today. In order to keep you safe I had to *kill* you. Your detective thinks you are dead." Justin looked down at his sandwich and then set it down.

Maddy stared at him in mock horror, "Why would you do such a thing? My God do you have any idea what kind of hell you are putting him through? Why? Just tell me why?" She wouldn't let on that she already knew the truth.

"I'm sorry. I had to save you. I had to keep you safe."

Maddy wrapped her sandwich back up and put it on the floor. "Safe from what? You? Them?"

Justin opened his water and took a small sip. "I have to protect you from... me."

Maddy sat quietly. He was he becoming aware of what he was. "I'm not quite sure what you are saying, but Justin, why punish Jack?"

"Maddy, he will know when they get the autopsy reports back it's not you. Don't you want to know why you need be protected from me?" He watched her.

Maddy brought her knees up to her chest. "I don't ever know what to say to you. Like right now...you are so normal. But I don't know if you are going to turn and start slapping me around or...kill me. Just like when I talked to you on the phone. You would tell me I had nothing to fear from you and then in the same breath you would make a veiled threat. I mean when we talk like this...why are you keeping me here?"

Justin laughed softly. "I can see where you are confused." He paused, "When God has given me commands in the past...it seemed so cut and dry. I mean one of his followers broke the faith, so she was chosen to be sacrificed. I understood that and followed his commands. But you have done nothing. Why does he feel you need to die? I don't agree. I thought if I gave him someone like you, maybe he would be satisfied."

Maddy stared at him in disbelief. "So you think you can fool God into thinking you killed me?"

"I am sure I will feel his wrath. I just pray it won't be through you."

"Why can't you let me go? Leave, get the hell away from here before they can bring you in."

Justin laughed, "You want me to believe you wouldn't send the hounds after me. Besides your watchdogs would hunt me down until the day I die. You have a FBI man who is in love with you. He has long reaching hands and I am sure he would reach with them to furthest stretch of the Earth for you. Besides you are safest with me. I can protect you."

"From you?" Maddy shook her head confused. "Okay, let's just let it go at that for now. But can you at least Jack know I am okay?" Maddy put her head against her knees. "Do you have any idea how many people you are hurting by doing this?"

"Would you rather be dead?"

"No."

"Let's just let it be. I am hoping with loss of you felt by others it will be enough for him." Justin stood up and stuffed his sandwich in the sack. "You done?"

"Yes, I lost my appetite." She handed him the partially eaten sandwich and the empty water bottle.

"I will leave you be. Get some rest," he said as he walked towards the door.

"What the hell else do you think I do in here?" she growled.

He turned momentarily, "I can always give you something to sleep."

"Never mind." She stretched out on the mattress. "The least you could do is get me a damn pillow."

"Goodnight Maddy," he turned and left locking her up.

Man this situation was so fucked up beyond belief. She wished she could talk to Jack about it but she couldn't spare her battery. She was only into this six of seven days. Hell she didn't know for sure when she spent most of the time knocked out. How was she ever going to get out of this alive? She had a man who sort of had a duel identity, one side wanting to kill her the other wanting to protect her. Who would be the stronger? She couldn't give Jack or Bryan any clues to where she was because she never saw anything beyond this hellhole.

She wasn't afraid, not when he was Justin, but Parsons...who the fuck knew about him. Then there was kind of a middleman within him, kind of a cross between the two characters. This one was conflicted.

She heard the lock turning. Justin came in with another bottle of water, a couple of aspirin and a worn out pillow from an old piece of furniture. "Sorry, it's the best I can do."

Maddy propped herself up, popped the aspirin in her mouth, and washed them down with the water. She drank down the whole bottle and handed it back to him.

Justin held out the pillow. "I know it kind of smells. I will see if I can secure a good one for you tomorrow. Goodnight Maddy."

After he left, she tried plumping up the pillow and laid down on it. He was right, it stunk. She sniffed it a few times. It had the pudgent odor of rubber...like you smell on new tires. She was in some kind of automotive repair or a tire store. There were tons of them in the city.

Maddy curled up in a ball on the mattress. She had thrown the pillow across the room. She pulled out her cell phone and called Jack. She knew her time was limited. Ultimately Parsons would prevail so she didn't care about using her battery.

Jack answered in matter of seconds. He could her crying softly into the phone. "Baby, what the matter? Did something happen? You're calling."

"It's getting close to my time," her voice quivered over the line.

"What do you mean?" Jack felt the panic curse through him like venom from snakebite.

"Parsons wants me dead. Justin won't be able to protect me much longer; the Parsons personality is much too strong. I'm scared Jack. I'm terrified. For the first time since being taken, I feel my impending death. What hurts the most, I will never get to see you again." Maddy sobbed, her heart breaking. "Jack...help me...find me, find me soon before its too late. I am in some kind of tire shop. I can smell it."

"Kitten, baby, try to calm down," he was trying to sound calm...for her. "You sure he's just not fucking with your head?"

"Justin killed the other girl hoping to appease Parsons, but he can't fool himself, his other ego and he wants me dead. The next time Parsons takes over, baby, he will kill me. He does what he sets out to do."

Maddy heard noise outside the door. "I have to go, Jack. He's coming."

"Maddy leave your phone on so we can triangulate it and find out where you are."

"If I don't ever get to see you again, I love you, Jack, so very, very much," she whispered.

"I love you, but we will be together, I promise. Leave the phone on Kitten." Jack heard a muffled sound and then nothing. His phone showed she was still connected.

Jack ran to the squad room to Derek. "Maddy has her phone on, can you trace where the signal is coming from?"

"The nearest tower. What do mean her phones on? Jack she's gone, you need to deal with it," Derek shook his head.

"Bullshit! I just got off the phone with her!" He held up his phone showing Maddy on the ID screen.

Derek looked at the phone, "And you talked to her? You sure it was her?"

"Yes, God damn it! Get moving on this. She doesn't have much time left and I don't know how much power is left on her battery." Jack wrote out her cell phone number and handed it to Derek. "Needless to say time is of the essences."

When Bryan returned Jack filled him in on the phone call. "Maddy said it was a tire shop. We should be able to exclude quite a few of our search sites because of that."

Bryan looked at his watch. 4:21 AM.

Justin entered Maddy's cell with a chair in his hand. "Maddy, are you awake."

Maddy refused to look at him. Her voice unsteady, her body quivering. "Yes."

"You know don't you?" he spoke softly.

"Yes, and you can't stop him. You're not strong enough." She sat up, "Please let me see Jack one more time, please..." she pleaded.

"I will see what I can do." He looked down at the floor. "I'm sorry Maddy. I tried, I really did."

Maddy studied him through her teary eyes. "Who are you? I mean really... you are not Justin Parsons and you are not a minister. You became Parsons after your demons got to you, after you started hearing the voice." It was last ditch effort, but maybe she would die hearing the truth. "What happened to you?"

Justin rocked back on his chair. "My name was Lucas Riley. That was before. My sister was raped and murder by Reverand Justin Parsons." He looked up at Maddy, a tear sliding down his cheek. "I killed him, Maddy...with my bare hands. I disposed of him by cutting up his body and spreading his parts around the wooded areas. As punishment for killing a man of the cloth, God came to me and commanded me to do his bidding. He is an unrelenting God, and I must do what he says. He is angry with me because I did not obey him and tried to fool him. Now we both must pay. I will cease to exist. If I can, I will try to make it merciful for you.

We are running out of time. Let's go see if we can make it so you can say good-bye. I will be back when I get it arranged." He stood up to leave and turned back to Maddy. "I don't know how long I can stay in control, you understand?"

"Why can't you just let me go?" she cried.

"You know I can't do that." He turned and he left.

Derek was narrowing down the triangulation of the towers Maddy was phone signal was bouncing off of. They had the area narrowed down to the lower west side. Parson's phone went off on Bryan's desk. "I want to talk to the detective," Parsons demanded.

Bryan called Jack over and handed him the phone. "Try to reason with him," he whispered.

"What hell you doing fucking with Maddy?" Jack said angrily into the phone. Bryan kicked him.

"Do you want to say goodbye to her or not?" Parsons said coldly. "This is her last request and I thought she should get it, but if you don't..."

"No, no...I want to talk to her...please," Jack felt a chill run through him so intense his body shook.

"Do what we did the other day. Go to your office, alone, sign on to the site," he instructed.

Jack looked up at Bryan. If this was to be goodbye he thought Bryan should be able to say goodbye too. He knew Maddy would want it that way. "I have the FBI agent with me. He is very close to Maddy. Can he be with me?"

There was a long pause before Parson's answered, "She has spoken of him. I will allow it. I will call you back in five minutes to allow you time to sign on. You and the agent, that's it." And he was gone.

Jack and Bryan rushed to his office. Jack pulled the blinds and locked the door. He booted up his computer and turned on the web cam. They waited for Parsons' call.

"Before? You want to explain this?" Bryan pointed to the computer.

"The other night he let Maddy talk to me via the webcam for five minutes," Jack explained as his fingers traced the shape of the phone.

"You lied to me...again."

"He told me if I told anyone he would never allow it again. Now shut up, I got you into this one didn't I?" The phone went off in his hand. "I'm ready."

Maddy's image came up on the screen. Jack swallowed hard when he saw her face. A new bruise was added to her sweet face. She was very pale, her eyes swollen and red. She was visible shaking. She was scared shitless.

"Hi baby, Mickey..." her voice cracked, a tear slid down her cheek. She reached out and touched the screen, her hand shaking.

Jack touched the image where her fingers were. "Kitten, I love you baby."

Maddy wiped her tears away, "I love you too, sweetheart. Hey Bryan, you know I love you too. I don't have long. He said I could only say goodbye." She paused. "I guess this is it. Remember me always...remember the good okay?" She looked at the screen as her composure crumbled.

"Say goodbye boys," the man's voice had turn edgy and cold. He had turned into Parsons.

Jack shook his head violently, "I can't. I can't say goodbye. Please don't do this, her life has barely started. You don't know what hell this woman has lived through."

Pasons smiled into the camera, "All the more reason to give her release. Say goodbye now, you'll never get the chance again."

Bryan knelt down so his face was in the camera range. "Minnie, I love you, forever and always. You got to know that."

Maddy nodded. "I know, I have always known. What might have been will never be, but then we already knew that," she said to the both of them. "Goodbye Mickey...Goodbye Jack."

Parsons ripped Maddy away from the computer. He failed to disconnect the feed. They could see pieces of what was happening. Parsons was throwing her around like a rag doll by her hair, slapping her face and backhanding her. Maddy never cried out. It wasn't until she was out of sight that Bryan and Jack heard a bloodcurdling scream. Jack shouted Maddy's name into the computer, knowing it was falling on deaf ears. When he heard her screaming, he bent over his trashcan and became physically sick.

Bryan stood up, his face ashen. He couldn't account for the feelings that were coursing through his body—anger, pain, sorrow, and desperation. Was there nothing they could do? Was this really goodbye for Maddy? For all three of them?

There was a knock on the door. Bryan let Derek in.

Derek's eyes went from Bryan to Jack. Jack was literally falling into pieces. Bryan was maintaining like he had seen many times before, but Derek could tell he was struggling. "What's going on?"

"He's killing Maddy. For real this time." Jack struggled to find his voice. "The phone...the God damn phone...where are we with the damn phone?"

Bryan knelt down beside Jack and put his arms around Jack. "Have faith buddy, somehow, some way. We will get to her. We have to."

Maddy felt numb from the beating, she put her wall up and did her best to maintain. Just like Justin/Lucus told her, Parson would take over and finish the job he was unable to finish. Parsons had duct taped her hands and mouth. She could taste the blood in her mouth. Her eyes were so swollen she could hardly see through them. He didn't speak a word to her.

He dragged her though a hallway leading out the back door where she was put into a waiting car. Damn it, he was moving her. Now they would never find her even with the cell phone tracking. This was really it. Her only consolation, if there were a God, a real God, she would be with her babies. Despite trying to shut her feelings down, the tears continued to fall.

She tried to struggle against her bondage. Parsons reached into a bag and pulled out a syringe and a small bottle of clear fluid. He filled the syringe, slowly pushed on the plunger letting a minute trace of the fluid squirt though the needle. Maddy screamed from behind her gag as he brought the needle to her skin and injected her. The last thing she was saw was Parsons laughing and saying. "It is your time, sweet Maddy."

Derek flew into Jack's office where Bryan was doing his best to keep Jack under control. "We got it—an abandon tire shop on West 7th. I've called for S.W.A.T to meet us there. Let's roll!"

When they arrived at the scene of the dilapidated building, S.W.A.T surrounded the parameter. Derek tried the front door. It was secured with a lock. An officer hit the door with a battering ram breaking it into splinters. Jack, Bryan and Derek entered the building with guns drawn. They went through it room-by-room, yelling clear as they did.

Jack was the first to find the room where Maddy had been held for over a week. A lone mattress was placed on the floor. Jack knelt down beside the mattress and ran his fingers along it. He felt the bulge on the inner side and pulled out Maddy's cell phone, still connected to his own.

"Jack," he heard Bryan yell. He followed his voice into another room where they found the computer, the feed still up and going. Just outside the room they found a splattering of blood on the floor and the wall. It was still damp to the touch. At least they knew Parsons didn't kill Maddy here.

Derek popped his head into the room. "She's not here. He moved her."

"Son of a bitch," Bryan tossed a chair across the room. "We were so fucking close!"

"Now what?" Jack asked quietly.

"We canvass, see if anyone saw them and get a description of the car.

When Maddy came to she was bound to a pole. The duct tape binding on her hands had been removed and replaced by barbed wire tightly bound around her wrists. With each minute movement a razor sharp barb cut into her tender flesh. Blood seeped from each cut. Her ankles were secured to the pole by another stretch of the wire.

When Maddy finally was able to focus on her surroundings, the room was flickering from the lights of hundreds of candles dancing off the walls. Her eyes were then drawn to the wall in front of her. A young woman with long blonde hair hung on a large wooden cross. A white gown draped loosely from her lifeless body. Barbed wire tightly secured her arms and legs. Another strand circled her slender throat like a necklace. Blood seeped from the tearing in her skin as the weight of her body gave way to gravity. Although the posture of her body appeared lifeless, the woman's pale blue eyes were wide open. The fear in her eyes pierced through Maddy's soul. The woman had been pumped full of ketamine...alert and powerless to witness her own torture. She knew the girl's fate and she was helpless to stop it. Maddy squeezed her eyes shut as the tears spilled from her eyes.

Parsons entered the room adorned in a long red robe. In his hand he held a wooden case, like the kind fine silverware would be stored in. He placed the case on a table off to her left. He pulled out what appeared to be a golden cross. The hilt was finely ornate, while the base was honed down to a sharp point. Then he removed another item. It too had an ornamental hilt, however the shaft was more blade like. This was a wide blade with a razor sharp edge on one side.

He turned to Maddy and laughed in this low guttural laugh saying, "I figured if you wanted to be so snoopy you might as well as have a front row seat, witness the Lord's work first hand. You will finally get the answer to the question you kept asking. How do I perform the ceremony? You already know why, because she is a chosen one and needs to be sacrificed to save her soul."

He brought the narrow knife to Maddy's throat letting the sharp point lightly graze her skin. Instinctively she tried to pull back but was unablel to move. "You won't be so lucky to receive the sacrificial rites. Your soul can't be saved."

Maddy turned her head away. Parsons grabbed her hair yanking her back to face him. "No sweet Maddy, you will watch. I want this to be the last thing you see before you meet your end."

Parsons left her and turned his attention to his victim. He opened a cupboard and pulled from it a clear ornamental bottle of something. He pulled the plug from it and flicked the water at the woman chanting illegible words as he did. Holy water. She didn't know the language but guessed it was probably Latin.

Parsons' eyes were fixed on the woman's as he reached for the narrow dagger. He saw the fear in her eyes then threw back his head and laughed, a cruel, evil laugh. The devil incarnate. He brought the knife to her heart. Maddy held her breath as he took the point of the knife and made a shallow cut through the material and into her yielding flesh. Blood seeped from the point of entry. A crimson stain spread across the white mesh material of the gown. Parsons looked back at Maddy, smiling as he turned back and brought the knife steadily down her body, slicing a bloody path down the girl's chest and torso. The girl's eyes fluttered and rolled back in her head.

Maddy felt the bile rise in her throat, but it had nowhere to go. She turned her head away from the torture only to have Parsons yank her back. "I said watch," he commanded coldly.

Maddy peered up at this poor woman's face. Her eyes were glazed; her skin had turned pale white. Maddy felt for her, felt her pain...and she prayed for release for this innocent woman whose only mistake was getting involved with Parsons.

Parsons took the dagger and made a horizontal incision entering just above the girl's breast and sliced across her chest chanting more gibberish as he did. He took the hilt of the knife smearing the blood into it. He held it up and made the sign of the cross then smeared the blood across his victim's forehead.

The material from the gown loosely draped down apart from the incisions, blood trickling from the gaping wounds. Parsons brought the sharp end of the knife to the girl's heart. He let it hover there while he chanted his ritual speak. He placed the tip of the knife in the intersecting point of the incision. He took the palm of his hand and pushed it into her flesh. Blood spurted from the small entrance wound the impact had created.

The woman's head went limp, her eyes glazed. Maddy knew that look; it was the same she had seen in her own son's eyes when the life had left his body.

Before Maddy realized what was happening, Parsons grabbed the wide knife, lifted the woman's head and in one quick motion slashed her throat. Blood spilled from the wide gash flooding the front of the gown. Parsons turned to her, the woman's blood had splashed his red robe leaving dark shadows where it made contact. His smile spread across his face, his eyes seemed almost glowing in the flickering light. He took the bloody knife and smeared the blood across Maddy's cheek.

Maddy could deal with no more of this horror and lost consciousness.

Witnesses reported an older model dark brown Crown Victoria often parked at the back of the tire shop. They described a man fitting Parsons description driving the vehicle. Lately the vehicle was parked there more frequently. How these people failed to notice he was the subject of a citywide manhunt was beyond Jack.

Jack sat back in Maddy's chair going through her drawers. He found a small bottle of perfume tucked away in the middle drawer. He took the lid off, closed his eyes and brought it to his nose. He breathed in deep the scent, visions of Maddy doing the crazy things he loved so much about her. The first time he met her two years ago, he hadn't been with this force for more than a month when she showed up in the doorway of his office. He smiled at the memory. There was nothing shy about her. She dove right in asking all sorts of questions about the case, a multiple stabbing. Then somehow she kept showing up at the crime scenes. She was relentless pestering him. She had a keen eye and a wicked sense of humor. The more time he spent with her, the more he looked forward to her company. He began to tip her off on cases just to have her around. He wondered if she ever figured that out.

Bryan sat down at his desk and watched Jack. He was somewhere else, somewhere in the past. He was lucky. He had recent fond memories of being with Maddy. He only had the pain he had caused over the course of the past decade. He mourned for the love of his life, but he refuse to let anyone see it. He would keep it inside him, bury it away like he did so much of the pain he felt in his life.

Jack came out of his revere and notice Bryan staring at him. His sorrow was written across his face. Jack found his behavior strange, but everyone dealt with... he didn't want to say it. If he said it, it would mean it was real. Even though he still felt Maddy's life force he couldn't deny the obvious. She was gone.

Jack handed Bryan the small bottle of perfume. "I want it back," he said quietly.

Bryan took the perfume and brought it to his nose. He set it down quickly and fled from the room.

Jack rose from the desk and followed him. They found themselves at the back entrance of the station sitting on the steps. Bryan pulled out a cigarette. His hands shook so bad as he tried to light it, Jack reached over and steadied his hand and then lit one up himself. He looked sideways at Bryan, seeing him wipe the tears from his eyes. "It's okay to loose it, Bryan. God knows I have."

"We were suppose to be protecting her," Bryan choked. "We failed and now she's...gone. This is my entire fault. If I had never come here, she never would have been put in the middle of this nightmare."

Jack inhaled his cigarette deeply, letting the sensation of the smoke burn his lungs and then let it out slowly. "I'm not going to dispute how she got in this mess, but what's done is done. It is what it is." He put his hand on Bryan's shoulder, "Are you letting your guilt consume you so you don't have to feel the pain."

Bryan glanced at him and smiled weakly, "That's why you're the top detective in this joint. She was finally getting back to being Maddy, the Maddy without all the demons haunting her. God, she was so brave right up until...the end."

"Do you mind if I take off for while. I need to go talk to my parents," Jack snuffed out his cigarette.

Bryan stood up and flicked his cigarette. "You go ahead. I am going to stay here in case we get word on the manhunt for Parsons." He turned and disappeared inside the building.

Jack walked around the building to the parking lot, got in his car and took off for his folks' house. He let his mind go numb yet the tears kept coming blurring his eyes as he drove. He tried blinking them away to no avail.

Alisha saw her son's car pull up and watched him get out of the car. His posture, normally so perfect, was slumped forward, his hands sunk deep in his pockets. This was not good. When he walked through the door all she had to do was look at his face, his eyes, and she knew. She went to him and pulled him close as he collapsed in her arms. Her baby was hurting tremendously and no words she could say could change that.

Edward Parker came into the kitchen and saw the two of them standing there. Alisha looked up and shook her head, her own eyes glistening. She led Jack over to a chair and motioned for him to sit down. Jack didn't argue with her. She poured him a cup of coffee and set it in front of him.

Edward shook his head, went to the cupboard, reached for a bottle of whiskey and poured a large tumbler and set in front of Jack.

Jack wrapped his hands around the tumbler and gave a soft laugh. "I gave Maddy whiskey to calm her nerves the night she got us the burial location of the last victim from the unsub. She got drunk." He downed the drink. Edward filled the glass again and then poured one for himself.

"Are you sure?" he asked quietly.

Jack took a deep breath. "We haven't found her but we're pretty sure. We were so fucking close!" He pounded his fist on the table. "We missed her by less than half an hour."

Eddie jumped up on the table and pushed his furry face against Jack's sleeve. He picked the kitten up and brought him to his face. He dropped his head and cried into the kitten's soft white fur.

Jack took the kitten up to his old room and lie on the bed. He held the kitten tight as he drifted off into a fitful sleep. When he woke his room was dark and still. He remained lying there letting himself feel his loss.

27

The shroud confined her numb limbs to Maddy's body. A thin vale was wrapped more loosely around her head. The distance above her was dark; she could see the night sky through the gauze. It was so cold. The ground beneath her felt damp and frigid. She could breath in the musty, earthy smell all around her. She was in a grave—a grave dug just for her.

A blinding light beamed into her eyes and she squinted against its glare. "It won't be long, sweet Maddy. Soon you will be set free." Parson's raspy voice spoke to her. She tried to protest but all that came from her was a whimper from within.

She heard the grating sound of metal scraping rocky soil. She felt the shovel full of dirt landing on her body repeatedly. She was being buried alive. The panic in her rose to a crescendo. She felt a needle piercing into her skin. A white fog descended on her.

Two teenage boys sat on a picnic table taking turns taking swigs out of a bottle of whiskey. The night was dark, stars lit up the sky, the fall night air was chilling, but the fiery liquid coursing through their veins gave them warmth.

One of the boys noticed a dim light shining in the not to far distance. "What's that?"

"I don't know" the other said, "but let's go fuck with them. I'm in the mood to give a good pounding." They walked towards the light laughing and joking. They peered through the bushes and saw a sight they were totally unprepared for. A man was shoveling dirt into a long hole covering an object placed in it.

"Hey fuck head, what the hell you doing?" One yelled at the man.

The man, dressed in dark clothing, stood up, looked at them and took off running across the grassy turf.

One of the boys went to check out what the man was doing. "Fuck man, call the cops. There's a woman in here!" He reached down with his hand and felt her skin. It was still warm. "I'm not sure, but I think she might be alive."

The other kid pulled out his cell phone and dialed 911. "Hey we found a grave in the east side of Grandview Park. I think the lady is still alive."

Bobby ran up to the squad room, panting heavily as he reached the door. Damn he was out of shape. "Where's Jack?" he said holding his stomach.

"He went home, what's going on?" Bryan demanded.

"A woman...body...grave...Grandview Park...still alive...maybe," forcing the words out of his mouth. "Ambulance...cars...on way."

Bryan picked up the phone. Jack was at his parents' house which was right beside Grandview Park.

Jack answered his phone, his voice low and without spirit. "Hello?"

"Get your ass over the east side of Grandview Park. I think they found Maddy...alive."

Jack didn't bother to answer Bryan. He tore off downstairs, past his parents without a word, flew outside to his car.

The eastside was only a couple of blocks from the house. He put the light on the top of the car and whizzed by all the traffic. He saw a kid standing in the street waving his hands. He pulled onto the grass following the kid as he ran to a bushy area of the park. He was the first on the scene.

"She's in there," he pointed to where a second kid was holding a lantern. Jack quickly pushed the bushes aside.

"Bring that over here," he said about the lantern. He looked down into the shallow grave. "Oh dear God, Maddy! Help me get this dirt off her," he directed the boys.

They both dove in scooping the dirt away from her body. Finally she was clear enough they helped Jack lift her body from the grave.

Jack ripped the cloth from her face and put his finger to her neck. He could feel the faint beat of her heart. "Maddy.... Come on Maddy....wake up, baby."

He could hear sirens approaching. "Get the ambulance over here." When the kid just stood there he yelled, "NOW!" The kid took off running.

Jack held Maddy in his arms face up. He couldn't feel her breathing. He lowered her back down to the ground and began to perform mouth to mouth on her. "Come baby, you aren't leaving me now. I won't let you!"

Two medics ran up behind him telling him to step aside.

"She's not breathing," Jack told them breathlessly. "Do something!"

One of the medics ran back the rescue squad while the other took over doing CPR. The first medic brought back a bag and the defibrillator. The second one put a stethoscope to Maddy chest. "No heart beat. Charge it up." The medic took some wires with tabs on it and stuck them to Maddy's chest. Two thin lines moved across the screen of the monitor. The other tech yelled clear, placing the paddles on her chest and shot the electrical charges through her body. Her body jumped as the electricity cursed through her chest cavity. "Nothing, do it again." It seemed like an eternity before the machine recharged and they shocked her again.

Jack watched as they did it then looked at the monitor. The lines began to jump, however slowly. He watched as one of the techs shot something into her.

"Her pulse is still thready. We need to get to the hospital ASAP." A gurney was brought over and they lifted Maddy's lifeless body. Even as they moved her to the ambulance they were hooking her up to an IV.

Jack hadn't realized he hadn't taken a breath until he felt a hand on his shoulder. He turned to find Bryan standing with him. He threw his arms around Bryan. "She's alive. Our Maddy is alive."

As the medics were loading up to leave Bryan asked them, "Where you taking her?"

"St. Luke's, it's closer." With that they left, the flashing red lights reflecting off the barren trees, the siren fading into the distance.

"You going to just standing there or are we going to hospital?" Bryan asked him a small smile playing upon his lips.

"Oh yeah," Jack moved into action.

Bryan threw his keys to one of the uniform cops. "Drop the Suburban off at St. Luke's." He turned to Jack. "Give me your keys. You're not driving."

Jack patted his pockets, "I think they're still in there." The adrenaline was coursing threw his veins so strong he thought he was going to pass out. He slid into the passenger side seat and laid his head back taking deep breaths."

Bryan chuckled, "You aren't going to do Maddy any good if you end in the hospital too."

"I'll be okay. God, I can't begin to explain to you what I am feeling at this moment." He turned to Bryan grabbed his arm with both hands and shook Bryan, "She's alive!"

"I don't want to dampen your spirit, Jack, but she's in pretty bad shape," Bryan told him softly as he kept his eyes on the road.

Jack turned to him, "Now you have to believe in God. He would never have brought her back to us if he meant to take her away again. God is not that cruel."

Bryan didn't reply. He had seen too much to agree with Jack's assumption. He had seen children raped and murdered, women tortured and slaughtered, people blown into little pieces...entire families massacred...like Maddy's. How could he still believe in God after seeing what the human race could do to each other? He didn't believe there was a God, but definitely believed in evil. He didn't want Jack to loose his faith just because he had. Maddy could still slip away on them. And if her body does survive would her mind?

When they arrived, Bryan dropped Jack off at the ER and went and parked the car. Jack ran into the ER straight to the desk and asked about the woman they just brought in. The nurse pointed to one of the bays but told him he couldn't go in because they were working on her. She pointed to the waiting area and told him to take a seat. When Bryan came in she directed him to do the same thing.

They were sitting there quietly, each in their own little world when Derek and Andy found them. "Is it her?"

Jack looked up, "Yep...their working on her...whatever the hell that means."

Andy sat down beside Jack. "How bad is she?"

"He beat the shit out of her, but I didn't see a lot of blood on her so at least he didn't mutilate her." Bryan said quietly without looking at them.

"She died out there—she quit breathing—her heart stopped. Thank God the ambulance made it time." Jack told them, also without looking at them.

"She'll be okay," Andy said anxiously. "I know she will. She's one tough broad."

Everyone looked at him and laughed. "Now you're the expert on her huh?" Jack asked.

Andy turned red and sat back in his chair. "Well she is."

Jack stood up and walked by the bay where Maddy was hoping to catch a peek at her. The bay was closed off to all view. He could hear the medical staff as they worked on her. He stepped outside and took out his cell phone and called home. "Dad...we found Maddy. She's alive."

"Oh thank God. I am so happy for you son. How is she?"

"Pretty beat up. Other than that I don't know. She's here at St. Luke's in the ER. They haven't told us anything. Dad...he buried her alive. If it hadn't been for a couple kids getting boozed up in the park...well I don't even want to think about it." His voice trailed off.

"You want us to come down, kid?" Edward asked, his voice full of concern.

"No, there is nothing you can do. Bryan and a couple of guys from the squad are here with me. I will let you know when I know more."

"Our prayers are with you and Maddy, son. Call if you need us. We love you."

"I know Dad, thanks." He closed his phone, went back in and sat down.

Jack gave a deep sigh, "What the fuck is taking so long?"

"Jack, I told you, she's in pretty bad shape. Let them do their job," Bryan said leaning back with his head resting against the wall with his eyes closed. "Derek, what's the status of Parsons?"

"Still on the lamb. Those kids scared him off. Lord knows where he is now."

"I don't imagine he will go back to where he was holding Maddy. He has another hideout somewhere where he moved her to. We need to have a uniform outside Maddy's hospital room. He failed, he might attempt again." Bryan said wearily.

Jack turned his head sharply, "Fuck, I hadn't thought of that. Well I can guarantee you I won't be leaving her side. Not again. And if they don't like it at the precinct, fuck 'em."

Bryan laughed, "I am sure under the circumstances they won't say a word."

Derek stood up, "Well were going to head back. Come on Andy. Give us a call when you know more."

"Get a couple of the other agents to stand guard at the fort. You guys get your asses back to the motel and get some sleep. You've been up for over forty-eight hours. And that's an order." Bryan said, his eyes still closed. God he was so tired himself. He couldn't remember that last time he slept. Maybe that's why he felt so numb, to tired to feel anything.

They must have sat there for over an hour waiting for any kind of word on Maddy. Bryan was lightly snoring beside him. Let him sleep, Lord knows he needed it. Finally an ER tech came out of the bay. Jack nudged Bryan awake.

"Are you two here for Miss Sheridan? What's your relationship to her?"

Bryan stood up. "Miss Sheridan is an agent with the FBI. I am Supervisor Special Agent Bryan Mayland and this Jackson Parker, my associate." Bryan pulled out his credentials and showed them to the tech.

"We are moving Miss Sheridan upstairs to a room. I can't give you the details of her condition; you will have to get that from her doctor. He will be up shortly if you want to wait up there. She'll be in room 503. The desk will need someone to fill out the paper work for admission." He pointed to the ER desk.

Bryan put his hand on Jack's shoulder. "You go on up. I will take care of this and join you when I get done."

Jack looked unsure of what to do. Bryan gave him a gentle nudge. "Go sit with your lady. She needs you."

Jack found the elevator and made his way to the fifth floor. He followed the signs to find Maddy's room. When he got there her room was full of hospital personnel setting up IV's and hooking her up to machines.

He waited until only a nurse was with her and went in. The nurse smiled at him. "Good evening. Are you related to Miss Sheridan?"

"Her fiancé," he answered quietly. Well it wasn't a lie—she had said yes, did she not? "How is she?"

"Stable. The doctor will tell you more." She showed Jack the call button if he should need it.

Jack pulled up a chair next to Maddy. Jesus she looked bad. Her face was covered in bruises, her lip was split and her eyes were bruised and swollen. He could see black and blue fingerprints up and down her arms. She was hooked up to all kinds of machines. He was not a medical person and all this hardware made him nervous. She was hooked up to a respirator and a heart monitor. Two IV's were attached to her arms. He reached for her hand and held it. It was limp to his touch. Her wrists were covered in bandages. He stood up and kissed her forehead then sat back down. He reached up with his free hand and softly stroked her hair. "Oh Kitten, baby...you've been through so much." He brought her hand up to his lips. "You got to fight baby. You got to come back to me. I'm not going anywhere, Kitten, I promise." He sat quietly watching as the respirator pump move up and down assisting Maddy with her breathing.

He looked up when Bryan came in the room. He saw the look of horror shadow Bryan's face. He hadn't seen her up close yet and had no idea the extent of her injuries.

"Jesus Christ, Jack, what the hell did he do to her? I'll kill the mother fucker with my bare hands if I get the opportunity." The anger in Bryan's voice sent a chill through Jack.

Jack had no emotional room for anger. Fear and hope superseded it. "Doctor hasn't been in yet. They just got her settled. All these machines...it's scary."

Bryan stood over Maddy, brushed her hair back and kissed the top of her forehead. He stood back gently feeling her scalp. "Fuck she's got bumps and stitches all over head. That son of bitch!"

"Yes, he really did a number on her." Jack and Bryan looked up to find the doctor walking in dressed in blue scrubs holding a clipboard in his hand.

Bryan stuck out his hand and introduced himself and Jack. "How is she?"

Doctor Baker flipped open the chart. "Maddy has a concussion, multiple contusions, but my biggest concern is the amount of kadamine we found in her blood stream. Its level is high enough it has raised her blood pressure to dangerous levels and impaired her respiratory system. Until we can counteract its effect on her she is unable to breath on her own. Internally she is in pretty good shape, no organ injuries. Luckily the fetal heart rate is strong and there appears no stress on the baby. With careful monitoring we hope that will continue." He shut the chart and looked at the two men. "Any questions?"

Bryan and Jack both heard what he said thinking they misheard that last part of it.

Jack shook his head confused. "Baby?"

"We run pregnancy tests as standard procedure when doing the initial exam. It is a good thing we did. We could have administered medications that could have been harmful to the baby."

"How far along?" Jack stammered, still not believing what he heard.

"Estimated six to eight weeks. Hard to tell without further examination." The doctor's beeper went off. He looked at it and excused himself.

Bryan ran into the hall, "Doctor, any evidence of sexual assault?"

"Nope," he replied and went on his way.

Bryan took a seat beside Jack, both staring at Maddy. Finally Bryan spoke, "Congratulations, Jack."

"Huh?"

"I said congratulations, you're going to be a daddy." He glanced over at Jack who was pale as a ghost.

Bryan laughed, "You should see your face."

"I don't understand, how did this happen?" His face was full of shock.

Bryan put his head in his hands and shaking it, chuckling, "Do I have to fill you in on the birds and the bees?"

"You don't know...it could be yours," Jack whispered staring at Maddy watching the rise and fall of her chest.

Bryan shook his head, "Nope, no way. I can't have children. I love them dearly but because of an injury it's just not possible. That's one of the reasons I don't give up on my stepson and fell in love with Scotty and Lexy. That baby is all yours, Jack."

"Jesus Bryan, what is this going to do to her? She's been nowhere emotionally ready to even think about having a child. We talked about it. She wasn't even sure she wanted another child. Said she didn't know if she was capable of loving one again." Jack said anxiously. "And now this..."

"Kid, she will be okay with it...better than okay. Trust me. You talked about kids? I hope you talked about marriage first," Bryan chuckled.

"We decided to move in together. She asked me about future hopes. I told her that eventually I would like to marry her and start a family."

Bryan was surprised that Maddy had agreed to move in with Jack. They hadn't been together that long. But then again, once their relationship was allowed to happen, thanks to his fuck up, it had rapidly moved along. Probably to the point it should have been if he hadn't interfered in the first place. "How did she feel about it all?"

"The marriage thing, she said probably someday if things progressed as well as they have been. The baby thing...that was way out there in the ball park." He glanced over at Bryan. "That night when Parsons let us talk for five minutes. She told me yes she would marry me and didn't want to wait along time. I know she said it under duress, so I wouldn't hold her to it, but it sure felt good hearing her say it."

Bryan played around with his chair discovering it would recline. "Cool, now I can get comfortable. She meant it Jack. Even under the conditions she was in, she wouldn't lie about that."

A nurse came in and checked Maddy's vitals. "What happened to her?" she asked.

"She was abducted by a serial killer and buried alive," Jack said flatly as if it was an everyday occurrence.

The nurse looked up, "The one I've been reading about in the papers?" She picked up Maddy's chart and read the name. "This is Maddy Sheridan, the reporter?"

Jack nodded.

She notice both men looked like they were ready to drop from exhaustion. "How long has it been since you guys have slept?"

"I had a nap this afternoon." He looked at Bryan who was half asleep. "Been days for him."

"Maddy is doing fine, all her vitals are good. Hopefully we'll be able to get her off this respirator tomorrow. I'm going to have them come in and set up a cot. I don't imagine you guys will be leaving anytime soon." She reached up and pulled the blanket around Maddy. She left and then returned with two more blankets and a couple of pillows. "In case you guys get cold."

Jack stepped out in the hall and made a call to Derek giving Maddy's status. Then he placed a call to his dad. "Hey it's me. They got her in a room. She's not doing very well. She's on a respirator and hooked up to all these wires and tubes. The asshole pumped her full of drugs that made her respiratory system fail."

"We'd be glad to come up and sit with you son." Jack could hear his mom in the background asking all kinds of questions. "Alisha, would you shut up long enough I can hear him?"

Jack smiled, "No, Bryan is up here with me. Maddy is unconscious anyhow so she wouldn't even know you were here. They're bringing a cot in for us if we need to sleep."

He went back in the room and sat down, taking Maddy's hand in his again. He wished she could squeeze his back so he knew she was in there somewhere.

Once they brought the cot in and had it set up, Jack nudged Bryan. Bryan lifted his head and Jack pointed to the cot and threw a pillow at him. "Go lay down...and that's an order."

Bryan smiled weakly, snatched the pillow and moved to the cot, "Yes boss." Bryan stretched out on his back and quickly dozed off.

Jack got up, grabbed one of the blankets and covered him up. He took the curtain and pulled it around the cot, then dimmed the overhead lights. He was amazed at how well Bryan held up over this whole ordeal. Bryan had credited it all to his FBI training, but he found it hard to believe given Bryan's emotional connection to Maddy. Jack figured that Bryan must be one of those people that can compartmentalize his emotions to keep them inside. He saw him weaken, even loose it, but he never broke down to the extent Jack did. He wondered if Bryan thought he was weak.

Jack pulled the reclining chair closer to Maddy and watched as she slept, or whatever it was she was doing. A baby. She was carrying his child. Wow. They hadn't used protection. It had never entered his mind, evidently not hers either. It didn't matter to him. The thought of them having a child together filled him with warmth...and apprehension. What would her reaction be when she found out. Maybe she wouldn't want to keep it. No, she would, he knew her better than that. He decided he would ask Bryan not to say anything to anyone. He felt Maddy should know before anyone else. And if something should happen where she lost the baby...Maddy would never have to know.

Jack slid the rail down on Maddy's bed. He leaned his head down so his cheek rested against her arm feeling the warmth of her body against him. He said a silent prayer thanking God for bringing her back and drifted off to sleep.

Bryan's eyes fluttered open. It took a couple of seconds to figure out where he was. He sat up, rubbed his eyes and quietly pulled back the curtains. Soft daylight filtered into the room from between the opening of the closed drapes. He looked towards Maddy. Jack was leaning over so his upper body was leaning on her bed, his head resting on her arm. His body was going to be hurting for that.

He left the room in search for coffee. As he walked out the door, Bobby greeted him. He was sitting on a chair outside Maddy's room. "I offered to take first shift," he smiled.

"Going for coffee, you want some?" he asked Bobby. Bobby told him that would be great and where the cafeteria was located. Bryan's body felt better and his mind alert. The sleep had done him wonders.

He found the cafeteria, bought three coffees and took a seat for a few minutes to get his head together. He thought about Maddy and Jack. He was honestly glad they had found each other. He only wanted her happiness and now she could have it all—a man she was crazy in love with, a man that returned her feelings, unconditionally, a pending marriage...and a child. Wow, it was a lot to take in. He wondered what would have happened if it hadn't been for that fateful night when he showed up at her house unannounced. On Sunday he felt they was as close as they had ever been. On Monday something changed. He couldn't put his finger on it but it did. A wall had come up and her attitude towards him totally changed. He sensed it when she talked to him on the phone while she was at Jack's house. She was distant, defensive and combative—and it went down hill from there. He knew then he was loosing her, at least subconsciously, probably why he showed up at Maddy's house...drunk beyond recognition. He had to take her back. Instead he ended up pushing her into Jack's arms. It was so far from what he initially planned. By setting her free from her demons he lost her. He should have known better. He blew his chance with her a long time ago. When this was all over, he would leave, but this time they would stay in contact and he would even make it a point to come see her. It's like she said, it didn't have to be goodbye.

Jack was rousted awake by one of the nurses. "Mr. Parker, would you mind stepping out for a moment. We need to check Maddy over."

Jack sat up and groaned, rubbing his neck. He looked over at the cot to find Bryan gone. He stepped outside the room. Bryan was standing talking to Bobby, drinking coffee from a Styrofoam cup. Bryan reached down, picked one up and handed it to him.

Jack nodded a thank you, took the lid off and blew on the steaming hot liquid before taking a sip. "Damn that's strong." He looked over at Bryan, "You look a hell of lot better. Now all you need is a hot shower and a shave."

Bryan smiled, "You looked in the mirror lately?"

Jack ran his hand over his face, "Yeah, I guess a shower and a shave would be in order." He turned to Bobby, "Any news on Parsons?"

"I was just telling Bryan they found his car abandon down on lower 7th, but no signs of him. Do you really think he would be dumb enough to stick around?'

Bryan answered for him, "He hasn't completed his mission, and he won't leave until he does."

Bryan's statement left Jack feeling sick. They weren't done with this sick fuck yet.

Bryan went back to his motel to take a quick shower and change. He would then come back so Jack could do the same. They decided one or the other would sit with Maddy at all times. It wasn't just for her protection, but they didn't want her to wake up alone, scared and confused.

Bryan returned about an hour and a half later looking no worse for wear. "Any change?"

Jack shook his head, his eyes never leaving Maddy. "She will come out of this won't she?"

"It just going to take time. Need to ask you something, Jack. When she does come out of it, are you prepared to deal with how her mental state might be? When she lost the kids...it wasn't good. This happened to *her*. I realize she was strong during the whole ordeal, but we have no idea what happened to her after our last contact with her...and then to be buried alive. I would bet with the ketamine she was aware of what was happening to her."

Jack hadn't thought about it. For some reason he thought she would just wake up and everything would be all right. Bryan had lost her because of her breakdown all those years ago. Could it happen to him? He didn't want to think about it. "We'll just have to see how the cards play out. We don't know what will happen. We can't let her slip away. And you noticed I said we."

"Take off and get your shower and shave in. You look like a bum. You sure as hell don't want to be looking like that when she wakes up," Bryan laughed. Jack was still covered in dirt from pulling Maddy out.

When Jack stepped into his parents' house, Alisha was there to greet him and bombarded him with questions. "What happened? How did you find her? She was drugged? Is she okay?"

"Damn Mom, give me a chance to breathe will you?" Jack said as he unbuttoned his shirt and threw it in the laundry room that was just off the kitchen. He took a deep breath and tried to explain without going into great detail about what happened. He didn't really want to relive it. "A couple of kids interrupted the guy in the process of burying her. When they checked it out, they discovered she was still alive so they called it in. When Bryan got the call, he called me knowing I was the closest. She was in pretty bad shape when they brought her to the hospital. He had beaten the hell out of her and drugged her. She's hooked up to a machine to help her breathe and she hasn't come to yet. Anything else?"

"Is she in coma?" Alisha's concern apparent.

"How the hell would I know? I said she was unconscious. That's all I know." He was still tired and edgy. He had done so much thinking in the last 24 hours his head hurt from it.

"Gee you're sure in a pissy mood, Jackson. But considering everything I will excuse it."

"That's the second time you called me Jackson in the last week. Knock it off. You know I hate it. I need to go shower and shave and get my ass back up the hospital. Bryan's sitting with her now."

When Jack returned to the kitchen Alisha had made him a sandwich and set out a glass of milk. He debated whether or not to take the time to eat, but then he thought better of it. His dad was sitting with his mother, both of them watching him closely.

"What?"

"We're just concerned about you. You seem all out of sorts, not like yourself." Alisha told him.

Jack took a deep sigh and looked at them in disbeilf , "Do you really need to wonder why? Christ Mom, look at everything I've been through these last few weeks, and now this. Don't worry about it. I'll be fine when things start settling down." He sat down, took a bite of the sandwich and drank some of the milk. His dad was still watching him.

"Now what?

"This Bryan guy, what is he to Maddy?"

Jack was getting real irritated with them. "What the fuck difference does it make? What does who he is have anything to do with any of this? But if you feel you must know, Bryan in Maddy's ex-boyfriend. They used to work together in the FBI several years ago. They are still close and he's been a damn good friend to Maddy and me. He is basically the one person that has held me together through all this." He looked at both of them. "Anything else?"

"No," Edward said calmly.

"Listen Mom, Dad, I am sorry I'm so bitchy. I just really have a lot on my mind right now. I am physically and emotionally run down with not a lot of patience." He popped the last of sandwich in his mouth and finished off the milk. "I have to get going." He gave his mom and hug and kiss. "I will call you if anything changes. See you later."

When Jack returned to the hospital he was surprised to find Maddy had been taken off the respirator, but she was still on oxygen. Bryan was flipping through a magazine and looked up at him when he entered.

"She's breathing on her on now, that's a good sign," he told Jack and went back to the magazine.

Jack went to her and kissed her forehead. It was nice to see that tube out of her. "No indication of her waking up?"

"Nope, no change. Don't worry; she's not in coma. They took her down and did and EEG on her. She has good brain activity, so she is in there somewhere. Doctor said her brain just might not be ready for her mind to cope with what happened. You know, like when people get into car accidents and can't remember what happened. The brain shuts out what the mind can't deal with. You also have to remember she has a concussion."

Jack sat down and took her hand in his. Some how he felt his touch would somehow get through to her. This waiting was killing him. He would give anything to see her beautiful eyes even though the skin around them was swollen, black and blue. The swelling had begun to go down a little. It would take several days before she would even begyn to start to look the least bit normal again.

Bryan stood up, "Listen kid, I am going to run down to the station see how things are going. I'll be back in a little while. Want me to bring you anything?"

Jack's eyes stayed on Maddy. "No, I'm good."

"Okay, see you later." Bryan slipped out of the room.

Bryan was restless and Jack didn't think he felt comfortable in hospitals. He guessed he had his reasons.

Jack stood and leaned over Maddy brushing the hair out of her face. He kissed her forehead and the softly kissed her lips. He straightened himself slightly and watched her face and then kissed her again. Well she wasn't sleeping beauty and he defiantly wasn't Prince Charming. He smiled slightly as he sat back down and took her hand in his and kissed it. "Hey Kitten," he laughed softly, "I tried. I guess I just don't have the magic. I wish I could tell you how much I miss you."

He brushed the back of his hand across her cheek. "I'm so sorry I let you down. I promise I will never let you down again."

He had no idea if she could hear him, but he figured what could it hurt. It made him feel better. He leaned forward bringing her hand to his chest. "I'm going to tell you something and I don't know how you are going to feel about. It means the world to me and I hope you will feel the same way. Maddy, sweetheart, we're going to have a baby. That's right, you and me. I pray you will find the joy in it that I do."

Jack laid his head down on the edge of the bed and said a silent prayer. He never had been real religious, but lately he depended more and more on God for strength to get through this. Jack's head shot up. He thought he felt movement in his hand and looked down. Maddy's fingers lightly curled around his. "Oh baby, that's it, come back to me." She stretched her fingers and entwined them between his. He watched her face thinking her eyes would flutter open. Nothing happened.

He grabbed the call button and pushed it. A nurse came in shortly after. "Look." He showed Maddy's hand entwined with his. "She did that, she's holding my hand."

The nurse smiled, "That is good news. It means she's coming back to us."

"How come she's not waking up?"

"Sometimes it's a slow process. Deep down she knows you are here even though she is still locked inside there somewhere. There is no real physical reason she hasn't woken up yet. The ketamine has worn off; her concussion is not that severe. Keep reaching for her. It's what she needs." The nurse looked at her watch. "Dr. Baker will be making his rounds in about another hour. He will able to tell you more about it.

"Okay, thanks." After she left, Jack turned his attention back to Maddy. "Kitten, can you hear me? If can show me a sign. Squeeze my hand tighter. Come on baby, you can do it." Jack wasn't sure if imagined it or not but he thought he felt her hand tense up. He smiled and kissed her hand. "I believe you can, Kitten." He felt a coolness on his cheek. When he reached up to touch it, it was wet. He wasn't even aware he was crying.

If she could hear him, she needed mental stimulation. She loved music. He placed a call to Bryan. "Hey when you come back, can you bring a CD player. Stop by my house. There is a key in my center desk drawer. Grab the CD's out of Maddy's car and bring them in."

"Sure, but what's going on?" Bryan asked.

"Bryan she is holding my hand, squeezing it. They told me to keep talking to her, trying to reach and to stimulate her. I thought her favorite music might help."

Bryan paused, "It's going to be awhile, Jack. We got reports of a sighting of Parsons we are following up on."

"How strong of a lead, I mean is it a positive ID?"

"Don't know that yet, that's what we're checking on. Jack...keep your eyes open," Bryan answered him quietly, "And Jack...about Maddy...this is good news."

Jack smiled, "Yeah it is. I'm not going to let anything happen to her so don't be worried on this end. I will just give my mom a call. The woman has been irritating the hell out of me lately, and I really don't want her here, but I guess something's you have to tolerate."

Bryan chuckled, "Live with it dude. I will see you in awhile. We will see what I can make her do."

"Fuck you," he laughed. "See you later."

Jack placed a call to his mom and asked her to pick up the CD's and a player for him. "And Mom, when you come, don't go all freaking out on me okay?"

Alisha acted shocked, "Have a little faith in me son, I will be there I a bit."

Dr. Baker arrived shortly after he placed the call. Jack reached out and shook his hand, not letting go of Maddy's hand.

"I understand we have some movement here. Can I see?" Jack moved back so he could see Maddy's hand snuggly wrapped in his. "Talk to her. Ask her for confirmation."

"I already did, but I will again." He leaned over Maddy, close to her ear. "Hey Kitten, I love you baby. Give me a sign if you can hear me, please. Squeeze my hand Kitten." He sat back and watched. Maddy's fingers released and then tightened them.

"Okay, now release her hand and let me try," Baker stood over them.

Jack tried to release her hand, Maddy held on. Jack secretly smiled. It was him she wanted to hang on to.

"Well," the doctor smiled, "That answers that. She is responsive to you."

Baker checked Maddy's vitals, listen to her heart, and then he shined a pen light in her eyes. "There appears to be no change anywhere else. She is still non-responsive."

Baker pulled up a chair next to Jack and sat back. "I understand Maddy was abducted by our resident serial killer which climaxed into the condition she is in now."

Jack nodded, "She held up pretty good until a couple of days ago when the guy snapped. We don't know exactly what happened except what you see there and ended with her being buried alive."

"That alone is enough to give her PTSD, but I am wondering if we have some underlying things going on. How much do you know about her psychological history?"

Jack took a deep breath and blew it out slowly. "I'm not the best person to be asking this to. Bryan is your man for that, but I will do my best. And mind you this is all what I have been told. Maddy is, and or was a FBI profiler so you know she's seen a lot of shit most people don't. Nine or so years ago, her children were killed in a home invasion, which she walked in on. She witnessed their murders and killed the perp. From what Bryan told me, she had a mental break and then blocked it all out for years. A few weeks ago we were at an active crime scene, and I guess the word is she triggered, bringing it all back. She's be working with it, coming to terms with the past. She recently told me she is bipolar which I know she is taking meds for."

He watched as the doctor jotting all this down in his notes. "So this is her second tramamatic event. I image the bipolar is a result of the first incident. Do you know what meds she's on?"

Jack shook his head, "Couldn't tell you. But she hasn't had them since she got abducted."

"Probably not such a bad thing for the baby. We will have to find out what she's on and modify it. I don't know Jack, I'm afraid Maddy has a long road ahead of her. From what it sounds like she has already suffered from PTSD. Have you witnessed any of the following? He spouted off a list of symptoms to which some Jack did know she had experienced. The rest, he couldn't answer.

"Like I said, Bryan is a the better person to ask about this. He was there. He knows what she's been through. What I have is just second hand. He will be here a little later if you want to talk to him."

Baker closed his file. "I won't be here, but I would like him to talk to a psychiatrist who I will be conferring with about Maddy."

"Maddy already has one, and a therapist," Jack informed him.

"You know who they are?"

"Nope, Bryan does though."

Baker laughed, "You really are the wrong person to talk to about this."

Jack smiled, "I told you that much."

There was a knock outside the door. Jack and the doctor looked up to see Alisha standing there with her arms full.

The doctor turned to Jack, "Thank you for your help and keep up on the good work. You're getting through to her." He turned and left.

"Come in Mom," Jack called to Alisha. "Set the stuff over there on the floor."

Alisha placed the CD player and CD's on the floor. She went to Maddy's bedside and lightly stroked her hair. "You poor sweet baby, what did that monster do to you?"

Jack noticed his mother tearing up. "I would come and give you a hug, but Maddy won't let go of my hand," he smiled up at her.

Alisha looked at Jack and then looked at Maddy. "Is this a good thing?"

"It's a very good thing, Mom. She's still got a long way to go, but I'm working on it."

Alisha looked back down at Maddy, stroked her hair again and shook her head. "It's hard to believe there could be someone out there who could be so cruel and vicious to do something like this to her. All your fears for her came true."

Jack looked down sadly, "Yeah, well it happened and there is nothing we can do to change it now."

"I noticed the cop sitting outside here. Is she still in danger?"

"As long as Parsons is out on the street, she is still at risk, but I won't let anything happen to her. Not ever again," he told her with a hint of anger in his voice.

Alisha knelt over him and kissed him on the cheek. "Honey, don't knock yourself out. Some things happen that are beyond our control no matter how hard we try. We'll just deal with it. You know you both have your dad's and my support through all of this. I am sorry you have to go through this. This nightmare will end and you and Maddy can move on and live a normal life. Maddy can finally live a normal life, honey." Alisha looked down at the CD player, "Do you want me to set that up for you...since you appear to have your hands full?" she grinned. "I'm assuming you think playing her favorite music will help?"

"That's the plan. If you could, I would appreciate it."

Alisha placed the CD player on the opposite side of the bed on a nightstand next to Maddy. "What disc?"

"Melissa Etheridge."

She sorted through Maddy's CD's, finding the right one and popped it in the player. She hit play and put the volume so it played softly.

Alisha kissed Maddy on the forehead and did the same to Jack. "Call me if you need anything sweetheart. Keep us posted."

Jack watched Maddy sleep. He decided to try something. He reluctantly released Maddy's hand from his. He closed the door to her room. He raised Maddy's bed into a semi upright position. He kicked off his shoes and carefully sat in the bed with her, sliding one arm underneath her so she was lying on his chest and leaned back. He circled his arms around her and held her. When he kissed the top of her head her hand slid up his chest and rested there. "That's my Kitten." He laid his head on hers and closed his eyes.

Bryan stood outside Maddy's door. "Medical people in there?" he asked the officer guarding Maddy's room.

"No, Jack brought music in for her. I think he shut the door so it wouldn't bother anyone."

Bryan slowly opened the door. Soft music filled the room and when he looked at Maddy's bed he smiled. Jack was holding Maddy in his arms. Maddy's arm was resting on his chest, her fingers clinging to his shirt. Jack's head was resting on Maddy's. He was sound asleep.

Bryan gently nudged Jack's arm and sat down in the chair next to them.

Jack's eyes fluttered open as he raised his head. He looked over at Bryan. "Hey." He said softly.

Bryan smiled and nodded toward Maddy's hand. Jack looked down to see her fingers tightly clinging to the material of his shirt.

"She wake up?" he whispered.

Jack shook his head, "No," he grinned. "It was an experiment and it worked."

Bryan brought his fingers together and pressed them back and forth, a smug smile on his face. "I see. Less than 24 hours and you're back in bed with her. Damn Jack, you are one smooth operator."

"Fuck you," Jack smiled. "I just wanted to see if she would respond to me on a little higher level, and she did. Her doctor stopped in, asked me a whole shit load of questions about her psychiatric past. I answered what I could, but told him he really needed talk to you. He kept talking about PTSD?"

Bryan nodded, "Post traumatic stress disorder. Fits her profile. Guess I never looked at the picture as a whole. What did he say about her condition now?"

"All he said was about her suffering two traumatic events and that she had a long road ahead of her. Not sure exactly what that means. The nurse said there was no physical reason she's not coming to, but since she is starting to respond it was good indication she is beginning to."

Bryan stood up, "Okay let me try."

Jack held Maddy possessively, "No fucking way," he laughed.

"No dumb ass, don't get your shorts in a knot. I am going to hold her other hand and see if she responds to me or if she's a one man woman." Bryan reached for Maddy's free hand. What if she didn't respond to him? Would that mean she was beyond his touch. One way to find out. He put her hand in his and stroked her hair as Jack watched. "Hey Minnie, its Mickey. Can you hear me hon?" He gently squeezed her hand and was rewarded by her fingers moving in the palm of his hand. A big smile crossed his face. "See," he looked smugly at Jack, "she still loves me too."

Jack kissed the top of her head, "Don't be a dick. We've known that all along." He looked over at Bryan, who continued to hold Maddy's hand. "Any luck with Parsons?"

"It was a positive ID. He is somewhere over on the west side. His other hideout must be over there somewhere—where he took Maddy after the tire shop. I don't image even Maddy would know because I am sure he knocked her out before he took her there. We have, however, been bringing in the remaining members of his flock. They have be very forthcoming considering how close they came to being one of his *chosen ones*. However, one of the ladies is missing, Cassandra Beech. Little blonde thing disappeared yesterday morning on her way to work.

Jack got a sick feeling in the pit of his stomach as he wrapped his arms tighter around Maddy.

Bryan quickly picked up on it, "What are you thinking, Jack?"

"One of the questions she repeatedly asked him was why he did what he did as far as the ritual went. I would bet he made her watch while he killed this one," Jack spoke softly into her hair.

Bryan released Maddy's hand and quietly sat back down in the chair. His heart was thudding in his chest, his respiratory rate increasing. He swallowed hard. "Is there no end to what hell Parsons put her through? Christ it's no wonder she don't want to wake up. And face that?"

Jack felt Maddy move in his arms Her body began to quiver, she moved her head slowly back and forth whimpering as she did. Her nails dug sharply into his skin. She cried out as tears began to fall from her eyes. "Maddy, honey," he held her close stroking her hair. "It's okay baby, Bryan and me are both here...you're safe."

Maddy was trapped, trapped in her own mind. She could hear Jack and Bryan's voices, but she couldn't understand what they were saying. Parsons...blood, blood everywhere...terror filled blue eyes...that evil smile...the glimmering of a gold cross. She wanted out...the grave...needed to get out. She thrashed out against her restraints.

Maddy was fighting against Jack's hold on her. "Jesus Christ, Bryan, get a nurse!"

Bryan ran out into the hallway yelling for help. A nurse came running from behind the nurse's station and followed Bryan into the room.

Maddy was screaming and kicking, her words were incoherent. Jack was doing his best to hang on to her.

"Can't you do something, give her something?" Bryan shouted at the nurse.

The nurse threw her hands up in the air. "I can't, I got strict orders, no medication. I'm sorry. I will see if I can reach Doctor Baker." The nurse turned and ran out of the room.

Jack took Maddy's head in his hands and forced her to look at him. "Maddy! Honey, I'm here. I am NOT going to let anything happen to you. Listen to me!" His voice was raised trying to reach her over her own screaming. Maddy's screaming subsided down to whimpering. Her breathing was still rapid, her body shaking. Jack looked into her eyes but could tell from the faraway look in them she couldn't see him. But she could hear him. "That's it Kitten. You're safe. Easy does it..." Maddy's body began to relax as she collapsed against Jack. She clung to him, breathing erratically. She laid her head against his chest, her eyelids fluttered shut. After a few of minutes her breathing returned to normal and her body was at peace again.

Through the blood and the smell of dirt, the sound of her screaming, she heard him, her beloved Jack, calling to her, telling her she was safe. She let the blanket of warmth take her in and surround her and she blissfully surrendered to it.

The nurse returned to the room, "Dr. Baker doesn't want to give her anything. He's afraid it will send her deeper into her state and doesn't want to put any more drugs in her system because of the baby. He said to try to....ride...it...out." She saw Maddy lying quietly in Jack's arm.

"No shit," he said bitterly.

The nurse took one of her wrist and checked her pulse rate. Maddy had pulled out all her IV's and ripped off the sensors for the monitor. "I'm going let her rest for a bit then we are going to have to put these back in her. I will be back in a little while."

Bryan put his hand on Jack's shoulder. "You okay buddy?"

Jack's hand trembled as he stroked Maddy's hair. "I looked into her eyes, Bryan. She couldn't see me...are we loosing her?"

Bryan took a deep breath, "I don't think so. She hears you. That's contact. I just think she was starting to surface far enough memories took over—very bad memories. Bad enough it kept her locked into them. Last time I couldn't touch her, Jack. Nothing I said or did would get through to her. And she wasn't even unconscious. She eventually came out of it, but like I said before, changed. Nothing like this ever happened. She just shut it off and moved on. Do you understand what I am trying to say?"

Jack leaned his cheek against her. "So you think this is good that just happened?"

"No, that's not what I said. Jack, we have no idea what happened to her, what she saw, what went through her head as Parsons was shoveling dirt on her. I don't know about you, but I can't image what horrors she endured. She was already in a weakened state by her breakthrough. I don't have the answers here. All we can do is hang on to her. Keep pushing contact with her so she can't slip away. We can't do what I did...give up on her."

Bryan's cell phone went off in his pocket. He pulled it out and answered it. After talking briefly he hung up. "I have to go, Jack. They recovered Cassandra Beech's body. He didn't even bother to bury it this time." Bryan stood up and kissed Maddy on the forehead. "I will stop in later, not sure when though."

"No problem...hey Bryan, what did you do with the unsub phone," Jack asked softly.

"Smashed the mother fucker with my bare hands," he said as he walked out the door. "I don't ever want to hear that bastard's voice again, and she sure as hell is not going to if I have anything to say about it."

Cassandra Beech's body was dumped in creek bed just off Gordon Drive. Parsons hadn't even bothered to clean her up and give her a rosary. When Bryan looked at her face, pale faded blue eyes stare back at him. Maybe he was imagining it, but he thought he could see the terror in her eyes. The woman had all the signatures of Parsons with a new twist. Where Vanessa Granger just had a shallow piercing at the crossroads of the chest wounds, Beech's pierced her heart. She was dressed in a white gown that had been cut from her torso. She had bled profusely from the chest, which Bryan guessed was the fatal wound. The slitting of the throat was just for show...a show for Maddy. He left CSU to clean up the mess. He had seen enough.

Maddy open her eyes. The room was dimly lit it with the blue hue of the florescent lights. Maddy knew where she was, in Jack's arms, a place she thought you would never be again. She reached up and tilted her head and kissed him tenderly. Jack was in the twilight zone of sleep. When he felt Maddy's lips on his, he responded in kind by capturing her mouth with his own. His hands slipped around her head and held her there while he returned her kiss. Maddy pulled away and laid her head on his chest again.

Jack looked down at her becoming fully awake. Did he imagine it or did she just kiss him? He touched his lips. It felt so real. Damn what a dream. He felt her hand moving over his chest. "Maddy?"

"Hmmm?" she answered hardly a whisper.

He turned her face to him. Her green eyes sparkled back at him. The only thing to hinder the beautiful sight of them was the swelling around them. "Kitten," he smiled. He let her put her head back down on his chest. "Do you know who I am?"

"My Jack," she mumbled.

He squeezed her gently. "That's right, Kitten. How do you feel?" He spoke softly as she felt timid in his arms.

"Safe." Maddy wished she could say more, but she couldn't make the words come and she didn't know why. She could hear him, feel him, but she had difficulty finding the words. "Love you..."

"I love you too, so very, very much. You have warmed my heart, baby, you don't know how glad I am to see you."

Maddy formed her words carefully, "Me too." She tilted her head and kissed him softly. "Want to go home."

"You can't, baby. You're not strong enough. You've been through a pretty rough trip. We need to get you stronger, then we will go home...your home or mine?" he asked.

"Our home," a tear slid down her cheek. "Want out...out of my head."

"Sweetie, we're working on it. You are doing so well. It's going to take time. But we're here, baby. Bryan has been here most of the time. We won't let you down." He stroked her hair.

"Bryan...where..."

Jack took a deep breath. How much should he tell her? If she wasn't ready to deal with what happened to her, he didn't want to provoke those memories. "He's at work doing his thing. You know him, work, work, work. But seriously, Kitten, he spends whatever time he has here with you."

"Tired...wake for Bryan..." She wanted to see him, needed to see him.

"I'm going to lay you back down, Sweetheart. I need to stretch." He laughed softly. "Been holding you for hours."

Maddy weakly nodded. Jack helped her slide back down in the bed. He lowered her down so she could sleep. "The nurses have to come in and put your IV's back in. You need them to build your strength. You okay with that?"

Maddy nodded, already drifting off to sleep. He gave her a light kiss and left her to rest.

Bryan met Jack out in the hall. He looked extremely stressed. So much for him loosening up this morning. Perhaps the good news would make him feel better. "Hey Bud, got some good news for you. Maddy woke up."

Bryan leaned against the wall. "That's wonderful," he smiled. "How is she... mentally?"

"Not real alert, knows her surroundings. She seems to be have difficulty speaking, not sure if its because of weakness, or something else going on. She asked about you. She wanted me to wake her up but she is resting now. Can you stick around for awhile?"

A small smile played up on Bryan's lips. "They can't pry me away. Derek can fill in for now."

"I really need a cigarette. Where the hell can we smoke in here?" Jack looked around.

"Nowhere, let's go out and sit in the truck. You could use some fresh air." Bryan turned to the officer on watch. "We're going to step out side for a few minutes. Keep a close eye on her."

"Will do, Sir," he replied.

The two of them walked silently down to the Suburban. Jack and Bryan lit up. Jack took a long drag of his smoke and let it out. "God, I needed this. We're going to have to watch what we say in there, she hears us and I don't want her upset. She doesn't give me the impression that she remembers or doesn't want to remember. She doesn't seem to be able to speak in whole sentences. She said she wanted to go home." He paused, "She said she wants out of her head."

Bryan flicked the ashes of his smoke out the window. "It's a lot to deal with. It would probably be too much to dump on her all at one time. How was she when she first came to?"

Jack grinned, "She kissed me. I had dozed off and woke up to her kissing me." He laughed, "I thought I imagined it." He glanced over at Bryan who was looking off into the distance. Something was bothering him in a big way. "I'm going to leave you two a lone for awhile. I'll go grab something to eat." When he still didn't say anything, "Okay, spill it. Was it that bad?"

Bryan smoked the last of his cigarette and pitched it out the window. "I think you were right about Parsons motive for butchering this last one. He just dumped her body in a creek bed, didn't do his usual clean up on the body, not even a rosary. He did it to make Maddy watch. Oh yeah, this one's cause of death...he pierced her heart. The slitting of the throat was anticlimactic. She was already dead. All that blood." He shook his head.

They went back upstairs and stood outside Maddy's room. "You go ahead," Jack told Bryan. "I'm going to go down to the cafeteria." He left Bryan standing at the door, who appeared hesitant to go in.

Bryan quietly entered the room. The IV's and the heart monitor had been placed back on Maddy. He stood over her and watched her sleep. She stirred and then opened her eyes and smiled weakly at him.

Bryan leaned over to kiss her. She reached out with her hand guiding him toward her kissing him tenderly. "Happy to see you," she whispered. "Come...hold me."

Bryan moved to the other side of the bed and raised the bed and slid in beside her. He gently pulled her into his arms and engulfed her in them. When she turned her head up to him, they kissed a long tender kiss. Bryan brushed her cheek with the back of his head. "You've made a bad day so much better, Minnie."

"Work too hard." She nuzzled down into his chest and kissed it.

"Yeah, we do what we have to, baby." His fingers softly stroked her skin. He eyed the bandages on her arms. The fucker bound her in barbed wire.

"Catch him?" she asked.

"We don't need to talk about it okay. I don't think you're ready."

"Catch him?" she repeated.

Bryan took a deep breath and let it out, "No baby, not yet. We're getting close."

"Need truth from you...Jack protecting. Not say anything."

He kissed the top of her head and then turned her face toward him, covering her mouth with his kissing her deeply. Maddy whimpered softly.

She softly stroked his cheek. "Love you, Mickey."

He kissed her again and smiled, "I love you too, Minnie."

Tears welled up in her eyes. "Love Jack...but often wonder..."

Bryan put his finger to her lips, "You don't have to say it, I know. I feel the same way. I know the way you love me and I feel the same. But we know how things have to be, baby. And it's okay. You and Jack, you're good together. You have a future with him. You wouldn't with me. We both know this. We will always have each other, what we have nothing can take away." He smiled down at her, "Besides, if Jack drops he ball, I will be waiting with open arms."

She smiled softly up at him. "Know won't happen."

He smiled and hugged her laughing softly, "I know, he's a good guy."

"Best...next to you."

"Tried to fight, too strong," her voice barely a whisper.

"I know you did, Maddy. You were so strong."

"Not...strong enough."

"Baby, you can't blame yourself for any of this. It was so far beyond your control. We should have been there more for you—protected you better. We dropped the ball."

"No...both were good. Enough of this...how are you...truth."

"Tired, sweetheart," he said in her hair, "So very tired. You know me, been keeping it bottled up inside. Jack was so torn apart. I couldn't let you or him down."

"Good friend to Jack."

Bryan chucked softly, "Yeah, well it has worked both ways."

There was knock at Maddy's doorway and Jack walked in. He smiled at them, "Hey in bed with my girl?" He sat in the chair beside them.

Maddy weakly smiled at him. "Share."

Jack reached out and gently pinched her, "To an extent, Kitten. So what have you two been talking about?"

Maddy looked up at Bryan and he nodded. "I will tell him. You need to save your strength." He looked at Jack, "She asked about Parsons."

Jack frowned, "I thought we agreed."

"No," Maddy shook her head lightly, "Not much, really. Know not ready."

"Good. We can't push this Maddy. One day at a time. We need to do this right...so you can heal." Jack ran his hand up and down her leg.

"Hard...nightmare...want to wake up." She began to cry. "Need meds."

Jack and Bryan exchanged looks. Should they tell her?

Bryan shrugged. "It's your call, Jack."

Jack looked down at his feet. This was not the way he wanted to tell her.

"Truth," Maddy said tearfully.

Bryan tilted Maddy's face and kissed her softly. "Jack and I need to trade places." Bryan helped her back down onto the bed.

Maddy was confused. They were acting so strangely. Her head was so fuzzy sometimes. About the here and now, it was okay. About the last few days, not so much. But what she did know, that was a good thing. "Tell me," she insisted.

Bryan slid off the bed. Jack propped the back of Maddy's bed up more so she could sit upright. He took Maddy's hands in his. He watched as she looked back and forth between he and Jack. "Maddy, I need to ask you, are you thinking clearly?"

Maddy nodded.

"Jack, would you like me to leave so you can do this alone?" Bryan stood up.

"No, its okay. It might be easier for her if you stayed." He stared into Maddy's eyes. She was afraid he was going to tell her something bad. He hoped she wouldn't think so. But before he told her about the baby, he was going to propose to her. He smiled to himself remembering Bryan said talk marriage before baby.

Jack brought Maddy's hands to his lips. "We've talked a little about this..."

"Tell me...please," she pleaded.

Bryan smiled; he knew what Jack was going to do. He just hoped Maddy gave him the right answer. When Jack glanced over at him nervously, he laughed. "Just do it."

Jack turned back to Maddy, "Oh hell, I'm not very good at this shit, and this is not the way I pictured it going...but...Maddy Sheridan, would you do me the honor of being my wife?"

A soft smile graced her lips, "Baby, already said yes. But yes again."

Jack leaned in and kissed her.

Bryan leaned back and reclined in the chair, "I told you she meant it."

Jack laughed and shot him a look, "You think you know her so well."

"I do," he replied smugly.

Jack turned back to Maddy still holding her hands in his. She picked up on his nervousness. "Jack...something more?"

He took a deep breath, "Okay...I honestly don't know how you are going to take this news...but it is what it is." He took another deep breath and glanced at Bryan again.

"Quit looking at him...tell me."

He reached out and softy touched her cheek. "We're going to have a baby... you're pregnant." He didn't know how she was going to react and he was scared shitless.

Maddy leaned her head back against her pillow, slowly taking in this totally unexpected knowledge. How the hell did this happen? When did it happen and how could she have not known? Wow...a baby. A sense of panic filled her, but she couldn't let Jack see. She knew he was thrilled with the idea of having a child, but she honestly didn't know how she felt. It was a moot point. She was pregnant, she knew it was Jack's child. She was just going to deal with it. This and how many other things? "Okay. Guess we start a family earlier than expected." She squeezed his hand weakly. Her eyes met his, "All this...nightmare...baby okay?"

Jack nodded. "Doctor said the heartbeat is strong and everything looks really good. He said six to eight weeks."

Maddy touched her stomach smiling softly. "This is good...giving me more reason to get better...faster." She reached out to Jack and he pulled her into his arms. She looked over Jack's shoulder at Bryan. He knew, but wanted to give her reassurance. He was smiling and nodding his approval. She mouthed "Thank you."

Jack looked back at Bryan, "I know this is kind of premature, but will you be my best man?"

Bryan threw his head back in surprise. "Wow." He laughed, "Now this is an extraordinary chain of events. Nine weeks ago we were rivals, now you want me to be your best man." He shook his head smiling.

"Well?" Jack looked at him expectantly.

"I would be honored, if that's okay with Maddy," he met Maddy's gaze.

Maddy smiled, "That or you could be my maid of honor."

Bryan chuckled, "I think the best man would be more appropriate."

28

Dr. Baker popped in just as Maddy was drifting off to sleep. Jack and Bryan were both dozing in their chairs. Bryan stirred in his chair and became aware of the doctor looking at them and smiling.

Bryan stood up and led the doctor out into the hall. "I'm not sure if you were made aware that Maddy woke up this afternoon."

"I see," the doctor said as he studied Bryan. "Were you present when she had her episode earlier?"

Bryan nodded. "Jack had been holding her. Maddy was responsive to him and then out the blue she started shaking, her eyes opened, she started kicking and screaming. Her words didn't make any sense. Jack said when she looked him she wasn't seeing him. Despite not being able to give anything for the attack, Jack did manage to settle her down. She went back to her sleeping nonresponsive state."

"And when she regained consciousness?"

"Jack had been holding her pretty much all day when she came out it. She's lucid, aware of her surroundings, able to communicate; however she is having problems with her speech. She tires quickly."

Baker was making notes, "Well that's to be expected. She's been through a major ordeal. Her speech should improve as time goes on, probably within few hours. Her memory of the events that led up to this?"

Bryan took a deep breath, "I think she does, but is not ready to go there. She is in a fragile state right now and she is quite aware of it and realizes she is not strong enough to deal with it. And I agree."

"You're Bryan right?"

"Yes."

"I understand you are the person I should be talking to about Maddy's psychiatric history." Baker inquired.

Bryan gave him the run down of Maddy's history over the past decade, leaving out the damage he did to her. He didn't feel it was relevant to the situation that they were dealing with now. He gave her the name of her psychiatrist, her therapist and a list of the medications she was on."

"Do you know if she was diagnosed with PTSD?"

"That I couldn't tell you for sure. I'm not privy to that information, but in looking back she does fit the profile. And yes, I was with her when she finally triggered into her break through a few weeks ago. She is working on dealing both with her doctors and personally." Bryan explained.

"How major do you think this event will affect her?"

Bryan looked at him dumfounded and his temper fared, "This event...this event? How the fuck do you think it's going to affect her? She was held captive by a serial killer for over a week, beaten the shit out of, had to witness the torture and murder of a woman and then buried alive, how the fuck is she suppose to handle it? You tell me?"

Bryan yelling at the doctor was loud enough Jack heard every word that was spoken in the latter part of the conversation.

So did Maddy. She woke up to the sound of Bryan's angry voice outside the hall. She heard his words over and over again, ringing through her head. With each cycle it brought the events into reality. She closed her eyes tight against the visions flashing before her. She sat up, brought her knees to chest, wrapped her arms around them and buried her head. Her body began to rock to and fro and she began whispering, "No...No...No..." repeatedly.

Jack had seen her like this once before and it wasn't pretty. He went to Maddy and pulled her into his arms. She fought him trying to pull away from him. "What the fuck do you guys think you're fucking doing? Bryan, get in here!"

Bryan stormed into the room, the doctor right behind her.

Jack looked up at Bryan frantically. "Help her, please, help her...do what you did before."

"No, Jack you're going to do it." Bryan picked Maddy up his arms, holding her as she struggled. "Get up on the bed behind her." "Maddy, honey, hang on, just hang on, you're okay; you're safe."

Jack climbed up on the bed. Bryan put Maddy across his lap. "Hold her, hold her real tight. Talk to her, bring her back."

Jack did as he was told but it didn't seem to be help. Maddy was crying uncontrollably. "Bryan please help her, I can't do this," Jack was panicking. "Please..."

"You hold her, keep talking to her, she needs to hear your voice." Bryan crawled up in front of her. He forced her head up and held it into his hands, making her look at him. She was gone. "Maddy!" he said sharply. "Come on baby, come back to me...look at me...we're here baby. Jack and Bryan...we're both here. Parsons can't hurt you Maddy." He repeatedly told her.

Jack held her and kept telling her how much he loved her and needed her come back them. He was frightened, were they loosing her? Would she go into that black hole and not come out?

"Talk to her, Jack, God damn it!" Bryan barked to Jack firmly.

Maddy heard them, heard them both calling to her. She desperately wanted to go to them, but she couldn't find her way. Parsons, he wouldn't leave her alone. His evil laugh, those penetrating eyes, the golden cross, the blood. Jack...calling to her...come back...he can't live with out her...Then she heard it "You have to be there for our baby."

Maddy fell back against Jack's chest, turning to him and burying her face into him. Her arms went up around his neck and clung to him for dear life. Sobbing. She felt Jack's arms holding her tightly whispering in her ear, "Maddy, sweetheart, my dear sweet Kitten, come back for us, me and our baby."

Bryan slid off the bed. Jack did it—he pulled her though. He hated to see Maddy in that much pain and he wanted to help, but ultimately it had to be Jack. More than likely this would happen again. It had to be Jack because he would no longer be there. Suddenly he was filled with a great sadness. The realization of his impending departure finally hit home.

Bryan turned and left the room. He needed to get some air and decided to go for a walk to clear his head.

The doctor followed him out and grabbed him by the shoulder to stop him. "What just happened in there?"

Bryan was still pissed off at this guy. He turned to him and decked him. "For fucking doctor, you aren't too bright. You need to find someone else to handle this case because you sure as the fuck aren't qualified to do it. She triggered all right? And what we did, we brought her back out of what could have been a very dangerous place for her. Don't be fucking with her or I will be fucking with you, you got that?" He turned and stormed out of the building.

Everybody within earshot stopped to stare at them and watched after Bryan as he left. Bobby was taking another shift guarding Maddy's room. He snickered under his breath but loud enough the nurses heard him, "That's why you don't piss off a chief FBI Agent."

Maddy started to catch her breath and calm down. Jack was still holding her tight. She could feel his body shaking. Her hands reached up and pulled his face down to hers and kissed him with a desperate urgency. Jack returned her kiss with the same urgency, their tears mingling.

Maddy pulled back and rested her head on his shoulder, she spoke, barely a whisper, "The whole time I was locked up...the one thing that kept me hanging on, that kept me sane, was you. I wasn't afraid of dying...I was afraid of never being able to hold you again."

Jack kissed the side of her face. "I have to tell you Kitten, I have never been so scared in my life. I just felt like I finally had everything I ever wanted...with you, and it was all getting taken away from me and I was helpless to do anything about it. I used to think I was a strong man, tough, able to take any kind of pressure. Quite honestly...I fell apart, Maddy. When I thought I lost you...I wanted to die."

"Don't ever say that, baby. One of the few times he left me without being drugged. I did a lot of soul searching. I came to terms with my past and knew what I wanted for my future...if I had one. My future...was to be married to you and have your children. Not this soon mind you, but it's okay." She smiled weakly up at him. "God must have heard my prayers, I am getting both."

He searched her face, "So you are happy about the baby?"

She smiled and nodded. She kissed him, a sweet, tender kiss. "I had quit believing in God, but he heard me."

They lay there quietly just holding each other when Jack laughed softly.

Maddy looked up at him, "What?"

"You got your voice back."

"Yeah I guess I did." She looked around the room. "Where's Bryan?"

"He was pretty pissed at the doctor. He either went out to beat the fuck out of him or went to smoke a cigarette and cool down."

Maddy sat up, "Maybe you should go talk to him."

Jack shook his head, "No Kitten, I'm not leaving you. He'll be back. Just give him some space okay? I couldn't have made it through this without Bryan, Maddy. I would put my life on the line for him and I honestly believe he would do the same for me. He was there for me, but I couldn't be there for him. For that I am sorry."

Maddy didn't answer him. She just lay quietly against him thinking about Bryan. Bryan was always out there on his own, always the protector, no one there to protect him. It hurt.

"Let's get you more comfortable. I don't know about you, but my back is killing me." Maddy moved so Jack could crawl out from behind her. They moved the head of the bed in the upright position and Maddy laid back. Jack stretched his back.

Maddy felt something trickling down her arms into her bandages. "Shit, I pulled out the damn IV's again." Maddy tugged on the bandages.

"Don't!" Jack said sharply.

Maddy regarded him, puzzled, "What?"

"I just don't think you should be looking at your wrist right now. One trigger a day is more than enough."

"Oh...will you call the nurse in then to change the dressing?" she asked. She was so tempted to look at her wounds. She didn't remember what happened to them. She shook her head; no she wouldn't go there. She wouldn't try to remember, not now.

The nurse came in and looked at Maddy's arms. "Girl you are hard on these IV's. I will check to see if we can leave them out since you are conscious now." She left and returned with some fresh bandages and started to unwind the old ones. Maddy looked at the ceiling while she did it.

The nurse gave a chuckle, "You're friend sure gave Dr. Baker an earful. Thought he was going to pee his pants right there. You'll be getting a new doctor tomorrow morning. Where is your friend? He's kind of cute."

Maddy laughed. "Yeah he is kind of hot when he's hot."

Jack watched as the nurse took off the gauze from her wrist. The gouges in her wrist were deep, angry, red and oozing. It was enough to make his stomach feel woozy. Which was stupid because he had seen a lot worse. He guessed it was knowing how she got these wounds and who gave them to her. It looked as if he must have wrapped the wire around a couple of times and bound them extremely tight. He saw Maddy trying to cop a peek. "Maddy! I said no."

She laid her head back down. "You are not very nice."

The nurse smiled, "No, he's being nice, sweetie." Maddy flinched as she smeared a topical antibiotic on the welts and replaced the bandage.

"How bad are they going to scar?" Maddy asked.

The nurse shook her head, "Bad, I'm afraid."

"Is there any kind of reconstructive surgery that will get rid of them?" Jack asked. He didn't want her to have a constant reminder of all this. They wanted to somehow put it all behind them.

"I can't answer that. There are some great plastic surgeons at Dakota Dunes. I'm sure your new doctor can refer you to one."

As the nurse went to leave, Bryan came back in. Maddy and Jack heard her giggle and whistle. They laughed.

Bryan stopped and looked behind him then looked back at them, "What the hell was that all about?"

"She thinks you're hot," Jack smiled.

A puzzled furrow creased his brow and he looked back towards he door. He shook his head, "Nah, looks too much like Donna."

Maddy smiled. "Heard you fired my doctor."

Bryan smiled and shook his head, "The quack is a dumb fuck." He went to Maddy and gave her a kiss. "You feeling better, Minnie?"

"Yes, Mickey, feeling better." She grabbed his hand and brought it to her lips. "Thanks."

"Don't thank me sweetie, it was Jack."

"I heard you calling down that black hole too, hon, so don't get all humble on me now. Come here," she held her arms out to him. He went to her and she hugged him extra tight. "Love you, Mickey."

He kissed her on the cheek, "Love you too, Minnie."

Bryan went around to the other side of the bed where the chairs were placed, "Parker, you're in my chair." When Jack started to get up, Bryan laughed, "Sit down, I was kidding."

"Oh I wasn't getting up," Jack smiled, "I was just adjusting my ass."

Maddy was exhausted, but she tried hard not to let on. She wanted to spend time with her guys. She missed them both, with the time she spent in Texas and the abduction, it was just over a month since she had spent time with them. She loved to listen to Jack and Bryan banter and tease each other.

Then Jack's parents showed up. Alisha came and gave her hug. "Maddy, so nice to see your smile."

Edward gave her toes a wiggle, "You look awfully tired hon, and we won't stay long. I just wanted to give you these." He held out a big arrangement of pink roses.

Maddy smiled weakly, "They're beautiful, thank you."

Jack slipped around the bed and led his mother out into the hallway. "Did you bring it?"

"Of course I did," she laughed. She handed him a red ring box. "Your grandmother's engagement ring. Are you going to give it to her now?"

Jack smiled. "I proposed to her this afternoon and she said yes...again. It is official," he opened up the box, "once I get this on her finger."

"Wait here a second." Jack ran down to the family room and bought a can of diet coke and then ran back. "Maddy can't have alcohol."

Maddy eyed Jack and Alisha suspiciously but kept quiet. She knew they were up to something. Jack wasn't very good at hiding surprises. She bet he sucked at Christmas time.

Bryan stood up, "Well I think I will leave you all to visit."

Jack stopped him, "No, I want you to be here. I'm sorry, I forgot to introduce you." He made the introductions. And then proceed to kneel beside Maddy's bed.

"What are you doing?" she laughed.

He opened the ring box and asked...again, "Will you marry me, Kitten?"

Maddy smiled at him, "What three times a charm? Yes, yes, and yes."

Jack slipped the ring on to her finger and kissed her tenderly. "Just wanted to make sure before I gave you my grandmother's engagement ring."

Maddy studied the ring on her finger. It was a beautiful ring of white gold with a modest diamond. Not small by any means, but modest. A ring of tiny diamonds surrounded the stone. The band look like it was finely braded close to the setting. "It's beautiful baby." She pulled him close and kissed him again.

Alisha pulled out a bottle of champagne and five glasses. She handed them around to everyone. When she gave Bryan his she said, "For Jack's best man," she smiled at him. She gave him the bottle. "Would you do us the honors, Bryan?"

Maddy saw Bryan turn a light shade of red. It was kind of funny because he felt about as comfortable in family situations as she did—something they both had in common.

Bryan popped the cork and began filling the glasses while Jack opened the diet coke and poured it in Maddy's glass. They all held up their glasses. Bryan made the toast "To Jack and Maddy, may their future be blessed with much happiness and tons of children."

Maddy and Jack both choked on their drinks and glared at Bryan. Bryan's face lit up and his eyes were gleaming. He winked at them both.

Maddy lie back on the pillow, barley being able to keep her eyes open. Jack picked up on it. She needed to sleep. "Well folks, it's been a long day for Maddy and she needs to get some rest."

Alisha gave Maddy a kiss on the cheek.

Maddy was really surprised when Edward kissed her too and whispered, "Welcome to the family, Maddy." He turned to Bryan and shook his hand. "It was a real pleasure to meet you, Bryan."

"Likewise," Bryan told him.

After the Parkers left, Bryan stood up. "Well kids, I'm going to head back to the station and check on things." He hugged and kissed Maddy. "I will be in tomorrow morning, Minnie. Love you."

"Love you to hon," Maddy yawned. "Sorry."

Bryan gave Jack a playful smack on the side of the head, "Use the cot and get some sleep."

Jack punched him on the arm, "Nice toast by the way."

Bryan laughed as he walked out the door. "I thought so."

Jack stood up, stretched, then went and shut the door. He turned down the lights and grabbed a pillow.

Jack lowered Maddy's bed down for a better sleeping position and propped the pillow next to Maddy's head.

"Aren't you going to sleep on the cot?" Maddy asked sleepily.

He kicked off his shoes, "Fuck no, scoot over."

Maddy slid over. Jack lie down beside her and put his arm around her and pulled her over so she was lying against his chest. He turned her face to him and kissed her deeply then kissed her nose. "This is where you are going to sleep for the rest of our lives, Kitten. In my arms." He reached over his head and pulled the light cord.

Jack lie awake in the stillness of the night listening to Maddy's soft breathing. This wasn't the case a short while ago. She cried and whimpered in her sleep, clinging to him as she did. Nightmares. How long would she have to endure them or would her nights always be filled with terror. He could protect her while she was awake, but who would watch out for her while she slept?

Maddy could feel Jack awake. The rhythm of his breathing changed slightly and it was that way now. She wished they were home in Jack's bed holding each other instead of this antiseptic prison. What she wouldn't give to feel Jack make love to her again. It had been over a month, too long. She longed to be close to him...as close as she could get.

Physically she felt pretty decent, banged up, but okay. Mentally, well, she didn't know about that but keeping her in a hospital wasn't going to change it. That wasn't anything being at home would change. She wanted out of here...and once again, she just wanted to go home, even if it were Jack's home.

Maddy slid her arms up around Jack's neck pulling his head down to hers. Her lips came down on his, parting them with her tongue kissing him deeply. She leaned back pulling him down on her as he responded to her kiss. Her heart began to beat faster when he entangled his fingers in her hair as he explored her mouth. He rested his body over hers pressing against her. She moaned softly.

Jack's heart was on fire as Maddy hungrily kissed him, touching him, making him ache. The feel of her body beneath him stirred the passion inside him. No...not here. He pulled back and rolled off of her, breathing heavily. "What the hell are you trying to do to me?" he asked her softly.

She leaned her head against his shoulder, softly stroking his arm with her fingertips. "I need you..."she whispered.

Jack was still trying to regain his composure. "I need you too, Maddy, but not here. We can't."

Maddy snickered, "What? You afraid of getting caught?"

Jack turned to her, a devilish grin on his face, "You wouldn't have the balls."

She threw herself back on the pillow and laughed, "I know I don't, but do you?"

Jack lie back smiling, "This is good."

"No sex? You call that good?" she laughed.

He propped his head up with his elbow. "No, no sex is never a good thing," he grinned, "but this...us being us...I likey."

Maddy leaned up and kissed him, "I likey too, but would likey it better in our own bed where we can really do stuff we likey."

Jack reached over with his other hand and cupped her face kissing her deeply and then looked in her twinkling eyes. "You like this don't you?"

She looked at him innocently, "Like what?"

"Having the power over me to drive me crazy with desire?" he smiled down at her.

She gave him a quick kiss, "Yes, me likey...and so do you. You could always push the cot up against the door."

He chuckled softly under his breath, "No." He took a deep breath. "We gotta get you bailed out of here, Kitten. I can't take much more of this."

When Bryan came into the room Jack was sitting in the chair reading the morning paper. He looked up at Bryan, smiled and brought his fingers to his lips and pointed at Maddy.

Bryan peered over at her to find her peacefully sleeping, her hands tucked up under her face.

He handed Jack a McDonalds sack and a glass of orange juice. "It's not the best, but will do in a pinch. How did last night go?"

Jack stuck a straw in the orange juice and took a sip. "Except for the nightmares pretty good. Damn she was full of it in the middle of the night." He smiled, "like her old self."

Bryan grinned, "That's good...I think. I wasn't sure how she was going to come out of this, but overall I think she is doing well. She is stronger this time."

"She's still sassy anyhow." Jack took a bite of his sandwich. "Thanks for the grub by the way. She wants to go home."

Bryan sat back in the chair, "What's new?"

Jack smiled, "This is true. But really I can't see any physical reason she can't, do you?"

"Depends on what her doctor says. She going to need close psychological monitoring, you know that don't you?"

"Yeah, I know, but the point is, so does she. She's not in denial and I think that is half the battle." He took another drink then wiped his mouth. "What do you think?"

Bryan studied Maddy as she slept. "I don't know...this time is so different. Based on past experience it makes me nervous, but today is a different day than yesterday."

Bryan glanced down at the paper Jack had laid off to the side. He picked it up and scanned the front page. There was an article about Parsons, Maddy's rescue (without the details), the discovery of Cassandra's body and the manhunt was continuing. Max Sutton was doing the writing. "I went to see Maddy's boss before I came here."

Jack looked up from his food, "You saw Chief? What did you tell him?"

Bryan folded up the paper. "Gave him an update."

"Did you tell him what happened?"

Bryan shook his head in doubt, "I don't know what she wants him to know. I did tell him about the circumstances she was found, off the record of course, and that I didn't know how long she was going to be gone. I figured it would be up to you guys to figure out who should know what."

Jack studied him closely. "You are starting to detach from us."

Bryan looked down and smoothed out an imaginary crease in his slacks. "I have to Jack. This is winding down and I will be leaving before too long."

"You don't have to. Quit and joined the force," Jack told him in all seriousness.

Bryan laughed, "Doing what?"

"Hell I don't know, I am sure we could find something."

Bryan shook his head, "No, I can't do that. You and Maddy need a clean start...without me. I will go back to Quantico, back to training. I've been offered a job in D.C. I might take. I don't know. Coming here was a big mistake, for everyone."

"Oh cut the bullshit. There were some good things that came out of you coming here. Aside from the Parsons nightmare, you made peace with Maddy. At least now you have some kind of relationship, which is more than you had before. And you made a damn good friend." Jack said as a matter of fact.

Bryan laughed, "Okay, you have me on that. But still I need to go back. I can retire on full benefits in a few years and do what I want to do then. Maybe then we will see about other prospects."

"We haven't set a date or anything, but you are coming back for the wedding right?"

"I'm still the best man aren't I?"

"Damn well better be. And I am sure Maddy, and me of course, will want you to come back when the baby is born," Jack told him honestly.

Bryan looked over at Maddy and smiled. "Getting a little presumptuous aren't you?"

"You mean to tell me you honestly don't know what a big part of her life you have become? I mean, damn Bryan, you are part of her, you just can't take that away from her."

Bryan met Jack's gaze, "You really think so?"

Jack smacked him along side the head, "I really know so, now quit being a wet blanket."

Maddy had been faking sleep for quite a bit of this conversation. At first she was alarmed about Bryan leaving but as he and Jack talked she felt better and more secure about it. There was no way in hell she was going to let Bryan out of her life now. She couldn't, it was like Jack said—he was part of her.

Maddy rolled over, "How the hell is a girl suppose to get some sleep around here with you two yakking your asses off over there?"

Jack and Bryan exchanged looks. "I told you she has her mouth back," Jack commented.

Maddy threw a pillow at him, "Fuck you."

Maddy's new doctor, Dr. Ryan Fuller stopped into see her with a psychiatrist, Dr. Rosario in tow. Jack and Bryan made their introductions.

Fuller stood back eying Bryan, "You're the one who decked Baker?"

Maddy looked at Bryan, her mouth dropped, "You decked him?"

Bryan looked all innocent and said, "His face got in the way of my fist, what can I say?" Then he turned to the doctor, "The guy was being a total jack ass and not looking out for Maddy's wellbeing. Isn't that what a doctor is suppose to do?"

Fuller smiled, "Well yeah, the guy is an ass." He turned to Maddy, "How are you feeling, Maddy?"

"Good, I want to go home."

Fuller checked her vitals, looked in her eyes, felt the bumps on her head, looked at her bruises and then said, "I want to see your wrists and your ankles. See how they are healing up." He called for a nurse to bring in supplies. "While I am doing that Maddy, Dr. Rosario is going to ask you a few questions."

She looked over the Psych doctor. The man looked to be in his thirties, obviously Italian, with dark eyes and dark hair, olive skin, overall not a bad looking guy. "I have a Psych doc," she told them.

Dr. Rosario pulled up a chair, "Yes, Maddy, I spoke with your Doctor, we are going to be working together with you. He doesn't have the experience in these kinds of cases that I do, so I will be assisting him and Lonnie McKenzie, your therapist. Now I just need to ask you some questions about your experience and if we get into an area that makes you feel uncomfortable and or causes you pain, you just tell me stop okay?"

He looked over at Bryan and Jack, "Maybe you two should step outside for a little bit."

"NO!" Maddy blurted out. "They stay or I won't talk."

Rosario made a face and nodded, "Okay, we'll do it your way." He turned to the guys, "I want the answers to come from her; no filling in the blanks you got it?" Then her turned back to Maddy, "No looking to them for the answers."

Maddy smiled, "Damn you got this down good don't you?"

Rosario cracked a smile, "That's my job. You ready?"

Maddy took a deep breath, "I guess so."

"We are just doing an exploratory interview here so you don't have to go into details, okay? Just give me a rough composite. Do you want to start at the beginning of the effects of this case on you or just with the abduction itself?"

Maddy thought about it. What happened prior to the abduction all seem irrelevant now, except maybe the phone calls, but they could go into that later. "The abduction, but only certain parts."

Rosario nodded, "Like I said, we are just testing waters here. If you just want to answer yes or no to some of the questions that's fine. I just need to figure out where your trigger spots are, and that's what we'll work on later. Okay, here we go. Do you remember everything that happened while you were being held captive?"

"No."

"How it happened?"

"In the parking lot across from the police station. Then he drugged me. Next thing I remember is coming to in my cell."

"Your cell?"

"Well the room he had me locked in."

"Did he get physical with you?"

"At first, he knocked me around a lot, but that's when Parsons was in control."

Rosario gave her a strange look and then looked back at the guys. They in turned shrugged their shoulders.

They knew a little of what she was talking about, but they never had the chance to learn what really happened; only what she told them via text.

Maddy went on to explain, "You see this guy, his real name is Lucus Riley. The real Justin Parsons raped and murdered his sister." She turned to Jack and Bryan, "That was his trigger by the way. He killed the real Parsons." Then she turned back to Rosario, "Anyway, Lucas believed that God was punishing him for killing a minister and was talking to him, telling him to do things. Lucas became Justin Parsons and it split his personality. Justin, that's what I call the good guy, Parsons is the monster. There was a middle guy to but I never named him. He was kind of mix of the two of them. He was the transitional guy. When Justin was in control, he took good care of me. He even allowed me to make contact with those two," she nodded to Jack and Bryan. "He made sure I had food and water. He would sit and talk with me. He felt guilty for keeping me hostage. He wouldn't let me go because he was afraid of Parsons. Later on he felt that he was protecting me from Parsons. That's why he killed that other girl—the red headed one.

He thought he could fool Parsons into thinking it was me. He said he had to let Jack and Bryan think I was dead because his God was watching. He never knew I had my cell phone and I would text the guys when I could. I let them know I was okay, but they had figured out the dead girl wasn't me already. Whenever Parsons was in control, he was cruel and violent. He seemed to really get off on slapping me around. Justin kept me sedated most of the time, said it was to protect me, from what I don't know." Maddy was rambling. "The last time I talked to Justin, he told me he was sorry, but he was too weak to stay in control and he was going to be gone...for good. Parsons had figured out what Justin had done. That's when I knew I was done for. I remember telling the guys goodbye. The rest is flashes I don't want to talk about." Maddy didn't really feel uncomfortable talking about what she said.

Jack and Bryan watched her, amazed by her recount of what happened.

Jack interrupted, "May I say something?"

Rosario looked over at him. "Let me ask you two something. Who are you two to Maddy?"

"I am a close friend of Maddy's and also her SSA," Bryan told him. No sense on going into the past or the role he played on putting her where she was.

"SSA?"

"Maddy reactivated into the FBI to work on this case, I was...am her supervising agent."

He turned back to Maddy, "You are a reporter and an FBI agent?"

"I'm a profiler," she told him.

"Holy shit," Rosario said under his breath. "So you know about all these psychology techniques?"

"Yep, abnormal and forensic."

"I got my work cut out for me," he smiled. Then he turned to Jack, "And you?"

Jack smiled, "It's complicated, I am the chief of detectives at SCPD and lead detective working on this case working under Bryan. Maddy used to shadow me on her crime beat. I am also her fiancé."

"Okay, what were you going to say?"

"Bryan believes it is Maddy's experience as a Profiler that allowed her to get into Parson, I mean Justin's head. I believe she has a gift, what I call her chameleon mode where she can adapt to situations around her making people trust her to talk to her. She uses it in her job as a reporter. You can figure out which ever you think it is for yourself I guess."

Rosario watched Maddy's reaction to what Jack was saying, "Which is it you feel you were, Maddy?"

Maddy shrugged, "I don't know, I just did what I felt I needed to do, be who I thought I need to be. I was one way with Justin, I was, how do I put, not so nice with Parsons."

"But you don't really believe these were different people?"

Maddy threw her head back and laughed, "Hell no! I told you it was like this guy was suffering from a psychosis which I believe to be dissociative identity disorder whose onset was caused by the real Parsons killing his sister."

Jack watched her, once again in awe. Wow. Who was this woman? He glanced over at Bryan to get a feel for his reaction. Bryan was making an odd face, slightly nodding his head. What the hell was that all about?

Bryan too was amazed by Maddy's report of her abduction. She was able to gather information and analyze what was going on around her. He still believed it was her keen skills of observation and ability to read people, the profiler. Damn, she was so good at her job, but not in a million years would he want her to continue profiling. It was just too much.

Dr. Fuller had removed her bandages and looked at the wounds, not allowing her to see them. At least this doctor was smart enough to know it might trigger a psychological response from them.

"Well Maddy, I want to run some tests to make sure the ketamine is out of your system and run some tests on the baby. If all turns out well I think you can go home on an out patient basis. I want you to come in here to have your bandages changed."

He turned to Rosario, "What do you think?"

"Are you having any nightmares? I understand you triggered yesterday."

Maddy looked at the guys. "Yes on both accounts. The nightmares, I can't help, but they guys are great pulling me out of mental states brought on by the triggers. Both of them have done it in the past."

"Okay, you have a green light from me, but I want to see you on a daily basis for awhile so we can work through all this. You are highly susceptible to PTSD, which from what your other Psych thought you were suffering with from a prior event but believes you have that under control. So are you willing to work with me on this? Do you feel comfortable enough with me?" He watched for her reaction.

Maddy actually liked this guy. He was a no bullshit kind of guy and she felt he wouldn't fuck with her. "Okay, you have my cooperation. So I get to go home?"

Fuller said, "After we run these tests and get the results back. You should be able to leave later this afternoon.

After the doctors left Bryan turned to Jack, "Why don't you run home and grab a shower. I will sit with Maddy."

"I can take one tonight when she's home," he started to protest but then realized Bryan wanted to talk to Maddy alone. "Maybe I will go grab a quick one and a shave. He rubbed his chin. "Getting kind of furry here."

"I will see you in a little while hon," he gave her a quick kiss and took off.

Maddy smiled at Bryan, "Way to run him off in a hurry. What's up?"

"His family is...quite friendly aren't they?" Bryan grimaced.

Maddy threw her head back and laughed, "No shit. Kind of overwhelming compared to what you and I are used to isn't?"

Bryan sat on the edge of the bed and leaned his head on hers.

"I know what you want to talk about and I don't want to," Maddy turned away from him.

"It's not going to go away, Minnie. It is getting closer and closer," he said softly.

Maddy started chewing on her lip. "I don't want to loose you...not ever."

"We promised, remember? You're not loosing me. We just won't be physically in the same place. Besides you have Jack now."

Maddy whipped her head around to face him, "Why do you always throw that up at me? It's not the same damn thing and you know it. You and Jack are two different people, and I need you both in different ways. Don't get me wrong, I love Jack with all my heart, but you...you are like my soul. You know me inside out. I don't have to say things to you because you already know. We are so much alike, the way we think, the way we feel, the way we see things. So don't give me this shit about I have Jack."

Bryan sat up. "Maddy, when it comes to a lot of things, we don't think alike. If we did, you would be with me. The way we feel, yeah, that I would say we are close. The way we see things, sadly, yeah we do. We both see how things have to be...especially now. This only goes to prove you are meant to be with Jack. This is how it should be. It was never meant for us to be together, if it had been it wouldn't have taken ten years for it to happen. Yeah, I am sure it's my fault, and I'm sorry, but I can't change what has already happened. But Maddy, as you so smartly pointed out, we can still be a part of each other's lives. And I damn well plan to keep my end. What about you?"

"You know I will. I just don't want to be with out you," she told him tearfully.

"Maddy, you went nine years without me. If I hadn't barged back into your life two years ago and this time, you would have done just fine without me."

She looked at him in disbelief. "You don't think you weren't always back there? That you didn't cross my mind all the time? Yes, granted they weren't always pleasant thoughts, but you never left me."

Bryan shook his head, "Hon, I have done nothing but cause you pain since the day I walked out on you."

"You didn't walk out on me damn it, I pushed you away. I left you!"

Bryan met her gaze, "Why are we fighting about this?"

Maddy sat quietly playing with Jack's ring on her finger. "This should have been us."

"In an alternate universe, yes. But it's not, and you can't say you're not happy with Jack. I can't give you what he can and you know it. I can't marry you; I can't give you a child. I can't give you hopes and dreams. I am a tired, worn out, jaded old man, Minnie." He smiled softly, "And quite frankly Maddy, I don't think I could keep up with you."

Maddy smiled weakly. "I don't know about that. You weren't doing too bad. And you're not old."

Bryan laughed, "I didn't mean just in that department, hon. I watch you. You are still so full of energy for life. You get so excited about things and get so animated. When you get pissed, damn, everybody better be ducking because things are going to fly. And sweetheart, when you hurt...it breaks my heart. I don't want to be the one doing the hurting. You see, yes we are soul mates, but because we are so much I think we have the power to hurt each other that much more and deeper than most people. Do you understand what I am saying?"

Maddy reluctantly nodded her head. "That doesn't mean I have to like it."

Bryan smiled, "I would be upset if you did, kiddo. We will find some way to make this work. We will talk often. I will fly out here and see you when I can as often as I can. As long as Jack will tolerate it anyhow. You're going to be getting so you can't fly so I won't expect as much from you." Bryan put his arm around her and held her.

"You promise? I mean you really, truly promise you will do what you just said?"

He held her chin up and kissed her softly, "I promise."

They sat quietly holding one another when Bryan asked her, "How do you really feel about having a baby hon?"

"Terrified."

Bryan nodded, "I thought maybe you would be. You know though, accepting a new child into your life doesn't mean you are taking away from the love you have for Lexy and Scotty right?"

"Part of me feels like I am betraying them." She looked up at him, "You won't repeat any of this to Jack will you?"

"Minnie, this is us. The part of us we don't share with anyone else."

"Sometimes I think about all this and I wonder what the hell happened. Two months ago, I was living my life the way I thought I wanted. I liked keeping my life separate. I liked that no one really knew who I was. It was safe." She leaned her head on his chest.

"Until I came along and fucked it all up, you mean?"

She smiled softly, "It wasn't just you. Jack was messing with my head too, and I image he would have kept doing it until I gave in. But you know, even if given the choice, I don't think I could go back to that life. After going through what I have been though, I realized the past controlled me, made me who I was, and I don't want to be that person anymore. Yeah, you came back in my life, but you did what you always have—you made me feel alive again. I think because of you not despite you, you made it so I was able to love Jack."

"Kiddo," Bryan chuckled, "he did that all on his own."

"You know something, I never noticed how high energy he is." She laughed, "He exhausts me."

"Maddy, you are high energy. Jack is just...I don't know quite how to put it."

"Anal," Maddy filled in for him.

Bryan threw his head back and laughed, "No, that was not the word I was looking for. He's thorough. He looks ahead all time and he anticipates, then he prepares. It's not a bad thing."

"He told me he couldn't have gotten through this without you. He feels bad he couldn't have been there for you."

Bryan took a deep breath and let it out. "You know how I am, Maddy. I am a control freak and when it comes to my emotions I am no different. We get that way in the profession we're in and you know that. At least you had the good enough sense to get out of it while you still had a soul."

She poked him gently in the ribs, "You have a soul, you have me."

He buried his face in her hair, "And sweetheart, I thought I lost that part of me. I was hurting just as bad as Jack. There is one of the major differences between Jack and I, he is capable of expressing his feelings...I am not."

"I don't know, you don't seem to be too bad expressing yourself when you're pissed off," she replied smugly.

It was his turn to poke her in the ribs, "We won't go there."

He pulled back away from her so he could see her face, "So are we okay about everything?"

Maddy leaned forward and kissed him tenderly. "We are okay as much as I can be without you staying here. But like you said, we will make it work."

"I'm going to go grab a smoke. I will be back in a few minutes okay?"

She grabbed him by his tie, pulled him back and kissed him again. "Okay."

As Bryan walked out he glanced to make sure there was an officer watching Maddy's door. The guy was reading the paper. Bryan told him good morning to which the officer mumbled a reply.

Maddy was lying on her side facing the windows thinking about the conversation she had just had with Bryan. It was nice they could now talk about things so honestly.

Maddy didn't hear her door closing or the man approaching her. But she got this queer feeling and the hair on the back of her neck stood up. She quit breathing—something here didn't feel right. Parsons. Oh God, would this be the ending to her nightmare?

"What? You don't think you did enough to me already you had to come back for more?" she spoke to him calmly. She didn't feel calm, not at all, but he loved the smell of fear and she wasn't going to give it to him.

"Oh sweet, sweet Maddy, did you really think I would let it end so easily? We were so rudely interrupted. Turn around so I can see you," Parsons' voice was raspy like it was that night in the park. That part she remembered quite well.

Maddy sat up in the bed. Her hand slipped along the side and hit the call button. She didn't know if she had actually pressed it hard enough before she released it but she prayed she did. Parsons was dressed as cop...the guard. That's how he got passed Bryan.

She looked at him squarely in the eye, "What the fuck do you want with me? Haven't you done enough? Because of you every time I look at my wrists I will be reminded of you. Every night when I sleep, you haunt me. Don't you think that is torture enough?"

Parsons reached behind him and pulled out a knife. The golden cross...everything came back to her in rush, that poor woman he slaughtered in front of her with those knives. She felt the blood leave her face.

"Now it's time to finish what we started."

"Why the hell didn't you just do it in the first place? You could have saved us all some trouble." She was stalling, praying Bryan or someone would come in and save her. She didn't want to die; she had too much to live for now.

"We need to save your soul, Maddy," he came towards her, that demonic smile on his face.

Parsons grabbed Maddy by her hair and literally pulled her out of the bed. He raised his hand, the blade of the knife loomed abover her. Maddy swallowed hard and waited for her fate.

As Bryan made his way to the parking lot, something about that guard was bothering him. He had never seen any of the others reading or doing things to distract them. "Oh shit!" he said out loud and took off running back to Maddy's room.

When he saw Maddy's door shut, he took out his gun and pushed the door open to find Parsons standing over Maddy with a knife raised above her chanting something.

"Freeze Parsons!" he shouted.

Parsons kicked out behind him sending the hospital bed table flying in Bryan's direction catching him off guard. His knife slashed into Bryan's chest as Bryan fell backward.

Parsons moved over Bryan's body and prepared to plunge the knife into him. Maddy acted without thinking. She grabbed the nearest thing she could find. She held the metal bedpan out and swung it screaming, "Not this time mother fucker!" and slammed it against Parsons head.

It only stunned him knocking him to the floor. He reached for Maddy's foot tripping her, pulling her to him. Pain shot up her leg as his grip tightened around the wounds around her ankle. Maddy struggled against him, kicking at him violently with her free foot. She caught sight of Bryan's gun. Her finger barley grazed it but she managed to pull it to her.

She twisted her body to face him, her eyes blazing and pointed the gun at him and pulled back against the firing mechanism. "Get up you bastard." She kicked at him and rose to her feet. "I said get up." She took a quick look at Bryan, seeing the front of his shirt covered in blood. Oh God, her Bryan. She turned back to Parsons and glared at him. "You are so going to pay for that."

Parsons stood up, the knife remaining on the floor. "Are you going to shoot an unarmed man, Maddy?"

"No," her voice was eerily calm. "I am going to put you in hell where you belong. But first I have something from your victims...your so-called chosen ones..." First she shot him in the kneecap. He fell to the floor. "That's for your first two." She got an errie thrill hearing his cries of pain. She shot him in the other knee, "and the next two." She the calmly shot him in both arms, "the last four."

She looked down at him lying on the floor, withering in pain. She kicked him in the shoulder, loving the sound of his wail echo throughout the room. "Damn...that looks like that hurts. Are you suffering?"

He whimpered.

"Good," she hissed. She knelt down to see his face up close. "How does it feel? How does it feel to know your impending death is upon you? Scream for me Parsons. " When he didn't oblige, she dug her heel into his bleeding shoulder. "I said scream! Beg me for mercy! Where is your almighty God now? You do his bidding yet he is not here to protect you." She pressed down on him harder. "Where is he?" she screamed.

"Your soul can not be saved," he gasped in jagged uneven breaths.

She brought the nose of the gun inches from his head, seeing the terror in his eyes, "Maybe so...but this one is from me, see you in hell!" and she fired sending his skull into shards across the floor.

"Maddy..." Bryan slowly moved on the floor. He was struggling to get up.

Maddy dropped the gun and ran to him. "Oh baby, thank God, I thought he killed you." She pulled him into her arms, tears running down her face.

He pushed himself up in a semi sitting position. He brought his hand up to his wound and flinched, "Just grazed...I think." He looked over at the bloody pool Parsons was laying in. "What the hell did you do?" he whispered between breaths.

Maddy looked in the direction of Parsons' body and recoiled at the bloody mass. "I killed him...I guess..." she replied without emotion.

Jack followed by several hospital staff rushed in. He looked at Bryan and Maddy then back at Parsons. "Jesus fucking Christ," he rushed to them and knelt down. He looked at Maddy, fear in his eyes. Maddy's face was covered in blood spatter and the front of her gown was crimson. "Are you okay?"

"I'm fine...help Bryan, please..." she whimpered.

Jack barked out orders to the nurses to get help for Bryan and pulled Maddy back away from him.

"No, I can't leave him," she reached out to Bryan.

"Maddy, they need to help him. Come on, come with me." He helped her up and led her from the room. As he turned to leave he told the others, "Throw a sheet over the body. Do not touch anything in this room. This is now a crime scene."

Jack stood with Maddy out in the hall making sure his instructions were followed.

They took Bryan out on a gurney. He made them stop and he reached out and took Maddy's hand. "Minnie, I'm okay," he smiled weakly. "This is nothing, sweetheart. Just need to get patched up and I'll be as good as new. You're safe now, kiddo, it's over."

Derek and Andy found Jack and Maddy sitting in another hospital room. Maddy had a blanket wrapped around her, Jack holding her tightly next to him. "I'm sorry Jack, but I need to ask Maddy some questions."

"Do you have to do it right this minute?" Jack asked coldly.

Derek looked at him, "Do you really need to ask?"

Maddy lifted her head, "It's okay."

"Can you tell me what happened?" Derek asked her softly. He didn't like doing this anymore than Jack wanted him to.

"Parsons came into my room. He was dressed as cop. What happened to the guy that was suppose to be there?" she asked.

"Lucky O'Brien. They found him in the parking lot. He had been stabbed, but he will live. Call it Karma. Anyway, what else?"

"Said he came in to finish what he started and was about to when Bryan walked in. He shoved one of those tables in to Bryan then stabbed him. I hit him over the head with a bedpan, took Bryan's gun and I shot him. I killed him and he can never hurt anyone again." Maddy said as if she were speaking off into the distance.

Derek met Jack's gaze. Jack pleading not to take it any further, but he also knew Derek had to. "Maddy, how many times did you fire the gun?"

Maddy shook her head, "I don't know, I can't remember, a lot."

"Okay Maddy. Thank you. Jack, can I see you out in the hall please?" Derek said as he walked towards the door.

"Sit here honey, I will be right back. Andy's here. He'll be with you."

Maddy looked up to see Andy. She hadn't seen him in weeks, "Hey," she smiled weakly.

"Hey," he smiled back and hugged her.

"Did you happen to see Parsons' body?" Derek asked Jack.

Jack shook his head, "Not closely, he wasn't my biggest concern when I got there. I had Bryan lying on the floor bleeding from his chest and Maddy, covered in blood kneeling over him crying her eyes out. I saw he was dead. That was good enough for me."

"Come with me." Derek led Jack back to Maddy's room. Parsons' body had not yet been moved. Derek asked the scene investigators to leave for a moment and he pulled back the bloody sheet from the body. "She shot him five times."

"So, it happens, she just kept shooting, gut reaction."

"No, you don't understand." Derek knelt near the body. "He was shot once in each knee, once in each shoulder and then right between the eyes. Maddy is an excellent marksman. She shoots what she aims for. She knew what she was doing."

Jack looked at him, anger slowly rising, "So what exactly are you saying, Derek?"

"I'm not saying she was conscious of what she was doing, I am just saying that while this was happening, she shot him how she did for a reason. It was definitely overkill. Look at him, Jack. How can you say otherwise?"

"Okay, cut to the chase. What are you getting at? She murdered him?"

Derek returned the sheet over the body then stood up, "That's not what I am saying at all. It was self-defense pure and simple. I am just saying that in the scheme of things, given what he put her through, it was a revenge killing at a very opportunistic time."

Jack looked at him with out blinking, "Murder."

"No it was self-defense and that's what it will read in the file. Her life, Bryan's life, they were in eminent danger. She defended them. It was justifiable. I guess what I am saying is...I know she is getting psychiatric care, I think this needs to be brought to the table when the time comes okay?" Derek leaned against the wall. "Do you really think I would put Maddy through anymore bullshit? Damn, I would have killed the motherfucker without it being self-defense."

Jack leaned his head back against the wall. "It's over Derek. It's finally over. Now we just have to pick up the pieces."

Derek sighed, "And that poor girl has the most to pick up...if she ever can."

Jack shook his head smiling slightly.

"What?"

"She hit him on the head with a bedpan."

Derek opened the door for them. "Yeah...well no one ever said she wasn't creative."

29

Jack left Maddy up in the room with Andy. Andy was catching Maddy up on his love life with Miranda. It was a neutral topic; one Andy felt she could deal with. He couldn't begin to comprehend what Maddy had been through in the last week or so and since he was prone to ask stupid questions he decided not to.

Jack talked to Maddy's doctor and informed him with or without his consent, he was taking Maddy home. Fuller signed off on the release with the condition she came to his office tomorrow for a blood work up and to have some test run on the baby. He gave Jack Rosario's phone number to get in contact about setting up an appointment for tomorrow and in light of what just happened, it wasn't a request.

Jack found Bryan had been taken down to the ER. He discovered what bay he was in and went in without asking.

Bryan looked at him and flinched as an intern was stitching his chest. "Hey Bud, how's our girl hanging in there."

Jack made a face and shrugged lightly. "I don't really know. She is kind of distant, detached."

"She's in shock, Jack. It's to be expected." Bryan watched the intern wipe away the seeping blood as he continued to stitch. "Mother fucker got me good. Four inches long, two inches deep. Had to stitch it in layers. Poor Maddy, I'm sure it was like reliving some things all over again."

Jack leaned against the wall. "Did you see what happened...after she cocked him with the bedpan?"

Bryan got quiet. "We'll talk about it later. They said I can leave here when they are done, but don't want me to be alone."

"That's simple enough to take care of, you will come and stay with us," Jack told him.

"It's your first night home. You need to be alone." He sucked in a breath as the intern squeeze the edges of the wound together, "God damn it! What the fuck are you doing?"

"Sorry Sir," the intern answered feebly.

"No Bryan, I think it would be easier for everyone involved if you did stay with us tonight. I know you said I needed to start handling these matters on my own. But I am lost here. It would be a big favor to me if you would."

Bryan studied Jack. This man was so self-confident in every part of his life except where Maddy was concerned. He was at a loss as to what do with her pain. He better wise up, she needed him to be strong. But for now, he would go stay with them, not for Jack's sake, but for Maddy's. "Go take her home and get her settled then you can come back for me. They won't let me drive. Stop by here on your way out so she can see for herself that I am okay."

"Will do." Jack turned and left.

He went out to his car and grabbed some clothing out of one of Maddy's suitcases, which had been in his car since the day Maddy was snatched when he took them out of the rental car. If Bryan had just let him take her back to his place like he wanted maybe none of this would have happened. But he knew blaming Bryan was just stupid. He never was one to play the blame game and felt things happened because it was they way it was meant to be.

Once he took the clothing up he gave it to Maddy so she could get cleaned up and get dressed. He signed the release papers and they were ready to go. She said nothing to him as they took the elevator down to the lower level. "Bryan wants you to stop in and see him before we leave. I'm going to take you home then come back and get him. He will be staying with us for a couple of days." He watched her reaction.

She just nodded and said "Okay."

When Maddy entered the ER bay, the intern was bandaging Bryan's chest. "Hey, Minnie," he smiled. "Finally you're getting to go home."

A flood of relief washed over her face seeing him smile. She thought they were lying to her, telling her he was okay and he wasn't. She stood over him and brushed the hair away from his eyes and kissed his forehead. "You really are alive."

Bryan chuckled, "Honey, you know damn well I have lived through worse." Then he looked down and looked back at her. "You save my life, Maddy," he said quietly. "I wouldn't be here if it weren't for you."

She bent over and softly kissed him on the lips, "No you saved my life by coming in when you did. I thought I was done for."

He reached out and touched her nose. "Let's just call it even okay?"

She smiled softly, "Okay, even."

"Let Jack take you home and get you settled, then he's going to come back and get me. We will talk more later okay...and Maddy, help him out a little. He doesn't know what we do. He hasn't seen what we have so he doesn't have a clue what it feels like. Do you understand what I am saying?" He squeezed her hand.

"I just feel numb right now. I mean I honestly feel nothing."

"It's shock honey. We'll get through it," he laughed half-heartedly, "Well you found away for me to stay a little longer, but you didn't have to go to this extreme."

Maddy laughed softly, "I didn't want you to stay that badly."

Jack popped his head in, "You ready Maddy?" He nodded at Bryan.

"Yeah, be right there." She leaned over and kissed Bryan. "I will see you soon, Mickey."

Jack led Maddy to his car and opened the door for her. She turned to him and pulled him close. "I'm sorry for all this. For the hell I've put you through."

Jack held her back away from him and searched her face, "What you put me through? Baby, none of this is your fault. You didn't do anything, it was done to you."

She slid her hands up his chest as she leaned her head against him. "I love you, Jack."

"I love you, too, Maddy." He held her head next to him as he looked off over the parking lot. Something just wasn't right with her. But then again what did he expect? He was glad Bryan would be there to help him.

They spoke little on the drive home. Maddy commented on the change in weather, how quickly summer had turned into fall. She felt like she had been put in this time capsule and had just been released. She didn't know how she felt. She didn't know what she thought...about anything.

Jack grabbed Maddy's bags out of the back of his car and set them on the kitchen floor.

Maddy looked around, searching, "Where's Eddie?"

"At Mom and Dad's. I will go get him tomorrow. You want something to eat? I don't have much for groceries. I will have to go shopping tomorrow."

Maddy shook her head. Food was the furthest thing from her mind. "You haven't been staying here?"

"No...I couldn't without you here," he told her softly.

She turned to him and smiled weakly, "Well, I'm home, sweetie, and I'm not going anywhere...ever again."

As she turned to walk away, Jack grabbed her hand, "Maddy, you are scaring me...is there anything I can do to help?"

She frowned and shook her head. "No...I just need to take in everything that's happened okay? I will be all right, I just need to process it and find a place for it. I'm going to go take a shower and lie down for a bit while you go get Bryan."

After Maddy finished her shower, she slipped into something comfortable and laid down on the bed. She breathed in the scent of it and smiled. A real bed, their bed, soft and cozy and so many good memories. She turned on her side and tucked her hands up under her face.

She remembered everything, no mental blocks, nothing. She knew the harsh reality of what happened to her. The only blanks were when she was drugged up. But why couldn't she feel anything? Why couldn't she find release? And if she couldn't, would she be able to let go of it?

Jack pulled his car next to the ER entrance and helped Bryan into his car. They had put his shoulder in a sling to keep the stress off the wound. They told Bryan he had to keep still to avoid pulling on the stitches.

Bryan groaned when he slid into the seat. "I am not wearing a fucking seat belt," he said half joking.

"We're cops, who gives a damn," Jack laughed.

Jack put the car in gear and they took off.

"Can you swing by the motel and pick up some clothes for me. Give us some time to talk." Bryan grimaced as he tried to make himself more comfortable.

Jack nodded in agreement. He paused then said, "Derek said Maddy..."

"Methodically killed Parsons?" Bryan looked at him with a raised eyebrow.

"I guess that would be one way to put it."

Bryan breathed in slowly, "That's what I wanted to talk to you about. I saw it, Jack, all of it. They were struggling on the floor. The next thing I knew Maddy had my gun in her hands. She could have grabbed my cuffs, but she didn't. She could have held him at bay until someone got there, but she didn't. Even if she had just shot him once..."

"But she didn't," Jack finished for him.

"She pointed the gun at him, ordered him to stand up. Her grip on that gun was steady, unflinching. She flat assed told him she was going to send him to hell. Then she methodically shot him. She took her time Jack. She wanted him totally aware of what she was doing and why she was doing it. Once she had him helpless on the floor, she brought the gun to his head. She asked him something like if it hurt, was he suffering, then said good. She said something else I didn't quite catch, then she said see you in hell and pulled the trigger." Bryan looked over at Jack trying to see his reaction. He was too hard to read. "Talk to me kid."

Jack bit his lower lip. "I don't know what to say. I feel what she did—he had it coming. Do I feel as an officer of the law it was justifiable...no, not according to the use unnecessary force. But Bryan, when it comes to this, I'm not a cop, I am me. He tortured her and tried to kill her twice. What would any sane person expect her to do? Act like a cop? I don't think so." He glanced at Bryan, "Derek called it a opportunistic revenge killing."

Bryan looked at him sharply. "Fuck, Derek said that? Is he going to file it like that?"

"No, he said it was a clear cut case of self-defense, and as far as how she did it, she must have snapped. Said she had been through enough." Jack paused, "Did she snap? I mean do you believe she was out of her mind when she did it?"

Jack had just pulled into the motel parking lot and turned to Bryan. "Tell me honestly."

Bryan looked out across the lot, "Would it make anything difference to you?"

Jack thought about it briefly. "You know, I almost would feel better about it if I thought she knew what she was doing, because that would be her choice, her in control, not some reaction out of being his victim. Does it make any sense and am I wrong thinking like this?"

Bryan looked at him square in the face. "Maddy knew exactly what she was doing. I believe it was the sanest thing she ever did." And he believed it with all his heart.

Jack helped Bryan into the house. "Can I get you something before I show you to your room?"

Bryan laughed, "Nice glass of that whiskey you have in the cupboard and a couple of my pain killers. That ought to put me out for a bit." He leaned against the counter and wiped off the sweat beading up on his forehead. He hurt like fucking hell.

He watched Jack pull out a couple of glasses and fill them with the amber liquid. He handed one to Bryan and set on in front him. "You look like hell."

Bryan took out a bottle of pills from his pants pockets and shook out two onto the counter. "Well that's good because I feel like hell. I would hate to waste it all for nothing." He popped the pills in his mouth and washed them down with the entire glass of whiskey. He felt the fire surge through him into his belly. What he really would have loved was to take that bottle and drink down the remainder, but that was not an option. "Okay, I'm ready."

"With the exception of thinking you were dead...she hasn't shed a tear."

"Huh?" Bryan looked over at him.

"Maddy, she hasn't cried. Does that mean she is building a wall?" Jack asked as he took a sip of the whiskey.

"Kid, I told you, she's in shock...Have you ever taken a life?"

"No."

"We have, both Maddy and I, on more than one occasion. You don't ever get used to it. You can't ever prepare yourself for it. And even though the person you killed deserved to die, it doesn't make it any easier. You still can't justify it to your conscience. It eats at you, each time worse then the last. Don't judge Maddy by how she acting. She's coping the only way she knows how. Give her time, just be there for her." Bryan held out his glass for Jack to fill. Now he wasn't so ready.

Jack swooshed the liquid around in his glass, "Maybe I'm not the one she needs," he said quietly. "Maybe I'm not strong enough to help her. Maybe it's you she needs to be with." Jack looked up at him.

Bryan took a deep breath and flinched. "You shouldn't say that too often, Jack, I might just start believing you...Now if you wouldn't mind showing me where I can crash I would appreciate it. These pills are taking affect quickly."

Jack grabbed Bryan's bag and helped him upstairs to one of the guest rooms. "Do you need any help getting into bed?"

"No, I can manage. Thanks." Jack turned to leave the room when Bryan spoke to him. "Jack, I am only going to tell you this once, Maddy loves *you*, she has agreed to marry *you*, and she is carrying *your* child. Get your head out of your ass and be the man she needs you to be. Goodnight...and thanks for letting me stay."

Jack slipped into his room. The only light in the room was the dim reflection of the yard light slipping between the partially opened blinds. It wasn't that late but it had been a long day and all he wanted to go do was to crawl in his bed and hold his woman. He kicked off his shoes, slipped off his socks. He stripped down to his shorts and crawled in next to Maddy.

She was curled up in the fetal position, her hands tucked neatly under her cheek. Her breath was soft and steady.

Maddy felt the bed give to Jack's weight as slipped in beside her. She waited for him to wrap his arms around her but he didn't. He just snuggled up to her back close enough she could feel his breath on her neck. She could smell the faint scent of whiskey and tobacco...and his cologne. She breathed it in deeply letting it fill her senses. She felt calming warmth spread through her. Thank God, she could feel something.

Maddy shifted her body to face him. He didn't move even though she knew he was awake. She sat up and gently pushed him on to his back. She lay across his chest, her face resting on her arms. "I love you."

Jack stroked her back softly with his fingertips, "I love you, Maddy, but is it enough?"

Maddy looked at him confused, "I'm not sure what you mean, what do you mean is it enough? Is your love enough?"

"Even though I love you more than life itself, what if my love is not enough to be what you need me to be?"

She could see his eyes looking down at her, searching. Maddy scooted her body up higher so they were face to face. "Jack, you are everything I will ever need. Don't ever doubt that. Where is this coming from?"

"I'm not what you need. You need Bryan. He is the one that gives you strength and support. He is the one who knows how to take care of you, to be there for you in any situation. I can love you, Maddy, but I can't protect you like he can."

Maddy sat up and looked at him in disbelief. "Are you trying to piss me off? Because if you are you are doing a damn good job at it." She smacked his chest, "How dare you. After everything we have been through, after everything I told you I thought while I was gone." She hit him again and the stood up. "I can't believe you!" She stormed out of the room, slamming the door behind screaming, "Asshole!" as she took off downstairs.

Jack got up looked down the hall making sure Maddy was nowhere around. He quietly walked down the hall and popped his head in on Bryan.

He could hear Bryan laughing, "Did it work?"

Jack smiled and chuckled, "Like a charm."

"Told you she can still feel, now go find her. Make-up sex will make her feel even better."

Jack heard him snicker and then give out a little yelp, "Son of bitch that hurt."

Maddy found her way into the den and crawled up on the window seat. She pulled her feet up underneath her and stared out the window. She was so angry with Jack. What the hell was he thinking? Where the hell did he get the idea she was better off with Bryan? She knew damn well it wasn't from Bryan. Was he testing her? What did she ever do to make him doubt her? She hadn't been with Bryan since they had been together. Or was it like Bryan had hinted to her earlier, Jack was insecure about what to do for her, to help her get through this. Jack hated feeling helpless and Lord knows he felt like that a lot lately. But still...

She turned her head and watched a shadowy figure move towards her. She knew that physique—that was her baby. She turned back towards the window. Asshole wasn't getting off that easy.

He came up to her silently, sat down on the edge of the seat, took her head in his hands and crushed her lips with his own. He tongue parted her lips, slipping it deep into her mouth.

Maddy pressed her hands against his chest, pushing half-heartedly against him. Her protest was short lived as he wound his fingers through her hair and continued to explore her mouth. She moaned softly as her arms crept up around his neck. She fervently returned his kiss, sliding her body into his.

Jack pulled back and stood up. He knelt down and scooped her up into his arms. Without speaking to her he carried her up to their bed and laid her down and slid in next to her. When Maddy opened her mouth to say something, he silenced her with a hungry kiss. He lifted his head, his hand stroked her hair as he looked into her eyes. "No more talking...no more doubts." His mouth returned to hers.

Maddy felt alive again in his arms. He had taken her breath away, her heart was beating wildly, and her desire to be completed by him was intense. So long... it had been so long since she felt him. She ran her fingers lightly grazing his chest and ran them over the smoothness of his back. When his hand slid beneath her top and cupped her breast she took a quick intake. She turned her head. "Wait..." She moved away from him long enough to peel her clothes off and threw them off to the side. She knelt on her knees and tugged on his shorts until they came off and joined hers on the floor. She slid her body up his; their naked skin touching sending shivers up through both of them.

Jack wrapped his arms around her and rolled them over so he was on top. She was his tonight, he was loving her, she did belong with him...to him. He claimed her mouth again as his hands searched out her breast. He felt Maddy's hand slid down over his hips. When she touched him her hands felt like fire searing into his skin. He gasped as her hands ran up the length of him. He was planning on making long sweet love to her, but he needed her, need to be part of her.

Once she touched Jack and felt his response her body ached with desire for him. She tore her mouth away from his, panting heavily. "Need you...now..." she pleaded between breaths.

As Jack moved between her legs and gently pushed inside her, he moaned. God she was so sweet. He loved the feel of her as she pushed into him creating a soft gentle rhythm. He braced himself with his arms so he could watch her face as he made love to her.

Maddy held on to his hips firmly, as if she were guiding him inside her. She softly whimpered each time he thrust into her. She wrapped her legs around his and arched her body into him so she could feel the full length of him. She felt the urgency building as he thrust more quickly and harder inside her. She dug her nails into him and cried out as he shuttered inside her.

Jack stayed where he was; not wanting to break the connection. Sweat glistened on their bodies; both were trying hard to catch their breath.

"Cramp...Cramp." Jack rolled over grabbing his calf.

Maddy laughed and crawled down to the end of the bed. She grabbed his foot and put her palms against the bottom of his foot. "Push against my hands."

"I can't...hurts too fucking much," he whined.

She slapped him. "Do what you're told," she ordered laughing.

He finally did what she told him to do and pushed his foot into her hand. She pushed up with one hand on the ball of his foot until the cramp subsided.

When Maddy felt him relaxed she crawled up in the bed beside and rested her head in the crook of his arm.

"Two nights ago I was in a grave, tonight, I'm in heaven" she said softly.

Jack leaned over and softly kissed her. "You are here with me now and you're not ever leaving."

"I killed a man today," she told him flatly. "And the scary part is, Jack, I took great pleasure in doing it. What does that say about me?" She turned her body to face him.

"You are not a monster, Kitten. You gave evil what he deserved. You should feel vindicated by all his victims. You gave them a voice they never had a chance to speak. Don't feel you need to punish yourself over it, okay?" he told as he pushed her hair behind her ear.

"You really believe that?"

He kissed her forehead, "Yes."

They were lying there when Maddy gasped. "Do you think Bryan heard us?"

Jack laughed softly, "So what if he did?" He glanced over at her seeing the look of horror on her face. He gave her a little squeeze, "Don't worry about it, Kitten, I put in the room at the far end of the hall."

"How is he...injury wise?"

"Parsons gave him a nasty gash, four inches long, two inches deep he said. They got him all stitched up, can't move around too much for a few days. So I guess we're stuck with him. Man that's gotta suck for you," he teased.

"The end is near," Maddy said softly.

"Not the end baby, just a new beginning."

"Maybe I should go talk to him," she started to get up.

Jack pulled her back down, "No, you're staying with me. He needs to rest, seriously. He was hurting pretty bad. He took some painkillers and couple of shots of whiskey. You can talk to him in the morning." He pulled the covers back. "Come Kitten, home is waiting for you."

Maddy woke up in the wee hours of the morning. She wanted to talk to Bryan. She slipped out of bed and slipped a nightshirt on and thought she was quietly slipping out of the room.

"If he's asleep, leave him be, otherwise don't be a pain in the ass," Jack mumbled as he rolled over.

"Damn, it's like you have radar," she whispered.

"I do. Come back to bed when you're done."

Maddy smiled, leaned over and kissed him on the cheek, "I love you."

"I know....now go."

Maddy left the door ajar and quietly crept down the hall. She slowly turned the door handle and opened the door. She softly slid onto the bed and snuggled up to Bryan leaning her head against his shoulder.

"Been a long time since I've had you in my bed, Minnie. Too bad I hurt too much to do anything about it," Bryan whispered. "Jack knows you're here? I don't want you to get into trouble."

"No, he knows. Is there something I can get you?"

"A glass of water and a couple of pills out of the bottle on the nightstand would be nice."

Maddy took off down the hall to get a glass of water. "Kitten?" she heard Jack call to her as she walked by the bedroom. She poked her head in, "Huh?"

"Is he okay?" he asked.

"Sounds like he's in a lot of pain. He doesn't look too good." She was a worried he was hurt more than they were telling her. "I'm getting him water so he can take his pills."

"You want me to go get it?"

Maddy laughed. "I think I'm capable. Go back to sleep, sweetie."

When she returned from the kitchen with a glass of ice water, she could hear Bryan softly moaning from the hallway. She turned the on lamp and quickly noticed a red stain on his bandage. "You're bleeding. Did they send extra bandages home with you?" She handed him the pills and the water.

He popped the pills in his mouth and washed them down. "Over there in my bag."

Maddy grabbed the bandages and the dressing, moved to his side of the bed and slowly removed the soiled bandages. "That mother fucker," she whispered as she saw the long gash still seeping blood. Maddy took off to the bathroom, grabbed a wet washcloth and towel and returned to the room. She dabbed the blood away, then lightly dabbed the wound with the towel. She places a couple of gauze pads across the cut then taped the bandage over top. "There, almost as good as new. I will let you get some sleep. We can talk later.

"Come lay with me until the pills kick in...please?" he asked her, his voice just a whisper.

Maddy moved to the other side of the bed. He held his arms up so she could lie in the crook of his arm. She gently put her arms across his stomach.

"I saw what you did today...to Parsons."

"How do you feel about it?" she asked.

"The point is, how do you feel about what you did?"

"Justified."

"Good."

"How much trouble am I in?"

"None, Derek wrote up as a justifiable homicide. Self defense."

"What about when the autopsy reports get back? You can't dispute the overkill."

"They will be lost in the paper work and never find their way into the file. The case is closed. We will protect you. Am getting really tired, sweetheart. Would you do me a favor?"

"Sure, what do you need?" she asked.

"A kiss from you, a real kiss, Minnie."

Maddy slid up along his arm being real careful not jar him around. She leaned in and tentatively kissed his soft lips. He reached up with his hand and held her head as he savored the tenderness of her lips. His mouth covered hers, prying it open with his tongue and took in her sweetness. Maddy responded, kissing him back with an undeniable passion. Her body was responding to him despite the fact she had just made love to Jack hours ago.

Bryan was the first to break the kiss. "Thank you, Minnie. Was just as I remembered. Go back to Jack now. We will talk more in the morning." He pulled her back down and kissed her deeply one more time. "Now go before I loose control and be less than honorable."

Maddy returned to her and Jack's room and slid beneath the covers snuggling up to Jack.

"How is he?" he mumbled.

"Asleep. Goodnight baby."

"Goodnight Kitten."

Jack stirred from his sleep, his arms wrapped around Maddy waist as she faced away from him. He ran his hand down her body and across her hips. He felt his desire for rise. His hand found its way up under her nightshirt. His fingers slipped under her panties and slowly removed them from her body. He watched to see if she was waking up. She hardly moved. He adjusted his body to hers and gently guided himself into her.

"Mmmmmm..." Maddy's hand came up behind her reaching out for his head as she felt him push inside her. She felt his strong, firm hands on her hips guiding, holding her as he thrust deep inside her. "Oh...baby..."she gasped. "What you are doing to me?" she moaned.

His hand slip up across her breast caressing her, his finger rubbing her nipple, "You likey?" he whispered in her ear smiling.

"Mmmmmhhmmm, me likey..." She felt him push deeper and faster inside her sending waves of electricity coursing through her. Her fingers frantically grabbed his hair and pulled his face down to her where she could kiss the side of his face.

The feel of Maddy response pushed his need for her even higher. Her body was compliant to his snuggling fit into his molding her body to him. She pushed into his body meeting his thrusts, their bodies moving as one. The sound of her moans and gasping sent him over the edge and he exploded inside her. She screamed out as her fingers dug into his hair.

He held her in place until the wave subsided and their breathing became more even, kissing her neck. Maddy moaned softly. "My Kitten purrs," he chuckled.

Maddy grasped his hand and brought it to her lips kissing his fingers one at a time. "Damn," she grinned. "That's all I can say...damn."

"I love you would be nice," he nuzzled her ear.

She leaned her head back to trying to look at his eyes, but it was too awkward in the position they were in. She turned in his arms so she was facing him. She kissed him softly, "I do love you. You're my baby."

His fingers reached out and brush the hair away from her eyes. "Speaking of baby...how long can we keep doing...this?"

Maddy laughed, "Making love? Honey, we can make love until the cows come home until it gets to be too uncomfortable." She watched his face and laughed again.

Jack felt the heat rise to his face, "Hell, Kitten, how would I know? I don't know anything about this shit."

Maddy laid back in the bed, "I'll buy you a book," she laughed.

When Jack came into the kitchen Maddy was trying to replace the bandages on her wrists and was having a hard time doing it.

"What are you doing?" he asked alarmed. "What did you take them off for? I told you I didn't want you seeing them."

"Oh for Christ sake Jack, how much worse can it be then what I saw and did yesterday. Help me out here." She held out the bandage and the tape.

Jack readjusted the gauze pads and began to wrap the bandage around her wrist. "I'm confused. You are handling this so much different than what everyone told me to expect. I mean this is good, I mean better than the alternative."

"People handle things in different ways, even from one situation to the next. What happened to me now isn't the same as what happened then. I watched as my children were senselessly murdered. I couldn't cope with that loss. This time what happened happened to me. What loss did I suffer? None. Yes, I endured some pretty horrific things, but I am okay, I lived through it. I know for fact he will never hurt me or anyone else ever again. I know that because *I* saw to it." She watched as Jack snipped the tape and secured it to the bandage and moved on to the next one.

"So you believe this is all done and over with? No repercussions? No triggers?" He eyed her above the bandage.

"I don't know. Probably not, I am sure I will have a lot of shit to deal with, but the point is I am not dysfunctional. I don't want to succumb to his evil and let it cripple me. For once in my life I have so much going for me. We need to get down to the station and formally close this investigation. I want to go down to the Journal and find out what's going on down there. We need to figure out how we're going to handle this living situation..."

"We need to plan a wedding," Jack added.

Maddy smiled at him. "Yeah that too." She paused, "I'd don't want to tell anyone I'm pregnant."

"Why? I thought you were happy about it. Or is it because we're not married?"

"No, silly, who care's about that? You never tell anyone until after the first trimester. It's bad luck."

"Why?"

"If something is going to go wrong, it's usually in the first trimester," she told him.

A shadow of doubt crossed Jack's face. Maddy laid her hand on his arm. "Baby, don't worry about it. If this kid made it through what I just went through, he is one tough kid. Nothing is going to happened to him."

Jack smiled, "Him?"

"Or her, don't get your hopes up just yet."

He secured the last of the tape. "How about your ankles?"

She pulled up her pant leg. "All taken care of. Are you going with me to the station?"

Bryan slowly came into the room, "Do you really think you should be going in? Christ Maddy, you just got out of the hospital."

Maddy poured him a cup of coffee and set it in front of him. "Why not? I just want to get these files closed up, put it to rest."

"And chase me out here that much quicker," he commented as he blew on his coffee.

Maddy frowned. "You know that's not true. Besides I thought we took care of that with your injury. You can't go anywhere for a little while right?"

"Maddy, I think you are pushing things a little too fast. Despite the way you are acting, and what you may be feelings, it's not real. You and I both know it." Bryan set his cup down.

Maddy poured herself a glass of juice, "If I don't think about it, don't deal with it, it's not there is it?" She looked at him with her eyebrows raised.

Jack watched the exchange between the two of them. Once again Bryan knew Maddy better than he did. He just took her at her word she was okay, not that she was in a state of denial. "I fucking give up. Damn it, Maddy if you can't be honest with me what the fuck is the point?" He grabbed he keys off the counter.

"Jack, wait! Where are you going?" Maddy reached for him.

He pulled away. "I don't fucking know, but I am tired of feeling like I'm the only one playing the game that's missing the game pieces and doesn't know the rules. Think about it, Maddy. You come completely clean with me about everything or when Bryan leaves...you leave with him. I'm done." He turned and slammed the door as left. She heard the garage door go up and him tear out of the garage.

Maddy sat quietly on the stool. "I'm sorry he doesn't know me the way you do. Christ, you and I have been through so much, you know me better than anyone. How can he think that he and I can be like that when we really haven't been together that long? Yeah, I told him I was okay, because I am okay. Why does everyone think I have to be an open book and nothing is my own to keep? I can't do this. He's got to believe in me or he doesn't. It's not going to work. I should have known I couldn't be someone I'm not, no matter how bad I want it." She slipped the ring off her finger and left it on the counter. She grabbed her bag.

"Maddy don't be irrational. Don't do something you're going to regret," Bryan called after her.

Bryan sat at the bar with his cup of coffee in front of him. "Ooooookay, now this is awkward."

Bryan was still sitting at the bar looking through the paper when he heard a vehicle pull in the garage. He had hoped it would be Maddy, but it was Jack.

Jack came in and set a bag of groceries on the counter. His eyes were drawn immediately to the ring laying on the counter. He picked it up, touching it with his fingers. What had he done going off on her like that? "Where is she?"

Bryan shook his head, "I don't know, kid. She's upset. She's back to that notion that she has the right to keep things to herself and deal with it on her own. She doesn't feel she's not being up front with you. She just wants to be a normal human being without everyone casting doubt over everything she does. She just wanted you to believe in her."

"Is that in her words or yours?"

"I don't know what the hell is going on with you. You have known all along how things are between Maddy and me. It's just the way we are. I can read her better than anyone. Don't get pissed at me and blame me for that. Would you rather I ignore what I see and let her just cover everything up just to blow up in her face years later or deal with it now? Don't threaten her, especially with her emotions," he pointed to the ring in his hand. "Or that is what you are going to get."

"So she chose you..." he stared at the ring.

"God damn it," Bryan slammed the palm of his hand down on the counter and flinched, "Fuck that hurt. She didn't choose me. It was never about choosing me. What she did, Jack, is something you are going to have to fix, and fix it fast, but what she chose—she chose to run."

Jack took out his cell, "Fuck, I can't even call her. She doesn't have her cell. Jesus, Bryan where do I start to look?"

Bryan slowly stood up. "Come on."

"Where?"

"The station. She's hell bent on formally closing this case. She is either there are heading home."

When they arrived at the station, Jack didn't wait for Bryan. He was on his own. He had to find Maddy and fix what he had fucked up.

He found her at the evidence board pulling pictures off and placing them in the box. She didn't look at him when he entered. "Can we talk?" he asked her softly.

"What's the point? I thought you pretty much said it all," she responded coldly as placed more photos in the box.

"I fucked up, I'm sorry. I just keep feeling that when it comes to you, what goes on inside your head...I'm not a part of it and you don't want me to be. That it's yours and Bryan's secret to keep. As long as he has that part of you, he has you," Jack tried to explain his actions.

Maddy leaned against her old desk. "He will always have that part of me, but he doesn't have me, you do. God, has nothing we've been through proven anything to you? I don't think I should have to keep proving to you how much I love you." She poked him in the chest, "you should damn well know it here!"

"I do know it," he snapped.

"Then act like it!"

"I'm scared, God damn it! I can't loose you and I'm afraid I am going to loose you..." he waved his had around the room. "to this...to him."

She studied him, "To Bryan?"

Jack shook his head slowly, "No...to Parsons."

Maddy took a deep breath. "He's dead. He can't hurt us anymore."

"But he is still alive in here," he touched her head.

"I promise Jack, I will deal with it."

"How? By pretending it never happened?"

"No! I will be a good little girl following my shrink's orders. Just let me live my life in the mean time, please..." she looked up at him, tears shimmering in her eyes.

He reached for her left hand, dug out the ring out of his pocket, and slipped it back on her finger. "Now leave it on. You're not walking away from me so easily. You have to help me out with this, Kitten. You have to be honest with me about how you're feeling, what's going through your head. I'm not Bryan, I can't read you and anticipate your needs. You have to let me know. He's not always going to be around to tell me, hon."

She looked away from him, "So everyone keeps reminding me." She got up and started ripping the pictures off the wall. "Where the hell is everybody?"

"It's Saturday, Babe. They were given the weekend off since there is no pending business. We don't have to be here either. Let me take you to your house. Get some peace."

"I don't want peace!" she snapped at him. "I have been stuck in a fucking hell hole for days...by myself. I don't want to be alone. I don't want to be left there to sit there and think about everything that happened. I can't do it, Jack, I just can't do it." She was so angry she could spit and she didn't even know where it was coming from. She thought when she killed Parsons she would be set free, but she wasn't free at all. She was stuck in this prison in her mind and she couldn't escape. And no she wasn't going to tell Jack, or Bryan either for all that matter.

"Maddy, you need to get a grip," Bryan said calmly as he came through the door. "You're out of control. Do you want to end up back in the hospital, but on a different floor?"

Maddy glared at him. She knew his meaning. "You wouldn't."

"If I thought it was best for you, I would do it a heartbeat."

"I am no danger to anyone or myself. You have no legal right to put me away," she said angrily.

"And who does Maddy? Your family? What family? I don't see anyone around looking out after your welfare. I am your supervisor. You're FBI. I own your ass legally."

Jack watched the exchange. Bryan was being just plain cruel. "What am I in all this? She's my fiancé."

Bryan turned to him, "Legally that don't mean shit. If I feel Maddy is mentally incapable of dealing with this shit on her own, I have the ability to have her committed."

Maddy shook her head violently, "Oh no you don't, not this time. You are not going to lock me away!"

"Oh just settle down. I didn't say I was going to...not yet. I am just putting you on notice."

Maddy looked down at the papers she was holding, "You're leaving and you won't have a fucking thing to say about it."

"Is this what this is about Maddy? Are you angry because I'm leaving? You knew it would be coming."

"No!" she threw the papers at him, "Because you are leaving me now! When I need you the most." She stormed out of the room.

"What the hell did you do that for? Christ, I was just getting her to communicate with me. You can't put her in a mental ward. How can you think that would do her any good? Besides, she is quitting. Then you have nothing to say about what she does," Jack argued.

"For Christ sake Jack, open up your eyes and see it for what it is. She's a powder keg waiting to blow. She needs to deal with reality and she's not. She's burying it. There's a lot more going on in that head of hers then she's letting on. You can't tell me anyone could go through what she's been through and be okay. Fuck, look how she went off on Parsons. That's not someone who has her shit together. Do you really want to wait until it's too late to help her?"

"What the fuck do you want me to do, Bryan? How can you help her if I she won't let me? And what did she mean do it to her again?

Bryan slowly sat in his chair, flinching as he did. "I was the one who signed the commitment papers to have her put in last time."

"You had her locked away in a mental institute? God, Bryan, it's a wonder she even trusts you." Jack shook his head.

"She trusts me because she knows I did the right thing. She was catatonic when it first happened. She wasn't in there very long. I didn't say I was going to do it again, but someone has to make her see she really does need to deal with this."

Derek popped his head in, "They found the crime scene where Parsons took Maddy."

"Where's Maddy. She's going with us," Bryan rose to his feet.

Jack swung his head around, "Why the hell would you do that to her?"

"Do you trust me?"

"Yeah, I guess."

"Then trust me on this. Please go find her, I can't. I hurt too fucking much. Don't tell her what we are doing." He turned to Derek. "Did someone pick up my truck?"

"Yeah, but you're not driving. I'll take us," Derek told them.

Jack found Maddy sitting on the back steps. She was still very angry and wouldn't even look at him when he sat down. "Damn, Maddy, I'm not the one who pissed you off." He pulled out a cigarette and lit it up.

"You're going to have to quit that if you're going to be around the baby. And yes you did," she said twisting the ring on her finger.

"It's not like I smoke in the house. They are waiting for us out front," he inhaled deeply and let it out slowly.

"Who?"

"Derek and Bryan."

"For what?"

"Guess we're going to go check some place out," he took another drag and then pitched it.

Maddy looked at him sideways, "Jack, you are a lousy liar."

"Okay, I'm not supposed to tell you." He stood up and offered his hand to help her up.

"Whatever," she took his hand.

Jack pulled her close and kissed her softly. "Kitten, are we okay?" Maddy turned away from him. He grabbed her chin and made her look at him. "Tell me you don't love me. Tell me you don't want to be with me anymore."

"You know I can't do that. I am just really, really pissed right now...at everyone—including you."

"Point is, Maddy, where is this anger coming from?"

She surrendered to him by laying her head on his shoulder, "I don't know Jack. It just feels like there is something inside me waiting to erupt."

"We need to call Rosario and get you in to see him. We were supposed to do it anyhow. And get you into see Fuller. Baby, you don't have to do this alone. I am here, I'm always going to be here." He brushed the back of her head with his hand. "Do you trust I will be?"

She nodded, "I guess we better get going. Bryan is already on my case. Don't know what crawled up his ass."

Jack laughed, "Hon, he's in a lot of pain, more than he's letting on. He is also pretty worried about you. Don't be angry at him because he cares."

Maddy flipped her hair over her shoulder, "I can be pissed at him if I want to be," she said snidely.

"Just don't let the anger you're feeling be taken out on him, okay?"

"If you say so."

He nudged her. "Stop it. You can be a real bitch when you want to be."

She laughed, "And you're just figuring that out?

Bryan and Derek were waiting for them in the Suburban. Maddy and Jack crawled in the back seat. Maddy decided saying nothing was better than opening her mouth and cause more problems.

As they drove across town closer to 7th Street, Maddy began to get edgy. She couldn't explain why, she just was. A sense of fear began washing over her. "What are we doing here? Where are we going?"

Jack picked up the tension in her voice. When he looked at her, she was turning pale. Her eyes had this frantic looked. "You okay?"

"I just don't know what we are doing down here."

Bryan wished he could turn to face her, but it was impossible. It even hurt too much to reach up and pull the visor down so he could see her from it. "This is Parson's turf. I thought maybe you would want to see it."

Maddy kicked him under the seat. "Why in the hell would you think that? Do you think I want to remember all this shit?"

"The key word here, Maddy...remember. You remember—you deal with it."

"Fuck you, Bryan. Why are you being so cruel to me?"

"Because I care."

"Bullshit. You are just a bully going out of your way to tourment me."

Derek pulled in front of an old dilapidated brick building. Once white, the paint was practically peeling in sheets. The windows were boarded up. A couple of patrol cars were parked in front of the entryway.

As soon as Maddy crossed the threshold she felt a coldness hit her face like a gust of wind. A chill ran up her spine and the hairs on the back of her neck stood up. Then that smell hit her like a slap in the face. The acrid metallic smell of blood. Maddy turned and ran from the building.

Jack followed her to find her around the side of the building throwing up. He pulled her hair back away from face until she stood up. Her eyes were watering, but he didn't know if was tears of from getting sick.

Bryan came out to check on her. "Are you ready to go back in?" he asked her.

Maddy wanted to beat on his chest, but instead she just glared at him. "Why are you making me do this? What do you hope to achieve?"

He reached out for her hand, "Have I ever done anything to be intentionally cruel to you?"

Maddy pulled her hand back, "Do you really want me to go there?"

He continued to hold out his hand, "Trust me, Maddy, please."

She reached her shaking hand out and took his. His hand was warm, firm and strong giving her strength. He led her back into the building. Jack put his hand on her shoulder and squeezed it reassuringly.

"I know where I am. It happened here. This is where he slaughtered all those women."

Derek handed them each a pair of latex gloves. "I know he's gone, but it's still a crime scene."

Maddy walked forward not knowing where she was going yet knew it by instinct.

Bryan held his good arm up keeping the others back, just like he did when she would do one of her crime scene reads.

She followed her nose to a room that smelled of burnt candles and rancid blood. She felt along one wall and found a light switch. When she entered, she entered alone. As she walked around the room, she did it with the eyes of a profiler. Looming in front her like a ghost was the large wooden cross. Gouges ripped into the tender wood where his victims were bound by the barbed wire. When she stepped in front of her she felt something sticky on the souls of her shoes. Drying blood, blood that had pooled as it drained from the last victim. She saw the candles, dozens of candles, long since melted down into little wax puddles. She moved to the cupboard. When she opened the first drawer, she found many small crystal bottles she knew contained holy water. Angrily, she yanked the drawer out sending the little bottles crashing to the floors splintering into hundreds of pieces. She opened the next drawer, one she hadn't seen Parsons open. Cell phones...the missing cell phones. She slowly closed the drawer.

Jack and Bryan watched her from the doorway. Bryan shook his head and whispered to Jack, "This is not the reaction I was hoping for."

Jack cocked his head toward him, "What do you want from her?"

"I want her to crack, I want her to show some emotion," he told Jack calmly. "More than just slamming glass bottles on the floor."

Maddy knelt down and pulled out a lower drawer. She found it—the wooden case. She pulled it out and set it up on the counter space. She ran her fingers down along the split seam. She flipped the gold latch open and with shaking hands opened the flaps. There it was, the home of the golden crosses. In a bed of red velvet they both had rested. The bladed one was missing. He had used it to slice Bryan and planned on using it to put an end to her. She subconsciously brought her hand to her throat. The dagger still lay nestled in its crimson home. Maddy reached in and grasped its hilt. She took it in her hands and turned seeing the chair she was strapped to. She could see traces of her own blood on the floor.

As if she had been taken over by a spell, Maddy sat down in the chair. She closed her eyes and stroked the hilt of the dagger tracing the ornamental lines.

Bryan smacked Jack on his arm. Jack threw him a dirty look. "What?"

"Here it comes."

She took the sharp point of the dagger and sliced along the bandage on her wrist letting it fall to the floor, then she repeated the process with her other wrist. The sharp point grazed her wounds causing her to flinch. She needed to feel the pain, the same pain she felt that night. She grasped the dagger with both hands bringing the hilt to her forehead. Parsons, the blonde woman, the terror in her eyes; those pleading eyes; his piercing eyes; that evil, evil laugh; his chants echoing in her ears; the flickering candlelight blinding her; the blood spilling from the young woman's chest as her eyes rolled back in her head; the golden cross, the thrusting of the golden cross; his voice resounding throughout her head, "Sweet, sweet Maddy". Maddy screamed "Die you son of bitch!" as she threw the dagger forward without opening her eyes. Her body slid to the floor as she surrendered to the pain and sorrow she had bottled up inside her.

Jack moved to go to her, but Bryan held him back. "Not yet.

Maddy began to sob uncontrollability. He hurt her, he robbed her of her freedom, he fucked with her mind; he tortured her by making her witness his satanic ritual. And then he couldn't even kill her right. If only he would have done it right, none of this would have mattered.

Bryan nodded for Jack to enter. Jack knelt down beside her. She looked up at him, her eyes shining.

Jack's face came into focus. Parsons was gone. "He deserved to die," she whimpered. "He deserved it. I killed him. I killed him for all off us. He had to die. He had to pay. We can't rest, we can't be free until he burns in hell..."

Jack wrapped his arms around her and brought her to her feet. "He's gone Kitten. You did it; you freed them all. He is burning in hell, baby." He led her out of the room.

Bryan entered the room, Derek right behind him. "Would you fucking look at that?" Derek pointed to the dagger. It had lodged itself at the intersecting point of the wooden cross. "Kind of creepy isn't it?"

Bryan shook his head, "There are no words for it. Have them do what ever they need to do to get rid of this place," he said as he turned to leave.

When he stepped out of the building the bright sunlight blinded him. He covered his eyes and saw Jack and Maddy standing beside the Suburban. Maddy's head rested against Jack's shoulder. He held her hand in his.

Bryan lightly stroked her hair, afraid to say anything to her for fear she hated him for putting her through this. He was surprised when she turned to him and buried her face in his chest. He held her with one arm and kissed the top of her head. "I'm sorry, Minnie. It was the only thing I could think of to do to bring you back. I'm so, so sorry."

Maddy's mind was fog. She didn't want to think, she didn't want to feel. She just wanted to feel safe in Bryan's arms. She tilted her head up and kissed him softly. When she ran her hands up his chest he flinched. She pulled back his jacket and saw a bloody stain on his shirt. "Honey, you're bleeding. Let's get you home and take care of that. Then you need to rest."

She helped him to the passenger seat. She turned to Jack and kissed him tenderly. "Thank you, baby, you were and are here for me."

Jack drove he and Bryan home, Maddy followed up the rear. She still refused to let herself think about what happened. She knew it was real. She still felt the rawness from the whole event. She wasn't angry with Bryan for making her face it. She knew why. She needed to break the spell Parsons had on her that was preventing to....freak out. Everything she had been doing was controlled, right down to blowing his head off. All she had been feeling was angry. Angry it happened in the first place. She put herself in place for him to abduct her. She was angry she even allowed herself to get involved in this mess. But most of all, she was angry with Parsons for being so damn evil under the ruse of God.

Bryan would soon be leaving. She thought she was prepared for it and could handle it, but the closer he came to leaving, the more her heart ached and she felt this sense of panic of being without him. She had come to depend on him for her deep emotional needs. She loved him, very much and that would never go away. Sometimes she thought about it...being with him one last time. But she would never, ever do that to Jack. For Christ sake she was carrying his baby. If she weren't, would she? She didn't want to think about it. She felt guilty just for it having entered her mind.

Jack already had Bryan in the house when she pulled in the garage. Bryan was sitting at the bar, a glass of whisky and a bottle of pills in front of him. When she looked at his face, she saw the weariness and pain in his eyes. He never should have been out running around today, but he did it for her. Everything he seemed to do, he did for her.

Maddy ran up to his room and went through his bag to find more bandages. She came across a photo in the bottom of his bag. She let out a little cry when she saw it. It was a picture of Bryan with his arms wrapped around her, Scotty and Lexy each holding on to one of his legs. She slid the photo back into his bag, grabbed the supplies and took off back down stairs. Maybe she would talk to him about it later. Maybe it was something he wanted to keep private.

Maddy helped him off with his jacket and his shirt. She carefully pulled off the bandage. The stitches were still holding, but they looked stressed. He probably should have stayed in the hospital, but she knew how badly he freaked out in them. It was amazing he spent as much time there when she was in there. She replaced the bandage without saying much. Actually she had hardly said a word since she got home. "Okay, now get your ass to bed."

Maddy walked him up to his bedroom and helped him lie down. "Come lie with me, Minnie," he requested softly.

She crawled onto the bed and lay in the crook of his arms. Her fingers lightly touched his bare chest. She felt little sparks fly through her. Bryan picked up on it instantly. He brought her face up to his and kissed her hungrily, urgently... desperately. Maddy returned his kiss with crazy emotions running through her.

Bryan ended the kiss. "We are going to get into trouble," he told her softly. "We can't do this to Jack, and I meant what I said, if I make love to you again, Maddy. I won't let you go. You will be with me." He brushed her cheek. "Do you understand what I am saying?"

She nodded, kissed him on the cheek and then slid off the bed. "Rest Mickey. We will talk later."

It seemed like it was taking forever for Maddy to come back down. What was going on up there? He was picking up some weird vibes from her, and it was making him nervous. He climbed the stairs, happened to look into his bedroom and found Maddy lying on the bed staring at the ceiling.

She glanced over at him. "Come and hold me baby, I need you."

He sat down on the bed. "Do you want to be with me, or are you having second thoughts about being with Bryan?"

Maddy propped her head up with her arm, "Why are you doing this? How many times today have you made reference to me being with Bryan? Where is this coming from?"

"You, him. I'm just picking up on something going on between you and him. You two aren't hard to read. I feel like you're pulling away from me and moving towards him."

"Jack, it's just the realization he will be leaving me soon. I am finding it hard to cope with. We all knew I would...ever since he came here. It's going to hurt, hurt like hell. But we will get through it...somehow. It doesn't mean I love you any different, that I don't want to be with you. We have so much to look forward to. We have a future. I could never have that with Bryan, you know it," Maddy tried to explain. Did he really pick up on something between her and Bryan? Twice now she had felt a desire to be with him, and twice they walked away from it. Well, Bryan had. If he hadn't stop would she have? She didn't want to go there. She would have to watch herself in the future.

"If you thought you could have a future with him would you go with him?"

Maddy sighed and lay back down. "You need to stop this, Jack. You're starting to piss me off. One of the things I have always admired in you was your self—confidence. Where is it because I'm not feeling it?"

"I don't know. I guess you are not the only one who has to find yourself again. Hopefully when things get back to normal..."

"Things will never be the same, you know that don't you?"

"I just want things to be the same between you and me," he said solemnly.

30

Jack made supper and he asked if Maddy wanted to bring it up to Bryan.

"No, you go ahead. I'm sure you and he have a lot to catch up on analyzing me," she replied picking at her chicken casserole.

Jack knocked on the door and entered when Bryan acknowledged him. He waited until Bryan struggled as he sat up in the bed. He placed the tray if front him and pulled up a chair next to the bed. "How you feeling?"

"Like getting shot would have been easier. I don't like being helpless. It's my controlling side kicking in. How's Maddy?"

"Irritable. I think she is getting real annoyed with me," he said as he played with a string fraying of the edge of his jean pant leg.

"Are you annoying her?"

"Yes, I'm letting self-doubt effect our relationship, and she's getting pissed."

Bryan swallowed a bite of food and wiped his mouth, "Doubting yourself about what?

Jack met Bryan's gaze. "You."

Bryan sat down his fork, "Why?

"I get the feeling you would like to...have her back."

Bryan took a deep breath, flinching as he did, "You are being paranoid. I'm going tell you something, and I do NOT want this repeated to Maddy. She will only take it personal and it's really got nothing to do with her. As soon as I get the okay to travel, I am leaving that same day. Jack, I have been living out of a motel for over two months. I have been on this emotional rollercoaster, same one as you, but you got the girl. I lost her. I was doing a job I was totally unprepared for and did a shitty job doing it. I want to go home, Jack. I need to get my life back on track and I don't want to delay it anymore. I need to find a place to live, get acclimated in my old position, I need to move on. I promised Maddy we would still have a relationship. I want it as much as she does. I have six weeks of vacation time coming and I will fly out to see you guys when I can and stay in touch with at least weekly phone calls. I will be there for her, but not like I am now. You will have to let me know when the wedding is so I can put in for time off. And yes I will try to be here when the baby comes. Does this make you feel better?"

It was Jack's turn to feel like an ass. "No, because it makes me see how selfish I have been. I never stopped to think about your side and what will happen for you when you leave. I'm sorry."

"Maddy has a lot on her plate, Jack. She's dealing with what she just experienced. She went from being in solitude, to not only having a boyfriend, but getting married and having a baby. All this in a very short amount of time. Cut her some slack, give her support. She doesn't need your unfounded doubts where she will feel she needs to prove her love for you. She's off her meds, it's going to play hell with her emotional stability...and she pregnant, mood swings galore," Bryan chuckled. "You got your work cut out for you."

Jack smiled, "Gee thanks for the words of encouragement. Okay, once again I will do what you say." He looked down at his feet and then looked back at Bryan. "I am going to miss you too. I've gotten pretty used to having you around. You've been a good friend and a worthy adversary."

Bryan laughed, "You cheated, you're younger and faster than me."

Jack threw his head back and laughed, "Yeah and you're older and wiser."

"And look where it got me." He handed Jack back his tray after finishing up his meal. "I'm going to rest for awhile, thanks for playing nurse maid. If Maddy wants to talk later that would be fine, but for now I would kind of like to be alone."

When Jack returned to kitchen Maddy was nowhere around. Her half eaten plate was still on the bar. "Maddy?"

"In here," she answered back from the bathroom off the side of the kitchen.

Jack peered in finding Maddy kneeling over the toilet throwing up. "What's wrong Kitten?" He sounded alarmed.

Maddy laughed weakly, "Baby, it's called morning sickness." She wretched again.

"But it's afternoon."

Maddy shook her head smiling, "You are such an innocent, so much to learn. They call it that, but it happens anytime of the day. Welcome to parenthood. Look forward to the next seven and a half months of hormonal bliss."

Jack leaned back against the doorframe and chuckled, "It'll be worth it."

"You damn well better think so!"

Derek showed up on their doorstep a little after 6:30 with a large brown envelope in his hand. Jack invited him puzzled by his appearance.

"I need to speak with Maddy." He was acting a little nervous. Derek wasn't the nervous type.

"She's upstairs lying down. What's going on?"

"I need to deliver this...in person."

"Give me a minute, I will go wake her up." He turned and left to get Maddy.

Maddy returned with him, wiping the sleep from her eyes, "Hey Derek, what's up?"

"This came in for you this afternoon." He paused, "It's from Quantico."

Maddy eyed him skeptically and took the envelope. She broke the seal and pulled out the paperwork. She read it over. "This can't be right."

"Afraid so. Got mine at the same time." Derek sat across from her on the loveseat.

Jack picked up the papers and skimmed through them not understanding what they were saying. "What does this all mean?"

Maddy picked up the papers again. "It's my orders. I am to return to Quantico for a briefing and then on to my next assignment."

Jack shook his head violently. "The hell you are. Maddy, you promised. You promised me as soon as this was over you were done with the FBI."

"This has got to be some kind of mistake."

Derek shook his head, "Nope, not until they get the paper work and it's processed. Until that time she has to follow orders."

"She can't! I will not allow it. For Christ sakes, she's just been through hell. She's pregnant. She's not going out in the field again."

"Jack!" Maddy snapped at him. "I told you to keep your mouth shut! Damn it."

"Well they have to know. You aren't going anywhere." He turned to Derek, "How do we get this straighten out?"

"Bryan has to fill out the proper forms and submit them. Then it takes awhile for them to process it," Derek explained.

"Bryan is in no condition to make the trip down to the station. Can you get the paperwork and bring it here?" Jack took the papers from Maddy, looking through them again.

Maddy watched as the whole thing played out. Funny how no one asked her what she wanted. No, she had no plans on staying in the FBI, but it wasn't the point. Shouldn't it be her choice? Her request? Wasn't life just peachy? It just kept getting better and better. And here she thought once this case was finished everything would calm down and be *normal*.

"Yeah, I can put in the request for the paper work and drop it off for Bryan to fill out." He stood up to leave then looked back at the couple, "Congratulations on the baby."

Maddy peeked her head into Bryan's room. He appeared to be sleeping so she started shutting the door.

"Come on in Minnie." He said groggily.

Maddy crawled up on the bed and laid beside him, her head on a pillow instead of on him. She didn't want to be tempted. "Hey Mickey, feeling any better?"

He smiled weakly, "As long as I don't move, I'm fine. You got that look, what's up?"

"Derek brought over my new assignment," she watched for his reaction.

His eyebrows raised briefly, "Wow, that didn't take long. Where are you supposedly going?"

"Quantico for a briefing then to Oregon." She frowned, "At least Derek and I are assigned to the same unit."

Bryan gave her a look, "You act like you're going. I really hope you're not considering this, Maddy."

She laughed, "Of course not. I just wanted to see what kind of rise I could get out of you. Sure got one out of Jack."

He poked her in the ribs. "I bet. You're not being very nice to a crippled old man."

"I want you to do something for me, and Jack can't know about this. Instead of processing my resignation, can you just file an extended leave of absence?"

He studied her closely. "Maddy you are not fit to go back out in the field and you know it. Why would you even consider it?"

"I liked the work, just not the personal involvement. I don't know if working at the paper will be enough for me anymore. I want to keep my options open. I will have until the baby is born to decide."

Bryan shook his head, "Honey, you can't do this to Jack. It's no kind of life to lead when you are married and with a young child. You know that. You are always going to be out in the field. And you would have to move. What's Jack going to do? Are you going to ask him to up and leave his job and family to move to a place you're never going to be? Think kiddo. You are forgetting what it was like before. Besides that, you would be deceiving Jack. That's no way to start a marriage. Am I getting through to you at all?"

Maddy laid there quietly staring at a picture on the wall thinking about everything he had said.

"Besides Maddy, you are in no mental condition to be making life altering decisions."

She turned on her side so she could see his face. "That's why the leave of absence. Hell, I will at least a year to think about it. There's the strongest possibility I'm not going to do it, but I want to leave my options open."

"Tell you what, you talk to Jack about this. If he agrees to it, and tells me himself because you are not above lying, I will do it. But if not, you're done with the Bureau."

"Fine," she leaned in and kissed him tenderly letting it linger. She applied a little more pressure until she felt him start to respond. She ran the palm of her hand on long his jaw line.

When he tried to pull away she continued to place light kisses around his lips. "Where is Jack?" he whispered, feeling himself begin to give in.

"Went to his folks to get the cat." Her mouth came down on his tasting his sweetness.

Bryan's hand came up behind her head and brought her closer to him as he took control of the kiss, parting her lips taking her all in. She was pushing him to the point where he really wanted her, to make her his own again. He gently pushed her back. "Minnie..." she kept kissing him..."Minnie, please. We can't."

"We're just kissing," she whispered breathlessly.

Bryan groaned, "We're not just kissing. At least that's not what it feels like for me."

"Just a little more....please..." She looked into his eyes. She could see the fire smoldering. Playing with fire? Yes. She wouldn't cheat on Jack. She just wanted to be close to Bryan. No more than kissing, anything else would be a mistake.

When Bryan searched her eyes, it wasn't passion he was seeing, it was love. His heart softened. He cupped her face and kissed her with a tenderness so intense his heart skipped a beat. He let it deepen only to the extent he thought he could maintain control. He would give anything to make love to her, but he knew it would destroy any kind hope for a relationship of any kind. It wasn't worth it.

Maddy followed his kiss by sweet tender kisses, and then kissed his cheek. "Do you have any idea how much I love you? How much I have always loved you." Her eyes were sparkling with tears.

Bryan gently bushed away her tears with the back of his hand, "You are scared aren't you. Scared of loosing me?"

She nodded tearfully. "I just found you, now I am loosing you again."

"It's not the same, Maddy. I will keep my promise to you, it will be different this time."

Maddy laid back on the bed trying to keep her tears in check. "I will see that you do."

"Maddy?" she heard Jack calling from the foot of the steps.

"Up hear hon," she called back.

Jack appeared at the doorway, kitten in hand. "I brought someone to see you." He noticed her eyes, she had been crying again. How was she ever going to handle it when Bryan actually did leave? He brought Eddie to her and laid him on her stomach.

"She bothering you again?" he smiled at Bryan.

"Yes." He held up the envelope.

"You can fix this right?"

Bryan glanced over at Maddy and she looked away from him.

"Okay, what's the deal? Spill it, Maddy." Jack asked as he sat on the side of the bed.

"I asked that Bryan just put in a leave of absence instead of a resignation," she answered him quietly.

Jack reached out and scratched the kitten behind his ear. The kitten arched his back into Jack's hand...just like his Kitten. "Would it make any difference if I said no?" His voice was low.

"Yes," Bryan and Maddy answered simultaneously.

Jack looked up at Maddy, searching her face, "What about us? What about our family? What about our future, Maddy?"

"Never mind, it was just a thought. Kind of a *what if* kind of dream. You guys are right. I have no business in the field. I get too carried away. I can't follow the rules. I'm reckless. I would never get away with the behavior I displayed in this case." She reached out for Jack's hand, "And what you think matters to me."

Bryan smacked her arm, "And what I think?" he laughed, "I told you no right off the bat."

Jack looked away from her, "I'm not going to tell you what to do, Maddy. This has to be your choice. Whatever you decide, I guess I will support your decision and we'll deal with it." He stood up and left the room.

Maddy met Bryan's gaze. "Damn it Maddy, see how much he loves you. He would rather die than see you pulled back into that life, but he left it up to you. He has a very unselfish love, which is more than I can say for me. Think about it when you are considering making this decision. Now go talk to him."

Maddy slid off the bed and went in search of Jack. She found him outside sitting in a patio chair. The sun had long since set, but she could see his shadowy figure and the glow of a cigarette. She moved behind him and circled him with her arms and kissed him on the top of his head. "I'm putting in my resignation. I love you, Jack. You and this baby are the most important things to me in the world. Me staying a profiler would make our lives hell, and I won't put us through it. I don't want to miss anything our baby does because I am out in the field. It would be selfish of me to put my whims over us and I won't do it." She positioned her head so she could kiss him on the cheek. "Thank you for letting it be my choice, even though you were totally against it."

Jack slid his hand up her arm, "I don't want you doing this just because you think it will make me happy."

"I'm not, I am doing it because it's the right thing to do. Besides, isn't that what you did? You agreed to let me do it because you thought it would make me happy. Bryan said I am acting irrational because of my mental state. I'm sure he is right."

Jack snuffed out his cigarette and pulled Maddy around by her arm so she was sitting on his lap. "Bryan is a wise man." He lightly kissed her lips. "I am going to really miss him when he leaves."

"You and me both." She leaned her head against him.

"I tried to talking him into staying. He still said no."

Maddy's head popped up. "You did?"

Jack smiled, "Not for you, but for me. He has become my best friend, my confidant."

Maddy kissed him softly and laughed. "You are so selfish."

"You know he has to do this for himself right?"

"What to get away from me?"

Jack laughed softly under his breath, "No, because he needs to put his life back together. We need to let him do it without pressuring him okay? That's what good friends would do."

"Come here, Kitten," he took her face in her hands and kissed her tenderly. "I love you and all I want is for you to be happy. I will do whatever it takes."

She covered his lips with hers and kissed him deeply. "You already have."

Maddy kept her doctor's appointments on Monday morning. Her blood test came out clean and her OB exam revealed the baby was in good health with a strong heartbeat. When they did a sonogram Maddy had to laugh at Jack's amazement with the tiny blob on the screen. His eyes lit up and he got so excited asking all kinds of questions. She thought it was going to be fun watching Jack over the course of this pregnancy. The man knew absolutely nothing about having a baby. She thought she would have plenty of opportunities to yank his chain.

When she met with Dr. Rosario, she went over the feelings and experiences she had felt during the last couple of days. She felt uncomfortable talking about the shooting. She really liked Rosario because he didn't push the issues and let her deal with things in her own time. They discussed her bipolar and treatment options during pregnancy. Maddy chose to go unmedicated during the pregnancy to avoid risks to her child even though it increased her chances of reoccurring relapses. She would deal with it. She hoped Jack could.

On the way back home Maddy smiled as Jack talked her ear off about the baby. He was so cute.

"Do you care if we stop at the Journal? I would love to see Chief," she asked with puppy dog eyes.

Jack laughed, "Sure, I don't see a problem with it."

Miranda's mouth dropped when she got a look at Maddy, "Holy shit, he really did a number on you." She never was one to mince words.

Maddy touched her face. She hadn't given a thought to the bruises that darkened her once smooth, unblemished skin. Maddy smiled weakly, "Yeah, well it's nothing a couple of weeks won't take care of. It's no big deal. So what's going on with Andy? He still sticking around?"

Miranda smiled meekly. "Yep, putting in his resignation within the next couple of days. He applied at the SCPD and with Jack's recommendation he should be able to get on there under Jack with no problem. We found a house to rent, so as soon as things settle down, he'll be moving up here."

Maddy smiled, "That's great news. It will be fun having him around. Keep me posted."

As Maddy and Jack entered the bullpen, they got plenty of stares.

Max Sutton stood up and actually gave Maddy a hug. "Maddy, it's so damn good to see you. You're looking none worse for ware," he grinned.

"Fuck you, Max," she laughed.

He chuckled and shook his head, "Never thought I would say this, but it will be good to have your smart ass back in here."

Maddy knocked on Chief's door and when he glanced up a huge smile spread across his face. He waved them in and met Maddy in front of his desk. He picked her up and swung her around.

"Damn," she said after he set her down. "I take it you're glad to see me!"

"Oh hell yeah," he reached over and shook Jack's hand. "I hear congratulations are in order. Finally reined this one in did ya, Jack?"

Jack glanced over at Maddy. "Well once I started working on her she couldn't help but to succumb to my charms."

"Ass," Maddy mumbled under her breath. "How'd you find out?"

"Agent Mayland told me when he stopped in Friday morning. Pretty decent guy when you actually sit down and talk to him." He pointed to the chairs, "Sit down and take a load off."

Chief leaned back in his chair and put his feet up on his desk. "When you coming back, Tiger?"

Maddy looked down as she twisted the ring on her finger, "Not sure yet. I have to be formally released by the Bureau and would like a little time to recuperate. In case you haven't notice, my appearance is a little less than stellar."

Her boss nodded in understanding. "You doing okay? Heard about what happened at the hospital. Damn sorry you had to go through that, sorry you had to go through any of it. You getting help dealing with it?"

"He's not the first person I've shot and killed," she said trying to sound nonchalant.

Chief raised an eyebrow at her response.

"But it will be her last," Jack said firmly.

"Listen Chief, I know I promised you a hell of a story when this was all done, but to be quite honest...I don't think I can do it."

Chief studied her closely. Despite her smart assy attitude, he could see the change in her. Whether she was aware of it or not, her spirit had been broken. Maybe not forever, but she would need time to heal. "I understand, kid. It's too personal and I don't feel you need to relive it for the sake of the readers. There are some things people don't need to know the details. But you still haven't answered me, are you getting help?"

Maddy smiled weakly, "Oh yes oh father figure. I am seeing a very good psych doctor who specializes in this kind of trauma. Max has done a good job filling in for me, do I even still have a job?"

Chief cracked a smiled, "He will be glad to give it back to you. Said his a columnist not a reporter. Said he's done his time and he doesn't have the contacts you do."

"Well Max was a big help, you need to give credit where credit is due."

"If he hadn't written that story the cop leaked you never would have been put at risk like that either," Chief told her.

"What's done is done," she replied quietly.

Jack stood up, "Well you if you don't mind I want to get this one home to get a little rest. We've got Bryan back at the house recovering, too, so we need to get back and check on him."

Chief shook Jack's hand again, "Take care of my girl. We need her back here soon."

"Will do, Sir."

He gave Maddy a hug. "You behave and stay out of trouble."

"Yeah right, like that's going to happen," Maddy shot off at him as she walked out the door.

As they walked through bullpen to leave Maddy stopped in front of her office. "Wait a sec." She searched in her bag for her keys and unlocked the door. It felt strange being in here. She sat down in her chair and leaned back thinking back on the last day she worked in here. The day Bryan offered her full disclosure. It seemed like a lifetime ago.

On her desk were the preliminary files she had put together on the first victims. The tip of the ice burg, hell it was hardly a snowflake. If she had known then what she knew now, would she still have gotten involved? She smiled faintly. Yeah, she would have, because that was just the kind of person she was. She always had to have the answers. She grabbed the files and walked over to the paper shredder, flipped the switch and fed the sheets one at a time watching them come out in little strips like hamster bedding on the other side. Gone but not forgotten.

Jack reached down and flipped the switch off. "Come on, Kitten. Let it go."

"I want all traces of this case gone when I come back. Chief has the original evidence packet. Would you see that it gets destroyed?"

"Yes, now let's get out of here." He helped her to her feet. When they stepped out of the office Jack took the keys from her and locked the door. Maddy was trying hard to mask her feelings, but he could see it and he could hear it in her voice.

"When you going to get your ass back to work?" Sutton yelled at her from behind his desk.

She waved at him over her shoulder, "In a couple of weeks. Try not to fuck everything up before I get back."

They decided to stop off at the station to see if the paper work was in yet for Bryan to fill out. Derek, Andy and couple of the other agents were finishing up the job she started Saturday. There were tagged boxes stacked along one of the walls.

When Andy saw her, he smiled shyly and gave her a hug.

"Miranda told me the good news. It will be great having you around and I know you will be a good asset to Jack's squad.

"Thanks. I've never been so glad for something to be over as I am this." He grabbed a box and placed it on the stack.

"Where are they putting all these?" she asked.

Jack put his hand on her shoulder. "In the archives." He handed her a folder.

"What's this?"

"The final report. Derek thought maybe you might want to see it."

Maddy skimmed through the report until she got to the part about the shooting. *In defense of SSA Bryan Mayland and herself, Agent Maddy Sheridan discharged Agent Mayland's firearm, firing five shots into the suspect Lucas Riely a/k/a Justin Parsons killing him. The shooting was ruled a clean kill and in self-defense.* The truth forever buried in red tape. Maddy handed the file back to Jack without saying anything.

Maddy opened her desk drawer and pulled out her badge and glock. She brought it to Derek and turned it over to him. "I know it's not formal, but I'm not taking these home with me." In returned Derek handed her the resignation forms.

"It's a shame you decided to do this. We would have made a good team, just like the old days, Fire Fox," he half joked.

Maddy shook her head and laughed softly, "Yeah the old days...better than the now days."

Derek gave her hug. "You'll pull through, hon. As Andy said, you're a tough broad."

Maddy laughed, "When did he say that?" She looked over at Andy who pretending to straighten up a stack of boxes.

"At the hospital the night they brought you in." he grinned.

Maddy shook her head, "Tough broad, I'll remember that Andy."

Jack put his arm around Maddy and kissed her on the cheek. "You ready to go?"

Maddy let her eyes rove around the room. It held a lot of memories. Some fun ones, mostly not so good ones. A sense of sadness washed over her. Working with Bryan and Jack before everything went to shit...that was fun. She ran her hand over the back of Bryan's chair. She would never see him in this chair again. There was no real reason for him to come back here. Man this really sucked. She noticed the target sheet pinned up on the wall behind his desk. She removed the pins and folded it up for him...if he still wanted it. She tucked it under her arm. "Okay, let's go."

She hugged Derek again, "I guess this is goodbye."

He smiled down at her, "I bet our paths will cross again someday."

Maddy smiled back at him, "Only if you're in the neighborhood. Feel free to stop in."

Jack shook his hand, and then they patted each other on the back. "Pleasure working with you Derek, even though you were a real hard ass sometimes."

Derek chuckled, "Some one had to be. You guys had Mayland wrapped around your fingers. Tell him bye for me and I will see him back at Quantico."

"Will do." He turned to Andy, "See you in a couple of weeks. Don't think I'm going to cut you any slack either."

"I won't. See you guys soon."

Jack put his arm around Maddy's shoulder as they walked to the elevator. "You okay, Kitten?"

"Yeah, its just all kind of sad in away."

Jack pushed the down button. While they were waiting Jack cupped Maddy's face and gently kissed her. The elevator door opened while he was kissing her.

They turned to enter and came face to face with Stella. Oh Jesus, Maddy thought. Like she needed this right now.

Stella's eyes looked from Jack to Maddy and back to Jack again. "Jack... Maddy," she greeted them coldly.

"Stella," Jack nodded. "You look beautiful as usual."

Maddy shot Jack a look. What the fuck? What a fucked up thing to say when she was standing there with fading bruises on her face. She wanted to kick him...hard.

Stella smiled sweetly, "Why thank you Jack. You're looking pretty scrumptious yourself."

Jack grabbed Maddy's left hand and brought it to his lips making sure the ring was visible to Stella's eyes. Maddy grinned, okay no kicking.

Stella grabbed Maddy's hand and looked at the ring. She looked back at Jack. You could see the anger rising in her. "You're engaged? You're marrying this slut?"

"I think you better stop, Stella. I don't want this to get ugly. I was trying to be pleasant."

Out of the blue Stella grabbed Maddy by the hair and pulled her away from Jack. "You whore, that ring should have been mine!"

Jack stood back. Oh shit, Stella should have never touched Maddy's hair, not the way Parsons yanked her around with it. He held his breath. He might have incited another murder.

Maddy grabbed Stella's hand and threw her up against the wall. She pinned her to the wall with her forearm and got right in Stella's face. "Listen you stupid ass bitch. Jack never loved you in the first place. You were just a steady fuck, and not even a good one at that." She pushed her arm further into Stella's neck. "I'm only going to tell you once, I killed a man less than four days ago. I'm not afraid to do it again. If you ever, and I mean ever lay another hand on me...let's just say... watch your back."

When she looked in Stella's brown eyes she saw the fear she had instilled. Frightened blue eyes...

Maddy released her and turned to Jack. "Let's get the hell out of her before I bust her face and no more Barbie doll."

They stepped into the elevator. Maddy smiled sweetly at Stella, "Have a nice day." And she hit the down button.

Jack tried to keep a straight face as the elevator descended. "Damn Maddy," he started laughing.

She kicked him.

"Ouch, what the fuck was that for?"

"Damn men getting off watching women fight, that's what that is for. You set that up and don't deny it."

Jack rubbed his shin still laughing, "I didn't know it would go that far. I just thought it would be a few nasty words."

Maddy turned to him angry, "She pulled my fucking hair! No one ever better pull my fucking hair again! She's lucky I didn't throw her down the damn elevator shaft!"

Jack stood up, looking away from her, suppressing a smile.

Maddy glanced over at him and started laughing. She kicked him again. "You are such an asshole!"

When they arrived home Bryan was sitting on a stool at the counter reading the paper. Although his shoulder was still touchy it was starting to heal nicely. Which also meant he would be leaving...his flight was scheduled for tomorrow morning.

"You missed a good cat fight," Jack laughed as he grabbed himself a Dr. Pepper.

Maddy kicked him again.

"Damn it Maddy, stop that, it hurts," he whined.

Bryan smiled. It was good to see them like this again. "What happened or do I dare ask?"

"We ran into Stella at the station," Jack started to tell him.

"And this asshole set it up so Stella would come after me. And the bitch grabbed my hair."

"Oh shit."

Jack cracked up, "Maddy pinned her against the wall and verbally shredded her to pieces."

Bryan smiled and shook his head. "That was cruel, Jack. Hilarious—however cruel."

Jack threw the manilla envelope in front of Bryan. "Maddy's resignation forms."

"Got a pen?" Bryan asked as he removed the forms from the envelope.

Jack grabbed one from the drawer and handed it to him. Bryan raised an eyebrow. Damn, Jack couldn't have this done fast enough. He proceeded to fill them out taking him about twenty minutes.

He looked them over. "Okay Maddy, sign on the dotted line." He slid the forms across the counter to her.

Maddy skimmed over it. Hell, it didn't mean anything to her, she was done. She took a deep breath. So much for her short lived FBI career. But it's the way she wanted it right? She scratched her name on the line and dated it. She slid the forms back to Bryan.

"Hey, I got something for you, I almost forgot." She ran out to the car to get the target sheet.

Bryan looked up to see what Jack was doing. He was snooping around in the cupboard for something. He flipped the forms back several pages. He marked the deactivation box, reason—injury and pregnancy. Duration—indefinite. He signed his name and dated it. He did it to her again. She would have her in without betraying Jack. He looked covertly around him and stuffed the papers into a fed ex envelope and sealed it. "Already to go, signed, sealed, just needs to be delivered."

Maddy jaunted into the kitchen and handed Bryan the sheet and smiled, "You can hang it behind your desk at Quantico and think of me."

Bryan hugged her tight and kissed her tenderly, "Like I wouldn't be thinking of you anyhow, but thanks for grabbing it. That was sweet."

"Ah here it is," Jack pulled a bottle of amber colored liquid from the top shelf of one of the cupboards. "Aged scotch." He pulled down three tumblers, went to the fridge and filled one with milk, filled the other two with the scotch. He placed the milk in front of Maddy, and the other glass in front of Bryan.

Maddy looked at their glasses and then back at hers. "Something doesn't seem very fair about this."

"Rules are rules," Bryan laughed. "Deal with it."

"As usual, fuck you," Maddy made a face at him.

Jack held his glass up, the other two followed suit. "To new beginnings and lasting friendships!"

"Here, here," Bryan said as he and Jack downed their drinks.

Maddy looked away. This was it, really it. She didn't feel like celebrating, she felt like crying. She didn't want to spoil things by making a scene. She took a sip of her milk. She was trying so hard not to blink so the tears would stay put.

She wasn't aware Jack and Bryan were both watching her. Bryan stood up, moved behind her and wrapped his arms around her. "Minnie, it's okay. Everything will be okay. Just think of all the mini vacations we will be taking. Jack said the back bedroom is my permanent room. I'm even going to leave some things there so you know I am coming back." He turned her so she was facing him. He held her chin up so she had to look at him. He wiped her tears away with his thumbs. "It's like Jack said, new beginnings and lasting friendships. That's us kiddo, the three of us." He pulled her close and whispered in her ear, "You know how much I love you, will always love you. That will never go away. You understand?"

She nodded and wrapped her arms around him being careful not to hug him to tight. "I love you...forever and always."

The three of them slept in the living room that night, Bryan's last night with them. Maddy slept in Bryan's arms. Jack curled up on the loveseat. He didn't mind sharing Maddy one last time.

Maddy was quiet as they drove Bryan to the airport. The guys left her in peace in her thoughts while Bryan told Jack about his job—training agents back at Quantico.

Maddy held Bryan's hand as they walked through the airport.

Jack held Maddy as Bryan went to check in. "You okay Kitten?"

"No, but I will be," she smiled weakly, "everything will be okay. You guys promised and you don't break your promises right?"

He kissed her softly, "Never in a million years, Kitten."

Bryan returned, "Well I guess this is it."

Jack and Bryan hugged and patted each other on the back. "Take care of my Minnie. Let me know when you set a date, and I will be here with bells on."

Maddy told herself she wouldn't cry. She buried her face into Bryan's chest breathing his scent in deeply. She kept telling her self, she would see him soon, they promised.

Bryan pulled back and lifted her face to his and kissed her tenderly and deeply. He smiled down at her, that heartbreaking smiled. "You take care of you and that baby. Behave Minnie, and don't be too hard on Jack. Don't go all hormonal on him," he laughed, "he's just an innocent." He kissed her again and pulled her close, "Remember, until we are together again, I love you, forever and always."

She nodded and whispered back, "until we are together again, I love you, Mickey, forever and always."

Bryan grabbed his carryon and walked through the checkpoint. Jack held Maddy from behind as they watched. Maddy thought about the old Irish folklore. As Bryan walked towards the gate, she whispered. "Please don't look back, please."

Just as he was about to disappear from view, Maddy saw his hand come up as he waved without looking back.

Epilog

The cold November wind whipped through Maddy's hair as they stepped out of Bryan's car. Bryan had kept his promise. They talked a couple of times a week, but this was the first trip taken to see each other. Jack and Maddy came to Bryan. There was just something Bryan and Maddy had to do before they could surrender the past.

Jack hugged and kissed Maddy then turned her over to Bryan.

Bryan took her hand, "You ready to do this?"

Maddy hugged him, "Yes, finally after ten years, two months and five days, I'm ready."

Jack leaned on the side of the car as he as watched the couple walked down the gentle rolling hill of the cemetery. The grass had a brownish hint to it as winter would soon be setting in.

Maddy held in her hand two wreaths of baby's breath and miniature roses. Bryan held a bag in his.

"They're over here, Minnie." He led her to two small tombstones.

Maddy knelt down and explored them with her hands. Each stone was that of an exquisitely detailed marble lamb sitting on a pedestal, a hint of a cross rose above the lamb's back. Her fingers traced the names on the stones. Lexi Elizabeth Sheridan, Scott Michael Sheridan. She smiled softly as a tear slid down her cheek. She brought her fingers to her lips, kissed them and touched each of the stones. She placed a wreath over the cross above each of the lambs.

Bryan knelt down beside her. She glanced over at him noticing his wet cheeks. She reached out for his hand and squeezed it. He pulled the bag in front of him and reached into it pulling out the first of two small objects. He placed a small sorrel stuffed pony; a tag was hanging from its neck, Simba. He wiped his eyes and placed the pony lovingly on by Scotty's stone. Maddy watched as he pulled out the next item, she gasped and smiled when she saw what he had. It was a tiny pair of red ballerina shoes with Lexi embroidered across the toes. He tied it to the wreath so they dangled freely. He put his arm around Maddy and kissed her on the top of her head and whispered, "The past is left to cherish, the present here to celebrate, but tomorrow is a toast to forever."

Made in the USA
Charleston, SC
23 February 2011